Praise for Bryan Thomas Schmidt's *The Saga of Davi Rhii* trilogy:

Honorable Mention for *The Worker Prince*, Barnes and Noble's Year's Best Science Fiction Releases—Paul Goat Allen.

*"THE WORKER PRINCE breathes dynamic new life into the space opera genre. Rich characters, wild action, and devious plotlines collide in a thoroughly entertaining book!"*

— Jonathan Maberry, New York Times bestselling author of *Predator One* and *Deadlands: Ghostwalkers.*

*"A brisk science fiction novel full of rich characters and settings, it embodies 'sense of wonder' in the best traditions of classic science fiction. Well worth your time!"*

– Robin Wayne Bailey, New York Times Bestselling author of *Dragonkin* and *Frost.*

*"I found myself thinking of stories that I read during my (misspent) youth, including Heinlein juveniles and the Jason January tales, as well as Star Trek and Star Wars."*

— Redstone SF.

*"Retro-with-a-twist SF brimming with an infectious enthusiasm!"*

— Saladin Ahmed, author of *Throne of the Crescent Moon.*

*"Bryan Thomas Schmidt's THE WORKER PRINCE will appeal to readers of all ages. Bryan deftly explores a world where those who believe in one God labor against oppressors, and a single man may have the power to change their situation for the better. But will he be able to rise above all that his powerful uncle has taught him?"*

— Brenda Cooper, Author of *Edge of Dark, The Silver Ship and the Sea* and *Mayan December.*

*"In THE WORKER PRINCE, Bryan Thomas Schmidt combines elements from the Biblical story of Moses with exciting outer space action to create a satisfying hero's journey that is well worth taking."*

— David Lee Summers, Author of *The Solar Sea,*
Editor of *Tales of the Talisman.*

*"Bryan Thomas Schmidt's love for Science Fiction comes through on every page. THE WORKER PRINCE is fun for any age."*

— Maurice Broaddus, Author of
*The Knights of Breton Court* and *King's Justice.*

*"Bryan Thomas Schmidt's debut novel is a fast-paced and deftly-told space opera adventure set in a well-envisioned political and social environment. It is classic space adventure in all the right ways, with plenty of action, twists, and characters with emotional depth."*

– Gary W. Olson, author of *Brutal Light.*

*"A very well written book, and a story very well told. It's nice to read a book where the heroes are heroes and the villains are villains. I thoroughly enjoyed the combination of the Moses story with the Sci-Fi themes…I would highly recommend it even if you are new to Sci-Fi."*

– Ben Love, First Million Words Podcast.

*"…Not a simple story, but a complex piece of work…the intricate plot alone is enough to carry the reader along….Bryan Thomas Schmidt depicts this absorbing world. Drawing on strong literary elements which are key to this type of fiction, the potential for the series is boundless."*

– Ricky Brown, Howell Book Examiner.

*"The Returning has romance, assassins, tension, both modern and classic science fiction notions, and very smooth writing. What more could you want? Bryan Thomas Schmidt keeps improving. As good as The Worker Prince WAS, The Returning is better."*

– Mike Resnick, Author, *Starship* and *Ivory*

*"The Returning blends themes of faith with classic space opera tropes and the result is a page-turning story that takes off like a rocket."*

– Paul S. Kemp, Author,
*Star Wars: Riptide, Star Wars: Deceived*

*"A fun space opera romp, complete with intrigues, treachery, dastardly villains, and flawed but moral heroes."*

– Howard Andrew Jones, Author, *The Desert Of Souls*

*"An exciting and satisfying conclusion to Bryan Thomas Schmidt's "Davi Rhii Saga." Schmidt capably balances a large cast of characters, keeping everyone who has survived the first two books in play throughout this conclusion in either major or subplot roles. And the book covers just about everything classic space opera should. One hell of a finale."*

– Anthony Cardno, Author, *The Many Tortures of Anthony Cardno*

# THE COMPLETE SAGA OF DAVI RHII

BRYAN THOMAS SCHMIDT

# ALSO BY BRYAN THOMAS SCHMIDT

## NOVELS

The Worker Prince (Saga of Davi Rhii 1)
The Returning (Saga of Davi Rhii 2)
The Exodus (Saga of Davi Rhii 3)
Simon Says (John Simon Thrillers)
The Sideman (John Simon Thrillers)
Common Source (John Simon Thrillers)
Milk Run (John Simon Thrillers, forthcoming)

## CHILDREN'S BOOKS

Abraham Lincoln Dinosaur Hunter: Land Of Legends
102 More Hilarious Dinosaur Jokes For Kids

## NONFICTION

How To Write A Novel: The Fundamentals of Fiction

## ANTHOLOGIES (AS EDITOR)

Robots Through The Ages (with Robert Silverberg) (forthcoming)
Aliens Vs. Predators: Ultimate Prey (forthcoming)
Surviving Tomorrow
Infinite Stars: Dark Frontiers
Joe Ledger: Unstoppable (with Jonathan Maberry)
Predator: If It Bleeds
Infinite Stars: Definitive Space Opera and Military Science Fiction
The Monster Hunter Files (with Larry Correia)
Maximum Velocity (with David Lee Summers, Carol Hightshoe, Dayton Ward, and Jennifer Brozek)
Little Green Men—Attack! (with Robin Wayne Bailey)
Decision Points
Galactic Games
Mission: Tomorrow
Shattered Shields (with Jennifer Brozek)
Raygun Chronicles: Space Opera For a New Age
Beyond The Sun
Space Battles: Full Throttle Space Tales

# THE COMPLETE SAGA OF DAVI RHII

Ottawa, KS

BORALIS BOOKS
Ottawa, KS 66067


*Rivalry on the Sky Course* first published in *Residential Aliens*, 2011
*The Worker Prince* first published by Diminished Media Group, 2011
*TheReturning* first published by Diminished Media Group, 2012
*The Exodus* first published by Wordfire Press, 2017
*The Hand of God* first published in *Space Battles: Full Throttle Space Tales 6*, 2012


ISBN-13: 978-1-62225-7904 hardcover
ISBN-13: 978-1-62225-7911 ebook

First Boralis Books Paperback Edition: September 2021
Printed in the United States of America

10 9 8 7 6 5 4 3 2 1

*Interior Design & Layout by Guy Anthony De Marco/PublicationEngineering.com*
*Cover Design: Audra Redington*
*Solar System Map: Jeana Clark*
*Borali Crest: Mitchell Davidson Bentley*
*Author Photo: Bryan Thomas Schmidt*

# Dedication

*For my parents*
*Who allowed me the freedom to dream*
*For Grandma Marie and Grandma Ethel*
*Whose support and gifts, along with their love,*
*made dreams possible*
*And For Lucy*

*To Griffin, Noah and Kyle*
*With encouragement to shoot for the stars*
*you can do anything if you believe in yourself*
*and work for it*
*I'll never doubt you*
*May all your dreams come true*

*To Al Girtz, who always believed*
*and made me believe, too.*
*And to Mike Resnick,*
*you can't spell my name,*
*but your help and support has been invaluable.*

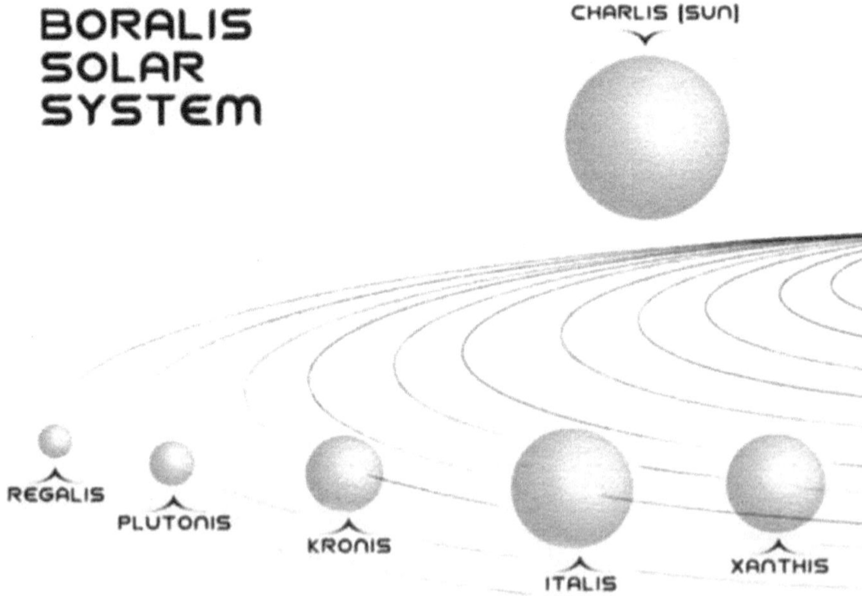
BORALIS
SOLAR
SYSTEM
CHARLIS (SUN)
REGALIS
PLUTONIS
KRONIS
ITALIS
XANTHIS

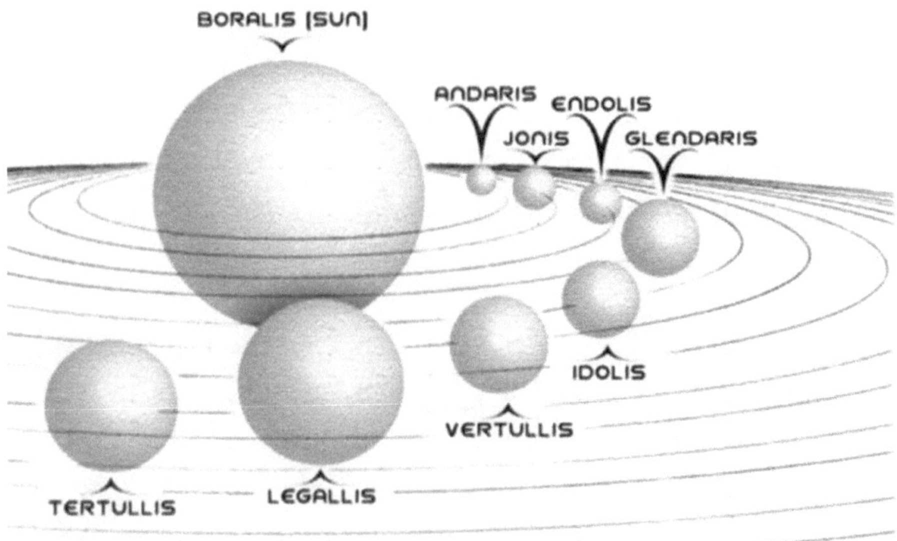

BORALIS (SUN)
ANDARIS
ENDOLIS
JONIS
GLENDARIS
IDOLIS
VERTULLIS
TERTULLIS
LEGALLIS

# Author's Introduction

It gives me great pleasure to release these books in hardcover, especially in a complete, chronological omnibus which tells the whole story as I've written it so far.

The original idea for the Davi Rhii novels was invented years ago in my basement bedroom at 1937 Starlight Drive in Salina, Kansas, by fifteen or sixteen-year-old me, who loved *Star Wars* and was steeped in biblical education from Sunday school and church. I wanted to combine the two into an epic miniseries like those I loved—*Roots, Shogun, Centennial, North and South.* The only character names to have stuck with me were Xalivar and Sol, but the concept never left my consciousness — nor did the opening line of *The Worker Prince*: "Sol climbed to the top of the rise and stared up at the twin suns as they climbed into the sky." Those items were part of the vision and I am pleased to have kept that connection to original dream, because a lot changed when I finally sat down to write the saga in 2008, many, many years later.

For one thing, my original vision was to tell the biblical Moses story set in space note for note, but I realized by the time I sat down to write it that doing that would be far less interesting than borrowing the structure and key elements and making it my own. I also realized that downplaying the religious aspects would open the story to a much larger audience, particularly in science fiction, and when I went back upon WordFire picking up the titles after my first publisher went defunct, I removed even more in polishing the first two books before writing the third. The result is a story with the basic Moses structure and key moments but without the stone tablets containing Ten Commandments, the parting of the Red Sea, and any miracles or plagues. Instead, I came up with other unique plotting devices to add twists and turns that I hope will keep readers interested. The fundamental theme of persecution over ideological differences remains. And in the days of cancel culture and great divide, that remains more relevant than ever, if you ask me. I hope the story speaks to readers on that.

But The Saga of Davi Rhii is much more about heroism and belief in good conquering evil than any message. It's about entertainment with humor, action, fun characters, and interesting settings. And that most of all is what I hope makes it memorable for you. This omnibus includes two short stories I wrote in the universe. One, the depiction of an incident hinted at in *The Worker Prince* during Davi's Academy days that sets up his rivalry with Bordox ("Rivalry On A Sky Course." The other, set a decade or more later, has only a small cameo at the end by Davi himself, but features Farien training a bunch of cadet pilots as they battle space pirates led by the mysterious Hand Of God. I know who the Hand Of God is. And so do readers. You will meet him in these pages. But the reveal of that is saved in case I ever want to revisit the Saga and write more stories. I had always intended to do that, but life happened and the series never took off, so I moved on to other stories. But who knows. I leave the door open, because I still very much like these characters and universe. Most of all, I am proud that I somehow captured the feel of the original Star Wars: A New Hope, because that was something I very much wanted and which made the story fun for readers of all ages.

One final thought is that I am a much better writer now. My craft has come a long way. After all, other than a few polishes made along the way, *The Worker Prince* was written in 2008-2009, 12 years ago, and *The Returning* shortly thereafter. I did do significant rewrites to *The Returning* for the WordFire version, which affected plot and outline quite a bit. But even still, you will notice a much more mature writer sat down to write *The Exodus* when I finally finished the saga in 2014-2015, a number of years later. And if you've read my John Simon thrillers, you'll see an even more mature writer now. I could go back and spend time revising and polishing this series but I chose not to. One, because showing my growth as a writer may serve as inspiration to new writers coming up after me who enjoy my work. Two, it's a reminder to myself of how far I've come. And Three, if I take time to sink myself into that, it will delay by months many new projects I have yet to write and want to release, and frankly, they seem like the better use of my time than fixing an old story that may have a few weaknesses and rough spots but remains a fun read. After all, it was that version that lead respected reviewer Paul Goat Allen to list the book Honorable Mention on Barnes and Noble's Year's Best Science Fiction in

2011, and led to all the blurbs you see on the back cover from popular writers. And it was that version that despite micropress release sold 1200 copies out the gate, a really sizable number for such an unknown small press at the time. Those accomplishments I remain proud of.

All this said, I hope you enjoy revisiting or visiting the story of Davi Rhii and his friends for the first time as a complete saga, and I appreciate your support and hope you'll check out my other works. Not all of them are as family friend as Davi was, but they all show the same sense of humor and desire for fun characters with a sense of humor and good action mixed together. Enjoy the adventures of Davi and friends, and remember, look out for Lord Xalivar! Happy Reading!

Bryan Thomas Schmidt
Ottawa, KS
August 2021

# RIVALRY ON THE SKY COURSE

**A Saga Of Davi Rhii Short Story**

# Rivalry on the Sky Course

BEEP! BEEP! The alarm on the targeting computer of his VS28 starfighter pounded Davi Rhii's ears as adrenaline throbbed through his veins. He glanced down to see several blips on the screen. "Incoming enemy craft," he announced into the comm, then switched on his shields and prepared for his second encounter with the enemy that day.

Body tensing and pressing back in the seat, he shifted weight and adjusted his controls as the sleek, black snub nose of another VS28 appeared beside him in the clouds, flying a little too close. "Bordox, aren't wingmen supposed to fly in formation behind their leader?"

Bordox's snapped back over the comm, "Yeah, so fall back and fly behind me then."

Davi bit back a retort and took a deep breath. "I have command, pilot."

The enemy craft appeared ahead, swooping down toward them. Davi rotated his VS28 and lined up on the lead attacker's fighter. His hands clasped the joystick as he let go with his lasers. He landed two hits on the attack leader's wings, sending him spinning toward the ground, smoke and debris trailing behind.

"Got him!" He whooped over the comm as another enemy fighter exploded nearby outside his blast shield.

"Lucky shot," Bordox sneered as another attacker's ship exploded on Davi's screen. "*That* was skill."

"Great, but stay in formation so we can protect each other," Davi ordered, but Bordox ignored him and dove off in another direction. He executed a roll with his VS28 and went in for another run. Breathing deliberately to keep himself relaxed—a trick his uncle had suggested—he fired three times in a row, sending another attacker into a smoking dive.

Bordox dove in from the opposite direction, but his lasers missed their target even as an enemy fighter braked and slid onto his tail.

Bordox cursed over the radio. "Get this guy off me, Rhii!"

"Oh, now you want teamwork," Davi snapped as he swooped down toward the fighter chasing Bordox but he was too late. The enemy fighter fired three times, hitting Bordox's engines and one of his ship's main wings. Bordox's fighter rocked and spun out of control toward the ground. Davi remained focused, lining up his sights and destroying the last two enemy fighters.

Then his console flashed and froze as klaxons blared and the cockpit shield rose automatically.

"Lights up!" Professor Orson Jonas called.

The reflector pods overhead lit the room with blinding light. Davi squinted and climbed out of the flight simulator. His best friends, Yao and Farien, raced over to pat him on the back, the shorter Farien's lighter white skin contrasting with their Tertullian friend's orangish tone, both aglow with Davi's victory.

"How many does that make?" Yao's purple eyes brightened against his dark orange-tinted skin. "Nine in a row by my count."

Davi's breathing returned to normal as he glanced over at Bordox struggling to extract his huge frame from the tight seat of another sim. "Who's counting? It's all in fun."

Bordox scowled as their eyes met.

Farien guffawed. "Don't show him any mercy he wouldn't show you."

"Just friendly competition," Davi said, figuring he'd already humiliated Bordox enough. Still, inside, his heart pounded in triumph and blood warmed his flesh.

The flight classroom was one of the largest on the military academy's campus. Occupying the bottom floor of an instruction building, it contained several rows of tan flight simulators with black seats and control panels identical to those of actual VS28 starfighters. A laser board covered most of the front wall.

Professor Orson Jonas stood behind a lectern, his black hair beginning to show strands of gray. He wore the gray uniform of the full military officer he had been until retiring to teach at the academy.

"Perhaps next time, Cadet Bordox will try and work with his leader instead of trying to compete with him and *actually* survive the battle," Professor Jonas said with a smile.

Bordox grimaced and slunk back to his desk in the classroom as Davi exchanged high fives with Yao and Farien.

"I failed the test!" Farien rested his dark hair on the dining hall table.

Davi chuckled and patted him on his bulky shoulder. Farien might be the shortest of the three, but he made up for it in muscle. "I think I failed, too. You're not the only one."

The glint of the gold buttons on their blue-gray uniforms teased Davi's eyes. Matching hats sat on the table next to their trays of brown Qiwi antelope meat, Gixi juice, and Jax fruit salad with fresh baked bread. They faced each other around one of the long, reddish brown tables that ran in rows down the middle of the dining hall.

Yao sipped his Gixi juice and his purplish eyes glinted as he smiled at the sweet taste Davi knew reminded him of home. "Don't be so dramatic, Farien. You could have joined the study group. We invited you several times."

"Easy for you to say, you're a genius at math," Farien growled as Yao and Davi laughed.

"Ignore him, Yao," Davi said. Farien needed to let off steam, and Davi knew better than to interfere.

"At least you're good at something." Farien lifted his head off the table, pulled his tray back from the middle, and took a bite of Qiwi. "You impressed Professor Jonas on the simulators today. I stink at that, too."

"Bordox didn't seem impressed." Yao grinned.

Davi licked his lips in anticipation as he sliced his Qiwi, pink juice flooding out to cover his fingers. "Bordox relies on his size to intimidate people instead of developing his skills."

"Speaking of Bordox." Yao nodded toward the door.

A huge, hulking cadet with light yellowish-brown skin and a dark beard, common to colonists who'd descended from Hispanic cultures on Old Earth, Bordox walked as if he owned the place. None of the cronies who followed him matched their leader's size, but all walked with the same swagger, the same smug look on their faces.

Davi turned and his green eyes met Bordox's for a moment. His rival's brown eyes held an anger Davi hadn't expected, but his smug face never faltered.

Swallowing, Farien smiled and waved at Bordox. "Hey, Bordox, nice job on the flight simulators. So good of you to show us all how not to do it!"

Bordox struggled to maintain his composure as the cadets around them smiled and guffawed.

"Don't egg him on, Farien," Yao said as Davi nodded in agreement. Bordox didn't appear in the mood for their usual hazing.

"Mock all you want, Farien," Bordox said in his scratchy baritone as he and his friends barreled across the room, stopping at the end of their table. "You're as inept at flying as you are at math." Bordox's buddies snickered.

Farien's muscles tensed and he jumped to his feet, rattling the bench. Davi put a hand on his arm. "I'm sure everyone could use extra time on the simulators."

Still shaking, Farien frowned and sat back down.

"Like your family will allow you to be put in danger, Prince." Bordox sneered. "You're only here because of special treatment."

"At the Academy, I'm your peer, not your Prince," Davi insisted, deliberately keeping his voice even despite the embarrassment that his rival had brought it up.

"Yes, your royal peerness," Bordox snapped, and his cronies cackled as they turned away and moved off toward the serving counter.

"I'm sick of that jerk!" Farien shuffled the food on his plate with a fork.

Davi shrugged as he chewed a bite of juicy Qiwi meat. "He's never liked to lose."

"If he keeps this up, he'll be drummed out of flight school," Yao said. "His focus should be on his studies rather than humiliating you."

"He still thinks my uncle stole the throne," Davi said amused by the absurdity of it. Would Bordox and his family never let that folk tale go? "I don't think his father makes it easy on him with all the failures, either."

Farien groaned. "Don't tell me you feel sorry for him! No one deserves your sympathy less than that moron!"

Davi and Yao exchanged amused glances as they turned back to their meals.

Professor Jonas pounded a fist on the lectern, motioning for the chattering students to quiet down. "Cadets, I'm pleased to announce our annual sky course competition has been scheduled for the end of the month. You'll want to work hard in the simulators over the next few weeks to avoid embarrassing yourselves in front of your family and friends. The High Lord Counselor, along with most of the Council, will be in attendance."

"Our little Prince had better sit this one out," Bordox said raising his voice and sneering as Davi grimaced, "so he won't publicly embarrass the

Royal family." Bordox and his friends guffawed as others in the class voiced their disagreement.

"I wonder what excuse your father will come up with, Bordox," Farien said, "to avoid having to see you humiliated again."

Bordox's face reddened as the cadets laughed at him again. "At least the Lords won't have to lower themselves by sitting next to commoners like your family, Farien." He and his friends sneered as Davi offered Farien a calming look.

"Cadet Bordox, Cadet Rhii followed orders well in the simulators last class, unlike yourself," Professor Jonas said, causing Bordox to sink down in the chair of his simulator. "Your own attitude and performance leave much to be desired."

Davi relished Bordox's discomfort as the other cadets snickered and elbowed each other through broad grins.

"I'd be happy to tutor him, Professor Jonas, if he'd like," Davi said with a smirk, provoking another round of laughter.

"Oh really, my Prince? You'd lower yourself to help little ole me?" Bordox said back, mimicking a small child. "Go back to your stolen palace, crown boy."

"Members of the Royal family are to be treated with respect!" Farien stood, chest puffing, fists clenched, as if preparing to rush Bordox at any moment.

Bordox's face turned dark. When their eyes met, his look was sharp as blades. "From what I hear, the royal prince's blood isn't so royal."

Yao stood and grabbed Farien's arm, trying to calm him as Davi smiled. Bordox must be really desperate to come up with something so absurd. "Who'd have known you're so fond of folk stories, Bordox."

"If it's a folk tale, I guess you're the folk lore prince," Bordox said. "A starport rumor about a baby who arrived in a courier craft from the stars and landed near the palace, adopted by a lonely princess with no offspring." Bordox's cronies chortled and sneered. "Maybe I should have my father look into it, just in case," Bordox said as Farien struggled against Yao's grip. Bordox's father, Lord Obed, headed the Lord's Special Police, an elite squad of soldiers dedicated to the High Lord Counselor's service.

"Enough!" Professor Jonas hollered then waited for them to quiet down. "Cadet Bordox, you're out of line. Impugning the reputation of another cadet without cause is enough for me to have you dismissed. Prince Rhii's heritage is not in doubt. Would you like me to take this matter before the Academic Council?"

Bordox tensed in his seat, fists clenched and just stared straight ahead but Davi felt the anger radiating from him in waves.

"Now pull up your texbooks to the chapter on flight patterns and pay attention!" the Professor ordered as Bordox sank down further into his seat. His eyes held a hatred like Davi had never seen.

The next night, Davi, Yao, and Farien gathered for dinner at the Promenade with three beautiful women they'd met at a park. Seated on the outdoor patio that overlooked a lake, the smooth, cool breeze urged them to relax and enjoy the time off.

"Would you ladies care to go for a stroll?" Warmth filled Davi as the last bite of his meal settled into his stomach.

"There he is, the adopted prince. It's sad, isn't it, hearing his blood isn't really royal? It's so charitable of the High Lord Counselor and Princess to take him in anyway so he can make something of himself."

Davi's blood temperature rose as he turned to see Bordox and his companions cackling nearby with dates of their own. People around them stared, making Davi and his friends' dates shift uncomfortably.

"A slave child sent into space in a courier to save his life adopted by a princess." Bordox's sarcasm cut Davi like shards of ice. "It really is a great story, isn't it? Almost like magic."

Davi heard more guffawing around them as Farien stiffened, his face whitening in anger. "You're pushing it too far, Bordox. I'm warning you."

"Or what? Your worker prince will call his uncle?" Bordox sneered as his friends chuckled.

"It must be really humiliating to watch him keep beating you on the sims," Yao said with a grin. "Especially since his family has a history of such victories against yours."

"Let's settle this right here!" Farien's chair squeaked as he pushed back from the table and stood, fists balling at his side.

Davi stood beside him. Public disparaging was too much. He had to defend his family's honor.

"Come on, ladies, don't listen to him," Yao said from behind them.

Farien and Davi turned as their dates hurried away down the promenade.

Bordox snickered, his eyes glowing in triumph, as he and his companions turned and walked away.

"Let's go!" Farien said, stepping forward.

"He's got too many people with him, Farien. You can't take them all on," Yao said, grabbing him by the arm.

Davi stood fuming, his body stiff with tension, as he watched Bordox and his cronies walk calmly past a skitter shop along the Promenade. His instincts matched Farien's. Private teasing was one thing, but spreading lies in public was another. Especially when it cost them their dates. Who knew how far the rumor would spread now? An idea popped into his head and he smiled. "I think what I have in mind will make you feel much better."

He turned and led the way toward the skitter shop, Yao and Farien following.

They rented skitters and took off down the promenade, hovering a few feet off the ground as they weaved through the scattered pedestrians. Experienced riders, the three manipulated their vehicles smoothly around light poles, people and other objects as they sped along. One man ground craft ridden like Old Earth motorcycles, skitters used manipulated air to hover and move above a planet's surface. They were sleek and fast, and favorites of both civilians and military.

As they rode, Davi spotted Bordox's group walking close to the edge of the water.

"There they are. Let's go say hello." The skitter's servos hummed as Davi accelerated, enjoying the vehicle's vibrations and gentle hum as he raced forward with Yao and Farien close behind.

Davi steered the skitter over behind Bordox's group. Others on the Promenade spotted them coming and jumped or stepped aside to clear a path. Davi revved the engines loudly as he came up fast from their rear, taking Bordox and his friends by surprise.

Trying to jump clear in panic, Bordox and several companions, including his date, lost their balance and fell into the river. They yelled as they fell, sputtering and cursing after splashing down in the water.

Amused by their version of revenge, Davi and his friends didn't even look back as they rode away.

"Your ideas really are the best," Farien said.

"I hope that water's cold," Yao said as they stopped and turned to watch Bordox's friends helping him and his disgusted date out of the water. "You know this will only make him madder." Yao looked at Davi.

Davi shrugged. "He's the one who made it personal. Besides, I feel better." Laughing with his friends, he revved his skitter's motor and accelerated again and they rode away.

Over the next several weeks, Davi and Bordox barely crossed paths; mostly during lectures or when cadets gathered and compared simulator results. Bordox jeered at him a couple of rare times when his scores outdid Davi's, but otherwise made no attempt to converse. In time, the tension between them receded to its normal level.

Two days before the competition, Davi and his fellow contestants gathered with Professor Jonas at the starport.

"You each get one practice run on the actual course before the competition," Professor Jonas explained. "You must destroy all the targets and avoid all the obstacles before reaching the finish line. Scores will be determined through combining how many obstacles and targets each of you defeats with your overall speed."

Davi glanced around at the grandstands scattered through the course, which wound over the city in a large oval. He could almost feel the history that had taken place there. Spectators could rent special goggles allowing them to see the course for the popular annual event. Adding to the challenge, the VS28s had been designed for spaceflight and didn't operate near as efficiently within the planet's atmosphere. The professors regarded it as a truer test of the cadets' piloting skills due to the added handicap.

Davi, Bordox, and Farien had been assigned to a group with six others. As they approached their fighters, Davi increased his pace to come alongside Bordox. "Good luck up there today."

Bordox looked at him a moment, as if evaluating his sincerity. "You too."

"I saw your sim scores. You've been working hard."

Bordox shrugged. "We'll see who's the hotshot pilot now."

Davi grinned and extended his hand. Bordox nodded as he shook it, then they hurried toward their assigned craft.

They launched from the starport and rendezvoused at the starting zone for the course, waiting for Professor Jonas' signal to start their run.

Davi's VS28 rose into the sky, its vibrations and hums not much different than the well-designed simulator's. Sunlight from solar system's twin suns warmed his neck and shoulders, making him feel like he belonged up here.

Listening to the hum of the engines ease as the ship's vibrations calmed beneath him, he settled onto his starting altitude and turned to each side, memorizing the wingspan and diameters. Although they'd been allowed some practice time over the past two weeks, the sky course would require them to fly in closer proximity than normal, and he wanted to feel out the fighter so he could run the actual competition on instinct. His concern for the day wasn't winning but learning how the fighter would respond and what would be required to succeed in navigating the course. He could always add speed later.

A long, high tone sounded over their comm channel as they accelerated onto the course, engine trails streaming behind them. Farien and two others accelerated far too fast for Davi's comfort. He relaxed and hung back, getting to know the fighter and the course. To his surprise, Bordox hung back with him.

Navigating the first few obstacles with ease, Davi hit three targets then accelerated, the force pushing him against his seatback.

Then his controls froze.

He wiggled the joystick and punched the fuel button. Control returned. He breathed a sigh of relief.

He'd lost sight of Bordox as they passed through some low clouds. As he emerged from the cloud cover, his controls froze again. His heartbeat pounded in his head like a bass drum, rushing adrenaline making it difficult to think and focus, even as his mind raced through troubleshooting checklists they'd memorized in class.

When every attempt he made failed to restore control, he keyed his comm. "Test Alpha Six, my controls are frozen." He breathed deeply and tried not to panic.

Professor Jonas' steady voice came back through the comm. "Test Alpha Six, attempt to reinitialize your flight computer and report the results."

Davi flipped the switches, starting the reinitialization sequence for his flight computer and controls. The whole process should take a couple of minutes, and as he waited, he flew into another series of clouds. His fighter jerked, tossing him about, and he heard metal shrieking. Turning back, he saw Bordox's fighter close on his wing, a cocky smirk on Bordox's face. Had their fighters touched?

Davi switched his comm to the private squadron channel. "Bordox, what are you doing?"

Bordox's voice came back sounding apologetic. "Sorry. It's hard to see through the clouds."

"Back off, Bordox," Farien scolded over the comm. "He's lost his controls."

Before Farien finished, Bordox accelerated up beside Davi so close, Davi feared an impact.

"More fun if I can see your eyes." Bordox looked over and smiled.

Davi tensed, glaring toward Bordox's cockpit. This wasn't the time to play.

"Test Alpha Eight," Professor Jonas said, using Bordox's call sign, "pull off so you don't get caught in the tractor beams."

Bordox sneered and put his ship into a gradual dive, allowing his left wing to scrape Davi's right wing. Startled and fearful, Davi shifted his joystick and accidentally sent his VS28 into a roll.

Davi's flight computer finished initializing and beeped, notify him it was ready. He struggled with the controls, trying to stop spinning and regain control. Instead, his fighter pointed straight at the ground.

The g-forces pushed him back harder against his seat with every second. He struggled with the stick to no avail, then pulled a hand off the joystick and keyed the comm again. "Test Alpha Six in trouble."

"Hang on Alpha Six," Professor Jonas responded, klaxons blaring in the control room behind him.

His fighter continued spinning out of control, the ground growing nearer as he gained speed. His pulse pounded and his breathing increased. He wondered how a pilot mentally prepared to die. The ground appeared as a smeared whirl through his blast shield.

Remembering the eject system, his hand shot toward it. The fighter rocked, sending his shoulder hard against the cockpit wall, and two VS28s flown by military officers pulled even with him on either side. His fighter jerked again and stopped spinning, suspended between the other two. They adjusted direction until all three flew straight again, then turned back toward the starport.

Davi had never experienced tractor beams before. His body relaxed in the seat, as he exhaled and released the controls then said a silent prayer thanking the gods.

That night in his dorm room, Davi leaned back on his bed as Farien paced beside the closed door. Yao watched from the chair near the desk.

"Bordox tampered with your fighter," Farien said, still angry.

"We don't know that for sure," Yao responded.

"What other explanation is there?" Davi exchanged a look with Yao then Farien, hoping.

Neither had one.

Davi breathed deeply, thankful it was over. "It's the first time he's ever apologized to me. He made a point of asking if I was okay. The fighters are harder to maneuver than the simulators. And you know how bad Bordox was on the sims."

"Did you see the look on his face at the starport after?" Farien continued.

"Tampering with fighters is serious," Davi didn't want to believe Bordox would take things so far. "Someone could get hurt or killed."

"His eyes said he knew," Farien said.

"Oh, you're an eye reader now, are you?" Yao teased.

"Come on. You both know what I mean." Farien stopped pacing and leaned against the back of the closed door, looking frustrated.

"Why would he go that far? He may be jealous of me. We give each other a hard time. But I could have been hurt or killed." Davi wondered when their friendly competition had gotten so distorted that Bordox would risk putting Davi in real danger of doing him harm? This was military training, not war.

"Bordox hates you," Farien answered. "Walz overheard him at the Bar Electric swearing he'd bring you down no matter what."

"Bordox always brags like that." Davi had heard Bordox's comments so often, he'd stopped caring. "It's just talk. He never acts on it."

"Lord Obed still claims your grandfather stole the throne." Yao was the best versed among them in history, his favorite subject.

"It's just silly jealousy." Davi scoffed at Yao's expression.

Yao shrugged. "It's a motive."

Bordox had deliberately flown too close on the practice run. That much was sure, but had the crashing been deliberate or just his usual incompetence? Davi sighed, hoping they were wrong. "Without proof there's nothing we can do."

"We can tell Professor Jonas," Farien said.

"And risk being accused of disparaging another cadet ourselves? You have enough demerits already." Yao looked at Farien, who sighed in defeat.

Davi took a slow breath, releasing tension from his body. "They always reassign fighters before the race. Professor Jonas promised to let me have another practice run alone tomorrow during afternoon break. Can you two keep Bordox occupied?"

"A request to stop by his father's office during afternoon break." His shoulders lifted as the corners of his mouth formed a smile.

"What?" Yao shook his head. "He wouldn't have time. He couldn't get to LSP headquarters and back before his break ended."

Farien nodded. "Right."

Yao stared quizzically at Farien. "You're planning to forge an official government communiqué?"

"Walz's specialty is intelligence," Farien said. "Forgeries are part of his training. He'd love to test his skills in a real life situation."

Davi laughed. "Sometimes I think you're too devious to be an officer, Farien."

Yao shook his head. "It could come back to haunt us."

"You've got a better idea?" Farien asked.

"No," Yao and Davi said together.

"Okay, let's go see Walz," Davi said as he stood.

Farien lit up and gleefully turned to the door.

On the day of the competition, Davi walked past the grandstands and saw his mother, Miri, and Uncle, Xalivar the High Lord Councilor, talking with Bordox's father and Yao's parents. His mother spotted him and waved, smiling with pride.

*Hope she's still smiling afterwards*, he thought nervously and struggled to focus, trying his uncle's deep breathing again.

The VS28s waited in smooth, perfectly aligned rows, their snub noses and three wings gleaming under the light of the twin suns overhead. The transparent cockpit blast shields waited open at ninety degree angles from the cockpits below as the pilots prepared to climb into their ships. Davi glanced over and saw Bordox sneering at him from nearby.

Professor Jonas approached. "Rhii, switch fighters with Bordox."

The smug smile vanished from Bordox's face as they both turned toward the professor. "What? Why?"

The Professor sounded irritated. "All the fighters are the same. What's the issue, Cadet?"

Davi kept his eyes on Bordox's face watching for a reaction. He saw the truth in his eyes. *You did it again, didn't you?*

Bordox ignored him, grumbling to himself.

Davi and Bordox both moved to the fighter to which the other had been assigned.

Yao climbed the ladder to help Davi strap in. "Maybe Professor Jonas suspects Bordox had something to do with what happened on your practice run."

Davi shrugged and smiled. "Doesn't matter. As long as the competition's fair, I'll leave him in the dust."

Yao grinned and climbed down, saluting with a wink of his purple eyes.

Davi's group went through their preflight checks, then launched in pairs through the launch tubes, rendezvousing again at the sky course starting zone. He greeted the twin suns like old friends. The sky seemed clearer than usual. *A good day for a race.*

When the signal came over their comm channel, they flew into the course as fast as they could.

Bordox kept his fighter even with Davi's as they dodged the first obstacles and shot several targets, then his speed dropped off as his ship began angling downward. Davi looked over, watching him struggle with the controls.

He keyed the private comm channel. "You need help over there, Bordox?" When he got no answer, he sped on through the course.

Five minutes later, Davi landed at the starport, riding the high from an almost perfect run. Once he'd gotten into it, he'd forgotten all about his competition and just done his job, enjoying the ride. Looking around, he realized Bordox and his fighter were nowhere in sight. Had he even completed the course?

Then he heard a whining overhead and turned as a VS28 arced in at an odd angle and slammed to the tarmac in a dangerously rough landing, Bordox still at the controls. The man had moxy, that was for sure. Davi would have ejected and let the ship crash. The fighters were rigged for ground activated self-destruct if their crash trajectory took them too close to any grandstands or populated areas.

As those around him gasped and mumbled, Bordox's hateful eyes locked on Davi's own from the cockpit.

Later, Professor Jonas announced the winners. Davi had the highest score by far. As he and his friends walked back toward the grandstands, Davi overheard a commotion down an alley between buildings. As they reached the alley's mouth, they stopped and peered in.

Bordox forced one of his friends back against a wall. "You were supposed to make the fighter slow, not unflyable. I could have been killed!"

"You're the one who didn't want him humiliating you again!" The friend said.

"It's not our fault the professor switched the fighters for the first time ever," another friend said.

"You humiliated me in front of my father!" Bordox pounded a fist against the wall above his frightened friend's head.

Davi and his friends exchanged a look then hurried past before anyone spotted them, continuing toward the grandstands.

"We're so proud of you," his mother, Miri, said as she wrapped Davi in a warm embrace. Her light blue eyes radiated warmth.

"Well done, Xander," Xalivar said with pride, addressing Davi by his given name, not the nickname Davi and his mother favored. Uncle Xalivar wore his usual gold robe with a white collar and cuffs. In the center by his neck lay the jewel known as the Emperor's eye. Shorter than Davi but taller than Miri, he had a dark beard.

Davi smiled. "Thanks for coming."

"We wouldn't have missed it," Miri assured him, pride almost bursting off her face.

Davi tried not to frown as Lord Obed and Bordox approached. Obed wore a ceremonial robe similar to Xalivar's. His skin had a light yellowish brown hue with the same intense brown eyes as his son. He smiled and extended his hand to Davi. "Congratulations, Prince Rhii. A great showing."

Davi shook the proffered hand, smiling. "Thank you, sir."

Lord Obed turned and looked at Bordox, who stood there looking down at his feet. "You've embarrassed me enough today," Obed growled.

Bordox sighed and extended his own hand. Davi had to hide his surprise as he shook it. "Congratulations, Rhii. You deserve it."

Obed led Bordox away as Yao stepped away from his parents and stopped next to Davi. "That had to hurt."

Davi nodded, continued to watch Bordox for a moment. He feared things had changed forever between them. He'd never wanted to make an enemy, but it hadn't been his fault.

"Come on," Farien called, waving him over, "we've got a party to get to!"

Their hands met in a high five as Davi joined them, and they hurried off for their favorite bar.

# THE WORKER PRINCE

The Saga Of Davi Rhii Book 1

# Prologue

Sol climbed to the top of the rise and stared up at the twin suns as they climbed into the sky. Yellows, reds, and oranges faded under the increasing blue of oncoming daylight, leaving a pinkish glow on the horizon, and the ever-present smell of chemicals and fuel filled his nostrils but he barely noticed.

For as long as he could remember, he'd started each day with an escape from the heavy, polluted air and the noise of people, factories, and traffic. The peaceful, quiet sunrises would usually calm him to face the day ahead, but today he had no sense of peace, and the silence of the city's edge drowned beneath the clamor within him.

*My precious son! My God, don't forsake us now!*

The wait had been interminable, punctured by endless prayers to God for a precious gift. Now they had to send him away—their Davi! Was there no justice in this universe?

He glanced at his chrono and sighed. *Wouldn't want to be late to serve the Borali Alliance!* After one last look at the twin suns, he turned and hurried back along the path toward Iraja and the starport filling the horizon near the city's edge below.

He labored more with each breath as heavy air filled his lungs. The depot occupied a strategic site at the center of the planet, ensuring easy access from all regions. Ignoring the droning soundtrack of the city awakening, Sol timed in on the chrono and greeted Aron, his co-worker and lifelong friend.

"Regallis," Aron said, smiling.

"Regallis?" Sol asked. It seemed so far away—one of the outer planets in the system.

Aron nodded. "It's perfect. Good population, frequent tourists, fertile plants, peaceful, no pollution. Best of all, no slavery. Davi should find a very happy life there." Sol smiled at the thought. "I plotted coordinates to the capital. Figured it would give him the best chance."

Sol clapped Aron on the shoulder, as the idea blossomed. "Thank you,

Aron. We knew we could count on you."

Aron, short and bulky, filled out the blue-green jumpsuit, leather boots, and tool belt comprising their mechanics' uniform more fully than his thinner, taller companion. They moved across a hangar toward their workstation, despite the deafening racket closing in around them—the constant hum of machinery, men shouting to be heard over it, the roar of engines, and the staccato hammering of tools. The sounds, the chaos of starships in all states of repair, and the smell of fuel and sweat combined to make the hangar a place most visitors preferred to avoid. Sol didn't even notice.

"What do you have left to do?" Aron asked as their eyes scanned the daily work assignments on their terminals.

"Test the seals, navigation system, and replace the injector. Then I need fuel." Sol sighed, ticking the tasks off on his fingers like always. There would be no time to work on the courier today.

"My friend at the fuel depot has leftover military fuel cells. They almost never ask for them back. He volunteered some for the courier."

Sol beamed. If he'd ever had a brother, he hoped it would have been someone like Aron. "What did I do to deserve a friend like you?"

Aron shrugged. "Some people are luckier than others."

Sol laughed at Aron's silly grin as they set to work on their assigned tasks. As he worked, Sol stared through the hangar's transparent roof at the clear blue sky overhead. Through a break in the gray, polluted clouds, the clean purity of a blue sky contrasted with his daily existence. He and Lura had adored every moment since the birth of their son. Every giggle, smile, or sign of personality sent waves of warm amazement coursing through him. There was not any more precious gift than that of this little creature who'd come from their love.

But Lord Xalivar's decree had taken the planet by storm. All first-born worker sons would be slaughtered for the gods. There were rumors that the crisis resulted from one of the High Lord Councilor's nightmares, but no one knew for sure. Xalivar didn't need a reason. Concerning the slaves, his word was law.

*The gods! Gods our people don't even believe in would dare to take away our Davi!* Sol and Lura desperately wondered what they could do to save their precious boy. After hours of discussion, they'd found a single choice.

The next morning, Sol had begun modifying the round, silver courier craft designed to carry supplies and papers between planets in the solar system. Being a mechanic at the depot put him in the perfect position. He installed a vacuum sealer and oxygen vents and hollowed out the cavity to hold the cushion on which he would place their tiny son for the journey.

Sol enlisted Aron, who had access to navigation charts for the entire system, knowing together they could find a place where Davi would be found and cared for. The courier's sub-light drive would cut travel time to no more than a day to anywhere in the solar system.

Lura wouldn't eat and barely slept, sitting with Davi and refusing to leave him. At least Sol's work kept him occupied. He couldn't bear watching her suffer, and if he didn't act, Davi would be sacrificed with the others. Healing would come when they knew he was safe. Sol was, even now, working on a tracking device, which would send back a signal to the depot when the craft landed. They might never see Davi again, but at least they would know he'd escaped to a new life.

As the suns' rays shone through the hanger's translucent roof and warmed the space where he stood, it comforted Sol to know their baby boy would see the same suns wherever he wound up. Shadows crept away like their quat, Luci, who loved to sneak around feeling invisible with her arched back and long tail. Luci would miss the little one, too. Sol offered a silent prayer of thanks for the time they'd had with their precious son then turned back to his tasks.

"LSP Squads are landing and moving toward our neighbor-hoods." A co-worker appeared beside Sol's worktable, his fearful eyes darting around like flies hovering over a corpse.

"We don't have much time," Sol said to Aron as the co-worker hurried off, and they abandoned the hulking barge to finish the courier.

Aron tested the navigation system, while Sol checked the seals. Less than thirty minutes later, the first reports of methodical killings came in—first-born males of all ages being slaughtered by LSP squads moving from home to home.

"I hope Lura heard the news." Sol couldn't stand still. And even as he said it he winced, wishing he could spare her. But if she heard it, she'd come, and that was their only chance.

"I'm sure everyone on the planet knows about it by now," Aron replied as both did their best to hurry without making any mistakes. "She's probably on her way here already."

Sol nodded, fighting the tension stiffening his limbs. His clammy hands slipped a bit as he worked, his breath bursting in and out as his heart pounded. Lura would follow their plan and head for the depot with

Davi. With his supervisors watching, he couldn't run home and warn her. He'd risk encountering the LSP squads, who tended to shoot first and ask questions later of citizens who interrupted them in action.

The supervisor was upon them within the hour. Tran hurried over waving the two lower arms extending from either side of his rounded, voluminous stomach. Two parallel arms extended out of his shoulders above them, one holding an electronic translator, which translated his words from his native Lhamor—a series of clicks and clacks—into the commonly used "Standard," the official language of the Alliance.

"There's no courier on your worksheets." His gray jumpsuit bore not a blemish or wrinkle, unlike theirs which were covered with grease and grit. The stare from the green-scaled supervisor's disproportionally large orange eyes might have been intimidating if Sol hadn't already grown used to it.

Sol's throat tightened, but Aron remained calm. "It's the courier for Estrela Industries, Tran," Aron said as he entered calculations into the navigation system's computer. "We got notification they've moved up the testing. It's for a top-secret program authorized by Lord Xalivar himself."

Sol and Aron had long ago devised the story about the courier belonging to an important defense contractor. They'd seen too many other workers killed just for failing to meet their quotas. Since couriers were a part of their regular routine, it was easy enough to excuse their working on it from time to time if anyone asked. Before now, no one had.

Tran mulled this over, staring at them as if he could read their minds.

"It's almost done—a few minor adjustments." Sol used a wrench to finish checking bolts on the courier's hatch.

"Well, you can't leave today without finishing your assignments." Tran's eyes reddened with suspicion before he whirled and marched away. At least they'd bought themselves time.

"If he goes to the manager—" Sol shuddered at the memory of past tortures for disobedience.

"He won't. He flinches at the mention of Xalivar's name," Aron reminded him, as they hurried back to work on the courier. Sol's breathing normalized again, and he hoped Lura was on her way there.

A clerk in a red jumpsuit appeared, handing Aron some parts for another project. As Aron signed the laser pad to acknowledge receipt, the co-worker looked at Sol. "They've started in your neighborhood. We just heard."

Sol and Aron exchanged a frightened glance as the co-worker slipped away. Sol's shoulders stiffened and his heartbeat climbed as sweat beaded on his upper lip. He jumped at the communicator's beep, and then double clicked the talk button. "Station sixty-five."

"Your wife is in the lobby," the auto-bot receptionist responded. The line went dead.

Sol's shoulders descended as he turned to Aron. "Get the pod to Test Pad Seventeen-A. We'll meet you there."

Aron nodded as Sol hurried off toward the lobby.

Lura waited with Davi wrapped in a blanket, rocking him in her arms. She wore a simple white jumpsuit and tan leather shoes, her long brown hair flowing down her back. As it had for fifteen years, her beauty took Sol's breath away. The most perfect human he'd ever met had chosen him. He'd never deserve her, and it just made him love her more.

Sol hugged his wife, seeing the fear in her hazel eyes. "Come with me." Grabbing her arm, he steered her away from the four-armed auto-bot, which sat permanently affixed before a huge communications console. He tried to relax, knowing it was a mech but as they neared the door, Davi began crying.

"Is that a baby?" Tran's voice came from behind them, and they turned to see him frowning as he approached.

"It's our son," Lura commented, then put a hand over her mouth as Tran reached for a communicator on the wall.

The clerk who'd delivered supplies to Sol and Aron earlier entered at a run. "Tran, Station Thirty-Four has no fuel."

Tran stopped reaching for the communicator and turned to face him. "What do you mean they have no fuel?"

As Sol pushed Lura through the door, Tran whirled back around, scowling before the door slammed shut behind them.

Lura's tears flowed as Sol dragged her by the arm, zigzagging through the chaotic hangar toward the test pads. They almost couldn't hear Davi crying above the din.

"I'm sorry …" Lura's hand shook as she clung to his arm.

"Let's hope Aron's got the courier ready." Sol tapped three numbers into a security door and it rose into a ceiling cavity with a loud, whooshing sound. He ushered her down a dimly lit corridor.

"I don't know if I can let him go," Lura said, as she had over and over since the decree's release.

"If we want our son to grow old, we have no choice, love." Sol's practiced emotional burying failed him and his voice cracked as they moved past numbered doors toward Test Pad Seventeen-A.

The dark walls and floor of the narrow corridor absorbed what little light the reflector pads overhead provided. If Sol hadn't known the way, they would have progressed more slowly. But in moments, they stopped before a gray door marked Seventeen-A as Sol entered another key code into the security pad.

The door swung up and Sol rushed Lura and Davi onto the test pad, where Aron was busy double-checking the courier's navigation system. Mounted on the launcher, the courier appeared bigger and taller than it actually was.

Upon seeing it, Lura clutched Davi tightly to her chest and let out a gasp.

Sol squeezed her hand as his eyes met hers with as much comfort as he could manage. "Lura, we must hurry!" Tiny daggers danced and sliced at the surface of Sol's pounding heart.

"I've got the coordinates programmed. And I borrowed fuel for the sub-light drive from Station Thirty-Four," Aron said and Sol winced. "It should take them a while before they miss it."

Sol climbed a small ladder and examined the courier one final time. "Tran's already been alerted. Why'd you do that?"

"There was no time to go anywhere else," Aron said, his face registering alarm.

Sol motioned to the courier. "Let's get the engines prepped. They don't know where we've gone."

Aron and Sol hurried about the final launch preparations as Lura held Davi and softly sobbed. After a few moments, Sol stepped down off the ladder to join her. "He's going to Regallis, Lura. Aron checked it out himself. He'll be in the capital. Someone will give him a life we never could." Tears flowed as his hands caressed the feathery down atop his son's head.

"How can this be happening?" Lura said through her sobs. "We've waited so long for a child!"

Sol's arms wrapped around her, holding his family for the last time. "We have to have faith, Lura. God will protect him. It's time for him to go." He reached for Davi. Lura resisted a moment, then kissed Davi's forehead and surrendered.

His infant son lay so light in his arms—soft and warm. The eyes looked into his with total trust, but instead of cuddling with him as he wanted, Sol hugged the tiny boy to his chest and hurried up the ladder to the courier.

Placing Davi in the molded cushion, he wrapped the safety straps around him, put the life support pad in place, and turned it on. Its LEDs lit up bright green as it began to hum. The note Sol had written for whoever found Davi rested secure in the info pouch on the side wall. Everything was good to go.

Lura rushed up the ladder beside him. She removed the treasured necklace his mother had given her before their joining ceremony and set it beside their son. Since the ceremony, Sol had never seen her without it. Tucking the family crest emblem inside the blanket where it couldn't float free and scratch their son, he reached for the hatch, bending down as he did to kiss Davi's head.

"Always remember we love you," he said, the last words his baby son heard before the hatch closed over him.

Sol clasped Lura's hand and led her down the steps. He nodded as Aron entered the launch code in the computer, and they all moved out of range to watch.

The courier's engines ignited, whining as they rose to full power in preparation for launch. The room vibrated around them as the courier's engines shot out twin columns of orange-red flame, rocking the pedestal upon which it rested, before launching with a lurch up a ramp and into the clear blue sky on its journey to the edge of the solar system.

Sol wrapped his arms around Lura as she collapsed against him, sobbing and Sol's own tears refused to be restrained any longer. Then armed starport security forces arrived, surrounding them, as Sol glimpsed Tran's angry orange eyes peering in from the doorway and sighed, resigned.

# Chapter One

Why do they keep staring at us?" Sweet, fruity perfumes contrasted with stale sweat from gyrating bodies afflicting Davi's nose.

Farien nodded toward the dance floor and Davi realized all eyes in the Bar Electric were focused on them.

"I told you we looked good in our uniforms," he joked as his eyes turned back to his friends. After twenty-one years, he'd never gotten used to it.

Farien stood shorter by almost a foot than his two friends, but made up for it in a bulk that filled out his gray uniform. The shiny gold buttons and shoulder insignia appeared ready to pop loose at any moment. Yao was the tallest, thinner than the others. A humanoid from the planet Tertullis, he would pass for human if it weren't for his dark-orange-tinted skin and purple eyes.

"I think they're staring at you, Prince Rhii," Yao said.

Like an old habit, Davi forced a grin and waved casually, the crowd watching his every move. "And to think I felt like just another cadet at the Academy." He looked around. "Serve-bot!"

Metal feet pounding on the floor mixed with flashing lights and the electronic tones of a recent pop hit blasting through speakers overhead. The robot waiter waded through the crowd toward their table. Other cadets, a few officers, and regular citizens filled the dance floor and tables as identical serve-bots worked the room with drinks and food.

The serve-bot stopped at their table on one corner of the dance floor. "How may I serve you, sir?"

"A round of drinks for everyone, on me," Davi instructed.

"On you, sir?"

Davi chuckled. Bots' vocabularies were simple, practical, and devoid of any colloquialisms or idioms. "Bill it to the Royal Palace, please."

"I'd need authorization—"

Davi sighed, holding up his ID. The serve-bot scanned it, its facial

LEDs lighting up with recognition. "Right away, Prince Rhii."

Yao and Farien chuckled as the serve-bot hurried off.

"Come on, Davi, when are you going to drop the childhood nickname and use your real name, like a man. Xander sounds much more mature than Davi." Farien's face was serious, yet Davi couldn't help but laugh.

"It may be a nickname, but it's one I like."

Farien rolled his eyes. "Haven't you been teased enough over it? Do you want to be taken seriously as an officer? We're not kids anymore. We're going into the world as adults."

"Let the man choose his own name, Farien," Yao scolded. "No one's asking you to change yours even though it sounds a little feminine." Yao and Davi exchanged a look and laughed.

Farien scowled. "It's not feminine! It's a family name!"

Davi and Yao just laughed harder as Farien took a huge gulp of his beer.

After a moment, Yao turned serious again. "Now that you've made the public happy, how are you going to deal with the other crisis?"

"What other?" Farien asked.

Davi and his friends had come to the bar to celebrate graduating from the Military Academy. After receiving congratu-lations and hugs from their friends and family, the three headed off to Bar Electric to discuss their assignments and dream about the future awaiting them—which meant Davi had skipped out on the celebratory dinner planned in his honor at the Palace by his mother and uncle, the High Lord Councilor.

"They'll get over it." Davi dismissed it with a wave.

"When have they ever gotten over it?" Yao asked with a knowing look.

Davi sighed. "Yeah, they'll make me pay, won't they?" They both laughed. "Let's make it worth it then!"

"Vertullis," Farien muttered as he took another sip of his favorite off-world beer. "Babysitting slaves, great."

Davi chuckled and sipped his own beer. "What did you expect—some grand adventure?"

"No, but maybe at least an assignment on one of the distant planets with breathing apparatuses, aliens to encounter …"

"We can make our own excitement, as usual." Davi grinned at Farien. Farien rolled his eyes and laughed as they gave each other a high five.

"You'll be there supervising work crew guards. I get to be supervised by some newbie fresh out of the Academy like you," Farien complained, a glint in his eye. "Funny how your Uncle couldn't pull strings to get you a cushier assignment."

"You're a newbie fresh out of the Academy," Yao reminded him, shaking his head as Farien grinned.

"You can shut up, mister star-student-professor," Farien answered. Yao had received the most prestigious assignment of all.

Uncle Xalivar's explanation was that Davi needed to earn the people's respect, not just count on it because of his uncle's favor or position. But Davi did sometimes wish his uncle would relax a bit and use his influence on his nephew's behalf. He was High Lord Councilor after all.

Seeing his friends staring, he brushed it off and reached over to squeeze Yao's shoulder. "Yes, congratulations, Yao, it's well deserved. The Presimion Academy is a fantastic school," Davi said, proud of his friend. The ceremony had consisted of the usual speeches, and faculty aggrandizing, but Yao had won recognition for his skills with math and sciences, and Davi had received the leadership medal.

"Instead of serving alongside newbies fresh out of the Academy, he gets to prepare pre-Academy newbies." Farien downed the last of his beer in one long sip, wiped his mouth on his sleeve, and stood. "Anyone else want another round?"

Davi and Yao shook their heads as Farien ambled toward the bar.

"We'd better slow him down or there'll be trouble," Yao commented.

Davi motioned to the door as three girls they'd seen in the front row at the graduation ceremony entered. "I think the diversion we need just walked in."

Yao turned toward the doorway as Davi stood, making his way toward the three beauties. He approached their table and smiled. "You all look even better than you looked at the graduation."

"You remember us?" the dark-skinned one asked as the girls exchanged shy looks.

Davi laughed. "Of course. Who wouldn't notice you three?"

The dance music swelled forcing Davi to yell as he asked their names and chatted with them a moment. Then he offered them his arms. They giggled as they stood, two of them looping their arms under his as he led them back toward the table.

"You know who I am, right?" he asked as they neared his table.

The girls all nodded. "Of course, Prince," the dark-skinned girl said.

Davi preferred the rare woman who didn't, but he nodded and bent to kiss her hand as they stopped at the table where Yao waited.

"Yao, these beautiful ladies are Bela, Jaqi, and Vivi," Davi said, helping the girls with their chairs. They smiled at Yao, ogling his uniform as Bela and Jaqi sat on either side of him. *What was it about Tertullians that seemed so irresistible to women?* Davi took the seat next to Jaqi. The sweet scents of the girls' perfumes found his nose and made him smile. Vivi sat down on his left, being sure to keep from touching him without permission as was custom with Royals.

"We saw you at the graduation," Yao said, smiling awkwardly as Jaqi slid her arm into his.

"Congratulations on your awards," Jaqi said. "You must be very smart."

Yao blushed. Despite the fact they seemed drawn to him, he'd never been as comfortable around females as his two friends. "Well, I studied hard."

"Yao's being modest. He's been appointed a professor at Presimion Academy," Davi interjected.

The girls exchanged a look, then Jaqi scooted closer to Yao, resting her head on his shoulder. They'd worn beautiful gowns at the ceremony, but now their form-fitting pants and low cut blouses flattered their impressive figures. Vivi's dark skin hinted at mixed racial blood, but Davi couldn't guess which.

Farien returned with another beer and smiled at Davi. "I see you two didn't waste any time."

"Meet Bela, Jaqi, and Vivi," Davi said as Farien took a seat between Bela and Jaqi.

"So pleased to make your acquaintance," Farien said, as he put his arm around Bela. She smiled, snuggling up to him.

"Are you going to be a professor, too?" Bela asked.

Farien grimaced as Davi and Yao stifled laughs. "I'll be serving on Vertullis, making sure our worker population continues to produce at proper capacity."

It came out with such bravado that Davi and Yao couldn't hold back and exploded with laughter.

"Oh, Vertullis. I always wanted to visit another planet," Bela said, looking impressed as Farien shot his guffawing friends an annoyed look.

"What about you, Prince Rhii?" Vivi smiled at Davi. Her accent was Southern with slow and precise words, a pattern he found both intriguing and attractive.

"Call him 'Davi.' He doesn't like formality." Ignoring sharp looks from Yao and Davi, he pressed on: "Our fearless leader will be leading the workers as well," Farien said, ignoring the fact that Davi would be his supervisor.

"Oh," Vivi said, her eyes sparkling. "I always wondered what the workers are like. I've never met one."

"Me neither," Davi chuckled. "We failed to offer you ladies libations. What can we get for you?"

As Davi turned to search for the nearest serve-bot, a group appeared in the doorway—Bordox and three of his cronies. A huge, hulking cadet with light yellow skin and a dark beard, he sneered as he spotted them, then led the way to a corner table across the dance floor. Davi frowned. He hadn't seen Bordox at Bar Electric in months. *Why today?*

His mind flashed back to an incident at the Academy after he'd beaten Bordox on the flight simulators. Bordox had let slip about a rumor claiming the "royal prince's blood wasn't so royal"—an attempt to rile Davi up and create a distraction.

Davi and his friends had demanded to know what Bordox meant.

"Who'd have known you're so fond of folk stories, Bordox."

"If it's a folk tale, I guess you're the folklore prince," Bordox had cracked. "A starport rumor about a baby who arrived in a courier craft from the stars and landed near the palace, adopted by a lonely princess with no offspring." Then he and his friends laughed loudly.

Farien had wanted to tackle him, but Yao and Davi managed to hold him off. It took their professor threatening to charge Bordox with impugning the reputation of another cadet without cause to end the incident, but Bordox had never really let it go. From that day forward, he and Davi became fierce rivals at everything. Bordox was not as smart or coordinated, and far less likable than Davi, but they each had their crowd and were very competitive. Since the incident, each set his goals of achievement at a level designed to ensure he could better himself over the other.

Davi sipped his beer and reached down to finger the necklace he'd worn around his neck since childhood. His mother had given it to him, insisting he never take it off, even though the symbolism of it was lost on him. He'd never gotten around to asking her about it, but he'd never seen another like it, and he knew many regarded it as a symbol of his Royal heritage.

"Would you like to dance?" Vivi's question broke him out of his reverie. He spotted Farien and Bela out on the dance floor, and Yao had taken Jaqi's hand and was leading her there.

Davi stood and extended his hand to Vivi. "Absolutely. I thought you'd never ask!" Vivi laughed and took his hand as he led her to an open spot on the floor.

They hadn't danced long when Bordox and his friends came onto the dance floor. Not finding immediate partners of their own, they began tapping the shoulders of other men, looking menacing if they showed any reluctance. Then, paired with the former partners of the frightened men, they maneuvered themselves over to the area surrounding Davi, Farien, and Yao.

Davi and his friends danced as if nothing mattered until the song ended, then Bordox smiled and leaned close to Davi. "So, folkloric prince, what assignment did you draw?"

"It's nothing as glamorous as yours," Davi replied, doing his best to ignore him. The music started again and Davi and Vivi resumed dancing.

"Lieutenant of the Lord's Special Police," Bordox responded with pride. The LSP was indeed a respectable assignment. Only the cadets deemed most loyal and sure to serve with lifelong honor at the High Lord's beck and call would ever be chosen. It didn't hurt that Bordox's father, Lord Obed, ran the LSP.

"We're going to Vertullis to keep the workers in line," Farien said, breaking the lull.

"Glorified babysitters. I wondered if they'd let you three do any real work," Bordox replied as he swung his reluctant partner around them. The girl seemed too afraid to do anything but try and keep up.

"Yao will be teaching math and sciences at Presimion Academy," Davi responded.

Bordox's smugness faded a moment, before he recovered. "Presimion, well, at least one of you was smart enough to draw a real assignment."

Davi wanted to reply but Yao and Farien maneuvered their dates between him and Bordox. He did his best to maintain his composure, but Bordox had gotten him fired up.

"Are you hungry?" Vivi asked as the song ended.

Davi smiled. Not many girls would be so direct knowing who he was. He liked this girl. "Yes, I am, as a matter of fact. Would you like to order something?" She smiled, then nodded and he led her back to their table. Farien and Yao followed with the others.

As he helped Jaqi into her chair, Yao leaned toward him. "Don't let him get to you. It's all petty jealousy. You've always bested him at every challenge."

Yao's eyes met Davi's as Yao slid into the opposite seat. Davi smiled, calming the raging storm within. It was true. Despite the constant challenges, Davi had always come out ahead. Bordox was still looking for an opportunity to prove himself better. Davi sighed, as he glanced over the menu. Perhaps Bordox's LSP assignment would keep him off their backs. At least Bordox could feel superior for the moment, if he wanted. He didn't have to know that Davi would have turned down the LSP if he'd been asked. It held little interest for him.

Davi saw Bordox motion for a serve-bot, as he and his companions requisitioned a nearby table. They threatened the occupants, who stood and hurried for the door, while Bordox and his friends helped themselves to the food and drinks the party left behind.

Davi glanced over to where the bar manager and bouncer-bot stood watching the events unfold. "Aren't they going to do anything about it?"

"His father's head of the LSP, remember?" Yao said. "They can pull bar licenses whenever they want."

Davi started to stand but Farien reached over and pulled him back down into his seat. Both of his friends shot him warning looks.

"Maybe you ladies would like to find somewhere more romantic to dine?" Davi suggested.

Their dates smiled. "That would be nice," Vivi said.

Davi and his friends stood, taking the ladies by the elbows and leading them toward the exit.

As they waited beside the air taxi post outside, Davi glanced through the Bar Electric's window and realized that Bordox and his friends had abandoned the requisitioned table. The blue air taxi arrived and Davi's group climbed onto the two benches behind the cab-bot driver. As the door shut, Bordox and his friends appeared at the taxi stand, waiting impatiently for another taxi.

"He never gives up, does he?" Farien asked.

"Let's make ourselves hard to follow," Davi replied. "Taxi, take us to the starport please."

"Of course, sir," the cab-bot's humanoid head whirled around to face front again and steered the auto taxi into the flow of traffic.

Their dates' faces lit up. "The starport, really?" Jaqi said.

"We're gonna take a little tour before we head to the restaurant," Yao said.

The cab-bot consisted of a torso with two arms and a head, on which LEDs lit up when it talked, attached to a seat facing the control panel at the front of the air taxi. Created to take over simple tasks like answering phones or loading cargo, newer bots now performed even more complicated tasks, including some trusted with the safety of humans.

Davi relaxed as the air taxi turned between a row of buildings and rose up onto the main artery running through Legon, the capital city. While Davi and the others enjoyed the ride, chatting with their dates, the auto taxi executed a few more twists and turns on the transportation corridor before turning onto an off ramp marked with signs for the starport.

"You're not gonna fly us to some remote star restaurant, are you?" Bela asked.

"Not really. We're just trying to lose our friends," Davi answered as the air taxi threw him forward hard against the safety bar and he grunted as their dates cried out in surprise. Then there was another bump as something hit them from behind.

They all whirled around to see another air taxi with the cab-bot disabled and Bordox at the wheel.

Farien cursed.

"You've got to be kidding me," Yao muttered.

Davi turned to the cab-bot. "Please outrun that taxi and take us to the north shore."

The cab-bot's facial LEDs lit up in the shape of a smile. "I am attempting to adjust our velocity, sir."

The taxi jerked as Bordox rammed them again. Davi leapt over the safety bar and pulled the manual override lever, pushing the cab-bot to one side and placing himself at the controls.

"Do you know how to drive this?" Vivi said, her face pale. Neither of her friends looked much better, tensed, and holding onto hand rests like their lives depended on it.

"Davi's the top pilot in our class," Farien said and smiled.

"Let's see how I do on the ground." Davi began pushing buttons, bringing the air taxi to a much faster speed.

Bordox launched another run at them, but Davi braked, and then slid in behind him, taking an onramp back up onto the air highway overhead. As he turned onto the onramp, Bordox's frustrated face appeared in the rearview mirror. His bulky body looked ridiculous behind the wheel of the air taxi. His dark beard couldn't hide his aggravation as he struggled to turn the air taxi around.

As they merged into traffic, Davi couldn't see Bordox behind them.

"Maybe we lost him," Bela said, hopefully.

"I doubt it," Yao said as he and Davi exchanged looks.

In a moment, Davi saw another taxi racing up from behind. "Here he comes."

Davi weaved their taxi in and out of traffic, trying to keep Bordox at a distance, but the other air taxi continued to close on them.

"What's his problem anyway? Why won't he leave us alone?" Vivi said, her voice shaking.

"It's a long story," Davi replied, braking and bringing their taxi in behind the other. "Who'd have thought he'd fall for that twice?"

Yao and Farien laughed as Bordox hit the brakes, forcing Davi to dodge and bringing them side by side.

Bordox glanced over—his face a mask of bitter resentment. His friends stared at them with sneers of contempt. Bordox and Davi wove their air taxis through traffic, each trying to keep the other at bay.

"We've gotta get away from this traffic before someone gets hurt—" Davi was silenced by a jolt as Bordox slid his air taxi in behind theirs and slammed into them again. The windows around them cracked loudly as veins creeped out in all directions covering the panes.

"Better get us down to the lower airways," Yao suggested, "before the windows disintegrate."

Davi nodded and dove onto the nearest off ramp. Bordox followed. Now, buildings surrounded them, but the traffic had thinned. A group of barges plodded along ahead of them. He aimed the air taxi straight at the rear of one of them and accelerated.

"Do you know what you're doing?" Yao inquired as he leaned over the safety bar close to Davi's ear.

"Just secure everybody back there, okay? I have an idea." Davi said.

"May the gods help us," Yao answered, shaking his head. "You ladies might want to get into those safety harnesses now," he said, motioning to the girls, as he and Farien began strapping themselves in. As the girls grabbed for their harnesses, and Yao and Farien turned to help secure and adjust them, Bordox rammed them again from behind.

The windows in both vehicles shattered, glass exploding around them with a deafening crash. The girls screamed. The wind blew against their faces, strengthened by their airspeed and pressing them back against the seats.

"Hold on," Davi shouted. Slowing a bit as they approached the rear barge, he suddenly accelerated and pulled the air taxi up over the top of the barge. His lips pursed with concentration, his movements were in perfect synch with the machine, just as if he were in his fighter's familiar cockpit.

Alarms blared from the speakers overhead. "Warning. Violation!" a computer voice screamed.

"Is this even safe?" Jaqi screeched.

"He knows what he's doing," Farien assured her. Both he and Yao showed no signs of fear or tension.

Bordox's air taxi cut across the incoming traffic lanes, zipping around the barge as Davi slipped between the two barges. In seconds, Bordox had squeezed in behind them again.

"I thought Bordox sucked at flying?"

"I guess he's been practicing," Farien said with a shrug.

Davi saw the first barge enter an intersection as Bordox accelerated toward them, and smiled. He had a plan. When the air taxi's front passed the corner, Davi made a sharp turn, whipping everyone to one side, and landed safely on a corridor to the side as the girls cried out in surprised protest.

Bordox's air taxi accelerated straight into the back of the second barge. Bordox and his friends looked shaken and confused, covered with blue Daken feathers from the barge's shipment of the frightened, squawking birds.

Davi and his friends exchanged high fives, laughing. "That ought to hold him for a while."

They watched as Bordox struggled to stand despite the slippery feathers all around him. His eyes met Davi's, his hateful stare barely visible amidst the feathers dangling from the sweat on his face.

"He doesn't look much different than he did before," Farien joked.

Yao and Davi laughed.

"Can we please get out now?" Vivi asked, trembling.

"Just a few more minutes. We know a great place on the north shore you ladies will love," Davi said casually, inwardly relieved as he accelerated again and turned onto another corridor.

The High Lord Councilor's Palace stood atop a rise at the center of Legon. An imposing landmark composed of white buildings of various shapes and sizes; it offered an unobstructed view of the entire city. When Davi arrived, he headed straight for his suite.

"Your uncle is not very happy with you for skipping your celebratory dinner." His mother's voice stopped him outside the lift. He turned as Miri approached him. She wore a beautiful evening gown, with light skin and light blue eyes which radiated warmth. Davi saw the disappointment in her frown.

Raised by his Uncle Xalivar to act like an officer, Davi had been told time and again he'd command great armies. Like all sons of High Lords, he'd followed the prescribed course of schooling and training, excelling in almost all of it. He'd risen to and stayed at the top of his class in every subject and every training regimen, such that any failure in discipline had become unacceptable to his mother and uncle.

"I'm sorry, mother. Yao, Farien, and I wanted to celebrate in our own way." Davi wondered what it was like to be an ordinary citizen of the Borali Alliance. Did they have more fun than he did? It's not that Davi didn't appreciate all the advantages his life had brought him, but always having to meet others' constant demands wearied him.

"The Vertullian ambassador was anxious to meet you. She might be very helpful to you in your new assignment," Miri responded, her voice softening from its previous scolding tone. He knew she adored him too much to stay mad at him for long, and the adoration was mutual.

"Is she staying at the palace? Perhaps I could meet her over breakfast," Davi said, as he leaned in and kissed her cheek.

"If you survive your uncle's wrath," she said, smiling.

Davi shot her a sheepish grin. "Maybe that can wait until morning, too."

"I hardly think so," said Xalivar's top aide, Manaen, from behind them. "Your uncle is requesting your presence in the throne room."

Davi and Miri turned to see Manaen standing in a nearby doorway. A member of Idolis' second most popular race, the Andorians, Manaen was tall and thin with blue skin and red eyes.

"How did he know I'm here?" Davi muttered, but he already knew the answer.

As always though, Manaen faithfully offered an explanation. "Little goes on at the Palace without your uncle's knowledge."

*Or permission*, Davi thought, but he kept it to himself.

"Of course," Miri said, motioning to Davi to go with Manaen. Davi turned with a sigh and followed Manaen back through the door. Miri followed close behind.

They stopped in a corridor. Each wall bore the shield of the Borali Alliance in embossed gold; a large door rose before them. They stepped inside the ornate throne room. The bejeweled throne stood centered on a raised dais set a few feet out from the far wall. A series of support pillars lined the sides of the long room with space in between for seating guests. The throne and the floor featured the same seal they'd seen in the corridor outside. As many times as he'd been here, Davi still found it impressive.

The High Lord Councilor waited beside a large window, staring out at the city, dressed in a gold robe with a white collar and cuffs. In the center by his neck lay the jewel known as the Lord's eye that matched a similar but larger jewel embedded in the center arch at the back of the throne. Shorter than Davi but taller than Miri, he had a dark beard.

Manaen stopped in the doorway, awaiting instructions as Miri and Davi moved into the room, a long, red carpet cushioning their steps. The carpet ran in a rectangular line to each corner then continued around pillars lining each side and ended behind the throne—creating a complete square frame around the room.

Xalivar turned to face them. Instead of angry, his brown was wrinkled and there were circles around his eyes. He motioned to Manaen. "That will be all, Manaen."

Manaen offered the expected salute with crossed fingers over a fist, then turned and exited, the door sliding shut behind him.

"The Vertullian ambassador was most disappointed she didn't get to meet you," his uncle said immediately.

"So mother explained. I'm sorry uncle. Perhaps over breakfast—"

"I decide the agenda in my palace, Xander. Not your mother, or you," Xalivar responded. The anger in his tone surprised Davi.

Davi's given name was Xander Rhii, son of Princess Miri Rhii, sister to Lord Xalivar, the High Lord Councilor of the Borali Alliance, but, for some reason, his mother had always called him Davi. He'd grown quite fond of the nickname himself. All the men in the line had names beginning with X—Xander, Xalivar, Xerses, Xonas—but Davi stood apart, making him unique. Davi had never been one to follow the crowd. In the court of the High Lords, it was hard to be unique.

While Lord Xalivar was a revered figure, both loved and feared by many throughout the Alliance, to Davi he had always been his kind, but sometimes stern uncle. It wasn't often their conversations reached the present intensity.

"You would do well to show proper respect to those who can help your advancement," Xalivar continued.

"Why is he being sent to oversee workers anyway?" Miri interjected. "It's a waste of his skills." She surprised Davi with the anger on her face. He hadn't realized she was against his assignment.

"I cannot afford to play favorites. He has to work his way up like everyone else, if we want to take him seriously and accord him the proper respect," Xalivar replied, softening somewhat.

"He is not like everyone else," Miri said.

"He is not yet a Lord, sister. Don't forget it."

"He will be," Miri held firm.

Xalivar looked at her as if trying to understand her concern. "You've never been to Vertullis. Service there is a respected part of officer training. Most graduates spend some of their career there," he said. "Why are you so fearful of it?"

Davi chuckled as he watched them. No matter what, they would always be brother and sister. His mother had always been gentle and soft with him, while Xalivar had been tougher and more serious, although he'd never lived up to his reputation among the other cadets as ruthless and cold. At least not with Davi. Many rumors continued to float around about his uncle, but Davi had always found them hard to believe.

"I welcome the assignment, mother," he said, hoping to put her at ease.

"You see? The boy knows something about honor and responsibility," Xalivar said with pride.

"He is no longer a boy," Miri said.

"All the more reason to not treat him as such," Xalivar chastised her.

Miri wilted. They all knew it was an argument she could not win.

"I will do my best to serve with distinction befitting our family," Davi said, hoping he could meet their expectations.

"We have no doubt you will. Perhaps you will also remember that gallivanting with your young friends—and using auto taxis for playthings—is not the proper behavior of an officer, especially a prince."

Davi glanced down, embarrassed. Somehow his uncle always seemed to know everything.

"You are quite lucky no citizens were hurt."

"Bordox was provoking us," Davi said.

"There are better ways to deal with your petty rivalries," Xalivar said, shooting Davi a stern look which stopped him from responding further.

"What happened?" Miri asked.

"Nothing to concern yourself with. Two auto taxis needing repair. A few soiled uniforms," Xalivar explained.

"None of them ours," Davi added with a smile.

Xalivar's eyes narrowed as he frowned at Davi. "You'll be having breakfast with the ambassador at nine sharp. Don't be late," he said.

It was more a warning than a request, Davi noted. Still, Davi suppressed a smile at the concession. "Yes, High Lord Councilor." He formed a fist and placed his other hand with crossed fingers on top.

Xalivar gave a slight nod at the salute as Davi turned and marched toward the door. "Congratulations on your awards today, Xander. We are very pleased," his uncle said as Davi waited for the door to open.

"Thank you," he responded as the door slid into the ceiling. Davi turned back to the corridor, his face beaming with pride, and marched out of the room.

Xalivar watched his nephew go, pride swelling within. His sister's son was the closest thing he had to a son of his own, his only heir. Up until today's events, everything had been proceeding according to his plans. Xalivar had long known he would train Davi as his successor, but the rebellious streak Davi had demonstrated today concerned him. He would have to keep a closer eye on things to ensure that kind of behavior didn't continue.

Miri kept watching him as the door slid shut behind Davi. "I need him near me," she said.

"I can arrange accommodations for you on Vertullis if you wish," Xalivar said.

Miri frowned.

Xalivar ignored her and pressed on. "It's the planet nearest to us. He will be well protected by my officers. If he is to be my heir, he must know about all aspects of the Alliance. And he must be able to gain respect on his own, not by relying on my power."

"He has a kind spirit," Miri said.

"Kindness is not a luxury rulers can easily afford," Xalivar said. Miri was too soft. "Perhaps this experience will disavow him of his fantasies. He could use a dose of reality."

Miri blanched, turning defensive. "He's not like you," Miri said. "He will never delight in their oppression."

Xalivar shrugged with disinterest. His failure to mold Davi into his own image was something she treasured rubbing in Xalivar's face. Miri was one of the few he would ever allow to be so direct with him. "Delight is not required, only recognition of the way things need to be."

Miri sighed and walked toward the door. Xalivar suspected his sister hoped her son would never be the kind of emperor he was. There had been many conquerors in the line preceding him, but Xalivar took special pride in his reputation as ruthless and arrogant. Except for Miri and Davi, no one dared question him on even the most routine of matters, and Xalivar liked it that way.

There would be no place for weakness in running an Alliance. One had to be firm and decisive, and given time, it would come as easily to Davi as it had to him. With the endorsement of the Council of Lords, Xalivar's family had led the Borali Alliance for generations. It ran in their blood.

Xalivar turned back toward his private suite, ready for some rest after a trying day. Davi would have to get used to that, too. The days of a ruler were full and demanding. Perhaps the assignment he was about to undertake would serve Davi well. He'd never understood his sister's insistence on using the nickname which even Davi himself seemed to prefer. The men in his line all had honorable names and Xander was quite respectable. He sighed, shaking his head. That too would have to change.

At breakfast the following morning, Davi joined Miri, Xalivar, and other distinguished guests. He sat next to Sinaia Quall, the Borali Alliance's Ambassador to Vertullis—who was less of a diplomat and more of an overseer in this case. A short, dark woman with her black hair in a bun, she chatted with him about the situation there, filling him in on the background and details about the planet he didn't already know. In the end, Davi found her charming and informative and appreciated the opportunity to get to know an important official on whom he could call if the need arose. Sinaia in turn assured him she would look after his well-being during his assignment there.

After he excused himself, Miri took him aside. His shuttle would depart in a few hours and he knew she wanted some mother-son time before he left. As they arrived in her chambers, she seemed overwhelmed with sadness.

"Mother, I'm worried about you," he said, noticing for the first time new lines around her eyes, the distance in her stare.

"You're worried about me? I think I'm the one who should be worried," Miri said, refusing to meet his gaze. Her eyes reddened as if she were near tears.

"Why? I graduated near the top of my class. I have been through years of training preparing for this. Uncle has a lot of people looking out for me. I know I will make you proud."

Miri smiled. "You've never done anything but make me proud, Davi. You know I adore you."

Davi put his arm around her shoulders and pulled her close. "And I you."

She tousled his hair. "I wish your assignment wasn't so far away. I like you close by."

"It's one planet away. Come and visit any time."

"Of course, I will." She smiled. "Do you have it?"

Davi gave her an inquisitive look. "What, mother? The necklace?"

She nodded as he pulled the chain over his collar and let it dangle on his chest. The necklace was round and silver colored with a blue-green crest at its center. The four sections of the crest bore distinct images: laborers, soldiers, farmers, and priests.

"Perhaps you could leave it with me for safe keeping—a remembrance of my son to comfort me in your absence," she said, stroking it.

"You know how much it's always meant to me. It's one of the first gifts you ever gave me."

"I know, son, but so many things can happen out in the field. If you lost it …"

"I won't lose it, mother." She'd always been very protective of the necklace, but she'd never before asked him to give it up. Davi was puzzled by the sudden change, increasing his worry.

"I would feel better if I had it with me," she said, sniffling a bit.

"But you've always insisted I wear it. I don't understand. Are you so worried I won't come back?" Davi looked into her eyes, wishing he could find the words to ease her worry.

Miri rushed into his arms, embracing him. "Never say that! I can't bear it!" She held him tight, her voice cracking.

"I'm sorry, mother. It was supposed to be a joke!" Davi held her, trying to reassure her.

"Never joke about such things," she said with tenderness. "I love you, son."

"I love you, too, mother." He would miss these times with her when they were apart. Tears flowed from her eyes. Davi stood there and held her a while, the necklace pressed against his chest by her embrace.

The small temple attached to the Palace was empty, as expected, when Miri led Davi through the Royal family's secret tunnels. As instructed, a priest had prepared libations and vestments and left them at the altar for the Royal family's use. Davi couldn't remember the last time he'd been here, and he knew his mother didn't come often either. But today, she had insisted they offer prayers and tribute for his safety and success before his departure, and so they'd come.

The priests kept the temple clean, free of dust and other odors, though Davi's nose did detect the few types of incense that had been burned recently in tribute. The altar consisted of a small, marble platform with a triple staircase leading up to it, all broad and wide with overarching ceilings as befit one coming into the presence of higher beings.

Miri led him straight to the altar and knelt, motioning Davi to her side as she began putting on one of the two ornate robes in preparation for their offering.

Davi put on the other then knelt beside her and joined her in the traditional recitations that preceded any proper offering. "Nehes, nehes, nehes, Nehes em hotep, Nehes em neferu. Nebet hotepet. Weben em hotep …" Together, they recited the ancient words any Boralian learned from birth, and Davi gently lifted the carafe of red wine, holding it ready for when Miri wanted it.

Miri's recitation sounded sincere and passionate, but Davi had enough trouble remembering the words that he couldn't quite manage to muster even a semblance of emotion in support of his mother. But she didn't look at him or offer comment.

After the opening indroit, Miri accepted the carafe and launched into specific prayers, asking the gods for wisdom, strength, courage, and protection for Davi. She poured the libations on a small dish she'd set centered on the altar cloths, her eyes closed and head bowed, and Davi bowed similarly, but kept his eyes open. He had long ago given up devotion to his people's religion, which seemed far more like silly ritual to him than anything profoundly spiritual or connected to another realm. He just didn't feel anything when he participated in it. It was all ritual motions, words, and actions, but he experienced no spiritual connection to go with it, no matter how hard he tried. Still, it comforted Miri, so he did his best to project a spirit of support and love to honor her as she prayed.

*Would any of this matter?* He asked himself and then heard Miri reciting the closing words and joined her in offering the traditional four-fingered salute to the pantheon.

Miri's shoulders sank with her sigh as she finished and looked over at him, warmly. They embraced, holding each other for another moment, then slowly stood and headed back into the passages that would return them to the Palace.

Whether any of it had been worth the effort for spiritual aid, Davi had doubts, but the confidence it gave his mother was more than worth the time. He hoped it would carry with her throughout the days ahead after they parted. He let his love for her flow back through the embrace. At least he could offer her that.

Davi and Farien arrived at the starport a few hours later, their gray uniforms neatly pressed, and shook hands with Yao. He'd shared so many fun times with his friends, and Davi knew he'd miss having them around. After a few moments, he pulled Yao aside. "I need you to look after mother for me."

"Of course. Anything I can do? Is she upset because you're leaving?"

Davi sighed, raising his hands in the air as he took a deep breath. "Yes. More than I expected. She seems more weak and frail than I've ever seen her. I'm not sure why."

"She's always adored you and kept you close. I'm sure this is hard for her," Yao said.

"It's hard for me as well, but she's really broken up about it. She even asked me to leave the necklace with her for safe keeping."

Yao's eyes widened and he took an involuntary step back. "The one she's always been after you to wear? Did she have a bad dream about something happening to you?"

"I don't know. She wouldn't say. Just check on her for me, will you?" Their eyes met and Davi saw recognition there of his depth of concern as his hand reached down to touch the crest where it rested beneath his uniform.

"Every day, if you want," Yao replied, eyes locked on Davi's.

Davi clapped him on the shoulder. "I don't think it's necessary, but I trust your judgment."

Yao smiled and they embraced. "You take care out there, okay? I want to hear all about your adventures," Yao teased.

"Oh yeah, and you make sure those future cadets are up to standards, all right?"

Yao laughed. "I'll be as hard on them as I was on you two." He twisted his face into a fierce expression.

"Do us a favor and be harder on them, okay?" Davi said with a grin. He glanced over at Farien, who frowned, pacing beside the shuttle ramp. They both laughed and shook hands one last time.

"Let's get this show rolling," Farien said, glancing at his watch. "Let the adventure begin!" He clapped them both on the back. Yao shook

Farien's hand before he and Davi boarded the shuttle.

As the shuttle pilots prepared for launch, the engines hummed and ignited. Contrasting with the shuttle's white exterior, the interior was light gray. The cockpit held two black chairs facing a transparent blast shield, surrounded by controls. It was separated by a bulkhead from the passenger compartment which contained four rows of seats—two lining each exterior wall and two back to back down the center. Each had its own safety harness. The sole decoration was a large Borali Alliance emblem centered above the seats on the ceiling. The cabin smelled stale, used; not fresh and clean like the royal shuttles always did.

Davi strapped on his safety harness and began mentally reviewing what he knew about Vertullis and his new assignment. From what he'd been told the planet's capital city, Iraja, was far from impressive when compared with Legon, but Iraja was also one of the Borali Alliance's major starports and the key shipping and receiving point for agricultural products in the solar system. His heart raced in his chest. He'd never been off planet before.

The thirteen planets in the star system all varied in size and shape, the outermost and innermost planets being the smallest. Three of the larger planets had several moons. Vertullis had two. While Vertullis, Tertullis, and Legallis alone had atmospheres suitable for human life, due to Borali scientists' determination and skill with terraforming, all but one of the system's planets had been inhabited, though some with populations consisting only of a few workers and military personnel. The planets revolved around the two suns, Boralis and Charlis, in an unusual orbital pattern due to the effect of the twin gravities. Because of the limitations in terraforming science, the four planets nearest to the suns had been surrendered as viable habitats for humans. Of the thirteen planets, Vertullis was the sole planet which had a surface containing fifty percent forest, and it had one other distinction. It remained the only planet in the solar system whose native citizens weren't free.

Slavery was a subject on which he'd never formed much of an opinion. He valued his own freedom, and human beings, to him, had always seemed deserving of such freedom. But he had never met a Vertullian. He had no idea what they would be like. Perhaps after spending time there, he would understand better. They might be great troublemakers, lazy, even subhuman as he'd been told. Throughout history, they'd been the enemies of his people, but beyond that, he decided it would be best to wait and see. Regardless of what he thought of them, Davi determined to treat them with fairness and dignity. He had read stories of abuse by past supervisors and guards, and he would not allow such things on his watch.

The shuttle accelerated, forcing him back against his seat as pressure closed around his head and chest. He took deliberate slow breaths as he'd been trained and looked straight ahead, trying to relax. He hadn't been on a shuttle since his early days at the Academy, and even though he'd flown VS28 starfighters in training, he'd never been out of Legallis' planetspace. Whatever else happened, he figured it would be an interesting challenge.

As twinkling stars filled the windows and the shuttle settled into its flight path, Farien snored beside him. Chuckling to himself, Davi leaned back and glanced out at the black void of space. The blue tinged globe he'd always consider home receded rapidly as the shuttle broke orbit and arced away from its surface. He'd never seen the planet from space before. It was far more spectacular than any of the pictures he'd seen. A new phase of life was beginning. He'd been dreaming of this for a very long time.

# Chapter Two

There has to be something better than this! Two weeks behind a desk shuffling papers is not what I had in mind!

Since arriving on Vertullis, Davi's only excuse to get out of his office had been occasional forays to check on operations. His days consisted of report after report from subordinates and superiors: requests for upped production times, reports on incidents involving workers or fellow soldiers, etc. Despite his responsibility for numerous squads of men supervising farm workers in the region south of Iraja, his big adventure had turned out to be anything but.

Never had Davi so wanted to blast off an e-post to his Uncle begging him to pull strings and get him out of there! He cringed at the thought of how his uncle might respond. Xalivar never responded well to any sign of weakness. Davi's head hurt from thinking about it all. *Either my head's going to explode or I'm going crazy.*

The communicator beeped. A major from Administration had invited him on a tour to show him around. *Finally, a chance to get out of this office!* Davi pushed his chair back from his desk like a rocket and stood, hurrying to meet his host.

He met Major Isak Zylo at the shuttle port near the administrative offices. As Davi appeared, Zylo smiled and extended his hand.

"Pleasure to see you again, Captain." Short with broad shoulders, Zylo's light skin seemed bright against the grayness of his uniform. His red hair and beard were both sleek and well groomed.

"Please, call me Davi. I think there's no need for such formalities among officers when they're alone," Davi said.

Zylo smiled, an impressed look in his eyes, and relaxed noticeably. "Indeed. Call me Isak. Shall we be off?" As Davi nodded, Zylo turned quickly and led him aboard the shuttle. Moments later, the doors closed.

Unlike the shuttles Davi had flown in before, this shuttle had been designed for in-atmosphere tours like theirs. Except for the thin framework, its top half consisted of transparent materials several inches thick, enabling passengers to enjoy an almost three-hundred-and-sixty degree view of the world around them. Davi and Zylo sat on swiveling chairs atop a raised dais in the center of the shuttle, enabling them to turn in any direction at a moment's notice with just the flick of a foot. The Ensign piloting followed a major artery out of the city and headed toward the agricultural fields to the south. Now that Davi had set the informal tone, Zylo seemed totally relaxed, but Davi found himself nervous and excited. His stomach fluttered and his throat grew dry. Ironic, given that usually others were more unsettled in his presence than he was in theirs.

Downtown high-rises slid past as they left the starport then gave way to residential neighborhoods. Houses of all shapes, sizes, and colors surrounded them, the streets here noticeably less hectic than those of the city center. The constant chattering of people mixed with music blasting from electronic billboards floating overhead. Moments later, they reached the outskirts of the city and the landscape changed. His ears filled with the sound of his and Zylo's breathing, the shuttle's flight computer, red zinga birds' gentle singing and eight-legged insectoid amblygids' chirping, forming a pleasant drone.

As they entered the agricultural region, buildings stood further apart amidst great stretches of farms and grazing land. Transportation corridors ran throughout linking buildings to each other and to the capital. Workers tended herds of gungor and daken, while others ran harvesting machines.

From what he'd seen, the Vertullians lived up to none of his expectations. The workers didn't seem lazy or troublesome or at all subhuman. Instead, they performed their tasks as if they enjoyed themselves and required very little supervision. If there hadn't been soldiers guarding key points and supervising some of the work sites, he might not have even remembered the Vertullians were slaves.

As Davi watched the workers, Zylo smiled. "Have you had much experience with workers?"

"Not really," Davi said, turning back toward his companion. "Nothing beyond some reports."

"Ah, yes, the workers' reports," Zylo said, his voice rising in pitch as irritation flashed in his eyes. "'The quotas are unreasonable and unfair. The Alliance's demands are abusive.' You shouldn't give much credence to most of what they say. These people love to complain." He shook his head, his mouth crinkling with disdain at every word.

"You think there's nothing to them?"

"I think we should expect nothing less from a people like the Vertullians," Zylo said.

The Major's defensiveness puzzled Davi. He'd studied the history of animosity between the Vertullians and his own people, and from what he'd read, it seemed his people had often provoked the Vertullians. In any case, they'd never put up much of a fight. Conquered time and again throughout history, they'd fled the Earth and settled on Vertullis when their ship developed an engine problem. Upon discovering who their neighbors were, they tried to forget the past and sue for peace, but the Legallians conquered them again. They'd been slaves ever since.

The history books overflowed with stories about the laziness of the troublemaking workers, but Davi knew enough to suspect at least some of it was propaganda. He refused to form an opinion about them yet.

Desiring him to think for himself rather than simply conforming to society's views, Miri had arranged special tutors to expose her son to the writings of classic philosophers from Old Earth like Holmes, Locke, and John Stuart Mill. He'd read Martin Luther and Erasmus and many others. From these books, he'd come to believe in the inherent dignity of man and man's right to free will and self-determination. While he also believed in the superiority of the Borali Alliance—the greatest society in the history of humankind—his exposure to life on Vertullis had him wrestling all over again with issues he'd debated over and over in his youth.

It wasn't like he had anything personal at stake. He'd never known any workers, but they seemed as human as he was. According to his professors, their continual failure to defend themselves reflected on their validity and equality as men. Still, he found himself wondering how they'd come to lose the freedom he believed all men deserved.

As they passed a clearing, he took in rows of workers assembled beside a barn to watch as soldiers administered punishment to another worker. The guilty man had been strapped to some sort of electrical wires which disappeared into the barn. The soldier questioning him shocked him every time he gave a dissatisfactory answer. Davi flinched, averting his gaze as his eyebrows lowered and pinched together. It disturbed him to see such a thing out in the open.

Zylo's hand on his shoulder drew Davi's focus away from the scene he'd been watching. "Sometimes we have to make examples of them so the others will learn."

"What could he have done to deserve that?" Davi wondered aloud, trying to conceal his horror.

"He was born a worker. They may be human but, trust me, they are not as evolved as our people. No sense of responsibility. They need to be motivated," Zylo said. Conviction dripped from him like sweat.

A group of soldiers leaned against the barn and laughed as they watched. To Davi, it seemed less about serious discipline and more about entertaining the soldiers at the workers' expense, but having heard Zylo's acceptance of it, he held his tongue.

"You know the history, of course. The Vertullians have long been the enemies of our people. Inferior thinkers—they have only one god, no respect for power, no ambition. The work gives their lives meaning. Left alone they'd all be aimless with no real purpose or direction," Zylo said. It was the standard justification historians and pundits used for the Boralian's treatment of their ancient enemies.

Davi stared out the window as the shuttle flew past the clearing and into a small city called Araial, landing near the small downtown.

"I thought you'd like to see more than the agricultural areas," Zylo said as they stepped out onto the tarmac. "Workers are also employed in factories and maintenance in most of the cities."

The first thing Davi noticed was that the air here seemed lighter, clean and refreshing, unlike in Iraja itself or in Legon where he'd grown up. Only the hiss of the wind blowing through the trees pierced the calm around him—a silence like he'd never experienced before.

They walked along between a row of buildings with eight or nine stories, instead of the minimum fifteen or twenty found in Iraja or on Legallis.

"Araial has a population around one hundred fifty thousand. It's small, but nice as outer cities go," Zylo said.

Davi followed Zylo around a corner and saw two soldiers with a worker backed against a wall between two buildings.

"For almost a week now you've failed to meet your quota," the taller soldier said.

"I try, sir, I do. The new quotas are impossible," the worker pleaded, his voice shaking, his face filled with fear.

"The Alliance sets the quotas, not the workers," said the shorter soldier with a cocky grin.

"Your job is to meet them," the taller soldier added.

Davi watched the worker's eyes. He didn't appear to be making excuses. Instead, he appeared to be struggling to remain upright.

The shorter soldier poked him hard in the chest. "Did you think you could stop doing your work and keep making us look bad without any consequences?"

The worker shook his head, confused. "No, I—"

"Maybe we need to teach you a lesson." The taller soldier rolled his eyes as both soldiers grinned.

"No, please. I'll work harder," the worker said, backing away.

The taller soldier took a club from his belt and started banging it on the wall, inches from the worker's head. Wood splintered under the impact as nearby windowpanes rattled. The worker trembled in fear.

"You've said the same thing every day this week!" the taller soldier responded as he swung the club again and again.

Davi tensed, his nostrils flaring as he started toward them, preparing to interfere.

Zylo grabbed his arm. "Let them handle this!"

Davi was shocked. "They're going to beat him!"

"He probably deserves it," Zylo said, unconcerned. "We get nothing but trouble from these workers."

"Nothing justifies cruel abuse of another human being," Davi snapped, yanking his arm free.

"These workers don't qualify for the term 'human,'" Zylo said with growing irritation. "You might want to know the situation before you decide to interfere with our soldiers doing their duty."

"Their duty is to make sure the workers stay on task, meet their quotas—"

"Their duty is to do whatever it takes to maintain the workers' production levels and focus," Zylo's cheeks reddened as he shot Davi a reproaching look. "Maybe someone who's been on the planet only a couple of weeks should observe first before rushing in. Lord Xalivar's order authorized whatever's necessary to keep the workers in line. The Prince of all people should know these policies come from the top."

Davi did know but he'd never imagined anything like what he was seeing. "He didn't mean *this*," he said, matching Zylo's accusing stare. He hadn't known about this specific order. Could his uncle have authorized such barbaric means? He wanted to respect his uncle, yet what he had seen conflicted with what he knew in his soul to be right and just.

"Come on. There are other things I wanted to show you." Zylo grabbed Davi's arm and led him on past the soldiers across a well-groomed lawn. Soft grass bent with each step, cushioning his feet. Davi ignored the hand on his arm, realizing that here he was just another officer, not a Royal whom touching casually was forbidden by law.

Clearly, he had a lot to get used to.

Over the next two hours, Zylo and Davi toured a few factories and then the city works warehouse where workers bore responsi-bility for keeping the city's parks and transportation corridors in top condition—picking up garbage, clearing debris, and tending landscaping and plants.

At his desk again, late that afternoon, Davi couldn't get his mind off what he'd witnessed. He stared at a plant on the windowsill next to his framed diploma from the military Academy. They amounted to the only decorating he'd had time for. Sparse light reflected off the standard gray paint common to government offices. His standard chair sat next to a standard desk buried under piles of files, in queue for the file cabinet behind him. Occupying space between stacks of papers were his computer terminal and communicator. The blandness of the room matched his mood, though he couldn't keep his eyes off the plant, a gift from the ambassador he'd met at the palace. It stood as the sole living object in the midst of dreary desolation.

His mother and teachers had taught him principles of law and ethics, intrinsic human rights, and the fundamental value of life. His uncle Xalivar seemed far from sympathetic, and they'd often had hearty debates during which he'd learned his uncle had a different perspective on the world than his. Even though their discussions had always ended with respect and understanding, Davi couldn't bring himself to respect orders calling for such cruel abuse. Perhaps the rumors he'd heard from other cadets had some basis in fact. How could the uncle who'd been like a father to him have hidden such a dark side all these years?

He turned on his computer terminal and fired off an e-post to his mother. She would know the truth. It amazed him she'd never spoken about it before. Did she agree with what was happening?

The next day, Davi travelled out to the farm where Farien oversaw a team of soldiers who supervised workers. The farm itself was larger than Davi had expected with acres of land stretching off for miles and dozens of barns, warehouses and processing buildings, giving Farien a great deal of responsibility, despite his disappointment at not being assigned to a higher position. Neither one of them seemed to be living a high adventure, but at least Farien got to work at the heart of things. Though they hadn't seen each other since their arrival on the planet, Davi hoped to keep their relationship friendly, despite the discomfort either might feel at Davi being Farien's supervisor.

Sounds of livestock, humming engines, and whining servos filled his ears as Davi stepped off the shuttle. Fresh air filled his lungs, as he found Farien leaning against a fence, watching two soldiers load injured workers into a hospital shuttle. Davi took care to move up behind him unnoticed.

"Neglecting your duties, Lieutenant?" Davi said, smiling. The smell of bean plants and grain filled his nose.

Farien snapped to attention on instinct, his face falling as he expected to be reprimanded. "We had an incident with some angry bulls today." Seeing it was Davi, he relaxed.

Davi laughed, stepping up beside his friend at the fence.

"Nothing which would keep them off task for more than a couple of days at best," Farien continued. "Little more exciting than the paper cuts and headaches you supervisors are prone to, Captain."

"Stop rubbing it in, okay?" He would always consider them peers.

Farien shrugged, suppressing a smile. "What are you doing here?"

Davi motioned for Farien to walk with him. Farien turned to the soldiers by the shuttle. "I want an incident report by the end of the hour, okay? Get back to your duties." From the look on his face and his tone of voice, Farien enjoyed being in command. "What's up?" He turned back to Davi as they walked along the fence together.

Davi began filling him in on his conversation with Zylo the day before and the things he'd witnessed. "I'm wondering if you've witnessed any incidents of abuse," he asked as he finished.

"Well, it would depend upon how you define abuse," Farien said. "These Vertullians seem very lazy to me. We have a number of them here who don't want to pull their own weight and meet quotas."

"New quotas demanded by the Alliance or the same quotas they've had?" Davi frowned at Farien's lack of concern.

"What's the difference? We're here to follow the Alliance's orders, aren't we?"

Davi had spent the afternoon before reviewing files on the administrative computer bank. The complaints and issues in the reports almost all related to workers who had failed to meet their quotas or filed complaints about mistreatment by soldiers. Davi had looked into several and found most of the quota problems related to increased demands by the Alliance, and, in some cases, the health of workers. Men could only be pushed so far, but that didn't stop the soldiers from employing any means necessary to coerce the workers into producing higher and higher results, however. And the result was abuse.

"Some of the quota increases I've seen seem unrealistic to me. A man can only do so much labor," Davi said. "Especially when he's ill."

They moved past the fence toward a large barn. As they entered, a worker approached with a datapad, handing it to Farien. He read it over, then used the laser stylus to approve it and handed it back as it beeped to acknowledge his signature.

"Have you been out here to see the operation before?" Farien asked as the worker scurried away.

Davi shook his head and watched workers loading grain and cut stalks into various machines which processed them and sealed them into shipping containers on the other end. He stood there a moment admiring the compactness of the machines.

"The machines do a lot of the work. They're all run by computers. All the workers have to do is supply the raw materials. The machines always seem to spend more time than they should every day waiting on the workers," Farien continued.

"Is it because they can't get the raw materials here fast enough from the field?" Davi asked.

"Not from what I've seen. Some of the workers just aren't hustling," Farien said.

"Switch their assignments then and get workers who are," Davi said. It seemed an obvious solution.

Farien lifted his hand in a lazy attempt at a salute. "Yes, Mr. Supervisor."

"Oh, come on. You know I didn't mean it like that!"

"Look, if you're asking me if I've seen soldiers get a little aggressive from time to time, yeah, I have. I've even been tempted to myself," Farien said. "But nothing out of hand."

"You'd tell me if it was, right?"

"Come on, you know me better than that!" Farien's voice rose in pitch as he tensed, sounding a little hurt.

"Sorry. You don't seem to think much of the workers," Davi said gently while inwardly hoping he'd read his friend all wrong.

"That doesn't mean I don't know what's right," Farien answered.

Davi put a hand on his shoulder. "Sorry, I should have remembered who I was talking to." He trusted Farien, but Farien saw the world through a different lens, tending to be less focused on issues of right and wrong or justice, than Davi. The average soldier didn't have to think about such things. He simply had to follow orders. But Davi wasn't the average soldier. Royals had much different expectations upon them.

"Yeah, don't let your higher position go to your head, Captain," Farien snapped.

Stung by the remark, Davi removed his hand from Farien's shoulder.

Then Farien laughed and broke into a wide grin. He'd been teasing. "Wanna see more?"

"Aren't I supposed to be the one giving instructions here?" Davi asked, struggling to recover from the weight of the thoughts filling his head. They both chuckled. Farien offered a silly salute and led him back out toward the landing pad.

Farien took Davi on a tour of the facilities in a floater, which hovered above the ground by using the planet's gravity to manipulate the air. It was a pleasant sensation both from the vehicle's gentle vibrations and the breeze caressing passengers' skin as it moved. The farm setup impressed Davi a lot, and they witnessed no incidents of abuse. In fact, everything seemed to be running quite smoothly.

Afterwards, they ate in the soldier's mess at the back of the barn they'd visited earlier. They took seats across from each other at the end of a long table as workers served them plates of hot gungor meat and Vertullian white bean salad. The presentation was professional, and the service as well-handled as any restaurant. One worker delivered their plates as another provided cutlery and poured them drinks; each moving off in turn to wait on other soldiers.

"Well?" Farien stared across the table at him, anxious for his response.

"It's quite the operation out here," Davi said, munching on delicious bread made from fruit and nuts. "Very well organized."

"Like I told you, nothing out of hand." Farien replied as Davi glanced down the table to where a worker was pouring drinks for some soldiers. A soldier stuck his foot out as the worker backed up. The worker tripped, struggling to keep his balance as the pitcher flew, spilling its contents on the floor and the uniform of another soldier.

"Hey! You watch it, slave!" The angry soldier said, shoving the horrified worker as he stood and wiped at his soiled uniform with a napkin.

"I'm sorry, sir. It was an accident," the frightened worker said, bowing his head.

"Looked to me like he did it on purpose," said the soldier who had tripped him.

The angry soldier began shoving the worker. "It's the truth, right? You think you can ruin my uniform without being reprimanded?"

"Of course not. I tripped. I'm very sorry," the worker said.

"You don't seem sincere to me," the angry soldier said, grabbing the worker by his collar and pulling him close so their faces almost touched.

The worker trembled, eyes frozen wide.

Davi stood up, trying to control his anger. "Soldier, he already said it was an accident and apologized."

The soldiers turned and glared, their faces changing as they spotted Davi's uniform insignia. He hurried over, Farien close behind.

"These slaves show no respect," said the soldier who had tripped the worker.

"Perhaps you should have a medical officer check your leg to see if it suffered any damage when you tripped him," Davi answered, shooting him a stern look.

The soldier reacted with surprise at being caught. "Can I help it if he's not watching where he steps?" the tripper responded, still trying to pretend it was accidental.

"No, you can't control that. What you can control is how you treat workers. Any soldier who treats workers without dignity and respect can expect to be reprimanded," Davi said.

"Ah, come on, Captain. It's a little harmless fun," said the soldier whose uniform was soiled.

"Go get these soldiers something so they can clean up the mess." Davi motioned to the worker, who nodded and hurried off, suppressing a smile.

"That's a worker's job!" The angry soldier objected.

"Not today it isn't. You made the mess. You clean it up," Davi ordered as they both scowled. "If you want, I am sure I can arrange to make cleanup a regular part of your duties." He glanced at Farien.

Their faces became apologetic and they shook their heads. Davi returned to his seat at the end of the table.

As Farien took his seat across from Davi, he glanced back down at the shocked soldiers. "Don't you think you were a little harsh?"

"Don't you think that's unprofessional?" Davi said right away.

"A few men trying to have a little fun? Like we did at the Academy?" Farien crinkled his mouth as he finished.

Farien, Davi, and Yao had had their antics but never at the expense of the service workers. But Davi didn't correct him. "At the worker's expense! It's cruel and unnecessary. It's your job to ensure it doesn't happen again," Davi said.

Farien bristled at the tone as the worker returned with cleaning materials. He offered them to the soldiers, who stood there in disbelief. Seeing Davi and Farien watching them, their attitudes changed and they set to work on the mess.

The worker started to leave but Davi motioned for him to stay and watch a moment as the soldiers knelt on the floor and used rags to soak up the liquid, then twist it out into a bucket. One of them glanced up at the worker with murderous intent.

Davi stood and stared the soldier down as the timid worker slipped away.

On the way back to the landing pad, Farien remained silent and distant. As they arrived and stepped off the floater, their eyes met.

"Am I supposed to protect that worker from those soldiers now?" Farien asked.

"If any harm comes to him, I want them brought up on charges. Warn them personally."

Farien frowned at the commanding tone in Davi's voice. "Soldiers deserve more respect than workers," Farien said.

"Workers are human beings, too," Davi said.

"They're not like us," Farien responded. "You don't know. You rarely see them."

Davi stiffened, struggling to control his rising anger. He stopped walking and turned to Farien in disbelief. "Tell me you're joking."

"Come on, Davi, you know what I mean."

"Yes, I do believe my ears are working perfectly. Being our subjects doesn't negate their worth as human beings," Davi said, angry at Farien for having such a narrow mind.

"Soldiers and workers have different places in society," Farien said, irritated. "Ask your Uncle!"

Davi ignored the jab and controlled his tone. "All the more reasons why soldiers should be more dignified, above reproach. How can we ask more of our subjects than we ask of ourselves?"

Farien shook his head, disgust on his face. "I guess we just don't see things the same, Davi."

"I guess we don't." Davi said.

"Maybe if you were out here in the field instead of being stuck in some administrative office, you'd understand better what we have to deal with," Farien snapped.

Davi shot him a look and snapped back, officer to charge. "You have your orders, and I know you'll follow them."

"What're you gonna do? Take on the whole army over this?"

"If need be, yes," Davi said.

Farien shook his head. "Maybe Bordox is right and your royal upbringing is going to your head!"

Davi fought the urge to punch his friend. Coming from Farien, the comment stung. He took a deep breath and relaxed his arms before replying. "Make sure it doesn't happen again!" He turned and marched toward his shuttle, feeling Farien's gaze boring a hole in his back the whole way.

As his pilot flew them back to Iraja, Davi sat in silence on the shuttle, his shoulders sunken in defeat, replaying his confrontation with Farien over and over in his mind. Why had he gotten so angry? Farien and Yao were his best friends. They'd grown up together. Sure, he and Farien had different views on how the world should work, but it had never led to angry discussions like this. Besides, Davi was a royal, born of privilege. Why was he so concerned about the lives of the lower class? Justice and fairness aside, he had never known any workers before. It wasn't like he'd given it a whole lot of thought before his arrival on Vertullis. It seemed obvious his anger had taken Farien by surprise as well. He'd have to apologize as soon as he could arrange another visit.

After the shuttle landed, he spent the rest of the afternoon handling paperwork in his office, wishing he could forget what he'd discovered that day. His computer terminal beeped, notifying him of an e-post. He clicked on his inbox to find an e-post from his mother:

To: AgriCptSouth@Federal.emp
From: HRHMRhii@Federal.emp
Subject: Your concerns

My dear son:

Your e-post brings me to a day I knew would come but had long dreaded. I raised you to be an independent thinker, not dependent on the Alliance or your family for forming opinions. I wanted this for you despite the fact so many in our Alliance have never been afforded it, and I offered it knowing that someday it might lead you to some conclusions about our

Alliance which might cause you pain or discomfort. If this is the case, please believe I am full of regret, for you know I would never do anything to cause you harm. But you were born for leadership and raised to lead, and good leaders must be able to make hard decisions. That cannot be done in an intellectual box. This day has come faster than I had hoped, but here we find it upon us, and so, as I have always done, I will respond with honesty to your questions.

Your uncle doesn't see the world through the same eyes we do. This is the result of both his years of isolation as the leader of the Alliance and the natural development of his personality and knowledge through various experiences. Our father was a very difficult man; though please don't hear this as making excuses. He tolerated no failure from his children or anyone else, and I am afraid the harshness he passed down has manifested itself in your uncle even more than it existed in himself. Whatever the case, I fear—as time passes and various events come to light from which you have in the past been shielded for your own good out of a mother's deep love—that you will more and more find yourself coming into conflict with both the ideas and ethics by which your uncle guides himself.

I beg you to be very careful in how you respond to these revelations. He is, after all, the High Lord Councilor, leader of the Borali Alliance. Our armies, Lord's Council, and population are sworn through oath of loyalty to serve him. Any criticisms you may have must be handled with great discretion. You can feel free to discuss them with me through our encrypted e-posts, but be very careful. Your uncle has many friends and spies. If you express yourself too directly, I fear how he might respond. You are like the son he never had, and I know he loves you dearly. This doesn't negate his lesser qualities, by any means, but please keep it in mind before passing judgment upon him. I too have long been disappointed by the Alliance's handling of the Vertullis situation, but I beg you to understand there is not much we can do to interfere. This pattern was established long before us and has the backing of the highest reaches of government. I long for a day soon when we can discuss these things with more freedom in person. In the meantime, know you forever have my adoration and love. I miss you dearly, my son.

Love,
Your adoring mother

Davi sat at his desk, stunned. His mother had always been candid, but the content of her missive left him at a loss. He'd expected her to remind him of his uncle's love and urge him to not be hasty in rushing to judgment, but he'd also expected her to tell him he did not yet have the full picture to understand the reasons behind the decisions his uncle had made in regard to Vertullis. Instead, she confirmed everything he had discovered and been wrestling with. What now? He winced at the headache developing behind his eyes. He was a simple Captain, who shouldn't have to worry about such pressures, right? Yet he couldn't bring himself to let it go.

Miri was right. He would have to be careful. Xalivar would indeed have spies and most people in the Alliance were loyal to him. Davi needed to control his feelings and consider each move. Would he take on the whole Borali Alliance as Farien had said? Not even his status as a member of the Royal Family ensured success. He would be fighting an entire system and way of life for his people, and he knew few would support him.

*Slow down, Davi, and remember your place.*

Needing to get out of this office and distract himself, he decided to explore areas of the capital he had yet to see. After all, for the time being, this would be home. It might be a good idea to get to know his environment. He deleted his mother's e-post from the server and shut his terminal, returned the paperwork he'd been reviewing to his inbox and headed out the door.

Outside the noise of the city assaulted his ears. As the twin suns sank toward the horizon, the late afternoon light began to fade, dressing the transportation corridors around him in a mix of colorful light and shadows. Just breathing the outside air, despite the city's pollution, invigorated him. From the smell of chemicals and fuels to that of flowers, restaurant kitchens, animals and people, his senses worked overtime. Past the end of a long block of administrative offices, he entered the narrower corridors of a residential district. The area surrounding the Borali Alliance's offices had become prime real estate and contained some of the largest houses in the city, most occupied by off-world government employees.

A few corridors over, a tall security fence sectioned off that neighborhood from the adjacent one. On the far side, the houses changed noticeably: three story apartment buildings mixed with small dwellings, the landscaping sparser, the corridors narrower. He heard even more noise here than in the area around the government center. People bustled around the corridors past shopkeepers on sidewalks drumming up business. It almost seemed like earlier in the day, rather than early evening. In such worker neighborhoods, life began when the people came home.

He wandered, pondering the juxtaposition between houses which seemed run down set between pristine, newer dwellings on either side. In other places, a thatch-roofed house would have added plants or laser displays on the sides, its small yard kept tidy and fresh, while vines ascended the walls of sleek modern transparent aluminum dwellings with overgrown yards. Finally, he reached a point where the corridor made a sharp turn.

Turning the bend, he found himself in the market with rows of stalls and tents of all shapes and sizes, bustling workers and vendors. A few saw his uniform and tensed, looking at him with wary glances but most went about their business as if he weren't even there. The smell of various perspirations mixed with manure and fresh meats and fruits assaulting his nose.

Vendors offered everything from standard vegetables like green heads of lettuce, orange carrots, and shiny red tomatoes to more exotic ones like feruca, gixi, and jax—fruits from other parts of the solar system. Feruca was black with a thin skin and soft pulp and was often served with various sauces. Gixi, a round, purple fruit grown in orchards on Vertullis and Italis had a delicious, tender pulp and sweet juice. Jax were blue and oblong with crispy pulp and a taste which went from bitter to sweet during boiling. All had been discovered when colonists first emigrated here centuries ago and now were regular staples of their diets.

Other vendors offered livestock for sale, everything from blue daken and goats to quats and qiwi, a long antlered creature from icy Plutonis. Dark brown with white spots lining either side of their spines, qiwi stood waist high on Davi and had four long legs ending in black hooves. Their antlers grew up to forty centimeters out of their skulls. He also spotted gungors, the six-legged brown animals with yellow manes raised for their tasty meat. Davi moved on past as vendors hollered prices and argued with customers, while the various animals brayed and moaned around them.

As he neared a tent, someone poked his arm—a smiling vendor who appeared half-human and half-Lhamor, gesturing with his bottom two arms when he spoke, his forked tongue giving him a strong lisp.

"'ello, Capt'in, my frien', wha'ever you nee', I can ge' for you," he said with the accent of Italis and patted Davi's back like they had been lifelong pals.

*There's a reason others of your race use translators.* "No thank you, just passing through," Davi said with forced politeness, moving on through quickly.

The market fascinated him. He saw many species and products he'd never seen before, realizing how big the Alliance really was. He hoped someday he might have time to explore it. When he was younger, he'd dreamed of going on a starship to see the planets in the outer solar system—alien species, plants, animals, alien languages. He'd spent so much time in the office, he hadn't even bothered to discover what awaited him on Vertullis. He dodged another eager vendor and ducked into an alleyway. Quats moaned and darted out of his path, scattering the trash crowding the walls as they ran.

*Might as well see what the neighborhoods are like on the other side.*

Entering a corridor so narrow it was restricted to pedestrian traffic, he set about exploring. The corridor and buildings curved, making it impossible to see one end from the other. He walked past doors and windows of one dwelling after another. Separate units shared outside walls like one long building. The area appeared deserted. *Everyone must be at the market or already inside.*

A woman screamed around the bend ahead.

He quickened his pace, rounding the corner to see an Alliance Captain the size of an air taxi with a worker girl backed into a corner. His gray uniform was dirty and wrinkled, his hair graying around the edges. The girl looked to be in her upper teens, almost a woman, her stance determined even as she trembled. The Captain struck her across the face with the back of his hand and was preparing to do it again.

"Please," the girl pleaded, almost a whimper, "let me go."

"You'll go, when I say you can go," the Captain responded, his voice like poison.

Neither had noticed Davi creeping toward them along a wall behind them. As he drew near, his nose crinkled at the overpowering smell of the Captain. He reeked of sweat and alcohol. Not even the sweet pollen drifting off nearby flowerbeds could overcome it.

"What do you want from me?" The girl's eyes darted around, looking for an escape as he breathing increased with her panic.

"I want you to show me the proper respect." The Captain swung his arm, but instead of hitting her face, which she turned away, he grabbed the collar of her blouse and ripped it open.

She slid along the wall, trying to get away. "I'm sorry, sir. I didn't mean to be disrespectful."

"Workers like you are always disrespectful," the Captain said. "Stop moving and come closer." She shook her head as he grabbed her and pulled her to him, trying to press his lips against hers. She kept wiggling and pushing.

"I'm gonna teach you what it means to obey now, slut," he said. Buttons popped as he ripped her blouse again and threw her to the ground, climbing on top of her and trying to force her legs apart. She cried out, struggling to free herself.

Davi rushed up behind him, grabbing the Captain by the shoulders and pulling him off. "Enough, Captain," Davi said.

The Captain swung to his feet and whirled around, pulling free with a power that sent Davi stepping back. The sobbing girl picked herself up and cowered against the wall behind him. "Who do you think you are?" the Captain sneered.

"A fellow officer concerned with a peer's professional conduct," Davi said.

"I'm off duty," the Captain said.

"You're in uniform," Davi said.

"I guess this worker slut's not the only one who needs a lesson in respect," the Captain said, looking Davi over. He towered over Davi, muscles bulging from his jacket.

Davi stepped back, hoping the man had slow reflexes like everyone else when he was drunk.

The Captain swung at him and Davi ducked, throwing a fist into the man's gut. His fist throbbed like it had hit an iron wall. He groaned, gritting his teeth against the sudden pain.

The Captain laughed. "Is that the best you can do?"

"Run," Davi said as his eyes met the worker girl's. "Get away now!"

The Captain swung at him again as the girl backed away. "Where you going?" The soldier asked, missing Davi as he whirled and reached for her. Her blouse pulled loose into his hands.

Davi glimpsed a necklace around her neck with a blue-green crest at its center. The Captain knocked him to his knees with a blow he hadn't seen coming. The man remained calm, relaxed, as if it required no effort, while Davi gasped for breath and struggled back to his feet.

*Where are my friends when I need them?*

The Captain swung again, and Davi dodged to one side. "You need to learn to mind your own business!" Keeping ahold of the girl with one hand, he swung again at Davi's midsection.

Davi ducked to one side as the girl tried to pull free. His adversary found himself pulled in two directions but managed to grab Davi's collar and jerk him roughly off his feet.

As the Captain pulled Davi closer and closer, the girl bit the Captain, who yelled and flinched, letting her go. Davi tried to use the moment to pull himself free, but the Captain pulled Davi's uniform collar tighter, causing Davi to slip and fall away from him and into wooden double doors which cracked loudly as they splintered from the force.

Seeing the girl slipping away, the Captain chased after her, turning his back on Davi.

Davi needed some kind of weapon. He thought for a moment of his blaster, but the Alliance had laws and he could think of none which would justify shooting a soldier, especially not to save a worker. Besides, the Captain had a blaster hanging on his hip.

As he climbed to his feet and stepped away from the door, part of it slipped back inside the house behind him. He examined the splintered wood and began pulling free a section he could use as a club. Wood creaked and snapped as he pulled.

"Why are you doing this to me?" the girl screamed, as she continued dodging the Captain.

"Because you're a worker," the Captain said, grunting with satisfaction as he grabbed her again and glanced around for something to tie her with.

Davi ran up behind him with the board. Seeing him out of the corner of his eye, the Captain turned, raising an arm, as Davi swung the board down hard atop his head.

The Captain's arm deflected the board, sending it hard against the side of his head. Sharp pain filled Davi's fingers and hands at the force of it, as he struggled to hang on. The Captain froze and emitted a loud gurgling sound, releasing the girl and falling to his knees as blood poured from his ears.

Davi pulled the board away and saw that a large spike had entered the man's head at the temple. The Captain fell over face down and lay still as the salty smell of warm blood rose into the air from a widening pool around his head. *Oh my gods! I killed him!*

"Is he dead?" the girl asked, petrified.

Davi knelt beside his opponent, feeling for breath. The strengthened stench almost made him gag but he swallowed hard. "I think so. I don't know." The Captain's chest wasn't moving.

The girl gasped. Davi saw her pointing at his chest where his ripped uniform revealed his own necklace—an exact duplicate of the one she wore around her neck.

"Where'd you get it?" the girl asked.

"I've had it since I was a baby," Davi responded.

The girl's eyes widened as she turned and ran back up the corridor.

"Wait! Come back here a moment!" Davi stood, desperate to ask her more.

But her footsteps faded into the night.

Davi glimpsed faces peering at him from nearby windows and heard footsteps behind him.

A worker stood in the splintered doorway as it finally sunk in—he'd killed an Alliance soldier. Davi tensed again, his heartbeat matching the pace of his breaths. Then he turned and raced off into the night.

Davi took dark side corridors all the way back to his quarters, ducking into alleyways every time anyone approached. Gasping for breath until his lungs were about to explode, he ran as fast as his feet would take him, his soaked clothes sticking to his skin. *I hope no one got a good look at my face. How am I going to explain this?*

# Chapter Three

When Aron had informed her that the courier craft malfunctioned, Lura thought she'd never find breath again. She'd collapsed on the floor of her home as visions of every worst-case scenario clouded her head. Perhaps it had burned more fuel than Sol and Aron's calculations anticipated, running out and leaving her only son to die in orbit or forever drift in space. Could it have been struck by an asteroid and disabled, or worse, exploded? Maybe the life support had failed and Davi had died inside. They had no way to know if it had landed, because its tracking device failed to maintain contact with the computer at the depot. Sol had been working on the device the day they rushed to launch the courier. Her only son was gone forever!

Worse, Sol had been arrested for treason and taken away. She'd heard rumors he'd been sent to a science planet somewhere, but she had also heard talk of his execution. She never really knew for sure. Just like that, she was alone.

Aron took care of her, taking her into his home to live with his family and treating her like a sister. His children even called her "auntie." But when the attention of government spies on his own activities made it impossible for him to remain, Aron and his family had gone into hiding, leaving Lura alone again.

After her brother-in-law's death in a tragic incident with soldiers, her sister came from the countryside with her children to live with Lura. She welcomed them. After five years of loneliness, she loved having a family again, and it seemed as fine a life as a Vertullian could expect. She still thought of her missing son and husband, but those thoughts were more fond these days and less dark and disturbing.

The whoosh of the opening door drew her attention. It slammed into the wall as Nila stumbled through the opening, her clothes torn, her face bruised. Blood dripped from a cut on her forehead.

Lura gasped. "Nila! Are you okay?" She rushed to help her.

It took her niece a few moments to catch her breath but then she nodded. "Two Captains … One tried to rape me … The other helped … Had a necklace … Like mine." Nila reached through her torn blouse and pulled out the family crest just like one Lura had placed in the courier beside her baby son before it launched, taking him away.

Surely her niece was mistaken. "A Borali Captain with our family crest?"

Nila's eyes widened and she smiled with glee. "It's him, Aunt Lura! Your Davi!"

Lura stepped back, stunned. *Could it be, after all this time, God's finally chosen to answer my prayers?*

After she'd cleaned Nila up and put her to bed, Lura sunk into a chair, feeling like she'd lost the power to stand. She couldn't believe it! She'd long ago given up the dream of ever seeing him again, and yet, according to her niece, the son she'd lost so long ago lived across the city? *My Davi!* She thought. *Could it really be you?* She tipped her head back against the back of the chair and screamed.

Her first instinct was to run and embrace him but it might not be well received. The last thing she wanted was to scare him off. *He has the necklace, sure, but does he know who he is?*

In fact, she had to be sure it was Davi. What if someone else had somehow wound up with the necklace, having no idea of its significance? It would be dangerous for her to inquire too openly, exposing herself to scrutiny from any Boralian officer or soldier. Especially after what had just happened to Nila.

She managed to kneel on the floor beside the table in prayer, seeking God's guidance about what to do next.

The knock on the door of his quarters almost sent him into a panic. *Could they be after him already?* Davi sighed and raised his shoulders, trying to calm himself. It had been twenty-four hours since the Captain's death and no one had come. *You're just being paranoid.* Straightening, he opened the door to find a humanoid smiling at him.

"What are you doing here?" Davi asked with surprise as he immediately relaxed.

"Is that any way to great your best friend?" Yao said with a laugh. "Can I come in?"

Davi chuckled, stepping aside and motioning for him to enter. "Of course. I'm sorry. I wasn't expecting you. School on a holiday?"

Yao stepped inside and the door slid shut behind him. "In a manner of speaking. Your mother sent me."

*My gods! Word had gotten to her already?*

Yao smiled. "About your e-post."

"Oh," Davi said, trying to hide his relief. "Of course."

"She told me you're finding things here harder than you'd expected," Yao said, looking concerned.

"Yeah, well, it's not the glorified adventure we all talked about," Davi said. "You want a beer?"

"Sure," Yao said as he settled onto a couch, leaning back. "She filled me in a little. You want to tell me more?"

"Okay, but first, how's Presimion?" Davi asked as he opened the cooling unit.

Yao straightened involuntarily, his enthusiasm obvious. "It's pretty terrific, actually. I wasn't going to bring it up. Didn't want to rub in my good fortune in light of—"

"It's not like it's the end of the world," Davi said, closing the cooling unit and returning with two beer bottles. He handed one to Yao. "Let's call it a rude awakening to the real world."

"Ah, I see. Like a rite of passage sort of thing?" Yao took the beer and opened it with a familiar hiss both barely noticed, savoring its scent as he waved the neck under his nose. His face lit up with delight. "Mmmm. Been too long since I had one of these. Teachers aren't allowed to drink on Academy grounds." He closed his eyes and smiled as he enjoyed a long first sip.

"Maybe you should get out more." Davi uttered a satisfied sigh as if to say he drank these all the time, though he didn't.

"Maybe I should," Yao laughed. "I've missed you."

"I've missed you, too," Davi said, smiling and sipping his own beer again, as he settled into a lounge chair across from his old friend.

"How's Farien?"

"Oh, you know Farien. Give him a few men to boss around and a little freedom, and he's on top of the world," Davi said.

They both laughed as they pictured it.

"Gods help those poor soldiers," Davi said with mock horror and they both laughed again.

"The worker-soldier thing has been going on for generations, Davi," Yao said, cutting to the chase. "It didn't develop overnight, and it won't change that fast either."

"Have you ever met a worker?" Davi asked. Yao shook his head. "I know the history. But book learning and reality are not the same when you're staring a fellow human being in the face and one of you is supposed to be superior over the other by birth."

Yao nodded. "You don't think a Tertullian can relate? Your ancestors wrestled with this issue eons ago on Earth." Always a history buff, he read voraciously in his spare time—anything he could get his hands on from history to the sciences.

"Oh yeah? What did they do about it?"

"Well, much of the world outlawed it in the nineteenth century, but reports continued of slavery in various places almost until the colonists began departing for other systems," Yao said.

"Sounds like they never really found a solution," Davi said.

Yao shrugged. "Not totally, no. You realize you'd have to take on the whole Alliance?"

Davi smiled. Sometimes the three knew each other too well. "Farien said the same thing."

"How'd that conversation go?"

"Not well." Their eyes met and Davi saw Yao already knew what was coming. "He didn't seem to understand my feelings. To him, it's like a natural course of events. He's too busy seeing the workers' faults to see their humanity. He's bought the Alliance's party line one hundred percent."

"Well, we both know Farien's no great thinker. He's got a lot of qualities which make him an ideal soldier, but intellect is not at the top of the list. He probably hasn't given it much thought. Most soldiers never do. They train us to obey, remember?" Yao paused and looked at him as Davi nodded. "On the other hand, I do see his point. You're treading a dangerous line here. You could lose everything if you fight this."

Davi stood and paced, his body stiff with tension. "So you think I should just ignore what's happening, get on with my life?"

"I can't tell you what to do, Davi, but it's a big risk."

"Now you sound just like Farien," Davi growled and drowned the words with another gulp from his beer.

Yao's purple eyes softened to violet with sympathy. "Hey, I'm on your side here, okay? One man can't change an entire culture."

Davi wiped his lips on his sleeve and met his friend's eyes again.

"This man has to try."

Yao sighed, sinking back into the couch again. "Why?"

Davi stared at him a moment, anger mixed with disgust. But Yao wasn't the bad guy. *You've got to tell him.* Ignoring his internal voice, he shrugged.

"Have you spoken to Farien since?" Yao asked.

"No. There hasn't been an occasion."

"Maybe we could pay him a visit," Yao said. "Be good to have the three musketeers back together again." Yao loved references to the classics. Along with history, he'd read many novels.

"Sure. Of course …" Davi's voice trailed off as he looked away, lost in thought. *Should I tell him?* He needed to confide in someone before he burst.

Yao's brow furrowed, his eyes narrowing. "You look as if you haven't slept. Your eyes seem as if they're carrying the weight of the world. What haven't you told me?"

*He's one of the only people you can trust*, Davi thought. If nothing else, he needed to talk through his options. After all, there had been a few witnesses, and sooner or later somebody would talk. *But he's a loyal officer of the Borali Alliance*, he reminded himself.

"Come on, Davi. It's me," Yao said, his eyes pleading as he sat forward with genuine interest again.

Davi could hold it in no longer. He recounted for Yao the events of the night before with the worker girl and the Captain.

When he'd finished, Yao looked stunned. "My gods! You're sure he was dead?"

Davi looked at the floor.

"They saw your face?"

"I don't know. It was getting dark, lots of shadows. But what if they did?" Panic set in again as Davi thought about it and every muscle in his body tensed.

"It was self-defense," Yao said as he deliberated. "Given your status and reputation, I think they'd have to take that into account."

"You know the law. I was defending a worker."

"I thought you said you weren't having much of an adventure here," Yao teased, trying to lighten the mood as they always did when one of them was under stress.

"What I said was not the glorified adventure we'd all talked about," Davi reminded him.

They both laughed as they flashed back to the naïve daydreams of their Academy days.

"Amazing how grown up you can feel a few months after graduation," Yao said.

Davi nodded.

"We've got to ask your mother for help. She has the power to protect you."

"I don't trust the communications channels. The government has spies everywhere," Davi said, but in that moment there was no one he wished he could talk to more than Miri.

"Sounding pretty paranoid for an officer of the Alliance," Yao said, but from the look in his dark eyes, Davi knew he understood. "Come on, let's fire off an e-post to Farien. Maybe he can come here and meet us. He might enjoy a night away from the field."

Davi chuckled, stood and led him to a nearby desk, where he sat again and turned on his terminal. "There'd sure be a lot more to do here than where he's stationed." He began typing an e-post as Yao looked on.

Wearing the best clothes they owned, so they wouldn't look like workers, Lura and Nila wound through the worker neighborhoods past the security fence and into the free neighborhoods of the city. They hung to the shadows as the twin suns peaked over the pinkish violet horizon to the west, hoping no one would try and stop them. They carried fruit as a gift for the barracks and hoped to catch a glimpse of Davi. Lura couldn't resist. Her heart had been skipping in her chest ever since Nila told her about the necklace. If this might really be Davi, she had to try. She'd waited so long, almost given up hope. Nila had insisted on coming along.

As they crossed the corridor from the residential districts, the government area looked deserted. The hum of transports and usual city smells filled their senses, but it seemed they'd chosen a good time to come and not be noticed. Lura had no idea how they would get the fruit to the soldiers without drawing attention, or even how she might be sure Davi himself would receive some fruit. But her mind was racing even as they walked the long block alongside the Alliance offices.

An air taxi pulled to a stop beside a small side gate up ahead, and three officers stepped out onto the sidewalk. Two were human, the third a dark humanoid with purple eyes.

Lura's heart began racing as she saw their faces. *It's him! My God! He looks like his father at his age!*

He wasn't the tallest of the three, but the middle one, average height and thin, so dashing in his uniform, with neatly combed light brown hair, and tanned skin. She fought the tears which welled up in her eyes. *Maybe we can talk to him.* The urge was so compelling.

She started rushing toward them, but Nila reached out and caught her arm, whispering urgently, "Auntie, wait!"

The three officers stepped through the gate as Lura and Nila approached. Two guards intercepted them, bur Lura's excitement got the better of her and she pushed forward against them, straining for another glimpse. *They're walking away from us. What can I do?*

"What's your business here?" the taller of the two guards asked, shoving Lura back.

"We brought some fruit for the soldiers," Nila said, her voice wobbling in fear. She extended the basket she carried toward him.

*Take it*, Lura urged him with all her heart as its thumping beat filled her ears.

"Soldiers can't accept gifts here," the other guard said, looking them over with suspicion.

"We're sorry. It's some fruit from the market. To thank them," Nila said. Neither of them knew what else to say.

Lura's eyes stayed locked on Davi as he receded further into the barracks.

The guard knocked the basket from Nila's hands, spilling the contents. "No gifts! Go away!"

Davi stopped and whirled around, drawn by the commotion. His eyes fixed upon Nila, recognition dawning there.

*He's coming back!*

Davi's companions reacted with surprise as he hurried toward them. "Hold it there," Davi called out as he approached.

"You know these women?" the taller guard asked.

"I know her," David said, indicating Nila. He stepped back through the gate and stood face to face with them.

Lura thought her heart might explode from her chest.

"They were trying to bring gifts here, Captain. You know our policies," the other guard began explaining.

Davi smiled, hoping to reassure him. "I'm sure they meant no harm. Please allow us a moment."

The two guards shrugged and turned back to their post as Davi pulled Nila and Lura off to the side.

"You remember me?" Nila said, fearful.

"We remember each other," Davi said as she nodded. "You ran away so fast the other night, I never got to ask you about this." He reached under his uniform collar and pulled a chain hanging around his neck. "It's just like yours."

Lura's eyes widened as the blue-green crest appeared, and her knees felt weak but she leaned against Nila to steady herself. All four were there—the laborers, the soldiers, the farmers, and the priests. She couldn't help but reach out and stroke it gently with her hand.

"I know. I saw." Nila said, seeing Davi's surprise at Lura's forward behavior.

"I wanted to ask you about the symbol on it," Davi said.

*Speak to him. He's your son.* Lura kept telling herself, as tears welled at the corners of her eyes. She'd waited so long, dreamed of this moment, but now she couldn't formulate the words.

"It's our family crest," Nila said. "Where did you get it?"

"My mother gave it to me when I was a baby. I've always worn it," Davi said.

Behind them, a police cruiser dropped down from overhead and parked nearby, lights flashing. As two officers climbed out, one of the guards motioned toward the women. "It's those women there."

Davi's face turned red with anger as he turned to the guards. "There's been a big misunderstanding. They've done no harm."

Nila grabbed Lura's arm with an alarmed look and pulled her back the way they'd come. "Run, Auntie! Run!"

*Police! We're going to be arrested!* Lura snapped out of it, realizing what was happening.

Nila dragged her, picking up pace as she went, while Davi stepped between them and the police. "Auntie Lura! Hurry!"

Lura forced her eyes away from Davi and turned back around, running as fast as she could. Voices rose as men argued behind them, but no one seemed to be chasing them.

Davi followed Yao and Farien to his quarters and the door slid shut behind them. They both shot hum puzzled looks.

"What was that all about?" Yao asked.

"It was the girl from two nights ago," Davi said.

Yao squinted with understanding.

"What happened two nights ago?" Farien asked, glancing between them in confusion. Davi and Yao had already decided Farien wasn't ready to know about the attempted rape and its consequences.

"Why'd she come here?" Yao asked, puzzled.

"I don't know, but the necklace she wears is identical to mine," Davi said, pointing to the chain around his neck.

"I've seen you wearing that. Where'd you get it?" Farien asked, forgetting his earlier question.

"My mother gave it to me when I was young," Davi said.

"I've never seen you without it. What does the symbol mean?" Farien asked.

"The girl said it's her family crest," Davi answered, watching them both for a reaction.

"Why would your mother have you wear the crest of a worker family?" Farien said, more puzzled than ever.

Davi turned to Yao, who seemed lost in thought. "Do you remember that rumor Bordox brought up at the Academy about me?"

"The starport's full of rumors." Yao shrugged dismissively.

"What if it was more than just a rumor?" Davi knew how farfetched it sounded.

His friends' faces filled with a mix of worry, dread, and disbelief.

"Are you saying you're the child of workers?" Farien struggled to even form the question.

"It seems rather odd for it to be pure coincidence," Davi said, still unsure what to believe himself. "But I've never known my mother to lie to me."

"Yet given who your uncle is, she would want to protect you," Yao replied, clearly starting to put the pieces together.

Davi nodded.

"You two can't be serious? He's a member of the Royal family," Farien said.

"An only child of a mother who never married," Yao said.

Farien kept looking back and forth between them in disbelief. "Single mothers are not that uncommon, especially in official families. You read all those history books."

Yao and Davi chuckled.

"Good thing since I carried you through history at the Academy," Yao teased.

Farien scoffed. "But this is crazy."

"Maybe, but I have to find out for sure," Davi said. "They ran off. I don't know where they live."

"If they came on foot, it must not be far," Yao said.

"Think about the consequences if that were true," Farien said, shaking his head as he turned away.

"I have to know the truth, Farien," Davi said. The potential consequences had been haunting him since he saved the girl and saw her necklace. But this was about knowing who he was. How could he live without being certain? He had to find those women again somehow.

Then he remembered the security camera. Maybe he could get prints of their faces off the databanks and ask around. Someone had to know them—maybe someone at the market. But then who would want to talk to an Alliance Captain? He had to try or it would always haunt him.

"Farien, not a word of this goes outside this room," Yao said. "When Davi finds out the truth, he'll let us know. It would be very dangerous for him if certain people found out about this."

Farien nodded. "Come on. I've been his friend all my life. You can trust me."

Yao and Davi exchanged uncertain looks. Can we trust him?

Farien began frowning until Davi put his hand on his arm, squeezing firmly. "I know I can."

He hoped he was right.

Getting images of the two women off the security tapes proved relatively simple. Tracking them down proved even harder than Davi had imagined.

His first two trips to the market produced no leads. As he'd feared, few people there wanted to talk to an Alliance officer. On his third attempt, he came there out of uniform. A couple of vendors recognized the women from the vidprints, but only knew the approximate area where they might live; nothing definite.

Davi wandered through worker residential zones, hoping for another chance encounter with them. His feet moved in time with the droning noise of the city around him. Because the workers' diets consisted of different foods than he'd grown up with, he discovered new scents of warm meats and sweet fruits as he passed by their houses. Some delighted his nose, while others caused him to cringe. Since Yao and Farien had returned to their duties, he conducted his search alone, on foot, using air taxis a few times to get from his office to the areas he wanted to search. Though the civilian clothes helped a bit, his military haircut and accent still raised suspicion. He made no progress even with those who thought they recognized the women.

After a week, he'd covered most of the areas mentioned by those who'd recognized the women at the market. Almost ready to quit in frustration, he decided to check one last neighborhood. Because he had a meeting at a nearby factory, he stopped there during work hours, in uniform. He knew it might hinder him a bit, but at this point it didn't seem to matter.

He wandered through one corridor after another, enduring the suspicious glances of the workers he passed. He'd about given up, when he realized he'd been so preoccupied with his thoughts that he'd failed to keep track of the twists and turns he'd taken to reach his present position. He knew he'd crossed the corridor parallel to the one he was on, so, seeing a walkway cut between two buildings, he decided to see where it led.

Entering a courtyard between two buildings, he passed a cart stacked with crates of groceries as a few chickens squawked and scattered at his feet. Then he saw her. At the end of the courtyard, sweeping outside a door stood the woman who'd come to the barracks with the rape victim.

Davi stopped, staring, his mouth dry as worst-case scenarios played in his head. She hadn't seen him yet but what if she ran? What if she refused to talk to him? He'd treated them nicely before, yes, but he was a Boralian officer, the enemy. Besides, he didn't know either of the women's names. *What can I say? Come on, think of something!*

Then she turned, saw him, and stopped sweeping.

At first, she stiffened, blinking rapidly at the sight of his uniform, but then, recognizing him, she broke into a smile. She mumbled something, raising her palm to the sky as if offering some kind of prayer, then set the broom aside and moved toward him, almost bouncing like a young girl.

"I was hoping you'd come," she said, motioning toward the door in front of which she'd been sweeping. "Please. Come into my home so we can talk."

Davi had the sense she had restrained the urge to hug him. He smiled and moved toward her. "Thank you."

The dwelling was small and intimate, permeated by the smell of candles mixed with dust. Wooden beams from the frame shown through the white stucco walls at the ceiling and corners. A simple table and chairs sat at one end of the room next to a cooking area with a hotpad and microwave. At the far end, a small entertainment console hung on the wall with a couch and chairs arranged around it. Everything looked much more primitive than Davi was used to. In fact, the building itself appeared as if it might have been built during the earliest days of the planet's colonization. A few pictures hung on the cooling unit with magnets and one solitary painting decorated the wall opposite the door. Light came from a single reflector pad in the center of the ceiling, with more leaking through the door and a window along the wall near the table. A single candle at the center of the table flickered from air slipping in through a crack in the door.

The woman motioned him toward a chair by the table, smiling. "Welcome to our home."

Davi nodded, as he took it all in and forced a smile. "Thank you. My name is Captain Xander Rhii. I'm the officer in charge of the Southwest farming district. My friends call me Davi."

The woman's eyes sparkled at hearing his nickname. "It's so good to see you again Davi. My name is Lura. Can I offer you any refreshment?" Again, she bounced lightly with every word as if she might burst any moment.

"Thank you, yes. I am thirsty."

She opened the cooling unit. "I'm afraid our options are quite limited. I do have some tea and juices."

"Anything would be fine, Lura. Surprise me," Davi said, smiling again.

She returned with a can of gixi juice and handed it to him.

As she sat across from him, he popped the lid open and took in the sweet scent. "Mmmm. One of my favorites. It's been a while, too. Thank you."

Lura seemed delighted. "I'm so glad we found something you like. What brings an Alliance officer to our humble courtyard?"

"I came to find you—either you or the girl who was with you at the barracks," Davi said as he savored the sweet, smooth taste of the gixi juice.

"Ah yes, my niece, Nila. Thank you for saving her from that soldier," Lura said, placing her soft hand over his atop the table as if she couldn't help herself. "Why us?"

Davi hesitated a moment, surprised by her forwardness. "Well, I wanted to be sure you were okay after what happened at the barracks. And I wanted to know more about this," Davi said. Removing his hand from Lura's, he pulled out his necklace and let it hang down the front of his uniform. "What can you tell me about it? Before the police chased you off, Nila mentioned a family crest?"

Lura pulled her hand back, staring at the necklace. "There are only a few like it in existence."

Davi nodded. "How would my mother have come to have one?"

"I don't know. Who's your mother?" Lura asked with curiosity.

"I was raised by Princess Miri Rhii, sister to Lord Xalivar," Davi said.

At the mention of his uncle's name, her face turned white and her voice shook. "Legallis? The Royal Family?"

"Yes," Davi said as he nodded. He wondered if all workers had the same reaction to the High Lord Councilor's name. He sipped his juice again as she considered what he'd said.

"My God, I never imagined," she said, almost as if talking to herself. "When we sent you away, it was supposed to be Regallis." Her voice faded as she realized she was speaking her thoughts out loud.

"Sent me away? What do you mean? Have we met before?"

Lura stood and walked over to one of the pictures hanging on the cooling unit. She removed the magnet with great care and carried the picture back to the table like a precious treasure, setting it before him. "This is a picture of my husband Sol."

Davi stared at the picture. The man staring back at him had light brown hair and tanned skin similar to his own, and the same nose and green eyes that looked back at him in the mirror. *My gods! The resemblance is startling. Could this really be?* The resemblance was amazing. No wonder Lura had been excited. Anyone who saw the two men together might guess they were related.

Seeing the look on his face, Lura's eyes showed her concern. "I'm sorry. I know this must be shocking for you to hear."

"No, please. Tell me everything," Davi said, leaning back in his chair and doing his best to relax his face and sound reassuring.

"Twenty-one years ago, there was a decree ordering all first-born sons to be killed. The High Lord Councilor had a dream a worker child would arise to overthrow him," Lura explained. "The Death Squads began killing all first-born males among our people, on every planet of the solar system."

Davi searched his mind. His recollection of the history of the Borali Alliance brought back no recollection of such an incident.

"My husband and I only had one child, a baby boy born right before the decree. We couldn't bear the thought of losing him, after so many years of waiting and hoping," Lura continued. "My husband worked at the depot, repairing starcraft. He was able to modify a small courier to transport our child to another planet in the solar system. We hoped he would be found by someone who would raise him as their own and give him a good life."

*Courier craft. A child sent to the stars. My gods!*

"The courier malfunctioned sometime soon after its launch. Its tracking device failed, so we had no idea where it ended up or if it even finished the journey," Lura said.

"So you think I'm the son you sent to the stars?" Davi asked.

Mistaking his question for total disbelief, Lura shrugged and looked away. "I know it must sound crazy to you. Like a fairy tale or something."

"My mother is a good woman. I've never known her to lie to me," Davi said, thinking out loud.

"I'm sure she's a wonderful woman," Lura smiled, a bit puzzled by his second sentence. "May I ask you how you came to be called Davi?"

"I don't really know. It's like a nickname my mother gave me at birth. Everyone except for my Uncle and a few instructors has always called me by it," Davi said.

Lura deliberated a moment, before her hazel eyes found his again. "My husband placed a letter to whoever might find our child. It contained his name and a note asking them to take care of him and raise him as their own. Our child's name was Davi," she said.

*My gods! It has to be true!* He didn't see how there could be any more doubt. *But why would mother have lied to me?* "How would my mother have come by the necklace?"

"Moments before the courier launched, I placed my necklace next to our child, hoping whoever found him would give it to him," she said.

"I don't know what to say," Davi responded, his mind racing along with his heart. He swallowed hard, possessed of both excitement and a sudden urge to get away. He had to talk to his mother about this! He dreaded hurting her, but it couldn't be a mere coincidence. What motive would Lura have for making up such a story? She'd had no idea he was a Royal before he told her—it seemed obvious from her reaction when she learned his identity. "Do you live here with your husband?"

Lura's face turned sad and she looked at the photograph. "The Special Police took him away after we launched the courier. I don't know what happened to him."

*No wonder she reacted that way to Xalivar's name! Could my uncle really be so different from the man I thought I knew?* "I'm so sorry for your loss," Davi said, taking a deep breath and straightening as he placed his hands atop hers on the table again.

She smiled. "You are such a kind soul. We're not used to finding such kindness in Boralian officers."

"I'm not like most Alliance officers," Davi said.

"No, you're not," she said with a laugh. "You're special!"

Davi pulled his hand away, finishing off the gixi juice. "Please don't be offended if I take some time to think about all this."

"I'm just happy to have had the chance to meet you," Lura said, with a reassuring smile as he scooted the chair back and stood. "I hope I'll see you again."

"I'm sure you will," Davi said. He moved around the table, standing next to her, then took her hand in his and kissed it. "Thank you for your generous hospitality."

"Thank you for your kindness to Nila," Lura said as she stood.

Davi bowed slightly and walked to the door. "I'd appreciate it if my visit here stayed between us for now," he said, turning back toward her.

"Of course," Lura smiled again. Her face lit up every time she did. She was a striking woman with long, flowing brown hair. Feeling sorry for the hardness her life must have been, he returned the smile then turned walked out the door.

As Davi crossed the courtyard and entered the tunnel, he struggled to keep his pace steady while his mind raced. This was almost beyond belief! His whole life had unraveled before his eyes—everything he thought he knew about the world, about his family, about who he was.

His mind filled with question after question. Why didn't his mother ever tell him? Protecting him as a child was one thing, but he was far from a child now. She must have expected him to wonder about the necklace and his nickname. He'd always been one to ask a lot of questions. How much did his uncle know? Would the High Lord Councilor actually accept a worker child as his heir apparent? Based on what he'd been learning about his uncle, he doubted it. How would his friends and colleagues react if they found out? Certain his whole life would change, he wasn't sure he was ready for it.

He meandered through the neighborhoods for a while before realizing he needed to get back to the office. He was already late. Stopping on a main artery, his eyes darted around for a familiar landmark. He spotted the market ahead through some arches. It would be easy to find his way back from there.

He headed in that direction; ignoring the stares of the people he passed. *Can they know by looking at me that I'm one of them?* He shook off the idea. The stares had been because of his uniform, as always. *Boy, I really am getting paranoid!*

Passing beneath an arch onto another corridor, he glimpsed the tents and booths of the market up ahead. *Thank the gods, I know where I am.* He quickened his pace as he entered the market and the familiar smells and sounds assaulted his senses. The market seemed less crowded. It was mid-afternoon, and most of the workers would be at their jobs. Raised voices came from up ahead. He rounded a corner between rows of booths to find the humanoid vendor he'd asked about Lura and Nila, arguing with two workers.

"It's a fair price!" The vendor's purple eyes glowed with rage.

"This fruit is not even ripe," said one worker, tossing two gixis back at him.

"I provide the highest quality," the vendor insisted.

"You should be ashamed ripping off people!" The other worker said with disgust. "Give us back our money!"

The vendor spotted Davi passing and motioned to him. "Captain, please. You've been here before. You know my product."

Davi sighed. *Don't get me involved in this.* He turned to the vendor and smiled. He had bought some fruit there two days before and it was fine. "I didn't have any complaints."

"Well, he's an off-worlder. How would he know when gixi are at their ripest?" the first worker said.

"Don't you men have jobs to attend to?" Davi asked. They showed no fear, despite his uniform.

"Our supervisor won't pay us if the gixi isn't ripe," the second worker said. His face formed a question. He examined Davi like he knew him from somewhere.

The first worker angrily grabbed the vendor by the collar, his eyes still locked on Davi. "Stay out of this. It's a dispute between us. We want our money back!"

Davi stepped forward and put his hand on the first worker's muscular arm. He could feel the man's strength through his sleeve. "Let him go."

The second worker's eyes went wide with recognition. Davi couldn't imagine how they knew each other.

"What are you going to do? Kill us like you killed that Captain last week?" the second worker said loudly.

The words hit Davi like a rocket and the hair lifted at the nape of his neck as his hands suddenly felt clammy. *My gods, how did he know?*

"I saw you on my corridor, Captain. I saw you real good," the second worker said staring at him. The vendor and the other worker eyed Davi with worried looks.

Davi recognized the second worker as the man who'd stood in the doorway as he fled the corridor where the Captain lay dead. Davi pulled his hand off the first worker, turned and ran as fast as he could. *People are talking about it now. It's only a matter of time before the police come for me!*

He passed the end of the row of stalls, making his way along the transportation corridor ringing the market toward a nearby residential corridor. He ran as fast as he could—his footsteps pounding the pavement so loud he feared the entire city might hear—drawing even more stares from the people he passed. Dwellings flew by in a flash as he wondered if the stares had been about more than his uniform. He tried to remember how many workers he'd seen peering out at him in the alley. The gasps of his breathing echoed loudly off the walls around him as his eyes stung from perspiration falling off his forehead.

Passing through the security gate separating the worker districts from the finer homes, he continued around a corner as his eyes locked on the outline of the government buildings ahead of him. The intersection separating the government sector from the residential areas was quiet, so he hurried across and up the transportation corridor toward the barracks gate where he'd encountered Lura and Nila.

Activity near the gate ahead drew his attention. Lord's Security Police officers were talking with the guards. Two police vehicles sat nearby with lights flashing. Then he saw a face he recognized–Bordox in full LSP uniform.

Bordox spotted him too, and raised his arm to point. "There he is!"

The Security Police and barracks guards all turned to stare at him. Bordox and the LSP officers began rushing toward him, pulling their blasters from their holsters.

Davi turned and ran back the way he'd come, his chest tingling even as he began feeling dizzy. *Where can I go? Quick! Think!* As he passed the end of the block, the sirens of LSP cruisers drew nearer. Spotting an air taxi at the curb, he hurried over and jumped inside.

"Residential Sector Four, fast, please."

The cab-bot beeped, as the door slid shut. "Of course, sir." The air taxi accelerated.

Catching his own scent for the first time, he felt relieved the cab-bot had no sensory abilities. His uniform was soaked with sweat. "Turn here," Davi insisted.

The cab-bot complied, making a sharp turn into the finer residential area. The transportation corridors became narrower. The air taxi would soon run out of room.

"My computer maps show limited access to Residential Sector Four from this corridor, sir," the cab-bot informed him.

"Can't you just fly over the buildings until we're closer?"

"It's against regulations, sir. Emergency vehicles only per ordinance—"

"I can get out and walk. Please get me as close as you can," Davi said, not waiting for the cab-bot to finish, his own voice revealing his panicked state. Hearing sirens behind him, he glanced back. The LSP vehicles had not turned. He wasn't even sure if they could fit.

"Of course, sir," the cab-bot responded.

Davi saw LSP men exiting a vehicle at the entrance to the corridor and chasing after the air taxi.

The cab-bot turned a corner, winding the taxi through the narrow corridors. At the security gates leading to the worker residential areas, the air taxi pulled to a stop. "This is it, sir."

Davi slid his cab card through the slot near the door as it slid open. "Thank you. Please move on right away."

He rushed from the cab and out into the worker district again, squinting as he ran and flinching at every noise. He hoped to lose himself in the numerous narrow corridors surrounding the market.

The air taxi departed behind him. *Did the LSP men see where the taxi stopped?* He prayed they hadn't.

Quats hissed and scattered as he ducked onto a side corridor. He continued, unsure where he was going, knowing he had to get away. He heard sirens as the LSP vehicles raced around the edges of the district looking for another entrance.

He ducked through an archway like the ones leading to the market, running as fast as he could, until his uniform dripped. His feet pounded the pavement like beating drums. Then someone called his name.

"Davi!"

*Since when can Bordox run that fast?* His mind registered the voice was female as he forced himself to stop and turned around.

Lura motioned to him from a nearby doorway. "Come this way!" She smiled reassuringly. *Where did she come from?*

He didn't hesitate, hurrying inside as she shut the door behind them. It was a small interior corridor with dwelling doors scattered on each side. He started to apologize for his appearance and smell but Lura motioned for him to be quiet.

Outside feet shuffled as someone ran past. *They're going to find me.* And then it was silent again until the sirens began moving away. No more commotion came from outside. Could he really have escaped?

Lura took his hand, leading him further down the corridor. "Were the Police chasing you?"

He nodded, out of breath. "Word has spread about Nila and the Captain."

"Oh no!" Lura pulled him behind her. "Follow me. We can get back to my house through the tunnels."

"How?" He hadn't heard of any tunnels.

She nodded, pulling open a small wooden door on the corner of a building. Stairs descended.

*Tunnels under the city?*

"They run underground throughout the worker areas. Officers aren't supposed to know about them."

As soon as they entered, she closed the door behind them. It was dark and damp as they headed down. Every footstep echoed like thunder interrupting the droning rasp of his breathing and the thumping of his heart. He had no idea where they'd wind up, but he followed as fast as he could.

# Chapter Four

Manaen's red eyes moved back and forth while he read the report aloud off the datapad as Xalivar and Miri listened.

"If he wants our help, why is he running away?" Xalivar asked, his anger growing.

"Bordox is his rival from the Academy. They have a long history. Maybe if someone else had come after him—"

Xalivar cut Miri off. "I can't control which LSP officers answer such warrants. I didn't even know about it until this morning. How can we help him if we don't know where he is?"

Xalivar fumed when he learned his own nephew was assisting workers, no matter what the circumstances. His chest tightened and his fists clenched at the very thought of it. They were the Lord's ancient enemies and deserved no mercy. He cursed Miri for making Davi weak. Xalivar had done his best to harden the boy, but there hadn't been enough time. Besides, it had been clear to Xalivar his nephew was far too sensitive to handle the reality of certain types of situations and decisions. He had always protected the boy from exposure, hoping he would come around in time. Now he wondered if Miri had succeeded in ruining her son for the throne.

"I'm sure he's looking for a way to get in touch with us," Miri said, pacing anxiously. "He knows we'll help him."

"What business does he have involving himself with helping workers? The workers are our enemies!" The last sentence came out like cursing, and as far as Xalivar was concerned that was appropriate.

Miri recoiled at Xalivar's anger. "Is it wrong to show com-passion to fellow human beings?" Miri asked, sounded as if she herself were wounded by his words. She had always been too soft.

"The term only applies to them by natural default. They are not our equals," Xalivar said, annoyed at having to remind her of it after so many years. He turned quickly to his majordomo. "Manaen, get me Major Zylo and Lieutenant Bordox. I want to see them as soon as possible. In the meantime, any further reports on this come to me right away."

Manaen nodded, hurrying for the door. "Yes, my Lord!"

Xalivar waited until the door slid shut behind his aide before turning back to scold Miri. "He was raised to lead and you made him soft, Miri. Leaders must be hard. They cannot afford to be blinded by compassion."

"Human beings cannot afford to be totally blinded to concern for others as you are, brother," Miri said, anger rising as her body tensed.

Xalivar rolled his eyes. *Not this conversation again!* He and his sister had always been different. Miri always wanted to appear sympathetic in front of the help, for example, and she had protected Davi just as their own father had protected her. As a result, neither Davi nor Miri understood the harsh realities of leadership. "If he is to rule one day, he will have to learn to make difficult decisions," Xalivar responded, tired of spoon-feeding his sister. Time for her to grow up.

"You think he killed an Alliance soldier in haste? Perhaps he had no other choice! Perhaps it was an accident!" Miri threw her hands in the air.

"Whatever the circumstances," Xalivar said, softening his tone in an attempt to inspire her cooperation, "we both know the law. He will have to answer to the Tribunal of Lords. We will do all we can to help him, of course. If there is a good explanation, they will show him mercy. Have you had any contact with him since he's been on Vertullis?"

"One e-post to let me know he had arrived," Miri replied.

Her gentle blue eyes caused him to doubt her. They always darkened when she felt uncertainty. She and Davi had always been close. Why would they not continue to be? The distance would slow them down, but electronic communications between Legallis and Vertullis were fast, especially for officers like Davi with access to Borali Alliance channels.

"Nothing else?"

"I already told you," she said, still angry.

"You will, of course, let me know if you hear from him?"

"Of course," she said.

Xalivar offered a warm smile but made a mental note to have her e-posts monitored. He hated to resort to spying on his own family. In the past, Miri's correspondence had been of no relevance, but this was different. Davi was Xalivar's known heir and he had to stay informed about all developments. Besides, he didn't believe her promise for a moment. Grunting to himself, he turned away to hide the doubt in his eyes and moved to the window behind the throne, staring out at the starport. He hoped Zylo and Bordox would have good news for him.

Davi sat in Lura's kitchen, lost in thought, as life spun on around him. He'd run fearing how Bordox might treat him, but soon he would have return to Legon and face this. He'd been over and over it in his mind and decided turning himself in to the LSP would create all sorts of problems. The best route would be to contact his mother and go straight to his family first. They could determine together what to do next. Beyond the issues of the Captain's death, he needed to resolve the issues of his heritage or it would eat away at him. He had to know who he was.

At Lura's, he reconnected with Nila again and met Lura's sister, Rena. They were all very kind to him, convinced he was their long-lost relative. Their warmth touched him and he returned it in kind, but butterflies still danced in his stomach and he had to defy the urge to blanch several times. He couldn't be sure how to respond until he'd cleared it all up with Miri.

He'd attempted to sneak back to the barracks and send an e-post, but the LSP had been there waiting for him. Instead, he sent a message from a kiosk on the sidewalk. Afterwards, he proceeded across a public park to a ritzy neighborhood he hadn't visited since his second week on the planet. The home of Sinaia Quall, the Borali Alliance's Ambassador to Vertullis, stood in a cul-de-sac at the end of a palm tree-lined corridor—the black iron fence declaring its separation from the world outside.

After the guard admitted him, the Ambassador's majordomo escorted him to her office. The opulence still impressed him despite the fact he'd been there once before—the red curtains, gold-embossed furniture and fixtures, the fine Regallian carpets and paintings from artists around the solar system. The smell of papers from her crowded desk mixed with incense and her flowery perfume. Yet this was the world he was used to, far different from that of military life and Lura and her family. It evoked happy memories and strong feelings from his childhood and earlier life.

Sinaia Quall smiled and stood behind her desk as he entered. Despite the height of the dark hair she kept permanently affixed in a bun atop her head, most people towered over her, but she compensated for it with intense self-confidence. She wore a blue suit, neatly pressed, as if appearance counted even when she was alone in her home. Her grip was firm as she shook his hand.

"Captain Rhii," she said with a warm smile, "I've been meaning to have you over again since the dinner right after you arrived, but I'm afraid the diplomats have kept me rather busy."

Davi smiled. "I'm sorry I haven't managed to drop by either. I've appreciated your kindness to me."

She shrugged as if it were nothing. "Your uncle has been a good friend. What brings you here today?"

After Davi explained what had happened with the Captain and the LSP soldiers, she agreed that going to his family first was the wisest course.

"I don't like to take advantage of my status as a Royal," Davi said, starting to apologize.

"Nonsense!" the ambassador said. "Imprisoning a Royal would be as bad for the Alliance itself as it would be for your family, and my job is to serve the Alliance. I'm pleased you came to me."

After ordering supper and drinks from her servants, she excused herself and headed for the communications room down the hall. An hour later, a shuttle picked him up in the park down the corridor. Once they'd cleared the planet, the pilot slipped into sub-light taking them to Legallis in just under ten hours' time. Upon landing, he headed straight to his mother's chambers at the Palace, and she accompanied him to see Xalivar.

"You seem to have made a name for yourself in the most undesirable ways," Xalivar said, stepping down from the throne as the door shut behind them, his voice tired and face annoyed.

"It was not intentional," Davi said.

"Of course not!" Miri said, but stopped as her face reverted to a worried expression. She looked at Davi, anxious for answers.

"Murder they're saying." Xalivar's look also urged him to explain.

Davi hesitated. He'd known the moment was here from the time he boarded the shuttle, yet standing before them, his throat grew dry and heavy as his muscles tensed, and he found it challenging to formulate the words. After a moment, he forced the words out.

"I came upon the Captain as he was about to commit a violation against a female. When I interfered, he turned on me. In trying to subdue him, I inadvertently killed him." He offered a silent prayer to the gods, hoping they'd understand.

Xalivar almost spat the words out: "Why are you helping workers? They are ancient enemies of our people."

Davi was shocked by the fierceness of his uncle's tone. "Alliance soldiers raping helpless young girls does not qualify to me as subduing our subjects."

"You think they deserve better?" Xalivar asked, irritated.

"They don't deserve to be treated worse than animals," Davi said. If his uncle didn't understand, he hoped his mother would.

"We do what we must," Xalivar said.

"Then we act dishonorably," Davi replied, his resolve unwavering.

Xalivar's cutting look warned him to mind his words. "One day, if you lead the Alliance, you'll understand the hard decisions which have to be made."

"I don't know if I could ever understand this!" Davi said.

Miri shot a look at Xalivar, making it clear she agreed.

Xalivar stared at them a moment as if collecting his words and thoughts. When he spoke, his tone became softer again. "Inadvertently?" Xalivar raised an eyebrow.

"He was very strong. I tried to use a board to knock him unconscious, but a spike entered his brain and killed him," Davi explained. "His death was an accident."

"What an unfortunate thing," Miri said and wrapped her hands softly around Davi's upper arm, her voice full of concern.

"You know the law?" Xalivar asked.

"I would hope the law would account for accidents," Davi replied, beginning to doubt he could count on his uncle for help.

"There were witnesses?" Xalivar asked.

"A few workers, yes," Davi said.

"You will, of course, write up a full report, Captain?"

Davi nodded. "Of course."

"Good. As soon as possible. Then I can go to the Council and get the arrest warrant revoked before real harm is done."

"You believe they will show mercy?" Miri said, hopeful.

"I believe they will consider the circumstances. I make no promises, but he is a Royal, and he has come himself to face it," Xalivar said.

"You are the High Lord Councilor," Miri said, releasing Davi's arm and straightening to glare at her brother.

"I know who I am. But I am not a dictator," Xalivar said. "This is a matter for the Council."

Davi and Miri exchanged a look. They both knew Xalivar had heavy influence with the Council.

"The Council on which you serve," Miri said.

"As one of twelve members, and I must recuse myself from this," Xalivar said. "The Council will be fair."

Davi's heart sunk. He'd hoped his uncle's influence might serve to keep the matter private. Xalivar's look told him the discussion was over.

"You dislike your duty assignment."

It was more of a statement than a question. "I have learned many things I did not know, uncle," Davi answered.

Xalivar smiled. "Ah, I see you do indeed still have the heart of a diplomat, Xander." He laughed. "You will find life is full of hard choices."

"He has known this for a long time," Miri said, her irritation still obvious.

Xalivar sigh loudly and shot her a stern look again. "The choices faced by a leader are different." Turning back to Davi again, he smiled. "We have much to talk about. Your education has barely begun." He reached over and pressed a button on a pillar to his right.

Davi did his best to hide his disappointment. "I understand."

The door slid open behind Davi and Miri as Manaen entered and stood at attention.

"Go with your mother. I believe she has missed you. I have some things to attend to, but I'll join you when I can," Xalivar said, his eyes locking on Davi's with reassurance.

Miri smiled warmly at Davi as he saluted his uncle. "Yes, High Lord Councilor." Then they turned and walked out together.

Miri's suite was a section of rooms smaller than Xalivar's on the opposite wing of the Palace. The main room resembled the throne room with pillars lining the two long walls. A raised dais ran around the room with the largest section of the floor in the center, set down by several inches. Two couches sat angled around an entertainment center with a vidscreen. There was a desk in the corner with a terminal. Four rooms led off the main at each corner—a bedroom, closet, kitchen and dining area, and cleansing room.

Miri led her son there and embraced him as soon as they arrived. For a moment, she held him like she'd never let go. She wished she didn't have to.

"When Yao told me what happened, I was so afraid for you," Miri said, still reeling from her brother's refusal to protect her son.

"I'm sorry to worry you," Davi said apologetically as he stepped off the dais onto the center floor.

"When you had expressed your concerns by e-post, I should have arranged time for us to talk sooner. I'm sorry," Miri said, following him.

"It's not right, mother. If the general public knew about this—" Davi said.

Miri put her fingers over his lips. "Keep your voice down."

"We're in the Royal Palace, in your private quarters," Davi said.

"Which doesn't mean we can't be overheard," Miri said, tensing even as she fought the urge to look around. Her brother spied on friends as well as enemies.

"When I was younger, he was always there for me. I never would have imagined he'd sanction such—"

Miri shushed him again. "We always did our best to protect you."

"From what? Reality?"

She winced at the intensity of his tone. "From things which might hurt you," Miri said, her eyes pleading. *Please don't ask for details.*

"I'm not the one who's being hurt here," Davi said, his brow furrowing in frustration.

"Yes, you are. You're feeling disoriented, as if this isn't the world you thought you knew," Miri said with gentle calm she hoped would ease her son's mood. "That's much the same way I felt when I discovered it."

"You didn't know it either?"

"When I was younger, about your age, my father protected me, too," Miri said.

"What about uncle, was he also protected?" Davi asked.

"Your uncle was raised to lead. He didn't have to be protected," Miri said. Their father had been very hard with Xalivar.

"I'm his heir, yet I was protected," Davi said, still confused.

"You're not his son," Miri said.

"He acted as if I was," Davi said.

"He's very fond of you, but the role of an uncle is different," Miri said.

"He protected me because of you, didn't he?" She saw by his expression that her face had answered for her.

As Davi turned away, Miri stepped toward him, reaching to touch his arm, but hesitating. "It was for your own good. I didn't want you to be like him." She'd brought him up to be compassionate, like her.

"I'd like to think I would never be that cold." Davi grimaced as he said it.

"You believe what you're taught to believe," Miri said, hoping some justification might ease the pain of discovering his uncle's cruel nature.

Davi turned back to her, shaking his head. "Humans are capable of intelligence. They can think for themselves, make their own decisions.

You ensured I would learn that."

"Yes, but your decisions are based on your sense of morality and justice. Xalivar believes slavery is the right thing for the workers," Miri said.

"Because he doesn't know any different?" Davi's expression told her he refused to accept it.

"Because it's the way it's always been," Miri said with a sigh. *Please, my son, no good can come of this attitude.*

"A few select history lessons of the evils of the Vertullians, skipping, of course, our own mistakes or abuses, and any human being can be trained not to think about it?" Disgust filled her son's face.

"This occurs in any society," she said, sinking into one of the couches.

"Which makes it right?" Davi's voice was loud as he fought to control his anger.

Miri glanced toward the door.

"What are you afraid he might hear, mother? About a baby sent from the stars perhaps? Events you raised your son to be ignorant of?"

Miri froze, her heart stilled within at his words. She couldn't remember the last time she'd been this scared. *Please, gods, I don't want to lose him.* She paused a moment wondering how to disguise her fear when she answered. "What are you talking about?" Her voice shook as she spoke.

"About this." He reached below his uniform collar and pulled out the necklace. "A baby who came from the stars, a courier craft which crashed—we both know the story," Davi said.

Miri's face fell as she saw he knew the truth. Tears flowed from her eyes like rain and her shoulders sank, her knees weak. I *should have known it would cost me and kept that damn necklace to myself! Why didn't I just take it before you left for Vertullis?* She took a deep breath to quelch the swelling desperation and anger inside.

"Isn't that how it goes?"

"I'm sorry," was all she could say between sobs.

"Why didn't you ever tell me?"

"I didn't know how," Miri said. "I dreamed of a child of my own for so long, and there you were, a beautiful baby boy. The note asked whoever found you to raise you as their own—I love you." She wanted to throw herself at his feet, beg his forgiveness, hold him and never stop.

"I've never doubted it," he said. Collapsing onto the sofa, he put his face in his hands. "Everything I thought I knew about myself, about my world—it's changed now. Who am I?"

"I'm still your mother. I raised you," Miri said. She'd been so blessed when she found him and wanted to honor the gift of his birth parents' sacrifice, so she'd given him the necklace and nickname. She'd never imagined they would find each other one day. More than once she'd wanted to tell him, not wanting there to be any secrets between them, but each time, she couldn't bring herself to do it. If only she'd never seen the necklace or the note that told her his name.

"I met her," Davi said, and she knew he meant his birth mother. "The girl the Captain tried to rape is my cousin."

Miri collapsed on the sofa beside him, unable to control her tears. Even now all she felt in his presence was an overwhelming love for him. "I'm sorry you never had cousins or siblings …"

"I don't care. I had lots of friends," Davi said.

"Is she nice?" She wasn't sure she wanted to know.

"Yes. And beautiful!"

Miri smiled, wiping at her tears. "I always did what I did because I love you. I want what's best for you."

"We both do." Xalivar's booming voice startled them both as they turned toward the door.

He stepped out of the shadows. *How long has he been there?* Miri wondered. *How much did he hear? Why didn't we hear the door?*

"You come here to my quarters unannounced—" Miri said, standing to confront Xalivar. Despite knowing his penchant for spying on people, she felt betrayed, disrespected.

"It's my palace. I go where I please, when I please," Xalivar said. "A worker boy raised in my own house!" He almost screamed it and she knew then: *He'd heard it all.*

His fists clenched as he whirled to face her. "You had no right to keep this from me. To make this decision—"

"It's the Borali Alliance's palace, and I am your sister, not your subject," Miri snapped. Her posture stiffened as the muscles tightened at the corners of her jaw.

"Stop acting as if you are the one who should feel betrayed," Xalivar snarled. "He does not belong here!" His fists clenched and unclenched at his side, something he always did when he was furious. Davi winced at his uncle's every word.

"He's an outsider! In my palace, Miri! Have you no loyalty to your family?"

"Have you no loyalty to yours?" Miri demanded. "He's been like a son to you his whole life. You loved him, as I do!!"

"Based on your lies—"

"I never lied," Miri said. She'd never lied. She just hadn't told him everything. The distinction had allowed her to feel she'd never misled him.

"You never told the truth," Xalivar said, eyes narrowing as he glared coldly at her.

"And you never asked," she reminded him.

"Have I been such a terrible nephew?" Davi demanded, his voice filled with pain. "For you to hate me so much ..."

"You are an enemy of our people," Xalivar said, frowning as his eyes met Davi's.

"He is a human being!" Miri's voice grew, getting louder, along with her desperation. How could Xalivar be so cold to his own nephew? She knew he loved him. Witnessing Xalivar with Davi over the years had been her only proof that her brother was even capable of love.

"He will never belong here!" Xalivar punched a button on a wall communicator near the door. "Manaen!"

Miri ran to him and fell to her knees, grabbing his arm in desperation. "Please, Xalivar. He's my only son."

"He just told you about meeting his real mother," Xalivar said, emphasizing the last two words to make them sting.

Miri looked away, fighting tears again. "I need him!"

"Then pack your things!" Xalivar said, pushing her away. She collapsed into a ball on the floor at Xalivar's feet as his fists clenched again.

"Don't touch her!" Davi said, stepping forward. The door opened and Manaen appeared.

"The Captain is to be reassigned to Alpha Base on Plutonis at once. Get him suitable clothes and notify the commander," Xalivar ordered as Manaen and Miri reacted, confused.

"He is wanted for murder, my lord, as we discussed—" Manaen said.

"Let the Council go to him, if they wish," Xalivar said, with a dismissive wave toward his aide.

Miri screamed and grabbed Manaen by the leg. "No! He's my son! Don't send him away!"

"He's sworn to serve the Alliance," Xalivar said, "As are you," then turned and marched through the door.

Manean motioned to Davi. "Come with me." Pulling free of Miri, he turned toward the door. Davi followed reluctantly. The door whooshed shut behind them.

Miri collapsed on the sofa again, sobs bursting from her like gasps for breath. Everything that mattered had just been stolen from her.

Plutonis? The ice planet? Things had not gone the way any of the possible scenarios had played out in Davi's mind. He was being banished, but not for the reasons he'd expected. Maybe he'd been wrong about Xalivar. By sending him away, Xalivar had protected him from discovery. It would be hard for Miri, sure, but at least he wasn't being thrown out of the Alliance.

He'd feared the worst once his heritage came out, wondered if his uncle loved him the way he'd always thought he did. Now Davi hoped maybe his fears had been misplaced. Maybe Xalivar would make the murder charges disappear, too. Despite his anger and disappointment, Xalivar was taking care of his family. And Davi hoped Alpha Base would be a better adventure than Vertullis had been.

He couldn't get the worker's situation out of his mind. He had to find a way to change things. If Xalivar cared about him despite the revelations of his heritage, maybe there was hope he'd be open to considering that, too. It would take time, and it wouldn't be easy, but Davi intended to e-post him about it as soon as he got settled on Plutonis. He was sure his mother would help, too. He reminded himself he had two mothers now. He would also have to let Lura know what had happened. She had been so worried when he returned to Legallis. He would e-post her, too.

He was still trying to wrap his mind around his new identity. It was a big change, and he had a lot to learn. He knew nothing of the workers' religious beliefs, history, etc. Outside of anything he'd studied about them in school—mostly negative due to the Alliance's slant—he knew very little about them, which needed to change. He would ask Lura for resources to begin his reeducation. It would be strange at first, but he had to start thinking of himself as a worker now. Everybody else would. That would be hard as well. At least, he didn't have to change his name.

Xalivar had gone to Miri's quarters after going over some reports with Manaen. Instead of the corridors, he'd taken a private passage only Royals knew about. He entered Miri's main room through the back of her closet, slipping in unnoticed, to hear Miri and Davi's conversation. Their words took him by surprise. And he'd never had to work harder to control his fury. *My designated heir sympathetic to the Alliance's enemies! One of them!*

Xalivar raged at Miri for allowing such a betrayal. Lonely and barren or not, she had no right to make a decision which put the Royal family at risk without consulting him! If word got out, it could jeopardize everything the family had worked for since his grandfather's reign. He had to protect the family as well as the Alliance. So he'd isolate Davi in a remote part of the system until his true loyalty could be ascertained and full damage control achieved.

Damage control started with select, trusted operatives searching Davi's quarters and office on Vertullis, clearing them of all personal belongings and references to Davi and his interactions with others. They then set about trying to locate anyone who knew the truth about Davi's identity. It would take longer and be difficult, because interrogations would have to occur with neither the interrogator nor the subject knowing the full details. They couldn't know. He wanted to control damage, not spread it. Davi's worker family would have to be dealt with as well. He should have ordered Davi to tell him their names, but it could wait until his nephew settled in on Plutonis. He took care not to act in a way that might create distrust. He needed Davi to trust him now more than ever.

He sat gathering his thoughts, when Miri burst through the Royal passage, unannounced, into his chambers and pounded her fists against his chest. "How dare you send him away?"

"How dare you leave me no choice," Xalivar responded. She always was far too emotional for her own good.

"Plutonis is the edge of the Alliance!" Miri said as he caught and held her fists before she struck him again. She shot him a cold stare.

Xalivar was glad then that he'd never married. He'd spent little time with women outside of a few social interactions and found himself unburdened by the guilt men always associated with such female stares. "Which makes it all the more likely he'll be safer there," he said.

"Safe from whom? You? The Council?" It was an accusation meant to cut him, but Xalivar fought the urge to laugh.

"Do you realize what would happen if his heritage became public knowledge?" Xalivar said, instead filling his voice with concern that might reach her. "We could lose the throne! It could undo everything our family has been working so hard for over the past five decades!"

"No one has to find out," Miri said.

"How long do you think we could keep a secret like this with Xander on Vertullis, interacting with his newfound family?" Her ignorance sometimes amazed him. "I did what's best for this family and the Alliance."

"He's my son. I should have a say," Miri said.

"You're not the High Lord Councilor. I am," Xalivar snapped, turning away. "You'll never understand the difficult decisions I am forced to make on a daily basis." He cursed his father again for allowing her to be soft.

"I understand the difficulty, just not the choices," Miri said, then whirled and disappeared back into the passageway. Xalivar sighed and hit the button on the communicator to page Manaen. It was time to find out if everything had been arranged per his instructions.

Alpha Base was the outermost post in the solar system for the Borali Alliance. Close enough to protect tourist haven Regallis with regular fighter patrols, Plutonis also had few inhabitants and even fewer visitors, thus fewer prying eyes to protect military secrets from. Even the base itself was hidden deep within a man-made cave created by terraform scientists whose technology wasn't up to the challenge Plutonis posed them.

Snowdrifts filled the surrounding landscape like a white desert, and the cold was almost overbearing. To Davi, it felt like being nowhere, because that's pretty much where Plutonis was—in deep space far from anything important. Inside the base, Davi and his companions lived as they always had because the computers generated an atmosphere suitable for humans. But when they ventured outside, they had to strap on breathing apparatuses and an assortment of heavy winter clothes. The air was cold and thick and hung heavy in their lungs. And the frosty air was so thick, they couldn't see more than a few yards around them at any time.

Plutonis only had two native species. The antlered qiwi it was well known for and the humanoid aliens calling themselves Plutonians. Their skin was bluish green, and they had three eyes and four arms. The qiwi and the Plutonians were the two known species in the system that could live on the planet without breathing apparatuses.

The surprising thing about the antelope was their ability to adapt to other environments. They had long been loved for their meat, but merchants also transported live specimens for sale on other planets. If they were transported on a ship on which the air quality in the hold was adjusted gradually over the course of the voyage, they could adapt themselves to survive in the environment of any planet. Thus, Davi had seen them for sale at the market on Vertullis. He had heard of some on Legallis as well. The Plutonians were not so adaptable. Outside their home planet, they required space suits, because the heavier atmospheres wore them out so much that their hearts would sometimes simply fail.

While Davi found the planet itself unpleasant, his duties as a squadron leader thrilled him. The squadron of eight would break into pairs on patrols, spreading themselves out to cover the outer reaches of the system. While they never experienced much excitement, Davi enjoyed the exploration and the thrill of being in flight. It gave him lots of time to think and to continue wrestling through all the revelations he'd been hit with in the weeks before his reassignment.

He e-posted Xalivar after his first two weeks on base to thank him for protecting him and to remind him to take care of Miri. He also suggested he would welcome more discussion on the worker problem, but Xalivar's reply had not mentioned it. His uncle simply said Miri was doing fine and he'd been glad to hear of Davi's taking to his assignment. Davi had not written his uncle since. Instead, he formulated a plan, hoping to offer Xalivar at least a starting point.

His correspondence with Miri occurred with more frequency. Yao continued to look in on her once a week as Davi had requested. Miri worried about Davi, sad to be so far apart, but seemed to be handling it well otherwise, much to Davi's relief. Davi also e-posted Lura to reassure her of his safety and let her know things had worked out well. He'd heard no more about the Captain's death, though he wasn't yet sure what his uncle's negotiations might have produced on that front. No LSP had come looking for him. He would have to inquire about that as well.

To his surprise, he encountered a small team of worker mechanics on Plutonis. He knew Vertullians had mechanical aptitude. Lura told him his own father had been a mechanic at the depot on Vertullis. But he hadn't realized the Alliance shipped worker mechanics to all major outposts and trusted them with responsibility for the maintenance of all starcraft. Unlike his squadron mates, Davi took time to engage the workers in conversation. For them, lives as slaves on an outpost were much better than lives on their home planet. Here, at least, while facing some restrictions and the usual discriminatory attitude from soldiers and pilots, they were pretty much left alone to do their work and lead their lives. Several of them said such assignments were very competitive.

Seeing the workers every time he entered the launch bay set him to thinking again about his own heritage. It had been unsettling at twenty years of age to realize he wasn't who he'd thought he was. He was thankful for the rest he'd gotten during the voyage to Plutonis. The voyage had taken four days, and instead of spending his time wrestling with his thoughts, Davi had slept. Like his uncle, Miri offered little comment on the new realities in her e-posts, instead reassuring him that Xalivar had things under control and urging him to relax. As much as he enjoyed being a pilot again, it continued to weigh on him that his blood relatives still lived as slaves on another planet. He had to do something to help them. He just didn't know what.

After a long patrol, Davi sent another e-post to Xalivar and Miri reminding them he'd lost sleep worrying about Lura and other family members. The situation needed to be addressed. *I'd expect you of all people to understand the importance of family*, he wrote.

Miri's reply startled him:

To: AgriCptSouth@Federal.emp
From: HRHMRhii@Federal.emp
Subject: Your concerns

My dear son:

While I fully respect your feelings toward these people, what I cannot understand, after all the love and support we have provided, is why you think these people still have rights to your love and devotion. They launched you into unknown space on a dangerous, makeshift craft. I think they forfeited their parenting rights and any claim to you with such an act. We are the ones who have raised you, supported you, and helped you for twenty years. We are the ones you should be concerned about, not the worker family whose only tie to you is genetic.

Wanting always what's best for you,
Your loving mother

Xalivar's e-post was short and to the point, reading:

I concur with your mother.

Both letters left him feeling deflated and frustrated. Davi knew his mother to be a caring person. Although this must be hard for her, he couldn't simply ignore people who were his family. After all, they had not given him up out of a lack of desire. They had done it to save his life from Xalivar's decree. And Miri and Xalivar were the ones who had taught him the value of family for most of his life. Davi realized he couldn't fight this battle from six planets away. He had to go back and confront things face to face.

Miri had taught him not to use his Royal status for special treatment, and Davi had done his best to avoid it. But when he filed a request with his commander for emergency family leave, and his commander grumbled a bit about granting a leave to someone who'd arrived only a few weeks before, Davi used his status as Royal. He was granted leave and passage on a transport two days later.

Not wanting to give them time to argue, Davi did not notify Miri and Xalivar. Xalivar might well get word of it through military channels anyhow. Besides, Davi had asked his commander for passage to Vertullis—something he didn't want to have to explain just yet.

A week later, he arrived at Lura's door. Once she overcame her shock at seeing him, she embraced him joyfully. "I've been so worried about you. Thank you for the kind e-posts. I cherished every one!"

Davi smiled, returning her warm embrace. "I'm sorry to have caused you any worry."

"Well, you should know by now that mothers worry. We can't help it," she said with a laugh. Thinking of Miri, Davi realized mothers on every planet must be the same and laughed with her.

"How was Plutonis?"

Davi told her about the antelope, the Plutonians, the worker mechanics, and life as a pilot. He spoke with great passion, and she seemed enraptured by his story. When he had finished, he apologized. "I know it must not be as exciting for you as I make it sound."

"Sounds like a fascinating adventure," Lura said, her face sincere. She patted his arm. "Are you hungry from your journey?"

"I spent most of the time asleep," Davi said. "But I wouldn't mind a good home-cooked meal."

"Didn't you go to Legallis first?" she asked as if she expected it.

"No. I came to see you."

She smiled, surprised. "I'm so honored." Then she moved to the kitchen, opened the cooling unit and began preparing a meal.

"I had something very important I needed to tell you," Davi said slow and deliberately, choosing his words with care.

Seeing the look on his face, Lura stopped what she was doing and their eyes met. "What is it?"

Davi took a deep breath, knowing once he admitted it, he could never go back. Then he lowered his shoulders, forcing the tension from his body and confessed, "I know the truth now, mother. I'm sorry if I caused you pain taking so long to accept it."

Lura smiled bigger than he'd ever seen and rushed to embrace him. "The hardest part was over the day we met. Welcome home, Son!"

He hugged her back as their tears flowed. It felt so natural to be in her arms, as if they'd always known each other. A little bit like coming home.

# Chapter Five

Before he'd finished reading the report, Xalivar's head already throbbed. Manaen had already tactfully disap-peared. *The little rat reads my dispatches*, he noted with displeasure. *I should have known. Maybe it's time to find a new majordomo.*

After all he had done for Davi, this was how his nephew repaid him—betrayal. It hadn't been easy to get the Council to ignore the murder of a soldier. Xalivar had explained the circumstances to the members a few at a time in private, and all agreed it was bad for both the Royal Family and the Alliance to proceed with any charges. The few who were reluctant had been convinced with careful reminders of their own families' secrets. Now, here Davi was, trying to undo everything in one fell swoop!

*What is the boy thinking, taking a leave without my permission? I am not just his uncle! I am High Lord Councilor! I should have never allowed Miri to raise the boy herself. I should have stepped in the moment I settled on Davi as my heir. This would not be happening if the boy had a proper sense of his responsibility to the Alliance and his place in it.*

Xalivar cursed Xander and the foolishness of youth. Then he thought of his own father and grandfather dressing him down for his own enthusiasm. He'd been a young man of action, too, and that had led to him being in their disfavor after the Delta V disaster. Their relationship had never recovered. He'd always determined not to make the same mistakes with his nephew, but now the boy turned out to be an imposter! That would be dealt with accordingly, all in good time. But for now, Xalivar had to find him.

To make matters worse, Davi hadn't gone to Legallis. Emergency family leave to Vertullis meant one thing—the boy was up to something with his worker family. Why couldn't he let it be? Didn't he know the risks? Didn't he know his uncle was trying to do what was best for him, despite the betrayal? So rebellious and independent! Just like a worker!

Maybe he had been too harsh in what he'd said when he learned of

Davi's heritage, but he'd been shocked and dismayed by the discovery. He'd protected him in the end, hadn't he?

Xalivar punched a communicator on the arm of the throne. Manaen's voice came back right away. "Yes, my Lord?"

"Find him this instant and get him here! I don't care what it takes!" Xalivar demanded.

"Yes, Lord," Manaen replied as the communicator went dead. And to think, Xalivar hadn't even begun playing hardball. Perhaps the time had come.

Davi sat at Lura's table as she set out the food she'd prepared. He'd had a few days of getting to know family members. They were all very nice people, and warm and welcoming and supportive, but after the initial emotions wore off, the place just didn't feel like home.

"Have you spoken with your mother, since you came back?" Lura quietly asked. He looked at her, confused. "Princess Miri?"

"No. I need to. I wanted a few days with you here first," Davi said.

"I imagine she's worried about you. Don't wait too long," Lura said, sounding almost like Miri.

Davi laughed. "Hmmmm. Maybe this having two mothers thing isn't such a good idea after all."

Lura laughed, then tousled his hair before going back to retrieve another serving dish. "All mothers worry."

Her concern for Miri touched him. It pleased him to know Lura was sensitive to the feelings of his other family. It meant she'd understand when he had to take time with sorting things out, and he felt a little less pressure as a result. "Maybe I should send her an e-post then after lunch," Davi said.

"Sounds good. There's a kiosk near the park a few blocks from here," Lura told him.

"Yes, mother," Davi said, with a wry grin.

Lura laughed. He was enjoying this time with her. It already seemed like they'd known each other longer. She appeared to be enjoying the time with him, too.

Lura brought the last of the dishes to the table, and then sat down across from him. "Do you want to say grace?"

"I'm still not sure I know what to say," Davi said. He was not used to talking to one god or even saying prayers, despite occasional visits to the temple with his mother. The only prayers he knew were those memorized from birth by all Boralians and used for sacrifices offered at official ceremonies. Some people did their own private worship services from time to time for one or another of the pantheon of gods, but the workers' personal religion was all new to him.

"It's easy," Lura said. "You talk to Father God like he's a person. I'll show you." She bowed her head and Davi did as well. "Father God, we thank you for the reunion with our long lost boy, Davi. We thank you for life and breath and the food on this table, all of which we know you've provided. Bless us now and lead us in your will. Amen." She smiled at him. "Is that so hard?"

"I don't know all the right phrases and words," Davi said.

"The good thing about prayer is there are no rules for how you say it. It's the attitude in your heart which matters to God," Lura said. Davi pondered her words, realizing he had a lot to learn. "Well, don't wait for it to get cold now." She began scooping servings onto his plate.

Later, at the kiosk near the park, he found a message waiting for him when he logged into his e-post account.

To: CptSQuad4Alpha@Federal.emp
From: HLC@Federal.emp
Subject: Where are you?

Nephew:

Your decision to go gallivanting about could cost this family and the Alliance dearly! You are to report to me at once upon reading this missive!

Xalivar

Davi sighed, shifting nervously. Time had run out. He had to go and talk with his Royal family, but he still had no idea what he was going to say. Regardless, they deserved an explanation.

*You'd better find the words in a hurry, Davi.*

He e-posted for a Royal shuttle to be sent then headed back to Lura's to tell her his plans.

Manaen escorted Davi as far as the throne room, but let him enter alone. Xalivar stood stiffly beside a window, staring out at the city.

"I gave you your orders," Xalivar said, without turning to face him. Davi heard the anger in his voice.

"I can explain—"

Xalivar continued staring out at the city as he cut him off, "Soldiers obey orders or they are disciplined. Don't think because I'm your uncle, you'll be given special treatment."

"I've already been given special treatment," Davi said.

Xalivar whirled around, glaring at him as his fists clenched. "Do you know what I had to go through to get the Council not to pursue murder charges against you?"

"I appreciate everything you've done for me."

"And this is how you show your gratitude?" Xalivar turned away again.

"I serve you best by being honest with you, don't I?"

"You serve me best by doing as I instruct you without raising unnecessary questions," Xalivar said.

Davi flinched at his uncle's anger. What could he say to make him understand? "I've been reading history. I don't understand why things are the way they are," Davi said.

"Maybe it's not your job to understand."

"Before the colonists left Earth to settle on other planets, the Legallians and Vertullians were at peace for twelve years," Davi continued. "When the Vertullians discovered they'd settled the planet next door to us, they didn't fight, they sued for peace. Instead, we conquered them and turned them into slaves."

Xalivar turned back to him. Their eyes met. "They cannot be trusted."

"They sued for peace and we betrayed them, yet they can't be trusted?" Davi saw from his uncle's eyes that Xalivar really believed it.

"Twelve years of peace during a time when everyone was distracted by other concerns," Xalivar said. "After hundreds of years of wars."

"Extremists and terrorists brought us together. Why would we forget all that when we settled here?"

"Do you know how many of our people have died at their hands? How many communities they destroyed?" Xalivar demanded, his passion evident. He didn't just know the history, he believed these things to his core.

"How many of them have we killed? Can't the past ever be the past?" Davi asked. He'd begun to wonder. His uncle's anger seemed pretty intense over something that happened so long ago. "Twenty years ago, I was supposed to die because of your decree, yet here I am. You let it go and protected me, because I'm your nephew."

Xalivar's face changed when Davi mentioned the decree. Had he forgotten? *Maybe he wishes I hadn't survived.*

"I protected you, yes, and here you are trying to undo everything I've done!" Xalivar threw up his hands in dismay as his pupils narrowed and his face turned gray with worry.

"How can I stand by when my own family is living in slavery?" Davi asked quietly.

"Do you wish so badly to join them in their plight?" Xalivar said, whirling so his eyes locked on his nephew's. "Everything I've worked for, everything my father and grandfather worked for could be undone by this, Xander! Do you not care about this family any longer since you've found a new one?" They both turned at the sound of the door opening behind them.

Miri's feet shuffled on the carpet as she rushed in. "Why didn't you tell me you were here?" she said, looking at Davi.

"I didn't have the chance yet, Mother," Davi said.

"He was too busy arguing the evils of our oppressive Alliance with his uncle," Xalivar said. "He won't let this go. I should have raised him myself, disavowed him of his moral illusions." He stared accusingly at Miri.

"I raised him to think for himself," Miri said proudly.

"Well, he's decided this family is the enemy now," Xalivar said, fists clenching again.

"You're still my family. I care about you," Davi said with genuine emotion. Did his uncle really not believe that?

Xalivar waved dismissively to Miri. "I cannot do what he asks. You talk sense into him." He turned and stopped beside the door to his private chambers, punching a code. The door slid up and Xalivar disappeared inside, leaving them alone.

"You're trying to fight a system which has been in place for generations, Davi," Miri said.

"It's wrong, mother."

"It won't change overnight," Miri said, her voice almost pleading.

Davi knew she was right but was convinced he had to try. "Someone has to speak for the workers. People know who I am; maybe I can make them listen."

"Or you will make more enemies than you ever imagined," Miri said.

Davi's frustration overrode his control again. "So you would have me stand by and do nothing?"

"No, but I would have you recognize there will be more to convince than just your uncle," Miri said. It was a warning.

"I have to start somewhere." Davi turned away, knowing she was right. "I won't give up. I can't."

"Do you want to go to prison? Do you want to be killed?" Miri's voice was tinged with desperation; worry filled her eyes.

"I'm willing to do what it takes to change things for my people," Davi said as their eyes met.

"The Lords or the workers?"

"Both, Mother. I belong to both," he said with a sigh.

"I can't protect you." Her voice was pained.

"I know. I would never hurt you, mother; I hope you know that." He looked at her with love and smiled.

"I only want what's best for you. Your uncle, too," Miri pleaded.

"Can't you see I have to do this?" Davi said, as tears ran down her cheeks. He hurt for her. He raised his arms and she rushed into his embrace. They stayed there holding each other awhile.

Xalivar watched the Royal Shuttle depart with Davi aboard from his private quarters. How could he have been so blind? He'd forgotten all about the decree! He'd forgotten all about the nightmares which kept him awake, night after night. He'd never given much credence to dreams, but after his scientists had reported an increase in male births on Vertullis, Xalivar had issued a decree and sent his Special Police squads to destroy all first-born males. They'd seemed so real to him then, but twenty-one years had passed. No one had arisen to challenge him in the decade that followed. He'd ultimately come to believe the dreams had been nonsense, but now …

Xander's mention of it had shocked him. He'd barely been able to maintain control. His throat had gone instantly dry, his limbs stiffened, almost freezing him in place. Somehow he'd recovered enough to hide it but his mind was a flutter with panic and worst-case scenarios. How could he have been so wrong? He would do whatever it took to protect the Alliance. He loved the boy, but love wasn't enough sometimes. Davi would have to be watched, although he didn't want him harmed. Not yet. He hoped it wouldn't come to that, but he was prepared to do what was necessary. Miri would object, of course, but neither she nor her son really grasped what was at stake. Anyone was expendable if they rebelled. It couldn't be tolerated.

The Council was scheduled to meet that afternoon, and he knew what must be done. He had to keep Davi close, and he had the perfect means right under his nose. Funny, he'd almost failed to see that, too. He'd been almost ready to order Davi back to Plutonis. *I must be growing weary. I need to get more rest. I have to stay on top of such things.*

And then he knew he had it and he smiled. Yes, it was the perfect plan. So perfect, it would almost seem like a natural course of events beyond even Xalivar's control.

"Let me get this straight," Lord Tarkanius said, leaning forward in his chair at the head of the table. "You now support the Council in prosecuting your own nephew for murder?"

Xalivar and Tarkanius sat atop a large dais, as officiators of the meeting. The other Council members were seated at rows of tables facing them. All wore the embossed white robes customary for Council meetings. Located in the Council Building, across the government complex from the Palace, the chamber itself was modeled after the US Senate back on old Earth but smaller.

"Having now learned other details of the incident, yes," Xalivar said, looking at Tarkanius with sincere determination.

He heard several Lords' grumbles from around the room. They were all surprised by his change of heart. But Xalivar had them right where he wanted them as usual.

"You are no longer concerned about the scandal this could cause?" Lord Hachim asked from halfway down the aisle on Xalivar's right.

"There will be talk, of course. But we believe we can contain it," Xalivar said.

"I hear rumors your nephew abandoned his post at Alpha Base and traveled back to Vertullis," Lord Niger said. He was seated near Hachim, his skin and hair dark, reflecting his Old Earth African ancestry. "Why would he do that?"

"His sympathy for the workers has driven him to unpredictable behavior," Xalivar said, adding a touch of sadness to his tone. "It is quite disturbing even to hear him discuss it."

"Yes, I can imagine it would be," Lord Obed said from Xalivar's left.

His skin had a light olive hue, common to people of Hispanic backgrounds on Old Earth, and his brown eyes were intense like his son's. The overseer of the Lord's Special Police, Obed's and Xalivar's families had been rivals since their grandfathers' days.

*You'd love to see me go down, wouldn't you, Obed? Not today.*

Xalivar smiled to himself. The special session was off limits to visitors. No one would witness him setting his plan in motion. He was free to manipulate the Council just as he'd planned.

Xalivar could see the questions in the Lords' eyes and feel their distrust. They feared betrayal; good! He liked keeping them off balance. It gave him more power. "Given the circumstances, I have no choice but to support the Council in upholding the law. Our sense of justice must prevail."

"And how will your dear sister react to this?" Lord Tarkanius asked.

"Miri has always been far too weak to govern," Xalivar said, dismissing her with a sympathetic tone. "She takes these matters personally and doesn't see the bigger picture."

"Will she hold her tongue?" Lord Niger asked.

"I will assist her, as required," Xalivar said.

A couple of Lords frowned with distaste.

"The younger generation is harder to bring into line these days," Xalivar continued. "Many of you have first-hand knowledge of this from your own offspring."

Several Lords nodded and groaned.

"Well, with your support we cannot refuse," Hachim said, leaning back in his chair with a satisfied look.

Others around him began nodding and mumbling agreement.

Tarkanius observed the responses and then sighed, his eyes scanning the room. "All right, let us take a vote then to reissue the arrest warrant," Tarkanius said. "All in favor, say aye."

When the votes were tallied, the decision was unanimous. Despite their reservations, none were willing to quarrel with the High Lord Councilor. Some, like Obed, couldn't resist the chance to do his reputation damage. Others feared his power. None of this bothered him. He had manipulated them as he'd planned, and he would deal with whatever came next.

"Lord Obed, send your Special Police again to locate and arrest the Prince," Tarkanius said with clear regret.

"I am reinstating the orders as we speak," Obed said as he typed on the terminal in front of him.

Xalivar suppressed a smile, as a warmth filled his veins. He found it amazing how easy it was.

Davi sat at Lura's table again and described his discussions with Xalivar and Miri. "Did you expect them to change their minds simply because you asked?" Lura asked, her brow furrowing at his frustration.

"I guess not," Davi said. "I expected them to listen at least."

"Xalivar's father was on the Council when they voted to enslave us," Lura said. "His grandfather started the war. And Xalivar himself has always been against us." For her, Xalivar never evoked a sympathetic figure and it was very odd hearing Davi talk about him as he did.

"I hoped it was different now," Davi said with growing sadness.

"It's hard for people to change," Lura said. "For the Council, the stakes are very high. And hatred for us amongst many Boralians has existed for generations and runs deep." Many Vertulians also returned that hatred, but she'd never really understood why. To blame individuals for their actions, yes, that she understood, but to blame everyone seemed ridiculous.

"Of course," Davi said, "But my mother raised me to believe in humanity's right to self-determination, and even she argued with me about it." He understood that Miri worried, but he'd still expected more support from her.

"The Lords don't see workers as human," Lura said.

Davi turned away and shook his head. He couldn't bear to look at her when he acknowledged such things. And he desperately wanted to help her. "I can't accept it," Davi said.

"None of us have any choice," Lura said, rubbing his back. "Don't be sad, my son. None of this is a surprise for me. I've lived with it all my life." The pain had lessened over the years to a degree with acceptance of the way things were, but it flared up in situations like those with Nila, or whenever she thought of Sol, and now watching her son hurt over it, too.

She had prepared another wonderful meal. They ate together in silence, as Davi struggled to come to terms with what had happened. Even the delicious dessert of fresh gixi pie couldn't overcome his somber mood.

Afterwards, Davi helped Lura clear the table and wash the dishes. "Who'd have ever thought I'd have a Prince drying my dishes?" Lura teased, still amazed that her son had come back to her.

Davi chuckled. "I've never done it before. Hope I'm doing it right." He seemed to be enjoying the experience of feeling normal for once.

"You're doing just fine," she said and joined in.

When they'd finished, Lura took Davi out for a walk. "There's someone I think you should meet," she said as they wound their way through the residential corridors and across the park where Davi had used the kiosk.

The fresh air, such as it existed in Iraja, improved Davi's mood. He had been feeling cooped up of late, being sent off to live in the stuffy base on Plutonis, hiding from the LSP before that, and it felt good to just walk under the open sky again.

On the other side of the park, they entered a residential district with several streets of nothing but apartments, then came to a cul-de-sac with houses which seemed larger than most worker houses he'd seen. Lura stopped at the door of a large blue house, designed in the nouveau deco style so popular a decade before, and pushed the doorbell.

A gray-haired woman wearing a flowery apron wrinkled and stained from years of work answered the door and smiled when she saw Lura. "Lura! Welcome! It's been months!"

The two women embraced and the woman waved them inside, letting the door shut behind them.

"Calla, I want you to meet my son, Davi," Lura said.

Emotion exploded off Calla's face. Her eyes lit up and her smile was blinding. She hugged Lura again and swung her around like they were dancing. "Davi? After all these years?"

Lura nodded as Davi extended his hand. Calla laughed and embraced him with passion. "If you think your Aunt Calla will settle for a handshake after twenty-one years, you are quite mistaken."

"Is Aron in?" Lura asked as she watched them, amused.

Calla released Davi and motioned with her head toward the corridor. "Of course. He's in the study."

"Come." She led them into the house and down a corridor which seemed endless—not at all what Davi had expected from a worker's home. Another corridor appeared, almost out of thin air, and they turned right and stopped beside a door, where Calla punched in a code. This was no ordinary worker's home.

The door opened, admitting them into a large office. A gray-haired man sat behind a desk, reading something on his terminal. He looked up, smiling as he saw both Lura and Calla.

"You'll never guess who this is," Calla said, motioning to Davi. Joy radiated like a sun's rays from her face.

The man stood and moved around his desk. He was short and bulky, with hands that showed signs of years of manual labor. He moved toward them, looking Davi over. "He looks so much like his father."

As he drew closer, Davi saw a face more youthful than he'd expected from one with such gray hair.

Calla smiled, pleased. "Yes, he does."

Davi extended his hand as the man chuckled, looking pleased. "Nice to meet you."

"This is your father's oldest friend, Aron," Lura said. Lura had told him about Aron's help with the courier.

Aron shook Davi's hand with a grip full of strength, his large hand surrounding Davi's like a glove. "After all these years to see you again … Sol would be so happy."

"Aron helped your father prepare the craft in which we sent you away," Lura reminded him.

Davi nodded. He was overwhelmed again meeting people who seemed to know and care so much about him despite having thought him dead or missing for so many years.

Aron frowned. "Only we made a mistake in preparing it." His face turned sad as he recalled it.

"He is safe and sound," Calla said, placing her arm reassuringly around his shoulder.

"We never saw your father again after that day," Aron said, remaining dour. "Such dark times," Aron continued, lost in memories. He regained his composure after a moment and motioned toward two couches and chairs arranged in a square. "Please. Sit."

"Mother told me he disappeared, but does anyone know where?" Davi asked, as he sat in a chair, wondering if he'd ever get the chance to meet his father.

Aron sat in the other chair, while Calla and Lura sat together on a couch. "None of us knows. But when the LSP take people away, they are never heard from again," Aron said.

"Davi was raised on Legallis, in the Royal Palace," Lura said, saying it with a mix of magic and fearfulness. Her friends reacted similarly.

"The Royal Palace? I guess our little courier's malfunction was not so disastrous after all," Aron said, chuckling.

They all laughed.

"He's a Captain in the military," Lura said with pride.

"I recognized his Alliance accent and wondered," Aron said. "Are you a pilot?"

"Top of his class," Lura said, smiling at him.

Davi blushed, her unabashed praise reminding him a bit of the Royal groupies he'd avoided as a youth. "I am certified in flight, yes."

"Davi has been working hard to convince Lord Xalivar to free our people," Lura said.

"A Borali Alliance officer questioning the High Lord Councilor?" Aron laughed, raising his eyebrows as he lexamined Davi again. "How's that gone?"

"Not as well as I'd hoped," Davi said, turning away. He'd never felt so useless.

Aron put a gentle hand on Davi's shoulder. "It's hard to reverse hundreds of years of oppression, as history has shown," Aron said. "You are not the first to try."

"I won't go back to my assignment until I find a way to make them listen," Davi said, turning to face them again. "I can't accept it." He feared he had no choice. He was running out of options.

"Many in the Alliance won't appreciate your attitude," Aron said.

"I know. But I was raised to believe man has a right to be free," Davi said, knowing he'd had more privileges than any of them.

"Raised to believe this in the Royal Palace right under Xalivar's nose?" Aron laughed. Calla and Lura joined him. "He must be quite disturbed by that. How did that happen?"

"Davi's mother is Princess Miri," Lura said.

Davi nodded. "She hired the best tutors and made sure I read broadly. She wanted me to think for myself."

Aron smiled. "Well, good for her." He exchanged looks with Calla and Lura. "Maybe I should take you with me to meet some friends of ours."

Lura nodded in agreement.

"You might like to hear their thoughts on the worker situation. And they yours."

"Anything I can do to help," Davi said, smiling.

Aron patted him on the arm, smiling back. "Your father would be proud to hear you talk this way."

Xalivar waited with Zylo for Bordox to arrive. After the Council meeting he had summoned them, wanting men he could trust to lead the search for his fugitive nephew. Neither man had been told why he'd been called to the Palace, so Xalivar could evaluate them, in addition to their military records, by how they responded to the assignment.

The Council meeting couldn't have gone smoother, and Xalivar was feeling relieved and excited that his new plan was coming together so well.

The door slid open and Manaen entered, followed by Bordox, who seemed overwhelmed. He'd never been in the throne room before. He took it all in, and then turned back toward Xalivar, as if afraid to turn away.

*Might as well enjoy this*, Xalivar thought, making his way back to the throne as the door slid closed behind Bordox. He sat down. He always looked more imposing sitting there. "Lieutenant Bordox, welcome to the Royal Palace." Tall like his father, Lord Obed, Bordox towered over both Zylo and Manaen.

*He'd tower over me, too, if I wasn't on this dais.* Xalivar could see why Bordox inspired fear in some. *And yet you don't fear Davi, do you?* His nephew didn't seem the type to inspire much fear.

"Thank you, Lord," Bordox said with a slight bow as his index and middle and fourth and fifth fingers crossed in the salute. His gray uniform was pressed and neat, like he'd wanted to make the best impression.

"I have been admiring your work on behalf of the Alliance. A very impressive record," Xalivar said.

"It's an honor to serve, my Lord," Bordox said, his legs wobbling a bit from nerves as he stood at attention.

*I see none of the cockiness I'd heard about. At least he knows how to show proper respect.* Xalivar reminded himself this was the same cadet who had been Davi's rival at the Academy. Not to forget that he'd surely been raised knowing the history of the old rivalry between their families. "This is Major Isak Zylo," Xalivar said.

Zylo nodded to Bordox. "Pleasure to meet you, Lieutenant."

"You, too, sir," Bordox replied, continuing to wobble.

*I just complimented your record. You'd think you'd relax.* "I've called you both here for a special assignment. The Council has announced murder charges against Captain Xander Rhii, my nephew."

Bordox didn't react, but Zylo's face showed surprise. "Captain Rhii, sir? I served with him on Vertullis."

"He was involved in an altercation with a fellow Captain. That

Captain was killed," Xalivar explained.

*Ah, there it is, Bordox, in your eyes—is that excitement I see? Good. Perhaps your resentment will serve me well.* "Major Zylo will head the intelligence gathering. Lieutenant Bordox will lead in the field."

*Ah, yes, your eyes seem pleased, Lieutenant. I hope your personal feelings won't keep you from obeying orders.*

"Yes, my Lord," Zylo and Bordox replied in unison.

"I want him brought in unharmed. His last known whereabouts was Vertullis." Xalivar couldn't resist playing with Bordox a bit. "I'm assuming your competitive spirit won't interfere with your understanding of orders, Lieutenant?"

Bordox's brown eyes showed surprise and he shifted on his feet. "Innocent competition between classmates, my Lord."

His eyes revealed he was lying but Xalivar smiled, admiring his resolve. "Good, Lieutenant. We're already three weeks behind him. You should both get started at once."

Both officers saluted again then turned toward the door as Manaen opened it for them. As they exited, Manaen turned back to Xalivar, his red eyes attentive.

"I want constant reports of their progress, Manaen," Xalivar said.

"Yes, my Lord," Manaen nodded then turned and followed the officers.

Xalivar stepped down from the throne and moved toward the window, as the door closed behind Manaen. *Miri will have to be dealt with.* He dreaded it. *I wish it hadn't come to this, but she's left me no choice.* He wondered why he was so conflicted. Perhaps he, too, had gotten soft. Hmmm. He'd have to work on that.

A week after their first meeting, Aron invited Davi to accompany him to a gathering of friends. Davi went expecting a small meeting in a private house, not anything like what he found. The meeting took place in a large square in one of the residential districts on the edge of Iraja. Hundreds of workers attended. They all seemed so relaxed and enthusiastic given the fact that mass gatherings of workers were forbidden. No one there seemed concerned about possible repercussions.

A makeshift wooden platform stood in the center of the square, and the crowd had gathered in a large circle around it. Davi and Aron wound their way through the chattering crowd toward the platform. Davi overheard people wondering what this meeting was about. Others chatted about their work and lives. Still others complained about there being too many people for the space. Volunteers handed out buttons with the initials WFR on them.

As they drew near, a pretty young blonde woman standing on the platform waved at Aron and ran to the edge to meet them. She wore a colorful dress bearing a WFR pin like the ones being handed to the crowd. Offering her hand, she helped first Aron and then Davi onto the platform. Davi was surprised by her strength. *Perhaps years spent as manual laborers did have its benefits.*

Aron introduced the girl as Brie. They were soon joined by a young man named Dru and another woman named Tela. Brie and Dru seemed like they had to be in their teens. Tela was around Davi's age and quite pretty. She had long brown hair and an attractive curved figure, medium height with blue eyes which sparkled. He had to force himself to take his eyes off of her. She didn't seem to notice his stare and continued talking with Aron, reviewing the agenda.

Brie smiled, taking his arm and pointing him toward some chairs on the platform. "Let me show you to your seat, Mr. Rhii." Was she flirting with him?

"Please, call me Davi," he said, smiling back.

Brie seemed to blush a bit at his smile and looked away. "Okay, Davi. Such an exciting day for the Resistance!"

*Yep, definitely flirting.* He glanced back toward Tela, hoping she hadn't noticed. Tela took no note of them. "Which Resistance?"

She laughed as if he were teasing. "The Workers Freedom Resistance, of course." She pulled one of the WFR buttons from her pocket and pinned it to his shirt, letting their eyes meet a moment. She'd leaned so close her breath warmed his cheek. Again he found himself glancing toward Tela. Again she took no notice. No woman had ever shown so little interest in him. He turned back as Brie smiled. She seemed plenty interested. In fact, for a moment, he actually thought she might kiss him. *Forget Tela. Brie's rather cute.* Then she stepped back and hurried off to return to other duties.

As Davi watched Brie go, Tela cleared her throat into a microphone. "Hello, friends! Welcome to the first gathering of the Workers Freedom Resistance! It's an exciting day for workers all over the solar system!"

The crowd quieted to hear what she was saying. Her enthusiasm was contagious; her lilting voice arrested everyone's attention. Davi couldn't take his eyes off of her.

"We have with us today a man whom many of you know and respect, a man who has provided leadership to us through difficult days. I give you Aron Tal!"

Brie, Dru, and Tela applauded. A few in the crowd joined in as Aron took the microphone. Perhaps Aron's characterization of this as a "gathering of friends" had been hyperbole. Many in the crowd looked as if they didn't know who he was.

"My good people, it gives me great pleasure to see you here today. For many generations, we have lived at the mercy of our old enemy and rival, whose sole mission has been to control and oppress us. But an opportunity has presented itself to bring about changes. Many of you know me as a man of patience and reason, but I tell you today—my patience has run out! The time for reasoning is very short. We must become a people of action and demand what we deserve—our freedom, our dignity, our planet."

Shouts erupted from all around them—showing the crowd shared his sentiments, though the looks on their faces made it clear most doubted his veracity. They applauded and cheered for a few moments before Aron continued.

"The Borali Alliance has refused to talk with us. The Lords deem us unworthy of their time and consideration. They treat us worse than they treat their animals, but I believe in part we are to blame for this."

Mumbles of doubt and surprise issued from the crowd.

"It's easy for us to blame the Lords, while we continue to do nothing but complain. Over the years there have been many voices, but no action. The time has come for us to work together. Only united can we take action that will have true impact. By uniting together with the same focus we give to our jobs, we can force them to listen."

This brought more cheers and applause. A few men near the front began to chant. "Freedom! Freedom!" Others joined in.

"Yes, my friends. Freedom can be ours!" Aron said, stirring the fervor among them.

Davi watched an older woman push her way to the front. "Freedom for what? To be crushed by the Alliance? To be beaten? To be debased? Humiliated as we have been so many times before? It will merely lead to greater oppression," she shouted.

"Which is why we must work together. We outnumber them here on our own planet. If we stand together, they cannot hope to defeat us," Aron assured her, smiling warmly.

Davi saw more of the crowd was getting into the idea now. More joined the chant, crying: "Freedom! Freedom!"

Aron spoke for a few more minutes, followed by a speech from Dru aimed at the younger people in the crowd. Afterwards, Tela got up and invited them to sign a petition supporting the Resistance.

As the crowd dispersed, volunteers stood with databoards awaiting signatures, but few agreed to sign. Several expressed doubts like those of the older woman and walked away. In the end, the young WFR leaders looked discouraged.

"Change cannot happen overnight," Aron said, trying to reassure them. "We must remain firm in our resolve."

"How can they yell so much and yet walk away so indifferent?" Tela asked.

"We have to inspire them to hope again," Aron said. "Those impulses have been smashed for years by the Alliance. They need to believe again. And they will in time." He embraced them each in turn, and then started home with Davi.

"What did you think?" Aron asked as they walked.

"You're trying to start a movement?"

"We're trying to unite our people, and get the Alliance's attention," Aron said.

"Large gatherings of workers will no doubt get their attention, and they'll send soldiers to arrest and detain you," Davi said, fearing for them, though he admired the man's resolve.

"They have to find us first," Aron said with confidence. "We don't gather often like that and worker neighborhoods are usually so quiet. They wouldn't have expected it. We never meet long enough for them to organize a major response." He certainly seemed confident that the WFR had thought it all through.

As they walked back toward Lura's house, Davi became quite disoriented. He couldn't have found his way back to the square, let alone anywhere else. The location had been well chosen. Its narrow corridors and arches were barely wide enough for pedestrian traffic. It would indeed be hard for the Alliance to move troops and vehicles in and surround them. Nonetheless, he knew the Alliance would find a way, even if they had to drop troops in on top of them.

Over the next two weeks, Aron took him to meetings in other parts of the city, some inside, some in similarly hard to reach squares. The crowds varied in size, but they gradually gathered signatures for their petition. Davi thought the speeches grew better and better each time. Brie, Dru and Tela seemed encouraged and started treating Davi like one of the gang. He even got a smile from Tela once or twice—moments he wished would last forever. He determined to do whatever he could to help them.

At the end of the month, the WFR core appeared on an underground comm-channel show to present their message, and Aron asked Davi to say a few words. He stumbled through them, but they seemed pleased with what he'd said.

"You came along at the right time, Davi," Aron said as they walked back to Lura's. "We needed to make the Resistance public, get people stirred up."

"I don't understand why the Alliance hasn't sent troops to arrest you or break up the gatherings," Davi said.

"We publicize by word of mouth," Aron said. "I've been using the underground comm-channel to spread our message a while now. It's enough to bring people out to hear what I have to say."

"Whatever you're doing it seems to be working," Davi said as they entered the courtyard near Lura's house.

They both stopped under the arch, staring at what was left of her front door. The wood had shattered into splinters. Davi stiffened and fear spread through him, as he raced toward the house.

"Wait! We don't know what's happened," Aron called after him.

Davi burst inside to find Lura and Nila being nursed by Nila's mother, Rena. "What happened?"

Davi and Aron halted in the doorway. Both Lura and Nila had cuts and bruises. Their dresses were torn.

"Soldiers came," Rena said.

Davi's heart stopped. Had the officials somehow connected Lura with the WFR's activities?

"Soldiers? What did they want?" Aron asked.

"They wanted Davi," Lura said, tears rolling down her cheeks.

*This was about him?* Davi couldn't believe it. *I thought the warrant had been dismissed.* "My gods, what did they do to you?" Davi rushed to her side, gently caressing her head.

She grasped his hand in hers, smiling. "It looks far worse than it is."

He tried to act as if he believed her, but his face gave him away.

Rena explained, "The Council reinstated murder charges against you."

"They had an arrest warrant for you," Lura said, her face full of fear.

"One of them said he knew you," Nila said. "His name was Bord-something."

Davi stood there, incredulous. *No, it couldn't be.*

"An LSP Lieutenant," Rena added.

"Bordox?" Davi asked as they both nodded. He turned away. Had his uncle changed his mind? He thought the matter was settled. Was Bordox acting on his own out of hatred and revenge? "How did they find you?"

The moment he asked the question, Calla appeared at the door out of breath. "Death Squads are going house to house, searching for Davi. He's wanted for murder!"

"We've got to hide you," Lura said. "They could come back any moment!"

Panic rose within Davi. Where could he hide?

Aron nodded. "We have the perfect place. Let me call Tela." He hurried to the communicator on the wall near the kitchen, dialed several numbers, and then clicked it off. "Now we wait, and pray."

Davi looked at Lura and Nila and was overcome with regret. He hated being the cause of more hurt for them. Bordox would never stop searching, and if Bordox found him, there was no telling what would happen. He couldn't call his mother for fear his uncle might hear and notify the LSP.

*So much for special treatment, mother.* He had nowhere to run. They would have notified the starport. For the first time in his life, Davi felt helpless.

# Chapter Six

They waited what seemed like hours at Aron and Calla's, but when the shuttle arrived, Davi glanced at his chrono—ninety minutes had passed. As the shuttle door slid open, he couldn't believe his eyes. Tela stepped out onto the ramp and smiled at them.

*She's a pilot?* She'd handled the shuttle with smooth ease. There was a stirring in his stomach and his heart hammered in his chest as his eyes locked on her. *I have to get to know this girl!*

They hurried aboard. The shuttle was an older model Davi hadn't seen in years. It had a gray exterior, instead of the white of recent models. Its interior had the four rows of chairs and harnesses in the passenger cabin and two in the cockpit facing the blast shield and controls.

Tela flew them to the far side of Vertullis over thick and undeveloped forest. It appeared that both the Vertullians and the Alliance kept busy enough with the existing agricultural and urban areas. The forest appeared mostly undisturbed. Tall cedars stretched around them as far as the eye could see. Wood had low value in the system—used mostly for making old-style furniture. Still, when Tela swung the shuttle in amongst them for a landing, it surprised him. Even more so when a portion of a rock wall opened to reveal a large hangar, into which they dove to land.

Stepping off the shuttle, Davi stopped and stared at what lay before him—a genuine Vertullian underground military base. Shuttles and a few skitters were scattered all around amidst the tool kits, instruments and personnel needed to keep them operational. Mech-bots of various colors and sizes rolled around performing tasks from delivering supplies to starcraft maintenance. Everyone went about their business with a precision and seriousness rivaling any post in the Borali Alliance. It took his breath away. How could they have built all this under the Boralians noses?

As he took it all in, Tela turned to the group and smiled. "Welcome to the Workers Freedom Resistance." Her face lit up with pride as did Aron's and Calla's.

Davi took is all in and smiled. "I had no idea you could fly."

"Why? Women aren't up to the challenge?" Tela snapped, frowning.

Davi raised a hand. "Wait. That's not what I meant at all—"

"You fighter jocks are all the same!" Irritated, Tela turned before he could say another word and headed off toward a group of mechanics working nearby.

Heat rose inside him. Women had affected him before, but not like this. She was clearly passionate, though he regretted making her so angry. "I think it's great," he called after her, but she was already busy chatting with the mechanics.

"I knew you'd been busy with the Resistance, Aron, but I had no idea …" Lura said, amazed.

Aron smiled. "It's a well-kept secret whose time has finally come. We've launched a campaign to gather support among our people, and we hope Davi can offer assistance in moving another aspect of the program forward."

*What do they want me for?* His mind filled with questions. "How can an operation like this remain undetected?" Davi asked.

"Radar coverage is difficult to deploy due to the density of the forest. Plus, once they clear the forest, our shuttles blend into intraplanetary traffic, and the Alliance hardly expects workers to have starcraft," Aron said.

The Borali Alliance rarely monitored intraplanetary traffic. "It must have taken years to build this," Davi said, full of admiration. He knew the Alliance took for granted that the workers were no threat, but they'd never imagined this. "How do you acquire starcraft?"

"Well, since we're the ones who repair them, when one gets written off as unworthy of repair, we find a use for it," Aron said.

Davi couldn't believe the Alliance would be so careless in disposing of starcraft. Then again, he'd seen how they disposed of old equipment in the Academy and on Plutonis—once they had no more use for it, what became of it wasn't considered a priority. "How do you get it here without detection?"

"Our mechanics send it out for one final test flight to ensure its status," Aron said. "When old shuttles designated for destruction disappear, they aren't deemed worthy of much investigation."

*They do seem to have figured out the loopholes.* "You have an actual hidden starbase here," Davi realized he sounded like a schoolboy and started to blush.

Aron laughed and patted his shoulder. "This is only the beginning.

Let's see to your mother and Nila first, and then I'll show you around."

"Of course," Davi said, excited about seeing more.

Aron took Lura's arm and led them through the landing bay toward a corridor carved out of the rock at the far end.

After seeing Lura and Nila to a makeshift medical bay, Aron escorted Davi on a tour through corridors cut out of rock.

The base had been built using existing caves. Corridors had been either dug out from scratch or expanded from existing tunnels between caves. Other than the hangar, dormitories, and the medical bay, a lot of the caves remained in various stages of development. Digging out the corridors and stringing the reflector pads to light everything alone had taken years.

Their tour ended in a large cavern containing the command center. It was as well developed as any area Davi had yet seen, including computer terminals, radar banks, various displays, a very large vidscreen, and consoles spread through the center in a U-shape. Everything centered around the vidscreen and a large radar monitor table in the center for monitoring battles.

"How did you get all this equipment?" Davi said, still taking it all in with awe.

"It's taken us years," a man nearby said, turning at the sound of his voice and smiling when he saw Aron. "We salvaged things wherever we could from old parts, things which had been discarded. A few things, like the radar table, were built from scratch to our own specifications."

Aron nodded as the man extended his hand to Davi. "Davi, this is Joram, one of our military technical experts."

Davi shook Joram's hand. "I didn't expect there would be a lot of military experts among the workers."

Joram laughed. "We've had to keep our knowledge secret, for sure. I'm well versed in military and cultural history. I also come from a long line of former military men, so I've tried to stay up on the latest materials. Nothing top secret for the Alliance, of course, but the web does provide quite a lot if you have the time to search for it."

Davi chuckled, truly impressed. "It's amazing what you've done here!" His friends at the Academy would never believe it.

"You can see why we've taken great lengths to conceal it," Aron said.

Another man joined them near the radar table, handing Aron a datapad. "Aron, we got those reports in on the repair depots."

"Wonderful," Aron said, turning to Davi. "We know the locations of all depots in the Borali Alliance where workers have been assigned."

"I guess some of the Alliance's secrets are easier to crack than others," Davi said.

The new man smiled. "Our intelligence network gets more and more advanced each day."

"Davi, meet Uzah, head of intelligence and military strategy for the WFR," Aron said.

Davi shook Uzah's outstretched hand. Their organizational structure was as impressive as their facilities and equipment. "This is great, but what do you plan to do with it? A full-scale military?"

Uzah and Joram looked at Aron, as if to ask if Davi could be trusted. Aron nodded.

"We plan to do whatever it takes to free our people," Joram said.

"We're hoping you'll be willing to assist us," Aron said.

"I don't know what I can do for you," Davi said, recalling his conversations with Xalivar. "I don't seem to have much influence."

"Within the Alliance, perhaps not anymore, but you do have something which we have great need of here," Aron said. Davi had no idea what he meant. "Flight training." Aron turned to the others as he continued: "Davi was a leading graduate of the Borali Alliance's military Academy."

Joram and Uzah's reactions told him right away what Aron had in mind. "I've never done much teaching," Davi said.

"I'm sure our pilot candidates will be eager to learn whatever information you can offer," Uzah said.

"You've already met several of them," Aron said. "Why don't we set up a class for you tomorrow so you can meet them?"

"I wouldn't know where to begin," Davi said, flustered. He had never imagined himself as a flight instructor.

"Begin where your instructors began at the Academy," Uzah said with an encouraging look. "We can train them on shuttles, and we've rebuilt several old simulators and placed them in a classroom. We also have a number of skitters, which can be used for training in the forest."

Shuttle training would only offer experience at flight. Shuttles and fighters were too dissimilar for it to be of much use in the long run. Skitters were one-man ground craft which operated on a system allowing them to fly above the planet's surface. They were sleek and fast and easy to maneuver through trees and other obstacles. They also had similar controls and handling to Alliance VS28 starfighters.

"Skitters and simulators are fine, but they can't replace actual flight time. If we have no fighters, how can we provide proper training?" Davi asked.

Uzah, Aron, and Joram exchanged a look and smiled.

"Don't worry. We have plans in place to acquire some," Joram said.

Aron slapped Davi on the back. "Let's take it a step at a time. They must first be ready for such training, yes?"

Davi nodded, still wondering how they would ever get a fleet of fighters here.

"Good. As you can see, we have anticipated all of our needs so far. Everything else will come together in time," Aron assured him.

Davi was starting to believe them. He decided to stop asking questions and see how things played out.

Xalivar had so far managed to keep Miri in the dark about the hunt for Davi, but her persistent questions about his whereabouts were getting on his nerves. It had been a matter of time before someone let slip to her about the reinstated murder charges. And given Bordox and Zylo's failure to track his nephew down quickly, he'd decided not to sit around waiting but to do some investigating himself.

The communicator on the wall of his inner chamber beeped twice. Manaen was coming. Good. He would bring with him some visitors who might provide some answers.

When Xalivar stepped into the throne room, he found Manaen waiting with Farien and Yao. Both had put on their finest dress uniforms, as Bordox had done. They stood at attention. He smiled. They knew him, because of their long friendship with Davi; still, they'd never managed to feel at home around him—a fact which suited Xalivar just fine. He liked keeping people off guard, particularly when he wanted information from them.

Seeing Yao in his full dress uniform reminded him of his dislike for aliens, especially those who'd been accorded equal status with humans with the support of the Council. Yet another thing Xalivar would change if given a chance. Aliens were fine for subordinate positions like Manaen held, but they would never be humans' equals.

He managed to conceal his displeasure as he turned to Manaen. "Leave us." Manaen bowed and turned back toward the exit.

Xalivar waited until the door slid shut behind him. "I have been following reports of your diligent work on the Alliance's behalf with great satisfaction. You are serving with honor."

"Thank you, sir," they said in perfect unison.

*Such good little soldier boys. Let's see how loyal to the Borali Alliance you really are.* "Have you been pleased with your assignments?" Xalivar asked.

"Yes, sir," they said in unison again.

"Good. Davi also seems to have enjoyed his assignments. Have you kept in touch?"

"From time to time, Lord," Yao said.

"We saw each other a couple of times before he transferred to Alpha Base," Farien said.

Xalivar took note of the look they exchanged upon the mention of Davi's name, as if asking each other how much they should say. "Perhaps you hadn't heard, but my nephew has fallen into some difficulties. He's wanted for questioning in the death of a Captain on Vertullis. Did you hear anything about it?"

Farien shrugged. "A couple of rumors."

"I saw the warrant on the web, my Lord," Yao said. His purple eyes almost seemed to glow a moment.

*One or both of you are lying. I can see it in your eyes.* "If you hear from him, you will, of course, report it right away?"

Both nodded. "Yes, Lord."

Xalivar knew nothing would be gained from attempting to force information from them. He could wait until another time. For now, knowing he would be watching might be enough to make them think twice if Davi contacted them. His voice changed to a tone of concern. "If you think of anything, anything at all which I should know about, I am very concerned about him, of course. He is my only nephew and designated heir."

They both nodded.

*It's still there in your eyes.*

"We are, too, my Lord," Yao said.

"Yes, I imagine you are," Xalivar said, doing his best to sound sympathetic.

"We will help in any way we can," Farien said.

*That's what I'm counting on, and why you'll be constantly watched.* "Thank you for your service to the Alliance," Xalivar said.

They both knelt, offering him the expected salute.

"Be sure and take some time to visit your families while you're here. Family is important. Dismissed."

They nodded, and then turned for the door. Xalivar watched them go, hoping they would somehow lead him to Davi.

Yao and Farien avoided discussing their meeting with Xalivar until they were alone at Yao's parents' house that evening. After some time with both sets of parents, who'd gathered there for a dinner together, they snuck away to the game room and turned the stereo up so they couldn't be overheard. Both were still tense and worried.

"Have you heard from him?" Yao asked as they played a game of virtual chess. He wondered why Farien always wanted to play. Yao beat him every time. And tonight, as distracted as they both were, he was making it easy.

"Other than a couple of friendly e-posts, no," Farien said as he moved his pieces quickly without much thought, setting up several opportunities for Yao to make important captures.

"Well, let's keep it that way as far as Xalivar is concerned, okay?" Yao said, noting his friend's surprise as he captured Farien's bishop.

"You expect me to hide information from the High Lord Councilor?" Farien asked as he deliberated over his next move.

"I didn't say to hide it," Yao said, "but don't volunteer it." He enjoyed watching Farien strain his brain for the right move.

Farien shook his head. "I don't know about this."

"I have my doubts, too, but he's our oldest friend." Yao couldn't believe Farien was even questioning it.

"And that means I should let my career go down the tubes for him?" Farien slid his rook across the board, threatening Yao's knight.

"Xalivar didn't threaten us," Yao said, his eyes urging Farien to cooperate. Even as he did, he thought again about all they had to lose. He took the rook with his own rook, watching as Farien frowned in frustration.

"Oh sure, I totally bought all his friendly chit-chat," Farien said, his eyes tired, his voice strained. "If he's allowing the Council to issue a warrant for Davi, he's not on Davi's side."

"I'm not saying he is," Yao said. "Don't you think we owe Davi the benefit of the doubt?"

"What I think is I don't want to get mixed up in this mess," Farien said, irritably. "I've worked too hard to get where I am, and this could really screw things up for me."

Yao shook his head. "It's sure screwing things up for our friend Davi." Despite his own doubts, he was disappointed Farien had such a narrow view of things. *Maybe I need to talk to Miri about this.* He'd send her an e-post as soon as they were finished.

"Maybe he brought this on himself by killing an Alliance Captain," Farien said, with surprising coldness.

*My Gods, has our friendship come to this?* "It was an accident. He told us the circumstances," Yao reminded him.

"If he wants to blow his whole career getting mixed up with workers, it's his problem. He can't expect me to blow mine!" Farien's nostrils flared. He was angry at Davi for putting them in this position, it seemed.

"Gods, Farien, no one's asking you to ruin your career, just to look out for a friend a little," Yao said, frowning as their eyes met.

"A friend who's wanted by the Council and the High Lord Councilor," Farien said. "I'm not making any promises, and if you ask me, I don't think Davi would expect me to."

"Fine. You keep looking out for yourself as usual," Yao snapped. He turned and punched a code in the panel next to the door, waiting until it slid open with a whoosh. "You seem to be very good at it."

He left Farien standing there, staring after him.

Not wanting to go near the Palace, Yao arranged to meet Miri at the city's largest public park. She came alone by air taxi, her face haggard with worry.

"Thank you so much for contacting me. I've been so worried about Davi," she said as she embraced Yao warmly. "I haven't heard from him since right after he took emergency leave from Alpha Base, and Xalivar won't tell me anything."

"I'm afraid the Council has charged him with murder," Yao said.

"What? Xalivar promised he would make sure that didn't happen!" Miri said, stiffening as her blue eyes filling with anger.

"I don't want to speak ill of the High Lord Councilor, but he called Farien and I in and asked about Davi. I got the impression he wasn't going to interfere with the Council's decision," Yao said, filled with regret.

Miri's face registered a mix of shock and rage. "What is he thinking? My gods! Davi came to us and asked about the workers. I'm afraid a startling discovery about his past has upset him."

"What discovery?"

Miri hesitated a moment, as if she were unsure how Yao would react. "He discovered I adopted him years ago from a worker family."

Miri clearly expected Yao to react with shock, but instead he nodded. "We heard a rumor about it two years ago at the Academy."

"A rumor? So long ago? It was supposed to be secret," Miri said with surprise and worry.

"We heard it from a cadet who never liked Davi. We figured he was trying to make waves, but Davi told Farien and I two months ago on Vertullis that he suspected it might be more than a rumor," Yao said.

Miri looked at her feet. "It's true." Her eyes met his and she was pleading. "Please don't hate him for it. I know it's a shock to everyone, but it's not his fault. I raised him as my own, because it never mattered to me, and it shouldn't matter to you."

Yao smiled, putting a hand on her arm. "He's the best friend I've got. He can't get rid me so easily. Besides, I don't know any workers. I have nothing personal against them."

Miri let out s slow breath, her body relaxing. "I wish more in the Alliance thought as you do." Relieved tears rolled down her cheeks. "If there was a rumor, how many know?" Her eyes widened as the implications sunk in.

"When it came up back then, no one believed it," Yao assured her, his eyes locked on hers. "I promise. We all thought Bordox was just making trouble."

Miri's shoulders relaxed as she sighed. "Bordox. I don't know why he hates Davi so much." Then she sobbed softly, overcome.

Yao pulled her to him in an embrace. "It's okay, Princess. I'd do anything I can to help him. I'll let you know as soon as I hear from him."

Yao meant it, although he wasn't sure what he'd do if the help asked involved things which might be deemed traitorous to the Alliance.

"Thank you. You know you're like family to me," Miri said, sniffling as she looked up at his face and subconsciously straightened a loose bang on his forehead just like his own mother would.

He dried her tears with his handkerchief. "You are to me, too," he said.

"Thank you for your support of Davi," she said, smiling as she recovered her composure. "And me."

"If there's anything you need, don't hesitate to ask," Yao said. "But be careful about Farien. He fears his association with Davi could hurt his career." Yao's might as well, but Davi was more important.

"There'll be many others, I'm afraid. Even Xalivar is more concerned for himself than anyone else," she said, her face graying with sadness. They both stood there a moment, pondering the gravity of it all.

Aron had skipped the flight-training classroom on the tour. Located on the opposite side of the hangar from the command center, it was clearly intended to serve a dual purpose as a ready room for pilots once training was completed. A rather large chamber, it contained four simulators on one side and rows of chairs and desks on the other. A laser board and vidscreen hung side by side on the front wall, behind a plexiglass podium.

Davi arrived to find twenty eager trainees seated and waiting for him. He was surprised to see Tela, Nila, Brie, and Dru among them. The moment he saw Tela, his heart accelerated in volume and pace. He feared the whole room could hear it. *I guess I should've guessed she'd sign up for this. Maybe I can make up for upsetting her the other day.*

He walked to the front of the room, taking a closer look at the students as he moved up the aisle. *They look like kids, all of them. Most can't even be my age yet.* Of course, he'd started flying at sixteen and graduated from the Academy at twenty-one. For some reason, he found himself feeling so much older now.

Stepping behind the podium, he turned and smiled. "Welcome class. Good to see so many future pilots here!" He turned to Tela: "And one very talented pilot already. How many of you have ever done any flying, besides, of course, Tela?"

Tela frowned as a few trainees in the back raised their hands, but none he knew by name.

He swallowed, moistening his suddenly dry throat and glanced around. Several others were looking warily, even angrily, at him. "Okay, we have our work cut out for us. Without fighters to train in, we'll be doing a lot of training on the simulators and then using skitters to get you used to the speed and feel as much as possible."

Brie raised her hand.

"Yes, Brie?"

"Skitters don't fly," she said, a puzzled look on her face.

Davi nodded. "Well, yes, that's true, but they do handle similarly to fighters."

Dru raised his hand.

Davi nodded at him.

"What about laser target practice?" Dru asked. "They don't have lasers either."

"Alliance skitters do," Tela interjected. Davi smiled at her in appreciation but she just looked away again.

"We'll have to do it all on the simulators for now," Davi said.

Brie raised her hand again.

"Yes?" *Would they always be like this?*

"When are we getting fighters?"

"I don't know." He was beginning to wonder if giving some of these people access to fighters would be a good idea. They seemed too eager. Brie and Dru seemed disappointed with his answer. "There're going to be a lot of things we'll have to figure out as we go along."

Several of the trainees sighed, frustrated. "How do we know they'll ever allow us to fly them?" a dark-skinned cadet said from the back row.

"That's what I'm here for," Davi answered as everyone in the room waited with anticipation for his reaction.

"Yeah, right," the cadet next to the other said, smirking at their buddies. "A Borali Alliance officer training workers against his own people."

A few other cadets chuckled in agreement.

"Not just a Borali Alliance officer! The Prince himself!" said the dark-skinned cadet. Now even Tela and Dru were giving Davi suspicious looks.

"Jorek! Virun! Cut it out!" Nila scolded, frowning at them.

"Look," Davi said, "I'm on your side. Why would your leaders send me here, if they didn't trust me?"

"Did your Uncle order them to?" Virun said with a smirk as his friends laughed.

Davi sighed. For the first time, he found being known as a Royal made him very uncomfortable. He fought the urge to snap back, instead chuckling and smiling at Virun. "Without the resources of the Borali Alliance, we do face some challenges."

The cadets mumbled in acknowledgement, some still staring at him as if he were to blame.

"However, when I was in flight school, we also didn't have experienced pilots in the class either, and you have the good fortune to have two."

Tela shot him an annoyed look. *What did I do now?* Several of the others were looking at her now. She looked away, shifting behind her desk.

"Okay, well, perhaps we should cover a few basics of flight first." *Going to leave her alone and hope she gets over it. For a pilot, she seems kind of sensitive. Hope she has the endurance to do this.* He made a note to keep the question to himself, flipped on the laser board, and began lecturing.

An hour and a half later, he wrapped up what he thought was a pretty decent lecture on the basics of flight and the trainees dispersed. He found Tela waiting for him in the corridor, eyes fuming.

*Might as well confront this head on.* "Tela, I'm glad you're here. I wanted to apologize to you for offending you when we landed yesterday—"

She didn't even wait for him to finish. "Don't single me out in front of everyone! They're already intimidated enough and they're my friends."

"Look, I'm sorry if I made you uncomfortable. I really meant it as a compliment. You're a very good pilot. You can help them learn." The heat rose in him just being near her.

"As what? Teacher's pet? They'll resent me for it!" She was clearly not appeased.

"Well, to be honest, if you were going for teacher's pet, you'd have to be nicer to me," he joked. She didn't even smile. *What is it with this girl?*

"You fighter jocks are all the same," she said. "Or maybe it's just you princes!" She stared at him, disgusted, then turned and marched up the corridor.

Davi had to run to keep up with her. "What's that supposed to mean?"

"Over-confident braggarts, who think all you have to do is come in the room and the women will start swooning," Tela snapped.

"Wait a minute! We don't really know each other. I'm not like that at all," Davi said, trying to hide his own growing irritation. She was making so many assumptions which just weren't true. Sure, women had been impressed by his Royal status, but he'd tried not to take advantage of it. Then he remembered the girls at Bar Electric. *Most of the time.*

"Yes, you are. I've been around your type my whole life!"

"Really? You know some other princes?"

She scowled and rolled her eyes, hurrying off again, but he grabbed her arm.

"You really are something, aren't you? Judging people without even bothering to get to know them? It seems to me I'm not the one here who's full of himself!" He sighed, regretting the outburst, even though it was true.

"Oh stuff it up your flight suit, air jockey!" She turned and stormed off, leaving him disconcerted. He'd never had problems talking to women before. Why this one? And why did it turn him on so much?

Bordox had searched the entire planet for Xander with little to show for it. He had no idea why Rhii was helping the workers. There'd been a rumor when they were at the Academy about Xander being found in a courier, a worker child, and he'd helped spread it, but Bordox never really believed that. It was Xander Rhii after all. The little Prince had always been soft. What Bordox couldn't fathom was how he'd survived five years at the Academy. Bordox had what it took. Rhii didn't. Now, Rhii's actions proved his success at the Academy was a fluke. The Prince had sailed through on his family name, charming the faculty and administration, or, at least, revealing their hypocrisy. Bordox knew he was ten times the soldier Xander Rhii would ever hope to be, and on this mission, he would prove it.

He arrived early for his appointment with Zylo at the Regional Office of the LSP. They'd decided to put their heads together and regroup. But Bordox was wondering if a head butt might not be the best plan. Zylo's intelligence was worthless. Every lead he'd provided had turned up a dead end. Bordox was doing all the work, and he wasn't about to bust his butt to see Zylo get all the credit. It always worked that way with higher-level officers. The lower level guys did the work, while the higher-level guys got the glory. Not this time! This was his chance to show Xalivar, the High Lord Councilor himself, who the best soldier in the Alliance really was. At last, Bordox would get the recognition he deserved!

Zylo even seemed to feel sorry for Rhii. Bordox wanted to laugh when Zylo expressed sympathy for the little rat. *Pathetic loser.* Such softness would never get in Bordox's way. He made his way to the conference room where Zylo was already waiting for him. *Sigh.*

"We've generated a bunch of new leads for you," Zylo said, tossing a memory card across the table at him.

"I hope they're better than the previous garbage you guys sent me," Bordox said.

Zylo didn't bother to hide his annoyance. "Intelligence gathering is not an exact science, especially when it comes to workers. They have no reason to cooperate with us. We do our best to fill in as many of the pieces as we can before we send the data to you. Your tactics haven't helped the results."

Bordox stared at him, hiding his contempt. *Not more of this bleeding heart softie crap!* "We're trained to use whatever it takes to complete our mission," Bordox said.

"No wonder the citizens call you Death Squads instead of LSP," Zylo said.

Bordox fought to control his anger. That was a moniker used to cut down and disrespect men who served a higher cause in Borali society. Bordox hated that moniker. His anger won and he exploded: "If you don't want to work with me, feel free to request reassignment! I'm sure Lord Xalivar will be very sympathetic!"

"Watch your tone! I'm your superior officer!"

*Not for long!* "Are we done yet? I have work to attend to." Bordox stood and moved to the window, looking out across the city at the great view. Someday maybe he'd be in charge of an entire planet, an assignment far worthier of his talents. He knew he deserved more than bowing down to idiots like this.

"Xalivar gave us the names of two officers he wants us to monitor," Zylo slid a photo pod across the table.

Bordox grabbed it and looked at the pictures. *Farien and Yao!* He hated them, too. "Nothing but low-talent hangers on who followed Xander Rhii like puppies at the Academy."

"One of them is an instructor at Presimion Academy," Zylo noted as Bordox turned back to the window. "I assigned top operatives to keep watch on the one stationed on Vertullis. The Legallis office will handle Presimion."

Bordox made a silent note of the fact that Farien was still around. *I think I'd better go pay him a visit myself.* He didn't trust anyone else. None of them had the talent he had. Better to make sure what needed to be done got done right. "Shouldn't we question them?"

"The High Lord Councilor already did. He wants their activities monitored in case the subject makes contact," Zylo said. "I assigned our best operatives."

*I'm your best operative, you fool! It's why the High Lord Councilor assigned me to find his nephew not sit on some inconsequential wannabes like them.* How could Bordox continue to tolerate even weasels like Zylo failing to recognize his true abilities?

"He wants you to coordinate monitoring of all passenger traffic at the starport. Everyone who comes and goes from this planet is to be monitored, their records checked thoroughly. Someone's hiding him, and we need to find out whom."

*This guy ought to be a worker, with a brain like that!* "I'll take care of it. I'd also like to pay another visit to some of the workers we already interviewed. There's a woman and a girl who know more than they told me."

"You can do what you want with whatever time you have left after the starport's in order," Zylo said, standing. The meeting was over.

*Thank the gods! Such a waste of time being here with this idiot! I have my destiny to fulfill!* They both headed off in opposite directions.

The trio met Miri in the back room of a little-known restaurant on the outskirts of the city. Arriving separately to avoid drawing attention to themselves, each used separate entrances to ensure they wouldn't be seen together.

Restaurant staff escorted them to a private room in the back, where Miri sat waiting for them. They gathered around a long table, waiting for her to explain. Instead of the usual white robes they wore to official meetings, each wore comfortable cotton slacks and shirts. Miri had never seen Lord Hachim, who took particular pride in his official role, dressed like a civilian. He looked at her only for a second, his mouth a thin line, and fumbled with the collar of his robe. Tarkanius and Kray appeared more relaxed. All of them knew her, but Lord Kray, one of the few females on the Council, was Miri's childhood friend.

As waiters took their orders, Miri passed around memory cards. After the waiters had served their beverages, the door closed, and Miri stood, smiling.

"Thank you all for coming. I called you here because we're all loyal to the Alliance, and I have important information about recent events which should cause you concern."

"Why are we meeting all the way out here and not at the government center or in the Palace?" Lord Tarkanius asked.

"Because this involves highly confidential matters, and I ask you to keep it that way, until we've determined a course of action," Miri said.

They all exchanged looks wondering what she was about to say.

"You've all known my character and loyalty to my family. So you'll understand what I am about to say comes out of deep concern for both my family and the Alliance."

"Of course, Miri," Lord Kray said. "What's going on?" She sipped from her Talis, a warm beverage brewed from beans grown on Vertullis—somewhat like the old Earth beverage coffee.

"I don't know how aware you are of the situation on Vertullis," Miri said, "but events have taken place which, I believe, have created a crisis there. These events have occurred with the full support and consent of the High Lord Councilor and have resulted in treatment of the workers which I believe is unacceptable. These memory cards contain evidence I wish you to review relating to these events."

"Are you saying there has been mistreatment of workers?" Lord Hachim asked.

"Mistreatment, subhuman conditions, and abuses of power," Miri said, nodding. *Please gods let them believe me.*

The three Lords exchanged looks of both surprise and concern. "The workers are not like us. We all know the history of their attacks against our people," Lord Tarkanius said.

"Yet the Borali Alliance has always stood for fair treatment of those under our rule," Miri said. "We set certain standards, which are not being upheld now under my brother."

"How much does your bringing this to our attention have to do with the murder charges your brother asked us to reinstate against your own son?" Lord Hachim asked, leaning back in his chair and watching her for a reaction.

*Xalivar asked them to charge Davi?* It hit her hard hearing it, though she tried not to let it show. "My son was charged because he questioned the Borali Alliance's treatment of workers. He documented a long line of abuses, bringing the evidence to Xalivar, who was not receptive. Anyone who questions my brother is at risk. He refuses to respond to inquiries. He believes the workers are subhuman, lower than animals, unworthy of trust or respect." *And most other people, too.*

"Many in the Alliance would agree with him," Lord Tarkanius said, sipping his Talis.

"Then how can we blame the workers for calling us tyrannical?" Lord Kray asked, her brow furrowed with concern.

"Xalivar is consolidating his own power, taking on more and more responsibilities himself and relying less and less on your counsel," Miri said, hoping they'd noticed.

"He appears before the Council to make regular reports," Lord Hachim said.

"The Council began meeting every two months instead of monthly at whose request?" Miri asked.

The three Lords exchanged a look. "The High Lord Councilor requested it, due to increased obligations," Lord Kray answered for them.

Miri nodded. "I believe Xalivar wants to make the High Lord Councilor more like a kingship and less dependent on the Council. He has become more and more powerful and makes more and more decisions alone. If the Council doesn't take action soon, it will be too late."

"He has done nothing the Council doesn't approve of," Lord Tarkanius said, leaning forward in his chair.

"You'll change your opinion after you've viewed these memory cards," Miri said with anticipation.

"What are you proposing?" Lord Hachim asked.

"I believe it may be time for a change of leadership … for the High Lord Councilor's office to be returned to someone who respects both its powers and its limits," Miri said.

As expected they looked shocked to hear this from her. Stiffening and locking their eyes on hers, they examined her as if trying to determine how serious she was, but Miri made sure her expression never wavered.

"We will, of course, consider the evidence on these memory cards with great care," Lord Tarkanius said, leaning back in his seat again after taking a final sip of his Talis.

Miri smiled. "Thank you. Please keep this meeting confidential until we've had a chance to discuss your reactions."

They nodded. "Of course we will," Lord Kray said. "Thank you for bringing this to our attention, Miri."

"I love the Alliance and respect the Council," Miri said. "It is my duty."

"The Council has always appreciated your faithfulness," Lord Hachim said as they stood, placing the memory cards in their pockets.

Miri watched as they departed one at a time, leaving her alone. She knew the risks of revealing this to the Council, but she had grown increasingly concerned about Xalivar's activities after learning what Davi had uncovered on Vertullis. Xalivar's refusal to be questioned about it by her or anyone else had convinced her that someone had to step up and call him to account. She was in the best position to do so.

She'd chosen the members of the Council to which she gave the evidence with great care. She knew their influence on the Council would help her case. She would wait for their response, and continue gathering evidence. In the meantime, she had a plan that would bring the abuses to the attention of the public.

*Xalivar had asked the Council to charge Davi with murder! My gods, how could he do that?* His betrayal was the last straw. Any second thoughts she had, faded away. Fine. If Xalivar had no loyalty to her or his family, so be it. She would not feel it necessary to be loyal to him. The Borali Alliance itself was more important, and she knew in her heart even their father would disapprove of Xalivar's excesses.

# Chapter Seven

alivar had always had a soft place in his heart for his sister, but these days she was driving him mad—going on and on about Davi this, Davi that. Xalivar had a lot of responsibilities besides babying his worrywart sister.

The nightmares had come again. A kind he hadn't had in twenty years—ones that continued to haunt him, even in daylight. Now, Miri had stormed into his private chamber like a charging bull, heading straight toward him. He sighed loudly, but she paid no attention.

"You asked the Council to reinstate murder charges against your own nephew? I knew you could sink low, Xalivar, but—"

"Where did you hear that?" He asked, cutting her off.

"I have friends on the Council like you do," Miri said.

"Your son is determined to create problems for me where none existed. I did my best to reason with him, but he won't leave it alone!" Xalivar was not in the mood for her angry tone. He had responsibilities she would never understand.

"He's your nephew! You could have tried harder."

"He's an officer in the army, sworn to serve me. He refuses to serve. He's also a subject of the Borali Alliance," Xalivar said. "He's always shied away from special treatment, so I'm treating him like anyone else."

"Don't give me more lies, Xalivar. I'm your sister. I've known you all my life," Miri said. "You're singling him out because he defied you." She turned away, close to tears, staring out the window at the stars.

"He needs to know his place," Xalivar said, unmoved by her tears. *Always so dramatic.*

"You need to know yours!" She whirled around, pointing her finger in his face.

Xalivar had never wanted to hit Miri before, but he had to restrain himself this time. "You'd prefer I let him create a huge public scandal and bring the wrath of the entire Alliance down on him? I'm bringing him in, so we can keep this situation from getting out of control."

"You're so sure everyone in the Alliance would agree with you, aren't you?" Miri said. "I know for a fact many do not!"

"General public opinion is not my concern. I answer to the Council," Xalivar said. *And I don't really care what you or they think either, sister.*

"And answer you shall if you turn your back on your family," Miri said. "You sent his archrival to hunt him down like some kind of outlaw! Do you care nothing about his reputation? His safety?"

*Since when did Miri grow claws? Did she really have the nerve?* "Don't threaten me!"

"Don't threaten my son!" Miri turned around and marched back to the door. After a moment, it slid shut behind her.

Xalivar cursed whoever had betrayed him. He wasn't sure who'd told Miri, but he would find out. He would not tolerate people playing politics with his family. Perhaps it had been a matter of time, but he didn't need her enflamed emotions leading her to interfere in his business. He had enough to worry about. *They will learn what it means to cross Xalivar.*

The nightmares had reminded him of something he'd written off as inconsequential. He was starting to worry. He wanted Davi back under his nose where he could keep an eye on him. He would instruct Zylo and Bordox to retrace their steps. The search was taking too long. They needed to find Davi—and now.

A week after their argument in the corridor, Davi found Tela sitting at the controls of her shuttle, reading through maintenance charts. He took care to make noise as he entered the cockpit so as not to sneak up on her. She turned her head and frowned when she saw him.

"We seem to have gotten off on the wrong foot," Davi said, sitting down beside her in the copilot's seat. "I've been trying to figure out how it happened."

"Maybe your charms won't work on me," Tela said, not bothering to look up as she continued her work. "I'm pretty good at seeing through people. Especially men."

"Well, that's just it. You seem to have taken some of the things I've said the wrong way," Davi said, hoping she'd reconsider.

"Like what?" Her eyes remained on the charts.

"I didn't bring up your name in class to isolate you from the other trainees," Davi said. "I was trying to pay you a compliment. I'm impressed with the way you flew the shuttle."

"Well, thank you," she said, still avoiding eye contact, focused on her charts. "But the last thing I need is people thinking you're showing me special treatment. I'm there to learn the same as them."

"And I'm there to teach you," Davi said, "but someone with your flight experience is an asset for the entire class. You can help me to help them learn what they need to know."

"I didn't sign on to be a tutor," Tela said.

"I won't ask you to be, if you don't want to," Davi said. "All I'm asking is if they don't understand something I'm trying to explain, maybe you can jump in and help me clarify it."

"See?" She said, looking up for a moment. "You're asking me to teach. No thanks."

Her eyes turned back to the charts as Davi wondered why he always seemed to choose the wrong words when he talked to her. A familiar buzz filled his stomach as heat rose within. And why was he always so attracted to her when she was mad at him? "Whatever you feel comfortable with," Davi said. "The last thing I need is someone getting killed because they didn't understand."

"I wouldn't let that happen," Tela said.

"Good. I can use all the help I can get," Davi said. "I've never been an instructor before. And I've never been a worker either. It's all new to me. I pretty much have to relearn who I am." *I wish someone would teach me how to talk to you!*

"You're doing fine. You explain things well," Tela said, her blue eyes meeting his for a moment.

"Was that a compliment?" Davi melted inside like icicles in a desert. He smiled. "I might have to write that down. It might be ages before I ever get another compliment from you."

She laughed, rolling her eyes. "Don't get too cocky, okay? There's always room for improvement."

"Okay, so don't get mad at me when I suggest areas you can improve," Davi said. "It's my job as your teacher."

"You can't improve on perfection," she said, smiling slyly as she went back to her charts again. Was she joking?

"Now who's cocky?" He teased and this time she laughed.

He added, "Some of the cadets seem to resent me because of my past. They don't seem to realize, I'm on your side."

"Can you really blame them? You're the Prince."

Davi sighed, disappointed. "No, I suppose not."

She slid back in the chair and her face softened a bit as their eyes met again. "Give them time. They'll come around."

"I don't suppose you could put in a good word for me?"

Tela's face crinkled. "First I have to convince myself."

"But you saw me at the rallies! Do you really believe—"

He stopped as Tela broke into laughter. "You're giving me trouble?"

She smiled and nodded. "I couldn't resist."

"Well, I'd better let you get back to your work here. I wouldn't want anyone to know we actually had a civil conversation."

She smiled at him and his heart fluttered. "You like making jokes, don't you?"

"When it makes you smile like that," Davi said.

Her eyes darted quickly back to her charts.

After a moment, he slid from the copilot's seat. "Okay, well, thanks for letting me explain."

She nodded. "See you in class, professor." It sounded so formal. He contorted his face, and she laughed again, twirling strands of her hair around her index finger. "I'm trying to work here."

He nodded and backed out of the cockpit. The conversation went better than he'd expected. She'd laughed and joked with him. It was a start. And she'd twirled her hair—was she flirting with him? Best not to make too much of it. For some reason, all the way back to the command center, he found himself whistling a happy song.

"Retrace my steps and see if I missed anything?" Bordox groused as he sat in the military shuttle next to Corsi and reviewed Xalivar's orders for the tenth time. "I'm sick of that miscreant always making me look bad! Not this time!" He cursed Xander Rhii under his breath for the millionth time and growled.

They hadn't even covered a third of the worker community. Plenty of places to hide remained, yet his mission had already been deemed a failure. He cursed inside. He'd been given a chance to best his old rival, and he was determined to come out ahead. Revisiting areas they'd already covered would just slow him down. But after Zylo's inaccurate reporting of Bordox's activities, it's exactly what Xalivar had ordered him to do.

On their previous visit to one worker neighborhood, he'd found a photo of a man who looked very much like Xander Rhii in one of the houses. He had no idea why workers would have such a photo, but then again, he'd learned from interrogating the neighbors that a man who resembled Xander had been seen there a number of times. The woman had told him the picture was her husband, who'd disappeared twenty years before. In spite of his interrogation techniques, the woman and girl gave him nothing. Still, he'd never been able to shake the feeling they knew more than they'd told him.

When Bordox reviewed security tapes from the officers' barracks, he'd spotted the woman and girl on it, chatting with Rhii. All three had a friendly demeanor throughout. This time Bordox wouldn't let them off so easily. They knew where to find Rhii, and he would find out everything they knew.

"Why would a Royal be so friendly with workers?" he asked aloud, forgetting Corsi was sitting beside him. Bile rose in his throat at the thought and he swallowed hard, coughing after to clear the taste. "It makes no sense. Xalivar has always led the oppression of the workers. Of course that weak, overconfident Prince has never made sense. He's totally unfit for military service. Too nice. Too sympathetic. Too independent."

Ignoring Corsi's nod, Bordox turned toward the window, lost in thought. Xander had been given opportunities which should have gone to Bordox. Now Bordox had the opportunity to put an end to the undeserved favoritism. And end it he would. No matter what it took. Proving once and for all that Rhii was the imposter and scum Bordox had always known him to be.

He arrived with a squad of five men at the courtyard outside the house in question. Everything appeared the same as it had the last time he'd been there. He approached the door to the house and waited while his sergeant knocked.

"LSP, open!" Sergeant Corsi shouted.

A frightened woman opened the door, two wide-eyed young children hiding amidst the folds of her skirt. Bordox and his men pushed their way inside, looking around. No one else was in the house except the woman and children, who had not been there during his previous visit. The house had been arranged differently inside then—much of the furniture remained standard worker issue, but the pictures and personal knick-knacks had all changed—someone else lived there.

"Where are the people who lived here before?" Bordox demanded.

The woman shook with fear. Her children started crying. "I—I don't know," she said with great effort, so frightened she couldn't speak. *Good. Be afraid of me!*

Corsi and two soldiers returned from searching the back room. "No one's here, sir. And everything is different than the last time."

Bordox bared his teeth and uttered a guttural roar. He had to find these people—more certain now than ever that they had the answers he needed. Grabbing the woman's arm so hard she cried out, he pulled her outside. "That's it. I want all the neighbors in the square right now!"

He shoved the woman away from the house and then roughly carried her crying kids outside into the square as his men rushed to knock on the neighbors' doors.

In a few moments, eight others stood trembling in the yard. Bordox walked among them as his men searched their houses. They all looked as frightened as the first woman. "Some of you I recognize. You remember me from before." He glanced around at the fearful expressions.

A few found the strength to nod.

He sneered. "Good, then maybe you'll tell me what I want to know!"

Corsi came back with reports from the men. "All clear, sir."

Bordox grabbed an old man from the line and pointed his blaster at the man's temple. "I want to know right now where the previous tenants of that house are!"

The workers looked at each other, eyes darting around but remained silent, as if they didn't know what to say. Bordox didn't believe them. Someone had to know something. An older woman stepped forward. "They moved out right after you were here before. We don't know where they are."

"What do you know?" Bordox said, blaster still held to the man's forehead. Fear had always been his favorite tactic.

"Please," another man said, "we do our work. We make no problems for the Alliance."

"You're making a problem for the Alliance right now! Tell me what I want to know." Bordox said.

"We don't know anything!" The first woman said, as her two kids cried and continued clinging to her skirt. "Please, we have no reason not to tell you. I don't even know those people."

"You might not, but these people were here before. They were your neighbors," Bordox said, ignoring the woman and looking at the others with no effort to hide his irritation.

"They never mentioned where they were going," the older woman said. "All I know is the woman who lived there worked at Celedine Technology near the starport."

Bordox released the old man, who collapsed to his knees. He walked up the line, stopping a few inches from each of them to stare into their eyes. *They really don't know.* He cursed inside. Xalivar had warned him about excessive killings of workers. It would draw too much negative attention. He had to be discreet—the only reason these people still lived.

"If any of you see or hear anything, you will contact the LSP right away. Don't make me have to come back here!" He met each one's eyes in turn with a cold glare.

They all nodded, fear evident on their faces.

"Squad, move out!"

Bordox led his men back through the corridors of the worker district. They would go to Celedine Technology. He knew where it was. The more trouble it became locating Xander, the more determined he became to win. He would not have his career ruined by that incompetent fool ever again. He would bring him in, no matter what it took. Too bad Xalivar wanted him alive. Bordox would relish ending Xander Rhii's miserable existence.

When Miri arrived, the Legallis starport hummed with motion—bustling crowds, a buffet of noise, constant activity. The small diner lay out of the way on the end of one of the numerous corridors, which wound their way out from the landing platforms. The only evidence leading to it were the smells of grease, cooking meat and eggs, and other wonderful kitchen scents one's nose might be tempted by in the surrounding corridors. It would be easy to go unnoticed there. Besides, this time it was just the two of them, and meetings between old friends were not so unusual.

Kray examined Miri as soon as she sat down across the table. "You've lost weight."

"I'm fine," Miri said, deliberately leaning back to appear relaxed. She hated lying to an old friend, but Kray couldn't do anything about her sleepless nights in the Palace; her mind working overtime.

"Don't lie to me, Miri. I'm your oldest friend," Kray said.

Miri smiled. She'd been so busy the past few weeks; she'd had almost no time to actually relax. Sitting here for a moment gave her a much-needed break. "The life of a Princess is always busy." Even more so with her determination to uncover the truth about what was going on with the workers on Vertullis.

"Yes, and you've never been one to stay bored long," Kray said, nodding. "Promise me it's not because of worrying."

"A mother always worries, as you know," Miri said. Kray had three children herself. "But since we last met, I've been so preoccupied with other things; I haven't had much time for that."

As the waitress arrived to bring them mugs of Talis, Miri realized it was true. She'd been so focused on saving Davi, she'd had little time to sit around and worry about his circumstances.

"The information you provided was quite startling, as you said," Kray said, sipping her Talis. "We have discussed it quite often since reviewing it."

"I appreciate your willingness to take the time," Miri said, leaning forward as her hope rose within.

"You have our support," Kray said, her eyes not leaving Miri's. "But it will require a lot more evidence to validate an impeachment."

Miri nodded. "Public opinion will soon be on our side."

Kray looked at her with concern. "You must be very careful, Miri. As the Princess, your movements do not go unnoticed, above all when you interact with members of the media. Xalivar has many friends."

"So do I, Kray," Miri said smiling. "It will be handled with the same discretion as our meeting, I promise." Miri had not involved anyone associated with the Palace. She wanted no chance of leaks, but she knew she would also need to take other precautions.

"I hope so. Don't let the fact that Xalivar is your brother blind you in regards to your safety," Kray said. "He's never been kind to those who betray him."

Miri had seen plenty of evidence of this in the past. She nodded, sipping her own Talis. "I'm taking extra care, Kray. Really." Miri reached across the table to gently lay her hand across her friend's.

Kray's eyes stayed locked on hers for a moment before Kray smiled, relaxing a bit. "Good. There are few females at our level of power, you know. I need someone around who understands what it's like." They both laughed.

"I have always cherished our friendship," Miri said, squeezing Kray's hand atop the table. "So tell me about the children. How are they, these days?"

They continued chatting at the table for close to an hour as people came and went around them—two old friends talking about life and family. It did them both good to escape like this from the concerns of their lives—Miri from her worries about Davi and Xalivar, and Kray from the weight of government decisions. Miri realized they had not done this enough. She vowed to try and correct that in the future.

After two weeks spent covering the basics of flight, Davi allowed the first of his students on the simulators. His class had increased in size since it started, with Aron and the leaders adding more and more candidates with each new rally. Davi had done his best to keep the new students up to speed with the others. Some of them had the advantage of prior flight experience, while others had skill with skitters. He still had neophytes to train, but at least some had a head start.

At the moment, Dru, Brie, Nila and another boy their age occupied the four simulators. Tela and the other students sat at desks behind Davi, observing as he took them through their first mock battle. Each student pilot sat in a mock cockpit, with controls similar to those of VS28 fighters—a screen where the blastshield would be simulated stars and incoming enemy fighter craft. The simulator itself moved as the trainees moved the joystick. Combined, the effect was a sensation reminiscent of being in an actual fighter during a battle. Watching them evoked fond memories of his Academy days.

"Keep your tails up there," Davi instructed. "Easy on the joystick, Brie. It's sensitive, designed to move as one with your body. Dru, you've got one on your tail. Evasive action!"

The trainees reacted to his instructions. Dru tried hard to stay out of the fire of the enemy on his tail as explosions flashed in front of him on the screen with each hit.

Brie steered her fighter toward the enemy behind Dru. "I got him!"

Davi realized that her excitement was distracting her. She was coming in at an odd angle and way too fast. "Slow down, Brie! You're going to hit him!" Too late.

Brie's screen erupted in flashes of yellow light and her console went dead. "What happened?" Brie asked, confused.

"You're dead," Tela said.

"You got him off my tail though. Thanks," Dru said, chuckling.

Brie stuck out her tongue at him. "You're welcome." She turned to Davi with a sheepish grin. "I'm not getting it, am I?"

Davi smiled. "It takes practice." *For some more than others.*

Brie cocked her head to one side in a flirty way. "Can you show me one more time please?"

Davi smiled. "Okay. Look." He leaned over her from behind, holding his hand around hers on the joystick as he ignored the flowery scent of the perfume she always wore around him. "Pull back a tiny bit, like this. Enough to make her go the direction you want to go. Not too hard though."

Brie smiled, looking up at him. "Oh, right. I gotta practice it." Davi let go and she tried what he'd showed her. "Like that?"

Davi nodded, ignoring her flirting. "Much better. Keep practicing."

He turned back to the other students and saw Tela shaking her head and heading out the door. Virun and a couple of others followed her.

"Wait a minute! Class isn't over. Where's everyone going?"

The others looked at him and shrugged.

*What's wrong with her?*

Brie and the others climbed out of the simulators as other trainees took their place.

"Okay," Davi said, "let's try this again."

The second group was better than the first. A third did better still. At the end of the session though, Davi walked away discouraged. Some of the students would improve with practice, but others had him wondering if they weren't wasting their time. He wished Tela had participated. She would have handled herself quite well, he imagined. Her performance would have at least been more encouraging.

He left the classroom confused and wondering why she'd disappeared.

Tired of watching Brie throwing herself at Davi, Tela had stormed out of the training room. It was disgusting, shameless—totally inappropriate in the classroom. She'd grown more and more irritated, until deciding she needed a breath of fresh air.

As she wound her way through the corridors, she started feeling silly. Why did it bother her so much? *You don't like him, remember?* She'd known women who acted like Brie before. It wasn't like she had any claim to Davi. They were barely friends.

Sure, things between them had settled down since they'd talked in the shuttle. He'd asked Tela's opinion from time to time, and she'd done as he requested, helping him explain things when the trainees didn't understand. So why did seeing Brie flirting with him like that make her so tense? What was the big deal? Brie had every right to flirt with him. She'd acted like a fool. Why did she have such a tendency to do that when Davi was around?

She spent a few moments calming down, then turned back toward the classroom. Rounding a corner near the classroom, she spotted Davi exiting and heading up the corridor away from her. He looked very discouraged. She hoped not because of her.

She followed him across the hangar and into a smaller cave on the far side, where the skitters sat parked in several rows.

Long slender bodies topped with leather seats and two handlebars attached to a control panel, skitters had been designed for recreational use, but were so fast and easy to handle, they'd been adapted for other uses. Borali Alliance ground patrols used them on a regular basis.

She stood in the shadows as he began looking them over. Two mech-bots entered through another tunnel and began working on some of the skitters behind him. As she stepped out of the shadows into the cave, Davi glanced up at her.

"Hey," she said, with a slight wave and a smile.

"Hey," he said, going back to examining the skitters.

"How'd the rest of the session go?"

He shrugged. "We have a lot of work ahead of us."

Not even eye contact. So maybe he was upset with her. "Sorry I left. I needed some air."

"I was disappointed you didn't stay for your turn," Davi said as he examined another skitter. "Seeing someone actually succeed on the simulators would have been encouraging. I sure could've used it." His voice sounded tired.

"Was it really so bad?"

"You tell me. You saw how some of the students did," Davi slid into the seat of a skitter, fiddling with the controls.

"Some of them are a long way from being flight-worthy," Tela said, watching the mech-bots working behind him.

"Some make me wonder if they ever will be. Sometimes I wonder if Brie actually thinks she can flirt her way out of trouble with the enemy." He rolled his eyes.

Tela laughed. The flirting bothered him? Good. Still, it saddened her to see him so discouraged. He had always been so positive and supportive of the students. She wanted to do something to cheer him up. She took a seat on another skitter and turned it on, hearing the steady hum of the engine and feeling it rise up off the floor to float on the air as she adjusted the controls.

"Come with me."

"For a joy ride?"

Tela smiled. "Sure. There's something I want to show you." She waved toward the skitter he'd been examining.

He shrugged, climbing onto the skitter. The engine hummed as it rose into the air. "Okay. Lead the way."

She slid the skitter into gear and drove it out of the cave into a small tunnel. Davi accelerated his own skitter and followed along behind her.

They emerged into the dense forest along a path. Sunlight streamed through the tall cedars, creating a patchwork of dark and light areas on the ground. The chirping of birds and insects blended with the hum of the skitters as a light breeze tousled their hair and the sweet smell of cedars filled her nose.

Tela sped up, forcing Davi to speed up behind her. She admired the fluidness with which he maneuvered the skitter. She'd never seen him fly, of course, but it seemed to her he must be as skilled as the commanders said. She doubted he'd had much time to explore the forest around the base yet. She hadn't seen him in the skitter bay, but then she hadn't been there much until the past few days herself.

She led him through several twists and turns then around a bend into a clearing where she pulled to a stop and waited for him to come alongside.

Amid cedars at the edge of the course on both sides there were several wood pylons with various markings. As his skitter pulled alongside hers and stopped, the scent of his sweat and cologne mixed with the pollen from the cedars and she smiled. It was not altogether displeasing. Looking around, she nodded. "Well, here it is."

"What is it?" Davi said, trying to make sense of the pylons and markers.

"Our skitter training course," Tela said proudly as she watched him. "Aron asked me to set one up." Why was she so anxious waiting for his response?

Davi looked around and smiled. "You did all this yourself?"

"Well, I may have borrowed some from a schematic of one of the Alliance's training courses. With a few minor adjustments to compensate for ours being on land and not in outer space." She had to admit it had been enjoyable working on the course.

Davi nodded, looking pleased. "This is impressive. You amaze me."

*He's impressed!* She almost blushed. Why did she care so much what he thought? She'd never had time for men, not since her father's disappearance. She'd been too busy for much of a social life.

She took a breath, trying to hide how pleased she was. "Thanks. Wanna give it a try?" She opened the side pocket on her skitter and pulled out a helmet. "Gotta put on the helmet to see how it works."

She slid the helmet on as Davi opened the pocket on his own skitter and retrieved the helmet. As he began to put it on, Tela flipped the switch to activate the weapons simulator on her skitter.

After they'd both adjusted their helmets, Davi nodded. "Ready."

Tela accelerated and took off like a flash, zigzagging in and out between the pylons. Wind nipped at the skin of her face like tiny bugs. Trees passed almost as a blur as she focused on the markers and pylons. All her senses were a blur as she went and she loved the sensation. Glancing down at her control panel, she verified that the weapons simulator was fully charged. The visor of her helmet showed a targeting frame as she passed the next pylon. Everything seemed to be working right.

The next pylon she came to, she maneuvered the frame to aim at the pylon and then hit the fire button. The visor image flashed as she hit the target.

She flipped her communicator on and keyed the switch. "Flip the red switch on to activate the targeting simulator. The black button on the joystick is for firing."

She slowed down, allowing Davi to pull alongside as he fiddled with the controls. "Do you see it?"

"Yeah," his voice came in through the helmet. "You did all this?"

"Well, I had some help. Go for a run," Tela said, accelerating again and aiming as she came to each target.

Davi raced his skitter alongside hers, also aiming and firing. He broke into a huge grin as they raced in and out of the pylons, keeping pace with each other. The visor kept count in the bottom right corner of hits and misses. So far she had been dead on.

The total time for the course at full speed was less than four minutes. They reached the end in what seemed like a few seconds. She pulled to a stop as Davi stopped beside her, looking pleased.

"How'd you do?" she asked.

"Missed two," he admitted.

She smiled. "I didn't miss any."

"Well, you designed it. It's my first time." He said with a shrug, but she saw disappointment in his green eyes.

With an exaggerated shrug, she laughed. "Excuses, excuses."

He scowled. "Wanna go again?"

*Gotcha.* She grinned and accelerated her skitter like a rocket.

Davi raced to catch up with her.

They followed a curving path which took them back to the start of the course, and then both launched into it again. Davi gave it his best effort. She had to accelerate a few times to keep up with him.

As they neared the end of the course, he zipped in front of her. Her skitter misfired. She groaned in frustration, pulling back alongside and getting back on course. He laughed as they raced onward, finishing the course in less than four minutes.

"Perfect score," he said with a smirk.

*That's the Davi I know.* She shook her head. "I missed because you distracted me." But she knew his move to cut her off hadn't been the only distraction. She had butterflies in her stomach.

"Oh right, like the enemy won't ever try that," he said, shooting her a look.

She laughed. He was right. They couldn't count on total focus in a real battle. Maybe there were some things he could teach her on her own course after all.

"Shall we go again?" he asked, shifting excitedly on his seat. His voice had regained its usual energy, and she noticed the usual sparkle had returned to his eyes. The smell of adrenaline mixed with sweat wafted to her nose, adding to her excitement.

"Wanna switch sides?"

He nodded. "Catch me if you can!" He took off like a rocket.

She raced to catch up, determined that this time she'd be ready for any distractions.

Bordox arrived at the LSP office early the next morning, anxious to see the results of the e-post logs he'd asked Corsi to locate from public kiosks near the worker house they'd searched. He'd noticed a terminal nearby in a park both times they'd been there. Maybe something would turn up.

They'd gone to Celedine after searching the house and coming up empty. A woman from the address had worked there for a time, but disappeared after Bordox's first visit to the house. The owners, loyal to the Alliance, had no idea where to locate her. Bordox was sick of dead ends.

He entered the office to find Zylo and Corsi already there.

"I found some reports of suspicious activity in the forest on the far side of the planet," Zylo said.

"The forest? What kind of activity?" Bordox asked.

Zylo gave a slight shrug. "A few farmers reported shuttle flights, voices in the trees from time to time."

Bordos pursed his lips. "I thought the forest was undeveloped."

"It is. We haven't even deployed full radar there," Zylo said. "And gods know the farmers are always reporting unknown flying objects out there. It's low priority intel, but Xalivar insists we check all possible leads."

Bordox nodded. He expected it would be another dead end, but then at least it would get him out of the office and away from Zylo and they hadn't been that far south yet. He'd make a pass or two down there as soon as he'd finished retracing the areas they'd already visited.

He logged onto his terminal and found a folder with the log records waiting for him. He double clicked to open it and began scanning the lists. Xander's worker name popped up several times in the weeks before Bordox's team had first searched the house. What had he been doing in that neighborhood so much? Hiding out? Living there? How was he connected to those people? Someone had to know something. Who hadn't he talked to yet? His eyes continued searching the e-post list. *There!* Xander had sent an e-post to Presimion Academy. *Of course!* Xander was always in touch with those two.

Bordox turned to Corsi who sat at a terminal nearby. "Corsi, get me files on all duty assignments for officers overseeing guards in the agricultural districts."

"All of them?"

Bordox whirled around so fast his chair squeaked. "Stop asking questions and do it."

Corsi hurried back to the other terminal as Bordox turned back to his vidscreen. He didn't expect Farien to volunteer any information. Farien and Yao disliked him as much as their buddy Davi did. Nonetheless, Bordox had the authority to question anyone he deemed necessary. Yes, indeed, he would enjoy this, though he knew Farien wouldn't.

He smiled at the thought of Farien's reaction upon seeing him again and energy filled his veins. "Look for the name of Lieutenant Farien," he said to Corsi.

Tela arrived at the command center conference room to find Aron, Joram, Uzah, and General Matheu waiting for her around the table. Commander of the Workers' military, General Matheu's uniform breast bore medals and ribbons he'd earned over a career spanning back to the Delta V tragedy. Although the Vertullians had no formal military much of that time, certain veterans had none-theless created medals to recognize their fellows' achievements and remind those who encountered them of their service and sacrifice. And now the General had an opportunity to wear them properly again. His hair was dark with graying ends and his stomach had thickened in a way common for men of his age. But the eyes which met hers showed the same strength and focus she'd seen in him for years.

"Tela," Aron said with a smile, "so glad you could join us." He motioned to an empty seat at the table.

The others nodded as she moved toward the chair. The room carried the usual scents of military areas: men's sweat, musty uniforms, and dust. It was so familiar she barely noticed. Matheu stood and closed the door behind her before returning to his seat.

"How's the flight training going?" Joram asked.

Tela shrugged, searching their eyes for a clue as to why she'd been summoned. "It's proceeding slowly for sure, but we are making progress. Except, some of the students are questioning whether they can trust the instructor."

"They're not alone," Matheu groused in his scratchy baritone.

Uzah nodded. "We have doubts of our own."

"Not all of us," Aron corrected.

"He spoke passionately at several rallies," Tela said. "We didn't have any trouble."

"How do you know he wasn't just trying to earn your trust so he could gather information for the Alliance?" Matheu asked.

"If he was going to betray us," Joram said, "he would have done so already."

"I've told you time again," Aron added, "I've known his family for many years."

"His worker family or the Royals?" Matheu snapped.

Tela knew his years of military disappointments had left him skeptical and extremely cautious. She couldn't blame him.

"The longer he remains here, the more information he can gather," Uzah said.

"I vouch for him," Aron said. "That ought to mean something."

"It does, Aron," Uzah said, his voice softening. "No one here doubts your character, but we worry your love for his family may be blinding you where he's concerned."

"You trust him too much," Matheu added. "He already knows the location of our base, the numbers and make of our starcraft. How much more can we afford to let him see?"

"He's done nothing to cause suspicion," Aron argued. "Being adopted by the princess doesn't automatically make him a spy. He had no idea about his true heritage until recently."

"It does bring his loyalty into question," Uzah said.

"The Alliance is the only family he's ever known," Matheu said. "Why would he turn against them after twenty years?"

Tela found it hard to understand the vitriol she was hearing in Matheu and Uzah's voices. "He may be arrogant, but he made it obvious in his speeches at the rallies that he doesn't approve of how the Alliance has been treating workers. And he's been teaching us a lot about Alliance tactics in class."

"How do you know it's accurate?" Matheu asked.

"Because a lot of it matches the information already programmed into the simulators," Tela said. "A lot of it confirms what we'd already gathered ourselves, too. He's also given us information we didn't know."

"Simulators can be reprogrammed," Matheu said.

"We won't be able to confirm the information is accurate until the fighting begins," Uzah said. "Can we really afford to wait until then to determine if he can be trusted?"

"Do you really think he reprogrammed every simulator?" Tela asked, feeling her irritation growing.

"The Boralians' one goal is to keep us enslaved," Matheu said. "They'll do anything to make sure that happens."

"Have you spent any time with him, General?" Tela asked testily.

"I don't need time with him!" Matheu snapped.

"Oh? So you're like one of the Old Testament prophets then," Tela responded. "Sorry. I didn't know."

"I am your superior officer!" Matheu jumped up from the table.

"We're all on the same side here," Aron said gently, raising a hand to calm them.

"The General's right," Uzah said. "None of us know him well enough to risk so much."

"I know him, and so does Aron." The anger in her voice surprised her. She softened her tone. "We have spent time with him, and you know us. At some point, we all have to trust each other as we grow. No one can vet everyone." Tela lowered her eyes to the table and took a deep breath. Why was she defending him so strongly? Okay, so they'd been getting along, and his attitude did seem to be softening. *But why do I care so much?*

"This is an officer in a position of importance," Matheu snapped.

Aron raised a hand to stop them. "This fighting solves nothing,"

Aron said, looking as frustrated as Tela felt. "I've staked my reputation on him, and I'm confident I'm right."

"What if you're not?" Uzah asked.

"What do you want to do?" Joram asked. "Send him back and risk him going to the Alliance with everything he knows? At least here we can keep an eye on him."

"We can test him," Tela suggested. "Feed him false information and see how the Alliance reacts."

"We don't have time for such games," Matheu said.

"Well, he's here, General," Tela said, as she stood from the table. "And without him, we'll never be ready to fly those starfighters into battle. Trust him or not, we need him."

"We monitor all communications in and out of the base," Joram said. "We'll know if he makes contact with the enemy."

When no one responded, Tela nodded and headed for the door, wondering when Davi had managed to win her over.

Just as Miri had planned it, the package left the Palace with the Royal garbage, wrapped in a discarded towel inside a bag tied with a red ribbon. The garbage traveled on the garbage skiff to a central dump, where it was unloaded and sat, waiting to be sorted for either incineration or a launch into space.

The courier had no trouble getting access to the garbage dock. Month's end was a busy time, and no one was around to intercept him. He saw the red ribbon right away, untied it and found the package. He removed it before slipping the ribbon back in place, then disappeared.

An hour later, the courier dropped the package at a newsstand in the starport, leaving it taped to the underside of one of the many news monitors before disappearing into the crowd.

The second courier came ten minutes later, reaching under the monitor to find the package and quickly removed it before also disappearing. He dropped it at a flower stand outside the offices of Media Corp., an independent national broadcasting company on Legallis.

Miri's package sat under a vase at the flower stand marked with a small piece of red tape for five minutes before Orson Sterling arrived to claim it. A burly, slightly overweight man in his early forties with disheveled hair, he bought the vase, careful to place his hand flat on the bottom as he carried it back inside Media Corp.'s offices to his cubicle.

He eagerly opened the package at his desk and popped the memory card into his vidscreen. Reporters waited a lifetime for a story like this—and it had come to him signed, sealed, and delivered. He alone knew the source. He'd been contacted a few days before by coded e-post from a special communications center, not the Royal Palace. Miri had been very careful. Orson Sterling would be forever grateful to her.

# Chapter Eight

Xalivar shut off the vidscreen with his fist. After two weeks, it had gotten so he couldn't even watch the news nets any more. He cursed whoever had betrayed him by leaking these stories.

At first, he'd pretended it didn't matter. One story on one network was nothing to worry about. Orson Sterling was an overinflated loudmouthed reporter. Media Corp. reporters always slammed the government. But then it spread to every channel except the Federal one. Citizen groups formed in protest—Worker Rights Party, Worker Freedom Party, Lords for Workers; it sickened him. Didn't these people know what was best for them? Didn't they know that the government—that he, Xalivar—was making decisions with their needs in mind?

To make matters worse, there were rumors the Council was discussing a special hearing about atrocities against workers. Xalivar cursed the citizens and the Council. He cursed Orson Sterling, too. Bunch of idiots who didn't have a clue! His mouth twisted with disgust and his nostrils flared.

Bordox and Zylo continued to turn up nothing in their search. Xalivar couldn't remember encountering such incompetence since the Delta V disaster twenty-five years earlier. He'd hand-chosen rising stars to head that one, too. Could he be losing his touch? He used to be able to predict military stars and exploit them through special opportunities which built their loyalty to him. But now, he couldn't seem to pick winners. He sighed, glancing at the chrono. Time for another daily report from Manaen.

At least no one would see the worst footage. Xalivar had hidden the tapes in the Royal archive and supervised the destruction of any copies himself. What had been released seemed like light bruises compared to what those tapes revealed. He knew he needed to go to the Royal archives and destroy the tapes. Just in case.

He stood, straightened his clothes, and hit the button on the door, taking a deep breath to regain his composure. By now, Manaen would be waiting for him.

On his way to a meeting at the command center conference room, Davi ran into Aron heading the same way. "Good morning."

Aron smiled. "Good morning indeed. How are our trainees doing?"

"They're working hard and they need it."

Aron laughed. "If anyone can whip them into shape, you can."

Davi smiled, wishing he had the same confidence. "Some of them may never be flight-worthy. I have to show them the same things over and over. Others resent me for my past. They don't want to learn from me." He hesitated, wondering how honest he should be with Aron.

Aron noted the look on his face and reached up to squeeze Davi's shoulder as they walked. "Well, don't give up," Aron said. "They're all we've got."

"Maybe with several months' training I could bring them along," Davi said.

"We don't have several months. I wish we did." Aron said as they entered the bustling command center and found the conference room already packed.

"I'm no miracle worker," Davi said as they reached the door.

"Become one. You don't have a choice," Aron said sincerely.

"The untrusting are among the most talented. I could really use their help with the others."

"It's hard for some here to trust you. Even some of the leaders have questioned me about it. But I believe in you. They'll come around." He smiled, putting a hand on Davi's arm.

Entering the conference room, they both found their way to empty chairs. *What is that supposed to mean?* If this were the Borali Alliance, the weight of his status as a Royal would have prevented his opinion from being so easily brushed aside, but he hadn't carried that weight amongst the WFR from day one, and he was convinced he never would. He didn't miss it most of the time. This was an exception. Before he had time to think about it, the meeting began.

"Thank you all for coming," Joram said from the head of the table. "As you may know, Vertullis has an energy shield designed to protect the entire planet. Like similar shields deployed around Legallis and Regallis, this protects the planet from incoming laser weapons and starcraft. To pass through, starcraft must first enter a clearance code to lower a portion of the shield along their flight path. The Alliance put it in place to protect the planet if the need arose, but because there has been no external threat, they've never deployed it. For months now, we have observed the control station where Vertullis' energy shield is operated. The plan we have devised involves a multi-front assault. General Matheu has the overview."

Joram stepped aside as General Matheu moved to the head of the table. Around Aron's age and in a full dress uniform—dark blue, unlike the Borali Alliance army's gray, his face was hard, expressionless; his eyes intense like a man who had lived through many difficulties. Davi had heard rumors he'd been a hero of the Delta V revolt years before.

"Our flight team will be broken into two teams—one to assault the starport at Legallis, the other, the starport on Vertullis. Infantry assaults will occur simultaneously at multiple locations on Vertullis—the government complex, the starport, and the energy shield control center. At the same time, the mechanics core at all Boralian starports will disable any grounded Alliance ships, preventing their launch. Our goal will be to capture Alliance fighters and return them here, while taking control of the energy shield around Vertullis."

"If the shield has never been used," a woman near the far end of the table said, "how do we know it even works?"

"It has been tested every year since its inception," Joram said. "We have confirmed that it's been functional during those tests."

Davi hadn't known Vertullis even had a shield. Having never flown there himself, he'd never had to ask for clearance to land.

"What happens when the Alliance sends fighters from other bases to attack us?" the woman asked again.

"As long as the energy shield is activated, fighters will be ineffective," Joram said. "Any fighters we launch can be cleared through the shield to engage them."

"You expect to steal fighters from both Vertullis and Legallis? Do we have enough pilots?" asked a man seated across the table from Davi.

"We have forty trainees in Captain Rhii's flight training class at present," Aron said. "He can better inform you as to their status and capabilities."

All eyes turned to Davi, who met their stares with false confidence as his mind raced. *What am I supposed to tell them—that their plan is a complete bust? There's no way my trainees can be ready any time soon! They'll probably think I'm stalling because of torn loyalties or something.*

He stood, smiling, and doing his best to hide his feelings. "It remains to be seen if all forty trainees can even qualify as flight-worthy," he said. "Some of them have little if any experience with land craft, let alone starcraft."

"But you must have seen some progress over the past two weeks," Uzah said.

"Some are progressing quite well, yes," Davi said. "But I have concerns about certifying all of them without months more of training." He cleared his throat as he felt an empty feeling in his stomach.

"We don't have months," General Matheu said sternly. "They'll have to do the best they can." Curt and direct. Of all the WFR leaders, Matheu was the one who'd distrusted Davi from the start. Every conversation they'd had since his arrival had dripped with tension.

"With all due respect, it won't do us any good to take fighters and have them crash on the way back or get lost out in space," Davi said with as much authority as he could facing such a commanding opponent.

"You'll have to double the training time and work harder to prepare them," General Matheu responded, his look making it clear he wouldn't accept excuses.

"Half the candidates had prior flight experience," Joram said. "Those should be able to defend the others. The rest merely need to be able to follow their leader back to this base."

"I'm doing the best I can, but I can't guarantee they will be ready," Davi said.

Aron put a hand on his arm. "Captain Rhii is one of the most qualified pilots to graduate from the Borali Alliance Military Academy in the past five years. I'm sure he'll find a way to bring them up to speed." He smiled at Davi, motioning with his head for Davi to sit down.

Davi sighed and sat back down in the chair, relieved to have a moment to gather himself again.

"Besides the pilot issue," the woman said again, "do we even have enough infantry for these coordinated assaults?"

Uzah stood, smiling. "Our recruiting efforts have been quite successful. We have five hundred men in various stages of training."

"Various stages don't guarantee they'll be ready." The woman's stream of questions reminded Davi of Brie.

"They'll be ready. I'm quite confident," Uzah said, his face determined, but Davi wondered how he felt inside. *It seems to me they're taking a very fly-by-the-seat-of-your-pants approach. Do they really expect to succeed?*

"Once we control the shield, the military outposts on Vertullis, and have VS28 fighters, we will be able to protect and defend the planet,"

General Matheu said, sounding as if he had no doubts.

"And what if we fail?" The man across from Davi wondered.

"We cannot fail. Our people's lives depend on it," General Matheu said. They didn't need the look he proffered to convince them he meant it.

After the meeting, Davi walked out with Aron, more worried than before. The military leaders were clearly knowledgeable but their overconfidence worried him. Was it all bravado? That would at least be better than ignorance. "Do any of you realize we're attempting the impossible?"

Aron smiled. "Our people have a saying: Nothing is impossible with God."

"We risk losing so many in the process," Davi said.

"How many of our people have already died at the hands of the Borali Alliance?" Aron asked. "It's a matter of time before we're discovered here. Word is spreading. They can die trying or wait for the Alliance to come here and destroy them. Either way, the risk is the same."

Davi couldn't argue. He knew the workers' future depended on their success. He felt that pressure every class with his pilot trainees. And it was a heavy burden.

Aron smiled, patting his arm. "Do the best you can. You've been well-trained. I have faith in you."

The trainees had progressed over the past month, but Davi didn't want the responsibility for qualifying anyone who wasn't ready. Flying came easy to him, but when it came to the safety of others, he was more cautious. Davi appreciated Aron's encouragement. He just wished he had the same faith in himself.

A few minutes after Farien returned on a floater from reviewing the activity in the fields, Bordox and his men entered his makeshift office in one of the barns.

The floater was a blue floating platform with two seats facing a control panel at the front. The largest floaters had benches which held as many as twenty troops—more if ten more stood in the middle. Smaller models, like this one, held four or five passengers. Floaters moved by manipulating the air underneath as they floated along above the ground.

Farien sat at his desk, cocky and smirking as Bordox stared down at him with a serious look on his face, saying nothing. Farien fought the urge to laugh at the intensity of their old rival's stare. They hadn't seen each other in almost a year, yet Bordox's scowl evoked so many memories of their youths.

"Hello Bordox. How have you been?" Farien said after a moment.

Bordox nodded. "Have you heard anything new from our old friend Xander?"

*Not wasting any time, are you?* "Why do you want to know?"

Bordox frowned. "The High Lord Councilor wants to know." He said it as if it were a threat but Farien didn't even blink.

"I'm sure the High Lord Councilor, being his uncle, knows where he is," Farien said, his face making it clear he was unimpressed by Bordox's angry expression and tone.

"Your friend is a criminal wanted by the Borali Alliance for murder. If the High Lord Councilor knew where to find him, he'd be under arrest," Bordox said.

"I know all about the murder charges. It was self-defense," Farien said. "I'm sure he's out gathering evidence before he turns himself in."

"When was the last contact you had with him?"

"Look, Bordox, you've been giving us trouble for years. Why in the world would I tell you anything?" Farien said as he leaned back in his chair and turned his attention dismissively to the reports on his vidscreen.

"Because it's your duty to the Alliance," Bordox said, his breathing louder, his lips curling back with each word.

*You're angry. Ha! Good.* "Do the Alliance a favor and go back to whatever box you crawled out of and seal it," Farien said, turning away and punching a button on his datapad.

Bordox came around the desk so fast, Farien didn't have time to react. The brute dragged him from his chair, before his hand wrapped around Farien's neck. He fought for breath a moment before Bordox relaxed his grip while still holding Farien firmly off the ground.

"How about I let you live and you tell me everything you know?"

"You can't just go around killing people, no matter what authority you claim is behind you," Farien said, coughing. Would he really do it?

"I can make you wish you were dead," Bordox said.

A sharp pain shot through Farien unlike anything he'd ever experienced. He wanted to cry out, but couldn't catch his breath. Tears welled in his eyes, as Bordox pulled the shock device away from the small of his back. Farien collapsed to his knees.

"When was the last contact you had with him?" Bordox demanded.

"I saw him during Yao's visit a month or so back," Farien said. The words slipped out against his will, almost as if someone else had spoken.

"Good. That's better. Now, tell me why your friend is spending so much time with workers?"

"Because he's assigned to Vertullis, genius," Farien said. Shock waves hit again, causing him to writhe with pain. Every muscle in his body tensed as if they might pull apart into pieces.

"Since I'm here with the full support of the High Lord Councilor, you might want to show me a modicum of respect, Lieutenant," Bordox said.

"Look, he's been investigating some incidents of abuse, trying to gather the facts," Farien said as he gasped for breath and stared up into Bordox's cold face.

As expected, Bordox was unmoved. "We found evidence of him spending a lot of time in a particular worker's home. There was a photo there of a man to whom he bears a strong resemblance. What's his connection to those workers?"

"Why don't you ask him when you find him?" Farien said. "I don't know whom you're referring to."

Bordox shocked him again and again.

Farien couldn't breathe or think or move. Finally, he screamed, "Gods! I told you I don't know, Bordox!"

"I don't believe you," Bordox said, swinging the shock device toward him again.

This time Farien cried out, but stopped when the pain became overwhelming.

"Answer the question."

"His mother and her sister's family," Farien finally said. He cursed himself for being weak, but he couldn't take more of the pain.

"His mother lives on Legallis in the Royal Palace." The shock waves coursed through him again.

Farien managed to scream. "For the love of the gods! Stop! Please! He was adopted by Miri. His real family were workers, like you said at the Academy."

Bordox cursed as his fist hit the desk inches from where Farien's head had fallen in exhaustion. "It's true?"

Humiliation washed over Farien like wave. He couldn't believe he'd betrayed his friend. Bordox hadn't known the truth. What would he say to Davi? What would Bordox do to him?

Bordox pulled the shock device away, fastening it to his belt. "The Alliance appreciates your cooperation." He turned with his men and disappeared as fast as he'd appeared.

*My gods, the pain!* Farien lay there beside his desk, trying to shake it off. He might have died for a moment, he thought, but then he was alone, lying on the floor and wondering if he'd ever move again.

After a month on the simulators, Davi decided to give the trainees time on the skitters. When they'd gathered in the skitter cave for class, he began reviewing the controls as the students bustled excitedly around him.

"Any questions so far?" Davi asked, wondering how much they'd heard through their own whispering.

Brie smiled at him, cocking her head to one side flirtatiously. "So the way you make it go is this button here?" She pointed to the joystick as a few others around her groaned. It was a question they all knew the answer to.

Tela frowned, shifting weight to her left foot.

Davi did his best to keep his distance from Brie, nodding. "Yes, Brie. You'll need to get used to it. It's easy to push it too hard and accelerate out of control."

"Okay, I'll be careful then," she said, smiling at him again.

Davi nodded. "Okay, let's take them out for a trial run on the course Tela's set up for us. Keep your speed slow until you get used to the controls and the feel of the skitters."

He watched as, one by one, the excitable trainees started their skitters and accelerated into the tunnel. Tela, the only calm one amongst them, took off first, followed by several of the more experienced trainees. The rest followed. Only Dru, Brie, Nila and Davi remained.

Dru started out being cautious but seemed to feel comfortable by the time he entered the tunnel. Nila accelerated next, fumbling a bit, then recovered and disappeared into the tunnel.

"Well, here I go." Brie smiled sheepishly, starting to accelerate, wobbling a bit, slow then fast. After a few moments, she managed to steer the skitter toward the tunnel. As she neared the tunnel entrance, Davi winced, gritting his teeth. It looked like she might miss the opening and hit the wall, but, at the last minute, she steered to the right and entered the tunnel. Davi breathed a sigh of relief and followed.

As he left the tunnel, the sweet smell of cedars and wild berries filled his nose. Trees surrounded them now, filling every space around the skitter course and trails. The sounds of insects and birds rose above the hum of the skitters—a constant drone, which faded into the background after a few moments as their ears adjusted.

Davi pulled alongside Brie, smiling. "You did it. Good job."

"Thanks," she said, looking pleased with herself.

They rode past Tela, who waited outside the tunnel entrance. She shot Davi a cold stare. *What did I do now?* He met her stare and smiled. "All right, Tela, please take us through the course."

She turned away, avoiding eye contact and headed toward the front of the group, who waited at the start of the course. One by one, they followed her. Some of them seemed quite confident and steady, others more cautious and uncertain. Dru had moved up a few places, feeling more confident. That left Davi, Nila, and Brie.

"All right, Nila. Go ahead," Davi called to his cousin, who was reviewing her skitter's control panel on the far side of the clearing.

Nila nodded. "Okay." She accelerated with more confidence this time, following the others.

Brie accelerated full force and shot toward Nila like a rocket, her face in a panic.

Davi tensed, trying to decide whether to chase after her or call out instructions. "Let go of the handle, Brie!" he called after her, and then realized she was trying but couldn't do it.

As she closed fast on the unsuspecting Nila, Davi accelerated his skitter and chased after her. He pulled alongside, reached over and tried to pull her hand free. Her sleeve had gotten pinched in the small space between the joystick and the arm of the skitter. As she panicked, her fists clenched, triggering the accelerator. Her face morphed into a grimace as her speed increased and the wind pricked her face.

Nila rode a few feet in front of them, so focused on controlling her skitter she hadn't noticed the activity behind her. Brie's eyes widened, full of panic. Davi pulled his skitter closer to hers and reached past her, leaning way over to one side, controlling his skitter with one hand as he did. His fingers touched the start pin on Brie's skitter, but he couldn't quite grab it. He stretched further, adrenaline energizing every move, and popped it out.

Brie's skitter stopped instantly, almost throwing her off. Davi skidded to a stop, dismounted and ran over to pull her sleeve free, then lifted the shaken Brie off the skitter. For a moment, she lay in his arms staring up at him with relief as both caught their breath.

Tela pulled up nearby. She'd come back to check on how things were going. Seeing Brie in his arms, she scowled, then turned and sped away again along the course with Nila following.

Davi started calling after her, then realized she couldn't hear him. He set Brie on the ground. "Are you okay?"

"Yes, thank you. My hero!" she said, smiling.

"Try and be more careful. Maybe roll up your sleeves," Davi instructed.

Brie nodded. "Okay, right." She rolled up her sleeves.

Davi reminded himself to inquire about the status of uniforms again. Brie and several other trainees had not yet received theirs, and he didn't want a repeat of this incident.

For the rest of the afternoon, they worked the course with no further problems. Some of class could already race through the course at a decent pace.

Soon Virun and his friends began fiddling around with the targeting system, although Davi hadn't demonstrated it yet. Rather than scolding them, he watched, wanting to see how they handled it. And as he did, he concluded some of them might be ready now for the mission, if they could just learn to obey orders.

"Very good, you men," Davi said, after they'd finished the course for the fourth time. "Why don't you let me show you how that works?"

"I think we've got it," Jorek said as the rest of his friends ignored Davi.

"The course can only show you so much. In a combat situation—"

"In a combat situation, we may be on opposite sides," Virun snapped. With that, the group revved their skitters and headed back to the course again.

Davi sighed. *How can I get through to them?* He had no idea. As he mulled it over, Brie and Nila arrived at the finish line looking more relaxed than they had at the start. They seemed to grow more confident with each run. By the end of the class, they maneuvered their skitters with much more ease. They didn't seem to have the aptitude. The learning curve was too high. How would he get them ready? It would be impossible in the next few weeks.

*This would be so much easier, if I didn't care so much. Pilots die. It's part of the risk.* But these weren't any pilots. He was responsible for them. He walked away discouraged again.

That night, as he had often the past two weeks, he spent time in the Library studying the history and beliefs of his new people.

Miri had raised him to believe service to the higher cause of helping others was more important than service to one's self. Though the workers' religious rites seemed strange to him, in reading about them, they seemed to make sense. He started feeling more and more comfortable praying to their God and participating in services. In fact, he had plans to attend with Lura the following morning.

The workers believed God was with them at all times and working His will in their lives daily; that He was involved in everything that happened to them and was always working for their good. They committed their plans to Him and sought His blessing on their actions. Davi couldn't help but be drawn to a God who got so involved and cared so much. He found himself wanting to know more and more.

Tela ordered a Tertullian Hammer and settled into a booth at the pub to wait for her drink, enjoying the feel of the cool leather against her skin as she breathed gently and relaxed from a long day. Through the dome overhead, she watched the sky fade from purple to gray as the planet's two moons started their nightly climb. It was a view she'd enjoyed taking in ever since she was a young girl, and seeing it here evoked so many memories. It was hard to believe she'd wound up in such an unexpected place. She enjoyed it for a few moments before her mind turned to the day's events.

Again, Brie had flirted with Davi. And again, it had really set her off, though she couldn't understand why. She and Davi were just friends. She didn't have time for men right now. There were the coming battles to think about and, ever since her father had disappeared, she'd decided love was a waste of time. So why would her heart not get with the program?

She couldn't get Davi out of her mind—the way he smiled at her when the other trainees were making progress, the way he laughed at his own silly jokes, the serious look his face took on when deep in thought or lecturing on something intense. And how good he looked in that spiffy new WFR uniform. She supposed the form fitting uniforms made most of them look good, at least those who were in shape, but Davi was the only one she'd really noticed. Why did she pay so much attention anyway? She'd already decided he wasn't for her.

As the waiter arrived with her drink, she spotted Davi behind him, coming in the door. Handing the waiter a few credits, she watched Davi make his away across the room as the waiter disappeared. He hadn't seen her yet as he scanned the room, nodding at various acquaintances.

Why hadn't he seen her yet? She was right in front of him. *Oh great!*

*That bothers me, too! What's wrong with me?*

Then he saw her and smiled, waving. *He's coming over!* She tried to be nonchalant, relaxing in her seat as she sipped her drink and savored the smooth, fruity liquid warming her throat.

Davi came right to the table. "Imagine finding you here, Lieutenant."

There it came—his smile. She returned it. "Another long day." The butterflies danced in her stomach again.

He nodded. "For me, too. Are you alone?"

*Say no! Say no!* "Yes." *What's wrong with me?*

He sat across from her. "Hope you don't mind company."

She shook her head. "No."

"We had a real near miss today with Brie," Davi said.

*Ah, there it is! He's going to go right to it!* "Yes, it was a good thing you were prepared." It came off colder than she'd meant and she silently chastised herself for not controlling her emotions better.

"I wasn't. I almost panicked," Davi said. "Then I remembered the start pin acts as a kill switch. I haven't been around skitters much in a while."

She smiled. "Thank goodness you remembered."

The waiter returned, and she watched as Davi ordered a Regallian Smoothie. She admired the way his chin curved down from his head, the smoothness of his skin, the way he looked with his late-day shadow of a beard. Mmmm, and as he leaned back she could see the way his uniform hugged his well-toned chest and thighs. *Oh my God, stop!*

Davi turned to her as the waiter left. "I don't think we can get them all ready. There isn't time." He frowned, discouraged.

"We'll do our best," she said, trying to sound positive.

His shoulders drooped, his eyes red and empty. *Why do I want so much to encourage him? I can't bear seeing him so sad.* She searched for words that would encourage him somehow. "Some of them only need to fly well enough to follow others back here. They should be able to learn enough for that."

"I'm not sure Brie can learn much of anything," Davi said.

Tela laughed.

He covered his eyes with his hand, embarrassed. "I'm sorry. Terrible thing to say."

Tela laughed again.

He grinned. "She's so naïve."

They both laughed.

"Yeah, very naïve," she agreed. *What's this? He's not attracted to her?*

"She's like a little kid sometimes, too. So young and innocent," Davi said.

Tela did a cartwheel in her head. *Yes!*

"Several of them are," he continued. "It's hard to believe they're in flight training."

"It wasn't so many years ago, we were their age," Tela said, doing her best to hide her relief.

Davi laughed. "I guess you're right. I feel so much older after all that's happened."

The waiter returned with his smoothie. He sipped it for a bit, lost in thought. "I feel so responsible for them. If they go up there and become easy targets ..."

The waiter disappeared again.

"That's a risk for any one of us," Tela said. "In war, people die."

Davi nodded, his face taking on a somber expression as he sipped the smoothie. "I don't have to like it."

Tela laughed.

"What's so funny?"

*You. You're adorable.* "Nothing. I'm sorry. You're sipping a sweet drink looking like they're already dead. It's funny!"

Davi took another sip of his smoothie and shrugged. "Sometimes I let whatever's on my mind come out of my mouth."

Tela smiled. "It's okay. It's one of the things I actually like about you." *I can't believe I just said that.*

His eyes brightened as they met hers. "You mean there's actually something you like about me? Wow! Big progress!"

She sighed and turned away. "You cocky fighter jocks!"

They both laughed again.

She turned back, her face serious again. "No one wants people to die, but we have to remember the loss will be worth the price of freedom. We have been slaves too long!"

Davi nodded. "I know. I've been spending time in the Library learning the history of our people. I really believe in what we're doing."
Tela couldn't help being impressed by his effort. "That doesn't make it any easier to think about sending kids to their possible deaths."

"Some of them may surprise you," Tela said.

Davi nodded. "I hope all of them do." He took another sip, savoring the fruity taste a moment.

On impulse, she placed her hand on his atop the table. "Me, too." She fought the urge to yank it back when she realized what she'd done. Yet he hadn't tried to pull his hand away. Did he like this? She hated being so transparent, but then touching him like this felt so nice.

She slowly withdrew her hand. "We'll have to work harder with them."

Davi nodded. "I've been thinking the same thing." He took one last long sip of his smoothie, and then set the empty glass back on the table. "I guess I should head back and start working up a more intense lesson plan."

Tela joined him as he stood. "Do you want some help?"

Davi gave her a puzzled look. "Really?"

She shrugged. "Sure, why not? I can come up with some decent ideas."

He shifted in his chair, looking embarrassed that he'd offended her. "I didn't mean it like that."

Tela smiled. "I know." He was so cute sometimes.

Davi nodded and tossed some credits on the table. "Okay, let's go."

She had an impulse. "Wait."

"What?"

"One more thing."

Without thinking, she rushed around the table, and, before either understood what was happening, she kissed him.

After a moment, she pulled away, straightened her clothes and headed for the door. "Let's go."

Davi stood there stunned and watched her go.

She turned back in the doorway. "You coming?"

He nodded, moving toward her.

*Oh my God!* She fought to control her expression. *Why did I do that? This is just what I need.* But then she realized she hadn't wanted to stop.

The next morning, Davi and Lura attended a worship service in the base chapel led by Chaplain Timoteo. As Davi sat down, he noticed Tela across the aisle. She looked over and smiled. He smiled back. He'd thought she had no interest at all, but then she'd kissed him. He still couldn't believe it. Right before the service began, she slid across the aisle to sit beside him. For a moment, he half-hoped she'd kiss him again, right then and there, then he choked it back, fighting to keep from blushing.

The service was simple, with less elaborate rituals and show than he'd seen at the temples on Legallis. It focused more on God than on anything the believers had done, and the sacrifice demanded was a willing heart and life, not some physical object. The Lords' religion focused a series of rituals and sacrifices, and while they varied some from god to god, there were often many similarities. Followers offered sacrifices to the various gods to obtain something the believer wanted—forgiveness for some wrong done, help for some impending action, revenge, love, health, strength, etc. It focused on what the gods could do for the believers, rather than what the believers could do for the gods. It assumed the gods served the worshipers, not the other way around.

The workers' religion asked believers to offer their God worship for all He had already done for them, to embark on a personal journey of faith discovery. He'd never understood how gods so powerful existed to serve man's needs. This God knew His place in the universe. The history of this God interwove with the history of his people, a history which, as he learned about it, made sense to Davi and appealed to him far more than the Lords' religion ever had.

Service concluded with a time of prayer. Davi thanked God for his family–two wonderful mothers and so many cousins, uncles, and aunts. He thought about Miri and Xalivar and hoped they were well. He prayed they could forgive him for the betrayal they perceived. He prayed for his trainees, to teach and lead them well; for wisdom and for their safety. And he prayed for the battle, for God's blessings and guidance of the plans of His people. He'd read about the workers' ancestors fighting with God on their side. He knew they would need God to achieve their goal.

He also prayed for Farien and Yao, whom he hadn't seen in a while. He hoped they were well and would forgive his betrayal of the Alliance. He thanked God for Tela and their budding romance and asked blessings and protection on them through the fighting ahead.

In conclusion, he prayed for his father, wherever he was. Then he asked for forgiveness for the dead Captain and blessings on his family. Davi hoped the God of the Vertullians would forgive him for something he couldn't forgive of himself.

When he'd finished, Davi was amazed how peaceful he felt. A burden had been lifted from him, as if everything was under control—much different than he'd experienced after worshipping the Lords' gods. He'd never found himself praying so spontaneously to them and finding any comfort in prayers, but now he did, on occasion. He'd seen the comfort it provided Lura and Tela and the others, and he'd wanted to see for himself. It had made a difference, even if he still had doubts. He'd experienced something, though he wasn't sure what. And for the first time in his life, he found himself believing that perhaps gods or a God might exist, that religion might be more than just a construct of man.

Miri had not been down to the Royal Archives in almost a year. Located deep beneath the planet's surface in one of several caves dug out with lasers to create secure storage for important government materials, the Archives had very limited access. Besides the archivist himself, Xalivar, Miri, and their two most trusted aides alone had access to it, and the aides had to come together.

She went there straight after her morning prayer time at the temple. She'd begun praying again recently, a practice she hadn't engaged in for many years—the Rhii family had never been particularly dedicated to religion. But with all the things going on with Davi, she'd felt the urge and started going again every morning to pray for him, for Xalivar, and for others like Yao, Farien and Kray. Whether it had any effect, she had no idea, but she did find comfort in the rituals themselves, and the peace that brought her alone made it worth the time.

The archivist showed no surprise when she stepped off the elevator. "Welcome to the Royal Archives, Princess Miri."

She returned his smile as she placed her palm on the sensor. It beeped and the gate clicked, allowing her to step inside. "Good afternoon." Her heart fluttered a bit as she pondered what she was about to do. But no one had any reason to be suspicious, after all. She was a Royal and this was her family archive. Still, taking the action openly made her feel a tinge of nervous guilt and fear which she did her best to hide.

"Was there anything I might help you with?" The archivist asked.

She shook her head as casually as she could manage. "No thank you. I'm going over some old family papers."

"All right. Let me know if there's anything I can do."

"Thank you, I will."

Miri moved around the desk, forcing herself to remain at a normal, casual pace, and weaved down the aisles between white metal shelves, making her way to a vault in the very back of the cave. Here she stopped, pulling up information on her datapad. She had never used the combination before. She entered the combination on the keypad then waited until she heard several loud clicks and the door slid open. She almost chuckled with relief that she'd managed it the first time, then caught herself lest she be overheard and pulled the thick door wider then stepped inside.

Since her father and Xalivar alone had used this particular vault, she had no idea what she'd find there. She saw more metal shelving, faded gray. There were rows of old Earth books, some computer tapes and memory cards, some older royal vestments from past special occasions, such as her father's coronation robe and crown, her mother's wedding gown, and other similar items.

The label on a box of memory cards caught her eye. It read: "Vertullis Revolt." She grabbed one of the boxes and popped the top open. Retrieving the first card, she inserted it into her datapad.

She heard the sounds first—people yelling and screaming, laser fire. After a moment, the video appeared. Alliance soldiers used laser weapons to mow down slaves lined up in front of large pits dug in the earth. As one row fell into the pit, the next row stepped forward to be mowed down; their bodies falling into the pit on top of the others. This happened again and again to seemingly endless numbers of slaves.

Miri glanced away, grabbing the memory card and pulling it free. The next card showed more of the same at a different location. She had to look away at times, a pain piercing her heart, her head pounding as the images sunk in. She'd known about revolts being put down, but never heard of massacres.

She found it difficult to accept what she'd seen—Xalivar, in full military uniform, directing the troops himself and firing his own laser weapon in unison with them as worker after worker fell dead or wounded. *Xalivar not only ordered the massacres, he participated in them. My gods!*

Grabbing the boxes of memory tapes off the shelf, she looked around for something to conceal them in. A couple of large hats on a nearby shelf caught her eye. She chose the most modern, a hat her mother had worn on a ceremonial tour of the star system, slid the memory card boxes inside, then grabbed a scarf from the clothing rack, and stuffed it in and around the boxes—fiddling nervously until it was just right—so the archivist wouldn't see them.

She stepped out of the vault as casually as she could, shut the door behind her, and entered the code to trigger the lock. Hearing the clicks, she tugged on the door to be sure it had locked, then headed back through the aisles the way she'd come, again reminding herself to walk normally every step of the way.

# Chapter Nine

Xalivar's jaw dropped to the floor as his eyes registered what he was seeing, and he flicked on the sound with the remote control.

"These images are of Alliance soldiers committing mass murder of workers during the worker revolt ten years ago," Orson Sterling was saying.

Xalivar frowned as he watched himself on the screen, firing his weapon.

"As you can see, the High Lord Councilor himself led the massacres."

*How can this be? The Delta V footage was hidden in the private Royal vault! Copies were destroyed.*

He punched a button on the remote and changed the vidscreen to a private channel then entered a password. He chose one of the dates shown at random and began fast forwarding through the footage. It showed an empty vault. Could one of his servants have betrayed him after all this time?

On the third day he selected, he saw her. Miri was in the vault, viewing one of the memory cards he'd hidden there. Seeing her reaction, he knew right away. *Miri removed the tapes! My gods! Betrayed by his own sister!*

An old proverb came to mind: **Gods defend me from my friends; from my enemies I can defend myself.**

He swore, fists clenching as his entire body tensed and he fought to control the rage rising inside him. Miri had been leaking footage to Media Corp.? *For the gods' sake!* No wonder she'd made herself so scarce the past few weeks. *What have you done to our family, sister?* He buzzed for Manaen.

The door slid open and Manaen hurried into his chamber. "Yes, my Lord?"

"Where is the Princess at the moment?" Xalivar demanded, almost yelling as his majordomo flinched.

"She's gone into the city, my Lord." Manaen said, handing him a datapad full of reports.

Xalivar almost smiled at the delightful smell of his aide's fear. Instead, he took a deep breath and locked his eyes on his frightened aide's. "I need to see her as soon as she returns."

Manaen bowed deferentially. "Of course, my Lord."

"And what time is the Council meeting today?"

"Just past mid-day."

"Has the Council requested my attendance?"

"They have, my Lord."

Xalivar cursed to himself as he dismissed Manaen with a wave. The majordomo saluted and walked out the door. It slid shut with a whoosh behind him. He turned off the vidscreen and began reviewing the reports on the datapad Manaen had given him. One came from Bordox, going on and on about Davi being the child of workers. Xalivar cursed again. It would be impossible to keep the Council from seeing it. *I'm ruined! My gods! Is everyone turning against me now?*

He searched his mind for a way he could use this to his advantage. If he took the report to the Council first himself, perhaps he could lessen the damage. After all, hadn't he instigated the search for Davi himself? He'd protected the Alliance's best interests without favoritism for his nephew. And the Council needed to know more about their missing murder suspect, didn't they?

He smiled to himself. *Yes!* They needed to know Davi was not like them—a worker! *Yes!* Let Miri try and protect her son once the fact became public knowledge! Xalivar would present it as a surprise to himself. Miri had deceived all of them! She had betrayed the Alliance, acted alone. He found it unacceptable and he knew the Council would also. *Yes!* Let Miri's friends on the Council hear this.

For a moment, he wondered if they'd been involved with the news leaks, too. He doubted it. They would not want footage of the massacres getting out. The Council had been involved in ordering the suppression of the revolts. No. She must be negotiating with them for leniency for her son.

*Yes, my sister! See how much support you get when I am through with the Council. No one will dare to support you after this. No, my sister, soon you and I can discuss your activities alone.* He laughed, pleased with himself.

Davi took the trainees out on skitters for the third time in a week. Leaving Tela to start them off, he raced through the course to the halfway point, and then stopped to watch as the trainees passed by.

They'd made marked improvement. All of them could at least navigate the course to the end now, most practicing with the targeting system. All the trainees looked slick in their new dark blue uniforms. It seemed to boost their confidence. Good! They would need all the confidence they could get in the fight ahead.

He chuckled at the sight of the cloth protectors each wore dangling in front of their lower faces to protect from the bite of the wind. Practicality had overcome their initial resistance. It was time to shake it up a bit and take them out on trails. He needed to see how they handled things outside of a course they'd almost memorized. He waited until the last trainee passed, then followed along through the blur of the trees.

The spicy odor of cedars filled his nose as the drone of insects and birds blended with the hum of the skitter in his ears. He found his trainees waiting for him in the large clearing at the end of the course, chattering excitedly. They were all smiling as he pulled to a stop.

"Well done today. Definite improvements," Davi said, removing the cloth protector from his face so it wouldn't muffle his voice.

"Getting so we could do it blindfolded," Dru said, growing cocky.

Davi knew Dru was still struggling but smiled. "Good! Confidence is the right attitude. How about we shake it up a bit?"

"Try it backwards?" Nila asked, her expression sincere.

Davi laughed. "No. Let's try some of the forest trails. It's important to learn how to handle your craft under a variety of circumstances. In battle, there is no preset course to follow."

"Can we have a mock battle?" Dru asked eagerly.

"Let's try the forest trails first, okay? One step at a time." Davi smiled. "You wanna pick a trail?"

Dru smiled, pleased. "Sure. Can I lead the way?"

Davi nodded and Dru took off, struggling for balance a bit after accelerating too fast. A few of the other more skilled trainees grumbled at the idea of following him, but one by one, they followed him onto a trail through the forest. As usual, Brie and Nila brought up the rear.

Tela hung back to join Davi.

"Nice job on the course, Tela," Davi said. "It's making a world of difference." She'd become such an asset.

"Glad I could help," she said and smiled.

They'd been spending a lot of time together since their night at the bar. They clearly both enjoyed each other's company and they'd certainly kissed a few more times since then, even cuddling a bit. Though they'd both done their best to keep their growing romance secret from the rest of the trainees, sometimes Davi avoided looking at her for fear it would show on his face. But more and more, he wanted to shout it for the whole world to hear.

Bordox and Corsi rode together on skitters through a forest clearing. So far their search of the forest hadn't turned up anything. Even the local farmers who'd reported seeing activity here wouldn't talk to them at the sight of LSP uniforms. Bordox had grown bored and frustrated. How could Xander Rhii be so hard to locate?

A couple of his men rode back toward them, pulling up alongside. "No activity in that direction, sir."

"How far did you go?" he demanded. He'd gotten tougher and tougher with them, assuming that a good part of his failure rested with their incompetence.

"Twenty kilometers. The forest goes on forever," the soldier said over the hum of the skitters and the chirping of the insects and birds.

The chirping annoyed Bordox, even more than the smell of the cedar. More than once he'd fantasized about picking the birds off one by one with his blaster then frying the insects. Bordox frowned, irritated. "You'll search every centimeter of it, if I ask you to." How could someone as stupid as Rhii hide so well?

The soldier nodded, "Yes, sir."

"Try another direction for now," Bordox said.

The soldiers turned and rode off, disappearing into the cedars to the west.

"The trees are so dense, the scanner is having difficulty," Corsi said, tapping the device attached to his control panel.

"I'm getting the feeling Zylo sent us on another wild gungor chase," Bordox said.

"Gungors would be easier to find," Corsi mumbled.

Bordox nodded and swore. Even his men knew it was a waste of time.

As they followed the trail, Nila's skitter sputtered, a big cloud of smoke emerging from its motivator and trailing along behind them. Moments later, it stopped.

Davi pulled to a stop alongside her. "What happened?"

Nila shrugged. "No idea. It lost power and then stopped."

"Maybe the motivator is bad," Tela said as she stopped nearby, waving her arms to clear the smoke drifting toward her face.

"Can we fix it here?" Davi asked.

Tela thought for a moment and shook her head. "I'd have to ride in for another one. It would take a while."

"Can we tow it?"

"We might be able to rig something up," Tela said with a shrug. She started to dismount but Davi stopped her with a wave.

"You catch up with the others and let them know what's happened. Then ride back and see what you can find at the base," Davi said. "I'll stay with her and see what we can manage."

Tela nodded, looking around—just Nila and Davi. Brie had gone on ahead. *Good!*

Davi chuckled at the relief on her face as she said, "You be careful, okay?"

Tela blushed a bit. How could she still be jealous of Brie after all the time they'd been spending together?

"We can handle it," Davi reassured her.

Tela settled back on her skitter and nodded in confirmation, then started it up and rode away after the others.

Bordox and Corsi followed a winding trail through the forest, until they saw flashes ahead.

Bordox perked up, eyes locked on the direction the flashes had come from. "What was that?"

"Looked like lasers," Corsi said.

"It came from up ahead." Bordox accelerated his skitter and sped around a bend in the trail as Corsi hurried to keep up with him.

Davi and Nila had used their blasters to cut large vines from the thick canopy of the forest to make a makeshift tow line. As they finished tying the vines into longer ropes then began attaching the two skitters together with Davi's in front.

"We won't be able to go very fast, but it'll get us there," Davi said as they finished. He stood admiring their work as Nila smiled. His Academy training had paid off.

"Where'd you learn how to do all this stuff?" she asked.

Davi laughed. "Military Academies teach all kinds of skills. You never know what you're going to need."

Nila smirked. "Bet you never thought you'd be towing a skitter."

Davi shrugged. "There are a lot of things I've done on this planet I never thought I'd be doing. Including training my cousin to fly." He winked at her and she smiled again. "Let's mount up and get going."

Nila climbed onto her skitter as Davi settled back onto his.

"Might be a bit rough at first so hang on," he warned her then took his time accelerating. Nila did her best to match his steering.

Bordox stopped in a clearing as Corsi pulled up alongside. He couldn't believe what he saw.

On a trail to the west, Xander rode a skitter and towed a girl on another skitter behind him.

*My gods! I found him!* He ducked down, motioning to Corsi. "Keep your head down!"

"Is it him?" Corsi asked.

Bordox motioned urgently. "Let's get in front of him and surprise him. Call in the men. Quietly!"

Corsi nodded, reaching for his communicator.

Bordox smiled, his body tingling with excitement as he activated his skitter's weapons system. At last, he would get his revenge!

Davi stopped a moment and adjusted the vines. He'd strung them too loose the first time, making the ride rougher for Nila than he wanted. He cut them in half and retied the ends so the skitters would ride closer together. This time, he attached them with four lines instead of two, checking to be sure the knots were tight.

"That should be better." *I wish Tela would hurry back with that motivator.*

"I'm sure it's fine," Nila said. Her eagerness to learn and willingness to do whatever it took made up for the fact she sometimes took longer than the others to get up to speed during training. And he was proud of her progress.

Davi settled back onto his skitter. "All right. Here we go again."

He accelerated again, looking back to check on Nila.

She smiled at him, offering a thumbs up.

*Good. Maybe this time we can make some progress.*

Bordox quickly divided his men into groups and sent them in various directions, while he and Corsi continued on the same trail as Xander. He was so excited; he had to force himself not to move in before his men were ready. He couldn't risk allowing Davi to escape. This would be the highlight of his career to date. Not only could he take down his own rival, but he'd also be ruining the reputation of his family's rival clan at the same time.

He started humming a favorite song as he rode along.

Davi stopped a moment, scanning maps of the forest on his datapad. The vines and brush were thicker here, filling in space between the trees almost like a wall. "This side trail should be a short cut," he said to Nila. "Shall we give it a try?"

She shrugged, relaxed on her skitter with complete trust in him. "I follow orders. You're the officer."

He laughed, clipping the datapad back onto his belt before accelerating off the main trail onto the short cut. "I wish all soldiers were this easy to please," he joked.

"I'm saving my demands for when it matters," Nila teased.

They both laughed.

Bordox ordered his men to move in from all directions on Rhii and his companion. Bordox grinned as he and Corsi accelerated around a bend in the trees. Verifying his weapons had fully charged, he spotted his men closing in ahead. But his heart sank. Xander wasn't there. Bordox cursed.

"Where could he have gone?" Corsi asked, looking puzzled.

"Search the whole area! Quickly!" Bordox yelled.

Corsi winced and began issuing orders over the comm.

"He can't be allowed to escape!" Bordox fumed as the men scattered. "You, too, Corsi! Go! Go!"

Corsi nodded, accelerating his skitter up a side trail.

Bordox cursed again and examined the ground. How could Xander keep slipping through his grasp? They'd tear every inch of this forest apart if that's what it took. He had to be out here somewhere. He would not let Xander Rhii humiliate him again.

"Not this time Rhii!" he shouted. "You're mine!"

As Davi and Nila pulled their skitters to a stop inside the cave, Tela rushed toward them.

As soon as Davi stepped off his skitter, she embraced him. "Thank God you're back. We've had reports of LSP troops searching the forest."

"LSP troops here?" Davi couldn't believe it. His body stiffened with worry and his jaw tightened, his mind racing for a plan. "How'd they find us?"

"I don't know, but we'd better be careful on the trails from now on," Tela said.

Davi nodded. Tela was still holding onto him. He liked it. "So, does this mean we're going public then?"

Tela rolled her eyes, letting go and looking around. Nila had already disappeared. They were alone.

"Is it that embarrassing?" Davi raised an eyebrow at her.

"No, of course not." She sighed. "It's complicated. We're about to start a war. And since my father disappeared, I haven't wanted to get involved."

"Your father disappeared?" Davi hadn't known.

Her face turned sadder as she explained. "My father was a scientist. He made some discoveries the Alliance deemed threatening. They sent him to the top-secret prison on Legallis. Another worker spy, they claimed."

"Top secret prison on Legallis? Must not be too secret if you know about it," Davi said.

She shrugged. "I have no idea where it's located, but it's known to exist. A secret prison there for workers declared a threat to the Borali Alliance."

Davi's mind started racing. Could his father be there? He had to make some inquiries. Maybe Yao or Farien could find something out for him. "How long ago?"

Tela shrugged. "I was a little girl. Twelve years, I think."

"Your father is still alive?"

Tela's eyes brightened as she nodded. "Before she died, my mother had contact with a man who'd been making deliveries on Legallis and encountered my father working at the dock. They sometimes use the prisoners for various projects, and then send them back to the prison."

Davi's heart pounded with excited thoughts about his father. He promised himself not to say anything to Lura until he'd had the chance to get more information. He turned and started back toward his quarters.

"What's the matter? Did I say something wrong?" Tela called after him, but he didn't hear her.

Xalivar timed his arrival at the Council chamber so he could make a grand entrance when the meeting was well underway. To increase the Council's anticipation, he'd had Manaen send a message to Lord Tarkanius about Xalivar receiving shocking news of great import to the Council, which he would deliver in person.

All eyes fixed on him as he entered the chamber, and the session ground to an immediate halt. Lord Niger had been addressing the Council, but seeing Xalivar, he stopped and returned to his seat.

Xalivar smiled inside, his exterior expression remaining very grave. He could smell the tension of prideful men, their rivalries, bitterness, and drive for power, and it energized him as it always did when he entered their presence. All the more so when their every eye focused on him. "I apologize for my lateness to the proceedings," he said, making his way to the dais.

Tarkanius nodded. "Your aide notified us you would be late. You have important news for us?"

"Yes," Xalivar said, mentally preparing as he set his facial expression with the appropriate tone—a mix of shock, sadness, rage and worry. "I recently uncovered a shocking conspiracy against the Borali Alliance which has compromised the Royal Family," Xalivar said.

He heard gasps and watched the shocked reactions from those present.

"The Royal Family has been implicated?" Lord Hachim asked.

Xalivar blanched internally at the choice of words but maintained his composure and nodded. "I'm afraid so. The conspiracy was led by my own sister, Princess Miri," Xalivar said.

More gasps and shocked reactions.

"Princess Miri has been a loyal member of the Borali Alliance her whole life," Lord Kray said, her eyes already denying it could be true.

Xalivar fought the urge to scowl. Kray always sided with Miri. They were the oldest of friends. *Well, let's see her argue with this!*

"I have uncovered evidence that my own nephew, Prince Xander Rhii, was adopted by Miri from workers." He waited for the gasps and shocked reactions. "This illegal act occurred completely without my knowledge and remained hidden from me, until LSP forces, under my command, uncovered the plot during their search for the fugitive, Xander Rhii."

"Your own sister raised a worker child in your household, and you didn't know?" Lord Niger asked.

He saw others' faces fill with a mixture of doubt, disbelief, and challenge.

"Not until now. I was quite shocked and disturbed by the revelation," Xalivar said, ignoring Kray's icy stare.

"He's an officer in the Borali Alliance military, an Academy graduate … the entire Alliance may be compromised," Lord Obed said, angrily fanning the flames. Since Obed's son had written the report, Xalivar wondered how much he already knew.

Xalivar stared at the floor, forcing as much sadness onto his face as he could muster. "I fear it is so. My own men have informed me they are closing in on him now."

"And what of the Princess? What does she have to say about this?" Tarkanius asked.

Xalivar knew Tarkanius was among those who had met with Miri in private, causing Xalivar to question his loyalty. *All will be brought to light soon enough, Tarkanius. And those who betrayed me will answer for it.*

"She's away from the Palace, but she will be found and brought to me. I rushed here to inform the Council as soon as the evidence came to light."

"Your aide managed to come and go over twenty-five minutes ago," Lord Obed interjected with an accusing tone.

"This is a very serious accusation you are making," Lord Simeon said, ignoring his colleague. "We will initiate a full investigation."

*Another possible traitor heard from.* "I will assist you in any way I can," Xalivar said.

"Thank you for bringing this matter to our attention, High Lord Councilor." Only Tarkanius seemed to maintain his composure at the news. He nodded from the dais. "Your forthrightness before the Council exemplifies the honor with which you serve."

*Too little, too late, Tarkanius, my old friend. You've already proven where your loyalties lie.* Xalivar nodded back. This was going far better than he'd imagined. "Thank you, Lord Tarkanius."

"As soon as the Princess and her son are found, they must be brought before the Council," Lord Obed said, his face a cold stare.

"Of course," Xalivar said. "Now, if you will excuse me, I have urgent matters to attend to."

Tarkanius offered a sympathetic look. "Of course. Please keep the Council informed."

Xalivar returned the look and smiled as he turned and hurried down the aisle again. Several Lords nodded warmly as he passed them. When the door closed behind him, he heard the room explode in chatter.

*Good. Let them discuss it. Let them become distracted from whatever plans Miri set afoot. None can dare trust her now!* He smiled and quickened his pace. Despite Obed's attempts, it had gone so perfectly. He didn't even notice the bounce in his own steps.

To:HRHMRhii@Federal.emp;
YBrahma@PresimionAcademy.edu
From: DRhii@vertullisonline.com
Subject: I am safe

Dear Mother & Yao:

I hope this letter finds you well. I want you to know that I am fine, but I miss you both and long for the day when I can see you again. I have been very busy with many activities I am not at liberty to discuss at this time. But I assure you, all will be revealed in time, and I am working hard to make you proud of me.

In the meantime, it was brought to my attention that many worker prisoners are being kept in a secret government prison somewhere on Legallis. I have reason to believe my biological father, Sol, is among those prisoners. There is also a man called Telamon, who would be there. I know the prison is top-secret, but perhaps you can make inquiries through channels for me. I would like to know its location and attempt to confirm the presence of these two men there.

Again, I cannot tell you what I plan to do with the information you provide, but hope that my past actions and behavior would serve to reassure you I will continue acting with honor in all I do.

Please know you are in my thoughts and prayers.

With love and fondness,
Davi

Davi clicked send and hoped the e-post would arrive undetected. His mother would be very worried about him. It had been too long since they'd had contact and she'd be relieved to get any message. He promised himself when things got better, he'd set aside extra time to spend with her. He treasured her love and devotion to him. It was something he never wanted to lose.

He wondered how Yao would receive his message. Yao knew of his heritage, and perhaps also knew by now about the warrant and his involvement with the workers. He hoped their deep friendship would supersede Yao's loyalty as an Alliance officer. Yao had always been a free thinker, more sympathetic to his own sensibilities than the strict order of the law. Either way, the e-post had been sent through public servers with special encoding. It could not be traced to his location at the WFR base. Even if it did get intercepted or their sympathies for him had been tempered, he still bore little risk of discovery.

He'd asked around about the prison after his conversation with Tela. Many had heard the rumors of its existence, but few knew any facts. He'd concluded the only way for him to find out if his father lived would be to seek help through more official channels. He felt confident that Yao and Miri would be discreet and careful. If they decided not to help him, his inquiring of them would not raise great alarm.

He sat there for a few moments longer, before checking his inbox in a rush. Nothing. And then he realized how stiff with tension he'd become and chuckled. *Of course, they couldn't respond this fast. Give them time on this, Davi. It won't be easy to uncover information.*

One of his greatest longings, ever since he'd discovered his true identity, had been to know his father. He'd never had a father and always dreamed about it. From what everyone told him about Sol, he was a great man. Davi longed to know him, and he knew Lura longed to see him again, too. At the very least, he wanted to know what had happened to him.

He said a silent prayer asking for God's blessing on both his father and his quest. When had he stopped praying to gods and started praying to the workers' God alone? He couldn't remember exactly. He'd changed so much in such a short time. He'd never have imagined it when he left Legallis for Vertullis. He headed back to his classroom for another session with the simulators.

Lords Tarkanius, Kray, and Hachim convened in the back room of a lounge near the Council's offices. Tarkanius had arranged this meeting after the revelations at the Council meeting earlier in the day.

"As you both know, disturbing facts were presented to us at the Council meeting," Tarkanius began. "I thought it wise, given recent discussions, for us to have the chance to express how we feel about Miri's request for our help in light of these new revelations."

Both Hachim and Kray looked at him with uncertainty. They, like Tarkanius, were wrestling with what to do. Everyone on the Council knew Xalivar had never been a credible witness. He would lie about his own mother if it served his political ambitions. But at the same time, having read Bordox's report after the meeting, they all knew the facts were not in question. Despite their uncertainty about Miri's motives, she'd played a major part in the deception, and it didn't bode well for the Alliance's Royal Family to be infiltrated by a worker.

"I'm sure Miri had good reasons for her decisions," Kray said, remaining loyal to Miri as expected. Tarkanius knew she above all had never liked or trusted Xalivar. And her reaction to his accusations in the chamber had confirmed that opinion remained unchanged.

"I'm sure the reasons seemed valid to her at the time," Hachim said. "But that doesn't mean her decisions were made with the Alliance's best interests in mind. Given the facts, it would appear not."

"Being born a worker does not make him a spy," Kray said. "He may have just discovered his own heritage for all we know."

"It is possible," Tarkanius said. "His education and opportunities all came as a gift of the Alliance. I'm sure he has not forgotten. Davi is known as a man of good character, honesty, and integrity. But he's also been questioning the actions of the Alliance toward workers, which, combined with his newly discovered heritage, makes him far more sympathetic to them than he might have been in the past." Tarkanius wished the circumstances were different. He'd always liked the Prince, but he had to protect the Alliance.

"Maybe he's right to question the Alliance's actions?" Kray said.

"Given the news reports of late, there's much even the Council did not know and cannot approve of."

"The recent revelations are disturbing. Even the public is beginning to voice their objections," Hachim said. They all stiffened as they considered it. "But we, the Council, approved some of those actions; therefore, we will be held accountable for them as much as Xalivar and his troops."

"We must protect the Council from further negative associations and minimize the impact," Tarkanius said, agreeing with Hachim's assessment.

"At the cost of betraying a loyal friend?" Kray said, clearly angered by the thought.

"At the cost of putting aside our personal loyalties and emotions and acting with the objectivity and integrity demanded of us when we took our oaths of service," Tarkanius said, forcing a calm tone despite his reservations. He had no intention of ignoring what he knew about Xalivar, but Miri's role could not be downplayed either. Perhaps the Royals were turning against each other. He didn't want the Council to be destroyed in the process, so he would do his best to keep them all on his side.

"Indeed. If we maintain our integrity above all, the Council can survive the scandal and remain free to serve the best interests of the Alliance," Hachim said.

"Go to Miri and let her know that, for now, her request cannot be honored," Tarkanius said to Kray.

Kray scowled, starting to object but he cut her off.

"We will make a full review and investigation of these matters and make our decision at a later time. If she needs anything of us, she is free to ask, and we will do what we can within the limits of our authority and the law," Tarkanius said.

Hachim nodded in agreement.

"I'd trust Miri any day over Xalivar," Kray said.

"Trust is not enough this time," Hachim said.

Kray sighed, then stood and disappeared through the door.

"Do you think Lord Kray'll be okay?" Hachim asked.

"She is as torn as we are," Tarkanius said. "She's known Miri all her life. But Kray will do the right thing."

Hachim nodded, accepting Tarkanius' reassurance. Tarkanius hoped he was right.

Davi stepped out of the classroom to find Joram and Uzah waiting for him with two armed security men.

"We need you to come with us," Uzah said. It was not a request.

"What's going on?" Davi asked, truly at a loss, as the security men grabbed his arms and dragged him down the corridor behind the two leaders. Neither said another word until they'd reached the command center conference room and the door had been sealed behind them.

"What's this about?" Davi demanded as Aron and Matheu joined the others in looking at him with somber stares.

"You sent an encoded transmission through Borali government channels," Matheu said, his glare ominous.

"I sent a request to my mother Miri and a friend for help locating a secret prison on Legallis," Davi replied. "I think my father might be held there." He scanned their faces, seeing no change there. "I can't very well have the High Lord Councilor intercepting that."

Aron's eyes showed palpable relief as his shoulders relaxed and he leaned back in his chair. "I knew there'd be a logical explanation." He smiled reassuringly at Davi.

"If he's telling the truth," Matheu growled, stiff and unconvinced.

Davi moved toward a nearby terminal. "I can show you the message."

Uzah blocked his path. "My men are decoding it now."

Davi frowned. He'd grown tired of being treated like a criminal. "If my word's not good enough, I'll gladly resign."

"If your word's not good, you won't have to," Matheu threatened.

Aron stepped forward, glaring at the others. "Enough! You have no proof to justify these accusations!"

"I warned you he couldn't be trusted," Matheu said, unfazed.

"And I assured you, he can," Aron replied, not backing down. "Until you have proof, he is one of our officers and deserves to be treated with respect and given due process."

Using the distraction, Davi slipped past Uzah and sat at the terminal, quickly pulling up his e-account and locating the message. "Here!"

He stood and backed away from the terminal as the others hurried over to read the message on the screen. Matheu sat at the terminal and began examining the meta data. Then he closed the email and examined Davi's outbox further.

"It's just as he said," Joram said.

"So it would seem," Uzah agreed.

"Messages can be altered," Matheu insisted. "We'll wait for your men."

Aron whirled around and walked to the door, punching in a code on the lock panel. "You're free to go." He motioned to Davi.

Davi examined the others' faces again. Joram and Uzah had softened but Matheu's expression remained as somber as before. Davi nodded to Aron and hurried out the door, relieved but frustrated that it was so hard to earn their trust. Yet could he blame them after years of mistreatment? Still, he thought he'd done a lot to prove himself. Would they ever soften toward him? He headed for his quarters wondering what they'd do next.

Miri left the Library walking on air. While doing some historical research to back up her case against Xalivar, she'd stopped to check her e-posts and found a message from Davi.

At last! She couldn't believe it! She'd been so worried about him. He was okay and it took him this long to let her know? Her excitement turned to anger. He would hear about this!

She read the e-post again—something about his birth father and a prison. She knew nothing about prisons. She didn't know how to find out either. With Xalivar keeping a close watch on her, she'd started spending more and more time away from the Palace. He'd copied Yao on the message. She thought Yao might have better connections than she did at the moment.

She arrived at the café in the starport five minutes late, making her way to the back room where Kray sat waiting for her.

"Sorry I'm late. Where are the others?" She slid onto the chair opposite Kray. Kray's face and stiff posture gave the answer. "They're not coming?"

Kray hesitated a moment, searching for words. "There's been a complication."

"A complication?" Had they changed their minds?

"Xalivar told the Council today about Davi's heritage," Kray explained as the breath froze in Miri's throat. "An illegal adoption from workers, without his knowledge …"

"My gods! He didn't!"

Kray nodded. "He did."

Xalivar had betrayed her and Davi! "You're looking at me as if I betrayed the Alliance, Kray."

"The Council was quite shocked by his allegations," Kray said.

Did her oldest friend really believe Xalivar's lies? "You know he'd sell out our mother to get ahead," Miri said. And Xalivar would turn on her in a minute if she wasn't careful.

Kray's face fell, her eyes red and glistening. "I know, but the Council took his remarks to heart. I'm afraid there won't be much support for you at this time."

"None of them? What about the evidence I provided of wrongdoing? The public sentiment?"

"There has been public outcry, but not enough to force the Council's hand. The Council ordered some of the actions which resulted in the tragedies you've leaked to the press. We are all at risk too," Kray said.

Miri couldn't believe it. She'd been sure they would help her. Xalivar must have discovered her plot. Why else would he betray her?

She stared out the window. "I was barren, with no husband. I wanted a son to call my own. He's a good boy; honorable, strong character—just the way I raised him."

"You don't have to explain to me, Miri, but you know how some feel about the workers ..." Kray said, her voice trailing off even as her eyes filled with sympathy and concern.

"He's a worker by blood. He's Royal by upbringing. He doesn't know their life, their ways. He's more one of us than one of them," Miri said, turning back to face Kray.

"That's not how the public will see it," Kray said, her brows furrowing as her fingers absentmindedly twisted and pulled at her hair.

"The public is ignorant. We are the Lords, the leaders. We have to tell them what's right to think and do," Miri said, her legs moving restlessly as her stomach churned.

"We cannot support you at this time. I'm sorry," Kray said. Miri read in her eyes that it pained her to say it.

Miri slid down in the chair, dismayed. Kray seemed to be searching for something to say, but remained quiet. After a couple of minutes, she slipped away, leaving Miri alone with her thoughts.

*He's my son! Everything I did was for him!* How could they not understand? They all had children, too. Xalivar had conned the Council yet again, and this time his con had painted her as the enemy. Her mind raced for what to do as time slowed to a stop around her. Even her dearest friend couldn't offer more than sympathetic looks. She cursed herself. She had only herself to blame, but still ... why did it seem Xalivar always came out ahead? She pounded her fist on the table, stood, and marched out the door.

Slipping out into the main mall, she wove her way through the chattering crowds. Someone was following her. She stopped and turned around. Two LSP Soldiers walked toward her.

She turned and hurried away from them as three more LSP Soldiers appeared ahead, looking straight at her. *My gods! I can't believe he's gone this far!*

She dodged down a corridor, but they moved fast to intercept her.

"I am a member of the Royal Family," she shouted, drawing the attention of witnesses on purpose.

"I'm afraid we've been ordered to place you under arrest," the LSP Sergeant said, as he and his men surrounded her.

"This is ridiculous. My brother is the High Lord Councilor! I am Princess Miri Rhii."

"The order came from the High Lord Councilor," the Sergeant said as his men grabbed her arms. They all paid no attention to the gathering crowds.

The Sergeant turned and led the way as they hurried her across the mall toward a nearby exit. Miri tried to steel her face against the stares, even as she shook with fear, wanting to cry. Could Xalivar have uncovered everything or did he simply suspect? What would he do with her?

The soldiers led her to a transport outside and locked her in the prisoner cell at the rear. Whatever her brother knew, she'd soon find out.

# Chapter Ten

iri paced back and forth in the cell energized solely by adrenaline and fear, until the door slid open and Xalivar appeared. She shot him dead with a furious look as he stepped inside and the door closed behind him.

"You have no right to lock me up in a cell like this!" she screamed.

"I have no right? You have been conspiring behind my back for weeks, and you want to talk about rights?" Xalivar smiled, amused.

*He knows.* Her heart sank. But she tightened her jaw and stared him down anyway. "I am a member of the Royal Family, Xalivar. Not some mere peasant!" Miri almost spat the words out.

"I am the High Lord Councilor," Xalivar scolded. "My authority extends over you as much as the rest. Leaking top-secret information to the media, conspiring behind my back to turn the Council against me, and receiving communication from a fugitive this afternoon!" his voice rose in intensity with each word until he almost spat the last two words.

Miri's tried to hide her surprise. He always seemed to know everything. She softened her face and voice, hoping to appeal to whatever caring for her he still had in him. "He's my son, Xalivar."

"He's wanted by the Alliance for murder, among other charges," Xalivar said. "You told me he had not communicated with you."

"This was the first time," Miri said.

"Which I had to learn about through other channels," Xalivar chided. His hands hung relaxed at his sides. Why was he so calm? What did he know that she didn't?

"I had not seen you yet," she replied.

"As if you couldn't have reached me if you wanted to." Xalivar's brown eyes met hers.

Miri looked away. "You're crazy. What would father think if he was here to see me locked up like this?"

"Father is dead, and he left me in charge," Xalivar said. "Your actions are a betrayal, not just of me, but of the Alliance itself. Whatever imbalance is occurring in that head of yours, I cannot allow it to continue. Do you wish to make a confession?"

"You are a power-hungry, deceitful, evil—" she spat the words, tensing with anger again.

"Save your whining for your women's brunch, Miri!" Xalivar shook his head. "I have protected this Alliance for almost thirty years; done whatever it takes."

Just once she wished she could see him perspire. "I question you as a citizen of the Borali Alliance. It's all the authority I need," Miri said. Xalivar's calmness had her worried. He never handled betrayal this well. What was going on in his demented mind?

"Your loyalty to your son has clouded your judgment. Your actions have disparaged our entire family line. I cannot allow it to continue," Xalivar turned back toward the door. It slid open and he stepped through.

Miri could see Manaen's red eyes outside. "What are you going to do with me, Xalivar?"

"Send you somewhere safe," Xalivar said as the door slid shut.

Miri rushed over and pounded her fists against the door as tears flowed down her face. What could she do now? She had to find a way to get a message to Davi. He would help her. He had to help her. And she had to warn him.

Davi and Tela moved the training course to the west side of the base, hoping to avoid further encounters with the LSP. They also installed an electronic sensor system around it to notify them of any unknown vehicles entering the area.

The trainees had made great progress on the course in the past week. Each had now completed several runs with the targeting system on. Most had landed at least one successful hit on one of the pylons. A few could hit the majority of the targets every time. Davi was impressed with both their determination and their dedication to their training. He'd heard no complaints about pushing them too hard or demanding extra hours.

Even Nila, Dru, and Brie were getting the hang of things at last. Of course, he still had doubts they would be able to maneuver a fighter, but they'd at least know enough to take off and follow someone else home. He assigned them to the team against the base on Vertullis and let the stronger trainees take on the Legallis base and fly the longer distances.

The trainees had all run the course three times with increasing success, when Virun and Jorek's group pulled up beside Davi and Tela.

"We're going to try the skitters on the trails now," Jorek said. His friends mumbled their agreement.

Davi and Tela exchanged a look. The group remained defiant of Davi's leadership, despite his repeated efforts. Tela had approached them as well to no avail. The only reason Davi hadn't kicked them from the program was their skills were sorely needed—they were amongst the best in the class. And a part of him still hoped to win them over somehow.

He exchanged a look with Tela. Neither knew how to stop them, yet Davi still wanted to project a sense of command. "As long as you stick to the square mile around the course," Davi insisted. The trainees nodded and headed off.

Some of the less skilled trainees watched them go. "We want to go, too," Dru said.

"You guys need more work on the course," Davi said.

"Can't you show us stuff on the regular trails which would help us with the course?" Dru asked.

"Yeah, doing the same thing over and over is boring," Brie said.

Nila and Dru groaned in agreement.

Davi looked at Tela, who shrugged. "Okay, look, we can try it for a half an hour or so, but you guys need to master the targeting on the course."

Brie, Dru, and Nila exchanged high fives.

"We're going as fast as we can," Nila said.

Dru sped off toward the trails with Nila and Brie close behind. Davi and Tela raced to catch up with them.

Although he would have preferred to keep the search to his own men, for fear word of his failure on the mission might spread, Bordox had called in more troops after realizing that the sooner he succeeded the better. In the long run, success always outweighed failure and the forest was just too big an area for them to cover effectively alone.

As soon as the alert code came over the comm-channel, Corsi called for a rendezvous of their forces at the scout's location, and then notified

Bordox, and they headed for the coordinates together.

Bordox's heart pounded faster and faster as they sped past row after row of cedars drawing closer to the rendezvous. The sweet smell of the pollen and trees matched the sweet taste of impending victory on his tongue. Chattering birds and insects seemed to cheer him on as he tensed and released his muscles, preparing himself and mentally reviewing what he might say when he finally stood face to face again with his longtime nemesis. After this, there would be no doubt who was superior. Rhii's career would be over! He'd be in prison. Bordox would have the favor of the High Lord Councilor and be awarded medals, perhaps even a promotion. Thinking about it excited him. He accelerated his skitter, ignoring the wind beating against his face, as Corsi struggled to remain alongside.

Davi and Tela followed Dru, Brie, and Nila, as they weaved along a trail through the trees. The wind whistled past Davi, rustling his hair. The air was fresh and clean. He enjoyed the sensation, the blur of the trees as they passed, and their spicy smell.

Dru and Nila delighted in swapping places on either side of Brie—one zipping in front of her, the other behind. Sometimes, they cut it a little close, startling Brie, who cried out.

"Hey! Watch it!" She would shoot them scolding looks as they slid back alongside her, and then all three would break into giggles.

*Ah, to be young*, Davi thought, relaxing as he watched it. They were all three skilled enough now to avoid near misses under these conditions. It was pure play and excitement. He exchanged a look with Tela, who chuckled and shook her head.

"Try not to damage the skitters, okay?" Davi called after them.

This just led to more laughter as Nila and Dru swapped places yet again.

"I don't think they're listening," Tela said, her blue eyes glistening with amusement.

"You got that idea, did you?" Davi said as she chuckled. "So much for military discipline!"

Tela laughed. "We have kept things pretty loose. We'd better start tightening things up."

The comms on the skitters beeped as a red light on the comm panel began flashing. They exchanged a look.

"The warning beacons," Davi said.

Tela nodded. "Better call in and see what they've got."

The brush behind them rustled and they heard a noise, turning back to see four LSP soldiers slip in to follow behind them on armed skitters. Davi and Tela exchanged looks of alarm, accelerating toward the trainees as the LSP men fired their lasers and the cedars exploded around them.

"So much for our early warning system," Tela groaned as they sped up to catch their trainees.

Hearing the explosions, Brie, Dru, and Nila turned around to look as Tela and Davi pulled alongside.

"Don't slow down! Go as fast as you can. Follow me!" Tela warned them. She pulled in front and they sped up to follow her.

Davi hung back to protect the rear, dodging fire from the LSP soldiers with jagged zigzagging maneuvers. All around, he heard laser blasts and explosions as LSP soldiers engaged the other trainees. The smell of burning wood and leaves thickened the air and debris from near misses fell around him as Davi flicked on his comm-channel.

"Attention trainees: do not go back to base. Lose them, and then hide until we can rendezvous."

His private channel beeped and he switched over, steering sharply to dodge another laser blast.

Tela's tense voice came over the headphones. "Right about now, I'm wishing we had armed skitters, too."

Davi reached down to the side pocket and pulled out his blaster, gritting his teeth with determination. "I'm going to try and lay down some counter fire, but my blaster won't do much against their skitters' guns."

"Can you keep them occupied while I go help the others?" Tela asked, drawing her own blaster from the side pocket of her skitter.

Without answering, Davi turned and started firing back toward the LSP soldiers, who dodged to avoid his blasts. Davi slammed on the brakes, and the LSP soldiers zipped right past him, their faces registering surprise. He slipped back in behind them and began firing at their flanks.

Tela fired two bolts from her blaster, then she and the trainees sped away, as the soldiers swerved to avoid more bolts from Davi's blaster.

Davi managed to land a couple of hits on one of the skitters, sending sparks flying, but causing more fear in the rider than damage to the machine. As the rider and his companions leaned back to inspect his skitter, Davi ducked off onto a side trail. His heart pounded as his body slickened with sweat and he tightened his hands on his blaster and controls, shifting to strengthen his balance.

In a few moments, the LSP soldiers slid back onto his tail again. Davi accelerated to full speed, zigzagging in and out between trees, jumping over rocks, diving under overhangs—keeping his target profile as small as possible. The wind buffeted him every time he emerged from the trees, forcing him to work harder to stay on the skitter. Then he rounded a bend to find more LSP soldiers joining the chase.

*Great! Are they all after me?* He groaned, hoping Tela was helping the other trainees. He was too busy to help them himself.

Around another bend, Bordox and his aide joined the chase. *Bordox. No wonder they're all after me.* Davi smiled, waving, as he dodged their fire. Outgunned, he searched his mind for a new tactic.

Bordox sped to the front of the LSP soldiers, close on Davi's tail. Davi, looked back over his shoulder as Bordox growled: "In the name of the High Lord Councilor, I order you to stop! You're under arrest!"

Davi braked and Bordox's aide wound up in front of him. Bordox remained alongside, as Davi fired several shots with his blaster at the aide, leaning close enough to Bordox to yell: "Give my uncle my regards!"

He ducked off onto another side trail as Bordox shot on past, cursing.

The other LSP soldiers followed Davi as he followed the turns of the side trail, staying just out of range of their lasers. He shifted in his seat, trying to stay comfortable but his sweaty body and uniform made that difficult.

As he shot into a clearing, he discovered Tela, Jorek, Virun, and four others waiting for them, blasters held at the ready. Davi spun his skitter into a one hundred and eighty degree spin and slid in alongside them, aiming his blaster as the first of the LSP soldiers came into view.

Davi's group opened fire and chaos erupted. Two LSP skitters collided as the soldiers tried to dodge the blaster fire. Another slammed into them from behind, while yet a fourth ducked to one side and crashed into a large cedar.

Davi and Tela motioned, accelerating on their skitters onto another trail with their trainees close behind. All continued firing blasts back at the LSP men behind them.

Tela took three trainees with her and split off onto another trail as Davi, Jorek, Virun, and two others continued on the present course.

"They're after you?" Jorek yelled, sounding surprised.

Davi nodded. "I told you before; I'm on your side." A laser blast exploded near them and Davi keyed the comm-channel button. "Try and get around behind them."

Tela's voice came over the radio. "Hang on, Davi, we've got a plan."

*A plan? Who'd had time to make a plan?* Most of the LSP soldiers stayed behind Davi and his group.

"Make it hard for them to lock their weapons on us," Davi said, as his group zigzagged in and out of the cedars in varied patterns, never leaving more than one of them on the trail at a time. Their skills impressed him. They had made a lot of progress.

Jorek and Virun slid to a stop amidst the trees, watching several LSP soldiers zoom past, then accelerated after them, firing their lasers.

Davi heard a rebel yell over the comm-channel. "You two be careful. They outnumber us." Davi warned.

Jorek's eager voice came back at him. "Best training exercise ever!"

Davi knew the feeling. He'd experienced it many times himself in training and since, but were they ready? He put a warning tone in his voice. "Don't get cocky. This is not a game."

"No problem, Captain. We can handle it," Virun said, ever confident.

Davi wondered if he'd heard right. None of them had ever called him Captain before.

Bordox and his aide pulled back into the lead behind Davi, firing blasts which exploded on either side of him. Too close for comfort.

Tela and her group shot out of the forest, firing at the LSP. Two more skitters crashed with mild explosions and flying debris and two others were damaged and smoking. The LSP soldiers slowed down and dissolved into chaos as they attempting to avoid fire from the lasers.

Another group of trainees shot out from a group of trees and surrounded them, firing.

"When did you have time to get all this organized?" Davi said into the comm-channel, as he glanced back at Tela.

"Quick thinking is a military necessity," Tela said, grinning. "They were all issued blasters with their uniforms, so …"

Davi smiled. "You've never been more beautiful."

He braked, sliding in between Bordox and his aide. As they passed him on either side, he swung a foot out and kicked at Bordox's skitter. Bordox struggled to regain control but flew off to one side, as Davi slipped in behind the aide and shot at his skitter with the blaster, singing the side of its engine compartment.

Bordox pulled alongside him again, his face a fierce grimace. "You can't escape this time, Rhii. We outnumber you." Menace mixed with arrogance. Bordox as usual expected to win.

"You're losing men fast," Davi said as Bordox leaned over and grabbed for his controls. Their skitters banged into each other as Davi struggled to push him away. His right sweat-soaked glove barely maintained its hold on the handlebars of the skitter.

"I always knew you were a traitor," Bordox said.

"I always knew you were a pompous blowhard," Davi said, freeing his leg and kicking hard.

Bordox cursed as he spun off to one side.

Then Tela zipped up, firing at Bordox as his aide and another LSP soldier slipped in behind Davi.

Bordox corrected his course and charged back toward Davi, ignoring Tela's blasts and somehow completely missing them.

Slowing and sliding upward with his skitter, Davi watched as Bordox's aide and the other soldier flew right underneath him. Distracted, both turned, crashing into each other as Davi dropped down to fire on them from behind.

Bordox headed straight for his nemesis again, but Davi rolled his skitter, dove off, and landed on his feet in the dirt. He aimed his blaster and fired at Bordox, forcing him to turn suddenly and crash his skitter into Davi's. The impact sent Bordox flying off into the cedars. Both skitters sputtered and smoked, amid a field of debris.

Tela turned her skitter back and slowed down beside Davi, who hopped on behind her as the other trainees raced up beside them. For the first time in several minutes, he could breathe a bit easier again. He wrapped his arms around her waist, enjoying the touch and smell of her sweat mixed with perfume.

"We've got them on the run," Virun said triumphantly.

"Want us to go back and finish this?" Jorek said, sounding a bit too eager.

"No, get the others and get back to the hangar," Davi said.

"At least they don't know where the base is," Tela said.

"They know enough to keep looking for us here," Davi said. "It'll be a matter of time. We have to warn everyone. The forest won't be our refuge much longer."

Tela nodded as the group brought their skitters to full speed and sped away, disappearing into the trees.

Davi looked back; no LSP soldiers were following them. He blinked, double checking his vision. He couldn't believe they'd gotten away. Maybe his trainees deserved more confidence than he'd had in them. He took a deep breath and leaned in close to Tela, enjoying the ride.

Virun and Jorek passed them, smiling and laughing and enjoying it more than they should. He didn't have time to worry about it now. He had to get back to the leaders at the base and warn them. Then Bordox's curses drifted through the nearby trees.

"Get after them! You know the High Lord Councilor's orders! I won't disappoint him again," Bordox shouted.

Davi felt torn. His own uncle had sent his worst rival after him—the one man who had hated him for years and tried to destroy him. Things would never be the same now, and his heart ached at the thought.

The revving of skitters and crashing through nearby brush shook him from his thoughts. He had to go before they found him again.

He tapped Tela on the shoulder and she turned the skitter, racing off across the forest trails, while inside, his mind raced through a gamut of emotions at what he'd learned.

Bordox gave up trying to dust off the dirt clinging to his sweaty uniform and looked around for his skitter. It was a disaster, destroyed along with Rhii's. His men were scattered everywhere. His body ached from bruises and scratches but he could walk, and he pounded his boots on the dirt as he went.

Corsi ran toward him. "Are you okay, sir?"

"Don't stop. Catch them!" Bordox's voice was full of frustration.

"It would be a little difficult at the moment," Corsi said, motioning to several crashed skitters.

"Get the men regrouped now and go after them!" Bordox yelled. *A bunch of untrained workers against LSP troops?* Bordox couldn't believe it. How could they have embarrassed him again? Furious, he drew his blaster and fired at a nearby cedar. He'd find the next available skitter and go after Rhii himself. Let the men fend for themselves.

"Yes, sir," Corsi nodded, but his face questioned whether it would matter.

Bordox ignored him and focused on finding a ride.

Davi entered the command center at a run, having left Tela behind to wait for and gather the others. It was busier than he'd ever seen it with technicians and workers occupying every chair, fiddling with dials, adjusting wires and screens, and talking on communicators. Final preparations were underway for what lay ahead.

He found General Matheu and the other leaders in the conference room. "Our training today was interrupted by LSP troops searching the forest," Davi blurted out as he entered almost out of breath.

"So we heard," Uzah said.

"What were they looking for?" Aron asked.

"Me," Davi said.

They all looked at him with wide eyes, breath catching.

"It's true," Tela confirmed, arriving out of breath as he answered and slipping into the room.

"Why would they be looking for you?" General Matheu asked.

"I'm wanted for questioning in the murder of a guard who was beating my cousin Nila. His death was accidental, but the Council brought charges." Davi sat in an open chair, trying to catch his breath. Tela sat next to him, as every eye in the room focused on them.

"Against a member of the Royal Family?" Joram said with surprise.

"One who questioned worker policies, yes," Davi said. "And I suppose I'm also wanted for betraying the Alliance." He wondered if the minds of those who'd doubted him would change now.

"It's clear your chance encounter with them during previous training was not forgotten. They must have been searching for weeks now," Aron said sympathetically.

"Which means we have been discovered. We must put our plan into action right away," General Matheu said, standing and walking over to examine some charts hanging on the wall.

"You're sure you didn't lead them back to the base?" Joram asked, as he moved over to join Matheu at the charts.

Davi whirled and glared at him. "What will it take for you to trust me?"

"We just need to know if they've discovered our location," Joram responded, blanching at Davi's harsh tone.

"I've been with you for months now, training pilots, and helping you. What's it gonna take to prove myself?"

"The decoders already confirmed your story about the e-post," Aron said, putting a hand on Davi's arm.

"You have our trust now," Uzah added with a nod.

Davi glanced around at the leaders. Even General Matheu looked supportive. Tela smiled reassuringly. He sighed, realizing he'd made an ass of himself and his shoulders sunk. "I'm sorry."

Uzah shook his head. "No. I think we deserved that."

"I didn't get a chance to tell you yet," Aron said. "I'm sorry."

"We're sorry, too," Joram added.

Davi met their eyes one by one and saw that they meant it, then took a deep breath, releasing the anger, and remembered he hadn't answered Joram's question. "It won't matter if they followed me or not. The man leading them is a rival of mine from the Academy. He won't stop until he captures or kills me."

"We can't wait until we're discovered," Aron said.

"We must prepare final plans and brief our teams," Uzah said as they all nodded in agreement.

Feeling guilty for being the cause of this, Davi looked away. Rushing into battle could cause extra loss of lives. He wished they had another way.

Aron noticed Davi's sullen face and put a hand on his shoulder. "It's not your fault, Davi. It was a matter of time." Davi still felt responsible.

"Yes, our time for execution was drawing near regardless. Now we will act while we can still hope for some element of surprise," General Matheu said.

The others all watched Davi with anxious smiles. "My trainees are ready," Davi said. "They now have actual experience in combat."

Aron laughed, patting him on the back. The others laughed too, encouraged at the thought.

"They're about to get a lot more," Matheu added, his narrowing eyes making it clear he hoped they were all ready.

"Let's commit our plans to the Lord and He will guide us," Uzah said.

The others mumbled agreement, bowing their heads.

The Leaders met for several hours, after which Davi joined Tela at Lura's quarters for dinner. His mother had prepared beef with gixi sauce, accompanied by fried gixi and fresh jax salad. The fruits added just the right sweetness to go with the beef and red wine.

As they finished the meal, Lura raised a glass in toast. "A salute to the brave men and women who will accompany you both into this battle."

Davi and Tela raised their glasses, clinking them against hers. "And to all those who support us here at home," Tela said.

"Hear! Hear!" Davi said, smiling, as they sipped their wine. It brought warmth to his whole body as it flowed down his throat. He wondered how long it would be until he could relax like this again.

"May God protect you and give you wisdom," Lura said.

"May God protect us all," Davi said, placing his hand over hers atop the table.

She smiled and squeezed his hand. "I'm very proud of you," Lura said.

"I'm proud to be your son," Davi said.

Lura's eyes grew moist, tears forming at their corners. "I wish your father were here, he would be so proud. He fought with Aron and Joram in the revolution twenty-five years ago."

The Vertullians always referred to the Delta V incident as The Revolution. In truth, it had been incited by a massacre in which Xalivar participated, footage of which had been all over the Boralian news nets lately. The actual revolution was the workers' armed response to the massacre, which although determined, had been quickly put down. "One day we'll find him," Davi said, knowing he would give it his best.

"It's more than I could hope for," Lura said.

For a moment, he considered sharing with her what Tela had told him, but then thought better of it. False hope would end up making things worse in the long run. "I'm sure he's here in spirit," Davi said, squeezing Lura's hand again. She smiled and nodded approvingly.

"I wish my father could be here as well," Tela said. "And my mother."

"What happened to them?" Lura wondered.

"Dad disappeared a while ago. Another one of those unanswered mysteries that we're just supposed to accept. Then Mom died in an accident two years ago." Tela refuse to make eye contact.

"So you're alone?" Lura reached over with her other hand and placed it on top of Tela's, squeezing. "We're your family now."

Tela smiled and exchanged a look with Davi, whose heart warmed at his mother's kindness. "I feel blessed." Tela said.

"We're all very blessed," Lura said, nodding.

They bowed their heads and prayed for the battle ahead, committing their actions and plans to God and asking for wisdom, guidance, and safety through whatever came.

Davi had difficulty accepting that the actions he and others made might lead to the deaths of many old friends. But he knew the higher cause always required sacrifice, and, in the end, it would be worth the losses for his people to be free again. He thought about Tela, wondering if their relationship would have a chance to flourish or if this war would mark the end of it. He brushed the thoughts away. He couldn't afford to be distracted at a time like this. He had to appreciate the time they had while hoping in the future God would provide for them, whatever it was. As their Scriptures said, God's plan was perfect: a future full of hope.

Davi kissed Tela goodbye moments before launch. They'd stopped hiding their relationship from anyone now. The trainees had overheard them in the forest anyhow, and it seemed pointless when there were much greater matters at hand to worry about.

As flight crews performed final pre-flight preparations on their shuttles, Davi went over and over the plan of attack. Uzah had obtained schedules of regular fighter patrols on both Vertullis and Legallis. The fighters were kept on the ground for several hours a week for routine maintenance. The attacks were timed to coincide with one of those periods. The ground assaults on the Vertullis starport, energy shield control center, and government center would be timed to coincide with the attacks at the starports.

Davi watched the first shuttle launch anxiously—excitement mixed with nervousness and fear—carrying Tela and her team toward the starport on Legallis. He had assigned her the majority of his most experienced pilots—Virun, Jorek, and seventeen others—since her mission would require the most flight skill and involved the most possible risk of counterattack. Davi assigned Nila, Dru, Brie and sixteen others to his team. The shuttles were being flown by experienced men who had once worked for Borali citizens as private pilots. Additional shuttles would carry Uzah and his troops to their attack points.

Tela's team had to fly into the Legallis starport under the cover of an emergency landing due to engine failure. Because there would be no WFR ground assaults like those on Vertullis, Alliance ground forces posed a serious threat. The shuttle bay and fighter bay were connected by short tunnels, so that if the team moved quickly, they could get in and out without engaging troops. He and Tela had been over the layout several times with her team.

The potential for success of the WFR's ground attacks on Vertullis had been increased by recent developments. Bordox's attempt to capture him had led to reassignment of great numbers of troops to search the forest. As a result, while the worker's base might be detected during the launch of the attacks, ground forces at the starport, energy shield control center and government center would be down to skeleton crews during the time of the attacks. Davi couldn't believe their good fortune. Aron and Tela had reminded him their God was behind them and had a hand in temporal events. Davi found it easier to have confidence in a God who played such a role in human affairs.

When his shuttle landed, Davi was already on his feet beside the door. "Go!" he shouted as his pilots filed out, blasters held at the ready.

As he stepped on the landing platform, he could already hear ground forces engaged in other areas of the base. By launching their attacks first, the ground forces hoped to draw troops away from the launch bays around the fighters. From what Davi could see, everything was proceeding according to plan.

Mechanics met them on the ground and pointed them to the twenty fighters which they'd prepped and readied for launch. On both Vertullis and Legallis, the mechanics had disassembled key parts to make counterattacks impossible. Only the exact number of VS28s the WFR would steal remained flight-worthy.

Special shifts had been selected at each starport, and those mechanics would return with the strike teams on the shuttles to avoid execution. Since the fighters were already scheduled for maintenance, it would take the Alliance time to call in another shift, let alone determine why their fighters weren't functional. By the time they knew, Vertullis would safely be under WFR control and protected by the energy shield and stolen fighters.

Everyone moved quickly, with the mechanics doing their work, while Davi's pilots climbed aboard the fighters and started preflight checks. The moment the fighters launched, the mechanics would board the shuttle and follow them out. Davi would launch last.

Venetian System's Model 28 fighters were sleek and black with snub noses and three wings–two longer wings on each side, and a third shorter wing standing vertically above the fighter's four engines. Each bore their squadron insignia, and a few bore a name painted on at the pilot's indulgence. There were laser cannons on each wing as well as in the nose. The cockpit lay beneath a gray, transparent blast shield through which the pilot could monitor the area outside the cockpit.

As the first fighters prepared to launch, Davi heard explosions near the shuttle. Interrupting his preflight check, Davi turned to see a few armed troops moving into the bay. He tensed and prepared himself. *Here we go!*

"Get your men to the shuttle!" he shouted to the head mechanic.

Alliance ground troops wore the same gray uniforms as the officers, but were equipped with black metal helmets instead of hats. They had matching black shields and armored vests, all three designed to withstand heavy blasts from lasers. Their black boots reached almost to their knees. Well-trained and disciplined, they were intimidating to watch, let alone face in battle. They began setting up laser cannons and firing at Davi and the mechanics as soon as they entered the bay.

As fighters launched, Davi climbed down onto the landing pad and returned fire with his blaster. An entire squad of enemy troops wound their way toward the shuttle. The lead mechanic began returning fire with a blaster as well. Davi didn't stop to ask where he'd obtained it. Their co-conspirators had prepared for the worst.

As the fighters continued to take off, Davi and the mechanic laid down cover fire, taking out a couple troopers at the front before the rest ducked behind machines and starcraft to avoid their laser blasts and fired back. Several blasts hit fighters as they took off, but the damage was minimal.

To Davi's right, a fighter lifted straight into the air and around toward the oncoming soldiers. Davi heard the whirl of laser cannons revving up to full power and then spotted Dru at the controls.

"Dru, what are you doing?" he asked over the comm-channel.

Dru opened fire with the VS28's laser cannons at the Alliance troops. Machines and starcraft exploded as debris flew around the bay. Enemy soldiers dove to the ground. Some were buried under falling debris. One took a hit in the arm. Others screamed or shouted.

Davi chuckled at the bravery and ingenuity of Dru's efforts as he turned and climbed back into his fighter. The necklace jangling against his chest reminded him what they were fighting for.

"Get the shuttle out of here," he said into his comm-channel as he lifted his own fighter and turned it to add his own lasers to Dru's barrage.

The shuttle's engines revved up as the lead mechanic dove on board. Moments after the door slid shut, the shuttle launched.

"Go, Dru, go!" Davi called into his comm-channel as he fired another round from his laser cannons.

Dru turned his fighter and flew into a launch chute. Davi followed moments later.

Most of the other fighters had already headed back toward base as Davi and Dru launched with the shuttle, but four fighters closed in around them. Davi noted with surprise that two of them were flown by Brie and Nila.

"I thought I ordered you two back to base," Davi said over the comm-channel.

"Did you think we could go without knowing you and Dru were safe?" Nila's voice rang in his ear.

"Yeah. What took you guys so long?" Brie teased.

The women's laughter filled the comm channel as the fighters slid into formation around the shuttle.

"Well done, team. Let's go home," Davi said tension easing to relief as he wondered how things were going for Tela.

As they flew over the city, Davi glimpsed gunfire near the starport and government center. WFR forces had begun engaging the skeleton Alliance crews left to defend them. From what Davi could see, their attack had been a success. His prayers had been answered. He hoped Tela and Uzah were being as blessed as he had been.

As laser fire exploded outside the building, Zylo received an urgent SOS from the captain in charge of the defense detail at the starport. Most of the regular defense detail had been reassigned to search the forest, in the wake of Bordox's failed capture of Davi. Bordox himself had been sent back to Legallis to answer to Xalivar, while Corsi and Zylo took over leadership of the search.

The defense captain's voice sounded terse. Zylo thought he heard laser fire behind him as well. "The starport is under attack. I demand the return of my men," the captain said.

"Your men are on the other side of the planet," Zylo said.

"We are under attack by unknown numbers of enemy forces both inside and outside the starport!" The captain said.

"The entire government center is under fire. I have already called back troops, but they won't be here for an hour," Zylo said, not liking the captain's tone.

"An hour will be too late! I need help now!" The captain screamed.

"You'll have to do the best you can," Zylo said, breaking the connection before the captain could launch another protest. There wasn't anything Zylo could do about it anyway.

Out the window, he saw from the size of the WFR force that his own men would soon be overrun. Alliance soldiers ran around in chaos, dodging explosions as debris flew. *A worker army on Vertullis?* No one had ever imagined organized military attacks by worker armies. The mere idea was frightening and he found he could not relax, but he refused to let fear paralyze him. His men were trained for this and far better than any workers could be.

The explosions outside the building drew nearer and nearer and the windows and walls rattled. Zylo wondered what else could go wrong.

Uzah led his forces in attacking the Shield Control Center—one hundred and thirty men against twenty-five Alliance soldiers and officers stationed there at the time of the attack. They fought an intense battle, before the few remaining defenders retreated behind locked doors and shielded walls.

Some of Uzah's men used the battle as cover for a sneak attack from the rear. The five guards stationed there were easily overcome, allowing WFR troops to enter the station. They exchanged fire with the defenders locked inside, but once WFR reinforcements arrived, the battle was over. To Uzah's delight, the workers now controlled the energy shield around Vertullis.

He found himself surprisingly relaxed throughout. Focusing on his task and strategies kept his mind off worries and other concerns. His military training also helped, and his experience in years past as well, but it felt good realizing that he could do this under real fire, and that confidence invigorated him as he led his troops. He only hoped his confidence would bolster his men.

The battle for the government complex, including the offices, barracks, and starport, took longer. Although most of the Alliance troops had been out on other duties, there were still one hundred and fifty soldiers spread throughout the complex. The three hundred and fifty WFR men under his command wounded or captured large numbers of enemy soldiers, leaving only a few strongholds.

The last holdouts surrendered after two hours of fighting, when WFR reinforcements arrived. Uzah immediately contacted the base.

"Legallis approach control, I say again, identify yourself."

Tela listened nervously as her pilot identified the shuttle for the third time. While emergency landings due to engine failure were not unheard of, the Alliance almost never allowed emergency landings by civilian craft in military areas, and the portmaster didn't seem inclined to allow this one.

"You've been cleared to land at the civilian dock on the eastside," the voice instructed for the third time.

Tela reached over the pilot's shoulder and keyed the comm-channel. "We've told you. We're losing power fast. We can barely control her as it is. We need to land now. We won't make it to the east side." She leant what she hoped was just the right amount of exasperation to her tone.

Tela heard the portmaster's sigh over the comm-channel. "Landing Bay Five-A. Do not leave your craft until given further instructions."

"Thank you!" Tela tried to disguise her relief with a cheerful tone, but they'd been delayed almost half an hour. The other attacks were already well underway.

The portmaster sent two officers to inspect the shuttle upon landing. The moment they stepped inside, Tela, Virun, and Jorek disarmed them and tied them up. However, the wait for their arrival and their capture slowed things down.

Several times during the ensuing battle, Tela wondered if Davi should have led the assault instead of her, but because too many people knew his face on Legallis, the leadership had thought it unwise to send him there.

Right away, the portmaster's men questioned why pilots were in fighters during the scheduled maintenance period, then military flight techs inquired about unscheduled launches. While Tela and the maintenance chief did their best to allay their concerns, military police came to investigate and several mechanics died in the ensuing laser battle.

Adrenaline filled her veins as Tela shouted orders to her squadron and exchanged fire with the police, ducking and dodging as best she could behind what little cover the hangar provided, all the time worried about damage to their ship. In the end, she and her pilots held off the police, with aid from armed mechanics, but five pilots died and the shuttle suffered exterior damage from the lasers. Altogether it was more stress than she'd ever experienced, and she realized now why adrenaline played such an important part in their training. On her own power, she'd have collapsed exhausted long ago. The energy filling her veins was the only thing keeping her going.

When the shuttle launched, it did so with half the remaining mechanics on board. The others stayed behind to provide cover fire for the launching starcraft.

Tela mourned the loss of the brave mechanics internally, while externally pushing her team to fly back to Vertullis at top speed and warn them. Her voice remained steady and commanding and her people responded exactly as she needed them to. It wouldn't take long for those on Legallis to figure out what had happened, even if they couldn't launch fighters to counterattack. Despite the successful capture of the fighters, the mission felt like a loss. She blamed herself and dreaded facing Davi and the other leaders with the news.

When Manaen rushed into the throne room in mid-afternoon and announced the attack at the starport with great urgency, the news caught Xalivar by complete surprise. Who would attack them? No one had attacked Legallis since the settlement of the planet.

As bits of information trickled in over the next two hours, Xalivar became more and more enraged. *Disabled fighters? Mutinying mechanics?* He knew right away Davi had to be involved.

He motioned to the vidscreen. "Get me the security videos from the launch bays!"

"Yes, my Lord!" Manaen typed on a terminal and the videos played.

Davi was nowhere to be seen. Trained pilots took off in the fighters. How could the workers have so many trained pilots? He ordered the few surviving mechanics interrogated as soon as possible. They would be pumped for everything they knew before being executed.

Still, Xalivar couldn't believe what he had seen. He ordered all off-duty mechanics to be called back to duty to get the fighters airworthy. Pilots would launch as soon as possible to chase down the fleeing intruders.

Later, Manaen delivered even worse news. "There were attacks on Vertullis as well, my Lord. Enemy forces captured fighters there too, leaving the rest disabled or damaged. They also captured the entire government complex, the starport, and the energy shield." Xalivar couldn't believe his ears. "Vertullis is no longer under Alliance control."

Xalivar screamed in frustration. *No! This can't be happening to me!* The fighters he'd sent after the retreating attackers had arrived after the stolen fighters had already disappeared behind the planet's energy shield. Xalivar pounded his fists into the wall.

*Is there no one competent in my entire military? How could they be caught with their pants down? The Council will have me for this! I will never hear the end of it. My gods, the greatest army in the Universe defeated by a ragtag worker army?*

It had to be the workers. That much seemed certain. Who else would dare attack the Lords at their capital like this? Xalivar ordered reinforcements sent from all over the system. They wouldn't get away with this. He would show them the power of the Alliance. They would not defeat him—the greatest High Lord Councilor in the history of his people.

He paced back and forth behind the throne, cursing Bordox's failure and his sister's betrayal. Had she fed intelligence information to Davi and his co-conspirators? He would have to question her again as soon as possible. Yes, all those involved would be brought to justice. They would feel the iron hand of the Alliance.

# Chapter Eleven

Davi pushed the joystick forward with a grunt and his VS28 fighter dove out of the cloud cover to rejoin the rest of his squadron. As he slid into the pole position, he glanced over at Tela in position off to his right. She smiled and waved.

"Imagine seeing you here," he said over the comm-channel with a smile. Despite the fact they were headed into battle, having her nearby gave him comfort. He knew militaries traditionally favored keeping lovers apart in duty assignments because of the fear they'd be too distracted worrying about each other. But Tela was one of the best pilots he had. If anything, he felt reassured knowing she'd be there and could protect his tail better than anyone else.

Tela laughed and offered a flirty wink, then they both switched back to serious mode as the squadron formed up around them, doing so without the usual chatter. Davi knew they were all as tired as he was.

It had been an amazing three weeks. After their capture of fighters and takeover of the planetary shield, the WFR stayed busy skirmishing with Alliance forces. So far, the energy shield had prevented enemy reinforcements and aerial attacks, but it would be a matter of time before the Alliance sent in star cruisers to break through the shield.

The success of the WFR's attack plan also yielded other benefits for Davi. Once the workers had control of their planet, those who had shown little interest in the Resistance signed up like wildfire. Experienced pilots from all over the system offered their services. Davi and Tela gave those who were local an immediate crash course on VS28 fighters, enabling squadrons to be in the air around the clock, thus allowing Davi and the others time to rest.

Already the constant tiredness of the past few weeks had begun to fade. Additional fighters had been requisitioned from the Vertullis starport and brought back to the base, but fighting persisted around the starport and the Alliance still had access to fighters there. Davi and Tela continued training new recruits, while additional units were trained and added to Uzah's troops as well.

At a leaders' meeting, Davi learned the WFR forces had gained enough ground to drive the remaining enemy troops into strongholds at the government center and starport. The Alliance had failed to recapture the energy shield control center but continued trying. Davi and the pilots reinforced the ground forces by air and destroyed enemy infrastructure and equipment.

His comm-channel beeped. "Squadron One, commander," he answered.

Uzah's yelling voice came through, struggling to be heard over explosions and laser blasts in the background. "Squadron One, we request immediate response. We have enemy forces pinned down on the east edge of the government complex. Please intercept vehicle traffic."

The Alliance had been making use of shuttles and floaters to launch attacks and move troops. His pilots strafed enemy launch sites as well as ground craft.

Davi keyed the comm-channel transmit button. "Roger, Ground Leader, ETA six minutes." Davi ran down the pilots' various skill levels and successes, devising a strategy he hoped would work. It all depended on the actual positions and activities of the enemy once they arrived.

The fighters glided over the tops of the buildings at close range, staying low to confuse the radar and maintain good line of sight with the ground. Davi divided the squadron into two groups of six fighters, assigning Tela to head the second group. "You go after ground weaponry emplacements first. We'll try and take out any vehicle traffic."

"Roger," she said. They exchanged one last look before steering their craft apart as their assigned groups formed up around them. Then each group vectored off toward their target areas.

A few minutes later, the government center came into view. Two columns of large floaters moved up parallel corridors, attempting to flank the WFR forces. Their dark blue coloring made them hard to spot through the smoke on the ground but the shiny Alliance emblems reflecting light on both sides gave them away.

"Dru and Virun, form behind me. We'll take the group to starboard. The rest of you form behind Jorek and take the group to port."

"Roger," the pilots responded in unison, all business now as they split into subsquads.

Davi smiled, remembering when Jorek and Virun had pulled him aside after the air raids on the enemy starports.

"We owe you an apology," Virun had said.

"We're sorry we gave you such a hard time," Jorek said. "It was just hard to believe we could trust you."

Since then, they'd become two of his strongest leaders and had started working with him like true pros.

"Go for their weapons capabilities first," Davi instructed.

"Ah come on, boss! Total destruction is much more satisfying," Jorek said over the comm-channel.

"You can destroy them after you're sure they can't fire back," Davi said, knowing that despite his enthusiasm, Jorek's focus never wavered.

"You got it," Jorek responded, not big on comm-channel protocol.

Both squads executed the plan perfectly, swooping in on the floaters from above, strafing them with laser fire. Outside his cockpit, multiple flashes appeared followed by booming explosions as Davi's blasts disabled the front vehicle in the column. The next floater in line swerved to avoid it, but the driver misjudged his position, running over troops fleeing the first floater to seek cover, before crashing into the third floater in line.

"Three down with one shot, not bad," Davi said to himself. He adjusted his targeting and fired again, this time aiming for the laser cannons on the three floaters. He shifted in his seat as the VS28 vibrated with each blast. The cockpit started feeling stuffy as the temperature rose along with his excitement and adrenaline.

Laser bolts flashed outside his blast shield, sending a few minor vibrations through his hull. Spotting rooftop snipers, he didn't even bother to dodge. Blasters wouldn't do much good against the VS28's shields even at close range. He circled around and watched Dru and Virun dispatch laser cannons on four more floaters. Several more bright explosions boomed before the floaters split up onto separate corridors in an attempt to avoid their fire.

"They're trying to keep it interesting for us, boys," Davi said over the comm-channel.

"Good. Moving targets are so much more fun," Dru responded. To Davi's amazement, Dru had become one of the better target shooters among the pilots.

Davi and three others swooped down in tight formation and fired. Laser blasts exploded around the floaters again. Davi's and Dru's blasts hit their marks, taking out more laser cannons. Virun's missed, but he aimed again and blasted the floater's engines, bringing it to a sudden stop.

Troops jumped clear, seeking cover as Virun chuckled over the comm-channel. "That had to hurt."

Virun's fighter rocked from an explosion and orange flashes appeared on its port wing. "What the—"

Davi glanced over to spot a laser cannon zeroing in on him again from the top of a nearby building. "Laser cannon, top of the Acron Industries building. I'm on him," Davi said over the comm-channel. G-forces slammed him back against his leather seat as he put his VS28 into a steep turn and dove down, targeting the rooftop of the office complex.

Jorek's voice came over the comm-channel. "Keep your eyes out for laser cannons on the rooftops."

"How'd we miss those?" Dru wondered aloud over the comm-channel.

"There will be others. He really did some damage," Virun warned them.

Davi's targeting computer lit up as it locked on the target. Lining up visually on the guides, he pressed his boots firmly against the floor to brace himself and strafed the rooftop. Alliance soldiers dove to each side as the laser cannon exploded. "One cannon down."

"Thanks, boss," Virun replied as Davi steered into position above Virun and to the right.

Virun's starboard wing had black burn marks from the impact and a tear in the metal. "The damage doesn't look unmanageable from here. Can you still control her?"

"I'm not out of this yet," Virun replied turning the fighter for another run.

Davi and Dru both maneuvered into formation around him. Without further chatter, knowing what to do, they took out the laser cannons on the four remaining floaters, and then targeted their engines.

As they circled around, Davi glimpsed Jorek's squad making similar runs. In a few more minutes, the remaining floaters had been disabled and the squadron reformed around Davi, heading to assist Tela's team. Davi brushed his clammy brow against the sleeve of his flight suit.

They arrived at the government center to find charred remains of more laser cannons and Alliance equipment. One of the barracks was smoldering. In the beginning, the WFR had hoped to preserve as much infrastructure as possible, but Alliance resistance had made it so difficult they'd decided to do what must be done and worry about it later. They could always rebuild.

"Leave anything for us?" Jorek said as they circled Tela's team.

"We were about to ask you the same question," Tela responded in a singsong tone as she joined their formation. The rest of her team formed up behind her.

A squadron of seven Alliance VS28 fighters appeared heading straight for them with laser cannons blazing. "Heads up, here they come!" Tela called over the comm-channel.

Davi spun his fighter into a dive as two laser blasts exploded off his starboard wing, vibrating his cockpit. "We need to capture that starport."

"Let's knock these boys out of the sky!" Brie said over the comm-channel.

Davi chuckled. She'd come a long way from the lost teenage girl he had known in training. Davi glanced over to see one of his fighters crashing into the top of another office building, as the Squadron divided itself into pairs and began targeting the enemy fighters.

"We lost Kinny," Tela said over the comm-channel.

Davi pounded a fist into the side of his fighter. Kinny was an experienced pilot who had joined after the initial attack. "Wingmen, cover your leaders!" They didn't really need the reminder, but losing one of his pilots switched him into teacher mode again.

Tela lined up on an Alliance fighter and unleashed a burst of fire from her cannons. The enemy fighter exploded, spiraling toward the ground. Tela let off a victory yell, "One down!"

Davi lined up another in his sights, firing several sloppy blasts through its wing. It spun out of control. "Make it two."

An enemy fighter swooped in from above, firing on Dru at close range. Explosions rocked the hull of his fighter.

Smoke trailed from it, and Davi could see the damage out his blast shield. "You okay, Dru?"

Dru sounded rattled. "She's a little shaky but I can still fly her."

Davi and Tela both dove in to provide cover, blasting in unison at the enemy fighter trying to escape. It disintegrated with a bright flash.

Dru's voice rose in excitement. "He won't do that again! Thanks, guys!"

"Don't mention it," Tela said.

"Let's clean this mess up!" Jorek called.

Davi watched as the enemy fighters retreated.

"They're running!" Nila cheered.

"Jorek, take the squadron and chase them down if you can. We're escorting Dru back to base," Davi said.

"You got it, boss," Jorek said.

"Don't let them lead you too close to the starport. They might launch reinforcements," Tela warned.

"Don't worry. We'll be okay." Jorek said as the others formed around him and peeled off after the enemy fighters, leaving Tela and Davi flanking Dru.

"I don't know about the rest of you, but I'm hungry," Dru said, still totally unphased by the near miss he'd just experienced.

Davi heard Tela's laugh over the comm-channel as he keyed the transmitter. "Let's go home." They flew in formation back toward the WFR base.

Xalivar arrived at the meeting with his military leaders feeling beyond frustrated. Never had such brilliant leadership been undermined by more incredible incompetence. He hadn't relaxed since the news of the first attacks, and the time had come to put an end to this folly.

General Lucius, General Pres, and Admiral Dek sat around the table in the High Lord Councilor's conference room, just down the hall from the throne room. The oldest of the three, Lucius led ground operations. He'd served first under Xalivar's father and had a long and prestigious record of service, marred solely by his involvement in the Delta V disaster. He had Xalivar's sympathy.

The two junior officers were two decades younger. Pres, the sole female to rise to the top of the Alliance military hierarchy, was descended from the people who once ruled the Eastern regions of Old Earth. The shape of her eyes and yellowish cast of her skin hinted at that history. She coordinated air defenses, from energy shields to in-atmosphere attack forces. Of the three, Dek looked most like a soldier—his hair closely cropped, his big-boned, muscular frame emphasized by the fit of the gray uniform. He led the extra-planetary air forces.

As Xalivar paced at the head of the table, Lucius broke the silence. "We've consolidated all remaining forces on Vertullis at the government center. We are seeking to regain ground and retake the starport."

"We sent reinforcements?" Xalivar turned his stare on Dek.

"Our men are waiting and ready," Dek responded, "but until we find a way through the energy shield, they cannot be deployed to the surface."

Xalivar whirled around, his anger rising. "What's taking so long? We designed the shield, didn't we? We need those forces on the ground!" He clenched his fists.

Dek flinched but managed to compose himself. "We designed the shields to protect against these types of invasions. Our attempts to weaken the shield with fighters and smaller craft have not been successful, exactly as the shields were intended to work. We're preparing larger cruisers for a full-scale assault."

"Our forces have coordinated attacks on the surface using shuttles, floaters, and the few VS28 starfighters not under WFR control," Pres said.

"The greatest Alliance in the galaxy is being brought to its knees by a bunch of fly-by-the-seat-of-their-pants workers?" Xalivar couldn't believe what he was hearing! Had the years of peace turned his once finely tuned military into incompetents?

"We've seen several gains in the last few days toward recapturing the shield control center," Lucius said, the only officer of the three who'd shown no reaction to Xalivar's angry outburst. Perhaps he'd been around so long he expected it. "We hope to regain control of it in the next two days."

"It's been three weeks already! What's taking so long?" Xalivar saw them all flinch at his screaming. "You told me we had the finest military in the galaxy!"

"Our training is top notch, my Lord, but our troops have limited experience with real warfare," Lucius said.

"Are you actually arguing, General Lucius, that years of peace have made us soft and incompetent?" Xalivar stared at him, knowing he wouldn't get an answer. Proud men like this could never admit their failures. He shook his head. "I want all cruisers in the star system recalled to attack that energy shield. All soldiers not essential to their posts are to be brought here and armed for battle. We must recapture Vertullis as soon as possible."

The three leaders nodded. "The cruisers have already been recalled," Dek said.

"We're refitting some light aircraft with better shields to allow increased attacks on enemy positions," Pres said.

"How long will this refitting take?"

"We can't send supplies through the shields either, my Lord," Pres said. "Our men have to reconnoiter and requisition required materials."

Xalivar cursed and pounded his fist on the table. "When am I going to stop hearing excuses and start seeing results?" He turned to the door as Manaen entered holding a data pad. "More bad news?"

Manaen nodded.

Xalivar whirled back to face the leaders. "I expect the next time we meet to be hearing actual progress reports, instead of more excuses for delays!" He grabbed the datapad out of Manaen's hands and stormed out into the corridor without another word.

Davi reported to the command center for debriefing an hour after landing. Matheu, Aron, and Joram had already assembled.

"We lost a fighter today and three others were damaged," Davi reported. "One of those was nearly shot down as well. Repairs on two of them can be done in a few days, but—"

Matheu nodded. "Casualties of war. It happens."

Davi fought to control his tongue. "Dead pilots are more to me than just numbers!" His face turned red with anger as he drew close to Matheu and stared him in the eye. How could he be so callous? Davi felt devastation at every loss, every injury, a feeling he hoped he never lost. Could Matheu really have seen so much that it didn't matter anymore?

Joram stepped between them. "They are to all of us. But people die in war. It's unavoidable."

Davi stepped back, trying to regain his composure. Taking deep breaths, he centered himself before continuing, "We'll need all the fighters we can get if we hope to continue this fight. It's only a matter of time before the Alliance brings in star cruisers to blast through the energy shield."

"We have to hope we can negotiate before it happens," Aron said from a nearby chair.

"With what leverage? We are one planet against the entire system." Davi said, sinking into a chair near Aron and wondering how they could feel so confident.

A communications panel beeped, distracting their attention a moment as a commtech ran to answer it.

"Not everyone in the system sides with the Alliance," Joram said. "They dominate by force, not by election."

"We're making gains daily," Aron said. "The Lord's Council and the citizens of the Alliance must take note of it. Pressure will be brought to bear on the High Lord Councilor. Especially in regard to the Alliance prisoners we're holding. Xalivar may not care about them but others will."

"The Alliance hasn't even used half the force available to them. If history has taught us anything, it's that they won't give up easily," Matheu said, his face locked in its usual grave expression. Did the man feel anything?

"The Borali Alliance hasn't fought in years," Aron said. "They quelled a few ill-thought-out worker Movements, yes. But none of those had the military organization and planning we have."

"They don't even see us as human beings," Davi said. "You can't assume their whole way of thinking will change right away."

"Not everyone in the Alliance thinks the same way. You didn't," Joram said.

Davi nodded. "Because my mother saw to it that I was given unique opportunities and a liberal education most in the Alliance never have. Even she doesn't think as I do."

"Most of them only remember the history of animosity between our peoples," Matheu said.

Davi couldn't believe he'd wound up on the same side in this argument with Matheu. The tension between them had eased since they'd started trusting him, but the General was cold and hard, unlike Davi. "It may be a long fight."

"As soon as the area around the government center is stable, we'll retrieve what's left of Kinny's fighter. Try to rebuild—" Joram said.

"If the Alliance doesn't get to it first," Davi snapped, cutting him off. "It crashed into a building. There won't be much left to salvage."

"We'll take what we can from it," Joram replied. "Like always."

Davi nodded as Aron stood and motioned for him to follow.

"We've been looking into the information your friend at Presimion sent you about the prison," Aron said as they moved away from the others.

Hope rose inside Davi. "You've found something?"

Aron shook his head. "Information on its defenses. It's hidden underground and very well protected. Besides the fact that it's on Legallis, there's no feasible assault plan we can conceive of."

Davi's shoulders sank with his heart. "I have to find a way to help Miri and my father."

"Maybe something can be worked out in the negotiations," Aron said, trying to encourage him. And the tension in the leader's eyes reminded Davi that Sol was his oldest friend. He wanted to save him as much as Davi and Lura did.

"We don't even know if there are going to be negotiations," Davi said, his voice rising in frustration.

"We don't know for certain Miri and your father are being held there," Aron reminded him. "But we're trying to get as much intel as we can, I promise."

Davi nodded then turned and headed toward the corridor, feeling a need to get away from military thinking for a while. Lura had invited him and Tela to dinner. He hoped to gods she could take their minds off what they all faced, at least for a few hours.

As they sat around the table in Lura's quarters that night, Tela and Lura chatting happily, Davi remained quiet, a lump in his throat. In his mind, he went over and over the issues he faced, searching for solutions. The battles had grown more and more risky. They'd lost fighters before, that was inevitable, but knowing it didn't make him feel any less responsible. These real people, young people like him. Real lives lost. Real futures aborted. He wished he could reason with Xalivar somehow, but he'd already tried that. If he could only think of a way to convince him that friendship and cooperation would be far more beneficial to both sides than war. If the workers could let go of the past, after all the Lords had put them through, why couldn't the Boralians? Why couldn't they find a way past so no more soldiers and pilots had to die in senseless fighting?

Head down as he offered silent prayers again for all those lost, his stomach felt heavy, the world slowed down almost to a stop around him. He almost didn't notice when Lura reached out to gently caress his arm.

As he looked up, she smiled. "You're a million miles away today, son. Don't worry. Everything will work out somehow. God always has a plan."

Davi didn't even look at her as she placed her hand on his atop the table.

"We lost a pilot today," Tela explained.

"Oh, Davi. I'm sure that's very hard. But it's not your fault," Lura said, eyes filling with sympathy. It had little effect.

"Loss is part of war, I get that," Davi said, looking at the women. "But I don't like it. And the longer this war drags out, the more losses we will sustain. We can ill afford them. We're already outnumbered."

"We're never outnumbered when God is on our side," Lura said with confidence.

Tela nodded, smiling. "Amen."

"Besides," Lura added, "Your father always told me any man who likes war is a very dangerous man because there must be something seriously wrong with his mind. War is terrible."

Davi shook his head. "I wish I had faith like you two do. The situation seems so hopeless to me."

"I once thought my husband was lost forever, but now I find I may see him again," Lura said. "There's always hope."

Davi looked at her, his voice cracking as he felt a pain in the back of his throat. "A heavily guarded prison on the enemy's capital planet—we have no way to reach him. We don't even know for sure he's there." He glanced down at his feet, absent-mindedly biting his lip and wiping his nose with the back of his hand.

Lura squeezed his hand. "I refuse to believe that. I know God will find a way." And in her eyes, he saw she absolutely meant it.

She had so much faith. Davi hated to let her down. He didn't yet share her confidence that God would work things out, that God cared about the little issues of human hearts, but he wanted so much for it to be true. She'd been hurt enough. He couldn't bear to be the cause of further pain.

And Tela, who had become such a blessing to him, had grown up without a father. He knew what that was like and didn't want to disappoint her either. He wished he still had the influence he'd had as the Prince; that he could hold people accountable, issue orders, garner even a modicum of the military's respect, but those days were behind him forever. He couldn't recall ever feeling so helpless or hopeless.

"Well, he'll have to because I'm out of ideas," Davi said bitterly, then stood and disappeared into the living room.

Tela ran after him. "Can you blame her for being so hopeful?"

"I don't blame her. I just worry about her setting herself up for more pain and loss. She's already had so much." Davi sighed as he sunk onto a sofa.

"And she knows how to deal with it," Tela said as she sat next to him and wrapped her arm around his shoulders gently. "Besides, despite your doubts, I share her faith: God cares about what happens to us and has plans for our good."

"I never knew what it was like to have a father," Davi said, turning away. "There's nothing I want more than to have him here with us."

"If it's God's will, it will happen," Tela said, placing her soft hand on his arm.

Davi turned, his eyes meeting hers. "Okay, I know you believe that, but it's not so easy for me. I can't bear to have her hoping I'll get my father back, because if it doesn't happen, it'll break her heart. I don't want to be responsible for that."

"You aren't," Tela said reassuring him, her eyes showed conviction as she nodded with the words. "I want my father back, too, but it's in God's hands."

"We could have lost two pilots today, maybe even three if Virun wasn't so skilled," Davi said. "I'm responsible for those people."

"In a way, yes, but they're responsible for themselves, too," Tela said. "You didn't force them to fight. They chose to. A leader can only do so much to protect his followers."

"How many pilots can we afford to lose?" Davi said, pain pounding inside him.

"Loss is a part of living, and we're at war," Tela said. "I wish I had a better, happier answer for you, but I don't."

Davi nodded, turning away. "I don't want to let everyone down."

Tela rested her head on his shoulder, her voice filled with compassion and pride. "You've never let me down. You're a great teacher, a great leader, and a great friend. You gave up your whole life, everything you knew because you saw an unjust situation and wanted to do the right thing. I don't know if I could ever do that."

"I did it because these are my people," Davi said. "And because once I knew the truth, I had to do what was right, no matter what it cost."

"And I admire that so much," Tela said. "I can't imagine how hard it is. The Boralians are your people, too. You lived among them twenty years. They will always be a part of you."

Davi took her hand from his shoulder and held it in his, staring into her eyes. "Are you trying to depress me?"

Tela laughed. "You know I didn't mean it like that. The best part of them is a part of you, not the worst."

"How can you be so sure? They trained me. They educated me. I never gave the workers a second thought until I ended up on Vertullis." Davi felt moved by her faith in him. "I spent years in blissful ignorance living as a prince. I heard rumors, but never cared to investigate them. I never had to."

"You didn't know the situation until you came to Vertullis," Tela said.

"I was too busy enjoying the perks of royalty, Tela," Davi said, turning his eyes away to hide his shame. "If I needed something, all I had to do was ask. The one thing I never asked for was the truth."

"And once you knew, you did what you had to. Nothing else matters."

He turned back toward her and their eyes met. The sincerity he saw there brought tears welling to the corners of his eyes. *How could she see so much good in him?* After a moment, he sighed, choking back the sadness. "Sometimes I feel like you only see the best in me."

"No, I see the worst too, sometimes," Tela teased. "But overall, you're a good guy, so why focus on the bad stuff?"

"And here I was counting on you to make me a better man," Davi teased.

"Oh, I'm not done fixing you, don't worry. But it can wait until we're past this war," Tela said, smiling.

They both laughed, until Davi leaned in and kissed her. She kissed back.

"You know we're not alone here, right?" He teased.

She made a face and punched him on the shoulder. "Keep being a wise guy and you can be," she said with a mock serious look.

Davi raised his hands in surrender and she laughed again. "All I know is God is in control, and if we trust Him, things will work out for the best."

Davi looked into her eyes. She really believed it. He wanted to believe it, too. He did know that just being near her was healing for him. It helped him cope, helped him to find strength and focus, and he was beginning to depend on it in ways he'd never imagined.

She locked her eyes on his for a moment, letting the love and concern there soak in and energize them both, then she reached for his hand. "Come on. Your mother's in there alone. Let's go give her some company."

He accepted her hand and followed her back to the dining room.

"As the days stretch on and our troops experience more and more defeat at the hands of the Resistance, the situation grows more and more dim," Orson Sterling said from behind a news desk at the Media Corp. bureau. Reporters and support staff bustled behind him in the background as vidscreens lit up with various images on the wall immediately behind his desk. "The public is starting to protest. Many wonder why we're at war with a people who have not done us harm in many generations."

Xalivar shut the vidscreen off before the man-on-the-street interviews began. He'd caught similar reports on every channel. What was wrong with these reporters, stirring up the people to treason? He could understand the average civilian's ignorance of history, but the news media consisted of people with far more education and intelligence. How could they have forgotten what the workers had done to their people? Did no one still realize these workers were not worthy of respect or even a second thought? Could people have so distanced themselves from history that they were willing to forgive the past and treat the workers as human beings?

He cracked his neck from side to side and let out a guttural roar. For days, he had been listening to news reports of growing protests and outcry to "let the workers go." Just thinking about it disgusted him.

Xalivar cursed Orson Sterling and the rest of the media under his breath, making a mental note to have him investigated and arrested if possible on whatever charges he could manage. He would not be the High Lord Councilor who gave in to such outcries of ignorance. He would never live it down if he did. If the workers achieved the freedom they were demanding, they would come to regret it. They could never be trusted. If left alone, they would return to their old ways. His people may have forgotten the past, but he knew the workers hadn't. No matter how nice they pretended to be, Xalivar knew what was really going on in their minds. This was a war for the future of his people, and he wasn't about to let ignorance rule the day.

The communicator beeped. He stepped to the wall and clicked the button. "Yes?"

Manaen sounded hesitant. "We are receiving calls about food shortages."

"What?" Xalivar screamed and sunk back on the throne in frustration.

"Several of the minor planets have not received their shipments from Vertullis in the past two weeks," Manaen explained.

"Shipments have only been stopped for the three weeks of fighting," Xalivar said, collecting himself. Transports to Regallis at the far end of the system would take over a month at their fastest speeds. Some should still be in route.

"The last transports left five days before the fighting started," Manaen said.

Xalivar smiled, feeling smug. *Aha! So someone is panicking prematurely.*

Then Manaen continued: "But those transports were for Legallis and Tertullis. The last transports for the outer system left two weeks before they did and arrived last week."

"So why are they panicking?" Xalivar frowned. "How can they be out of food?"

"The calls were from Xanthis and Certullis," Manaen said. Both planets were in the middle of the system. "Their last shipments arrived about the time fighting started. New transports would have left a few days later."

Xalivar cursed under his breath. "Order the emergency release of stocks from the royal surplus."

"Yes, my Lord," Manaen said, hesitating.

Xalivar waited for him to speak, hearing the line still open. "What is it?"

"The Royal surplus didn't receive a shipment either. We'll have enough left to feed Legallis for two months," Manaen said.

"By then this will all be over," Xalivar said, clicking off the communicator and returning to his ruminations. *Everyone is blowing this out of proportion, my gods! Am I the only rational one left in the Alliance?*

Davi's squadron circled the government center, anxiously awaiting the signal to join the battle raging below. The call had come less than an hour before. The Alliance had launched a major push to recapture the shield. Uzah's army had been engaging the enemy for the past two hours and needed air support.

As they circled the starport, Davi noticed a line of transports still sitting as they had since the fighting started almost a month before. Some of the food shipments would have begun to spoil by now. He wondered how long it would take for the Alliance to feel the pain of dwindling food supplies. Vertullis supplied eighty percent of the system's food, along with other key agricultural products. Shipments had been postponed ever since the fighting began.

As he turned his attention back to the battle, one transport took off. "Looks like the Plutonians are getting their food," Davi said over the comm-channel.

"They're gonna love that on Legallis," Tela said with a chuckle.

Since the Plutonians and their antelope were the only lifeforms capable of inhabiting the planet outside the false atmosphere of Alpha Base, they were one of the few alien species in the system with their own governor and council. These leaders reported to the Alliance, along with everyone else, but exercised a unique amount of control over local affairs. An envoy had approached the WFR the previous week, seeking to negotiate a special shipment of food. The WFR leadership knew when word got out of such a shipment, other interested parties would approach them, and such activity would only serve to increase the pressure on the Alliance and work in the WFR's favor, so the deal had been made.

As the squadron turned back toward the energy shield control center, Davi's comm-channel beeped on the combat frequency. "Squadron One, commander," he responded.

Davi heard explosions and laser fire in the background as Uzah spoke. "We have enemy fighters coming in from the south and west."

"Roger, Ground Leader, we're on our way," Davi said, switching back to his squadron channel. "Okay, everyone, incoming enemy fighters. Let's go occupy them." He switched to the main combat channel again. "All fighters commence attack. All fighters commence attack." And then he prayed silently that God would keep his pilots safe.

Davi switched on his targeting system and turned his shields on full, increasing speed. As the pressure pushed him against his seat, he counted several squads of Alliance fighters approaching the shield control center, probably all the fighters they still had available. This might be the chance they'd been looking for to eliminate them.

Davi keyed the comm-channel. "Okay, form up on Tela, Jorek, Virun, and me. We'll take them in quadrants. Wingmen, protect your leaders. Go for attack."

The squadron followed his instructions, splitting into groups of five each and forming on their designated leaders. As the formations settled, Davi took a quick head count, just to be sure. He winced at the reminder of how many he'd already lost. They were down by two dozen in under a month.

"Go in high so you can target them before they even realize we're there," Tela said.

"Won't their combat computers clue them in?" Brie asked.

"Not fast enough for them to react," Jorek said then let out a rebel yell.

Davi chuckled as he keyed the comm-channel. "Keep your focus. Let's make this one count." He'd said it as much for himself as anyone else, and took deep breaths; trying to relax some of the tension that stiffened his body automatically these days every time they went into combat. He fretted like a worried father fretting over his children, and in a way, he realized, that's exactly what he was. With a heavy sigh, he relaxed his hand on the joystick and shifted in his seat, letting the tension release. Then he settled back and focused again.

Davi's group flew in over the top of the enemy fighters, vectoring in, then letting loose with their laser cannons. Explosions battered the startled enemy fighters as they changed trajectory and began targeting Davi's squadron.

Orange and white flashes filled the corners of his eyes as Nila took a hit on her wing, struggling to keep control.

"You okay, Nila?" he asked over the comm, feeling panic starting to rise within.

"Yeah, I'm hit, but not bad," Nila said.

Dru swooped in over the top of her and blasted the enemy fighter into pieces. "One down," Dru said with a whoop.

"Thanks, Dru," Nila said, as he slid his VS28 into position to protect her. Nila closed the distance forming up behind Davi again.

Davi glanced over to see the other pilots engaged in heavy combat. "Divide. Brie and Nila, stay with me. Dru, you and Zid see if you can sneak underneath them. Let's come at them from both sides."

"Roger, boss," Dru said as he took off in another direction with his wingman.

Davi circled around for another run, angling up, with Brie and Nila in tight formation. Enemy fighters tried to intercept them, but Davi's group dove down at the last second and flew up under the enemy and onto their tails.

"Line 'em up, girls," Davi said.

Brie fired first, hitting an enemy fighter with three blasts from her cannons. Nila took out one of an enemy fighter's two engines. Davi fired on the enemy leader and watched as his two blasts landed on the enemy's blast shield. Explosions rocked the fighter causing its emergency eject system to initiate. The enemy leader ejected into space and floated by Davi's blast shield, his face locked in a final scream.

Davi chuckled. "Good shooting, you two!"

"You, too, boss," Brie said.

Ahead, a WFR fighter executed several maneuvers back and forth, attempting to ditch an Alliance fighter on its tail, and he realized it was Tela.

Her voice came over the comm-channel moments later. "I can't lose this guy."

Davi glanced around for her wingman, but he was nowhere in sight. He accelerated, turning in her direction and targeting the enemy fighter. "On my way!"

Davi glimpsed yellow and red flashes and heard an explosion off his port wing. He glanced back. An enemy fighter dropped down onto his tail. "Brie, Nila, I need some help here."

"We see him, boss," Nila said.

Two fighters tried to slide in behind them as he ignored his attacker and continued his trajectory toward Tela. His mind raced as he calculated moves which would allow him to blast the enemy attacking Tela and circle around to confront his own attacker. More explosions rocked his cockpit. His control panel lights blinked on and off as he vibrated in his seat but he still had control.

"You okay?" Nila asked as Davi slewed his fighter side to side, hoping to avoid further damages.

"Yeah. Get this guy off me." His target screen flashed and he fired instantly, sending three blasts from his cannons at the enemy fighter chasing Tela. Its starboard wing disintegrated as it spun out of control toward the ground below.

As the enemy fell away, Tela turned around, targeting the fighter tailing him. "Thanks, Davi."

Brie and Nila fired at the same time, taking out Davi's attackers' engines and sending him diving toward the ground.

Davi heard Brie's whoop over the comm-channel. "All clear, boss." He sighed in relief, relaxing again.

"Way to go, ladies!" Tela called as they all turned and headed back for the battle.

Davi grimaced as a WFR fighter exploded ahead of him, but noted the enemy had few fighters left. His pilots had done their job well.

Jorek and Virun's squads headed in for another run as Dru and Zid eliminated the last fighter of the group they'd been sparring with. The Borali Alliance's air forces on Vertullis were close to elimination.

Tela's voice came over a private channel. "That was close."

Davi took a quick glance at her fighter as she pulled alongside, noting a few scorch marks on her wings but no significant damage. "For both of us," he responded. Davi ran a quick system's check. There seemed to be no major damage from the hits he took. He whispered a prayer of thanks. "Let's clean up the last of these and go home."

He led them on one last run, and in a few moments, it was all over. The enemy destroyed another WFR fighter first but each of his groups took out an enemy fighter and Tela and Virun went into fancy dives to destroy the last two. The Alliance had no air support on Vertullis.

"Jorek and Tela, form up the Squadron and work on those ground attackers. Nila, let's take our fighters back to base and get the mechanics to look at them."

"Okay, boss," Nila said.

"Two more coming with you," Virun said as two more injured fighters slid into formation with Davi and Nila.

"Great work today, all," Davi said as he led his formation back toward home and he meant it. Their losses had been minimal and damage minor; the enemy's great. With no air defenses and dwindling ground troops, the Alliance would now have no choice but to break through the energy shield. He comm-channeled a preliminary report back to the command center, wondering for the first time if maybe the WFR should take the battle to the enemy.

# Chapter Twelve

Tarkanius watched as the Council chamber dissolved into chaos—Lords leaning or sitting on their tables, huddling around in various groups, tables buried underneath a mass of datapads and reports—far from the usual atmosphere at their official meetings. The meeting had already been one of the most boisterous in Tarkanius' memory—Lords shouting over each other, ignoring those speaking from the dais, debating every aspect and nuance of the situation with Vertullis. The word "war" was heard only in whispers. No one wanted to be the one to declare it to be the truth. They all still hoped the situation would go away. Altogether, it was giving Tarkanius a headache.

"We've already heard complaints of food shortages, on Tertullis in particular," Lord Niger said from a table near the front. "Vertullis is the most important agricultural supplier in the system. Our system cannot survive without it."

"We can cultivate new sources," Lord Obed argued from across an aisle. "There are other planets with available land and decent climates for agriculture."

"Not on the same level as Vertullis," Lord Niger said. "It would take generations to develop the same level of production."

"We don't have generations," Lord Kray said. She and Simeon sat together at a table a few rows back, across the aisle from Lord Hachim.

"Well said!" Lord Hachim said as other voices arose in agreement and concern.

"We must send an envoy to discuss the cessation of hostilities with the Resistance leadership," Lord Kray said. "They need us as much as we need them. Perhaps we can find a way to coexist and share resources."

"Why would they want to share with those who have enslaved them?"

Lord Obed asked in disbelief.

"Kray is right. Some kind of discussion must take place," Lord Simeon said. "A peaceful resolution is the best option for everyone."

"There can be no peace with the workers," Obed scoffed, his face crinkled in disgust. Loud arguments resumed, with various factions taking up stances against each other and struggling to be heard over the others. Tarkanius had had enough.

He pounded the gavel on his podium. "Please. Please. Everyone must have a chance to be heard. We all have concerns, I'm sure."

As the Lords grunted in acknowledgement and settled back into their places, the doors burst open and Xalivar affected his usual grand entrance. He strode to the front of the room and onto the dais. "Sorry, I'm late."

"We were just discussing the possibility of sending an envoy to seek a settlement with our enemy," Tarkanius said.

Xalivar stiffened and whirled toward him as if he might strike, clenching his fists. "We don't negotiate with workers!" His sounded angry, full of contempt, his fists clenching and unclenching at his sides.

"We have no choice when our planets start to run out of food," Kray said.

Voices rose in agreement.

"We still have surplus in the Royal storehouses," Xalivar said.

Other voices arose in support of Xalivar's resolve.

"At the rate we have been releasing it, Lord Kray is right. It will be a matter of weeks," Simeon said.

"A week or two is all we need," Xalivar said.

The Lords quieted, peering at him with interest.

He clenched his fists again. "A major task force is, at this very moment, assembling to attack the planet Vertullis and punch through the energy shield."

"Do you really think taking things back by force is necessary, when we haven't even attempted negotiations?" Lord Hachim asked.

Xalivar whirled toward him. "Have you so little memory of our history? We have never negotiated with those workers, and I won't be the first High Lord Councilor to allow it."

"You're not the only one making decisions. The Council has a say as well," Kray said.

"We are at war," Xalivar said. "The High Lord Councilor is the de facto leader in times of war by law. There are still options I have not exhausted." Xalivar had never spoken to the Council with such disrespect. No High Lord Councilor ever had.

"We have used force in the past and still we face the workers again," Simeon said. "Perhaps the time has come for a new tactic."

Several voices chimed in supporting the idea.

"I will inform you when the time has come for a new tactic," Xalivar said with bitterness. "It is my decision to make as military leader by law."

"The laws do grant the High Lord Councilor broad powers in time of war, true, but the Council is free to have input at any juncture," Tarkanius scolded, irritated by Xalivar's disrespectful demeanor and tone. "You are to present your assessment and allow us to question it as we see fit." Someone had to rein Xalivar in, and as leader of the Council the duty fell to him.

"You are questioning without all the facts. The war is far from lost," Xalivar said, fists opening and closing.

"Only skeleton forces remain on the planet. We've lost our air defenses, the starport, the shield," Hachim said in frustration. "What more facts do we need?"

"You will have all the facts, when I say you do," Xalivar said. "I don't have time for debate. I must prepare an assault plan. We have one of the greatest militaries in the known universe. Let them do what we trained them to do." He glanced around the room with a cold stare, daring anyone to question him. When no one spoke, Xalivar turned and marched back the way he'd come.

Tarkanius sighed. Miri's concerns about Xalivar consolidating his powers had been even more well-founded than he had realized. The Council would have to give considerable thought to the steps to be taken in response to the Vertullian crisis. And Tarkanius would have to use all of his authority and cunning to put the High Lord Councilor back into line.

Davi and WFR Squadron One raced through the hole in the defense shield and continued toward the incoming Alliance Transport. Bound from Legallis for Xanthis, it carried surplus food from the Royal storehouses. The WFR had decided to intercept any transports which passed through official Vertullian air space. The agricultural needs of the system were already putting pressure on the Alliance to settle the fighting, and the sooner things came to a head, the better.

Shortages were causing alarm, and the WFR had been hailed as heroes by making private deals to supply the people's needs. Several more deals were in the works, and a transport had already been sent to Tertullis. The situation had become a can't-lose proposition for the WFR. Of course, the decision to attack Alliance transports might change things, but they'd decided it would be worth the risk.

As they passed the Vertullian moon Agora, Davi led the squadron in a tight formation. Their targeting computers lit up with multiple blips.

"Okay, we've got six contacts," Davi said over the combat channel as he sat up straight and tightened his muscles. "Must be a fighter escort. Arm shields."

"Roger, boss," Dru responded as Davi flicked on his shields, knowing all the others were doing the same.

"They're not going to make this as easy as we'd hoped," Davi said. There were five fighters, not a full squadron, but enough to make things more difficult than they had planned.

"Keeps it interesting for us," Virun said.

For a moment, Davi wished he'd reconsidered Joram's suggestion to appoint a special squadron of top pilots for the raid. Tela had argued that they all had combat experience now, and transports had limited shields and gunnery. It would be good practice for everyone. Davi had sided with Tela but now feared he might end up regretting it.

As the large Alliance 250 transport and its escorts came into visual range, Davi ran through the scenarios in his mind. It was too late to initiate any complex maneuvers. The straight on approach seemed the wisest course. He prayed his pilots were all focused. If they could see the enemy, the enemy could see them. The gray transport dwarfed their VS28s, but it moved slower and was less maneuverable.

The transport's fighter escort shifted into a combat formation, placing themselves between Davi's incoming squadron and the transport.

"Look sharp, here we go," Davi said. "Two groups, Virun's to the left."

"Squad Two: form on me," Virun said as the Squadron divided.

"Let's show these guys the same way we showed their friends on the planet," Brie said with excitement.

"Light 'em up!" Nila said, letting out a rebel yell.

Davi laughed and swooped down in formation with Brie, Nila, and two others toward the enemy fighters as Virun's group flew around to the other side.

"Focus," Davi reminded them as the targeting system flashed and he fired his cannons. "Remember, we want to disable the transport, not destroy it."

The enemy fighters started firing right after he did, even as they took evasive maneuvers to avoid his cannon blasts.

As Davi and his team focused on the fighters and transport, a Battle Cruiser and five squadrons of enemy fighters rose up from the far side of the planet, racing toward them.

"Incoming!" Dru almost shouted into the comm-channel.

"A month ago you were begging for action," Davi muttered, focusing as he double-checked his targeting system.

"Not this much," Dru answered as Davi noted the numbers of the new arrivals on his radar. Dru had it right. They'd soon be in trouble.

"Just a few more seconds, and I'll have the Transport's engines," Virun said.

Davi spotted Virun moving in to targeting range, his wingman close behind him. "Make it quick. We're about to be outnumbered," Davi said.

He counted five enemy squadrons of fifteen fighters each. He fired off a couple more rounds at the enemy fighters protecting the transport, watching the explosions as one lost an engine and another suffered wing damage. Brie and Nila's shots missed as the fighters they were targeting dodged their fire with quick maneuvers.

Virun and his wingman fired at the transport. "It's away!" Virun said as they arched around and raced toward Davi's squad.

The transport's engines exploded with sparks and fire. At least one of them went dark.

"Let's head for home," Davi said, relieved they'd accomplished what they needed to so efficiently.

The squadron formed up on him, circling over the transport and back down toward the planet.

"Watch your tails," he warned as the enemy fighters raced after them.

A fighter near the back of their formation exploded as enemy cannon fire struck its engine compartment. Another good pilot lost, another friend dead.

"Form up on Virun," Davi said, ignoring the dagger to his heart as he fell back to protect the rear when the Squadron reformed around Virun. "Fly evasive patterns. Don't give them anything they can lock onto."

Flashes and explosions rocked his cockpit. Davi executed a quick spin and fired back at the closest attackers, forcing them to change course to evade. Another two minutes and his Squadron would be safely beyond the shield.

"Prepare to open the shield on my mark," he comm-channeled the base and continued circling and dodging as he exchanged fire with the enemy fighters, his boots pressing so firmly against the floor he thought they might push right on through the hull.

"Roger, Squadron One commander," Joram's voice came back at him.

Another WFR fighter turned back to engage the enemy. Davi keyed the comm. "Brie, what are you doing? We're almost home."

"Protecting my wingman," she said. She fired off a couple of shots, hitting an enemy fighter square in the wing. Orange and yellow flashes illuminated the fighter as debris separated from its wing and it spun out of control toward outer space.

"Nice shooting. Now turn around and hightail it," Davi said, firing off two more blasts from his cannons and racing after her. "Open Shield," he said, transmitting the code. He held his breath as he awaited the response.

"Open," Joram said.

Davi followed his squadron through at the specified coordinates, and without a sound or any visible sign, the shield closed behind them, but not before three enemy fighters followed them through.

"We have company," Nila said as she whirled around, attempting to target one of the enemies. The rest of the Squadron turned to engage them. Enemy lasers exploded off Nila's wing.

"Watch it, Nila!" Brie warned as Nila fired, hitting an enemy fighter square in the blast shield. Smoke trailed from the fighter as the pilot dove, but the blast shield did its job and Davi watched him circle back around.

"Good shooting, Nila," Dru said, as he targeted another enemy and sent it spiraling toward the planet below with two well-timed cannon blasts.

"You, too," Nila said, angling her fighter for another shot at the enemy she'd targeted as he came back around.

"Two to go," Brie said as Nila fired again, this time hitting the enemy on the wing.

At the same moment, Brie's engine exploded behind her, an enemy soaring past as she struggled to maintain control.

Davi swooped down alongside to check on her. "You okay, Brie?"

"Yeah, blast him!" Brie yelled, with fire in her voice.

Virun came in from above and blasted the enemy with two laser shots on each wing. The fighter spiraled out of control toward the ground. Davi heard Virun's rebel yell in the comm-channel.

"Way to go, Squadron!" Dru said.

"We almost failed the mission," Brie said.

"Any mission where we make it home is a success," Davi said as he led the Squadron back toward the base. But inside his cockpit he uttered a loud prayer of relief and thanks that they'd made it through.

What had the Battle Cruiser and its escort been up to? *They must be looking for a weakness in the energy shield.* It would be a matter of time before the Alliance launched a major attack to try and break through the shield. The WFR had better be ready.

Tarkanius gathered with three other Lords in a small study off his office in the upper west corridor of the Council building. Except for Lords Niger and Simeon, they included the same group who had met with Miri in private several months before. The topic was the same: Xalivar.

Lord Hachim had also been invited, but Tarkanius noticed, as he glanced at his chrono for the fifth time in an hour, that Hachim was running late—very late. It was not typical of him, and it had Tarkanius worried. His thoughts were interrupted by someone saying his name.

He looked up to find the others staring at him. Kray and Niger sat on opposite ends of a divan Tarkanius had imported from Regallis—as nice as anything the resort planet was famous for. Simeon occupied a lounge chair with fabric of matching colors, though it was Xanthian in design.

After a moment, he realized Niger had spoken to him. "I'm sorry. I was wondering about Hachim."

The office remained warm, despite the cold air outside. For some reason, the weather was unusually frigid for this time of year, but the climate controls in his office did their job well, and no one would have known it sitting inside.

"We wondered what you thought about the peace conference. Xalivar seems dead set against it, and he's right—historically, we have never negotiated," Niger said.

"But times have changed," Kray interjected. "The citizens are no longer against such negotiations. People no longer see the workers in the same way as they once did."

Tarkanius nodded. "This is true. What Xalivar always seems to forget is that we were elected to serve the people, not just our own concerns."

The others grunted in agreement.

A moment later, the door slid open and a harried Hachim hurried in, his face anxious.

"What's the matter, Hachim?" Simeon asked as soon as he saw him.

"One of my transports was intercepted by WFR fighters," Hachim said, throwing himself into a chair next to Simeon. "If it weren't for an assist by Alliance forces studying the Vertullian planetary shield, it might have been lost."

Kray put her hand on his arm. "But they're okay?"

Hachim smiled, looking at her. "The shipment is safe. The transport's engines were damaged, but they can be repaired."

Tarkanius had been running over the scenario in his mind. If the WFR were attacking their transports, it meant they were comfortable with the control they had over the planet. They also must have learned that the Boralians' food reserves were running low. Such news wouldn't be any surprise. The Vertullians were well aware of the role their planet played in the star system's economy. "What are the latest reports on the battles?" he asked.

"Our latest intelligence reports say Alliance resistance on Vertullis has been reduced to all but a few pockets of troops," Niger said.

Tarkanius sighed. It was like he'd suspected. "That's all the more reason for us to question Xalivar's refusal to negotiate."

"Xalivar is a stubborn fool," Kray said with contempt, her face a scowl.

"You'd best keep such comments to yourself," Niger warned.

"He wouldn't dare spy on the Council," Hachim said.

"I wouldn't put anything past him at this point," Kray said. "Remember Miri's warnings and look what happened to her."

The rest nodded, their expressions grave. Miri's disappearance was wide knowledge now, and they all suspected Xalivar had been responsible.

The room remained silent for several moments, as they all sat lost in thought. Tarkanius wondered if Xalivar had listening devices in his chambers. He'd always maintained a good relationship with Xalivar and found it hard to believe the High Lord Councilor would have regarded him as a threat. Then again, the mere suggestion of a peace conference had made Xalivar quite angry, and none of them had any idea what Miri's interrogators might have drawn out of her since her capture. Perhaps Xalivar knew about their private meeting.

"I think the Council has no choice but to force the conference to occur," Simeon said, breaking the silence.

"Force the conference? How?" Niger asked.

"What if we put out a press release announcing the Council has sent an envoy to arrange it?" Tarkanius said. "Once it's announced to the public, it would be very hard for Xalivar to interfere."

Simeon nodded. "We can send our own representative to ensure negotiations occur, even if Xalivar is reluctant."

"It's the High Lord Councilor's place to negotiate, according to law, even if the law's never been used," Tarkanius said, wondering how they would pull it off.

"Our representative can act as an observer and mediate if required," Kray said.

The others grunted their consent. The idea became more and more appealing by the moment.

"Xalivar's not going to like it," Hachim commented. For Tarkanius, that would be a plus.

"Xalivar's not going to have a choice," Kray said. "How much longer should we wait? Until half our system is starving and demanding peace?"

They exchanged knowing looks. That time was fast approaching.

"The Council does have the authority to arrange conferences with other governmental bodies," Niger said.

"Yes. And even though Xalivar must be the one to negotiate, if we set the agenda, he'll have little choice," Kray said. The others smiled and nodded, knowing what had to be done.

"Simeon and I will prepare the official release," Tarkanius said, feeling a sudden lightness coming over him now that they were finally doing something. "Say nothing of this meeting to anyone until we're ready. We need to hold a secret vote to approve it. Xalivar must not get wind of it before it's released."

The others' faces told him they all understood.

Two neat rows of reflector pads in the center of the ceiling reflected light off the white walls with a strength that would have been blinding if Miri weren't used to it by now. She spent endless hours pacing in an attempt to loosen up her rigid muscles, but within a few moments of relaxing, they hardened again, no matter how many times she tried. Except for daily trips to the sanitation room, she'd been imprisoned now for over a month—at the high security prison Centauri Two on the opposite side of Legallis from Legon.

Located on an island in the middle of a large sea with no land around for miles, it was approachable through a few select mine-free channels via water or air—its location and approach channels so secret, Miri only knew about them from discussions she'd overheard between Xalivar and others in the past. She wasn't supposed to have known the place existed until she arrived there.

She'd even grown accustomed to the bright red prison issue jumpsuit she had been forced to wear day in, day out since her arrival. A far cry from the usual wardrobe of a princess, at least it was comfortable and she didn't have to wear it out in public. It made her feel like a giant red Vertullian cherry.

As she ran a hand through her hair and flipped through channels on her vidscreen—her sole connection with the outside world—for the fifth time that day, she stopped at Orson Sterling's newscast.

*Ah, yes, Orson. I could sure use your help about now.* She used the remote to turn up the volume.

The words "Breaking Story" flashed on the screen as she heard: "The Peace Conference is scheduled to take place at the end of the week at Presimion Academy, the Borali Alliance's leading school for future military leaders. Depending, of course, on whether the leaders of the workers agree to it in their talks with the envoy sent by the Council."

*What? Peace Conference?*

"High Lord Councilor Xalivar has yet to comment on the idea of negotiations with the workers. But it's unprecedented in Boralian history. Perhaps since Worker's Freedom Resistance fighters today attacked an Alliance transport on its way to deliver food to Xanthis, times have changed. Most citizens of the Alliance seem unopposed to peace with the workers, and with food supplies dwindling, time is running out for military successes. Soon, it will be a matter of survival for our people. Xalivar himself is expected to lead the negotiations at the Conference."

Miri shook her head. Xalivar negotiating at a peace conference? How had anyone convinced him to do that? He would be dead set against it. The Council must have forced the issue. Xalivar would never have agreed to it on his own.

A message indicator flashed on the vidscreen—she had an e-post. She couldn't send e-posts out but could still receive them. Since he was the only person who knew her location, she knew it must be from Xalivar. She leaned forward with her stiff neck and used the remote to flick over and read the message.

**To: Prisoner157.83A@Centaurill.emp**
**From: HLC@Federal.emp**
**Subject: Status of Xander Rhii**

Hello dear sister,

I hope this finds you well. You'll be delighted to know the Council, in their infinite wisdom or ignorance, has declared a peace conference which I must attend. It won't surprise you to know I have special plans for Davi and his friends at this conference. They may soon be joining you in your lovely new home. Unless, of course, I decide to execute them on the spot.

Enjoy using your wonderful imagination to ponder what will happen to your son and his friends, my dear sister.

Your loving brother,
Xalivar

Miri couldn't believe her eyes. *Would Xalivar really openly defy the Council? Of course he would! What could they do about it after it was all over? And if he were successful at squelching the workers' Resistance in the process…?*

Alarms set off in her mind. *How can I get a message to Kray? I have to warn her! Council members must attend the Conference. Farien!* She ran to the door of the cell and hit the buzzer to call one of the guards.

Farien had arrived there two weeks before as Assistant to the Head of prison security, an assignment arranged by his father, who had several friends on the Council. The move was a slight demotion but still not the fall to disgrace he might have expected. Farien's work on Vertullis had gotten him high marks, despite his run in with Bordox, and he seemed grateful to still have an important job. Farien had always been fond of her, Miri knew, and they'd had some pleasant conversations since his arrival there. He'd told her about his encounter with Bordox, guilt ridden over his betrayal of Davi, feeling even worse because he had been more concerned about his own career than their friendship.

Hearing the facts, Miri had assured him Davi wouldn't blame him. She knew it would be wrong to exploit his guilt, but people's lives were at stake. Miri would beg him to break protocol this once and send a message for her. He was loyal to Davi, and when she explained the situation, he would be sympathetic. She hoped so. If not, she would make him realize the opportunity this provided for him to make amends.

She focused, preparing herself, and checked her hair and appearance in the mirror. She needed to be at her best for this meeting. As the lock clicked, she took a deep breath and hurried over. *Gods give me strength*, she prayed as Farien entered her cell.

His face was full of concern as he looked her over. She knew she appeared harried, as her sleep had been intermittent for weeks and she'd lost weight, too, either from stress or from skipping meals. Farien was too polite to comment but all of it registered in his eyes as he spoke, "I got an urgent message saying you needed to see me, Princess. Is everything okay?"

Miri smiled, wrapping her arm around his and turning on the charm. "Yes, I'm fine, but I need your help with something."

"I'll do what I can, of course," he said with a nod.

"I need you to get a message out for me," she said, pressing a folded slip of paper into his open hand.

Farien looked down at his hand a moment, shifting uncomfortably. "You know I'd do anything for you, but there are strict protocols here . . ."

"It's urgent," she pleaded, her blue eyes locking onto his. "Davi might be in danger."

Farien glanced at her a moment and she held his gaze. "I wouldn't know where to send him a message these days. Besides, after the way I betrayed him, why would he trust me?"

"The message is for Lord Kray," Miri said.

"Of the High Council?" Farien's eyes clouded as his eyebrows squished together with uncertainty..

Miri nodded. "Xalivar is planning to betray Davi and his friends at the peace conference." She grabbed the remote off her bed and pulled the e-post up on her vidscreen. "The Council must be warned."

Farien read the e-post off the screen, his face changing as he finished.

"You've been his lifelong friend, Farien," Miri said. "He needs us now more than ever. Please help me help him."

Farien's face filled with anger as he moved toward the door, offering only a curt nod.

Miri smiled, running over to embrace him. "Thank you, dear Farien!"

He nodded and rapped urgently on the door with the back of his hand.

Davi's stomach clinched and his skin tingled as Aron repeated it for the third time.

"An envoy from the Alliance is seeking to arrange a peace conference."

The WFR leaders sat around the table in the command center conference room in numb silence as they pondered it.

"It's totally unprecedented," Joram said. "The Borali Alliance has never asked for peace before, let alone agreed to sit down across the table with workers."

Davi could hardly believe it himself. The Xalivar he knew would never want this. "Xalivar wouldn't agree to this unless he had no choice." He'd been immediately suspicious and even after thinking about it, he remained unsettled. He glanced around. The room was in disarray resulting from constant use: full waste bins, discarded datacards on the floor, fingerprints on the surface of the table amidst the stain rings left by beverages.

"The announcement came from the Council, not the Palace," Uzah said. "They did, however, say the High Lord Councilor would attend."

"He has to, by law," Aron said. "It's his place to lead any negotiations. They've just never done it before."

"It's not the kind of precedent you'd expect Xalivar to set," Uzah said.

"So, it's a trap?" Joram wondered.

"Of course it is!" Matheu said. "We must not allow ourselves to be easily lulled." Davi had to agree.

"I agree," Uzah said. "A trap would be very much like Xalivar."

Grumbles of agreement came from others around the table. Several nodded, including Davi.

"At the same time, we can't afford to ignore it," Aron said. "Not if there's even the slightest chance that they're serious."

They all paused, eyes meeting across the table. Clearly Davi wasn't alone in having a hard time believing it. Still, he wanted to. Like everyone else, he wanted the fighting to end as soon as possible.

"The question then is, who do we risk having captured?" Matheu said sternly.

Davi leaned back in his chair as the eyes of the others fell on him. "He'll want me to be there," he said, "as a matter of personal pride." He dreaded the encounter, but knew he had to go. Xalivar would refuse to negotiate without him.

"We need you to lead the fighters. You can't be risked," Matheu said.

"We can't afford to risk any of our leadership, but we have no choice," Aron said. "Davi's right. Xalivar may well refuse to meet if he's not there."

"This war is not some personal family vendetta," Matheu said.

"Xalivar won't see it that way. To him, our Resistance and my rebellion are synonymous," Davi said.

"We can't afford to blow the conference by holding him back," Joram said.

"Agreed," said Aron.

A couple of others nodded and mumbled in agreement.

"I'm not afraid to go," Davi said. "It's time I faced him. Besides, if I ever want to put the issues between Xalivar and I behind me, I'll have to face him sooner or later."

"Of course," Uzah said as he poured himself some Xanthian tea from a pitcher on the table, "the question is whether this conference will be the best place for that."

Following his lead, others began filling their glasses as well. Xanthian tea was a traditional soothant, often used at important meetings and conferences to help people relax. Davi poured his glass with a smile. He needed to relax.

"May I suggest I meet with the envoy and hear the Alliance's expectations for the conference before we make any decision?" Aron suggested.

They all sat there a moment sipping their tea. Davi could feel a rush of calm winding through his body as the tea flowed down his throat into his stomach. It had been ages since he'd had Xanthian tea—once or twice as a child, if he recalled right. He liked it better than he'd remembered.

After a moment, General Matheu nodded. "Aron and Joram will meet with the envoy and return to us. Then we can make our decision."

Davi saw from everyone's faces that they were in agreement. Matheu dismissed the meeting without further discussion, and they all hurried back to their assigned tasks.

Xalivar entered his conference room like a hurricane. His military officials shrank back in their seats upon seeing his face. *Some warriors these are!*

He paced in a circle at the head of the table, feeling disgusted at the weakness of the Council, as they waited for him to speak. He'd known the public had become weaklings, but to see the once-great Lords of the Borali Alliance reduced to sniveling fools was too much. He must step forward and lead the Alliance back to its former glory. He would do whatever it took, even if it meant declaring martial law and dissolving the government. The thought of that made him smile.

*Yes. Yes! I am the leader with the courage and will it takes to restore the Alliance! And I will not quit until I do!* His fists clenched at his sides.

He turned back to the table. Lucius, Pres and Dek reacted to the smile on his face with surprise.

"You've all seen the news reports, I'm sure."

They nodded without speaking.

"The conference will take place at Presimion Academy in four days. Lucius and I will be in attendance, along with Lord Obed and our aides. I want the fleet assembled and ready to attack upon my orders before the conference commences."

"The Council has ordered us to negotiate," Dek said.

Xalivar silenced him with a cold stare, fists clenching again. "The Borali Alliance doesn't negotiate! If the Council has forgotten it, they are no longer fit to lead our people. The Council and the people have become weak. It threatens the entire foundation of our Alliance. We must have the strength to do what must be done."

"We live to serve you, my Lord," Pres said. "But how can we go up against the Council?"

"You answer to me, not the Council. So let me worry about the Council, while you worry about obeying my orders!" Xalivar's tone and expression made it clear he would entertain no arguments.

The leaders exchanged a look, then nodded.

"Of course, we will obey, my Lord," Lucius said.

"The fleet is close to being assembled," Dek said. "Everyone can be ready in time."

Xalivar smiled again, his hands relaxed and open. "Good, Admiral. I'm glad to hear it. Lord Obed will be arranging my security for the conference, in cooperation with Professor Yao Brohma of the Academy. Please make any resources you can spare available to him."

"The air forces will be at his disposal, my Lord," Pres said. "We can move several squadrons there as needed."

"I am sure two would be sufficient," Xalivar said.

"It will be done, my Lord," Pres said.

Xalivar nodded. He liked their attitudes—total compliance. The Alliance would need more people with the same attitude to regain their former glory. "Very good. General, Admiral, see to it, while General Lucius and I discuss more details of the conference."

Dek and Pres stood and saluted. "Yes, my Lord."

As they hurried out, Xalivar took a seat at the head of the table, nodding to Lucius.

"These are dark days for the Alliance, my Lord," Lucius said.

"Indeed they are," Xalivar agreed, his eyes narrowing with determination. "Let us work together to be a source of light."

Lucius nodded. "We will do what must be done, my Lord."

Xalivar pulled out a datacard and slid it across the table to Lucius. "These are the things which must be done, General."

Lucius began looking it over as Xalivar watched, anticipating the moment when his plan would finally unfold. The light from the reflector pads shone off the table with a sparkle matching the excitement inside him. All he had done before, all he had prepared for had led him to this moment. He knew the city outside carried on its daily business blissfully unaware of the pressures he faced. But his true greatness would soon be revealed.

# Chapter Thirteen

The Royal Shuttles waited at the spaceport to take them to Presimion Academy for the peace conference as Xalivar held one last meeting with his military leaders. He walked confidently into the conference room, hands flat at his sides, and smiled. The leaders waited in nervous silence, relaxing when they saw his calm expression.

"So, my dear friends, is everything ready?" Xalivar asked.

Dek nodded, a confident smile on his face. "The fleet is fully assembled and ready to attack upon your order, my Lord."

"Ground forces can be deployed as soon as the shield is neutralized. They're waiting and ready to launch at your command," Pres said.

They each spoke in a rush, as if anxious to please him. "Good, good," Xalivar sat down, leaning back in his chair at the head of the table. He could taste the victory. "General Lucius?"

"Lord Obed informs me all security arrangements for the conference are satisfactory, and I am ready to accompany you, my Lord," the General responded.

The enthusiasm in their voices matched his own excitement at the anticipated victory. *Yes, soon the Alliance's greatness will be restored!* "You have all done well, my friends. The Alliance will remember and honor your loyalty and dedication. Our finest moment has arrived!" At last, some officers worthy of his confidence.

"We are honored to serve, my Lord," Lucius said. The others nodded, then all three stood and saluted him.

"We will depart at once," Xalivar said to Lucius. "I want constant reports when the battle begins," he instructed the others.

"Of course, my Lord," Pres and Dek said in unison.

Xalivar stood and they saluted again. "May the gods be with us." He turned toward the door with Lucius following right behind him.

"May the gods be with us," he heard Lucius say.

Xalivar hadn't been so invigorated in years. At last, a major victory to remind the people who their hero ought to be. Yes, he would be hailed as the hero who restored the Borali Alliance! He picked up his pace, feeling his heart pounding—Lucius' footfalls behind him keeping time with it.

Aboard the small floater on the way to the starport, Xalivar lost himself in thought, warmth radiating through his chest. He felt lighter than he had in years. Soon the WFR leadership would be shattered. His rogue nephew would be imprisoned along with the other leaders. Morale would falter. The rest would fall apart at the Alliance's show of force. It would be a matter of hours before victory was his. Xalivar had no doubt. The best part of all was knowing none of the weaklings on the Council would have time to object. By the time they did, it would be too late. He chuckled at the thought. How they would whine and wail. He would see to their replacements after it was over. For now, let them whine. Xalivar had the upper hand.

Knowing all this would occur at his alma mater made it much sweeter. He was a distinguished alumnus already, but these events would make him a legend. For the first time in a long while, he experienced true happiness.

Bordox sat at the back of the shuttle behind his father, who'd instructed him to keep a low profile until the right moment. Xalivar might have objected to his presence, but Obed had been told to handle the arrangements, giving him the authority to choose his own men. So he'd chosen his own son for two reasons: he wanted Bordox to prove himself to Xalivar once and for all. He also wanted his son nearby should the opportunity arise to finally bring down his longtime rival. This scandal provided the best opportunity since the Delta V disaster to see their family returned to its proper place on the throne. Should Xalivar fail to make peace, Obed had confessed, it was sure Xalivar's family would lose the throne. Obed and his son would be front and center to save the day when that happened.

Bordox had cleaned and pressed his uniform, determined not to let his father down. He had a career to salvage, after the embarrassing failure on Vertullis. He cursed under his breath. He'd had enough of Xander

Rhii getting in the way of his success. The imbecile had been doing it since the Academy and it was time Bordox turned things around on him. He would do whatever was necessary to ensure his nemesis was tried for treason.

It gave him immense pleasure to know one of the last things his nemesis would see as a free man would be the wrong end of Bordox's blaster as he helped put an end to Rhii's freedom. In fact, he felt almost weightless at the thought of it.

While waiting for the shuttle to depart, Davi thought over how much his life had changed in the past few months.

He'd spent the prior evening at Lura's house, having dinner with Lura, Tela, Nila, and Nila's family. While Davi relaxed, confident the peace conference would come off without a problem, everyone else worried he would be walking into the arms of the enemy. He'd done his best to reassure them. He had known Xalivar his whole life. His uncle had always treated him like a son. Yes, Xalivar felt angry and betrayed by him, but Davi couldn't believe Xalivar would ever harm him. On top of everything else, the Council and population of the Alliance had been pressing for peace. Xalivar knew his options were limited. He would grouse and growl but some compromise had to be found.

Lura interrupted his thoughts by raising her glass of Talis to propose a toast. "Here's to Captain Davi Rhii, a true hero for our people." She choked up as she said it, and Nila reached over to hug her aunt to her.

"Here! Here!" the others said, as they tapped their glasses to hers.

Davi tried not to blush. "I've done what was right," he said. "I deserve no praise for it."

"You've risen well beyond the call of duty," Tela said. "We wouldn't have the air forces we have if it weren't for you."

"I know I would have never been able to fly," Nila said.

Davi smiled. "You succeeded because of your ability, not mine." He was so proud of his cousin.

"You taught me everything I know," Nila said, refusing to let him off the hook. They raised their glasses again and clanked them together.

"Your father would be very proud," Lura said. "We used to imagine the future, as we waited for you to be born. It was so hard for us, because we wanted a child very much but weren't sure what kind of world we'd be bringing you into. Life as a slave was not what we wanted for you."

Davi smiled. "Soon, none of us will have to live as slaves any longer."

"Thanks to you," Tela said.

Davi focused his eyes on his plate, embarrassed. They seemed determined to give him far too much credit. He hadn't acted alone.

Tela continued, "You've provided the leadership we needed to succeed. Without your knowledge and skills, we would have failed."

"All of the leaders are good men. I'm not so important," Davi said, sipping his own Talis and hoping the moment would pass.

"I wish your father could see you now," Lura said, her eyes growing misty. "You have become so much more than we could have ever imagined."

Davi stood and moved around the table toward her. "You'll see him again someday, I promise." They embraced as tears filled both of their eyes.

"From your mouth to God's ears," Lura said. "It's all I have left to hope for."

"I promise as soon as the peace conference is over, I'll find him," Davi said, meaning every word, and his chest felt lighter saying them. For a moment, he believed it was possible.

The others wiped their eyes, fighting back tears. "Wow, Captain, you sure know how to bring people down, don't you?" Tela teased.

They all laughed. Lura smiled, wiping her eyes. "And I can't wait for Sol to meet you, too, Tela. You'll make such a fine addition to our family."

Tela smiled. "Thank you." She looked straight at Davi, who tried not to meet her eyes as he moved back to his seat.

Nila chuckled, picking up on the cue. "Yes, so did you discuss it yet? You're joining?"

Tela laughed. "Before I met Davi, I never thought I'd ever want to be joined with anyone." Her eyes twinkled as she glanced at Davi.

Davi squirmed in his chair. "Can we try and get the war settled first?"

Everyone laughed. His aunt Rena patted his shoulder, enjoying Davi's discomfort.

"Are you saying the war is more important than me?" Tela teased. Davi blushed again. "Ah, the great military Academy graduate blushing, how wonderful. So strong you are!"

Davi pretended to punch her in the arm.

"Okay, okay, I'll stop."

Tela would be with him at the conference. Why weren't they worried about her? As he searched his mind for something interesting to distract them with, Lura pushed her chair back from the table and stood.

"Let us go before the Lord in prayer for the safety of our leadership and successful negotiations tomorrow," Lura said.

They bowed their heads as she led them in prayer.

Slipping out of the reverie, Davi glanced over at Tela, sitting next to him on the shuttle. Thankful to have her with him for this historic moment, he lifted up a silent prayer for God's protection, for Xalivar to be calm and reasonable, and for the hoped-for peace to become a reality. So much depended on this moment. *Please God, don't let us fail our people.*

Engines whirred and the shuttle accelerated, pushing him back in his seat. Tela held her breath beside him, meditating as she always did during a launch. The pressure eased as the shuttle entered its flight path. In a few hours, he would be face-to-face with the uncle he'd always adored. He hoped some of those fond memories and old feelings would make things easier as they met.

Rain fell as the shuttle landed on Eleni 1, the largest of Legallis' moons; a soft, silvery drizzle which draped itself over everything then slowly built to a slimy, slick coating. Davi and Tela stepped out and felt the cold rain against their cheeks; Davi hoped it wasn't a portent of things to come. A familiar dark-skinned humanoid stood waiting to escort them to the conference.

Davi grinned and raised his hand, hurrying to greet him. "Yao! Good to see you again!" They clasped hands and then embraced.

"You look pretty good—for a rebel." Yao said as they both laughed.

Davi turned to Tela, her eyes betraying her curiosity. He introduced Yao as a professor at Presimion. "Ah, so he's the one you leaned on to get you through the Academy," Tela teased.

"You have no idea," Yao said deadpan then laughed, turning to Davi again. "She has you figured out already?"

Davi smiled and introduced the other leaders.

Yao led them toward the cluster of buildings that composed the campus of Presimion Academy. Designed in a style befitting their age—Presimion was one of the oldest academies in the solar system—the buildings showed signs of improvement; modern touches to the windows combined with outdoor lighting and modern landscaping.

Yao led them toward a large building where a lighted sign beside the path declared: "Lord Killeen Library and Conference Center."

"The campus is quite impressive," Aron said with real admiration.

"Thank you," Yao said. "We're quite proud of it. It's the oldest Academy in the system. Many fine leaders have graduated from these hallowed halls." Yao stopped in front of double-paned sliding doors. "Welcome to Lord Killeen Library, friends," he said as the doors slid open.

They stepped inside into a reader's wonderland. In addition to rows of video terminals and data card storage shelves, the library also housed a large collection of Old Earth books—the kind actually printed on paper. These were housed on special shelves enclosed in see-through fiberglass-like walls to protect them from damage by the air and other impurities. They all stopped and took in the view with awe. The shelves and terminals stretched up seven stories, reachable by a series of lifts or spiral staircases designed to appear as if they floated on air. Light from large reflector pads sparkled off them like the glint of the morning suns' first rays upon a window. Combined with the ominous silence of the space surrounding them, it lent almost a fairy-tale atmosphere to the place.

"Hallowed halls, indeed," Davi mumbled, then heard it echo, amplified by the space.

Tela's eyes met Davi's. "I've never seen anything like this." Though she spoke at almost a whisper, the natural amplification made it sound like she'd leaned very close to his ear.

"It's reputed to be one of the finest libraries in the Alliance," Yao responded proudly. Davi's pride swelled as well. He'd always loved this place.

They moved on into the conference center part of the building—a stark contrast from the library. Here white walls reflected bright light from reflector pads, contrasted only by a drab gray tile floor. The doors were inset but also white and designed to slide into the wall when opening. Other than the Presimion Academy crest covering most of one wall, the walls were undecorated.

They turned a corner and stopped before large double doors. Davi looked around. Given the size of the doors and the wall into which they were cut, Davi guessed a sizable space lay behind them. Surprisingly, he'd never had reason to explore that when he was a cadet—a missed opportunity. He'd ask Yao about it later.

"I assisted with security arrangements," Yao said. "I hope Xalivar doesn't make things too hard on you."

Davi smiled. "He won't be happy, will he?"

Yao shook his head, chuckling.

Lord Obed appeared with a cordon of LSP men, surrounding them. "I'm afraid no security men can be allowed in the chamber."

Yao frowned. "That was not agreed upon."

"Plans have changed," Obed said with a stern look.

Yao glanced at Davi, confusion rife on his face.

"Will the High Lord Councilor's security be allowed inside?" Davi asked, frowning. Having Obed and the LSP in charge made him nervous. He could feel sweat beading on his forehead and under his arms already.

"You are in Boralian space," Obed said. "Alliance forces provide all security here."

The LSP troops began searching their escorts. Aron motioned for the WFR security men to allow the search, despite their worried expressions.

The doors slid open to reveal a large, elaborately decorated chamber with a long center table surrounded by chairs. A raised balcony circled the room above their heads, with bleacher seats in many rows.

"The rest of you may enter," Obed said with a wave.

Aron nodded and stepped forward into the room. Tela and Davi watched the LSP men a moment, feeling reticent about what had happened then followed Aron and Joram into the room.

Yao entered last. "I'm sorry. This was not supposed to happen."

"Perhaps the High Lord Councilor is already up to mischief," Tela whispered, her eyes nervous.

Davi tried to hide his own worries, wanting to reassure her but she reached out to squeeze his hand and he knew it wouldn't matter. "We'll find out soon enough," he said, watching as Aron and Joram took seats along the center of the table facing the door. He and Tela took the seats next to them as the few aides who'd been allowed in arranged themselves amongst the rest of the chairs.

A bar-bot appeared to take drink orders, its facial LEDs lit up in an electronic smile.

"Let me try and find out what's going on," Yao said, worried.

Davi shook his head. "You can't go up against Obed or Xalivar. Let's wait and see."

Aron nodded. "We have little choice."

"I'll be back," Yao insisted. The doors slid open and Yao disappeared into the corridor.

Xalivar's Royal Shuttle arrived on the opposite side of campus from where the WFR contingent had arrived. Instead of one shuttle, he came with two—the other filled with security men and aides.

As Xalivar and Lucius stepped onto the landing pad, Manaen and Lucius' aide rushed forward with rainguards to protect them from the weather. Xalivar looked around—a dreary day, indeed. Soon their mood at least would be brightened. He smiled. So far, everything had gone according to their well-thought-out plans.

As he stepped forward, he saw Lord Obed hurrying toward them with two aides, one of whom held a rainguard over Obed's head. Xalivar smiled thinking about how easy it had been to convince the Council to make Obed their representative at the peace conference.

"Everything has gone as planned, Lord Xalivar," Obed said with a smile as he stopped before them.

"They offered no argument?"

"Only your nephew and his friend seemed bothered," Obed said.

Xalivar smiled. *Of course they were.* "They are waiting in the chamber?"

Obed nodded. "Yes. And their escorts have already been sealed away in a secure location."

Xalivar chuckled, feeling a lightness in his steps. "Good, good." His hands clenched into fists and released again. "This will be a triumphant moment for us, Lord Obed. I'm pleased you can be a part of it."

"The honor is mine, Lord Xalivar," Obed said, joining them as they continued along the pathway.

Xalivar smiled. He had his most trusted people with him today. They were intensely loyal. The only one he'd questioned had been Lord Obed, but Obed had thrown his support behind Xalivar. It reassured him to have his rival nearby where Xalivar could keep an eye on him. Xalivar's grandfather had often said: "the safest place for your enemy is right beside you." It's why Xalivar had appointed Obed to head the LSP. Since the head of the LSP reported directly to the High Lord Councilor, Xalivar could keep a careful eye on him. If things went wrong somehow at the conference, Xalivar would be sure that Obed took the blame.

He glanced over at Lucius and their eyes met. Lucius nodded. The fleet was moving into position over Vertullis. Xalivar's fists clenched again. He could almost taste the sweetness of victory. He would make sure his former nephew and friends knew they had been beaten. He wanted them to taste the defeat even as it happened. It would make up in small part for the humiliations and frustrations they'd caused him over the past months. Soon, they'd have nothing but time to think about it.

The Alliance flagship Victory hovered in position off Jacote, Vertullis' largest moon, as Admiral Dek and General Pres stared out the bridge blast shield at the gathering fleet.

Dek smiled, feeling relieved to be on his bridge again, a far more comfortable and safer place than facing the wrath of the High Lord Councilor. Here, he was at home and in command, and he could already taste the victory that would soon be theirs. It had been a long time since he'd led a fleet into battle, and he had been much younger then. The only action he'd seen since had been during military exercises. How good it would be for his men to practice what they'd been learning. It would keep them fresh and ready, giving them greater confidence in their abilities and training.

Perhaps there would be a resurgence of reenlistments afterwards. The military had seen increased retirements and resignations over the past several years. They needed to renew the sense of pride and commitment in their forces—something a good victory would help ensure.

"Troop ships have launched and will arrive on schedule," Pres said, interrupting his thoughts.

Dek nodded. "Thank you, General. I am pleased you are here for this historic moment."

"I wouldn't miss it," Pres said, glancing at her chrono. "The negotiations should commence momentarily." She stood next to him, also looking at home and relaxed in the same way Dek himself was. She found Xalivar's moods just as difficult to endure. It felt good having her there. She'd become Dek's right hand and close friend, and although he knew she regarded him as a mentor, he'd come to trust her as a valued peer.

"And they will last but a few moments, I'm sure," Dek said with a grin. They both laughed at the thought of the disappointment and surprise the WFR leadership would experience.

"The planetary radar is jammed?" Pres asked.

"All the jamming ships are in position awaiting my command," Dek said with confidence.

Pres nodded. "We await your orders, Admiral."

Dek nodded, moving to the rail lining the walkway where they stood, looking down on the bridge. "Captain, order the Century ships to begin jamming the radar."

Below them on the command deck, Captain Colson turned to nod at them, his crisp, clean uniform so tight it fit him like an outer skin. "Lieutenant, issue the order."

"Yes, sir," a Lieutenant said from a nearby comm-panel. "Century craft: commence jamming at once," he said into the comm-channel, his face full of anticipation.

Captain Colson turned back to Pres and Dek, nodding.

"All ships full ahead," Dek ordered.

Colson turned to his men and repeated the order as the two leaders turned back to the screen. Soon it would all be over.

The WFR contingent waited around the large conference table for forty-five minutes before the doors opened and Xalivar entered. He wore the ceremonial robe he reserved for Council ceremonies and important events, walking as if he'd already won. He was accompanied by General Lucius, whom Davi had met at the Academy, as well as Lord Obed, Manaen, and other aides. They moved to the opposite side of the table and spread out—with Xalivar across the table from Davi and Aron.

Xalivar remained standing as the others sat, a smug smile on his face as his eyes met Davi's. "Well, the prodigal nephew returns. You look well. But I'm afraid I cannot say you've been making us proud, can I?"

Davi smiled. "It is good to see you again, un—" He stopped himself. *Don't call him that anymore.* "High Lord Councilor."

Xalivar frowned. "Ah, so soon we forget our family, is that how it is? A bitter sting upon my heart." He actually touched his fist to his chest a moment before sliding into his seat at the table, eyes still locked onto Davi's. "And after all our efforts to raise you with honor, give you the finest things in life …" His voice trailed off and a sad look came upon his face.

Davi knew the emotions were all for show. He tried to detect something in his voice—a clue to his frame of mind—but, as usual, Xalivar stayed controlled.

Davi allowed a bit of emotion to creep into his own voice. "I am grateful for all you have done for me, uncle. I have not forgotten. I owe you a great deal."

"Ah, I see, so you call me uncle when it's convenient then," Xalivar said. Davi kept his eyes locked on Xalivar, trying not to flinch. "You did, however, turn out to be somewhat of a disappointment." The last bit was pure accusation.

The words stung. "I'm sorry you feel that way," Davi said. "I have always tried to live by what you and mother taught me. My sole desire was to make you proud."

Xalivar laughed, his eyes sparkling with amusement. "Make me proud? By betraying the Alliance? Betraying your family? Betraying me?"

"By following my conscience, upholding my sense of honor, and serving with bravery and integrity," Davi said.

Xalivar's face changed to fury as he clenched his fists atop the table. "There can be no integrity in betrayal, Xander." He looked away, taking in the others.

"I can assure you, High Lord Councilor, your nephew has distinguished himself well by his service to us, as a pilot, an instructor, and a leader," Aron said with a smile. "You can be very proud."

Xalivar's head whirled toward Aron, locking eyes, fists clenching. "Honorable men take no pride in acts of rebellion!"

"I believe we have come to discuss the cessation of hostilities," Aron said, still smiling as if unphased. They'd expected Xalivar's hostility and his mental games, and Aron apparently was more prepared than Davi.

Xalivar pounded his fist onto the table. "I will decide what we do or don't discuss!" He glanced away a moment, appearing to collect himself. You could have heard a pin drop as everyone waited in silent anticipation, hesitating to even breathe. Xalivar turned back toward them. "You realize, of course, I could have you executed?"

"The peace conference was arranged by the Council of Lords," Davi said as firmly as he could manage. "You are in no position to even arrest us." His eyes locked on Xalivar's.

Xalivar's stare was like a knife slicing meat. "Do not tell me about my position, Captain."

"Why was our security contingent refused entry to this conference?" Aron asked, his voice revealing the tension inside him. "It was agreed upon in the terms."

"You are in Boralian space, not locked behind your stolen energy shield," Xalivar said. "I determine the arrangements for this conference, not you."

"So this conference was a ruse to lure us here under false pretenses?" Davi said, letting his frustration show.

"Ah, now who feels betrayed?" Xalivar said with a laugh. "The Borali Alliance does not negotiate with rebels. It's a long and proud tradition. I'm sure you studied it at the Academy."

The WFR contingent stood, chairs squeaking against the floor as they scooted back from the table. "In the name of interstellar law, we demand just treatment," Aron said, more irritated than Davi had ever seen him.

"Oh, you will receive just treatment for your actions," Xalivar said with a smile, "In prison. Take them into custody."

The doors opened and Bordox entered with a squad of LSP troops, weapons held at the ready. Davi's nemesis' sneer had never been bigger or more menacing.

Klaxons blared throughout the complex as controllers and technicians raced to their stations around Uzah and Matheu.

"What is it?" Uzah asked, the worry on his face matching his voice.

"The Alliance fleet just came around from the far side of Jacote," Matheu said.

Uzah's face showed immediate understanding. Jacote, the planet's largest moon, was the perfect place for a fleet to conceal itself before a surprise attack. "How many?"

"Four flagships, twenty Defenders, and thirty other craft of varying size," Matheu said, motioning to the large radar at the center of the room.

Uzah saw red blips on the screen moving toward the planet.

"Plus, whatever squadrons of fighters they can hold."

The moment they'd feared had arrived. Uzah hoped they were all ready. He took a deep breath and nodded, steeling himself. "Pilots to their fighters," Uzah ordered over the comm-channel on his headset. He heard the command repeated three times by the combat computer. "Our fighters won't be able to handle them all."

"They'll have to break through the shield first," Matheu said, raising his voice to be heard over the clamor around them as technicians and controllers exchanged data and checked their systems in preparation for the imminent attack.

"How long will it take them?" Uzah asked, dreading the answer.

"With a fleet that size? A matter of an hour or two, if we're lucky," Matheu said, his voice betrayed his lack of confidence—something Uzah had never seen before in the stern military man. Matheu had always been a steady source of strength among the leadership—his bitter past experiences fighting the Alliance hardening him to the realities of war.

"Ground troops are setting up the shield reinforcers at key points," a controller said from nearby.

"Very good," Matheu said, nodding to the controller. "They will help protect the shield control center once the Alliance breaks through. It's going to be a long night." He turned to a nearby controller who'd been motioning to them.

Uzah moved toward the communications center to his right. "Try and get a message out to our contingent at the peace conference."

"I've been trying, sir. They're jamming us," the controller said, shaking her head. *So it begins.*

Dek and Pres stood together on the bridge of the Alliance flagship Victory as the fleet moved into full view of the planet. "The shield is coming into solid range of our cannons now, sir," a radar technician nearby said.

Dek nodded at the man and smiled to Pres. "Let the fun begin." He was enjoying himself.

Pres chuckled. "I imagine the worker rebels must be in a bit of a panic already."

The Admiral laughed and raised his eyebrows. "It would be fun to see their faces, wouldn't it?"

Red lights flashed and klaxons blared as the battle stations alert sounded throughout the fleet. The command center filled with commotion. Everyone hurried about their final preparations for the attack.

Dek was proud to serve a leader with the strength and clarity to do what it takes. Those kinds of leaders had been the ones he'd always admired in history. Given the track record of the Borali Alliance over the past fifty years, he'd always doubted he would serve under one. He didn't know why others in the Alliance couldn't see how lucky they were.

*After this they all will see.*

He watched fighters launching from nearby ships. Victory was finally at hand.

"We hoped things would be handled with honor this time," Aron said staring defiantly at Xalivar.

It took Davi a moment to believe Xalivar would really betray them. He'd known Xalivar would be a tough negotiator, ruling with ruthless strength and determination. Xalivar had a reputation. But Davi had never seen this side of his uncle and he'd hoped for the best. Still, Xalivar had changed, and the evidence was clear. He'd sent Bordox, the most ruthless person he could choose, to hunt Davi down in the Vertullian jungles, clearly having sided with the Council to declare Davi a wanted criminal. Now here he was betraying his nephew yet again.

Bordox stood staring at him, his angry eyes never leaving Davi's face. *Oh yeah, you're enjoying this aren't you?*

He hadn't been surprised to see Bordox. After all, one of Xalivar's favorite tricks was exploiting the weaknesses of others. Davi had watched for years as Xalivar did it to Miri. And Xalivar would know how much glee Bordox would take in arresting his old rival, and how that might make Davi feel. Besides, Lord Obed would want to include his son in the scheme. Obed had always been the type of stern father Davi couldn't imagine growing up with. As a result, Bordox's hardness had never really surprised him. What happened next did.

"There can be no honor for traitors!" Xalivar unclenched his fists again and motioned to Davi. "Bring him with me. Take the rest of them to where we're holding the others."

*The others? Does he mean our security team and aides?* Davi didn't even have time to ask.

Bordox tore him out of the chair and shoved him toward the double doors. "Move, traitor!"

Davi stumbled but managed to stay on his feet. Glancing back, Bordox's smug smile showed he was enjoying this. "We demand treatment for prisoners of war as governed by military statute…"

Bordox cut him off by shoving him through the door. "Walk faster, Xander!" he said with a sneer.

"You will be treated as the workers you are," Xalivar said, his eyes cold, his face a sneer as he followed them into the corridor and moving ahead of Bordox. Manaen and two LSP men followed close behind.

"Where are you taking me?" Davi asked, his voice sounding stronger than he felt.

"You'll know soon enough," Xalivar said. Davi saw no sign of the old tenderness with which his uncle had once regarded him, even when he'd first raised the issue of the workers after beginning his assignment on Vertullis. Something had changed in the man, and his nephew barely recognized him. Davi felt even sadder at that realization.

Manaen's comlink beeped. Davi turned and watched as Manaen listened through his earpiece. "Thank you." Manaen raced up beside Xalivar, whispering soft enough so Davi couldn't hear.

"What are you going to do with us?" Davi asked again, with more firmness.

Bordox shoved him again as they turned a corner and moved down another corridor. It seemed like an endless tunnel of white walls.

"The same thing we're doing to your friends on Vertullis at this moment," Xalivar said, stopping and turning back with a smug smile. "Destroy you."

*Vertullis? What does he mean?* Seeing the question in Davi's eyes, Xalivar smiled triumphantly. "It will be a matter of moments before the fleet blasts through your precious energy shield," Xalivar said as he began walking again.

*A fleet? Attacking Vertullis? Of course! This would be perfect timing!* Davi did his best to hide his emotions but inside his heart and mind were racing. *We have to find a way to get a message to the base.* Uzah and Matheu would do everything possible to defend the planet. He had to get free so he could help Tela and the others.

"Who is it? Admiral Dek? General Pres?"

Xalivar smiled. "Ah yes, your old instructors are indeed participating in the destruction of your resistance."

Davi's mind raced to come up with something he could use to raise Xalivar's doubts. His uncle's greatest weakness had always been his paranoia. "Well, I hope they enjoy the surprise we have waiting for them," he said, trying to sound convincing.

"Your surprises are no match for us," Bordox said with a sneer.

"All those years in secret development at the hidden base," Davi said. "We've been hoping we'd have a chance to try it." Davi grinned, certain Xalivar's curiosity would get the best of him.

Xalivar stopped and turned back to face him.

"He's bluffing," Bordox said with mock confidence, his face betraying his doubts.

Xalivar's brown eyes locked on Davi's and they stood there staring at each other a moment. Davi didn't flinch. He had to win this bluff.

Uzah and Matheu stood at the large radar in the middle of the now chaotic command center. "The energy shield control center reported they're down to thirty percent. It can't hold much longer," Uzah said.

Matheu frowned in frustration and turned to the comm station behind them. "Launch all fighters! Prepare for enemy infiltration!"

The controller nodded and repeated the command. A klaxon sounded as Uzah and Matheu turned back to the radar.

"It took less time than we expected," Uzah said.

"They designed the shield, so they know how to exploit its weaknesses," Matheu said with a shrug as they watched blips representing the fighters launching on the radar.

A very relaxed Dek and Pres watched the attack through the bridge blast shield as a Lieutenant hurried toward them.

"Admiral, we've got two shuttles demanding clearance to land."

"Demanding clearance?" Dek frowned, his voice filled with disgust. "Who has the audacity to make demands of my ship?"

"Lord Tarkanius and members of the Council are said to be on board, sir," the Lieutenant responded.

Dek and Pres exchanged puzzled looks, frowning in unison. *Council members here?* Dek knew he had no choice. "Give them clearance, Lieutenant. And have them escorted here."

The Lieutenant nodded, hurrying away.

"Why would Council shuttles be out here?" Pres wondered aloud.

Dek shrugged. "I have no idea." *But this can't be good.* Unexpected surprises during battle rarely were. "Perhaps they want to see the victory first hand." He smiled as convincingly as he could.

Tela paced beside the conference table, worried about Davi. *Where have they taken him?* Davi being alone right now was not a good idea. Lord Obed stood in front of the double doors, smiling. *You're loving this, aren't you?*

She fought the urge to make a snide remark, as the doors burst open behind him and Yao appeared with a woman and two men in robes and a large number of armed soldiers.

"By order of the Council of Lords, you will release these people right now," the woman said to the surprised Obed.

"Lord Kray, what are you doing?" A truly shocked Obed demanded as two soldiers grabbed him and pushed him to the side. "Get your hands off me! I am a member of the Council!"

"By order of the Council, you are to be detained," Kray said, eyes full of confidence.

"This is an outrage!" Obed yelled, stiffening as he watched as Yao and other soldiers untied the hands of the WFR contingent.

Tela rubbed her wrists as the binders came loose. "Thank you. What's going on?"

"A slight change in roster for the peace negotiations," Yao said smiling.

A robed man stepped forward, his eyes warm and apologetic. "I am Lord Simeon of the Council of Lords. On behalf of the Council, we apologize for the way you've been treated here."

Aron smiled and nodded. "Thank you, Lord Simeon." He glanced at Tela. Things were getting very interesting indeed.

From the moment he saw Davi and the others in their blue WFR uniforms, Xalivar could barely hide his disgust. *Blue!* Blue represented the opposite of order—the expanse of ever changing blue skies, the blue of cresting waves, the icy tundra of Plutonis, chaos, sadness and the bitterness of Jax fruit. It seemed to him the perfect choice for worker scum. He continued staring at Davi for a moment, making a decision.

"In there." He motioned curtly toward a nearby door.

One of the LSP men opened the door and Bordox shoved Davi through. The others followed. As the door slid shut, Xalivar heard a commotion down the corridor. "See what's going on."

One of the LSP men nodded and hurried out of the room.

Xalivar turned to Davi, whose arms were being held behind his back by Bordox. "Secret weapons? A hidden base? You think one tiny planet can defeat an entire solar system?"

"With God on our side? Yes, I do," Davi said, nodding.

Xalivar clenched his fists, glaring at him. "Your false god is no match for the Alliance, Xander."

"We'll soon find out," Davi said without flinching. "And you can stop calling me that. My name's Davi now."

Xalivar's face grew angrier and he looked at Davi with a level of hatred that took his nephew aback. Xalivar turned to Bordox as Manaen reacted to something in his headset.

"My Lord—"

"What is it Manaen?" Xalivar snapped.

Manaen hurried forward, whispering in Xalivar's ear.

"Lord Kray? Lord Simeon? What?"

The LSP man returned out of breath. "There are soldiers everywhere. They're headed this way."

*What do they mean soldiers? Council members? Here? Had everyone gone mad?* His enemies seemed intent on ruining his plans, but he wouldn't allow it. He cursed, looking around them for another exit but finding none. "Bring him!"

He grabbed Bordox's blaster and aimed it at the large window along one wall. The others reacted to the sound of the laser as the glass exploded, flying everywhere.

"Bring him with me! Hurry!" Xalivar handed Bordox the blaster then stepped through the window frame, kicking glass aside with his boot as Bordox shoved Davi toward it.

Yao took a quick head count. Xalivar was missing, along with Bordox, Manaen, two guards and Davi.

"They took him down the corridor," Tela confirmed. "We have to find him."

Yao nodded, sharing her sense of urgency. He had none of the fear of his actions costing him his career one might expect at such a moment. He'd decided days ago he had no choice. This was something he had to do, the right thing to do. "Lord Kray—"

Kray motioned that she'd heard. "I'm coming, too."

Yao stopped in the doorway, motioning to a Lieutenant. "I need two squads of your best men, now."

The Lieutenant nodded, hurrying out into the corridor. Yao, Kray, and Tela followed.

Davi breathed in the fresh, clean, post-rain air as the twin suns broke through the clouds. He wondered what had happened to Tela, Yao, and his friends. His uncle's cruelty wasn't important. What mattered was their safety.

Xalivar and his officers led Davi across a broad lawn past trees and shrubs, almost at a run. Davi looked back and saw soldiers lined up in formation outside the Library entrance. Xalivar saw it too and quickened his pace.

"What are we running away from? I thought all of you are on the same side?" Davi asked, trying to unnerve his uncle. If only he could somehow reach the side of him that had once cared.

Bordox shoved him and Davi stumbled as they hurried along the pathway.

"You already know I have more enemies than friends," Xalivar said in a no-nonsense tone. "Extra precautions are always required. For your protection as well as my own."

*So, Xalivar and the Council have a rift?* When Xalivar had arrived and taken him into custody, Davi assumed the peace conference was a ruse. What if it wasn't? Had the WFR really succeeded?

"Where are you taking me?"

"We ask the questions, prisoner!" Bordox shoved him again.

Davi was getting tired of it. "Could you try and enjoy this a little less, Bordox?" Davi said, pulling his arm free of Bordox's grip and moving forward alongside Xalivar. "I'm talking to my uncle."

"We'll see how you refer to me, when we're safely aboard my ship," Xalivar said. Davi didn't find the tone reassuring.

Xalivar led them down a slope almost at a run, and Davi saw the Royal Shuttle waiting on a launch pad ahead.

Lord Kray appeared in front of the shuttle, and Xalivar frowned, hesitating. He stopped at the bottom of the slope, waving a finger in warning at Kray. "Don't interfere with me, Kray!"

"By order of the Council of Lords, you are to release the prisoner at once," she said.

"The Council has no authority here," Xalivar insisted.

"We do under the act of emergency powers," Kray said as Yao and Tela appeared, blasters at the ready, leading two armed squads of Alliance troops. Davi couldn't help but smile.

Bordox shoved him. "Stop smiling!"

"This is a family matter, Kray. It is not the business of the Council," Xalivar said.

"Yet it is the business of the LSP and Boralian military troops?" Yao scoffed, staring down Xalivar for the first time in his life. Davi was impressed.

"He is here as a member of a WFR contingent invited by the Council," Kray countered. "He cannot be detained."

Xalivar ignored her. "Step aside, Councilor!" He shoved Kray aside as Yao pointed a blaster at him.

"High Lord Councilor, I'm going to have to ask you to halt," Yao said.

Xalivar stopped and turned, staring at him. "I outrank all of you, Captain."

"The Council's orders override yours," Yao said, unwavering.

Bordox drew his blaster and shoved it into Davi's back. "You will allow us to pass or Xander here dies!"

Yao, Tela, and the soldiers aimed their blasters at Davi and Bordox.

"Let him go," Tela demanded, looking afraid.

"Slaves give no orders here!" Bordox shouted, pushing his blaster harder into Davi's back.

Davi winced. He'd never known Bordox to be so brave—defying the Council. Then he saw Obed being led across the campus under armed guard, wondering if Bordox had seen it, too.

"Lieutenant, you are violating Council orders," Kray said, in a commanding tone. "Drop your blaster now."

Bordox stared at her, glanced over his shoulder at Obed being led down a pathway across the campus from them, and then shook his head. "I can't do it, can I, Xander?"

Behind them, the Royal Shuttle's engines whined. They all turned to see Xalivar peering out of the cockpit, the shuttle doors now closed and locked behind him. He smiled as the shuttle lifted into the air.

"I told you—" Davi kicked backwards with his right foot, shoving his elbow back hard at the same moment. The foot caught Bordox's knee and the elbow dug into his ribs. Bordox cried out and stumbled backward and Davi dove to the ground. "—stop calling me that!"

Bordox hesitated a moment then aimed his blaster at Davi again. Tela and Yao fired. Bordox screamed and crumpled to the ground, grabbing his wounded leg. Davi dove and grabbed the blaster away from him, so near he could smell Bordox's charred flesh.

"Nooooo!" Bordox yelled through gritted teeth.

Soldiers surrounded Bordox as Yao reach down and helped Davi to his feet. "You okay?"

Davi smiled, reaching out to grasp his friend's shoulder. "Yes, and now I owe you my life!"

Yao shrugged. "Along with the answers for most of your tests at the Academy."

They both laughed as Tela rushed over to embrace Davi. "Thank God you're okay! I was scared for you," she said.

"Me, too," Davi admitted, enjoying her arms around him, the smell of her hair. It smelled like freedom.

Bordox struggled and two soldiers took him by the arms and led him away. "You'll regret this, Rhii! You haven't seen the last of me!"

Davi sighed and waved.

Lord Kray approached. "I'm sorry for the way you were treated."

Davi shrugged. "Nothing that won't heal, Councilor. Thank you for your help."

She smiled. "Your mother would be very proud of you."

Davi smiled, feeling sad. He wished Miri were here. "What about Xalivar?"

Kray shrugged. "Where can he go? The Council declared emergency powers hours ago. He'll be detained soon enough. You'll be negotiating with the Council now."

Davi nodded as Tela leaned her head on his shoulder. "I have no doubt the Council will be fair."

He could hardly believe it. With the Council's help, the WFR had won. He'd never dared imagine how it would feel. His heart jumped for joy as he and Tela walked with Kray and Yao back up the slope and across the campus toward the Library again.

# Epilogue

The starport on Vertullis bustled with activity as Davi, Tela, and Lura arrived. In the two weeks since the peace conference, things had returned to normal—transports, shuttles, and starfighters launching one after another. Workers and mech-bots hustled around loading, unloading and servicing the various craft. Passengers and ticket agents bustled around them. It was almost as if the war had never happened.

The Council of Lords had agreed to all of their demands. The workers would be free and treated as regular citizens of the Borali Alliance. Shipments had resumed from Vertullis bearing agricultural products out while other products were brought in. In the next month, Aron would join the Council as a full member to represent the planet. He would take the place of Lord Obed, who, along with the entire LSP, had come under suspicion.

Xalivar and Manaen had disappeared in the Royal Shuttle. They had not landed at any of the expected ports. Rumors had it they'd refueled at Alpha Base before word of the settlement and rearranged government had reached there, but no one was certain. High Lord Councilor Tarkanius had declared them wanted men. Though the Council had promised no sanctions at first if Xalivar relented and abided by their decisions, his flight left them outraged. It had been a sign of total disrespect and the Council would not stand for it. Xalivar's reign had been terminated, and Tarkanius had taken his place.

Davi accepted their decision not to choose him to replace Xalivar. The Council had always chosen the ruling family by election, and given what had occurred, he could understand their feeling that a change had been appropriate. His heritage was in question now, an issue which couldn't just be brushed aside despite the Council's new attitude toward their former slaves. Besides, he was too young to be a High Lord Councilor, and, at this point, there wasn't anything he thought he would miss about being Royal.

Davi, Lura, and Tela arrived at the designated platform, as the white shuttle from the Alliance Prison Centauri Two entered the landing bay. Lura seemed more nervous than he'd ever seen her.

"You okay, Mother?"

She nodded. "It's been so long."

"I'm sure he'll be as happy to see you as you are to see him," Tela said and Davi knew she was feeling much the same about seeing her father again.

Lura smiled. "I can't wait for you to meet him."

Davi turned away, feeling nervous. He couldn't believe this moment had arrived.

Aron approached and patted him on the back as the shuttle lowered onto the platform before them. "He'll be very proud of you."

"And very proud of you, too, no doubt," Davi said.

Aron shrugged. "A Lord on the Council! We never could have imagined it."

"It's well deserved," Tela said, squeezing Davi's hand.

Davi smiled, pulling her to him. "I'm proud of you both."

The shuttle's engines wound down and the door opened. The first person to step onto the platform was a young Lieutenant Davi recognized.

Farien kept his military posture, a stern expression on his face as he walked to where Davi and Tela were standing. He stopped there, examining Davi's blue uniform. "You look like a worker to me!"

Davi broke into a broad grin, and they embraced like brothers. "It's good to see you," Davi said.

"Guess you should have kept me around to keep you out of trouble," Farien said. They both laughed.

Miri stepped off the shuttle, spotting Davi and hurrying toward him. They embraced like two people who had been apart too long. "When I heard they were bringing us here, I wasn't sure what to expect. I missed you so!"

"You, too, Mother. I was worried about you," Davi said, silently thanking God she was safe. It felt good to be with her again.

"They told me you're a war hero? My own son, the Worker Prince," Miri said, looking him over in the way mothers inspect their children after a long absence.

"I've done what I could, Mother. Really. I'm fine." And looking around him at all those he loved, he knew he would be.

Miri smiled, embracing him again. "It's a mother's prerogative to be sure."

Over Miri's shoulder, Davi saw Lura embrace a man on the platform a few yards away as Tela greeted someone at the foot of the ramp.

"There're some people I want you to meet." Davi and Miri said in unison. Davi laughed.

"You first," Miri said.

Davi took her hand and led her toward Tela, who was embracing a man in his mid-fifties. His features were similar to Tela's, except he was taller, with graying hair.

"Davi, I'd like you to meet my father, Telanus."

Telanus smiled and clasped Davi's hand, his grip firm. "So this is the young man I have to thank for taking care of my little girl."

"She did a pretty good job of it herself, sir," Davi said. "In fact, you might say it was more the other way around."

Miri smiled, offering her hand to Tela. "Then it is I who must thank her, I suppose."

Tela grasped Miri's hand as Davi said: "Tela, this is my mother, Miri."

"I am so honored, Princess Miri," Tela said, reacting with surprise as Miri pulled her into an embrace.

"From what I hear, soon you may be calling me Mother as well," Miri said with a wink at Davi, who blushed.

Tela laughed.

Davi turned as Lura approached with a tall and thin man who bore a striking resemblance to Davi. His face and hands appeared hardened from manual labor, and his hair had turned gray but he walked with confidence. A familiar necklace hung around his neck.

"I never thought this day would come," Lura said, tears flowing down her cheeks. "This is your father, Sol."

Sol and Davi stood a moment, taking each other in, and then Sol grabbed Davi and pulled him into an embrace. Sol's eyes filled with tears as he spoke. "I have so dreamed of this day, my son."

"I have, too, father," Davi said, fighting back tears of his own.

"Your mother, Princess Miri, has told me so many stories in the past few days," Sol said, smiling at Miri, who was wiping her own eyes. "We are so grateful for all she's done for you."

"Thank you for taking care of our baby," Lura said, voice full of emotion as she grasped Miri's hands.

As the two mothers hugged, Sol continued, "We're also grateful for all you've done, and very proud."

Davi couldn't fight the tears any longer. They poured from his eyes as he embraced Sol again. "Thank you for saving my life!" It seemed to be the one thought out of several in his mind which he could manage to form into words right then.

They took another shuttle back to the WFR base where an elaborate banquet had been prepared for them in a large cavern. The WFR leadership, pilots, and other guests stood waiting for them. The banquet table contained a spread beyond imagination—every delectable delight they could have imagined and enough to feed an army. They all ate until their stomachs were ready to burst.

Everyone exchanged congratulations as they celebrated together. General Matheu even thanked Davi for his contributions and shook his hand.

Telanus, Miri, and Sol stared in amazement at what the workers had built, and it touched Davi to see the three of his parents—birth and adopted—getting along so well.

Later, he and Tela slipped off to one side and cuddled, watching them.

"I can't even begin to describe this," Tela said.

Davi nodded. "Me neither. It's so hard to believe, but somehow more than anything else, this feels like victory."

Tela smiled, pulling him close, and they kissed and then strode hand in hand back to rejoin the others.

# THE RETURNING

**The Saga Of Davi Rhii Book 2**

# Chapter One

Either his eyes were failing or the shadows were alive. Dru blinked as he listened to his fellow cadets breathing and snoring around him. He lay at the center of a row of seven bunks with seven more lining the opposite wall. All twenty-eight were occupied and no one else seemed to be stirring.

As he lifted his head, he saw a dark shape like a shadow, slinking down the center aisle. The figure moved quickly, sliding between the bunks on the opposite wall and leaning over one of them. He saw a sharp movement. Did the shadow have four arms? Who could it be? His mind raced for answers. His clothes stuck to his body, an odd feeling. He never sweated at night. There was a gargling, then he watched as the shadow shot upright and ran back the way it had come.

Dru heard wheezing coming from the bunk and sat up, planting his feet on the floor. What was happening with Cadet Kowl? He jumped up. "Kowl, are you ok?"

No sign of the shadow. A metallic smell filled his nostrils. Others stirred around him. He heard a click as reflector pads flicked on overhead.

Dru gasped and stepped back as he stared down at Cadet Kowl's slashed throat as blood drained from it into two pools on either side of his bunk on the floor. He shivered, a sudden chill coming over him.

"Gods! He's dead!" The cadet behind him sounded as shocked as Dru felt. Cadet Walz was it? Dru couldn't remember. Then chaos erupted as someone pulled the alarm and he was shoved aside by arriving instructors.

"Wonder what Dru's doing right now?" Davi's cousin Nila's voice crackled over the comm as his squadron flew in formation around him.

"Whatever he's doing, it's a lot better than sitting out here babysitting transports and going through the motions," Virun groused as the other VS28 fighters slid back into formation and continued along the course of their routine patrol.

"Keep the chatter down so Farien and Brie can give their report." Captain Davi Rhii fought back a laugh. He'd long ago grown used to the boredom of patrol. So what if Nila and her friends were always chattering during patrols? It lightened the mood and kept them alert. Besides, Dru's reassignment couldn't help but be a fascination for his friends. Especially since their current patrol route passed Eleni 1, the Legallian moon which Presimion Academy called home.

Dru and the others had trained together then fought for freedom against their enslavers with the Worker's Freedom Resistance. They beamed with pride when they mentioned his name. It was a huge honor having one of their own be one of the first ex-workers admitted to the most prestigious military school in the system.

"A junked freighter." Brie interrupted his thoughts as she began her report.

"Class Seven, Tertullian made," Farien added. "A ghost."

"What? They just leave them out here abandoned?" Jorek's voice dripped with disgust.

"Kinda big to just park somewhere on the ground," Farien answered. "Especially when there are plenty of pirates and scavengers around to do the work for them."

"And plenty of empty space." Davi glanced across the formation toward his old friend and grinned. As liaison, Farien functioned as a member of the squad, working alongside Davi to ensure the pilots were treated like every other Borali pilot, from training to uniforms to schedules. Having his old friend around to compare notes with lightened Davi's load, and Farien, for his part, seemed pleased to be working with Davi again. The promotion hadn't hurt his self-esteem either. Farien acted more confident and positive than Davi had ever seen him.

"What if it floats off into a planet or someone crashes into it?" Jorek was a fount of never-ending questions.

Farien snorted. "Then the legal people and politicians get to do what they love and argue and someone else gets to have a funeral."

Davi winced. Farien still needed to learn some tact.

"Exactly," Jorek said, as if he'd proved his point.

"There have been very few incidents of ghost ships colliding with other ships," Davi interjected. "And none of collisions with planets."

"Just a matter of time," Virun said, taking his best friend's side. "Somebody's nav system could malfunction." Jorek and Virun were two of the smartest pilots Davi knew, right up there with Tela. They reminded him of his own academy days with Yao and Farien: rarely seen apart; inseparable to all who knew them; top of the class in training, despite a propensity to let passion rule over reason.

"Well, back at base, you two can write up a nice report requesting an official salvage ship, ok?" Farien sent the images he and Brie had captured to the entire squadron via his ship's computer. "It will be one of many."

"Ech. Paperwork. No thanks." Davi could almost hear Virun's frown.

Sensors beeped in alarm, sending a familiar tingle up Davi's arms. Davi looked down and typed a command into his computer, sliding forward in his seat to force blood flow into his drowsy limbs and keep him alert.

"Incoming ship of unknown origin." Brie's speed impressed him. On the surface, she was the antithesis of a pilot: a short, cute blonde with girl-next-door looks, prone to using her wiles to get what she wanted by playing the weak female in need. She'd once been considered most likely to fail among his student pilots, along with Nila and Dru. But somehow they'd struggled through and become real pilots, equal to everyone else on the squad.

Almost even equal to Tela. He closed his eyes recalling the sparkle in her eyes when she smiled, the soft warmth of her hand holding his. Command had been giving her fewer rotations for reasons unknown. Davi hadn't had a chance to inquire about it, but he really needed to. Tela became agitated whenever they discussed it.

"Wish you could fly as fast as you type," Jorek teased, the banter breaking Davi out of his thoughts and back to the tension of the moment.

"Funny how you're usually the one chasing me," Brie teased. Nila and Brie's laughter filled the comm channel.

"Save the flirting for your dates," Davi instructed. "What are we looking at?" His eyes darted back and forth between the computer screen and the view out his blastshield as his scanners evaluated the target's course and position, firepower, shield strength and other factors.

"What the—?" Jorek's fighter suddenly dove and Brie darted right. A black shape raced through the space where they'd just been. Davi leaned forward, eyes straining to identify it.

"Shields!" Farien ordered.

"The computer says its components may be Lhamorian," Nila

reported as Davi's own computer returned the same results.

"Offensive formation," Davi ordered, hand tightening on his joystick. "Let's go give her a look."

The fighter's engines vibrated his cockpit as Davi accelerated. Circling back together, the pilots remained in tight formation. Davi took a moment to shift in his formfitting seat and stretch his legs. The one thing he did appreciate about long, quiet patrols was unsweaty cockpits. Being confined in a vacuum with his own body odor was something he'd never get used to, even with the distraction of combat.

"Heads up," Farien called. "There he is."

Davi sighed. The mystery ship accelerated away from Eleni 1 far too fast for a casual visitor, and so dark it was almost hidden by the starfield until the fighters moved in to surround it. Sleek and black starfighters with snub noses and three wings—two longer wings out of each side, and a third shorter wing extending vertically above the fighter's four engines—VS28s were dark black, but spotting each other was simple enough despite the gray, transparent blastshield. The squadron insignia on their sides helped, of course. This mystery ship, however, was tricky to see. It appeared designed that way. Line-of-sight stealth made little sense in space where sensory radar were relied upon to identify and track other craft, which meant the stealth was intended for something else. Plus the craft was unusually small, almost fighter-sized, yet appeared to have a passenger compartment behind the cockpit built to carry multiple passengers. Add to that the computer's dearth of information on its origins and that brought only two uses to mind: spying and smuggling. But spying on Eleni 1 made little sense.

Davi punched commands into the computer and the reports came up on his screen. "Sensors read one occupant. No weapons."

"The sensors didn't even find her until she was right up on us," Brie answered, her voice rising in pitch with the tension.

"We didn't see him either," Jorek barked, still clearly angry from the near miss.

"Whoever he is, he's not expecting trouble from us," Farien responded. *At least there's one voice of calm here.*

"Unless that's what he wants us to think," Nila added.

Davi smiled, pleased with his cousin. Her perceptiveness had developed with her flight skills. Davi had the same suspicion, and he knew Farien and others would, too, after hearing her voice it. Davi initiated another scan of the target. "Defensive formation." He switched his comm to a hailing channel. "This is Captain Davi Rhii of the Borali

Alliance, identify yourself immediately."

The radio remained silent for what seemed like forever.

"Weapons range, Captain," Virun reported as Davi watched his sensors flash the alert.

"I repeat. Identify yourself. This is Captain Davi Rhii of the Borali Alliance." So much for unsweaty cockpits.

"'ello, Capt'in, my ship's transpond'r 's malfuncti'ning." It was the same accent Davi had heard in the market on Vertullis many times. The accent of Itolis, a Lhamor. A Lhamor on Eleni 1? It had to be a merchant but why the stealth ship?

"Slow down immediately and maintain course," Davi ordered the stranger. "Identify. Who are you running from?"

The mystery ship slowed onto a steady course as the fighters slid in to surround her.

"Not runn'ng. 'erchant, Capt'in. Negotiat'r f'r Minist'y of Trade. I mean no h'rm. I he'd for X'nthis Depot for rep'irs."

Davi muted the channel and keyed the private squadron channel. "Ministry of Trade, right? He's a smuggler for sure." Nothing else made sense.

"Legallis Depot is closer," Farien responded.

"It's also expensive. He's probably trying to save some bucks, if his story's even true."

"You don't think it's a spy ship?" Jorek asked.

"What's there to spy on at Eleni 1?" Nila sounded amused.

"The Academy. Military tactics, weaponry..."

"There are easier ways to gather that data," Nila responded.

"What about the big agro firms?" Virun asked.

"They send spies for agriculture?" Brie sounded surprised.

"It's a competitive field," Virun responded. "Some firms have secrets."

Once one of them got going, the others followed. The questions rained like a storm. Davi winced. *Let's get some answers.* He keyed the hailing channel again. "Why Xanthis? The Depot on Legallis is closer."

"My boss h's a contr'ct with X'nthis. Leg'llis 's very expensive."

"By protocols, we should detain him," Brie said over the squadron channel.

"I say we do it for almost killing us," Jorek answered.

"If his employer is the trade minister, he'll raise hell." Farien wasn't arguing but his tone made it clear he wanted to let the ship go.

"He could be a spy!" Jorek and Virun clearly wanted to take this to the next level.

"You heard his accent. Why would Lhamors want to spy on the Academy?"

"Who knows why Lhamors do anything?" Virun answered. "They're not like humans. Not even very smart in my experience."

"It's a small transport, probably an interplanetary shuttle. He's unarmed. He's made no aggression toward us. Is it worth risking bad blood toward Vertullian pilots if it becomes an incident?"

Farien had a point. Davi keyed the hailing channel and ran a deep scan of the ship's holds and passenger compartment. "Do you carry any cargo?"

"Jus' mys'lf, Capt'in. C'me to negoti'te."

There wasn't enough to hold him without risk of elevating something minor into a major incident, and that was the last thing Davi and his squadron needed to get involved with. The scanner beeped—nothing beyond basic provisions and supplies. The VS28s matched the mystery ship's speed and heading, forming a reverse cone around it.

Davi chose caution. "My squadron will escort you to the next sector. Our companions there can see you safely to Xanthis."

"Th'nk you, Capt'in, for your kindn'ss."

"We're gonna let him go?" Brie sounded as frustrated as Jorek and Virun.

"We're going to see he's escorted the whole way to Xanthis," Davi answered. "If he behaves, he won't be bothered. Virun, radio ahead to the patrol in Sector Omega and fill them in on our friend here. We'll meet them at the border in a direct line to Xanthis."

"Yes, sir," Virun replied, followed by a click on the channel as he switched to another frequency.

Davi sighed and slid back in his seat again, his tension evaporating. "Maintain formation, squad. Let's see our friend here to the border."

The Council leadership convened in a small conference room in the High Lord Councilor's Palace over breakfast. Serve-bots took care of the serving as the Councilors focused on the agenda handed to them by High Lord Councilor Tarkanius. Although Aron wasn't on the Council leadership, he'd been included because he had a presentation to make on an important issue affecting Council decisions, and Tarkanius wanted the leadership to consider it first before he took it to the full Council. Aron felt as at home as a child at the opera. He was still adjusting to the idea of being an official member of the Council, let alone carrying the title 'Lord' before his name. Still, they'd issued him the official robe of a Council member and an apartment near the government complex where other Lords lived.

The chattering Councilors quieted and took their seats as their leader, Simeon, stood next to Tarkanius at the head of the table and motioned for attention. Taller and thinner than Tarkanius, Simeon had earned the gray hair that topped his head. Older, more experienced and harder working than the rest, everyone respected him. "This meeting was called at the request of Lord Aron to discuss a matter which has begun to draw notice throughout the Alliance: a Vertullian holiday called 'The Returning.'"

The room broke into chatter again. Aron had hoped including the topic on the agenda would quell some of the emotions of the announcement, but the ploy had failed.

"What is this 'Returning'?" Lord Niger shifted in his chair along the middle right side of the table. "Several of our security men requested time off, saying it was religious." The dark-skinned, dark-haired, overweight Lord had taken over responsibility for the Lord's Special Police and Security Forces after the resignation and disappearance of the disgraced Lord Obed.

"I've gotten reports from several sectors of similar requests," the Council's sole female member, Lord Kray, smiled at Aron, her face showing not a trace of wrinkles. Skinny, tall, with warm, yet determined eyes, she'd played a major role in overturning Xalivar's coup and freeing Aron's people. Yet with all she'd fought for, the absence of gray in her hair surprised him. "The agricultural sectors are particularly hard hit. The entire planet Vertullis will be shut down."

Seated next to her, Lord Hachim scowled. Olive-skinned, bearded, short and round, he and Niger were close friends. "If we shut down every time one of our gods had a holiday, nothing would get done." Others mumbled in agreement and nodded as all eyes turned to Aron.

Aron smiled, his white robe whooshing as he stood and typed into his datapad. "The information I'm sending you explains the historical and religious significance of the holiday." He continued as the others pulled up the information on their datapads and began scanning it. "It celebrates the day our Savior returned to heaven after his death and resurrection. It's our most important holiday. This will be our first chance to honor it fully since winning our freedom. As you can imagine, that's very important to us after generations spent celebrating in private."

"Your Savior isn't ours." Lord Niger's face crinkled as he scanned the data Aron had sent. "Old Testament God of Israel? This is Boralis, not Old Earth!"

"No one else takes religious holidays which affect work," Lord Hachim snapped. "First, you want to be accepted as our equals, now you want special treatment. It's a double standard!" Several others mumbled in agreement and nodded.

Tarkanius raised a hand to silence them. "Part of learning to accept others as full citizens is learning to accept their culture, their traditions, and their beliefs. Compromise is a necessity."

"I see no issue with it, as long as adequate warning can be given and proper arrangements made," Kray added.

"And what of those whose regular schedules must be adjusted to accommodate those requesting a holiday? Regular days off will need to be cancelled, schedules adjusted." Lord Niger exchanged a furious look with Lord Hachim. "It may engender hard feelings."

"Hard feelings can be overcome in time," Lord Simeon offered.

"They often are." Lord Kray smiled at him. "Do those required to work essential services resent it when we celebrate each New Year and Thanks Day?" Aron knew both as carryovers from Old Earth tradition.

"Those holidays are not associated with a particular people group nor religion." Hachim shot her a disappointed look.

"This could create renewed animosity between our peoples," Niger said. "Many are still adjusting to the idea of Vertullians being Boralian citizens as it is. Some of our own have lost jobs to former workers whose years of experience as slave labor made them more qualified for those positions. There's been an outcry about lost jobs. Cries of unfairness."

"All such integrations force changes in industry and labor markets," Tarkanius said. "It will even out in time and be forgotten."

"Then perhaps we should hold this proposal until the tensions die down a bit," Niger continued. "Right now, there's still a lot of resentment. Do you really want to risk inflaming old biases?"

"Old biases which have never died, lest we forget the news reports—graffiti campaigns, a few instances of bullying." Hachim stared at Aron. The news had been reporting anti-worker slurs written on the sides of buildings and on sidewalks for months. And there had been incidents of violence with workers being attacked in dark streets and schoolyards.

Aron's heart broke when he recalled it, yet he knew his people were better off now than they had been. He spotted it in their eyes when they met his; their stride as they passed him on the street. He paused as all eyes returned to him. "I think the Council declaring it an official holiday would send the right message. We are one people now. Some are always slow to accept change, but others will recognize this change is here to stay."

"I'm sure our people would love to join you in celebrating your private god." Hachim said. Was that a smile or a grimace? Sarcasm dripped off him like sweat.

"Some may," Niger added. "I personally resent it."

"No one's asking you to celebrate our God. Celebrate life, your families. Celebrate freedom. Anything and everything that matters to you. We won't hold it against you if you define the holiday in your own way." Aron smiled, feeling a tinge of hope that the suggestion would calm their fears, but Hachim and Niger frowned, as if they hadn't heard a word. And others refused to meet his eyes.

"It could give the impression your religion is the most important," Lord Qai said from the other end of the table. Young, yellow-skinned, descendent of colonists from the Eastern continents of the Earth, he had joined the leadership when Tarkanius became High Lord Councilor and Simeon became head of the Council.

"Only if you call it a religious holiday," Aron said. "If everyone has the holiday off, few will be concerned with how others use it." Explaining the significance of the day to people whose religion consisted of a series of rites rather than a deep personal relationship with their god had proved exhausting. But Aron kept trying.

"Word will spread of the special significance given the day by your people," Qai countered. "And certainly word of the Council's role will not be secret. People will draw the conclusion the two are related."

"Some people, perhaps, but not everyone." Lord Kray's eyes met Aron's with a look of reassurance. "The Lhamors have their Birthing Day Celebration. And don't the Xanthians have a holiday as well?"

"I believe it's a celebration of ancestors," Qai said with a nod.

"It only takes a loud few." Lord Niger crossed his arms over his chest.

"Lord Qai does have a point we must consider carefully," Lord Simeon said with a waved finger as Aron returned to his seat at the table. "If we recognize the holiday of one group, we have many others who will also want their holidays to be official."

"I can just see it now, an entire month with nothing happening because of holidays!" Hachim sat back in his chair and scowled as the others chuckled.

"Not all holidays occur in the same week, Lord Hachim," Kray said, her eyes bright with amusement.

"None of the other people groups have such a centralized religion," Tarkanius added. "We don't have to make a decision today. The holiday is not imminent."

"A free society cannot force people to work on days where they feel such a moral conflict," Simeon said with a nod. "If people do have religious reasons for objecting to working on a particular day, we must consider that carefully." Relief swept over Aron. At least a few of them understood.

"It's a privilege to have work; a privilege requiring sacrifices." Hachim remained firm in his resolve.

"Some research is suggested." Simeon panned the room, allowing his eyes to meet each of the others. "The High Lord Councillor and Lord Aron have done us a service by bringing this matter to our attention. Let us consider it carefully and not make a decision in haste. Lord Aron's suggestion about not emphasizing the Vertullians' connection is valid, and other cultures do celebrate official holidays. There were many on Old Earth, as I recall."

Aron read acknowledgement on the others' faces.

"Lord Kray, please send inquiries to the various planetary leadership inquiring about their cultural and religious holidays. We need to know what kind of resistance we might expect and who might campaign for their own holiday's recognition." Kray nodded and smiled as Simeon continued. "Niger and Hachim, research the potential economic impact of an official holiday. What real impact might there be on the economy." Hachim and Niger nodded, but their eyes never met Simeon's. "We'll all meet again and discuss this further later."

"I appreciate the leadership's willingness to consider my proposal," Aron said, resigned to whatever happened.

"Will your people refuse to work if we decide not to honor this holiday?" Lord Qai asked.

Aron couldn't answer for sure. Reestablishing this holiday had been an important topic among his people since their freedom was re-established and people longed for the day they could celebrate it openly again. Aron shared their joy. "I don't know, but many would be saddened and disheartened," he finally said.

"Perhaps some research of your own on that topic would be helpful," Simeon said. Aron nodded in agreement. "For now, this meeting is adjourned. Thank you for coming."

As the Lords scooted back from the table and resumed their chatter, Aron stayed seated, flickering like old reflector pads. This meant so much to his people, yet the Council couldn't afford to play favorites. How could he honor both his people's wishes and the needs of the larger citizenry?

A hand gently squeezed his shoulder. "Weighty decisions are the bane of a Lord's existence, Aron," Kray said, her eyes sympathetic. "Your suggestion was worthy. And the others will give it consideration and careful thought. Centuries of enmity don't disappear overnight."

Kray had been on the Council for a long time before Aron joined. She'd been one of his firmest supporters, helping him understand procedures and learn his way around the government complex, introducing him to contacts. And she also knew the others well. It reassured him having her as an advocate.

"Thank you, Kray. You've been a great support from the start." He remembered the look on Lord Obed's face when Kray and Simeon had burst into the Library Auditorium at Presimion Academy and overcome Lord Obed and the men holding the Vertullian peace envoys hostage there. "A good friend."

Kray laughed. "It's a pleasure to know you, Aron. You've taught us so much already about how wrong we were to let old rivalries turn our hearts and minds against your people." She squeezed his shoulder again and they both smiled.

By the time Yao arrived at the dorm, the Academy's poor semblance of an investigation was well underway. Presimion had no past experience with such investigations. In the school's storied history, no one had ever been murdered, or even assaulted, on the campus. He bristled as he took in the scene of the crime he'd only learned about after checking his messages. Cadet Kowl's skin was purpling and his body looked stiff. Yao should have been the first faculty member notified.

"Professor Brahma, I'm sorry we hadn't notified you yet." The Student Life Director looked dismayed as he approached, offering Yao a steaming cup of Talis.

Yao accepted it, sipping slowly. "I'm in charge of their assimilation, Alek. I should have been awoken immediately." For the premiere military institution in the system, Presimion was very behind the times in some important ways.

"We were a bit overwhelmed, as you can imagine."

*You're always overwhelmed*, Yao thought. His opinion of Alek Brak's capabilities would not have helped the man's curriculum vitae. "Where's the student who witnessed the murder?"

Alek motioned and Yao spotted the lanky, red-haired cadet sitting alone in the Dorm Attendant's small office, looking exhausted. "You okay?" he asked as he joined him.

Dru shook his head. "We switched beds."

"Switched? Cadet Kowl was in your bed?"

Dru nodded as his eyes dodged Yao's. "It used to be mine. We traded two weeks into the semester. Kowl had issues with the moonlight keeping him awake. Doesn't bother me." Dru's body shook as he spoke. He was a mass of fear.

Yao put a hand gently on his shoulder and knelt in front of him, trying to imagine how he'd have felt as a cadet if one his friends had been murdered across a dark room. "That doesn't have anything to do with this. Coincidence. I'm sorry about your friend."

Dru chuckled. "That's just it. We weren't really friends. I barely knew him. I just helped him out because someone had to. He was struggling a lot in classes. Why would anyone want him dead?"

Yao shook his head. "Things like this never make sense to sane people."

Dru shrugged. "Then I saw it." The cadet read the question on his instructor's face. "The message the killer left."

"The killer left a message?"

Dru pointed. "On the wall in the corridor. He was after me."

"Wait a minute. I'll be right back." Yao slid back out into the main room and hurried toward the corridor. The message jumped out at him right away. It was burned in the wall with a laser just outside the entrance to the students' sleep hall. The corridor still stank of smoke and charred paint.

YOU DON'T BELONG HERE

He knew immediately why Dru related it to himself. It was the most obvious motive for the attack. When ex-workers had arrived as students, Yao expected hazing; planned his response. But for the most part, it had been very minor and quelched quickly. Nothing like the schoolyard beatings in other parts of the system and none of the anti-worker graffiti seen in the cities. His memory flashed back to the controversy over his friend Davi's admission. He wondered how those who'd complained felt now that Davi's birth status as a Vertullian had been revealed. He'd suffered with his friend as Davi fought for acceptance.

"He's the Prince," the complaints said. "It's pure favoritism." There'd also been controversy when aliens like himself were first admitted and much of that vitriol had never really faded.

Still, Kowl wasn't Vertullian. It could be about something else—an old rivalry, Kowl's family's activities—they just didn't know. Vertullians weren't the only admissions people questioned. He stepped back into the office with Dru and leaned against the wall. "You don't know for sure what that means. It could mean a lot of things."

"Kowl was a nice guy. Who would want him dead?"

"Someone who hates his family. An old rival. It's hard to say. Davi's a nice guy, too, and he's got his share of enemies."

"Davi was once Prince. And he's no ordinary guy. Kowl was just ordinary." Dru reached up with his thumb to wipe tears from his right cheek. For a guy who'd slept over five hours, a lot at the academy, the cadet looked exhausted.

"There are still far too many unanswered questions to assume, okay? Have you eaten yet?"

Dru shook his head. "I'll make arrangements for you to stay with me for a while, okay? And I'm taking you to breakfast now, even if all you do is watch me eat. I'll order something strange only we Tertullians eat so you can stare."

Dru didn't even smile. He just nodded and stood, allowing Yao to lead him out the door.

Yao motioned to Alek as they entered the sleep hall. "I'm taking Cadet Dru with me. Have someone pack his things and send them to my apartment. He'll be staying with me for a while."

Alek nodded. "I can send the reports to your datapad as they develop, if you'd like."

"Do that. I'll be back soon to look into this more myself. Has anyone contacted Cadet Kowl's family?"

"Not yet."

"Don't, until I have time to investigate. We need to be sure we get this right. I take full responsibility for all notifications."

Alek shrugged. "That's fine with me."

Yao nodded, placing his hand on Dru's neck and leading him out. He deliberately turned so they wouldn't pass by the message as they walked through the corridor. It meant taking a longer route but that hardly mattered. He made a mental note to message Davi and Farien as soon as they'd ordered breakfast. Right now, he needed to help Dru get situated enough to function.

Tela flushed with warmth as she watched Davi's mothers, Miri and Lura, straightening furniture and artwork, discussing lighting and linens. She hadn't seen Miri so happy in months. The apartment was one formerly restricted for rental by government dignitaries, but Davi had been able to arrange with the government to open it for Miri. Sizable with a great view, it sat a block from the government center at Legon, the capital city of Legallis, not far from the Palace which had been Miri's life-long home. Across the street, amidst the high-rises, a preschool play-ground caught Tela's eye whenever she looked out the window.

The light blue-gray walls and lush navy carpet reflected light from the reflector pads overhead, lending a homey glow to the middle of each room. The central gathering, entertainment area sat like a hub amidst the spokes of the corridors leading to the kitchen, bedrooms, and sanitary facilities. The apartment also included an office which Miri used for a library. Altogether, the space wasn't really much smaller than Miri's suite at the Palace, even if it was less glamorous. Davi had often confided in Tela his worries about Miri's adjustment to civilian life, but from the vibe at her place, Tela thought Miri was doing fine.

She heard women's chattering coming from the kitchen as Davi's birth father, Sol, sat on a sofa, reading the news on a datapad. A hard worker who'd spent twenty years imprisoned away from his wife and son, Sol's skin was dark tan and his hands worn from years of manual labor. Still, he knew how to relax when he wasn't at the plant, and Tela found herself relieved that Sol and Tela's father, Telanus, had been given lighter duties these days.

"Tela, dear, come here, we'd like your opinion on this," Miri called in her singsong alto.

"Don't let them drag you into this, Tela," Sol teased, "Run for your life."

Tela chuckled and patted him on the shoulder as she moved past and climbed the stairs toward the kitchen. Lura and Miri stood huddled together beside the balcony, watching the twin suns paint the sky with their setting. Shades of orange and blue mixed with pinks, yellows and reds in a stunning display. It took Tela's breath away.

The women themselves were a contrast. Davi's birth mother, Lura, was shorter with tanned skin and long, brown hair the color of her son's, whereas Miri, his adoptive mother, stood taller, her light skin accented by her light-blue eyes and short-cut brown hair. Both women's hair had streaks of gray, though it was clear Miri made more effort to cover it up. She stood with the regalness one might expect from a former Royal, while Lura's demeanor remained humble, a legacy of so many years spent in slavery. Lura wore a round and silver-colored necklace with a blue-green crest at its center. The four sections of the crest bore distinct images: laborers, soldiers, farmers and priests. Tela had seen the family crest many times now. Davi and Nila each wore identical necklaces. She'd never seen any of the three without them. Despite their differences, Davi's birth and adoptive mothers had made a concerted effort toward befriending each other. It showed in the way they smiled at each other and Tela.

"You wanted my opinion on a sunset?"

Lura and Miri laughed. "No dear. Lura was just commenting how nice it would be if this balcony were bigger. It would be a beautiful location for a joining, don't you think?" Many adoptive mothers would have been devastated to have their son's birth parents come back into his life, especially mothers as close to their sons as Miri was to Davi. But Miri had remained supportive and dignified despite any inner turmoil she must have felt. Miri's strength was an inspiration, except for those times when it made her pushy, like now.

Tela smiled at their eager grins. They'd been hinting at the idea for months, hoping Davi and Tela would set a date. "We haven't really discussed it. We're enjoying just being together right now. Working out the rough edges, I guess."

"Working out a man's rough edges is a lifetime's endeavor, dear," Miri counseled. "He'll be much easier to mold once he's officially yours, as they say."

Lura grasped Tela's upper arm gently. "We're not trying to pressure you. You're just so good together and it makes us happy to see you both so in love."

Tela nodded, locking the smile onto her face. "We are in love. But love's never perfect. I'm waiting for Davi to get over some of his archaic ideas before I even think about taking that step."

"Archaic ideas?"

Tela continued before Miri could start lecturing on women's place in society. "It's a different age, Miri. Women may have once enjoyed sitting at home waiting for their man. That's just not who I am. I fell in love with your son as we fought together for freedom, side by side with the WFR. He showed me respect and appreciation. But I still think he'd prefer me safe at home in the kitchen."

Miri looked as if she couldn't understand the objection. Lura smiled.

"Davi's not like that. You mean the world to him. It's just that he worries about you. Can you blame him? You worry too."

"I worry sometimes, but we both love what we do, and I support him. I deserve the same consideration."

"Of course you do."

"I thought you were still flying patrol rotations?" Miri seemed confused.

"I am. But not as often as Davi is." That had been a decision by command, she realized, but Davi hadn't exactly jumped in to advocate on her behalf.

"Well, he's a Squadron commander. Their rotations are more frequent, naturally." Miri turned back to the sunset. "I worry about you both."

"Not much to worry about, Miri. We're at peace. The workers have their full citizenship. Patrols are pretty routine." So why did she miss them so much?

"Mothers can't breathe without worrying," Sol said as he came up behind them.

Tela and Lura chuckled as he wrapped his arms around Lura. "It gives us a purpose," Lura said as she caressed his arm.

"I'd be happy if you focused some of that attention on me." Sol leaned in and kissed her neck.

Lura blushed and pushed him away. "You're hardly neglected." Tela wondered if she and Davi would still be so affectionate if they made it twenty years together.

"You'd think after twenty years in prison, a man could get expect a warmer homecoming." Sol frowned, but the ends of his mouth jiggled, giving him away. When the women laughed, he gave up and joined them heartily.

"See what you have to look forward to in forty years, dear?" Lura said as she turned and kissed Sol's waiting lips.

Miri smiled and turned back toward the sunset. Another reason they weren't rushed was a shared concern about how Davi's adoptive mother would adjust to life alone. Eternally single, Miri had devoted her life to her son and her brother. Now, with her brother outcast and on the run and her son grown, Miri must be experiencing a loneliness she hadn't known in years. Both Davi and Tela wanted to be sure Miri never felt abandoned.

As Lura and Sol snuggled behind them, Tela put her arm around Miri. "It's really lucky you were able to get this apartment." After Sol's release, his lifelong friend Aron had arranged a new condo, courtesy of the government, for Sol and Lura on Vertullis, explaining it was the least the government could offer for the wrong it had done them.

Miri smiled, patting Tela's hand on her shoulder. “Yes. Davi's taking good care of me. All of you are. Sometimes I feel guilty for all the attention.”

“After all you've done for him, you deserve it.” She squeezed Miri's hand as it reached up and clasped hers.

“For all of us!” Lura echoed.

“I have a spare room available any time any of you want to visit.”

“We'll be taking you up on it often,” Sol said as he and Lura joined them beside the window.

“We're so close, we don't need a room at the moment, but you just try and keep us away,” Tela said. She and Davi each had apartments in the pilot complex near the starport. It was ten minutes away by air taxi.

Miri glanced at the chrono on the wall and turned back toward the food preparation counter. “We'd better get supper started. Davi's patrol should be back any time now.”

Lura and Tela hurried to help Miri as Sol watched them from his place at the window. “I'd love to know how a princess learned to cook so well.”

“Royal secret,” Miri teased as she handed Tela a plate of vegetables and reached back into the cooling unit for more ingredients. They all laughed once more as Sol escaped again to the other room, leaving the women to their task.

Bordox skimmed the Assassin's report as the man paced the opposite wall of the office. *Man? Funny to think of a four-armed freak that way.* He'd never liked Lhamors or any other aliens, but his present assignment required him to use whatever resources he could find and that included personnel.

“You got lucky with that patrol. I would have never let you go.”

The Lhamor's accent was almost a hiss, yet it penetrated the room like a loudspeaker was attached to his face. “T'ey'r' not as susp'cious as when you serv'd the Alli'nce. H'ving no enemies encour'ges relax'tion.”

Bordox's fist pounded the desk as he dropped the datapad. “What do you mean 'when I served?' I'm still serving the Alliance! I'm a true servant, unlike those imposters!”

“It w's not meant as critic'sm.”

"You'd be wise to consider your words more carefully." The Lhamor just stared at him in silence. "You're sure you got the right student?"

"He w's sleep'ng in the bunk you indic'ted."

"Did you use the photo image or not?"

"Hum'ns 'll l'k alike to us. Smell alike, too." The Lhamor's olfactory organ crinkled with distaste.

Bordox crinkled his nose. *As if you're one to talk.* "I don't need a four-armed freak criticizing how I smell. You'd best learn some respect."

"I don' work f'r you. You're just th' cont'ct."

"I'm empowered with authority to instruct you. That makes me your boss." Bordox frowned. He could swear the Lhamor was laughing. Nothing angered him like being mocked. He'd had enough of that in his life already. He'd suffered the greatest humiliation any man could at the hands of that idiot Xander "Davi" Rhii. The fullness of his rage rained over him. Revenge was coming. This was just the start.

He tossed a datacard across the desk toward the Lhamor. "Your next target's in Iraja. Go there immediately. I'll be out of contact for a few days. I have my own mission somewhere else."

"I won' need you until I'm finish'd." The Lhamor's top right hand reached down and clasped the datacard in its white-gloved fingers. The Assassins always insisted on wearing gloves, despite the fact they wore hardly any clothing over the rest of their insectoid-reptilian appearance. Disproportionally large, orange eyes glowed out of green-scaled skin which was stretched tight over a roundish frame. A rounded, capacious stomach lay between four arms, below the bottom set of which a brown belt held the translator which enabled their communication. Even the translator itself struggled to make sense of the gibberish the Lhamors called language, resulting in heavily accented translations. But without it, the Lhamor's native clicks and clacks would have been indecipherable for Bordox.

"Overconfidence can be a great weakness." The words brought to mind Rhii again. Oh, how it would feel to finally put the bastard in his place.

"Onl' where it's not merit'd." The Lhamor whirled and headed out the door into the corridor which led to the converted hangar the warehouse exterior concealed.

Bordox groaned and leaned back in his chair. Was success worth tolerating insolence and insults from an alien freak? He'd tolerated worse for sure, while hating every moment. He laughed. When it was over, he'd even get his revenge on the alien freaks. They'd all suffer. In time.

# Chapter Two

Davi's nose delighted in the cornucopia awaiting him at Miri's apartment—the hearty smell of boiled Gungor mixed with Gixi and a tart berry whose name he couldn't remember off the top of his head. Miri was becoming quite the cook these days, and, although the presence of both Tela and Lura hinted that she might have had help, he determined not to let on. Of the three, she needed the most encouragement at present.

"Mmmmm. Whatever that is, I can hardly wait!" He kissed Miri's forehead as he pulled her to him, wrapping her in his arms. The warmth of her embrace evoked memories of all the times she'd looked after him. She was the one doing the holding then. Now it was his turn to return the favor. "No time for chatter though. Let's eat!" He winked at Tela and the others as they laughed.

Miri pulled back and her eyes met his. "Don't tell me all that time in the cockpit has erased your memory of manners, Davi Rhii." Her scolding tone barely disguised her obvious delight at his compliment.

Davi released her and bent to kiss Lura on her cheek as his other mother hugged him.

"Welcome back, dear," Lura said with a wink. "Isn't it coming together nicely?"

Davi nodded as he pulled away to shake Sol's outstretched hand. "The condo's starting to feel like home as well," his father said, grip firm, the calluses starting to fade from lack of hard labor.

"Did they at least let you cut the Gungor?"

Sol smirked. "I picked angberries for hours, all by myself."

Davi and the women laughed as Sol winked and Davi turned to Tela.

Her form-fitting, black one-piece highlighted all her best places. Davi stopped to catch his breath before leaning in to embrace her.

"For a moment I thought you hadn't noticed me," she said as their lips met. Davi couldn't tell if she was teasing, until she tensed at his touch.

He relished her flowery scent, and soft, round lips on his. "Just obeying the scriptures and honoring my parents, Love," he answered, hoping to lighten her mood. Instead, she rolled her eyes and punched his arm with more force than he expected. "What? It's a commandment."

She forced a smile. "How was patrol?"

He knew it was serious when she failed to laugh at his teasing. They followed the others into a short corridor toward the dining area. Her hand grasped his and he winced as his fingers shifted under the firmness of her grip. "About as exciting as normal, until we got an emergency call from command."

She dropped his hand like it was poisoned and whirled to face him as the others turned to stare. "What happened?"

"A murder. One of the students at Presimion." He wished immediately he'd couched the information more gently.

Lura and Miri gasped. Tela looked as if he'd sucked the wind from her lungs. "Who? What happened?" she choked out.

Davi clasped Tela's hand in his. "Not a lot of details yet. Yao said it was no one we'd know. Farien was sent to assist in the investigation."

"Thanks be to God!" Lura said.

Everyone looked relieved except Miri. "So he won't be joining us then?" Since Farien's kindness during Miri's brief incarceration at the hands of her brother Xalivar, she'd treated him like a second son. Davi hated to disappoint her but shook his head.

"Let's not dwell on difficult things," Lura said in an obvious attempt to restore their former levity. "We can't let Miri and Sol's hard work go to waste." She winked at Sol, who shrugged guiltily as if he had her fooled. "Those are matters for others to be concerned with. You must be tired, Son."

Davi smiled as she put her hand on his arm and motioned toward the table. "I am, Mother. But it's good to be with all of you."

After they'd arranged themselves around the table, Sol said grace. Then the conversation turned to other matters and the food was passed. Hearty Gungor and angberry stew with fresh potatoes, carrots and beans mixed in, a rice casserole, and Gixi salad. Clearly they'd made an effort to prepare some of Davi's favorites.

"You know what would make things perfect now that I have so much free time?" Miri asked as she watched Davi savoring his first bite of her Gungor stew. "Grandchildren."

Davi coughed, struggling to keep from spitting out the food as Lura and Sol nodded. "That would be fantastic," Lura agreed.

"We're very much looking forward to it," Sol added.

Tela shook her head and chuckled as she patted Davi on the back as he coughed. Why did his throat feel so tight all of a sudden? "You three are relentless."

"This is what parents with grown children do." Miri smiled warmly as she took a bite of the Gixi.

Davi got control of the coughing and took a deep breath. "Sometimes I think patrol's less stressful," he said with a glare, but he couldn't hold it long and broke into laughter as they all joined in.

Gods, Xalivar hated Xanthis! Such a worthless lump of floating rock! It did have its advantages though. Only slightly more populated than its neighbor Italis, it was ice cold at night but pleasant during daylight hours. And its rocky plains were filled with hundreds of places to hide—cavern after cavern—making Xanthis the perfect place to keep a low profile while he put his plan into place.

After the humiliation on Eleni 1, Xalivar hadn't looked back. He'd stopped at the starport on Legallis and swapped from the Imperial shuttle to a private transport. The as-yet-uninformed Royal staff had met him there with the belongings and supplies he'd requested already loaded. He'd bid them adieu and headed off on his "Royal retreat." He could only imagine the confusion they later experienced upon learning he wouldn't be coming back. As stupid as Gungors. He wondered if they'd welcome him back if he just showed up at the Palace doors one day. He wished all the citizens treated him so warmly.

To be an outcast! Like some criminal in his own empire! His fists clenched at his sides as he pondered it. He would redeem his family's honor and name. His power and position would be restored. They hadn't seen the last of Xalivar!

As he made his way into the hollowed out chamber he now used as a conference room, the rest of his core allies sat waiting around an old wooden table they'd procured from the abandoned settlement nearby. Who knew how long the place had been abandoned? Xalivar was just pleased the settlers had left so many valuable resources behind. If they ever came back, they'd discover someone had raided them with flourish. Not much remained to come back to.

The others watched him as he made his way past toward the head of the chamber and the table itself. The walking space was lumpy rock, making passage challenging and causing him to slow his pace whenever his feet found questionable footing. He did his best to nonetheless look confident. This was no time to be seen as weak. Any one of these so-called "allies" would jump at the chance to usurp his role and leave him forgotten in their wake.

His majordomo, Manaen, waited for him beside the chair at the head of the table, smiling and handing Xalivar a datapad as he moved past. An Andorian from Idolis, Manaen's yellow teeth stood out against his blue skin and red eyes. He stepped back as Xalivar accepted the datapad and slid into his seat, facing the others. The chair's wooden arms sent a cold tingle up his arm. He deliberately kept the temperature in his chambers set at a level which made the others uncomfortable—first, because he liked keeping them on edge, and second, because whatever energy and air escaped was then less likely to draw attention from passing air or ground security patrols. An unexpected heat source in this barren region would draw attention Xalivar didn't need. So far, he'd had no interactions with the local authorities and he much preferred it stay that way.

"You have word from Bordox?" he asked as he panned the table, meeting the others' eyes each in turn.

Lord Obed nodded from a chair to his right. "The Academy leadership is baffled as to why anyone would murder one of their own. The mission's expanding to Iraja and Legon now. It'll be a matter of time before the press takes notice."

Xalivar smiled. "They are all too easy to manipulate, as expected."

"Perhaps not if they knew who was pulling their strings," Obed replied with a somber expression and tone.

Xalivar fought to contain his annoyance. Obed was the former chief of the Lord's Special Police under Xalivar, the most elite security forces of the Borali Alliance, yet he made no effort to conceal his identity in public, going about in his old Council robes as if he had not a care in the world. Everyone else had resigned themselves to new, less-noticeable wardrobes so as to maintain as much anonymity as possible. Obed refused. Xalivar had only allowed him to join the allies out of necessity and a desire to have a scapegoat for certain treacherous activities which might be required. He couldn't wait to be done with him.

Swallowing the bile which had arisen in his throat, he kept his voice even. "When done well, they always believe they are the ones doing the manipulating, my dear Obed."

"And no doubt they will again, my Lord," Admiral Dek said, shifting in his chair opposite Obed. It was only the second time since they'd launched their plans that Dek had been able to meet with them. As the new head of Borali Alliance military forces, he couldn't slip away easily without undue attention so he primarily communicated with them via coded transmissions. Despite his years of military experience, the Admiral became noticeably uncomfortable whenever tension flared between the two ex-Council members. Their history of rivalry was well known, and Xalivar had no doubt Obed's current alliance with him was by necessity, not loyalty. It's why he'd asked General Lucius, his chief of security, to keep a special eye on Lord Obed. And also why he'd made sure Obed was in charge of the field operations. It would make it all too easy later on to let the right information slip out and watch Obed take full blame for a series of actions which would disrupt both the harmony and the integrity of the Borali Alliance. Xalivar, of course, would move in to restore order and save the day. He chuckled as he imagined it. "Make sure the proper messages get left at each location," Xalivar reminded his rival and enjoyed watching his reaction.

"He's doing everything exactly as planned." Obed stiffened, leaning back in his chair with a look of annoyance. Obed's son was a known embarrassment, yet the father still bristled when anyone criticized him in public. Except, of course, Obed himself. Bordox was yet another reminder to Xalivar why he'd never wasted time having children.

Xalivar couldn't resist needling him a bit more. "Good. We don't want the same incompetence he evidenced the last time."

"He more than redeemed himself on Eleni 1. It's hardly his fault the Council chose to interfere."

Xalivar forced a smile and nodded. "Are we making any inroads with the government on Italis?"

General Lucius sighed. "We are increasing the pressure, but so far they remain noncommittal toward our request."

"They fail to see the advantages for them in the arrangement?"

"They remain determined to play a neutral role and avoid any commitments." Lucius slid a datacard down the table toward Xalivar, who inserted it into his datapad and began scanning the report.

"The time has come to widen our circle. We can only proceed in strength."

"Perhaps our strength is what they question." Obed's eyes cut into Xalivar like a sword.

"Your choice can be unchosen at any time, Lord Obed. Should you desire another arrangement, you need only give the word." Their eyes met in a cold, staring contest.

Finally, Obed looked away. "Of course not. I have chosen properly."

Xalivar smiled, his eyes narrowing into a warning. "You have so far."

"They will commence construction of the ships as planned at the end of the month," Dek continued. "We have secured investors to cover the initial phase, but the rest remain resistant until they see results from our campaign."

"Are they unconvinced of our sincerity?"

"They remain determined to move slowly."

"The time for action is upon us." Xalivar slammed his fist on the table for emphasis, watching Dek flinch, while the others remained undisturbed.

"Some would rather speak to you personally."

"You explained why that isn't possible?"

Lucius nodded. "They question whether you're even alive, my Lord."

Xalivar sighed. That meant part of his plan might be working a little too well. He'd been forced to reveal his involvement to entice the types of investors he would need, but at the same time refused to meet with them in person. If proof of his activities leaked out to the rest of the system, it would destroy the mystique surrounding his disappearance. He may have been mistaken in assuming the assurance of his known close associates, like Lucius and Lord Obed, would be enough to engage their sympathies. Some of these men hated uncertainty and the changes occurring in the Borali Alliance since Xalivar's departure had increased their nervousness and left them on edge.

"Perhaps when the first prototypes are ready, a meeting will be necessary. For now, General, let them wonder if we've lost interest. If they don't meet our needs, there are other options." Xalivar never trusted anyone. He always had backup plans.

Lucius leaned back in his chair. "As you wish, my Lord."

"But keep them under watch to be sure they don't reveal anything in the meantime."

"The sincerity of our desire to maintain anonymity did not escape their notice, my Lord."

Yes, these men knew all about secrets; they were used to living out much of their lives in secrecy. It's why he'd dared to trust them, yet still,

Xalivar never trusted anyone much. Not even men he knew had sworn their lives to his service. "And what of Phase I of the recruitment, Admiral?" He turned back to Dek. "We must maintain our schedule regardless of the status of any equipment."

"Indeed. The recruiters have found eager volunteers for the private militia, my Lord."

Xalivar laughed. Farm boys and poor laborers were as easy to manipulate as the media. Some things never changed. He leaned back in his own chair now, glancing around the table again. It pleased him to see that none of his allies looked as relaxed as he felt. That was the way he'd always liked it and he rued the day it might cease to be the case. Things were coming together just the way he'd envisioned it. The investors' hesitation was hardly a hiccup. Even they would become convinced in a matter of time.

He found he couldn't sit still. Such was his excitement at the thoughts of success racing through his mind. Adrenaline pumped through him as he spun around and reached for the remote to the broadcast channels. It was time they entertained themselves with news reports on the success of their activities. Nothing motivated men like watching their plans unfold perfectly. For the first time in his life, Xalivar reveled in creating chaos. It was the polar opposite of his previous drive for order in all things. But he knew this was only a phase. Soon this diversion would pass and order would be restored with Xalivar in the Palace again, right where he belonged.

Tela and Telanus crossed the street to the park opposite Miri's building, holding hands. With every word her father said to her, Tela fought the urge to giggle like a little girl. She was just so happy to have him back in her life after all those long years of not knowing if he was alive or dead while he was in prison. Now he was there with her to talk to, give her advice, hug her and cheer her on. He was so proud of her that it was almost embarrassing. But she, in turn, was just as proud of him. She couldn't believe she'd almost forgotten how great a man he was. She'd idealized him in his absence, of course, but now that he was here, she found the real thing surpassed her expectations. When he'd asked for a quick walk under the stars before racing back to Vertullis for his night shift with Sol, she'd been thrilled to oblige.

"What's bothering you?" he said as she shivered involuntarily.

She shrugged as their eyes met. "Nothing."

"Don't lie to me. You've been down all night." She looked away. "You've tried that on me since you could talk and I always see right through it." He looped his arm in hers as they strolled together along the sidewalk dividing the park from the street. The strength of his muscular arms brushing against hers made her feel so safe. She had her daddy back. She was a little girl all over again.

Tela giggled. "It's nothing. Just stuff."

"Stuff what? With you and Davi?"

How did he know that? Sometimes it scared her—like he could read her mind. She wasn't sure she wanted a father who could do that. "Yeah."

"He really loves you. It makes me so happy to see."

She sighed. "I know, Daddy. I love him, too."

Telanus laughed. "Then what's the problem, dear?"

"He treats me like some kind of glass doll or something. Like he has to protect me all the time."

"It's male instinct for us to protect our women. He doesn't mean any harm."

She stopped walking and frowned. They were standing near the preschool Tela could see from Miri's window. Miri had commented how much she loved watching the kids play in the playground. "I'm a soldier, too. Not some housewife." Pulling her arm from her father's, she gestured. "I'm strong, talented, well trained. I can outfly him."

Telanus grinned. "How many times have you proved that?"

Tela smiled. "A couple."

"Well, take me up sometime, okay?" He whispered like they were co-conspirators. "I'd really like to see that."

"I'm sure he'd love that." They both laughed and Telanus looped her arm in hers again as they resumed walking. Even his scent took her back. He smelled like Daddy, the way she remembered him. She'd thought she'd forgotten that smell.

"Look. He cares for you. So, of course, he wants to protect you. I want to protect you. Don't you want to protect him?"

She nodded. "Yes. And you, too." Their eyes met and she giggled again. Why was she acting like such a boob?

"I've missed this, you know? I wish we could do it every night."

"Me, too, Daddy!"

Telanus stopped again, pulling her around to face him and putting his hands firmly on her hips. "But you're all grown up, Tela. From now on, our moments are limited. You're an adult and you have to make your own life. And Davi's a big part of that."

Tela's eyes misted. "There's time. You can see me whenever you want. I'll come to Vertullis more often."

His fingers pressed to her lips to silence her. "Shh. You're not listening. I couldn't be happier for you two. He's a wonderful son and he'll make a terrific son-in-law someday. Now I know you'll be well taken care of no matter what happens. That's all any father could ever want for his little girl, Tela."

Tela hugged him, feeling the tears drip down her cheeks and onto his shirt at the shoulders. "I love you."

"I love you, too, Little Girl. And so does he. A whole lot. Don't let him get away."

His use of her childhood nickname gave her butterflies. For years, she'd never expected anyone to call her that again. Tela blinked then reached up with the back of her hand to clear away the tears. "It's just hard sometimes."

Telanus chortled. "Relationships are the hardest thing you'll ever do. But it's so worth it when you find the right one. And I know you, if I don't help him out a little, you'll keep pushing him away. You've always been so independent!" He pulled back and stared into her eyes. She giggled again. "Am I right?" Tela just smiled and nodded as their eyes met. He shook her gently as if knocking sense into her. "Okay then. Don't mess this up."

Tela stiffened and raised her hand to her forehead in a military salute. "Yes, sir!" They both laughed as he looped his arm in hers again and led her back the way they'd come.

Yao hurried through his kitchen to get the door, hoping the buzz of the bell hadn't disturbed Dru's sleep. The cadet was sprawled out on the couch, where he'd finally fallen asleep after hours spent fighting insomnia. The struggle had only added to his stress and Yao wanted to give him every opportunity to recharge after the events of the past twenty-four hours.

The door slid into its wall alcove to reveal a blonde Borali Military Captain in full dress, neatly groomed, waiting in the corridor. Yao smiled as he stepped forward and they embraced. Farien smelled as if he'd just showered and his appearance was textbook military formal. But his uniform bulged in a few spots, making him look healthier than he'd looked the last few times Yao had seen him. He seemed happier too, something in his eyes. Yao hoped that was the case "What are you doing here, Farien?"

Farien smiled with a new confidence. "Here to save your butt as usual."

"It's rare I'm the one who needs saving." Yao stepped aside and motioned for Farien to enter. Farien did and the door slid shut behind him as he followed Yao into the kitchen.

"Who's the kid?"

"Dru, one of Davi's pilots."

"The first Vertullian student? How's that going?"

Yao pulled two glass bottles from the cooling unit and popped the caps with an opener, offering one to Farien. "The students handle it pretty well. A little more hazing than usual, but the younger generation seems okay with it mostly, so those caught hazing get hazed themselves."

Farien finished a sip of his beer and broke into laughter. "Listen to you! The younger generation? We were there not so long ago ourselves."

Yao chuckled. "Yeah, but it seems like ages, doesn't it?"

Farien shrugged. "The whole world's changed."

Yao nodded and sipped his own beer. It was a cheaper brand he'd settled for when his favorite Tertullian brew hadn't arrived with the last supply shipment. It tasted dry and bitter but slid smoothly down his throat to warm his stomach. "So why are you really here?" One look from his friend and Yao knew. "The investigation?"

Farien straightened and offered a salute. "Captain Farien Noa at your service."

"Has command lost their minds?" Yao kept a straight face and sipped his beer.

Farien growled and punched him in the arm. "They like me now, since I helped save the Alliance and all."

"You helped send one message. I was on the ground keeping the Peace Conference from being destroyed." Yao laughed as Farien scowled. It felt good to be with his friend again.

"You got reinforced because of me, pal!"

Yao laughed. "Okay, okay, so your e-post helped a bit."

"They asked me to help coordinate resources. Presimion doesn't have much experience with this kind of thing."

Yao crinkled his face as he guffawed. "No experience is more like it. You and I may be the only ones who have any idea how to run this show."

"I ran a prison for a year. What's your experience with investigations?"

Yao chuckled to himself. Farien loved to inflate things when it made him look more important. Centauri Two had definitely been an important assignment. It was one of the most secure and formerly secret prisons in the Alliance. "It was seven months, and I've done a lot of reading." Seeing Farien like this after all his guilt over actions he'd taken during the WFR rebellion, Yao hoped his friend had finally turned a corner and gotten back on track.

Farien rolled his eyes. "Book learning'll only take you so far there, Professor."

"I thank the gods every day we have you fighter jocks to straighten us out."

Farien clinked his bottle to Yao's outstretched beer. "And cover your butt." He smirked.

Both sipped their beer in silence for a moment while Yao gathered his thoughts. He knew all he had were suspicions. Still, he'd spent the last fifteen hours doing nothing but working on the investigation and his suspicions were the only thing that made sense from what he'd learned. His shoulders sank under the weight of it all. It exhausted him just thinking about it. "We don't have a lot to go on." Yao leaned back against the counter with a sigh. "I *suspect* it may be worker-related. Dru's convinced it is. But the student killed wasn't an ex-worker."

"I thought you said the hazing wasn't extreme?"

"That's when I thought you were an outsider paying a social call. There's been a few more serious incidents. Not as many as I'd feared when the program was announced. But enough to stand out as abnormal."

"So you think a fellow Cadet murdered one of his own?"

Yao shook his head. "No, I doubt it." Farien stared at him in confusion, sipping his beer and waiting for more. Yao tipped back his beer and took a long swallow, allowing it to warm his insides for a bit before continuing. "A Cadet would have known the student involved had no association with workers. So, no, I think there may have been a mistake involved. But that bed was originally assigned to an ex-worker."

"Let me guess—our friend Dru there?" Farien tilted his head toward the corridor.

Yao nodded. "I dug into Cadet Kowl's past, his family history. He's clean. No enemies. No rivals. It doesn't make sense for him to be the target." Kowl's father was a former religious leader turned therapist who had a successful practice. Everyone who knew him had nothing but praise. And Cadet Kowl hadn't been exceptional, but hadn't been a problem either. He'd blended in to the middle ranks and gone unnoticed by all except his friends and a few classmates.

"Did you look into the past and families of all of your ex-workers?"

Yao grabbed a datapad off the counter and tossed it to Farien. All the relevant data had been downloaded to it. "There are only four so far. They're all pretty clean as well. But the hatred of workers doesn't need the extra incentive." *Some people hate just to hate.* He recalled Farien's past biases and wondered if his friend would understand. Given his close contact with workers since they won their freedom, Yao didn't see how Farien could still be harboring his old stereotyped views.

Farien shrugged as he skimmed the screen. "Sure, it's possible. We can start there. Maybe up the security for the ex-workers. Try to prevent a repeat of this. But we can't rule anything out yet."

"Of course not, but I don't think this is going to be the last."

"Cadet murdered?"

"Ex-worker murdered."

Farien sighed and set the datapad on the table, pulling a chair out and sitting with the back between his legs as he drained his beer in one last swallow. "Conspiracy already? The old school people fled with Xalivar, Yao. Workers are equal now, full citizens. It's a new Alliance. We can't just start raising accusations like that."

"No. We keep it quiet for now. But what other theory makes sense?"

Farien set his chin on the chair back and thought a moment. "I don't have one, no. But one step at a time, okay? By the book."

Yao smiled. "Of course. I'm so glad you're here to help. I need the support."

Farien laughed. "Just so long as you remember I'm in charge." Farien's face became serious, frozen into a pose he might use for an official military meeting or ceremony. For a moment, Yao wondered if he might be serious, but then he caught a gleam in his friend's eyes.

Yao nodded. "Okay, but I'm not saluting you."

Farien cracked, grinning ear-to-ear and snorting. "You will if I order you to. I outrank you at the moment."

"I'm up for Captain next month."

"I'll take whatever time I can get."

They stared at each other a moment then broke into laughter until Yao remembered Dru and waved his hand to shush Farien. "It's so good to see you again."

Farien whispered. "You, too."

Bordox fought his every instinct as he stepped off the shuttle into the starport landing bay on Legon. His mission required stealth, yet he stiffened at having to sneak around a place he'd once walked freely—admired and respected. Here he was, less than a year later, hiding in shadows like a wanted man. And there was only one person to blame: *Xander Rhii!*

He made his way through the pedestrian corridors and deliberately avoided areas frequented by pilots and maintenance crews with the hopes he'd be less likely to be recognized. The datacard in his pocket pressed against his leg with every step. He just needed to get to the flight data booths and insert it. The program it contained would do the rest, drawing out the desired intel from the systems, and he'd be on his way again.

"What's keeping you so quiet?"

He knew that voice, stopping to listen as it came from around the corner ahead of him.

"Nothing. I'm fine." A woman's voice answered. One he didn't recognize. He heard footsteps approaching and shrunk back into a shadowed doorway. "Just let me check the shuttle maintenance records for Aron and we'll be on our way."

"I know you, Tela. Something's upsetting you."

*Rhii!* Bordox gritted his teeth. His old enemy, the idiot who'd ruined his life, was coming toward him. What was he doing here this time of night? Last he'd heard Xander was a squadron commander. Military pilots didn't casually walk around this side of the starport.

Xander and the woman appeared around the corner and stopped as Xander jumped into her path so they were face to face. The woman was medium height, shorter than Xander, with long, brown hair and sparkling, blue eyes. Her pleasing curves stiffened in anger as Xander blocked her way. Both wore Borali Alliance flight uniforms with rank insignia on their shoulders and blasters holstered at their sides. Seeing Xander in uniform just launched him into a rage. Rhii had the career Bordox deserved.

"I know you, Tela," Xander said. "Why won't you talk to me about it?"

"Because it won't make any difference. We've tried before."

She stepped around him and continued down the corridor as he hurried after her.

"So it's about me then? What did I do?"

The woman, Tela, sighed. "I am not some delicate damsel in distress,

Davi Rhii. I'm a fully qualified Borali officer, just like you." Davi! Such a stupid nickname! A slave name. The idiot's preference for that alone was evidence of his incompetence.

Xander looked confused. "Of course you are. What are you talking about?"

She stopped and whirled to face him, hands on her hips. Her eyes narrowed with annoyance. "Are you the reason I keep finding myself left out of any risky missions? Did you have me reassigned?"

"There haven't exactly been a lot of risky missions lately, and I don't know why you were reassigned but there's a rule about couples not serving together when one's in command."

Tela growled. "A convenient excuse. I am not going to be the girl who sits at home and pines after you. I want to do my duty like anyone else. I don't want to be protected."

"I'm not protecting you."

"Yes, you are!"

She whirled and started up the corridor toward Bordox again. He slipped further back into the shadows, sliding his hood up over his head as he enjoyed the show. They were so distracted with each other he doubted they'd even notice him. Bordox began to relax from his rage a bit as he watched Xander Rhii get put in his place by a woman. The only thing better would be the day he finally did it himself. Like instinct, his hand felt for the blaster at his hip, closing around the handle, he squeezed it. All he had to do was draw and shoot and Rhii would be dead. They would never see it coming, totally taken by surprise. His fist clenched and unclenched around the handle as he fought the urge. He'd blow his mission. But he might never get a chance like this. The feel of the cold steel of the blaster against his palm got his adrenaline pumping.

"Okay, maybe I didn't rush to argue." Xander smiled as if that alone would charm her. Bordox wanted to step out and wipe that smarmy grin off his face with a fist, but he swallowed, silent and hard, and stayed frozen in place. "Look, I love you, okay? Guilty! It's my instinct to want to protect you."

"We fought side by side in the Resistance. Why can't we do that now?"

"Well, there aren't really any enemies at the moment for one. And we were just getting into things then. Now we're together."

"So I'm supposed to sit at home and worry about you while you get to relax and know I'm safe? That's *fair*."

Xander grinned and shrugged. "I'd feel good about it."

Tela groaned and punched him hard in the arm. "Well, I don't." She turned and marched on down and through the door into the landing bay as Xander raced after her, calling, "I was kidding!"

Bordox paused a moment, tempted to follow, but shook it off, remembering his mission and slid on down the corridor the way they'd come. There was more at stake. He had to remember that. Rhii's day would come. Just not today. In less than two minutes, he'd stepped into the data center and selected a private booth. He slipped the datacard from his pocket and inserted it into the terminal then watched as the screen exploded in thousands of numbers moving and changing at a pace so fast his eyes could barely recognize them. After another minute, the terminal beeped and the datacard ejected. He returned it to his pocket then slipped out and headed back the way he'd come.

Sol had arrived back at the Vertullis starport from Legallis just in time to make his night shift as a supervisor at the FTL components factory in Iraja. Both Lura and Davi had urged him to reconsider his desire to work after his release from prison, but for Sol the right to earn his way honestly was the greatest freedom of all.

"Aron's seen to it we have everything we need," Lura always said when the subject came up, caressing his arm with tenderness even as her eyes filled with worry.

"Everything except something to do with my hands," Sol would respond. "I've been a laborer all my life, and twenty-one years in prison didn't end my usefulness."

"It's not about being useful," Davi always argued when he took his mother's side. "No one would blame you for enjoying your life and freedom." But Davi had never done much manual labor and, without that common experience, didn't know the power a man felt when his sweat and brawn produced something useful to others. It made Sol's motives hard to explain.

"I want to contribute something. Our people fought for the right to full citizenship and a society can't thrive without the work of its citizens to make it better." For Sol, there was nothing left to say. He loved everything about working again—the uniform, the companionship, and the satisfaction of a task well done.

Telanus, Tela's father, felt the same way, and they'd gotten to know each other well serving side by side as supervisors on the night shift. "I may have been in prison, but I've got good years left" was Telanus' answer to Tela and Davi's questioning.

The warning came with a flashing light on their console and a beeping of the terminals in unison.

"What is it now?" Sol wondered aloud as he searched the terminal screen for answers. Probably some maintenance issue or routine malfunction. Nothing unusual ever happened there.

"Stoppage on the Third Line," Telanus responded as both typed codes on the keyboards and examined the data their terminals returned in response.

Sol sighed and nodded. "Doesn't look mechanical." The line had shut down two weeks prior due to sensor failures, but the bad sensors had been replaced and the rest reviewed and the system had worked fine since.

Telanus shrugged, picking up the comm. "We'd better call down and see what Reyna knows." His first call went unanswered and a second five minutes later also brought no response.

"Let's go," Sol said as they exchanged a look. Both men stood and hurried toward the door. Sol didn't panic. Reyna was reliable and her not checking in for the first time probably meant a quick bathroom run or that she'd already discovered the problem and gone out to fix it. It was just another routine night. What could go wrong?

The route to the Third Line operator's booth took them along catwalks and up and down ladders high above the factory floor. The supervisors used the routes to get a good look over the workers and machinery and avoid the obstacles which slowed anyone's movement when crossing the main floor. Their feet clattering on the metal catwalks combined with the humming and clacking of machinery, the chattering of workers, and the smell of smoke from lasers in the tubes below. Even at night the humid air up there was oppressive. The factory's ventilation system hadn't been replaced in decades. Sol remembered now why he avoided the catwalks as much as possible.

As they reached the final ladder and started down, Sol looked around for Reyna. The young worker was one of the newer employees, with an abundance of energy and positive attitude Sol admired. She had long, brown hair and light skin which reminded him of the way Lura had looked when they'd first met.

Reaching the bottom of the ladder, Sol hopped off and waited for Telanus to join him, before they moved off together toward the nearby booth. The air cooled immediately and Sol breathed it in deeply, relieved to be on the ground again.

Sol glanced around, still seeing no sign of the operator. "Reyna?" She'd never hear him over the noise of the floor.

Entering the booth, Telanus began checking the controls. "She must have gone out to check the vents for the source. Everything's normal here."

Sol nodded as both exited the booth again, then they moved along the tubes of the Third Line. The usual humming and vibrations were noticeably absent as they walked, finding no sign of opened vents and none of their coworker. The further they walked, the more concerned Sol became. Then as they drew near the end of the line, he spied strands of brown hair dangling through the bottom of the propulsion belt under the tube. Could Reyna have climbed inside to examine it? The vent wasn't open. Why would she have closed the hatch?

Sol and Telanus hurried to the vent and found the bolts fastened tight. "Reyna?" Sol called again as Telanus worked one side and he undid the other.

"Why would she have gone inside?" Telanus wondered aloud.

It took both of them, working together, to lift the vent cover. As it clattered to the floor beside them, the irony smell of blood struck their noses and glassy blue eyes and a bruised and bloodied face stared out at them. Reyna appeared to have been beaten, her right cheek and lower jaw smashed in.

Telanus gasped and turned away.

"Dear God, no!" Sol gritted his teeth to fight back tears. Written above the body in blood were two words:

YOU'RE NEXT

Tela and Davi rounded the corner of a corridor close to Aron's home. Why didn't Davi just let it go? She hated when he got like this: stubbornly focused on an issue until he got the answers he sought. It wasn't so bad when the issue didn't involve her, but this was all about her feelings and she didn't feel like talking about it yet. But he just wouldn't shut up.

"Come on, babe. What do I have to say? You know I never meant to make you feel like that."

"But you do—a lot."

Davi started to protest as they turned the corner and heard a scuffle ahead—a loud thump, boots on the floor, then heard voices.

"What do you want from me?"

It sounded like Aron. Tela's heart quickened as she and Davi exchanged a look then hurried around the corner.

Aron was backed against a wall as two figures in hoods confronted him. Each of them had four arms.

*Lhamors!*

"Please. I'm a friend to the Lhamors and all people of the Alliance."

On the wall nearby, a message had been begun in paint on the wall. So far, it was one word in all capital letters: LEARN.

Then the creatures' arms were in motion with one of the hooded Lhamors swinging two blades held evenly apart straight toward Aron while the other used two hands to swing a club at him from overhead. Aron shook as he lost his footing and sunk to his knees.

"Leave him alone!" The Lhamors whirled at the sound of Davi's voice as both he and Tela drew blasters from their holsters.

"Don' wan' you. Just th' t'rg't." The Lhamors voice was raspy, almost a whisper.

"If you hurt him, you'll answer to us," David said, his voice unwavering.

"We c'n kill 'll o' you," the other Lhamor said, whirling to face them, his blades at the ready.

"Why do you want to kill any of us? What have we done to you?" Aron stumbled back onto his feet, backing away from his attackers, attempting to slide past and join Davi and Tela.

"You 're en'mies o' the 'lli'nce." The larger Lharmor swung his club at Aron, who ducked then cringed as the club slammed noisily into the wall.

"The only ones here who will be dying are you," Tela aimed her blaster and fired it at the club. It disintegrated in the Lhamor assassin's hand as the laser struck, leaving a cloud of smoke and the smell of burning wood. She grasped the blaster tighter and aimed again.

The Lhamor dropped the remnants and drew sidearms of his own, four, one in each hand. "I 'm pr'p'red to die. 're you?" He jumped clear as Tela fired again, the recoil throwing her hand back and up as she did.

In unison, the Lhamors spun, the one with blades slicing backwards toward Aron with one hand and throwing the other blade in an arc toward Davi. Aron groaned as the blade sliced into his forearm, sending blood streaming toward his elbow. Davi ducked the other and fired as Tela took aim again and fired at the taller Lhamor. Laser bolts crisscrossed the hallway as the Lhamor returned fire.

Both blades clattered to the ground as their former bearer fell to his knees, struck by Davi's blaster. Davi rolled as he fired, narrowly missing being struck by bolts from the other Lhamor's blasters.

"Run, Aron!" Tela yelled as she dove and rolled the opposite direction, avoiding more lasers from the taller Lhamor, then screaming as one singed her upper shoulder. The laser stung as it burned into her flesh, but her arm was still functional and she aimed her blaster again as she landed, firing it at the Lhamor again. Davi fired seconds after and the Lhamor fell, just as Aron fell to his knees between them.

"Thank God you came!"

"Are you okay, Aron?" Tela quickly examined him. His arm was bleeding, but the cut didn't appear to have gone deep.

"I'm fine."

She heard Davi fire again and turned, ignoring the flare of pain in her arm as she aimed her own blaster and fired again. The remaining Lhamor's blasters clattered to the floor and he fell on his face, dead.

She and Davi quickly spun, backs touching, looking for other assailants. "Do you think there were only two?"

"They wouldn't expect to need more."

They turned at a thump to see Aron had fainted on the floor nearby. "Call for medics," Davi said as he hurried up the corridor to check the fallen Lhamors.

Tela nodded and knelt to examine Aron again. Her heart pounded as she set her blaster within reach on the floor and felt for a pulse. Then she keyed the comm on her shoulder. "We need emergency response. There's been an assassination attempt on Lord Aron. Outside his quarters on Level Seven, Corridor Six."

Davi kicked the weapons away from the Lhamors, sending them sliding down the hall toward her with scraping sounds as he bent to examine the bodies. Neither moved. His eyes met hers and he shook his head, sliding his blaster back in the holster at its side. Noticing something, he reached out and took a crumpled paper from one of the bladed Lhamor's fists. Unfolding it carefully, he read it over.

"What's it say?"

"I think it's the message he never finished." Davi's eyes met Tela's again as alarms sounded around them and footsteps and shouting voices drew toward them from nearby corridors. Davi held the note out so they both could see the words:

LEARN YOUR PLACE

# Chapter Three

Once the doctor informed them Aron was resting and would recover in a few weeks from his wounds, Davi finally relaxed and breathed normally again. He left Aron's wife, Calla, to tend to him and returned to Miri's study where Lura, Miri and Tela were waiting anxiously.

"He'll be fine," he assured them as Tela flipped a switch on a wall terminal and stepped back.

"I've got them on the line." It took Davi a moment to realize who she meant.

Three older men with graying hair appeared in the monitor. Two wore military uniforms but only one the uniform of the Borali military. The other's uniform was blue rather than gray and bore medals and other markings from the Workers' Freedom Resistance Army. The third man wore a green robe in a style common to planetary leaders or Council members like Aron.

"How is he?" The man in the robe asked. All three men's faces showed their concern.

Davi made eye contact with the men. "He's resting. Calla's with him. The doctor said the wounds would heal in a few weeks."

"Do you have any idea who the assassins were?" General Matheu's voice had a natural growl which made him all the more imposing in his blue uniform.

"Other than Lhamors? No." Tela kept standing and pacing around then sitting back down again.

"Well, there've been three deaths now and the attempt on Aron," the gray uniformed man said. "Coincidence seems unlikely."

"Three? We only knew about the one at Presimion." Davi and Tela exchanged a look.

"There was a housewife killed on Xanthis," Joram, the man in the green robe, explained. "Her husband was stationed there for an agricultural firm."

"And a technician was killed two hours ago at the FTL components factory," the gray uniformed officer said.

Davi's body tensed as his eyes met Tela's and she gasped.

"The factory where Sol and Telanus work?" Lura was on her feet in a minute with Miri rising beside her, grasping her arm with concern. For a moment, Davi considered pulling away from Tela to comfort Lura, but her legs remained steady and she continued staring at the screen with hopeful determination.

The man nodded. "Sol and Telanus found her."

"My God!" Tela pushed against Davi, allowing his arm to wrap around her as she buried her face in his shoulder.

"It's time for Aron to make the Council aware. Someone is orchestrating this." Matheu's face returned to his usual stern, emotionless stare, a look which annoyed Davi greatly when he'd dealt with Matheu during the Resistance. Matheu and Uzah had remained suspicious of Davi, forcing him to prove himself over time. But in the end, he knew he'd gained their admiration and full support.

"Why would the Lhamors start assassinating Vertullians? They've faced persecution themselves." Miri paced behind the couch where she'd been seated.

"We suspect they are mercenaries, not the orchestrators," Joram replied.

"The victims aren't connected in any way other than being Vertullians," Uzah added. "It would seem entirely random outside of that one fact."

"I'll contact Yao and Farien and see what their investigation has turned up." Davi took a deep breath and fought the urge to patch them in immediately. The Vertullian leaders didn't know his friends as well as he did and might not be comfortable sharing this conversation with outsiders at the moment.

"Are Sol and Telanus okay?" Lura's face had paled, her forehead creased with lines. Davi reached over and caressed her arm. He could find no words to say. She'd already been through so much.

"They're fine. The factory has been sealed and guards posted while we investigate." Lura looked relieved at Joram's response but still ready to rush out the door at any moment.

"I'll have my shuttle prepared to take you there immediately," Miri said, squeezing Lura's arm and hurrying toward a nearby corridor.

"You two may be safer right here." Davi didn't relish the idea of his mothers heading off alone into danger.

"I'm going too." Tela's tone muted any thought he had of arguing. Her eyes met Davi's with an intensity that caused him to nod and look away.

Miri disappeared into the corridor as he surrendered. "Just be careful, okay?"

"I know how to take care of myself." Her tone was terse, evoking memories of their earlier conversation. He sighed as his shoulders lowered in surrender.

"We need to handle this with great care," Joram had been elected President when the planet won its freedom. "Our status as citizens is still new. Old resentments remain. We must allow the authorities to do their jobs and not be seen as distrustful or accusing."

"At the same time, we have a duty to protect our own." As usual, General Matheu showed no concern for politics.

"We can do both for now." Joram's tone matched the General's in intensity.

"We will do what must be done. Together." Uzah was used to mediating between his strong-willed companions.

"Of course." Joram smiled and nodded to Uzah.

"You'll be on your way in an hour," Miri said as she returned.

"Check in with us please upon arrival," Uzah smiled, despite the worry in his eyes.

"You have enough to worry about without worrying about us," Tela answered.

"Save us the trouble of sending men to check on you," Joram said. The concern in his voice pleased Davi.

Tela looked ready to scold when Lura jumped in. "Of course. We appreciate your concern."

"I'll be in touch soon," Davi said as the three men nodded and the terminal went dark. He concealed his own internal panic until Tela and his mothers hurried off to prepare their things for the trip. Then Davi dialed into the military channels to see what information on the investigations had been made available.

Yao yawned as he poured another cup of Talis for Farien. The natural stimulants the drink was known for didn't seem to be doing their job. His body pleaded with him to lie down and sleep. The long hours they'd spent investigating Cadet Kowl's murder were catching up with them faster than either had hoped, and they were clearly losing the battle to stay awake.

"If you want me to go with you, I will," Farien said as he accepted the mug.

Yao shook his head. "It's my responsibility as the faculty member in charge of new student assimilation. Having an official from the military there might make it even more dramatic."

Farien nodded, sipping his Talis. "Either way. It won't be easy. Sorry you have to deal with that."

Yao closed his eyes as the warm liquid flowed down his throat to warm his stomach. "Thanks. I met the Kowls once at orientation. I'm actually glad it'll be someone they know."

"If word hasn't reached them already."

"That's why we've kept it quiet. It's only been three days. We wanted time to figure out what had happened and who might be involved." Only they hadn't learned anything yet. Yao had no idea what to tell them. He'd already dodged their calls twice, which was unfair, but so was giving them half-truths and guesses. He wanted more.

"What're you gonna tell them if they ask?"

"That the investigation is receiving all available resources. It won't be much comfort, but what else can I say?" He looked away, staring out the window as he wondered how he'd react to a professor showing up to tell him of his own child's death. The lack of information would just make it worse. All the Kowls knew at this point was that their son had been murdered, his throat cut. Who and why were still questions, and those were the kinds of things a parent would demand to know. Yao's head ached from a desire to have answers for them.

The comm beeped on the wall nearby and Yao turned and hurried to answer it. He pressed the brown button below the speaker. "Professor Brahma."

"Yao! Is Captain Noa with you?" Davi's smiling face appeared on the screen.

Yao felt some of the tension leave his body at the sight of his old friend. "Yeah, he's here causing all the trouble he can."

Farien walked over to stand beside him. "The trouble started long before I got here."

"This time." All three said it together and laughed.

Then Yao's thoughts went back to Kowl's waiting parents. "I hope you have good news for us. We could really use some."

"No progress on the investigation?"

"Not really."

"Well, I don't have good news, no, but I do have some information which may help." A seriousness filled Davi's face which Yao hadn't seen there since the Resistance.

"What's going on?" Farien's eyes met Yao's.

"We're up to three murders now and an attempt on Lord Aron's life." Davi leaned back in his chair, looking as tired as Yao and Farien. Yao leaned against the wall. He hadn't realized until now it was the middle of the night. Just realizing it brought an involuntary yawn.

"Who are the others?" Farien had his datapad out, prepared to take notes.

"A technician at the FTL factory on Vertullis."

Yao's eyes widened with concern. "The one your father works at?"

Davi nodded. "My father and Tela's father found the victim. Beaten and chewed up by the propulsion system of the line."

Yao cringed. "Poor thing."

"The other was a housewife stationed on Xanthis with her husband, who handles shipping for VerAgro."

Farien cursed as he typed into his datapad. "It's a conspiracy. Has to be!"

Davi nodded. "And the assassins are Lhamors—at least some of them."

Yao frowned. "Why would the Lhamors be after ex-workers? Surely they can understand what it's like to be persecuted."

"That's what Miri asked. We think they're mercenaries."

Yao turned away from the terminal, taking a deep sip from his glass again. *Come on, Talis! I need energy here.*

"You two look exhausted. You should get more rest." Davi didn't look much better. His eyes were hollow, his face haggard. Yao wanted to laugh but was too overcome with worry to manage it.

"Sol and Telanus are okay?" Yao felt Farien's stare at his back as his friend asked the question.

"They're fine. Just deeply worried."

Yao turned back to face the terminal and his friends. "So am I. This could be just the beginning. We have to get a fix on it fast."

Davi nodded. "I know. I wish I knew where to start."

"Bordox, Obed, Xalivar—I can give you a list of suspects." Farien counted them off on his fingers as he spoke.

"Xalivar's never liked aliens, we know that. But no one's seen or heard from him since the Peace Conference there. I can't imagine Obed getting involved in a murder plot. He used to head the Lord's Special Police."

"That doesn't make him honest," Yao countered. They all knew government police used lying and manipulation daily. They were skilled at it. "We can't just work on assumptions. We need real evidence."

"So we'll get some. Let me get on the Alliance database and call up those other investigation files." Farien moved toward the keyboard on a pull-out shelf in the wall beneath the terminal.

"I've already sent copies to you through e-post," Davi said with a smile. "I'll be back in touch tomorrow. Several high level meetings happening which may have impact on the information and resources available for the investigation."

"If command doesn't notify me first." Yao saw Farien stiffen, his eyes avoiding the screen.

Davi chuckled. "Relax, Captain. I'm just trying to help, not step on your toes."

Farien smiled. "Yeah, sorry. Just tired and stressed."

"Get some rest then. You'll need the energy."

Yao nodded. "We definitely will. Thanks for filling us in."

"You bet. How's Dru doing?"

"Better. Still recovering from the shock. But he went back to classes today."

Davi looked relieved. "Good. Tell him all his friends here are praying for him."

Yao smiled. "Of course."

"Hope we can talk in person soon about something a lot more pleasant." Davi smiled, but his slouched shoulders indicated he'd be headed for bed himself. "Rhii out."

The screen went blank as Farien hit a button and logged into e-post to retrieve the files Davi had sent. "Just let me look these over and I'll call it a night."

Yao yawned again. "I'll wait until morning. I wouldn't remember anything in them anyway as tired as I am. Don't stay up all night, ok?"

Farien rolled his eyes, attention still focused on the terminal as he typed in his login and password. When Farien got focused like this, he became oblivious to everything else. Best to leave him to do as he wanted.

He'd fill Yao in the next morning.

Yao patted his friend on the shoulder then turned and headed for his bedroom. He wondered if he'd be able to shut his mind down enough to get actual rest. Lately it had been working overtime, and he'd only slept fitfully. Combined with the Talis, he assumed he'd face the same this night. He looked in on Dru, who was snoring on the couch in the study. When had Yao and his friends lost their ability to sleep like that? Most cadets excelled at it. They'd only been out two years. It seemed like centuries. Who could have imagined how much they'd go through in that time? He sighed and continued down the hall.

From the outside, the rocky opening looked like any other mine shaft—an arced entrance laser-carved from rock which became quickly dark black within and required everyone who entered to wear special mining hats with lights. Everything appeared exactly the way it had been designed to. Xalivar was tempted to skip the lighted hat but dared not tip off any onlookers that the whole thing was just a ruse.

The entrance tunnel descended slowly to a dark metal door. So dark you couldn't see it until you were almost upon it, even wearing a lighted hat. It opened with a special cardkey General Lucius carried in a pouch on his belt. He slipped the cardkey into the slot then stepped back as the door opened before their eyes. Xalivar smiled. Lucius had always been one of his finest officers. He felt relief knowing at least one of his co-conspirators might be trustworthy or even up to the task.

They stepped inside and walked into the chamber. Within a minute the door beeped and swung shut on its own. No accidental discoveries. And no chance anyone who did manage to find their way here by accident would ever get out. Even if they managed to fake the cardkey to get in, you needed a separate device to get out, a microscopic chip injected by the medical team. So far only Lucius and Xalivar had it and Xalivar's had only been implanted that morning upon his arrival.

Despite its primitive state, Xalivar could picture it as it soon would be—a huge cavern for training and assemblies, surrounded by smaller cabins with barracks, dining and recreation. Above, his own quarters with a dais and balcony overlooking it all. Other chambers would be storage, weapons, and quarters for Xalivar's allies and the officers. He laughed, feeling good to be alive as Lucius watched him. Soon all those who'd written him off would find out how foolish they'd been.

As Xalivar spun slowly back toward him from surveying the room, Lucius extended a hand offering him a similar looking cardkey to the one he'd used to open the door. "Only two in existence. Some of the engineers have already complained, but I told them they'd be handed out when their need had been determined."

Xalivar accepted the card and looked it over. "Good, very good, Lucius. I can always count on you."

He could see the pleasure in the General's eyes as he saluted. "The tunnels are forty-percent complete. So far we've dug out only this cavern and one other, but we are increasing our workforce."

"Any trouble from the authorities?"

"Xanthis has seven moons and this one was long ago deemed worthless. It's far out and just a cold rock. They hardly took notice when we told them a TriLithium spur had been detected. I'm not even sure they believed it. They'll be delighted if it generates revenue. But they hardly care much until it does."

"They've left you alone then?"

"So far. An inspector or two might wander out here before we're finished, but I have some TriLithium samples on their way which should distract them from wasting time probing these chambers."

"Once training starts they won't survive their landing, of course," Xalivar had a plan to deal with the questions such deaths might bring, but that didn't need to be revealed yet. He intended to keep as many secrets for as long as he could. No matter how faithful Lucius was, the only person Xalivar trusted completely was himself. "And the recruitment?"

"Quiet inquiries are being made in the right places." Lucius waved a hand to indicate the far reaches of the system. "Your request to focus on human pilots does make things challenging."

"We can recruit alien pilots once the human leaders have been trained and integrated. The aliens will be disposable. The humans will not." Lucius nodded. "Any word from Pres on recruitment within the Alliance?"

Lucius turned slowly until their eyes met. He hesitated as if choosing his words, but Xalivar saw in his eyes he had displeasing news to relay. "Pres' loyalty is not easy to turn. I told you she might waiver."

Xalivar frowned, controlling the surging anger rising inside. "She's betrayed us already?"

Lucius shook his head. "No, my Lord. She's expressed some concerns. So far I have allayed them, but she's not made the amount of progress desired."

"Perhaps we should request a meeting then." Xalivar inwardly cursed the weakness of women. He should never trust another one! He'd trusted his own sister, Miri, and look where that got him.

Lucius sighed. "You know how difficult the last one was to arrange."

Xalivar smiled. "Great plans require great challenges, Lucius. If your fellow General needs reassurance, I should meet with her myself. You know well my powers of persuasion."

Lucius smiled. "I'm sure it would be most reassuring."

Xalivar began walking toward the tunnel at the far end of the chamber. "Good. Arrange it. Now I want to see the beginnings of our flight hangar."

Xalivar's bootsteps echoed off the rock walls as the General hurried to catch up with him. "The Xanthians will be quite humiliated at what we've pulled off right under their noses," Lucius said.

Xalivar laughed as Lucius led him into the darkness of another tunnel. *The whole Alliance will be shocked.* Ahhh to be making history again! It was so close, he could feel the power already.

The restaurant smelled of seafood and exotic potpourri, one emanating from the kitchen through the vents, the other pumped in deliberately for atmosphere. Together they just created an olfactory mess. Miri's midweek luncheon always met at the restaurant just east of the Palace in Legon's ritziest shopping district. It started fashionably late as usual with various women trying to assert their importance by arriving more fashionably late than their rivals. Miri arrived early compared to most and was well into her third Tertullian Hammer by the time the food was ordered. She hated all the presumptions and political maneuvering. She'd gotten more than enough to last a lifetime at the Palace. Now that she was a civilian, she just wanted to relax. The Hammer did its job, warming her blood and lessening her tension, and had her feeling pretty good by the time the serve-bots circled around them, some taking orders and others filling drinks, appetizer trays, etc.

Then the gossip began in earnest.

"Have you heard the rumors about the Council making that Worker holiday official?" Hachim's wife Irais had a voice that was almost like a squeal.

Abena's dark skin was a sharp contrast to her puffy white dress. She shook her head with disgust. "My Niger believes the public will never accept it. They're just not like us. Besides, they have such crazy beliefs!"

Selina Noa's hand came to rest gently on Miri's forearm. "Some of them are quite nice, when you get to know them. And they're not as different as we've been taught to believe." Farien's mother had always been close with Miri, the families united by their son's friendship.

Abena and Irais guffawed as they shot her disgusted looks. "Your bias toward them is well known, as is Miri's."

"We are biased, based on a great deal of experience, Abena," Selina responded calmly. "Experience few amongst us have."

Irais scowled, her double chin wrinkling in the process. "I have all the experience I need. History speaks volumes."

"A history written with bias and the intent to maintain the status quo," Miri finally said. "History is filled with lies."

"We'd expect that from you," Abena answered, "a woman who couldn't even adopt a quality child but instead stole one from workers!"

Tarkanius' wife Danae stood, raising her open palms to signal for calm. "Please. We've all been friends a long time here. There's no need for such talk." Older, with gray hair atop a gaunt face but with a warm smile and eyes, Danae was a respected friend to everyone.

Selina raised her Talis in salute. "Here! Here! Surely there are much more pleasant things to talk about." Her blue eyes sparkled to match her smile as her long, blonde curls framed her face.

"Those people want to shove their ludicrous ideas off on our children," Irais said. "That's the issue! And it's no laughing matter!"

Miri slammed her empty glass down hard on the table. "They want no such thing. They want to live in peace if only we'll let them. They have shown respect for our ways and our views. Why can't we have the maturity to do the same for them?" It was the first time any of her circle had treated her like less than an equal, and she didn't like it at all.

Irais coughed. "Maturity? This from a woman who never got serious enough to marry? Who tried her best to undermine our entire government and way of life?"

"I said 'enough!'" Now Danae sounded annoyed. "This is not the place for such discussions. Stop it at once!"

"We're just agreeing with our husbands that citizenship is one thing but full acceptance of their cultural views is a different matter." Abena looked to Irais who nodded vigorously.

*Your husbands side with whoever can give them the most power. They have no loyalty and no integrity, picking on the weak.* Miri despised them and their wives too. *Go on, Miri, tell her.* "Your husbands joined with me in fighting to change the old system," Miri said instead, not even meeting their eyes. "They seem to have forgotten the values they once stood for."

"Miri!" Danae looked at her with exasperation. "You know that all members of the Council have a track record of serving the public interest with honor and integrity. I'm sure any objections they may have are based on very real concerns for the safety of all citizens."

"Besides," Selina patted Miri on the arm, her eyes urging Denae to sit back down, "these matters are not ours to decide anyway. I, for one, want to hear about Irais' new granddaughter."

Several other ladies mumbled in excited accord at this.

Irais smiled, reaching for her datapad. "I brought plenty of photos."

"Send them around then! What are you waiting for?" Selina's smile was contagious.

Miri sighed and lowered herself back into her chair as a serve-bot retrieved her glass and began to refill it. She'd never before felt out of place amongst these women, even as their princess. Now most of them looked like strangers.

"When are Davi and Tela going to give you grandchildren?" Selina's voice was almost a whisper.

Miri saw in her eyes that her friend wanted to distract her. *Bless Selina for her gentle kindness.* "We have to convince them to marry first," Miri responded.

Selina laughed. "All things in time, dear."

Miri nodded as she took a sip of her refilled drink.

The military briefing took place in the officers' conference room at Alliance Command just off the starport on Legallis. Uzah and Davi hadn't even had time for lunch after his arrival, because a delay put his shuttle's arrival time too close to the meeting. They made their way to adjacent seats at the large, circular conference table and waited while other officers filed in, noisily chattering around them. The Borali military's emblem, a blue crest with images of crossed blaster bolts, fighters, and the twin suns, was lasered onto the ceiling under crystals which lent it a special sparkle when combined with light from the reflector pads lining each side wall. The table itself bore a smaller version of the logo as did the uniforms of all attendees. Everyone had worn their dress uniforms, crisp and clean. Uzah sat up straight and Davi did the same as they waited. Generals Pres and Grif were listed as running the meeting, and both were known for expecting their personnel to be shipshape and spotless, as per protocols.

The two generals arrived together and walked straight past Davi and Uzah toward the head of the table. Grif was tall and thin with graying hair at his temples and fuller, darker hair between. He looked like a kindly grandfather to Davi, but previous encounters had shown him to be serious and intense, not unlike General Matheu. Pres was medium height with a softer demeanor, her shoulder-length dark locks braided on each side. Both wore decorations earned from many years of distinguished service. Everyone who spoke of them did so with well-deserved respect.

The officers stood and saluted as the two Generals arrived at the head of the table. They nodded and saluted back. "At ease," Pres said and the officers lowered their hands and sat back down.

"A murder took place four nights ago at the Presimion Academy on Eleni 1," Grif began without preamble. He looked around making eye contact with the attendees as several muttered and others gasped with surprise. "A young cadet's throat was cut; a message left on the wall reading: YOU DON'T BELONG HERE. Since then, two other murders have occurred with similar messages and an attempt was made on Lord Aron's life."

"By the same criminals?" A female captain inquired from a seat near Davi, her voice dripping with rage.

Grif's eyes met hers. "We don't know yet." The captain looked away in disgust.

"It does appear that the murders are connected," Pres said. "Separate investigations are being coordinated and combined efforts employed to find out."

Grif nodded. "From this moment, I'm putting all Vertullian military personnel under special security."

"Special security?" the blonde colonel's voice crackled as he tried to hide a laugh. "Since when do military personnel need security? They are armed, aren't they?" Davi struggled to remember his name. The Colonel was Jansen, if he recalled right.

"Sure they are," said a red-faced major whose uniform barely fit his rotund frame. "They're just not very good shots." He and the Colonel cackled in unison, a few others joining.

"What about when they're off duty?" The same female captain asked the colonel, clearly annoyed by his crassness. "It'll take a large detail..."

"I carry my blaster everywhere," Colonel Jansen said, smirking at her. "So should they."

"Nevertheless, we're providing extra security—guards for their barracks and quarters and modified assignments when necessary. Is that okay with you, Colonel? Major?" General Grif's face was stern; his tone firm.

The two officers shifted uncomfortably in their chairs as the smile faded from their faces. "Yes, sir, General." Colonel Jansen nodded, not meeting the General's eyes. The Major glanced toward Davi, his face startlingly familiar for reasons Davi couldn't remember. Where had they met before? And why did he look at Davi with such anger?

"Have any of the murders been military?" the female captain asked.

"Just the cadet so far." Pres' look suggested she feared there would be more.

The Major turned to Davi and Uzah. "If you need special treatment, perhaps we should get you special armor, special starcraft, special uniforms..." Laughter came from other attendees as Colonel Jansen smiled and chuckled.

"We didn't request it, but since the assailants are unknown—"

The colonel cackled, cutting Davi off. "You Vertullians are the Council's new pet project, didn't you know? You don't have to ask for anything. They just give and give and give."

Davi opened his mouth to protest, but Uzah put a hand on his shoulder. "Do you feel you're being treated unfairly, Colonel?" Uzah asked, his brow furrowed as his voice shook with anger.

"No, you earned everything you've got, Lieutenant General." Colonel Jansen rolled his eyes and turned to glance around the table for sympathy.

"Far more than you did, Colonel Jansen," Grif barked as he stood stiffly and glared.

Several officers chuckled as the Colonel stiffened and straightened his uniform. "My family has a distinguished history of service to the Alliance."

"Their history of service has earned them their places, too," Grif replied. "If you have a problem with it, feel free to set up a meeting in my office to discuss a cut in rank."

"Or mine," Pres said, frowning as her eyes also focused on the Colonel. The Colonel's face reddened as he ignored the smirks of those around him and held his tongue.

Shifting in his chair, the major shrugged. "All military personnel should be prepared for danger at any moment. What makes this special?"

"The High Lord Councilor's orders for one. Three murders in four days for another." Grif relaxed his shoulders and turned back to take in the other attendees. "We all know there are some of our people, perhaps even in this room, who bear old grudges against the Vertullians, but those feelings must be put aside. They are full citizens now and deserve the same rights and protections as everyone else. Part of our job is to ensure they get them."

"Does this mean we won't be allowed to do our duty like anyone else?" Davi turned slightly, so he could see the Generals' eyes as he asked.

"For now, no. We just want to be sure extra security is around to help avoid unpleasant incidents." Pres smiled reassuringly.

"What kind of incidents? Anything besides murders?" the major kept a straight face, but his tone dripped of sarcasm.

"Hazing of any sort will not be tolerated," Pres answered. Both Generals stared at Colonel Jansen and the major, their eyes clearly implying they included the men's actions in that category.

"No one will bother them if they do their jobs." The major glowered at Davi and Uzah, but his anger had changed to raw hatred.

The annoyed female captain rolled her eyes. "Women have served for two decades and you still haze us."

"Friendly teasing." The Colonel waved in dismissal.

"Criminal charges will be brought against any and all violators. Would further explanation be required?" Pres and Grif looked directly at the Colonel as she finished.

His smile faded and he took a deep breath. "No, of course."

"Good." Pres smiled and turned away.

"I want immediate reports of any unusual incidents—of any kind. We have no idea who's responsible and we need to keep our people safe." Grif looked around for any questions or objections. All the attendees just stared at the Colonel.

"They'll be safe," Colonel Jansen said as if he answered for it personally.

Grif nodded and turned back to Pres. "Any resources you need can be asked for. Contact General Pres. In the meantime, I'm putting all units on alert. We may need to act quickly once the guilty parties have been identified to bring them to justice."

"Isn't that under the purview of the LSP?" the Major straightened in his chair as all eyes turned to him.

"We'll be available as needed, Major. Is that a problem?"

The Major shook his head. "No, sir."

Grif smiled. "Good. Ex-workers are to be treated the same as any other citizen. Violations will be punished to the full extent of military code."

"And what about the civilians, sir?" the female Captain met the General's gaze with no hesitation.

"Plans are in the works to protect them as well, Captain."

"Meaning you don't know, sir?" Davi watched her with curiosity, admiring her nerve.

"No one knows, Captain. But we intend to find out."

They were dismissed moments later and Davi and Uzah headed for the commissary at a casual pace. As they turned a corner, someone pushed between them roughly, in a hurry to pass. Davi recognized the Major from the meeting. Davi exchanged a look with Uzah as the major spun around.

"Sorry, sir," he nodded to Uzah, but his sneer was anything but apologetic. His eyes turned toward Davi's glare. "Did you want something, Captain?" He pronounced Davi's rank as if it were poison.

"No, sir," Davi answered, continuing to walk as their eyes met.

"Let me inspect your weapon, Captain."

Davi stopped, Uzah beside him. They exchanged a look. Davi didn't know whether to comply. What was the Major after? He couldn't shake the feeling they'd met in the past. Uzah motioned for him to hand over his weapon.

Davi pulled his blaster from the holster and grabbed it by the firing tube, offering it handle-first to the major. Officers were allowed to make flash inspections of their inferiors at any time. The major tore it from Davi's hand and looked it over carefully. "Are you fully trained in its use, Captain?"

"A crack shot, sir," Davi answered with a smile.

"You'd better be." The Major frowned. "If one of my men dies because you can't pull your weight, I'll have you up on charges."

Davi frowned, fighting the urge to snap back. "If you make one more such comment, Major, I'll have you up on charges," Uzah said, his voice rising in anger.

The Major merely glared as he offered Davi back the blaster, ignoring safety protocols and holding it out firing tube-first. Davi grabbed it angrily, and the Major turned without a word and started back down the corridor.

Davi pulled the trigger and a laser beam charred the floor between the Major's boot heels. The Major spun angrily around, raising a hand in accusation.

"Ooops. You handed it to me the wrong way, sir. It accidentally went off as I tried to holster it."

The Major looked at Uzah, who kept a straight face despite the sparkle in his eyes. Davi holstered the weapon and stood at attention. The Major's eyes met Davi in a warning before he turned again and headed back up the corridor at an even quicker pace.

Davi waited until he'd turned the corner then laughed as Uzah shook his head. "He could charge you with insubordination."

"You could charge him with harassment."

"Officers can inspect weapons of anyone they outrank with a moment's notice. Be careful, Davi. We have enough against us already. We don't need to make enemies."

Davi bristled. Why was Uzah taking the idiot's side? "Sorry, General."

Uzah smiled. "At least he knows you're a damn good shot." They both laughed as Uzah clapped him on the back and they started down the corridor again toward the commissary.

After several days spent bedridden at home under Calla's mothering eye, Aron escaped via an emergency Council session where he detailed the various facts of the attack. He found the other Councilor's reactions disappointing.

"Did you really expect no resistance to the idea of full citizenship for our former enemies?" Lord Hachim asked from a table in middle of the room as Aron finished.

"A few murders with the only connection between them being ties to Vertullis doesn't convince me of a conspiracy," Lord Niger added from a table across the aisle from Hachim. Others around them offered mumbled agreement.

"It's certainly cause for concern," Lord Kray said. Aron could see on her face she was furious at their indifference.

Simeon and Tarkanius officiated the session from atop a large dais facing rows of tables at which the other Council members were seated. All wore the embossed white robes customary for Council meetings. Aron stood at a podium before the dais, where he'd made his presentation and now faced the others' questions.

"Murders happen throughout the system. What you're asking is to divert resources which might prevent them from occurring in one area to another, to offer special treatment to a segment of the population who not too long ago forced us to war demanding their freedom." Hachim shook his head. "They have what they wanted. Now, they want more."

Kray's clenched fist slammed against the top of the desk where she was seated. "Are you suggesting we just let them die?"

"I'm suggesting we treat them like any other citizens."

"We will not stand by and allow our citizens to be murdered, if there's any chance we can prevent it," Tarkanius said sternly, frowning at Hachim.

"Of course not! But what makes you think you can prevent it?" Hachim looked at him as if the question were obvious.

Aron sighed. How could anyone aspiring so much to be a leader lack such basic compassion? "We don't know that we can, but there have been three attacks in a matter of days. Something must be done."

"And it will be," Niger answered. "What we're here to determine is what action is appropriate."

"Obviously more effort must be made to investigate," Lord Qui said from his seat beside Kray at a table near the front. "If there is a conspiracy, evidence will reveal it." Kray and several others mumbled in agreement.

"Investigate! Of course! But we shouldn't go jumping to conclusions about conspiracies and increasing security until we know something." Niger's voice remained calm but rose in pitch along with his passion as he spoke.

"No one wants any more deaths," Hachim said. "But as we discussed in our previous meeting, offering these Vertullians special treatment will only inflame the passions of those who resent the freedoms they've already been given."

"Like who, Lord Hachim?" Kray sounded exasperated. "Yourself and Lord Niger?"

Aron coughed into his hand to cover a laugh and several of those present looked at him with sympathy as Hachim and Niger chafed at the accusation, shaking their heads in offense. "We are honorable men."

Lord Niger nodded. "We both supported suing for peace. We have been supportive of the Vertullian's citizenship."

"Until their own enterprise competed with yours," Lord Kray hissed.

Simeon raised a hand from the dais. "Enough! Fighting amongst ourselves is not providing answers. I will coordinate with security forces to provide increased resources for the investigation while also ensuring extra security for our Vertullian neighbors. I have the authority as Head of the Council to do that, so if anyone wants to argue, you can come argue with me!"

He panned the room angrily as he finished, as if waiting for someone to raise a challenge. Aron wanted to call for them to stay, to try again to convince more of them, but he had no idea what he'd say. When the Lords remained silent, Simeon dismissed them with a wave and they hurried out, chattering amongst themselves.

As the others had left, Simeon, Tarkanius and Kray pulled Aron aside.

"We're putting you under increased security, too, Aron," Tarkanius said.

Aron shook his head, grateful Calla wasn't around as a witness. "I'm just fine. The doctor said I'll be full recovered in a few days."

"If they tried once, they'll try again," Simeon said, shaking his head. "You need to be protected. We can't have our Lords coming under attack."

Kray kept angrily shifting positions as she stood with them. "I cannot believe the attitude of those two! The deaths must be connected."

"They are only asking questions of us which the media and our citizens will, Kray," Simeon said, placing a hand on her arm. "We must follow proper steps and avoid any risk of making things worse."

Aron smiled at Kray. "What the people would appreciate most are a few Council members making an appearance in the capital to offer reassurance. Perhaps Lord Kray would like to accompany me?"

Kray nodded. "Of course."

"I'll come as well." Simon smiled. "I'm sure others will join us."

"We must be careful not to put the Councilors at risk as well," Tarkanius warned.

Aron chuckled. "We must take the same risk we ask of our citizens, my Lord." The others nodded in agreement. The support of the leadership was such an encouragement. When they'd agreed on a time for their appearance in Iraja, each returned to his or her office to concern themselves with other responsibilities.

Despite his insistence that he was well, Aron felt his energy waning after just two hours with the Council. The injury had been harder on him than he'd imagined, and although he did his best to hide the effects from others, including Calla, he knew he had to keep up on his rest if he hoped to heal quickly and put it behind him. He made a note to stay in regular touch with Davi and Uzah so he could stay abreast of any new discoveries. He had nothing else pressing at the moment, and he knew too many inquiries from him would just interfere with their focused efforts. Leaving the Council Chamber, he headed back to Miri's apartment, knowing Calla would be there waiting and worrying about him.

It was kind of Miri to let them remain there while she visited Vertullis with Tela and Lura, but he hoped the Council's decision to provide security meant they'd allow them to return to their own apartment soon. He always rested better in a familiar environment.

The Garden was so peaceful and beautiful. Davi had spent a lot of time there since being stationed at the Legallis starport. He couldn't believe he'd never visited as a child—such awesome natural wonder and beauty available for his enjoyment and he never took advantage. It was too public, he supposed. Still, the sweet scent of the Cherelia blossoms, with their poofy red petals and long, thick, green stems, the musty scent of the local blue moss at his feet, and the chirping of baby Taffitas amidst the branches filled him with delight. It was his favorite place to come and think.

*I wish Tela were here.* It was their weekly date night, yet she was on Vertullis with his family. He needed to go back and call them to see how things were going; to find out more about the worker killed at the factory where their fathers worked. It was hard to focus enough to choose a path home, however. His thoughts were so muddled in their rushed search to find answers. Was this truly his uncle's plot? Who else was involved? How many more would die? Why would God allow this to happen?

He hated that he and Tela had been fighting when she left. They'd been arguing a lot more the past few months and he had no idea why. The arguments always started over things they used to just talk about and resolve. Why had talking about them become so much harder now?

Feeling overwhelmed, he knelt in the soft, cool moss and offered a prayer. *God, please protect my loved ones—Tela, Lura, Miri, Sol. Please show us how to stop these killings. Help us to protect our people. Lead us well.* The thoughts came out in a jumble. He hoped somehow God could make sense of them. He felt like a child praying, so uncertain what to say, like he'd never done it before. *Help me talk to her, Lord. Give me the words to say. Help me to communicate well with all of them. And thank you for the many blessings you've showered on my life.*

As he finished, he felt a tingle on his spine. Was someone watching him? He glanced around the Gardens and saw no one. Then his eyes went to the observation booth high above. If someone was up there, he couldn't see them.

*Relax, Davi! You're being paranoid! Trust God! Have faith!*

He felt like a fool for having such doubt, but then who wouldn't, given the uncertainties? He wasn't alone in worrying about it. He hoped the combined efforts of his friends and coworkers would lead to answers soon.

Climbing back to his feet, he glanced once more at the observation booth then wound his way along the path again through the vegetation, taking note of whatever caught his eye. The curators had done an amazing job of collecting samples of native flora and fauna from each planet in the system, except a few outer ones where no such life was known. The combined colors, scents, shapes and sizes were a delight for the senses, and he took a moment to savor the divergent smells and sounds again as he reached the door.

*Thank you, God, for the beauty of your nature.* Such sights reminded him of God's ever-present spirit wherever he went. That presence was a great comfort to him right now. He glanced at his chrono and realized he had to call Tela before everyone went to bed. He pushed the button and waited as the door slid open before him, then stepped out into the steamy, noisy Legon night and headed for home.

Bordox slipped into the observation box above the Legon Botanical Garden quietly and found himself alone. He smiled. No one to recognize him. The lengths he'd gone to disguising himself might well be unnecessary. He'd retrieved and transmitted the information to his contacts on Xanthis without difficulty using a secure channel on his small transport. Then he'd landed again at the starport, claiming engine trouble and put his plan into motion. He could coordinate his assassins fine from anywhere. So far, except for the failed attempt on the slave Lord, they'd done their job well. A worker on the Council? He shuddered just thinking about it.

The time had come for him to take care of his own goals, not just those of his father and Xalivar. They'd isolated him away from them anyway, so they didn't need to know where he was or what he was doing. They'd both blow a vapor seal, of course. But Bordox was his own man. Sending the data instead of delivering it in person sent a strong message.

He watched Xander Rhii through the dark windows and smiled. His nemesis seemed deeply troubled. *Perhaps you're feeling a bit as you've made me feel, Rhii!* He chuckled at the thought. The hatred inside sent waves of warmth through his body. Rhii deserved to suffer as much as possible, and Bordox would make that happen, following his enemy wherever he went until the right opportunity to dispose of him presented itself. He wouldn't let the opportunity slip away like it had on Vertullis and Eleni 1. This time Xander Rhii would pay for what he'd done. Rhii paced amongst the foliage on a narrow path, looking lost in thought.

*Worried about your friends Yao and Farien? The woman? Your family? The slaves you call your people?* Bordox wouldn't stop at Rhii. He'd kill the woman and as many of Xander Rhii's loved ones as he could. If he got lucky, some would die before Rhii did, so Bordox could make him suffer. Others would be dealt with after. Perhaps even at the funeral. It hardly mattered as long as they all died.

He watched as Xander knelt on soft mossy soil beside the path and placed his hands together, his lips moving as he said a prayer.

"Gods, Rhii! A convert of their fool religion, too?!" Bordox laughed. "You will all see very soon that your God has no power to protect you!"

Bordox continued watching as Rhii finished his prayer then slowly turned and looked up at the observation booth. Bordox shrunk back from the window in panic, then remembered the booths can see out, but no one outside can see in. He was tired of hiding. Tired of Xander Rhii. He cursed Xalivar's orders. *Soon, Rhii, soon.*

Remaining in the shadows but still close enough to see, he continued watching his old rival until he left, slipping out quietly and unnoticed to follow him home.

# Chapter Four

A cool breeze had swept over Xalivar in the courtyard as he exercised under the rising twin suns. Tickling his skin like Daken down, it made him feel more alive than ever. Smiling as he finished, he strode inside, greeting Manaen and the minor staff as he passed them in the corridors. He chuckled at their surprise. Keeping people on edge delighted him. He was having a great morning...until Manaen brought the report. Bordox had decided to remain on Legallis, even though it was expressly against Xalivar's orders. The assassination attempt on Aron had been foiled by Xalivar's former nephew, Xander, and a female companion. Xalivar needed better people. Their standards for themselves weren't high enough.

His teeth ground together as he growled, tired of being disappointed. "What kind of incompetents can't dispose of an old man, a woman and a boy?" He whirled to face Obed and Lucius who sat quietly waiting. "Your maladroit son has decided he doesn't need to follow orders, Obed. I should have known not to give him any important duties."

Despite Obed's obvious attempt to hide his reaction, he wouldn't make eye contact with Xalivar. "I'm sure he has his reasons, Xalivar." No objection this time? So even Obed knew his idiot son had blown his mission.

Xalivar's fists clenched at his side. "I want him back here, and I mean now!" He spun back to reading the message. "He's gone after my derelict former nephew."

"The report says that?"

Xalivar scowled as his eyes met Obed's again. "He's let his desire for personal revenge cloud his judgment. I'm holding you responsible for assuring he gets his focus back."

"I don't control him, Xalivar, any more than you can control your nephew."

Xalivar's clenched right fist flew out against a nearby pillar. "You know nothing about that, Obed! My own sister let that slave in my house and hid his identity from me. When I discovered it, I made sure he was treated appropriately."

"Only when it was discovered by others." Obed's eyes filled with accusations.

"I personally asked the Council to order him apprehended," Xalivar reminded him. "I did my duty to protect the Alliance." Fury rose inside him when the doubt in Obed's eyes never wavered. He pointed an index finger. "Be careful, Obed."

Obed smiled, amused by the warning. "I know my duty, Xalivar. Do you know yours?"

How dare the insolent cretin question him like this! Xalivar wasn't the problem. Obed's son was!

Lucius spoke quietly from a chair in the corner. "Perhaps I can send someone to bring him back. Our plan is succeeding. The information he provided is exactly what we needed. The list of ex-workers in the Borali military gives us plenty of targets. And we can confirm the status and defensive capabilities of all military posts. Information we sorely needed to plan our attacks."

Xalivar looked down, remembering the morning breeze and relaxing his fists as he nodded at the General. "Everything will continue as planned. Obed will coordinate the assassins himself from now on." It was brilliant. Obed wanted to set Xalivar up, so now Xalivar would turn it around and put it all on him.

"He can continue to execute the plan from anywhere, Xalivar," Obed said, his voice still dripping with irritation. "You've given me other responsibilities."

"You will see to it that your son doesn't fail. Your other tasks can still be managed." Xalivar glared at him, his eyes allowing for no argument. "In the meantime, training and recruitment can be increased. With the base construction well on its way, it's time we begin the second phase."

Lucius nodded. "Admiral Dek has the recruiters out and some have already been successful. We've recruited several Borali officers and a number of foot soldiers as well."

"The disappearance of Alliance military personnel will not go unnoticed," Obed said. "Alliance Command will investigate."

"And find nothing. Their people will simply disappear." Xalivar smiled at the thought of their bafflement.

"They will no doubt be suspicious."

Xalivar brushed Obed's concerns aside with a wave of his arm. "And by the time they discover the cause, it will be too late." He nodded to the two men as his eyes met theirs. "You have your orders. I want regular reports."

Lucius nodded. "As always, my Lord."

Xalivar reread the report again in silence. After a moment, the others assumed he was done and quietly slipped out. Xalivar cursed his former nephew. *Miri will pay for all she's done. Miri and her bastard son!* Xalivar chuckled at the thought. Perhaps he'd even get to watch their faces as they died. Their father would be so disappointed in his daughter. She had thrown away everything their family had worked generations to achieve. *Sister dearest, how I wish I could see you now.* With Tarkanius now the High Lord Councilor, he wondered how she was enjoying life as an ordinary civilian. Miri had always prided herself in her royal status, always been special. Laughter rose from his belly like a wave, echoing off the walls until it filled the chamber around him.

The call to the High Lord Councilor's Palace took Davi by surprise. Atop a rise at the center of Legon, the Palace grounds held an imposing complex of white buildings of various shapes and sizes which offered an unobstructed view of the entire city. The meeting took place in the throne room. Davi hadn't been there since he joined the Worker's Resistance, and although the Palace had been his childhood home, he felt out of place being there again. Every corner he turned brought flooding memories. He'd known every inch of the place, even its secret passages. He'd explored them all in fantasy adventures of his childhood, fighting dragons and other fabled creatures to save the world time and again. Such foolishness it seemed now, yet how many times had he been called on to fight for his people? He'd imagined it as glorious then, but it hardly seemed so now.

Lord Tarkanius stood from the throne and greeted him as he entered, looking older than Davi had ever seen him. His slight paunch hung as if he hadn't the will to hold it in, and his kind eyes were filled with darkness that matched the worry creasing his brow. Davi was surprised to find Aron, Uzah, and Lords Kray and Simeon also in attendance. He'd had no idea why he'd been called there, but now he knew it was important. As he shook the High Lord Councilor's outstretched hand, then placed his right fist atop his left, crossing his right index and second, ring and fifth fingers to form the traditional salute, the others nodded in greeting, somber looks on their faces. Davi stood at attention, waiting expectantly.

"There's been another assassination," Aron said, in a breach of protocol. Usually the High Lord Councilor spoke first at such meetings. Yet Tarkanius didn't even react.

Davi turned to him. "Where?"

"Some sort of sabotage at the mechanic's depot in Alpha Base," Tarkanius answered. "Five mechanics were killed and seven others injured."

Davi couldn't believe it. He'd been stationed at Alpha Base briefly, by his Uncle Xalivar, to protect him when he was wanted for the accidental death of a Borali Sergeant. Located on Plutonis, an ice planet in the outer solar system, it was a remote and barely habitable region, and Davi couldn't imagine an assassin sneaking onto the base undetected.

"We've decided to ask you to represent the workers on the investigation," Tarkanius continued.

Davi looked at Tarkanius, surprised. "I thought Farien had been placed in charge."

"You will work with him and Yao Brahma as partners. Both have been temporarily reassigned to the investigation."

"We need a Vertullian on the team to assure our people it's handled properly," Aron said.

"We can't afford the possibility of any doubt," Lord Kray added.

Aron nodded. "You're one of the heroes of our people now. I'm afraid we must call on you again for service and whatever sacrifice it entails." Davi winced at the thought of being a hero. Certainly the idea would be far from the minds of his mothers and Tela when they heard of this mission. They'd gotten used to Davi being home a lot, in between quiet patrols, and wouldn't react well to Davi taking off on a dangerous assignment.

"It's my honor and privilege to serve my people and the Alliance," Davi responded, offering another salute. But he still worried about how Farien might react. He and Farien had come to loggerheads during Davi's time with the WFR and had just gotten back to a normal relationship. He didn't want to do anything to jeopardize that.

"You seem troubled? What's the matter?" Lord Kray's expression reminded him of Miri and Lura. He hadn't meant to wear his feelings so blatantly on his face.

"It's just Farien. He may see this as a lack of confidence in his abilities. We've managed to put past tensions behind us. I'd hoped to avoid any in the future." Farien had always had insecurities about his superior's confidence in him. This would just stir those up all over again. He didn't relish the thought of reigniting that old conflict with his friend.

"You three will be serving as equals on this assignment," Tarkanius said. "We're hoping your friendship will allow you to cooperate well in the investigation."

"We'll do our best, I can promise you." Davi forced a smile, despite his ongoing inner tension. Whatever his feelings, they weren't asking. The decision had been made. He took a deep breath and met their gazes.

Tarkanius smiled back. "We knew we could count on you."

Aron nodded. "We'll expect regular reports to the High Lord Councilor and me."

"Any resources you may need are at your disposal," Uzah said. "You have only to ask."

Despite any concerns about Farien, Davi felt a sense of relief. Having such support behind them could only make their challenging mission easier. And he wanted to know as much as anyone if his suspicions about Xalivar's responsibility for the attacks were correct. "I won't let you down."

One by one, they each stepped forward to shake his hand and utter words of encouragement. Then, seeing the meeting was over, Davi snapped to attention once more and saluted the High Lord Councilor before turning and marching out the door.

The lectures began from the moment he told them. The ladies followed him around as he packed, pecking at him like Daken hens at seed.

"Why you? There are other competent people," Miri said, hovering over him. "People with a lot more experience at investigations."

"They want to avoid the appearance of any impropriety." Davi folded his spare uniform just in case. "The Vertullian people are demanding answers."

"Of course we are!" Lura said, moving up beside Miri so close Davi almost couldn't move around as he packed. "Our people are being slaughtered."

Davi's eyes met hers. "And it's my job to find out who's responsible."

"How long will you be gone?" Tela asked from her position leaning against his bedroom doorway. Of the three, she was the most subdued, which really had him worried.

"As long as it takes."

All three ladies frowned. "You have no idea then?" Tela refused to make eye contact.

Davi finished neatly folding his uniform and placed it into his bag, then gently pushed between his mothers and crossed to her, putting his hands on her waist. "I'll be fine. I promise."

She brushed his hands away and straightened as she faced him. "You don't know that! These people have been committing murders. They won't be afraid of killing you."

"I have a duty to the Alliance."

"What about your duty to me?" She turned away, arms crossed over her chest.

"You know I love you. And I really need your support."

Tela's lips pursed and her brows knit as she turned back to face him. "And I love you, too, but I'm scared, Davi. We have our whole lives ahead of us. What about all our plans? Our dreams?"

"Those things will all happen, Tela. I want to spend the rest of my life with you. But I'm a soldier and these are orders from the High Lord Councilor."

"Maybe I should stop by the Palace and let the High Lord Councilor know how I feel about his orders then." She put her hands on her hips, her blue eyes darkening and lips puffing out as she said it. Her face was determined, but he saw in her eyes she was only bluffing.

"I'd certainly go with you," Miri said, her determination not wavering at all.

"For heaven's sake, leave the boy alone," Sol said from his position in the hallway. The women scowled as Sol and Telanus poked their heads through the doorway. "He's an excellent soldier. He knows what he's doing."

"Of course you men are behind this. You love nothing more than proving your manhood by fighting and killing." Miri glowered.

"I'd hope we don't have to fight or kill anyone," Davi said.

Miri looked at him and shook her head. "You know this won't end without a fight. Don't lie to your mother, Davi."

Lura rushed toward Davi and wrapped her arms around him. "You be careful."

She held on so tight he had trouble breathing for a moment, then he pushed her gently away as he hugged her back, nodding. "Of course I will." He let her head rest on his shoulders a moment before dropping his hands.

Miri embraced him next. "We expect regular reports of your welfare. Don't disappoint us."

"I'll communicate when I can."

"That's all anyone can ask," Telanus said as he put a comforting arm around Tela.

Davi extended his right hand first to Sol and then Telanus. Both shook it firmly. "We're very proud of you, son," Sol said with a warm smile.

Davi choked back tears as he turned to Tela. Moving towards her as Telanus lowered his arm, Davi embraced her, then reached up to wipe away the tears which rolled down her cheeks. "I've already requested that you lead the squadron while I'm away. Make me proud, okay?"

She sniffled and smiled. "You know I will."

He leaned forward and she leaned in to meet him. The kiss was passionate, almost as if all their emotions were channeled into it. They stayed with their foreheads touching after they finished, staring into each other's eyes. "You are my future."

Tela nodded, sniffling again. "Mine, too." It came out as a croak, barely audible.

Davi smiled. He kissed her again then gathered himself as he moved back toward his suitcase. "I have to finish packing. I'm to be on my way as soon as possible."

Tela hugged him again, then let go and moved toward the bed and began folding the rest of the clothes he'd laid out there in silence. They worked side by side for the next few minutes as their parents quietly slipped from the room. When they'd finished, Davi closed the suitcase. Tela reached over and grabbed his hand, squeezing it tightly. Then they embraced and kissed again, and Davi wished he'd never have to leave her.

Bordox watched from inside his shuttle across the landing bay as Xander went through pre-launch preparations in his fighter. From the quantity and type of cargo being loaded in the VS28s small hold, he could tell Xander was leaving on more than just a routine patrol.

"Where are we going, Rhii?" He said to himself, knowing wherever his nemesis went, he would follow. He was just awaiting the right opportunity to enact revenge.

He heard the hum of the fighter's engines as Xander initialized the pre-launch sequence. Bordox started his own shuttle and did the same.

When Xander launched a few minutes later, Bordox launched through the civilian launch tube and sped around until he spotted the VS28 and slid into position to follow. Xander was following the standard military flight path, so Bordox just blended into a civilian route that paralleled it and kept his sensor locked on the fighters' vapor trail. In their Academy days, Xander had proved the better pilot but no more. Bordox had been practicing, even getting coaching from a few mercenaries. He'd fly circles around him now. Maybe this trip would give him the chance.

As they passed through the atmosphere, Xander turned the fighter toward nearby Eleni 1. "Going to see your old friends, are you?" Bordox chortled at the possibility of enacting revenge on all three of the troublemakers. It would ensure Xander's friends never bothered him after Xander's death, leaving Bordox free to work his way back to prominence in the new Borali military under Xalivar's new government. There'd be no one to prevent him from taking his rightful place this time. He whistled as he matched the shuttle's speed to that of the VS28, then settled back to decide the safest place to land.

Voices echoed off the chamber walls as the assembled Lords chattered while awaiting the High Lord Councilor. Aron did his best to make small talk with Simeon and Kray, but he was too nervous to remember much of what they said. It was quarter past the hour when Tarkanius strode into the chamber. His mood was somber, and before he'd reached the podium, the conversations trailed off. Aron, Simeon and Kray rose from chairs atop the dais to stand behind Tarkanius. The announcement he was about to make was important and Aron hoped the Lords' reactions would not echo those the leaders expressed in regard to the Returning.

"I have just appointed a commission to oversee the investigation into the assassination of Vertullians throughout the system," Tarkanius said as he stood before the mic. "So far there have been four successful attacks, the last of which killed five mechanics at Alpha Base."

The Lords broke into chatter again, some expressing their shock, others proposing theories as to whom was responsible for the violent incidents. Tarkanius raised a hand to silence them.

"The commission will be overseen by Lords Kray and Aron. I have also appointed Lieutenant General Uzah from the Vertullian forces, General Grif from Alliance Command and, to investigate, Captains Davi Rhii and Farien Noa and Lieutenant Yao Brahma, a professor at

Presimion." This time the Lords held their chatter, waiting for him to continue. "The attacks seem to be systematic. At this point all that we know is that all of the victims, except one, were Vertullians. And we believe that was an accident and a Vertullian was the target. Attacks have occurred on Legallis, Vertullis, Plutonis, and Xanthis. The assassins in the attempt on Lord Aron were Lhamors. We have yet to confirm the identity of the attackers in the other incidents. I believe the time has come for the Boralians to pull together. The Vertullians are one with us now, our brothers and sisters. We must set an example and show unity and respect as a Council." Aron closed his eyes, offering a quick prayer. The moment had come. "Therefore, I am asking you to vote in favor of Lord Aron's proposal declaring The Returning an official holiday."

To Aron's surprise, the Lords' faces brimmed with support. Some even shouted it out or waved at him. Only a few, including Lords Hachim and Niger expressed their displeasure. The two Lords frowned and shouted in protest. Hachim crossed his arms over his chest while Niger stood and glared at the dais.

"Lord Kray's inquiries to the planetary leadership on all planets showed no serious resistance. And although in the short term some may object, I believe if we pull together in unity, they will come to accept it as we have." Tarkanius looked around the room, making eye contact with the Lords to see if any would object. Aron watched closely but no one stepped forward or voiced an objection. Niger and Hachim just stayed where they were, and Aron glimpsed in their eyes, they knew they'd lost.

Aron stepped forward and Tarkanius motioned him to the podium. He smiled, proud in this moment to be one of them, as he faced his fellow Lords. "I want to assure you all that I share your concerns about tension between our peoples. But we will do our best on Vertullis to earn your trust and respect and be good citizens of the Alliance. I hope you'll give us every opportunity to do so. Your support to this point has been admirable and a blessing, and, on behalf of my people, I thank you." Kray and Simeon began to applaud and soon the chamber filled with its echoes.

Aron nodded to Tarkanius as relief swept over him and took a step back as the High Lord Councilor reclaimed the podium. "I want any reports you receive about attacks on Vertullians given to me and Lords Aron and Kray immediately. And I expect each of you to cooperate fully in anything they may ask of you during your investigation."

Lord Simeon stepped forward to join Tarkanius. "The High Lord Councilor has my full support in this. Please make no public statements without running them by myself and the High Lord Councilor. This situation needs to be handled with great care so that no one says or does anything to jeopardize the investigation." He stepped back again to join Kray and Aron.

"All in favor of declaring The Returning an official holiday say 'aye.'" Tarkanius waited as the responses sounded from around the room. It was clear the Lords were overwhelmingly in favor of it. "Any opposed say 'nay.'"

Although he'd watched Lords Niger and Hachim stay silent while the others approved, both held their tongues, saying nothing now. The mood in the room was one of overwhelming support. Aron quelched an urge to smile. The last thing he needed was to rub his victory in the opposition's faces. But internally, tension rolled off him in waves.

"Congratulations, Lord Aron. Your proposal has been accepted." Tarkanius extended his hand to shake Aron's. Aron beamed. It was one of the proudest moments he could remember.

"Council dismissed," Lord Simeon said again from his seat atop the dais.

The Lords broke into chatter as they scattered. Several came forward to shake Aron's hand.

After bidding Davi goodbye, Miri returned to her chamber in sadness. He had a duty to obey his commanders. The High Lord Councilor himself had ordered this. But that meant seeing him go off toward danger again. She'd already lost him once when he joined the Resistance and fought for the Vertullian's freedom. He'd told her later of his many near misses. And she'd been relieved when his recent duties involved quiet patrols with little action. Now, still reeling from the animosity she'd encountered amongst her friends at the brunch, her son was being sent off to risk his life. All she'd tried to do was the right thing. Why was it costing her so much?

As the door slid shut and sealed behind her, the lights automatically came on and she moved to her terminal to search for the latest news. A flashing e-post alert filled the screen. She clicked the e-post but it was from an unknown sender. For a moment she was tempted to ignore it, then curiosity got the better of her and she opened it. Her heart raced as she read:

To: MRhii@Federal.emp
From: Unknown
My dearest sister,

It's been too long since we spoke. I'm sure you miss my delightful presence. Don't you? How's my precious nephew? I'd hate it if something happened to him before we meet again. Oh how I miss your voice, the lies, the betrayal. I imagine you hoped you were done with me. But I'm afraid your wishes won't be granted in this case. Soon, my beloved sister, we will be reunited. I hope you're as anxious for that day as I am.

Your loving brother,
Xalivar

Miri couldn't believe it. She'd known Xalivar was alive when he'd disappeared, escaping the wrath of the Council after his betrayal. But no one had seen or heard from him. Until now. Where was he? She reread the message and felt a chill, her skin tingling. The threat was implicit. Xalivar was bent on revenge. She'd hoped she'd never see him again. She suspected the assassinations of the Vertullians were his handiwork. Maybe it was time to notify the Council. Many of them thought Xalivar was gone with the past, but they didn't know her brother like she did. Xalivar was capable of anything. They had to stop him no matter what.

Davi brought his VS28 in for a landing on the small landing pad near Presimion Academy and made his way across the campus toward the Library. The campus looked much the same as it had almost a year before when the Peace Conference between the Vertullians and Borali Alliance took place. His prior visit had been during the rainy season, but now the Ambrose lilies were abloom, their intoxicating perfume filling the air, and Astreu Vermelho trees wore vibrant leaves of many colors. It was here that his Uncle had tried to arrest him and here that Bordox, his old rival, tried to kill him. It was here that his people won their freedom and the whole world changed.

As he reflected back on all that had happened, he spotted a familiar figure waiting for him outside the Library—a tall, humanoid with dark, orangish-tinted skin and purple eyes. Davi smiled as their eyes met. His old friend offered a wave and a grin.

"They notified me you'd landed. Word of your assignment just came over the military channel." Yao patted Davi on the back. "It's good to see you."

"It's good to see you, too. How'd Farien take the news?"

Yao shrugged. "You know Farien. He'll get over it once we're all together."

Davi shook his head. "We used to be a team, the three of us, helping each other through. When did it become a competition?"

"It's not unless you make it one." Yao was right. Farien would get over it if Davi just focused on what he'd been sent here to do. Yao stepped toward the Library and the large doors slid open, allowing them to walk inside. As they walked side by side through rows of video terminals and data card storage shelves, Davi ignored the activity on the lifts and staircases which connected the seven-story shelves housing a collection of old Earth paper books.

"How's the investigation going?"

"We've reached a dead end locally," Yao said. "Farien took a trip to Vertullis to interview your father and Tela's about the worker killed at their factory. The next step is a trip out to Xanthis and then Alpha Base."

Davi nodded and followed Yao as he zigzagged through study cubes and long tables drowning in stacks of books and papers deposited by the cadets and research assistants who came and went from them like butterflies. "We'll all go together."

Yao shook his head. "I have duties here, classes to teach."

"You've been temporarily reassigned. Someone else will fill in for you."

Yao frowned. "I haven't received any orders."

"Don't they send them through the Provost? They come from the High Lord Councilor himself, so the Provost won't have a choice."

Yao smiled. "The Three Musketeers together again?" Yao loved references to the Old Earth classics he'd read so many of in his spare time.

"You know I keep meaning to read that..."

"You and Farien have no appreciation for the history of the arts."

Davi laughed as they left the Library's main collection and moved into a series of white corridors toward the rear of the building. He squinted at the bright reflector pad glow bouncing off the walls and floor as they passed through. "Since when did they move your office here?"

"It's the only place they had space for Farien. I'm working here temporarily so we can stay easily in touch as things develop."

"How's Dru?"

"Improving. He's back to classes now, but he's not the same positive, carefree kid he used to be. He feels a lot of guilt over Cadet Kowl's death. He thinks it was meant to be him."

"What do you think?"

Yao stopped outside a door, his finger poised on the button. "It's probably not coincidence that Dru's original bunk assignment was the one where Cadet Kowl was killed." He pushed the button and the door slid open.

Davi saw Farien bearing a frustrated scowl as he scanned data on a monitor. "Look who I found." Yao's voice was cheerful in an obvious effort to diffuse any tension.

Davi strode forward and extended his hand. "They tell me you've done a great job here, Farien. I promise I'll do my best to be an asset and stay out of your way."

"We're all listed as equal by command. I'm told the High Lord Councilor himself ordered it."

Davi nodded. "The Council wants a Vertullian representative on the investigation to assure the people it's been handled fairly."

Farien glared. "I've served the Alliance with integrity. They have no reason to doubt me." The reaction Davi had expected. Yao sighed as he and Davi exchanged a look.

"No one's doubting you, Farien," Davi said. "But you served as an overseer of worker labor on Vertullis."

Farien spun toward him in rage. "I was always fair in my treatment of them!" For a moment, Davi half expected him to leap from his chair but Farien stayed there, seated, staring up at them.

"No one's saying you weren't, but there are political implications to this."

"What about all I did to help the workers and you since then? Does that count for anything?"

"Of course it does. This isn't about you."

Farien ignored him. "I have everything under control."

"I'm sure you do. And I'm counting on you to bring me up to speed."

"Come on, Farien," Yao said with a smile. "It's just like old times, right?"

Farien frowned at him. "Oh yeah, Xalivar threatening us, Bordox causing trouble, trying to kill us—"

"Actually, it was usually me he wanted to kill," Davi said with a grin.

"Bordox torturing me...oh yeah, good times." Farien's face remained stern, but Davi detected a glint in his eyes.

"Bordox and Obed arrested by the Council," Yao inserted.

Farien raised a hand to stop them. "Please, you're making me tear up." He broke into a grin. "That last part was well deserved." Davi and Yao laughed.

"Agreed," Yao said. "We don't get many excuses to pal around these days. It'll be just like old times."

Farien brushed it off with a wave. "We have no choice. We're under orders from the Palace."

He was starting to sound like the old Farien. Davi grinned.

Farien motioned to a datacard file box on the desk beside his monitor. "All the information we've gathered so far is on these cards. It would be easiest if you spent some time reviewing them. Yao and I can answer any questions you have."

"Can't one of you brief me a bit—"

Farien frowned. "Stop wasting time and get to reading, Captain."

Davi laughed. "What about all that stuff you said about the three of us being equals?"

"I'll treat you like an equal when you start pulling your weight. You can't do that until you're up to speed, so get busy."

Davi offered a mock salute. "Yes, sir." Yao laughed as Farien held out the data card file to Davi.

"There's another terminal next door you can use," Yao said as Davi accepted the file from Farien. "I'll get you set up in there."

It was heavier than he'd expected, forcing Davi to balance it against an arm as he carried it. Davi followed Yao back out into the corridor.

After some quick talking to get through military patrols, Bordox landed his shuttle in a clearing outside Eleni 1's capital city, Joia, in an agricultural district far enough out not to draw ground security forces' attention. He'd been allowed to land by blending in with farm traffic, and the last thing he needed was further attention, even if it meant he'd have to find a transport into the city to locate Xander and his friends.

His lungs felt heavier as he stepped off the shuttle. Although the atmosphere on the moon was comparable to that of Legallis, where he'd grown up, Bordox had spent so much time lately in the thin atmosphere of Xanthis and other planets that it would take a bit for his body to adjust. If he got lucky, he'd be inside the domed city long before it mattered. Joia kept the atmosphere inside its dome much closer to that of Legallis than the outer areas. He wondered if natives had difficulty with the changes every time they stepped outside the dome.

Making his way through the dense foliage and tall Dalee trees surrounding the clearing, he heard the calls of Eleni falcons as they circled hunting their prey somewhere overhead. The grunts and whines of Eleni bovines sounded around him in call and response patterns almost resembling echoes as the animals talked to each other. The bovines were called Krikatrus officially but nicknamed Krikees by locals if he recalled—a stupid nickname appropriate to a planet full of stupid people. He heard rustling in nearby Mrobi bushes and saw shadows skittering between branches. One of the falcons' intended victims was on the run.

"Run, little ones," he mumbled with a grin. *Real hunters will chase you to moon's end.* Bordox was a real hunter. No matter how far or fast Xander Rhii fled, he knew he would eventually find and defeat him. Moving on, he kept his eyes peeled for a road busy enough for him to flag down an air taxi into the city.

Davi spotted a tuft of red hair before they found Dru studying in a cube on the third level of the Library. His face was a mix of surprise and delight at seeing Davi. "What are you doing here?!"

Davi shrugged. "I hear you've been nothing but trouble. Someone had to come and straighten you out." He laughed as Dru embraced him like a long-lost brother. The young cadet looked haggard and his energy was lower than usual.

"You know me, trouble seems to find me. I don't even have to look for it."

Davi rolled his eyes. "That sounds so familiar." He turned serious even as Dru laughed. "I'm sorry about your friend."

Dru nodded and looked away. "It shouldn't have been him."

"It shouldn't have been any of you, and we're going to find who's responsible. I promise."

Dru nodded, his eyes avoiding Davi's as he sat back down at a desk and fiddled with the buttons on the keyboard.

"The professors said you've been doing better in your classes." Yao shot Davi a sympathetic look.

Dru dismissed it with a wave. "I can focus better, for what that's worth."

"I'm sure I can get everything I need from the reports Yao and Farien have already written, but if you need anything, I'll be working with them on the investigation, okay?"

Dru looked up and smiled. "It's good to see you, Captain."

"The whole squadron misses you," Davi said with a grin. "They keep complaining about how much more fun your life here must be compared to our patrols."

Dru guffawed. "They have no idea, do they?"

Davi shook his head. Dru turned back to his studies, chuckling to himself as Yao and Davi slipped quietly away.

"We have a lead on Xanthis," Yao said. "We're planning to head out there in a couple of days."

Davi nodded. "Good. I've never been there. Should be interesting." He kept staring back at Dru, wondering if the boy he'd once trained would ever be the same. Dru was focused at the terminal now but stood out from the students around him with the face of a kid with a whole world weighing him down.

"He'll be fine. Trust me. It's just the shock and fear. He's taken it harder than most of the others, but he'll recover in time." It was Yao's turn to pat Davi reassuringly on the back.

"So it's either depressed Dru or angry Farien. Not many good options for us, huh?"

Yao chuckled. "We could stop for a draft in the faculty lounge. I mean, if I left that off the tour, it would be sheer neglect."

"And horrible manners." Davi led the way.

Finding a place to connect the data interceptor Xalivar had provided proved easy. Bordox simply walked into the data center at Joia's small starport, signed in under his fake name for an available private cube, and plugged it into the terminal's port. The data center had ten private cubes lining the walls around two long counters containing rows of open terminals. Only four of the private and six of the open terminals were occupied, so Bordox was just another traveler checking in with the office back home or making arrangements he didn't want to be public. He couldn't have blended in better if he'd tried.

Despite its status as the home of a premiere preparation school for future Borali military officers, Eleni 1 was hardly a major destination and Joia's starport was its major point of entry. It took only a few simple commands before Bordox had the interceptor feeding him data from all sorts of sources, and, within five minutes, he'd isolated it down to the Academy itself and begun searching for Xander, Farien, and Yao's signatures. *Amateurs.*

So far their investigation seemed to be going nowhere. Bordox amused himself imagining their rising frustration. He saw the orders assigning Xander to join the investigation team. No doubt Farien would view that as a sign of distrust by his superiors. *He always was paranoid. Idiot.* But then Bordox didn't trust anyone either. Only his father and two loyal friends. He'd been betrayed enough to know that only a foolish man put his faith in his fellow humankind. He couldn't blame Farien for being wary, but Farien didn't even trust those who'd shown him loyalty and dedication his entire life. Farien had many more people like that than Bordox. It showed Farien was weak and lacked the timber of a true officer.

His mind filled with images of their frustrated faces. Bordox settled in and sent an e-post for an order of food to be delivered. He hoped his wait wouldn't be a long one, but he had no intention of wandering anywhere he might be noticed or, gods forbid, recognized. Better to just settle in here and make like any other traveling businessman using Joia's blip-on-the-map port to take care of important business dispatches and other activities on his way to somewhere far more important.

Farien's e-post arrived even before his food did—a notification to command of his plan to travel with Yao and Xander to Xanthis to investigate the Lhamori assassins. The mention of Xanthis raised his blood pressure. Could Xalivar's operation have been given away somehow? No, it was too well hidden. Farien's report mentioned only the attack on a worker couple there and suspicions about the assassins for which Xanthis had a known underground market. His old rivals were going to the heart of the matter and they didn't even know? Bordox laughed. He couldn't wait for his assassins to give them a surprise. If he were lucky, none of the three would make it to Xanthis.

Bordox relaxed as he finished reading. They had nothing to go on. The trip was routine and predictable. Since the assassins had been hired through an off-planet contact from Xanthis and neither Bordox, Obed, nor Xalivar had been involved, they would be impossible to trace. Bordox's first contact with them had been through comm-links, and, at the starport on Legallis, he hadn't even told them his name. *Alien freaks!*

Who cared if they got caught? Lhamori assassins were notorious for killing themselves before interrogators' techniques ever extracted anything useful. His old classmates' trip to Xanthis would prove to be another disappointing dead end. They were total incompetents. Farien even outlined their travel plans in his e-post, a security breach only an amateur would make, but then Farien never had been the smartest, and neither the investigators nor their superiors would ever suspect spies intercepting such routine communications. None of it would matter anyway.

He typed a command and the interceptor sent the travel data to its memory card. Bordox would send all three assassins. Only two of the three were traveling by VS28 fighters. Yao would be in a military transport, so he could be easily dispatched first, leaving the three assassins to deal with two distraught friends who'd be taken totally by surprise. It would all be over too quickly. Bordox's only disappointment was that he himself couldn't take part in it. *Just to see the look on your face, Rhii, that would be worth it.* He'd have the assassins record all audio channels on the off chance they'd intercept something he could replay and enjoy later as he celebrated the end of his troublemaking rival.

The last thing he did before ejecting the data card was initiate the script Xalivar had installed there. Bordox had no idea what the script would do, but he'd deliberately put it off for last to avoid the risk of detection. The script only took seconds to run; the terminal beeped as it finished. Bordox hit the eject button and grabbed the datacard, sliding it back into place in his bag as he hurried out the door.

"I want to go with you."

Davi turned his head and looked down from the cockpit of his VS28 to see Dru faced off with Yao beside the transport, looking tense and confrontational. Yao wore a blue flight suit similar to Davi's while Dru wore his old red WFR flight suit.

"It's an official Alliance investigation. You're not a military officer. Besides, you have school work that's important."

Dru shook his head, his eyes never leaving Yao's. "I need to go with you. I need to find who did this."

Yao lifted a hand and placed it on Dru's shoulder in an attempt to calm him. "I understand how you feel, but you'll just be in the way. We can't worry about protecting you and find the killer at the same time."

"I fought in the Resistance. I have the training. You don't need to protect me."

"You can't come. That's the end of it!" Farien's voice came from Davi's right, filled with irritation.

Dru whirled around, looking for Farien, who was in the cockpit of his own VS28. "You can't order me like some soldier."

"You're training to be a soldier. If you can't follow orders, might as well quit." Farien didn't even look up as he said it, his face stern. "Cadets aren't allowed on official missions."

Davi stood in his cockpit and made his way down the ladder, drawing Dru's attention. "We know how you feel, Dru, but we'd need permission from command, and that's really unlikely. On top of that, you're in no condition to help."

Dru's hands went to his hips, his chin lifting as his legs spread in defiance. "I worked hard to get where I am! To not be cut out of important missions!"

Davi nodded. "I know. You're on an important mission. The first of our people to be admitted. A role model for everyone who follows. We need you here, doing well, focused."

Dru shook his head. "I can't focus on anything right now but getting the bastards who are killing our people."

Davi closed his eyes, taking a deep breath. It was so hard to refuse. He knew he'd feel the same way if their roles were reversed. "You can't, Dru. I'm sorry."

Dru's eyes filled with fury as he spun and marched back the way he'd come.

The look still haunted Davi as he flew in formation with Farien's VS28 and Yao's transport. Designed for as many as two pilots and four passengers, military transports were similar to shuttles except for armament and FTL capabilities, and the restraints attached to each passenger seat in case prisoners were along. They were also dark with only small official seals on the hatches indicating their official nature.

"You didn't have to be so hard on him." Davi keyed his comm and glanced over at Farien.

"If he wants to be an officer, he has to learn the chain of command." Farien showed not even the slightest sympathy. Why was he so wound up? Still angry about Davi being assigned to his team?

"Look, I know you're upset about the decision to send me here, but don't punish him."

Farien glanced over, his eyes squinting at Davi. "I'm not mad. I have a mission. And that's my sole focus."

"He'll get over it, Davi," Yao said from the transport. "Dru does need to learn how to accept orders, even when he doesn't like them. And you're right, he belongs at school. It'll take all of his focus to catch up as it is."

A beep on his console distracted Davi before he could respond. Three incoming contacts of unknown origin. "You guys seeing this?" He punched a button and put his computer to work with its usual scans: speed, shields, firepower, etc. The sparse results looked all too familiar.

"Yeah. Type unknown. Who are they?" Yao's voice shook with tension as Davi reached down and flipped on his shields. His friend had never flown in real combat before, just simulations at the Academy, and to be alone in a transport with only manual turrets now wouldn't help things. Davi would have to keep a close eye on him.

"Better find out." Farien didn't wait for an answer, sending his fighter into an arc and looping back toward the targets. "You stay with, Yao. I'll be right back."

"Three against one? Better to stay together," Davi warned, but Farien was already gone. He closed in with Yao, tightening formation. Moments later, they heard an explosion over the comm.

"Farien? What's going on?" Yao sounded alarmed.

Davi wished Yao still had a fighter. A military transport needed a gunner to be effective in a dogfight. It was up to Farien and him. "Get ahead of us, while we head them off. You can't do much good alone."

"Do I have a choice? Why can't professors have fighters?" The transport's engines flared as Yao accelerated, speeding on ahead. "You two be careful."

"Farien, what are we up against?" An explosion to portside rocked the fighter. Davi had been so distracted he hadn't seen the target approach. His scanner showed an enemy ship locked onto his tail. He accelerated and began evasive maneuvers. "Damn it, Farien! Where are you?"

"I'm a little busy right now with some old friends!" Farien's ship came into view on the scanner with two targets tailing him. He went into a dive, then arced around on top of the contacts and fired at them, hitting one in the wing.

Davi watched through his blastshield as one of the targets locked back onto his friend's tail. The ship looked familiar, so dark it was almost hidden against the starfield—a stealth ship like they'd encountered on patrol!

"Just like the one we questioned with the squadron."

"Yep. Only this one brought buddies along." Davi saw Farien's fighter go into a dive again. "They're fast, too."

"Hang on while I give you a hand," Davi answered, turning his ship toward the others, as his cockpit shook from another blast exploding off his right wing. The targets were moving so fast, his computer couldn't provide useful tactical alternatives.

"You've got troubles of your own," Farien said, turning his fighter toward Davi.

For the next few minutes, the five ships shifted position like checkers on a board, explosions beating them back and forth, but no one managing to score any direct hits or damage beyond singed fuselages and frayed nerves. The ships zigzagged in and out, switching places with the enemy on Davi and Farien's tails and then Davi and Farien on theirs. Davi banked right, then hard left, the move jostling him so hard against the cockpit wall, he feared his whole left side would be black and blue. He felt a sharp pain as the family necklace he always wore under his flight suit jabbed his flesh. Ignoring the sweat sliding down his forehead, he blinked, trying to regain focus as it stung his eyes. The target was coming straight at him. They both fired within seconds of each other. The target banked at the last moment, sending the blast from Davi's fighter's triple canons wide to explode in empty space, but the target's own blast raked a line down Davi's fighter's right wing.

Davi slammed his joystick forward and went into a dive to avoid further shots, glancing over at his damaged wing. The VS28 still handled well, but it wouldn't stay that way with a few more hits like that. Growling, he rolled the fighter and dove back up to reengage, attempting to lock onto his attacker's tail. The pilot dodged his every attempt, staying just out of range.

"They're fast. You're right. Who are these guys?" he mumbled into the comm as he saw Farien land a hit. The enemy scurried away as smoke peeled from a charred hole just below his blastshield, but the damage didn't affect his ship's ability to maneuver.

"You okay?" Farien turned back to inspect the damage to Davi's fighter.

"For now, yeah, but that one hurt."

Then one of the targets whizzed between them and both fired. Farien's shots hit the blastshield and ricocheted off and away. Davi's missed and exploded near Farien's engines. "Shoot them, not me!"

Davi chuckled, mumbling, "You make it so tempting though." Davi lined up on the ship chasing Farien and saw the targeting screens flash as his weapons locked on. "Got him!"

He fired again, using both his nose and twin wing cannons again, and watched his lasers travel straight for the target's engines. Farien lined up on the ship following Davi and fired, but his shots missed as the target behind him exploded.

"Nice shot," Farien said. "Give me a moment and I'll try again." But he was too late.

The enemy tailing Davi had already fired again. Davi tried to evade but was jolted back in his seat when the laser bolts exploded inside one of his engines. Davi heard Farien curse over the comm as he ran a diagnostic to check the damage. "That oughta slow me down."

"Good thing there are only two of them left."

Davi checked the scanner and saw only one blip. "Only one on the scanner. Where's the third one?"

Both he and Farien spun their heads, scanning through their blast-shields. Davi reset his scanner with the same results. The lone enemy stayed locked on Davi's tail as Davi swung his ship in wide arcs and jerky turns in an attempt to stay out of target range. "Would you take him out before he hits my other engine?" The scanner beeped and Davi looked around, spotting Yao's transport circling back with the third ship on its tail.

"I need a little help here, guys!" Yao called. With his ship's minimal systems, Davi guessed Yao must be having to do all targeting and evasives manually. He couldn't keep it up long against this enemy's speed.

"I'm coming." Farien switched direction, turning his fighter toward Yao. Davi's fighter rocked as the ship tailing him landed a hit on his left wing.

"You okay, Davi?" Yao sounded worried.

Davi's eyes scanned his instruments. "Yeah, just a scratch. But the next one will hurt me."

He dove, evading the tailing ship's next shots, but the enemy stayed with him, diving back into position at his rear. Suddenly a panel atop the transport opened and a laser turret appeared, firing at the ship chasing Davi.

"You can control the turrets like that?" Davi's voice shook as an enemy shot exploded outside his blastshield. Beads of sweat started dripping on his brow.

Yao sounded confused. "No. Not sure what's happening."

The turret fired again and the ship chasing Davi exploded.

"That was a hell of a shot!" Farien sounded as impressed as Davi was.

"What shot? It wasn't me. I'm a little busy flying."

Farien's fighter dove in and fired at the ship tailing Yao, but it abruptly changed direction and accelerated, fleeing for safety as Farien maneuvered and gave chase.

"Who's there?" Yao's question was drowned out by cursing from Farien.

"You missed?"

"I'm a better shot than that!" Farien cursed again.

Davi watched, relieved as his friend's fighter turned and circled back toward them.

"Forget it for now. Let's find a place to land and inspect the damage." And find out who's on board Yao's transport. Davi had a pretty good idea, and Farien was going to be furious. He only hoped he could get there first and mediate. Tension left his body, as slid down to relax again in his cockpit seat, stretching his limbs.

Farien rejoined them and they headed toward the outer moon, Zeeri, which was vacant except for a storage facility. The dock had just enough room to land their three ships and take off again. He hoped they'd be ready. Especially Dru.

# Chapter Five

"You had no business sneaking aboard that transport!" Davi thought Farien might actually pace himself right into the wall. Unless his head exploded first. He wouldn't make eye contact with any of them and Davi expected to see steam rising off of him any moment.

"I told you, I need to do this!" Dru stood defiantly, staring him down in the landing bay of the supply depot on Zeeri. The techs there had been quite surprised to receive an emergency landing request from three military vessels. The bay barely had room for them to land and take off, but after examining it closely, Davi knew his VS28 wasn't going anywhere without repairs. Three of the techs were pouring over the fighter doing all they could but parts would have to be brought from the nearest depot.

"You were given a direct order!" Farien whirled and tapped his index finger hard against the cadet's chest.

"I don't take orders from you yet!" Dru pushed the finger away, defiantly.

Farien lifted his arm, causing Davi and Yao to jump between them for fear Farien might strike the young cadet. "Calm down, Farien. He saved our butts out there!"

Farien's eyes stung Davi's face like a sunray as his friend whirled to glare at him. "We would have been fine!"

"You said: 'That was a hell of a shot!' I heard it on the comm!" At Dru's comment, Farien froze, anger boiling again, refusing to look at him.

"It was a great shot," Yao agreed with a smile, then turned somber as he saw Dru's glowing reaction. "But you're in the Academy preparing to enter the military. If you can't learn to obey orders, whether you like them or not, you might as well quit."

Dru groaned. "You're all three welcome, ok? I'm not going back!" The cadet had no understanding of why they were so concerned.

"Yes, you are! I'm calling in another transport to pick you up!" Farien nodded for emphasis, looking at Davi and Yao for backup. But Dru's excited gaze never faltered.

"I can just steal a ship and follow, you know? I know how to fly."

"Not many ships around here to steal, so good luck finding one!" Farien turned toward his VS28. Davi's hand on his arm stopped him.

Davi turned back to Dru, forcing back his own frustration to speak with a calm tone. "It's not so easy stealing military ships. Get caught and your career's over. Plus you just announced that plan to everyone here." Mechanics around the hangar gaped at them. Davi's eyes met Dru's as he assessed his former trainee. "Don't you want to catch whoever did this? We can't have an emotional victim interfering while we investigate." Dru's persistence was a character trait which served him well during their flight training. But Davi wasn't so sure it was a good thing in this situation.

"You're emotional, too. Your friend was attacked." Dru's eyes darted away from Davi's stare. Davi could see his mind racing.

Davi smiled, acquiescing. "Yes. And our people are being killed. None of us like that. But this is far more personal for you. The last thing we need is you going off half-cocked on a witness or suspect and threatening our investigation."

"I can help you, Davi! If you'd just think about it." Dru's eyes flitted between Davi and Yao, trying to win them over. "You're military men, officers. You stand out in a crowd. I'm just a kid. No one takes me seriously. I can lurk around unobserved in places you can't; talk with people who'd be uncomfortable talking with you."

Davi and Yao exchanged a look—he was right.

"What about your classes?" Yao frowned at Dru, playing the concerned professor.

"Field experience is more important than classroom learning. You told us that during orientation." Dru's tone changed, his expression turning thoughtful.

Yao grimaced, looking at Davi. "How did I know I'd come to regret that?"

Dru smiled, all enthusiasm again. "See? We listen to you. Come on! I want to help catch whoever killed Cadet Kowl." He looked first at Yao, then Davi, then back to Yao, hopeful as a baby Qiwi.

Yao shrugged at Davi and both turned to Farien, who was pacing along a nearby wall.

"I can get you excused from classes for the week, but if you miss much more than that, you'll never catch—" Yao stopped, drowned out by Dru's whoop.

Farien turned and shook his head vehemently. "Uh-uh. No way. I'm running this investigation."

"I'll take all responsibility," Yao said.

"He and I both," Davi echoed.

"You're damn right you will!" Farien growled. "If that kid screws up, they're not hanging this one on me!" Farien slammed his fist against a nearby beam then cringed with the pain.

Dru practically bounced as he headed for the transport, his body language showing he knew he'd won.

"If we're partners, how come you two aren't backing me up?" Farien looked at the others, cutting them with cold eyes as he rubbed his sore hand.

Davi shrugged, amused. "We could wait days for another transport, Farien. Besides, Yao's the one who actually said he could come." Farien winced again.

Yao coughed, stifling a laugh and waved a finger at Davi. "You didn't object to it!"

"Can you two sort this out later?" Farien frowned. "Let's get the parts ordered for the VS28 and get back in the air, ok?" Exchanging amused looks, Davi and Yao saluted Farien. "Don't make me write a report asking command to put me officially in charge of you."

Farien motioned toward Davi's damaged fighter. Davi yawned, covering a laugh and hurried over to get back to cataloging the damage. His fighter's right engine was a charred, melted mass. It would need to be replaced and the scorching to the surrounding fuselage would require replacement panels and a new paint job. On closer inspection, his wing was also worse than he'd thought. The dark streaks he'd seen from the cockpit concealed tears in the fuselage which had to be repaired. He was lucky he'd been able to land where he did, instead of winding up stranded in deep space.

An hour later, a request had been sent to command for a maintenance shuttle to drop in on the supply depot and assist with the repairs, and Davi joined Yao at the controls of the transport as Farien started launch preparations nearby in his VS28. The supply techs didn't seem sorry to see them go. They left Dru to himself in the passenger compartment and followed Farien out of the atmosphere and back on course for Xanthis.

Xalivar's fists clenched as he finished the report and then started reading it all over again. Once or twice his datapad almost popped out from between his tightening fingers but he caught himself, relaxing his grip so it slid back down into place as he continued. Xalivar hated whiners.

Assassins of unknown origin had attacked Xander Rhii and two companions as they left Eleni 1 to fly to Xanthis. So Xander Rhii was coming to him? Xalivar smiled at the thought of an encounter. But that pleasure would have to wait. First, he would have to calm Pres who was convinced the attack had been ordered by Xalivar and feared that the peak in official interest it brought would lead to the discovery of her communication with Xalivar and the entire plot. Xalivar cursed her for being so weak minded. Why couldn't she trust that he had many safeguards in place? Borali officialdom would only discover what he wanted them to discover, when he wanted them to discover it.

"You sent for us, my Lord?" Lucius entered with Obed, interrupting his thoughts at just the right moment. The last thing he needed was to lose focus in anger.

He whirled to face them as they came to a stop a few feet away. "Your son's revenge scheme could jeopardize everything we've worked for," he said, pointing an accusing finger at Obed.

"My son will soon be back with us," Obed said with confidence.

"You've made contact?"

Obed shook his head, still smug. "No, but I sent an inquiry through personal channels. And when he responds, he won't dare disobey me."

"Disobey you how? By launching personal attacks on Borali military pilots in flight perhaps?" Xalivar watched Obed carefully. The wavering appeared first in the former Councilor's eyes. "Three assassins attacked two VS28s and a transport en route to Xanthis from Eleni 1, only hours ago. Do you suppose the identity of those pilots might make me suspect your son?"

"Who were they?" Obed frowned.

Xalivar locked his eyes on Obed as he responded, "Captains Farien Noa, Xander...Davi Rhii, and Professor Yao Brahma."

Obed's eyes avoided Xalivar's. "He knows them, yes, but they've all three made many enemies betraying our people."

"Your son goes rogue and his lead rivals from the Academy are attacked, and you want me to believe it is coincidence? You take me for a fool, Obed!" Obed simply stood where he was, stiff as if at attention. "Worry not, though. I'll deal with it. If you can't control your own son, I have men who can fulfill that responsibility." He glared at Obed, who finally met his eyes. Both knew the meaning of the threat.

"I will leave at once to bring him back," Obed said, his determination weakening.

"If you even know where to find him." Xalivar waved dismissively as Obed hurried out. "General, see to it our people not only stop Bordox, but bring me Davi Rhii alive. What happens to Bordox and Rhii's friends is immaterial to me. It's Rhii I want."

Lucius nodded. "Of course, my Lord."

"The training?"

"We have the first platoon assembled, my Lord. They shall begin exercises tomorrow. More will be arriving in the next few days."

Xalivar smiled. "Be sure the transports are handled properly. We cannot risk discovery until the time is right. What of the funds for our fleet?" Xalivar clasped his hands behind his back as he paced and thought.

"Our contacts have not come through with further funding," Lucius replied, looking frustrated. "Perhaps it's time to motivate them in other ways."

Xalivar growled. "They'll be plenty motivated when I'm back in power and they've lost my favor. I think instead it's time to implement the other option we discussed."

Lucius nodded. Only the two of them knew of the secondary plan. Xalivar had entrusted Lucius to make the inquiries and prepare the plan for implementation at a moment's notice. It had risks, but the time had come.

Lucius snapped to attention and saluted. "I won't fail you, my Lord."

Xalivar nodded, pleased, then turned back toward the General. "You never have. You're my best man, Lucius, and very soon you shall be rewarded for it."

Lucius remained rigid, his military training engrained, but his eyes gleamed with pleasure. "Thank you, my Lord."

"And set a meeting with Pres. Her lack of confidence is starting to disturb me. It's time we talked face to face and put her fears to rest."

Lucius' face showed understanding. "It will be difficult for her to get away, my Lord."

Xalivar jerked his head and gave a choppy wave. "Convince her then." Their eyes locked and Lucius nodded, acknowledging the message. "Give her a story about inspecting some facility in a neutral location. I can meet her half way."

"Shall I plan to come along, Lord?"

"No. I'll go personally." If Xalivar couldn't get results, she'd never return from their meeting. Lucius saluted again.

Xalivar took a deep breath and turned away, and Lucius took it as his cue to leave quietly. Miri's face popped into his mind. She hadn't responded to his earlier missive, but he smiled at the thought of her reaction. Alas, he couldn't give his location away. But he could taunt her. He laughed as the idea came into focus in his head. His most cutting betrayer, his own sister, would soon find out how alive and powerful her departed brother still was.

One woman would have been enough to drive Sol crazy, but Lura and Tela had both been treating him and Telanus like children for the past week. Both men had made excuses about overtime at work and other errands just to get away, and one or another of the women always insisted on going with them on the errands or calling to check on them at work. The only time they'd truly gotten away from them was during questioning by Farien, when they'd been taken inside the command center at the starport. After a week, Sol was on edge.

"Stop treating us like we were victims! You're driving us nuts!" He sipped a beer to help him relax.

"The assassin could have killed the both of you if you'd been in the wrong place," Lura said, shaking her head.

"We've got enough pressure already with Boralians accusing us of lax security at the plant," Telanus added as the women attempted to stare them down. "They're trying to maneuver back into positions once held only by Boralians and get many of us demoted." He watched the foam settle on his own mug, then tipped it back for a long swallow.

"Well, that's not going to happen," Tela said, her voice sharp with irritation, "because it wasn't your fault. Professional assassins like these could have gotten past security at any plant in the system."

"They don't care about the facts, Tela," Telanus answered. "Just the appearance of incompetence is enough."

Sol nodded. "And this is just one case. I hear they're making similar moves at all locations where workers dominate the workforce. We've heard complaints of unfairness for months, but no one's tried to force change until now."

"It's despicable to use the deaths of workers to make such power plays," Tela said as her face reddened. "They ought to be ashamed!"

"People will use every opportunity, dear," Lura said with sadness. The effect all the stress was having on her was what worried Sol the most. She'd been through so much already between his time in prison and Davi's disappearance. He never wanted to be the cause of any more heart-ache for her. "...with little regard for circumstances. It's human nature to compete. And since we stood up and fought against unfair treatment, why shouldn't they?" Sometimes Sol wondered how his gentle, sweet wife survived all the trouble they'd faced over their lifetimes.

"This is different and you know it," Tela frowned. "I hope the Council can make some headway quickly. They need to nip this animosity in the bud."

"It will take more than Council edicts for that," Sol said. "You cannot legislate people's fears and emotions." If you could, he had no doubt they'd have already done it. Politicians loved control, but more than that, they hated chaos and the world was roiling with it at the moment.

"Thank God the military's been spared most of that drama," Tela said with a sigh, as she relaxed back onto a chair beside the comm panel and sipped a cold glass of Talis.

"Let's hope it stays that way," Lura said with a smile and slid her arm around Sol's waist. Sol and Telanus mumbled in agreement, sipping again as the comm panel beeped.

Tela turned and typed commands into the terminal. "Incoming message from Uzah. It's marked urgent."

"What now?" Lura shot a worried glance at Sol, who stepped forward to wrap his arms around her as if he could shield her from any concerns.

Tela typed on the keyboard, pulling up the message. Her brow creased with worry as she read.

"What is it, dear?"

Tela turned to meet Lura's gaze. "Davi and his friends were attacked on their way to Xanthis."

Sol winced as Lura gasped and rushed toward Tela. "Oh no! Are they okay?"

"Attacked by whom?" Sol asked as he and Telanus moved closer, reading the missive over her shoulder. As he came alongside her, Lura reached over and put her arm around his waist. He pulled her closer.

"Lhamorian assassins, it says." Tela scanned the message again quickly. Sol could see she was close to exploding.

"Thanks be to God, they're okay." Telanus said with relief. He and Sol clinked their mugs in a toast.

Tela stood again with a loud sigh and began pacing along the wall.

"How could they know? His mission wasn't public knowledge. Someone's intercepting communications." Sol's gladness faded quickly.

"Someone inside command?" Telanus' words made Sol's heart pound faster in his chest. Lura's hand slipped from Sol's waist as her shoulders sank with worry.

"Will we ever be free of this? Davi's in danger again? Who now? Why do so many resent him?" Tela's words matched the choppiness of her paced steps as she zigzagged back and forth in front of the wall.

Lura drew near and put a gentle hand on Tela's arm. "It takes time to erase years of enmity, dear. It won't happen overnight."

Tela stopped pacing and turned to face her. "Private resentment, a few public complaints, okay, but people are getting murdered now! The Council has to put a stop to it!"

"No doubt they're trying to do that very thing," Telanus said, moving over to wrap his arm around Tela. "That too will take time."

"Well, I hope we have time. I'm not ready to lose Davi yet!" Tela slipped from his grasp and started pacing again.

"Neither are we," Sol said as his eyes met Lura's. Lura winced at the thought and Sol moved to her again to offer what comfort he could. He wondered if the warmth of his closeness relaxed her as much as having her close relaxed him. Just holding her clarified his thoughts. He was torn between wishing the military were less informative and feeling thankful they had the connections to stay abreast of such events. He didn't know which was easier: knowing or not knowing? Either way, the worry he felt lay across his heart like a storm cloud blocking the suns. Concerns about his job suddenly became less important.

Uzah and Matheu entered the command center just in time for the morning briefing and found it in chaos. Technicians checked equipment as controllers reviewed data on their screens, everyone chattering loudly. Louder voices coming from the Conference Room quickly drew their attention. As they dodged scurrying techs and hurried toward it, a worried Joram appeared in the doorway.

"What's going on here?" Matheu demanded.

Joram shook his head. "Some kind of computer glitch with the assignments."

"What kind of glitch?" It made no sense to Uzah. The system had been generating assignments with a well-worn algorithm for ages and no one had ever complained. "What happened?" He turned to Joram who'd followed him inside with Matheu. Officers, of both Vertullian and Boralian birth, were arguing and pointing at the various terminals, their faces heated.

"What happened is favoritism!" a Borali Colonel said, turning from a nearby confrontation. Uzah recognized Jansen from the briefing a few days past with Grif and Pres. "All the best assignments given to your people, with total disregard for seniority!"

"Forget seniority! Simple protocol!" a Borali Captain from the same group said, nodding in agreement as many in the room turned toward the new arrivals.

"Officers of all seniorities rotate through the various positions over time," Uzah said, still puzzled as he pushed forward toward the wall terminal around which they'd all gathered.

"Not like this!" Jansen said. "Now all our people get the all night shifts, the crappy locations all at once, for an entire month?"

"The rotation cycle is two weeks as always," Matheu said.

The Captain slammed his fist hard against the wall, narrowly missing a terminal. "Check the list yourself! It's a whole month and it's every assignment!"

"Our people have faced a similar situation in the past," a Vertullian Major said from Uzah's right.

"Not for an entire month!" The Captain said, angrily, his red face whitening with the cresting of his anger. "Some of us already served the past two weeks on nights. Aren't we allowed to see our families, too, or do just you 'chosen people' deserve that?"

"Look! Enough of this talk of their people and our people!" Joram said, his face whitening as his temper flared. "We are one people now. All equals and serving in a united military."

"Easy to say when the favoritism's on your side!" Colonel Jansen's sarcasm assaulted Uzah like a series of shells. "We should have seen it coming. More and more of our best men relegated to irrelevant roles as your own people got priority. Why is it you always assume the worst where we're concerned?"

Uzah put a hand on Joram's shoulder to calm him. As he checked and double checked the assignments, their complaints matched the data on the list, but he could detect no errors in the program. "It's done by an algorithm in the computer as always!" he insisted. "I'm sure it won't happen again."

"Or maybe it'll be a regular thing! I'm not waiting to find out!" Jansen turned and marched angrily from the room as the officers exploded back into loud arguing.

Matheu's voice cut through the room like a blaster bolt. "Are you men officers or not?! Enough of this bickering! We have a chain of command and you will follow it or be brought up on charges! Am I clear?!" Despite his rank, Matheu's uniform stood out all the more for its lack of medals comparable to those of the Borali officers surrounding them. The same was true for all of the Vertullians, whose time in service hadn't been long enough to earn them such accolades. Matheu glowered at them, his eyes as commanding as his glare.

The arguments died in moments as the other officers watched Matheu, their anger only in check, not faded.

"You'll be expected to discharge your duties as always or I will hear about it!" Matheu didn't even blink as he panned the room, staring them down.

Gradually, the officers lost their nerve—some sighing, others shoulder's slumping—a few offered weak salutes and mumbled acquiescence. Uzah was once again thankful Matheu found the thought of retiring insulting.

Matheu turned to Uzah. "We'll send the briefing report to your datapads. I want everyone to their stations right now!"

It only took a moment for the room to clear, but Uzah and Matheu were already reviewing the assignments again on the terminal.

"It is highly irregular," Joram noted as he read the lists on the terminal next to Uzah.

Uzah nodded. "Unfortunately, yes, it does seem odd. I'll get command on the frequency. We should at least request that they check the algorithm." Joram nodded and followed Uzah and Matheu into the command center.

"Soldiers do not question orders!" Matheu groused.

"I think it has less to do with orders and more to do with other recent tensions," Uzah answered, shaking his head. "Either way, command needs to be made aware of it."

Matheu nodded, his frown showing his distaste. "I will write up any officer who fails to obey orders under my command." He turned and hurried toward a corridor as Uzah sighed and headed for the communications station. He couldn't remember a day of service without some sort of crisis arising.

Pres felt grateful she'd been assigned to work with Admiral Dek after the debacle of the loss against the Workers. She and her fellow leaders could have easily been brought up on charges by the Council, but General Lucius' disappearance, combined with the new High Lord Councilor's desire to integrate the military and return things to normal as quickly as possible, conspired to make experienced leadership invaluable. Thus, Dek and Pres had been given a second chance. All soldier, Dek's hair was close cropped and his muscular frame highlighted by the fit of his gray uniform.

It was times like the present when Pres counted on Dek's experience to see them through a crisis. The computers responsible for duty assignments had been in place for decades, running an algorithm developed long ago; one which had never drawn complaints until now. She and Dek had arrived that morning to face a near mutiny of angry officers and men complaining that worker counterparts had been given favored assignments over them, and not just for the usual two week duty cycle but an entire month. In all her years, Pres had never experienced such hostility from other personnel, most especially command personnel she'd served with much of her career. Dek handled it with precision and calm she could only admire. It didn't bother him in the slightest. She was surprised later, when he actually confessed in private his frustration at having to deal with such a situation.

"We got a call from General Uzah on Vertullis, while you were talking with them," Pres answered. "They arrived to a similar crisis this morning."

Dek shook his head. "Call the techs and have the computers checked. It may just be an odd coincidence, the rare probabilities come to pass, but I'd rather be sure. And see if they can work on reprogramming the algorithm to avoid it in the future. We cannot have such routine matters threatening our morale."

Pres nodded as she headed for her terminal. "You handled that situation with such calm. I didn't know where to begin when we arrived."

"To maintain command, you must always give the appearance of being in control, even amidst chaos," Dek said with a chuckle. "I could have thrown up my hands in frustration, but that would have solved nothing. It would have only encouraged even more lax discipline from the personnel, and that's the last thing we need."

Pres nodded, her fingers bouncing off the keys in a barrage of clicks as she typed commands instructing the terminal to search for the contact information required. "I'm thankful we're still working together after all that's happened. Your experience is invaluable, especially at times like these."

Dek sighed and leaned against a nearby pillar, looking sullen. "We're both lucky to be working at all after that fool Xalivar's personal vendetta overtook his common sense."

"I thought we all agreed with him at the time?"

Dek sighed. "Well, my sentiments have never been favorable toward the Vertullians. But it was foolish to defy the Council on such an important matter, especially when the Council was in line with the will of the populace. It should have cost us our careers."

"Thank the gods it didn't." Dek nodded in agreement then turned away as Pres went back to her terminal. An alert flashed at the corner of her screen. An incoming message on her private secure channel. Forgetting the search, she clicked a button to open the comm, patching it to the earpiece she and all officers wore as part of their uniforms.

"Link 78A6," the message said in a droning computer voice, then repeated again.

Pres froze. It was a code few but she knew. It meant she had a private message even Dek couldn't be allowed to see. She pressed a button to delete the alert, then hurried back to her search. Finding the name of the Head Technician, she sent him and his senior officer the instructions, marking them as urgent and top priority. She struggled throughout to maintain a relaxed routine. Inside, her heartbeat soared and she found her eyes wandering, darting around with her thoughts. As soon as she'd finished, she stood and turned to where Dek was already conferring with a newly arrived junior officer on other matters.

"I missed my morning Talis. Can I get you any?"

He shrugged her off with a wave, not even noticing as she disappeared into the corridor. Hurrying to a private terminal at the nearest comm station, she logged onto the secret database and then clicked the secure link. After entering a few more code combinations, the message resolved onto her screen. She felt relief as she began to read:

*Meeting. 1100 hrs. Starport. Talekyn.*

In two days? Italis' moon was a long distance for her to go on such short notice. Xalivar and Lucius were threatening her credibility. What excuse could she use for an emergency?

She erased the message quickly and weighed it over in her mind all the way back to the command center. Dek was waiting for her. "What happened to the Talis?"

She suddenly realized her hands were empty. She struggled to stay relaxed, not give any reaction. "I got distracted by some more officers arguing about their assignments."

Dek smiled sympathetically. "It's happening everywhere. I need you to go out to Italis. They've had a particularly bad incident there with an officer threatening to shoot Vertullian soldiers if his assignment wasn't revised. He's to be court martialed. I want you to address the men personally. Go among them, make a personal connection, remind them the chain of command is doing its job, etc."

"Why not go yourself?"

"A cold hearted old warmonger stands far less chance of success than a beautiful female officer, Pres."

She fought a smile as blood rushed to her face. Had the environmental systems failed? The room felt hotter. "I hardly think they'll look at me like that."

"Regardless, you have a gentler manner and spirit than I." Dek said, the glint in his eye revealing his enjoyment of her discomfort. "The Alliance needs you to use it. We cannot have our ranks falling apart. Appear commanding, in control, but concerned."

"I'll do my best, of course, Admiral." Pres couldn't believe her luck. Could Xalivar have arranged it?

Dek nodded. "Your shuttle's being prepared. I'll expect you back in four days."

She nodded and turned toward the door. "I'll be in my quarters if needed."

The Admiral had turned back to other business before she'd finished spinning back toward the door. She couldn't stop his words from repeating over and over in her mind: "a beautiful female officer, Pres." And each time it repeated, her heart fluttered and she smiled.

The ninth planet from the sun Boralis, Xanthis was even drearier than Davi had expected. Known for its cold nights, Xanthis had few habitation centers and few natural mineral deposits. Spaces which appeared to have once held vast oceans were now filled with scattered lakes of craters filled during the scattered rainfall, a spelunker's paradise. Skimming the surface side by side, shuttle and fighter, on their way into the capital city, Nasyru, Davi and his companions chattered about the landscape.

"Like nothing I've seen," Farien commented.

"I've read about other desolate planets but it's hard to imagine people live here," Yao responded.

Dru just stared silently out the window even as the towering buildings of the city appeared on the horizon. Nasyru's buildings were of all shapes and sizes and the city itself looked fairly modern except for the barren, reddish-brown soil surrounding everything.

"Not even an attempt at artificial landscaping," Farien noted. "Must not be too proud of their city then." The few sections of open land they saw were scattered rocks and clay with occasional patches of sand. Davi found it surprising no effort had been made to add foliage or flowers, or wouldn't they grow here?

"Maybe some species take value in different aesthetics, Farien," Yao said. It made sense. It was hard to imagine anyone who didn't take pride in their capital city.

Davi and Farien made arrangements with the starport for a private military landing bay and led the way in.

A hurried city official met them there. His long dark-red robe ran from neck to toe, fitting his body like a second skin. Other than his blue-green skin, he appeared human, with dark-grayish hair and a slurred accent, and a bone structure reminding Davi of lightning-thin models in commercials he'd seen on the networks. "If we'd known you were coming, the Planetary Governor himself would have come..."

"We're on a classified mission," Farien said. "We don't want that kind of attention."

The official nodded. "It's rare we have military officers in the city itself. Most of them stay to the bases and landing strips on the other side of the planet." He looked to them as if he expected some sort of reaction then waved his arms, palms up as if shrugging it off.

"They say Xanthis is a rough place," Farien said.

Davi watched the official's blue-green skin darken, the Xanthian version of a blush perhaps. "Rumors exaggerate. Please allow us to give you a proper impression." Davi and his friends nodded politely as the official led them toward a large sliding door, presumably leading out of the bay. "A military attaché has been requested and will meet you at your hotel."

"We don't need him!"

Farien's words struck the official like missiles, causing him to grimace and shrink back. "Just someone to see to any needs which may arise; show you around and such."

"I'm sure any assistance would be very helpful, thank you," Davi said.

The last thing they needed was Farien's lack of tact causing any drama with local officials.

"Our mission is not very important, I'm afraid," Yao added. "We're here about recruitment for Presimion Academy. Now that Vertullians are successfully entering service, we've had discussion about admitting other groups as well."

The official brightened, looking at Yao and Davi rather than Farien this time. "How wonderful. A grand opportunity for our people to contribute to the Alliance's defense. We will be most proud to serve."

The door slid open, almost silently, with only a slight hum to be heard. Davi and his team followed the official into a well-lit corridor with patterned walls resembling a large three-dimensional relief map—squares, rectangles, circles of various lengths and sizes scattered across the surface of the walls like buildings on a planet's surface. Davi wondered if the pattern had any significance but wasn't sure this would be the time to ask. The official kept walking and they followed.

"We've heard of an unsettling incident in one of your residential districts," Farien said.

The official nodded. "The incident with the Vertullian woman, I presume?"

Davi met the official's look with a nod of his own. "There's been many other incidents throughout the system. Very sad."

The official looked down. "A most unfortunate situation. Our condolences go out to all citizens. We can assure you all efforts will be made to prevent further incidents."

"Given Xanthis' reputation as a recruiting point for assassins, I'd imagine that'll be a hard promise to keep." Yao and Davi both shot Farien a look.

"All planets in the system share similar concerns for our Vertullian brothers and sisters," Yao jumped in. "The Alliance is prepared to offer you any support you need."

"Thank you. A most kind gesture." The official's expression returned from shock at Farien's boldness to a welcoming smile. "We've arranged quarters for you at the city center."

"We have our own arrangements—"

Davi cut Farien off with a chuckle "But yours sound so much nicer. We are forever in your debt."

The official's palms came together as he smiled and offered a slight bow of pleasure. They walked on in silence, passing various other Xanthian workers, administrators, and other visitors as they wound their way through the corridors of the starport. To Davi's surprise, he saw only two humans, mercenary types if he had to guess. Both glared at them as they passed, showing an aversion to their military uniforms. A portent of the challenges awaiting them. Davi knew they would need to use extra caution here. He'd be sure to speak with Farien about it as soon as they were alone.

The official escorted them out onto a dusty street and into an air taxi which rose above the city and took them on a scenic ride to the city center as Davi and his companions assessed the city around them. It looked like most big cities, constant motion on the main avenues, quieter residential streets to the side, culminating in the center city. But this city had a dark underbelly which mostly showed at night. Davi knew he and his friends would see more of it than they wanted before their time in Nasyru was done.

The invitation had been Danae's idea, an attempt by the new lady of the Palace to ease the growing uselessness her predecessor felt in her new lesser role, Miri assumed. The gesture was appreciated, but coming so close after the incident at her brunch, Miri couldn't help feeling restless, even a little trepidation about what might occur.

"You'll do fine," Danae said with a reassuring smile and a gentle nudge to Miri's right shoulder. "To them, you're still a princess."

Miri's smile never wavered as she sat next to Danae on the dais awaiting introductions. "I hope their reaction isn't like those of our circle." She fidgeted in the hard-backed chair, trying to get comfortable.

Danae's eyes darkened. "Of course not. These people don't have bias acquired from years of special privilege. These are the everyday citizens, the kind who can most relate to the Vertullians' plight."

As his peer finished the announcements and vacated the podium, their host stepped to the mic, smiling as he panned the room with delight. "So many good people here today—people who are the heart and soul of this Alliance. The work you do keeps the Alliance strong; keeps it moving. Gods know you don't get recognized for it enough, but today, this Commission celebrates you for it. Just as we celebrate all the little people who matter a lot everywhere in this Alliance. Our next guest knows the value of those people as much as anyone. Her own adopted son is a fine example of a person rising above his station to great heights, disproving the assumptions that genetics determine one's fate, perhaps."

With that, he glanced over to Miri and Danae and smiled. Miri held her smile firm, nodding, as he gave a slight bow before continuing. She knew he'd meant it as a compliment but still felt, as any mother might, that he'd stated it in a way that cut Davi down. She hoped her own words could rectify that.

"The daughter of a once mighty dynasty of great leaders, High Lord Councilors, Lords all, Miri Rhii has lived a life of service to others, making many sacrifices. Every time we needed her strength, she never failed us, including during our most recent difficulties, a time of great change. Miri Rhii has always been there for us, loving us as her people, her extended family perhaps. And she's here today to tell us more about some who are new among us but have now joined the family. Let's welcome Princess Miri!" He turned, applauding as the attendees joined him from tables placed around the room. It was a modest-sized ballroom and modestly appointed, appropriate to the status of those present, except perhaps Danae and Miri herself.

With a nod from Danae, who joined the applause, Miri stood, smoothing her dress and stepping forward to take her place at the podium. Those present seemed delighted to see her, their faces filled with anticipation. Most even offered warm smiles. As the applause faded, she surveyed the room, smiling at the mostly adoring faces. A few toward the back looked bored, as expected, but the warmth of the reception thrilled her after her experience the previous week. She closed her eyes, took a breath and began.

"Good afternoon, my friends. It's so good to be here with you today and share with you about some new friends who are now part of us. We all know the history, the years of animosity and fighting between our peoples. I think I speak for generations of mothers when I express my joy and relief that those days are finally behind us for good."

She paused as new applause broke out around her from most of the tables. The bored onlookers toward the back remained indifferent.

"You're no strangers to hard work, like our new friends. They too have worked hard for generations."

Then it happened. A deep voice from the shadows in a back corner rose: "Not hard enough, and not long enough, I'd say."

Pain stabbed at her insides like a knife and Miri struggled to maintain her composure as her eyes sought the source of the voice. "Why do you say that, my friend? Are not all humans worthy of appreciating benefits from their labor, including times of rest?"

"All they do is rest these days," the taunter said, stepping forward, "while we do all the work!" His hair was graying at his temples, but his body had a muscular form. He was obviously a man used to hard work, not far from Miri's own age. His eyes and wrinkles added depth to his countenance. And he spoke with an authority and confidence, as if no one could dare disagree.

"We are all doing our part, my friend," Miri answered, averting her eyes from his hateful glare.

"Since when are we friends?" he snapped.

She ignored him and continued: "They share our labor, work alongside us as equals, with the same demanded of them."

"In appearance it would seem," the man said, "but how long 'til it changes? We've seen the beginnings of it now." Grumbles of agreement came from the tables around him.

Miri breathed deeply and glanced to Danae for reassurance but saw her friend was at a loss.

"They're already starting to get priority, the best assignments, favoritism clearly!"

This time some of the grumbles were decipherable: "That's right!" "You tell her!" "Send them back where they belong!" Miri stepped back from the podium as her host and Danae rushed to her side.

"Please, we are not here for negativity," the host said, leaning to the microphone. "This is a time to recognize our common achievements."

"Achievements like betraying our people? Let our speaker speak to that. She's an expert!" The taunter raised a fist in triumph as several others jumped to their feet around him, applauding.

"I did no such thing. I only wanted the best for us all," Miri mumbled, her voice cracking, the microphone barely picking it up. She felt small all of a sudden, a tightness in her chest making it harder to breathe.

"They are not like us," a woman near the front shouted. "You are kind hearted, because of your son, Princess. But it can be exploited. And those tricksters are masters of exploiting us!"

"Yes!" Several shouted at various points around the room.

Miri stepped back in a daze as the host looked panicked. Clearly the room was out of control, and he had no idea how to respond to it.

"The people supported this," Danae shouted over them, stepping to the podium. "Your Council acceded to your demand to end the slavery, to make peace."

"There can be no peace with their kind!" A well-dressed young man raised his fist in solidarity with the taunter at a table in the middle of the room. Fists rose into the air around him.

"My gods," Danae whispered as she lost her resolve and stepped back to stand beside Miri. Miri didn't look at her, focusing instead on fighting back tears. She refused to let these people see her cry.

"We cannot change hundreds of years of hate overnight," Miri reminded her.

"But the public outcry during the fighting was in favor of freedom. Now they demand the opposite. What would they have us do?"

Then their host was before them, his eyes pleading forgiveness as he gently waved them toward the back of the dais. "I'm so sorry, my Ladies. Perhaps it's best if you go to a safer location. We must address their fears, open a dialogue, but I fear their animosity may be a threat to you."

Several of his companions joined him, circling Miri and Danae and leading them toward the stairs at the back as the host turned back toward the podium. Both women walked in silence, but, for the first time, Miri felt truly afraid. Drops formed at the edge of her eyes, and she quickly dispatched them with her finger. Would she never again know the respect and endearment in which she was so long held? Had she thrown it all away? How could the people's hearts be so different from her own? She ached to go back, to speak with them, win them over, but then doors slid open and they were ushered through and the noise and commotion were but a memory.

Later, as they passed through the Lobby, many people who had attended apologized, warming Miri's heart. It was a relief to realize that not everyone shared the sentiments of those vocalizing it. Could she dare to hope it was a minority? Regardless, the fact that such strong, anti-worker sentiments existed left Miri feeling cold and concerned.

"Steps must be taken to change the stereotypes, the misconceptions," she whispered as she and Danae settled onto the Royal Shuttle which had brought them there. "We have no hope of really being one people, unless we can accept each other and put the past to rest."

Danae nodded. "Tarkanius and I and many others share your concerns. Conversations and plans are being made. Staying strong and holding firm in your message is invaluable, Miri. I intend to ask you to speak again, if you're willing."

"As always, I live to serve the Alliance." Miri forced out the answer, but inside she wondered if she had the strength.

Tela had found Uzah in the command center, during the quiet of mid-afternoon, pouring over reports on a datapad. He'd always been supportive of her and Davi but, this time, it didn't take long for them to wind up on opposite sides.

"You can't let personal feelings dictate assignments," Uzah responded to her request. "If anything, this is all the more reason why you shouldn't get involved."

Tela fought to control the anger she felt swelling inside. "He's my future husband. And he could be in danger!"

"We're all in danger. It goes with the job. Gallivanting off to protect your lover is not one of your duties, I'm sorry."

"This is not a normal situation. Assassins are attacking our people—"

"And our job is to protect them. That goes for Davi and everyone else! We have to put our personal feelings aside and do that duty, Lieutenant. I'm sorry." With that, he coldly turned back to his datapad, making it clear the conversation was over. She was tempted to punch him. No understanding or respect for women or their needs!

For a moment, Tela had toyed with approaching Joram about it, but planetary Governors never overruled their military commanders on assignments. She even briefly entertained the idea of General Matheu, but he was so hard-nosed about such things, she feared a bad reaction could harm her career. In the end, she went back to meet her friends for dinner, depressed and worried and feeling worse for the effort put forth.

"What's wrong, Tela?"

The voice jolted Tela back to the restaurant and she looked up to find them all staring at her—Nila and Virun, Jorek and Brie, the two couples. If command knew, they wouldn't be allowed to serve together. Tela wished she and Davi had kept their relationship secret now. It just hadn't been anything to worry about at the time. She shook off her thoughts and smiled at Nila. "Nothing. I'm fine."

"Fine for someone who looks like a Gungor just tore apart her pet." Nila shook her head. "We know you too well. What is it?"

Tela sighed, moving the food around on her plate with a fork. Couples and groups chatted and laughed at nearby tables, enjoying their food and camaraderie. She felt even more alone. "Davi. There was another attempt on them on their way to Xanthis."

Her friends perked up. "Assassins?" Even Brie's jovial tone softened, deeper with worry.

"Probably. Lhamorians."

"They're out there alone? Just the three of them?" Virun pulled his arm away as Nila reached across the table and put her hand atop Tela's.

"It's supposed to be a low profile secret."

"So we have a leak?" Jorek's temper was already flaring, she could see.

"I just want them safe. And there are people hunting them."

Virun finished his Zizi, a fruity beer made on Tertullis, and slammed the glass down on the table. "Let's go."

"I'm in!" The others all spoke in unison.

Tela shook her head, hiding the joy she felt knowing they were always there for her. "We can't."

"We have ships. We'll just file a flight plan—"

Tela's eyes met Virun's. "We've been ordered not to." She had responsibility for the safety of her people. She was a military officer. Davi could take care of himself. Her head knew this. But her heart...

"You asked already?" Brie sounded surprised.

Tela sighed. She didn't want to rehash it by repeating the whole story.

"And they ordered you not to go?" Blood rose to Jorek's face.

"Not specifically, but it was clear they don't support the idea."

"They misunderstood." Virun and Brie mumbled agreement with Nila.

"They understood. 'Danger goes with the job. Gallivanting off to protect your lover is not one of your duties.'" She cut to the chase. Davi was important, not just as her fiancé, but as a hero to his people. There was a reason command picked him for so many choice assignments; a reason he'd risen so quickly to a position of trust. But what if he needed her? Would she ever forgive herself for not being there?

"Uzah forbade you?" Jorek's mind was clearly racing to formulate a plan.

Virun smiled. "Not forbade, discouraged."

Jorek nodded, as if their minds were one. "And he's second in command to Matheu over the Army. But technically, we're still under Air Defenses, which is—"

Tela saw it coming and raised a hand in protest. "He acts as our commander and coordinates with Air Defenses on Legallis. He has the authority—"

"But he never issued the order," Virun said with a grin.

Jorek grinned back and nodded. "We also have standing orders to defend our fellow pilots when one of them gets in trouble."

Virun nodded as they all looked at Tela.

"That refers to pilots in our immediate airspace, not three planets away." Tela felt a headache coming on. They were saying all the things she wanted to hear. Still, mutiny was the last thing they needed to involve themselves in right now.

"We have a long patrol tomorrow night. No one defines how long." Virun chuckled, raising a hand to high five Jorek.

"We can't do it!" She was their superior. It was her job to set an example and enforce discipline despite her personal feelings.

"Nav computers make errors. It's happened." Brie smiled, clearly enjoying being a part of the men's scheme.

Nila nodded. "It happened on that long range patrol last month, remember?"

Tela tried to hide it, but they laughed when they saw her grin.

"We're just going to check it out while we're in the vicinity," Jorek said. "You know, once we realize where we are."

"We'll be short on fuel and provisions—"

"When we get lost, we'll stop and refuel." Nila shot Tela an urging look.

"They could court martial all of us."

"Better to go out together than alone. Davi needs us." Virun raised his glass. The others quickly followed suit, looking to Tela.

Nila pointed an accusing finger at Tela's glass.

Tela laughed, shaking her head again. Who could resist friends like these? They were right. She had to go. If Davi were in trouble, no one else was going to back him up. The assignment was dangerous. If they found he was okay, they'd just be out a little longer on patrol because of it. They'd come right back. She had to know. She raised her glass and they all clinked theirs together. "So much for our short-lived military careers."

# Chapter Six

The Council Chambers were abuzz as Aron entered for the second time since the attempt on his life. A few Lords took notice and nodded in greeting, but mostly his arrival went unacknowledged as he made his way to his usual spot at a table in the center section along the right aisle. Assigned seating for the Lords had not been intentional, but came about through a combination of personal preference, political rivalries and friendships. Tarkanius had chosen Aron's spot himself, negotiating for the previous occupant to relocate. Since Aron was the first Vertullian to serve on the Council, the High Lord Councilor wanted him to see and be seen, a reminder for others of the Vertullian's new status as full citizens of the Alliance and an opportunity for Aron to observe well and learn the Council's proceedings.

"This decision smacks of favoritism and a total disregard for the tensions dividing our citizens," Hachim was yelling, his finger pointed at Tarkanius and Kray, who stood on the floor before the dais, facing him. "The vote was rushed. Not enough consideration was given to the issues and repercussions. The price is being paid for that!" Since the vote, those opposed to the holiday had become even more vocal in their protests, to Aron's discouragement.

"I will not allow this Council nor my Palace to be held hostage by terrorists and bullies, Hachim. I won this seat on a platform of unifying the populace, and I intend to do it. No matter what's required!"

Hachim shook his head as Niger joined him. "You cannot force a unified opinion. Too many people have objections, and those are more often than not leading to violent outcries or actions against others. We must squelch this resistance first before we make decisions which will only serve to raise tensions further."

Niger nodded. "This Council's always been about serving the people, not just ourselves."

"It is in the people's best interests that I push these decisions forward," Tarkanius said, his brow furrowed with frustration.

"Xalivar said the same thing, and we impeached him for treason because of it!" Hachim's eyes bore into Tarkanius as Niger grunted his agreement. Tarkanius cringed from the comparison, which Aron thought was quite unfair.

"Xalivar's decisions were self-serving and against the wishes of the majority," Kray said. "The majority of our people want slavery to end." Her voice seemed to rise above the pitch around them until Aron realized many of the other conversations had stopped as people tuned in to this one.

"Well, you wouldn't know it from the broadcasts of protests and attacks airing constantly," Niger said.

"We warned you when this idea first came up," Hachim looked around him, meeting the eyes of other Lords as he gauged their support, "and the issues have escalated daily since then. Anti-worker sentiment is on the rise. That cannot be ignored." Several Lords around them grunted in agreement.

"If we allow them to bully us, to control our actions, we encourage them," Kray argued, shooting challenging looks at some of the grunters. "Do we want to be known as the pet Council of such men?"

"Don't oversimplify, Lord Kray." Lord Qai stepped forward shaking his head. "If we base our actions on only one set of voices, we ignore our duty to represent the entire citizenry, not just the ones whose hearts match our own."

"But what if they're wrong?" Kray looked around, dismayed at the lack of support.

"It seems clear we cannot take any action without first addressing the realities of violence and protest," Lord Simeon said. "But it is difficult to know how to do that."

"There are many precedents from the history of forefathers on Old Earth," Aron said as all eyes turned to him. "Slavery in the nineteenth century there almost divided an entire nation and caused much strife on several continents. We so often look back on them as primitive and unenlightened because of our knowledge and technology, but what have we really learned, when we ourselves allowed slavery to exist in our midst?"

"Perhaps yours is not the voice to provide such commentary," Qai said. For a moment, Aron thought he was being scolded, but their eyes met and he saw a sparkle in the other Lord's eyes. "So let me add my own. This abomination we have tolerated for generations must be abolished. We can no longer call ourselves higher society, or even civilized, if we allow it to exist. But changing the hearts and minds of our people is not a simple matter. It cannot be accomplished merely by the power of a High Lord Councilor's will or that of the Council. It requires a long-term plan to reeducate our people. It will involve not just relearning history with new perspectives but the kind of one on one experience which can only come through personal exposure of our peoples to one another." The words impacted Aron and he saw he was not alone.

"And if our people refuse to be taught such things?" Hachim raised his hands to emphasize the question.

"There will always be some who will, which is why such a program will take years to succeed." Qai looked Hachim and Niger in the eyes one at a time, challenging them to resist, but neither held his gaze for long. "It begins with us, the members of this Council. We must demonstrate with our own actions and attitudes our unity and common belief. If we cannot do that, we cannot hope to lead the people to a similar conclusion."

Hachim sighed. "I will not be intimidated into following a program. I'll continue to stand against any policy which favors old enemies over our own people, which is unjust to our own in favor of welcoming another."

"Perhaps your definition of justice should be on trial then, Lord Hachim," Kray said bitterly.

Hachim's cheeks flushed as Tarkanius stepped forward. "Our brother Lord Qai is most wise. And it shall begin with us. We will continue to discuss our differences and educate ourselves first, before we impart these lessons to our people. And we will stand together, unified always in this matter. Beginning this week."

He stopped a moment, glancing around to meet as many eyes as he could. "I will go personally to Vertullis to announce that 'the Returning' is to become a people's holiday. A committee will be formed led by Lords Qai and Aron to make recommendations how this can best be implemented. I invite all of you to travel with me to make this announcement, but to those who refuse, I say, I will tolerate no dissention. Any questions or complaints shall not leave this room. We will settle this matter amongst ourselves, not through public debate. Is that clear?"

"The High Lord Councilor does not control this Council!" One of the senior members, Lord Kretzu, shouted.

"Hear, hear!" his tablemate, Lord Elul, echoed.

Tarkanius remained undeterred. "Part of serving the people is leading by example. How can we expect them to unite, when we ourselves are divided?"

"Then let us settle our differences first, before we address them," Kretzu said.

"My responsibility to the people includes the responsibility to insert order into chaos," Tarkanius said. "With the violence, rumors, and divisions center stage, they need a reminder that we are all one people and our future is a common cause."

"It will take more than words this time," Elul responded. Several Lords, including Kretzu, Hachim and Niger, grunted in agreement. Aron feared they were right.

"Which is why we must take action and stand together," Tarkanius answered. He looked around again for any who might disagree but Hachim, Niger, and those known to support them refused to meet his eyes. He nodded. "Very well then. I'll have my aides make travel arrangements with your offices. I look forward to seeing you then."

"Let us postpone our official meeting then until after our return," Simeon said, stepping up beside Tarkanius to show his support.

The Council immediately dispersed, with Lords resuming private conversations with friends and adversaries as they cleared the room.

"It's a dangerous game to force their hand, Tarkanius," Simeon said, when only Kray, Aron and Tarkanius remained with him.

"I lead them the way I expect them to lead the people. We are not leaders if we are not firm in our course and confident in our wisdom."

Simeon nodded. "Nonetheless, we must be prepared to meet any resistance with equal determination as that we have toward our own success."

"I am prepared for any necessary course," Tarkanius said.

"Even if that course takes you down paths similar to those your predecessor trod?"

Tarkanius turned, his eyes meeting Simeon. Simeon didn't flinch. And Aron realized then he was not alone in his fears of what might be required to make unity work. "I hope it never comes to that."

Simeon nodded. "You must be prepared lest it does."

Kray put her hand gently on Tarkanius' arm. "We have much to consider and much work to do. Together. You won't be alone in it."

Aron smiled. "Indeed. I will support you in whatever must be done." He extended his hands, forming the traditional salute with his fingers crossed atop his fist. It was ordinarily a custom only military officers followed when entering and leaving the High Lord Councilor's presence.

To Aron's pleasure, Simeon joined him in it. "As will I."

Kray's hands echoed theirs as she too offered the salute.

Tarkanius' eyes closed as he took a deep breath in gratitude then started slowly up the aisle, the others following close behind him. Aron hoped the line would be far longer at the gathering on Vertullis.

Tela yawned then flinched. Telanus looked much too awake for this hour as he smiled at her from the terminal beside her bed. His smile almost sparkled. "Morning, Little Girl."

"You should not be this cheerful this early in the morning." Tela rubbed her eyes. What time was it anyway? Why was he waking her up? She sighed.

"You know I'm always cheery when I get to see my girl's beautiful face," Telanus winked then beamed at her. "Besides, it's midday. Check your chrono."

She frowned. Midday? Rolling over, she checked the chrono on the wall. He was right. Crazy pilot hours. It felt like the middle of the night, as if she'd just gotten to sleep. She yawned again. "You know if anyone's making it hard for Davi, it's you. Spoiling me with such sweet talk. I wish he talked like that."

Telanus laughed. "I'll have a word with him. We can fix that."

"Don't you dare!" She had patrol call in two hours and briefing in ninety minutes. She had to wake up. She searched his eyes and saw he was teasing then stretched her arms and planted her feet on the floor, willing her body to get up. Instead, every cell shouted at her: "More sleep!"

"Hey! What else can a father-in-law worry about but making sure his daughter's spoiled properly?"

"We're not married, Daddy."

He brushed it off with a wave. "You will be."

"You're relentless."

"Your mother said that, too." He laughed.

She forced herself to sit up. "Look, I have patrol soon. So I'd better get busy preparing. Thanks for calling, Daddy." She ignored the voices of protest inside and took a deep breath.

"You be careful out there."

She nodded. "I always am."

"I love you, Little Girl."

"I love you, too." The terminal went blank as she stretched again with another yawn and grabbed her uniform, heading for the cleansing room. Today was the last day of her short-lived military career.

The meeting took place in the back room of a warehouse beside the starport on Talekyn, Italis' largest moon. After taking her command shuttle to the starport on Italis herself and then insisting her crew remain with the shuttle, Pres had slipped out under the pretense of contacting command, gone to the civilian areas and changed clothes, then hired a private shuttle to take her to the rendezvous. The whole thing wasted a lot of time and she knew her command crew would be searching for her by now, but secrecy had to be maintained and it seemed the only way to prevent discovery. Even the private shuttle had been instructed to leave her at Talekyn's starport and disappear. She'd walked the rest of the way on foot. Talekyn's starport hardly qualified for the name. It was basically a one-room arrival hall with one corridor dedicated to ticketing kiosks, a fact that made further precautions unnecessary once she'd stepped off the shuttle.

Using her datapad to hone in on the coordinates given her, she found the nondescript, gray building. The warehouse appeared to be rarely used, and its insides smelled of dust with scattered bits of crates and cardboard decorating the floor. Entering via the northeast door, as she'd been instructed, she made her way to the center of the storage space and waited. At the top of the hour, a cloaked figure appeared out of the shadows.

The figure approached until they were almost face to face before removing his hood. Xalivar stared at her, his expression unreadable. She knew better than to speak first, so she waited for him to finish assessing or intimidating her, whichever this was.

"I'm told you have...questions?"

Pres nodded, hesitating to ensure he really expected an answer before speaking. "The High Lord Councilor has put security on high alert due to recent attacks on ex-workers—"

"They won't be for long."

"Pardon me?"

"Ex-workers. Soon they will be returned to their former duties, as will we all." Xalivar smiled, the embodiment of confidence as usual.

"While they remain citizens, recruiting has become a highly risky endeavor," Pres continued. "It cannot be done by normal means for risk of detection."

"I left the means up to you and others," Xalivar answered. "It's the results I care about."

"We all face great risks while we remain there—"

"You shant remain there long, either. Get me my men and you'll have no more to worry about."

"You intend to call them to training immediately?"

Xalivar shrugged. "The time is ripe to escalate and commence with our plan. Everything is in place except personnel. I am depending on you to provide them." Pres nodded, surprised at how quickly Xalivar's other efforts must have succeeded. "Can I count on you, General?"

Pres stiffened, her fists balling as her fingers crossed in salute. "Of course, my Lord. I have always been your servant." Xalivar's confidence had always been inspiring to those who followed him, and it was no different now. Her fears and doubts just faded away in the face of his passion.

Xalivar nodded. "Good. I have need of loyal officers. I'd hate to be forced to make other arrangements so late into our plan. Don't worry, in a few weeks, you will be back safe on the right side again."

"Of course, my Lord."

Xalivar laughed. "The High Lord Councilor looks like a baby Gungor who's lost his way. He's beside himself with confusion. Everything is going exactly as I foresaw. Enjoy this, Pres. It will be a great triumph for us all."

Pres nodded. "I won't let you down, my Lord."

Xalivar turned his back to her, his hands crossed behind him. "How are General Grif and Admiral Dek responding to this new crisis?"

"They do the best they can. We've had mutiny in our ranks of late to deal with as well."

Xalivar smiled, turning back toward her. "All according to plan, General. And it's working wonderfully so far, I'd say, wouldn't you?"

Pres had no idea how Xalivar could have interfered with the computer algorithms for duty assignments, but she'd suspected he was behind it. He seemed quite pleased with himself as always. She nodded and smiled. "Indeed, sir. We're investigating the cause now."

"By the time anything is discovered, you'll be safely elsewhere, fear not. In the meantime, you must prepare to leave. Two weeks from now at this very hour, your recruits will depart with you for their new training base. I expect everything to be ready."

"Sneaking soldiers out under the Alliance's nose is going to pose a great challenge—"

"You will not have to sneak. You will merely correct the course once you depart. Just make sure the ship is loaded with men loyal to you and me."

Pres nodded, stiffening to attention again. "Of course, my Lord."

Xalivar stopped a moment, his eyes cutting into her again, like a medical scanner. He seemed to be looking past or even through her as his eyes moved up and down. "We can tolerate no more delays. Bear that in mind." With that he spun on his heels, the hood sliding back over his head again, and walked away, disappearing into the shadows from which he'd come.

Despite the veiled threat in them, Xalivar's words reassured her. He was firmly in control, and when Xalivar was in control, he made things happen. Nothing less than success. She'd chosen the right side, and she felt more confident than ever. She wished she could be open with Dek. She hated the idea of facing him as enemies when the time came.

Pres waited a few moments before turning and making her way back to the civilian shuttles, her eyes searching the departure lists for Italis.

Tela and her friends arrived at the launch bay fifteen minutes before their scheduled departure time to find the mechanics finishing final pre-flight checks.

"That's not regulation," one of them noted as Tela added extra provisions to the pocket behind the seat of her VS28.

Tela smiled at him as she slid the seat back into place and climbed into the cockpit. "You never know these days what might happen on these patrols. With all the attacks on workers, we might be at risk too. Being pilots isn't exactly low profile."

The mechanic shrugged, thinking it over. "I sure hope it doesn't come to that, but I guess it doesn't hurt to be prepared."

Tela nodded. "I ordered everyone to carry extra just in case. Long patrols cut through a lot of isolated areas. You never know who you might run into."

The mechanic accepted it with a look that assured Tela she'd planted a seed to sway any doubts from others who might have made similar observations. She strapped on the belts securing her in place as the mechanic checked each one, adjusting them to fit smugly around her.

"Good luck. Come back bored and ready for excitement, okay?"

Tela laughed. "Not too much excitement, ok?"

The mechanic joined her laughter as she glanced over to see Nila and the others settling into their own cockpits. The mechanic disappeared down the ladder as Tela initiated preflight checks, reviewing the fuel tank indicators and long range scanners first just to be sure.

Then she switched on the private squadron channel. "We ready?"

"For what? The last act of our official military careers?" Tela could hear the grin in Virun's voice.

"Let's cut that kind of chatter, ok? You never know who might be listening," Brie's voice sounded far fiercer than the timid young girl had ever appeared.

"Yes, ma'am," Virun said, his and Jorek's chuckles blending on the comm channel.

"Let's get rolling," Nila said, shifting nervously in her seat as Tela glanced over.

Tela smiled. She'd always admired their constant enthusiasm, sometimes wishing her own could match it. As much as she loved flying, these days she found herself more and more longing for legs on the ground, a side effect, she supposed, of being relegated to less exciting duties. Still, she wasn't about to admit it to anyone. "Squadron, start your engines."

Just then alarms blared overhead as an alert flashed on her cockpit screen.

"What's going on?" Jorek sounded as confused as Tela felt.

"I have no idea. Squadron Alpha Six Leader to flight control." Tela muted the alarm klaxon on her control panel as she waited for a response.

"Alpha Six Leader, this is flight control, launch cancelled."

"Launch cancelled?" Jorek's voice rose as it always did when he was irritated.

"Hold on." Tela tensed in her seat and switched comm channels, keying the mic. "Squadron Alpha Six Leader to command. Is General Uzah there?"

Uzah's voice came back immediately, almost as if he'd been expecting her call. "Alpha Six Leader, we have a situation. Report to flight control for further instructions."

"What's going on, General?" For a moment, she panicked. Had command overheard Jorek's comment? Or perhaps someone at the restaurant?

"We need every available hand for protection duty. The High Lord

Councilor's making a speech this afternoon."

"The High Lord Councilor's coming to Vertullis?"

"He's supposed to announce 'The Returning' as a new official holiday."

Tela frowned, despite her relief. "Just what we need—more inspiration for those who already hate us."

"Lord Aron proposed it. They want to make a show of unified support. I need your team to lead the protection detail. Another squadron's covering the patrol."

Tela muted her comm so he wouldn't hear her fist slam into the arm of her chair.

He continued, unaware of the rising temperature inside her head. "We didn't get any notice, Tela. You're one of my most experienced officers. I need you to report as soon as possible."

Tela sighed, switching the mic back on. "Yes, sir. We'll be there in moments." Her fingers flew across the control panel as she hit switches to shut down the fighter. The servos whined overhead as the cockpit blastshield slid back up. Tearing off her straps, she began climbing out of the cockpit, glancing up as her feet hit the floor to see the rest of her team emulating her. Once they'd joined her, she led them out toward the elevator.

"What's going on?" Nila asked.

"We're security for Tarkanius' visit. 'The Returning' is about to become an official holiday."

"That oughta rile the nutjobs up," Virun mumbled.

"You're always saying you want more action," Jorek teased. Nila cut him off with an elbow to the ribs as she nodded toward Tela, who punched the elevator button and paced in front of the doors as they waited.

"We'll find him as soon as we can, don't worry." Brie's eyes were full of worry.

"If this announcement has the effect we're all imagining, we might not be slipping away for anything in the near future." She rushed aboard the elevator as the doors open.

"Well, I hope you're wrong about that," Nila said as the others followed her onto the elevator and Jorek punched the button for Flight Control.

"Me, too," Tela mumbled, her head racing with thoughts of Davi and his friends. She said a silent prayer for safety as the doors shut and the elevator rumbled into motion. Uzah had been right. It was personal. She couldn't shake the feeling Davi was in danger, and just like him, her instincts were to protect her mate. Problems aside, she cared about him and if anything happened to him, she'd never forgive herself for not taking action. Still, she was under orders to protect the High Lord Councilor. There was no way to slip away. She just had to pray and focus on her duty. Why did that thought feel so impossible at the moment?

Xalivar relaxed in his cabin aboard the small freighter as it crossed deep space from Talekyn back to Xanthis. To pass the time, he turned on the broadcast nets and watched with delight as Orson Sterling and the other talking heads replayed over and over Miri's disastrous speech and the riotous aftermath. He chuckled at her dismay and at Danae and their host's uncertainty at how to respond.

"It couldn't have gone any better if we'd planned it ourselves," Lucius said from the seat beside him.

Xalivar nodded. "Perhaps we did plan it." He glanced over as Lucius shot him a startled expression. Xalivar laughed. "Don't think just because you've earned my trust that I'm going to enlighten you with every detail of my plan. It's got many facets, and many teams will be involved in its success. Including some who have only to disrupt life whenever they can."

Lucius smiled. "Forgive me, my Lord. I should have remembered your facility for thoroughness."

Xalivar nodded, his grin widening. "Many wish they could forget all about it. Some may even think they have. The time is upon us for them to be disavowed of such treacherous notions. And the first amongst them shall be my beloved sister, Miri."

"Her life is not what it once was," Lucius said, almost looking sympathetic. "I imagine she has many regrets."

"She destroyed our family's legacy." Xalivar frowned. "She hasn't begun to know the amount of regret due her."

Xalivar stood and left Lucius to watch the broadcasts as he took a seat at a terminal on the cabin wall.

*Time for another missive from your dear brother, Miri.* He winced as an image of their childhood flashed into his mind. They'd always been so close, and it had broken his heart when he'd discovered Miri's deceit and betrayal. Still, Xalivar had long ago learned to control his emotions, and he'd quickly brushed it aside to focus on doing what he must. Still, Miri and her bastard son managed to ruin everything the family had worked generations for, but Xalivar would restore it. He would bring the Rhii name back to glory and set the Alliance back on its proper course. Even if it meant total destruction of every worker, young and old, he would do it. And nothing—no one—would stand in his way this time.

His fingers clacked on the keys as he began to compose the e-post. Taunting her might be seen by some as childish, but Xalivar enjoyed the clever wordplay, especially knowing how it upset her and threw her off balance. Unlike him, Miri had not trained in controlling her emotions. They ran rampant, and, as a result, they dominated and controlled her in ways that made her weak and easily preyed upon. For the first time, Xalivar found himself pleased at the thought of it.

*You're no longer my liability, dear sister. Your relationship with this family is in name only. You'll have no part in our new glory.*

As he typed, he chuckled at the thought of Miri whiling away her last days in seclusion and poverty while he returned to the Palace. Oh, how that would eat away at her.

*A well-deserved ending for a turncoat, father would agree.*

He smiled again as he considered the perfect ending for his post, then typed it in and punched send. His only regret was that he wouldn't be able to be there to watch her open it.

*Soon, my dear sister. Our day will be soon.*

Farien pushed the joystick forward, racing to catch Davi. Hot air pounded his skin as the g-forces threatened to pull his hands free of the controls. Clearly the time spent training worker pilots in the forests of Vertullis was paying off, as Davi had taken the previous corner so sharply Farien couldn't believe he'd stayed aboard his Skitter.

As Farien slowed and pulled alongside, Davi glanced back at Yao who was trailing them. "Well, we haven't lost him yet."

Farien grinned, shaking his head. "It wouldn't be hard." He keyed the comm. "Come on, Brahma, you fly like your grandmother!"

"My grandmother's survived this long for a reason—no one in our family's insane." Yao's tone was one of patient calm. By now, his friends' antics didn't cause him any stress.

"Well, try to keep up, okay?" Davi said. "The streets are getting narrower and none of us know the city."

"Plus, the blackmarket could be dangerous," Farien added. "Wouldn't want you left alone."

"Don't worry, I'll find the impact crater or crashed-in wall easily enough," Yao said, unaffected.

Davi and Farien laughed as both slowed down for their friend to catch them. The streets were getting more crowded anyway, and they needed to work together to make sense of the Skitters' cheap nav system's directions. Sleek and fast one-man ground craft operating on a system allowed them to float above the planet's surface, Skitters' controls and handling resembled those of a VS28, but their nav systems didn't come close.

"You don't really expect anyone to tell us anything?" Yao pulled between them, his pace constant as if it were up to them to stay with him, not the other way around.

"Just stick to the cover story and we'll see what happens," Farien said.

Farien wondered how long it would take for Dru to get himself into trouble back at their lodgings. He'd only agreed to stay behind, after Farien threatened to send him back to Eleni 1 on the next shuttle. The black market would be rough enough for the three officers without them having to worry about a cadet, especially when it seemed Dru couldn't keep himself out of trouble for very long.

Davi pulled to a stop at the next intersection, checking his nav computer. "It looks like it should be on the next block west of here."

Fairen and Yao halted their Skitters beside his. All three glanced around. Yao looked particularly alarmed. "I really hope this cover story works. This doesn't look like a place we want to be identified as military officers."

Farien didn't remember them being this soft at the Academy. He rolled his eyes at Davi, then frowned at Yao. "Just let us do the talking, okay? Chances are you'll blend in with the other non-humans around here just fine."

Davi nodded. "Yao's right, though. We need to be really careful. If this place is half as dangerous as the rumors say—"

"I can't believe we went to the same Academy. You two sound like scared kids. Just watch my back and I'll handle it." Farien accelerated the Skitter, turning left and heading for the next intersection as his friends hurried to follow him.

"Be cool, Farien. The last thing we need is to set anyone off."

Farien sighed into the comm, cutting Davi off. "I'm leading this team, remember? Trust me."

"That's what worries us," Yao replied.

Ignoring them, Farien turned onto the next street which dead ended at a large open field covered with ramshackle buildings and scattered canopies. A potpourri of scents struck his nose—fruits, raw meat, smoke, sweat, oils, perfumes. A handmade sign read "Xanthis Independent Market." Farien parked and climbed off his Skitter as Davi and Yao stopped nearby. Already shady-looking characters gawked at them from the aisles between the market's buildings. Farien saw Xanthians mixed with rough looking humans, a couple Tertullians like Yao, an Idolian and two Lhamors. He nodded his head toward the Lhamors, looking at Davi and Yao.

Farien strode past the sign and up the aisle, passing right past the Lhamors as if they weren't there. Davi and Yao hurried after him.

The signage was scarce and buildings not well marked. Finding anything here would be an accident. He debated the risks of splitting them up until a solution presented itself. A young Xanthian appeared, offering himself as guide. "Just a small fee for my services is all," he responded to Farien's inquiry about what he charged. The Xanthian wore ragged, mis-matched clothes and clearly was overdue for a cleansing. Not to be trusted.

"We'll figure it out on our own," Farien replied as Davi hurriedly handed the youth some credits.

"It's been a while since we visited the market," Davi said, shooting Farien a look. "Your help will be most beneficial."

Farien sighed and motioned for the guide to lead the way. He shot Davi a look that said: *Your responsibility!* The youth pocketed the newly counted credits and smiled, walking as if he owned the place. "My name's Qajuan. Whatever you need, I can find it for you, just ask."

"Right now, we're looking for something special," Farien said, his memory racing to recall terms he'd heard used in stories of the market. You couldn't just outright ask for assassins. There was a proper slang here, and one had to use it or be seen as an outsider who couldn't be trusted.

"Lots of special things here," Qajuan replied. "Anything you can imagine. A little more specific and we'll find it for you."

"Specialists," Davi whispered, using the term Farien had been searching for.

Qajuan whirled and stared at him, his face indifferent. "Ah, many we have. Depends on your needs."

"The three-armed kind," Farien said.

Qajuan frowned. "Those kind are very rare, very expensive. Haven't seen many here lately, but we have many others. Perhaps one of them can solve your problem."

"Take us to someone who can arrange for any type we want," Farien suggested.

Qajuan smiled, satisfied, then whirled around and started up an aisle to the right.

They wound through rows and rows of tables offering everything from Qiwi and Gungor meat to fruits like Feruca and Gixi, various dried beans and leaves and powders both medicinal and for brewing. The scents mixed together, a kind of pungent sweet, dusty smell filling Farien's nose.

They passed into another section and here were various items of clothing and household goods—furniture handmade from high quality Vertullian wood, Idolian sand weavings with their intricate patterns of colored sand speaking messages from some mysterious religion long forgotten, Tertullian cloth of all shapes, sizes and colors. Farien had seen similar items in museums as a student and spent little time examining them, hurrying after their guide who seemed confident of the path he'd chosen.

They passed under a narrow archway between two canopied booths and Farien stopped dead. Stretching before him were endless tables of every weapon and armament imaginable, from the blasters he and his fellow cadets trained on to the more sophisticated blasters he and his friends carried as officers to the laser rifles sharpshooters carried into battle and the tiny weapons those with ill intentions hid in various nooks and crevices of their bodies. Yao and Davi shot him a look of warning as they passed him nonchalantly, following Qajuan. Farien stepped forward, moving slower but keeping pace. Then they rounded a corner and he saw military-issue laser targeting systems, the most sophisticated, restricted type. Troops trained for months just to learn how to operate them. No one outside the military was supposed to have access to them. He couldn't believe his eyes. He knew stolen military weapons made it to the blackmarkets, but to so openly sell them?

Noting his interest, the dealer stepped forward. He was dressed in khaki from head to foot—pants and a shirt, even his shoes a light tan. His face was long, odd shaped, and at first Farien wasn't sure if the man was human or some other species. Then he smiled and his teeth were a cornucopia of colors—Idolian. The teeth always gave them away. Their skin and hair colors often quite matched humans but with the long faces and arms and colored teeth, you could always tell. "How can I help you, my friend?"

The accent was sharp but the words understandable. "Just passing through."

"These are very special," he said, reaching his elongated arm out to stroke one of the targeting units. He leaned forward as if sharing a secret, his grin widening. "No one outside the military has them, except for me."

Farien took a deep breath, tensing with the urge to arrest the man on the spot. "You must be very well connected."

The man laughed, nodding. "Yes, I am. It's very fortunate you've made my acquaintance."

"How much?"

The man rubbed his hands together, stroking the target system while keeping his eyes locked on Farien. "How many?"

Farien glanced up to see Yao and Davi waving impatiently as Qajuan waited behind them.

"How many do you have?"

The vendor raised his hands in a questioning gesture. "I can get you more than you can afford."

Davi cleared his throat. "Other matters await us."

"Please," the vendor frowned and waved dismissively without even glancing away from his new customer, "we don't rush here. There's always time."

Then, amidst the shadows, Farien thought he saw a familiar blue face, red eyes staring at him. He blinked, looking more intensely and saw a tall, thin figure hurrying away. Hurrying to follow, he pushed the vendor roughly aside, sending him back into a table as two targeting units fell to the ground. Farien heard a cracking sound but didn't look back.

"That's no way to do business here!"

But Farien was off and winding through narrow alleys between buildings and canopies. He barely noticed Yao and Davi following, with Qajuan bringing up the rear. "Where are you going? The man you need is not this way!"

Farien increased his pace, seeing the tall, thin figure bobbing in and out ahead of him in the dense crowd. For mid-afternoon, the market was hopping.

"Where are we going?" Davi's breaths were heavy as he hurried to catch up with Farien.

"Does that guy look familiar?"

"Which one?"

"The tall, thin one. Andorian maybe?"

"Andorian?" Davi stretched up to get a better look as he struggled to keep up.

"It's Manaen."

"You saw his face?"

Farien shook his head. "No, blue skin, red eyes."

"That describes every Andorian. Why are we chasing him?"

The Andorian slowed ahead, trapped by a shoulder-to-shoulder crowd watching a demonstration. He turned slightly and Farien caught a glimpse of his face. He motioned to Davi. "Look! Manaen!"

The Andorian shrunk into the shadows as Farien called, then suddenly disappeared into a building.

"Cover the back. Let's find out for sure!" Farien hurried toward the front of the building as Davi and Yao hurried to cover the sides and back, Qajuan shooting them a puzzled look as he hung back.

Farien burst into a dark room, tables covering every available space, with only narrow aisles between. He slowed as his eyes adjusted—the Andorian nowhere in sight. A startled Xanthian vendor turned from negotiating with a Tertullian couple over some Gungor carcasses. His nose caught a slight hint of rot mixed with dust and curing solutions. Their purple eyes lit up the darkness, reminding Farien of Yao outside. Farien ignored them, winding around and past tables. He heard a shuffling from behind a curtain and pushed through.

"You cannot go there!"

The vendor's voice faded as Farien entered a narrow corridor lined with stacked goods, hurrying onward. And then he burst through the back door and into shadows between buildings. Davi whirled, his blaster drawn as Farien waved. "Where'd he go?"

Yao appeared, shaking his head. "We never saw him."

Davi relaxed and started sliding his blaster back inside his shirt when the Xanthian vendor rushed through the back door with his Tertullian clients.

The Idolian vendor appeared around the corner behind Davi, pointing and motioning. "There they are!"

Two burly Lhamors followed close behind with another Xanthian, who carried himself like some sort of official.

"He has a blaster!" The Xanthian vendor pointed at the bulge in Davi's shirt.

The Lhamors slowed, fumbling with all four hands for weapons of their own.

Farien hurried to Yao and Davi, forming a defensive circle as they backed toward the opposite corner.

"No weapons! A misunderstanding." Yao smiled, his voice its usual calm. But the new arrivals continued staring at Davi with menace.

"We were negotiating, then he shoved me aside and ran off!" The Idolian's teeth flared with rage.

"I was only looking." Farien raised his hands to proclaim his innocence.

"You're making a lot of trouble for men we've never seen here before," the Xanthian official said. "Identify yourselves!" The Lhamor guards waved their weapons menacingly behind him.

Then Qajuan appeared between them. "They're with me. Here to see Beauran."

"Beauran?" The official and the vendors exchanged worried looks as the Lhamors' weapons lowered slightly.

"They damaged two expensive items," the Idolian said. "Who will pay for that?"

"It was an accident," Yao said with an apologetic look.

"They're not easy to replace!"

"They thought they saw an old friend." Qajuan offered a wave of dismissal. "They just wanted to catch up with him."

"At what cost to me?"

"Send the bill to Beauran," Qajuan said. "He'll see that you're compensated." Who or what was Beauran? A person? A place? All the locals reacted to it each time with recognition and fear.

The Idolian shrunk back, his face changing, as if it suddenly wasn't so important. "Just tell them to be careful. We don't need trouble here!"

Qajuan smiled. "Of course."

The Idolian turned and disappeared back the way he'd come as the Lhamors holstered their weapons and the Xanthian and Tertullian customers disappeared back inside his shop.

Qajuan nodded to the Xanthian official and moved past them, motion-ing for Farien and his friends to follow.

Within moments, he'd led them out a gate to the street and hurried around a bend where Farien could see the parked Skitters. "What about this Beauran?"

Qajuan laughed and continued on toward where they'd first met. "You can't go anywhere near him after what happened. Word spreads quickly. No one will trust you, least of all Beauran."

"We came here for information," Farien frowned, his voice rising with his irritation.

"I can tell you what you want to know." Qajuan stopped a few feet from the Skitters and turned back to face them. "An Andorian hired the Lhamors. The one you saw."

"How do you know it's the same one?" Davi asked, before Farien had the chance. Despite recent tensions, it felt good to be back working with people who knew him so well.

"The Andorian represents powerful interests. He's seen here often."

"Who are these powerful interests?" Farien asked.

"I don't know. But all treat him with respect." His look told Farien he meant fear.

"What's the Andorian's name?" Davi jumped in again before Qajuan could answer. "Have you ever heard the name Manaen?"

Qajuan shook his head, then glanced around to make sure no one would overhear. "I only know he buys what he wants and no one cheats him."

"If Manaen's here..." Yao's eyes met Davi and he didn't even finish the thought.

Davi turned back to Qajuan. "Can you get his name?"

Qajuan shrugged. "I don't know. Take me with you."

"We're on an official mission," Farien protested.

Qajuan shook his head. "I can't be here when Beauran hears of this. I'll explain when we're far from here." His eyes darted around them and back toward the market.

Davi nodded, helping Qajuan onto the back of his Skitter, then climbing on and firing the turbos as Farien and Yao did the same. The Xanthian youth held on to Davi's waist, looking grateful, but his eyes remained peeled for trouble.

"How do we know we can trust him?" Farien looked at Yao and Davi, ignoring the boy.

"He saved our lives," Yao said with a shrug.

"Let's discuss this later," Davi pushed the joystick and his Skitter begin moving as Farien followed his glance. The Xanthian official and Lhamor guards had arrived and headed toward them again. Yao accelerated after Davi and Farien followed, aiming straight at a crowd of Xanthians walking along the side of the street. They scattered, chattering angrily and blocking the official and his thugs from view.

# Chapter Seven

Tela and her team finalized security arrangements for the High Lord Councilor's visit to Vertullis the day before the Royal Shuttle arrived. It felt different being on her home planet on official military duty. Since joining the Alliance pilot corps, Tela hadn't been home much and now here she was in charge of security for an important historical visit. She'd never seen Telanus so proud, walking around beaming from ear-to-ear, treating her like she was the princess herself. No matter how many times she scolded him for making such a fuss about her, he kept it up, unable to help himself. The one good thing about her present assignment was it distracted her from worrying about Davi. He was still out there somewhere. She checked in daily with friends on the command crew, but no new reports had come in of any altercations. She prayed he was fine and all her worrying was for nothing.

They'd had only a few days to prepare for the High Lord Councilor's visit and the entire Borali leadership, including Joram and Uzah on Vertullis, remained determined to ensure no protests would occur. This was to be a day of great historical significance. They'd given her a big responsibility but one she'd thrown herself into entirely. She'd asked Uzah why more senior people from Legallis hadn't been put in charge. He told her it was a chance for the Vertullians to prove themselves worthy, and, with Davi gone, she was the best person for the job. As flattered as she felt, she also resented the pressure.

Fortunately, most of the pressure was manufactured by politicians. The actual preparations went smoothly with few hitches. A few angry citizens maneuvered for better seats and special passes, but that was normal politics. Overall, when the day came for Tarkanius' speech, Tela felt confident there would be no problems.

The morning of the event, she had breakfast with Telanus, who frowned at her silence and worried expression. "Is it Davi or the speech you're so worried about?"

Tela sighed, continuing to run her fork aimlessly through her food. "A little of both?"

Telanus smiled. "You worry too much, Little Girl. You are such an amazing officer. I couldn't be more proud."

"They picked me because Davi is off God knows where, in God knows what danger—forgetting all about anyone here who might give a damn about him." She flicked some eggs to the side at a nearby bush.

Telanus reached out and put a hand atop hers, in an attempt to calm her. "Stop it. They picked you because you're good at what you do. And because they trust you. And I'm sure Davi is fine but just too busy to communicate. Trust God to care for him, Tela."

Tela's eyes met his, but she quickly looked away. He loved her so much. Yet as good as it felt after growing up mostly without her father, it also scared her a little. So much of her life he'd missed. So much of his, she'd missed. She sometimes wished they could drop everything and just spend their time getting to know each other.

"You always were high strung, even as a child," her father continued, his brow creased with concern. "That's something your mother and I always wished we could have changed about you."

She took a deep breath and reminded herself there was still plenty of time. "I'm trying, Daddy. Really."

Telanus chuckled, relaxing his hand and resting it beside his plate on the table again. "I love when you call me that."

Tela blushed as she saw his grin, turning away again. "Stop it."

Telanus shrugged. "Sorry. It's just now that you're all grown up, I didn't expect you'd still call me that."

"It's what you are to me. What you'll always be." Turning back, she reached across the table and squeezed his hand.

"For what it's worth, I'm sure Davi's as worried about you as you are about him."

Tela sighed. "I hope so." If Davi knew the responsibility she'd been given, perhaps he would be worried, more than he might be at the moment. Her father was right. Davi cared about her. And he could truly be out of communications range. She glanced at her chrono. "But I'm late. I have to be there early to make sure everything's done right."

Telanus squeezed her hand back and smiled. "I'm proud of you. Go show them how amazing you are."

Tela felt herself blushing again. "Stop embarrassing me."

"Can't a father be proud?"

Tela stood, hesitating, then walked around the table and leaned in to kiss his forehead. "I love you, Daddy."

"I love you, too, Little Girl. See you soon."

She felt a shiver up her spine as he said those words. Every time. So many years she'd given up hope of ever seeing him again. The warmth of his smile stayed with her as she turned and hurried off.

One of the largest crowds ever assembled on the planet gathered for the event. It was the first time Vertullians would have the chance to see a High Lord Councilor in the flesh in decades, and as full-fledged citizens, that had special meaning for her people. She scanned their multi-colored faces, filled with excitement and awe—Vertullians of all Old Earth races and backgrounds united in anticipation of what the High Lord Councilor would say. The dais was packed with dignitaries. A majority of the Council accompanied their leader with Simeon seated immediately to Tarkanius' right and the others arranged in order of seniority around them. Military leaders were present as well, including Uzah, Matheu, and various leaders from Legallis. Representing senior command was General Grif, whom Tela met for the first time. She'd seen him on broadcasts and in passing but had never actually spoken to him until now. She was surprised to find he knew a lot about her. He was tall and thin, hair graying at his temples and initially came across almost like a grandpa in the way he spoke to her. But Tela had heard from Davi and others that he was quite serious and intense about military matters, much like Matheu.

Joram and Matheu made brief speeches, followed by Simeon, before Joram introduced Tarkanius. She'd never seen Joram looking so proud. It reminded her of the way Telanus had been looking at her since she got the security assignment. She chuckled a bit as he shifted nervously before the mic, then backed away, as if afraid to dishonor Tarkanius with his back, as the High Lord Councilor took center stage.

"My dear people," Tarkanius began, scanning the crowd with a broad smile that let them know he considered them his own. Tela felt a chill run up her spine as he said it. Hearing him say it on the nets was one thing, but in person it was electrifying. It had the same effect on the crowd. He won them over immediately, the rest of his speech interrupted with cheers and spontaneous applause throughout. He spoke for around thirty minutes, assuring them that the extension of citizenship had come because they'd earned respect, that it was long overdue and that it was permanent. He spoke of the significance of unity and service and then addressed 'The Returning.'

"In a way, you, joint citizens with us of a former age on Old Earth, are now returning to your proper place at our sides." Cheers and applause broke out all around him. Tarkanius smiled warmly, waiting for it to subside before continuing. "And it with this thought in mind that we are honored to declare 'The Returning' an official holiday for all of us."

The explosions came as the cheering and applause commenced again. Flashes of oranges and yellows from the corners of the podium and back in the crowd. Loud explosive reports blended with people's screams as the crowd began to scatter. Smoke rose from beneath the podium. The dignitaries on the platform looked like frightened Gungors caught in spotlights of a night hunt. Some stood and looked around, unsure what to do. Others cowered in their seats. A few fled the shaking dais.

Tela's breath caught in her throat as Tarkanius fell to his knees. A piece of the dais had split apart beneath his feet. For a moment, she thought his leg was trapped. The podium wobbled as if it might fall back on him. Then the personal security detail she'd assigned swept in, lifted him to his feet and raced him to safety. The comm channel remained a constant stream of agitated voices in her ear. Reports flew in so fast her mind hardly registered the details: sightings of possible suspects; suspicious packages; locations of possible explosives; endless questions. Just as her team reached the stairs with Tarkanius, the entire dais collapsed, sinking to the ground. The dignitaries all joined the chaos, scrambling for safety, mixing with the scattering crowd. Tela and her people quickly lost control, concentrating their efforts on the Council members and leader-ship. The comm channels continued with endless streams of reports. Virun and Jorek claimed to have found someone with detonators running away amidst the crowd. A couple of other security personnel found others with suspicious residue on their clothes. She ordered them all rounded up and taken for interrogation, waiting until Brie and Nila finished the count and assured her all the dignitaries and leaders were safe with only a few minor scrapes, bruises and burns amongst those closest to the edge of the platform.

Tela saw Joram, Uzah, Tarkanius and Simeon looking at her and wished she could crawl back into the shadows. She had no idea what to say to them. She'd failed in her most important assignment ever. How could this have happened? Everyone had been checked so carefully, the whole area swept. She knew she'd be busy for a while sorting all that out. She grimaced as Tarkanius led the others toward her. His ceremonial robe was singed at the bottom, his hair disheveled a bit, but he appeared otherwise fine.

He stopped, facing her, and smiled. "Don't worry, Tela. I'm okay.

We're all okay."

She struggled to fight back the tears welling at the corners of her eyes. "I don't know how this could have happened. We were so careful."

"Those who want to harm us are always more determined than we are to protect ourselves," Tarkanius said, putting a hand on her shoulder.

Uzah's face was a mixture of anger and embarrassment. "We will get to the bottom of it, my Lord. It's unacceptable!" He turned to Tela. "I hear rumors workers were involved?"

"We don't know yet. There were some people with residue on their clothing and others with detonators. They're being rounded up."

"I want answers right away!"

Tarkanius winked at Tela then turned to Uzah. "General, answers in such cases can take a while to become clear. We all want them, but let's not ask the impossible of our dedicated men and women, all right? I'm sure they'll all do their best."

Uzah looked as if he'd been called into court martial. Joram forced a smile and nodded. "Of course, my Lord. We all will. All we want is to ensure your safety."

Tarkanius sighed. "Right now, I have fear for the safety of all of us, not just me."

"It was a good speech, my Lord," Tela finally said.

Tarkanius smiled. "With an explosive ending." He laughed and soon the others joined him, nervously. Tela relaxed a bit, grateful for his generosity, then excused herself and hurried off to question the suspects her people had taken to the command base.

Xalivar closed his eyes and took a deep breath after hearing Manaen report seeing Xander and his friends at the black market on Xanthis. Xander and his friends were getting too close. They knew where to go and who to talk to. How was that possible unless someone had left too many clues? When he'd heard they were coming, he'd expected them to be chasing rumors, but this... He knew their encounter with Manaen had been pure coincidence but it exposed his operations to risks he couldn't afford. Xalivar whirled back around as his fists unclenched at his sides. "Get Obed now!"

Manaen nodded and hurried off, looking relieved to have an excuse to be away from his master. Lucius remained silent in a nearby chair, waiting.

"That idiot son of his should have never been allowed into this! He seems intent on doing everything he can to thwart our plans!"

Lucius nodded. "He's incompetent and careless, but I doubt it's intentional. He doesn't have the brains, from everything I've read in his file."

Xalivar paced, fists continuing to clench. "I want them eliminated, Lucius. All except my former nephew. I want him alive! Now!"

Lucius stood, hands closing to form the salute. "Yes, my Lord, I'll see to it."

Lucius hurried out as Manaen appeared in the doorway, waving Obed past him. Obed's face remained casual, but Xalivar saw a glint of irritation in his eyes. "Oh, I'm disturbing you?"

"Nothing that can't be resumed later."

Xalivar stopped pacing and turned to face his old rival, noting Manaen had disappeared with Lucius. "My former nephew and his friends are here."

"Davi Rhii? On Xanthis?" Obed seemed genuinely surprised.

Xalivar nodded. "Yes. And asking questions of the wrong people. The result, no doubt, of the foolish carelessness of your son."

"Bordox would never jeopardize this operation. He's as invested in this as the rest of us."

"You've wanted for years to ruin me, Obed. Don't take me for a fool."

"I want my family restored to its rightful place, yes," Obed said, straightening with pride instead of shrinking back as most would when facing Xalivar's wrath. "But I joined you in this plan because we share a common goal."

"I'd better not find out otherwise."

"Are you threatening me?"

"You and your son, yes!"

Obed coughed. "Don't be a fool. You have few allies in this. You need me."

"I trust no one but myself."

They stood a moment staring into each other's eyes, neither blinking nor looking away. Then Obed motioned, the wave of a hand. "I'll have someone deal with your former protégée, don't worry. He won't get off Xanthis alive."

"Lucius is seeing to it. You'll do nothing except find your son and bring him here. I want him now!"

"Fine. I will find him. But we did not betray you."

"You've waited for an opportunity for decades!"

"Serving you! I led your Special Police! How dare you question my honor. I won't stand for it!" Obed pointed a finger at Xalivar in warning.

"Then sit down where you can remember your place." Xalivar's fist clenched as he glared coldly at Obed, daring him to respond. After a moment, Obed turned and walked out the door.

*Your day will come, my old enemy! When all this is finished, I will deal with you. But first, my young Xander, you will answer to me!*

Imagining Xander's reaction to the death of his friends lit Xalivar's heart like laser lights and he chuckled to himself. There were few things Xalivar enjoyed more than enacting revenge.

When news of the bombing flooded the comm channels, Pres knew it was time to move. Xalivar had promised a distraction—an incident requiring military mobilization in response. The pretense was a call to respond, but while they'd depart under the same orders and headings as responders, she and her team would slip off course and disappear. She went quickly about her duties as required, sending out various orders via comm and e-post. Mixed among them, she sent the code ordering her recruits to meet at the transport in half an hour. By the time they were discovered, they'd have safely disappeared on FTL routes. The chaos surrounding the attack on the High Lord Councilor took some of the pressure off. Although they'd be missed, no one would have time to really search for them right away, allowing them time to put distance between the transport and anyone who might give chase.

Confirmation codes flooded her inbox, as she continued coordinating troops sent to escort the Royal Shuttle, seeing to the wounded, and investigating the assassination attempt. She glanced across the command cnter to where Dek was also busily coordinating the flood of calls. He stayed so cool under pressure. She thought back to when things fell apart over Vertullis. Even then he'd been calm, while she'd struggled just to stay on her feet. She glanced away before he noticed her stare. He could read her well after all the hours spent working together. She couldn't let him read the message in her eyes now. She was about to leave him, probably forever. If they did see each other again, she wondered if they'd ever do so as friends. Dek was an honorable man. He didn't tolerate betrayal or dereliction of duty. She hated to disappoint him and hoped someday she'd get the chance to explain.

As the last confirmation code came in, she ran the calculations. Three hundred officers and troops, including a tech she could see across from her in command. The last challenge was to slip away herself. Dek had already announced plans to leave for the surface within the hour, leaving her in charge. So her betrayal of him began with an unavoidable lie. She waited a moment, taking a few calming breaths, then stood and approached Dek.

"I've got a crisis to handle down at the launch bays. A few angry pilots wanting to take off and wreak revenge on the entire planet for attacking the High Lord Councilor."

Dek sighed. "I've had a few of those myself. Take names. We need to keep track of these people."

She nodded. "I'll be back as soon as I can."

"Of course, Pres. I have every confidence in you."

It took all her strength not to cringe at his last remark. Instead, she forced a smile, turned on her heels and hurried out, motioning for the tech to follow. "Come with me and bring your datapad."

The tech nodded, looking relieved that her quick thinking saved him from making his own excuse. He followed on her heels out the door.

The café looked abandoned as Hachim entered and made his way toward the back room. A waitress and a cook barely looked up from their conversation as he slipped past, saying nothing before returning to their gossip. Niger had arranged the location the day before, based on information from a friend serving in the military here. The spaceport was not its usual bustle today due to the speech. Even the assassination attempt didn't have people rushing for transports. Hachim looked around a moment before pushing the door and disappearing inside.

"Tell me you didn't rent this room under your name," he said to Niger as he entered.

Niger sat at a round table. Seated beside him was a Borali major, whose bright red hair stood out despite the low lighting, his uniform appearing stretched to the max over his rotund frame. Lords Elul and Kretzu occupied the other seats with one left for Hachim. He slid into it quickly as he sighed, noting the others were already savoring cups of wine.

"It's under the name of our lead employee, Ner Zebah," Niger answered.

Hachim searched his mind. "A man captured by the authorities?"

Niger smiled. "It's perfect, Hachim. His co-conspirators met without him. Only by the time they discover this reservation, there'll be no one who can identify them."

"Employees saw us enter," Hachim reminded him.

"They'll soon be hiring new staff," the major said.

Hachim scowled. The implication was clear. "My gods, you plan to murder them?"

"The major will make sure they don't talk," Niger said. "I leave the details to him."

"Our plan worked perfectly," Lord Kretzu interjected. "The dignitaries were traumatized. The people terrorized. The blame on Vertullians."

"We don't know that for sure yet." Hachim shot him a look. Kretzu didn't waiver. Older, tall, and thin with a narrow mustache, he'd been on the Council almost as long as Simeon. So long that he'd seen many crises and it wasn't easy to rattle him.

"Stay calm, Hachim. This was your idea after all." Lord Elul was almost as large as the Major but from fat instead of muscle. His robe bulged in all the wrong places and his puffy face reddened with annoyance. The looks the others gave Hachim were warnings to stop protesting and play along. Any one of them would gladly reveal his involvement and pin him with public blame if he dared rebel. The Major sneered and slid a cup over toward him.

Niger nodded, chuckling at Hachim. He reached across the table with a pitcher to fill Hachim's cup with wine. "It will happen, Hachim. The blame will be placed on those who clearly perpetrated the crime. We have nothing to fear."

"We must be very careful," Hachim answered. "Our goal is to increase the divide between Boralians and Workers. Protestors at speeches for a former princess, carefully planned bombings intended to injure and alarm. We cannot let ourselves lose focus."

"We also cannot allow ourselves to risk detection," Niger said. "We'll do what must be done for the glory of our people and the Alliance." He raised his cup and the others joined him in toast, sipping wine and laughing. Hachim raised his last, forcing a smile.

"Tarkanius wasn't even wounded. Your employees failed their task."

Niger shook his head. "Wounding Tarkanius would have been a bonus. Showing him incompetent and not in control was the goal, and that we accomplished quite well."

Kretzu nodded. "Indeed. We have only to await another such opportunity and strike again."

"We have an opportunity here to ruin their leadership," the Major said. "Men like Lord Aron, General Matheu, Governor Joram, and Davi Rhii should be implicated, their reputations clouded."

"Aron and Rhii are particularly known for their integrity. They fought hard to create this union, why would they destroy it?" Hachim stared at the Major, who would neither meet his eyes nor offer an explanation.

"We don't have to actually prove their involvement, just hint at ties," Elul said. "The confusion would be enough to cause damage, question their trustworthiness."

"Only those who don't personally know them would ever believe it," Hachim said, shaking his head.

Niger frowned, irritatedly, and glared at Hachim. "You've been against every idea Lord Aron has presented since he joined the Council. Why are you defending him?"

"I am commenting on his character. He won't be easily slandered. His reputation for loyalty and integrity is widely known."

"What about Rhii?" the Major asked.

"The Vertullian people's hero? Oh, yes, he'll be easily discredited." Hachim rolled his eyes.

"Discrediting them is not of any importance to the plan. As long as we sway public opinion in our favor, our mission will succeed." Niger looked at them one by one for agreement. None objected, although the Major never met his eyes. "Your doubts, Hachim, only discredit *you.* I suggest you reconsider your attitude immediately." His eyes met Hachim's.

Hachim and Niger had known each other since childhood. Was it a threat or an advisement? Either way, Niger's face made it clear he wouldn't tolerate argument. Hachim sighed and stood. "Let's get out of here before we're seen together." He quickly downed the rest of his wine, needing to calm his nerves.

"I can handle any witnesses," the major said.

Hachim looked sadly at Niger and hurried out the door. It had been his idea, but he'd wanted mild diversions—enough to increase the tensions and throw doubt on the integrity of the workers. He hadn't really intended to get anyone killed. He should have known things would get out of hand with the co-conspirators they'd chosen.

He kept to the shadows and took the nearest exit, not spotting anyone taking notice of him, then hurried back out toward the city.

The bar was a dive. There was no better way to describe it. Bordox supposed he should be used to it given his new life, but this place was a new low. His father sat there as if it was completely normal for men of their status to be in such a place. "Can you at least try to look relaxed? We don't want to draw attention to ourselves."

Bordox fought the urge to scowl as he carefully set his glass down on top of a stack of paper napkins, checking it for balance before releasing it. "Not my kind of place."

"It is if you don't want anyone to know about this meeting. So act like this is perfectly normal for us." Obed's eyes darkened in disappointment.

Bordox's anger rose with every disapproving word. He was tired of being treated like a total failure, his accomplishments going unrecognized. No wonder his military superiors never acknowledged his genius when his own father couldn't.

"Xalivar was quite angry to discover Rhii and his friends here on Xanthis," Obed continued with a smile. "Your leaks were most effective."

Was that a compliment? He couldn't remember the last time he'd heard one from his father. "Steps are already being taken to deal with them."

"Xalivar's sending his own people as well."

Bordox bristled, fumbling for his cup as he glanced away in an attempt to hide it. He had this situation handled. Why couldn't they just let him deal with it?

"Rhii and his friends saw the majordomo at the market. Xalivar blames you for revealing his location."

"They caught Manaen? Spoke with him?"

"No. He got away. They may not even be sure it was Manaen."

Bordox gulped his beer, almost choking. He coughed. "I hope we did reveal his location as planned. I hope the whole Alliance comes down on him!"

Obed frowned, glancing around. "Keep your voice down. This isn't a place Alliance talk would be welcomed." Bordox shrunk back in his seat, sipping slower this time. Obed's eyes scanned the room. But the few other patrons paid them no notice, chattering and eating as before. After a moment, when no one seemed to have taken notice of them, he relaxed again. "Xalivar will get what's coming to him, don't worry. Just stick to the plan."

"I want Rhii!" Bordox whispered it, but his voice sounded much louder because of the intensity.

"Rhii will get what's coming to him, too. He and all his kind will soon be back where they belong—as slaves. It's the only reason we're here with Xalivar."

"He blames us for everything that goes wrong. Treats us like idiots, like we're worthless."

"Our perceived alliance with him is a means to end, Son. That's all. You need to learn to better control your emotions. They've brought you much trouble."

Bordox wanted to shout at him but managed to restrain himself. "How can you tolerate being brushed aside as irrelevant? After all your hard work?"

"It is a passing phase, Bordox. Soon, they will be the irrelevant ones."

Both whirled at the sound of Orson Sterling giving a broadcast. The bartender had raised the volume and it now filled screens scattered around the room.

"—the attack today on the High Lord Councilor, while he was giving a speech in the Vertullian capital of Iraja. This unprovoked attempt to assassinate our leader appears to have been perpetrated by disgruntled Vertullians. Authorities made several arrests in the incident and the suspects are being interrogated now. Fortunately, the injuries for those present were relatively minor."

The chatter in the restaurant had died as everyone gaped transfixed at the broadcasts. Bordox couldn't believe his ears. "Workers tried to assassinate Tarkanius?"

Obed smiled, eyes locked on a monitor with delight. "Xalivar's lust for power knows no bounds."

"Why would workers help Xalivar?" He took a long draw from his beer and waited.

Obed finally turned back to face him. "His powers of manipulation are legendary. Don't underestimate him. This attack will help us."

"It will certainly inflame anti-worker sentiment—"

"It will do more than that. As I already told you, there are many on the Council who share our sentiments. This will mobilize them; make them good potential Allies for us. They have no love for Xalivar either." Obed sat back on the bench, looking excited. "Soon, my Son, we will restore our family's greatness. Just control your emotions and stick with the plan."

Bordox nodded, as he continued nursing his beer. He'd do what he had been doing and prove himself to his father and everyone else. Even Xander Rhii.

Xalivar reran the recording of Orson Sterling's report—an assassination attempt on the High Lord Councilor. He cringed at hearing someone else's name given that title. Soon enough it would be his again. Someone else was working to undo the tragedy that had befallen their people at Tarkanius' hands. Just before the broadcast, his own people had reported back. The protestors at Miri's speech were not his. Someone else had been responsible. And now the attack on Tarkanius, in which he had no hand. Lucius hadn't even needed to initiate their backup plan. This attack had provided all the cover they needed. *I have allies I didn't know about.* He chuckled at the thought: people who would hail him as a returning hero—likely members of the Council themselves. As long as they continued to aid his cause, he would be sure to reward them when the time came.

*Too bad you weren't even injured, Tarkanius.*

Still, it would be all too easy to overthrow the imposter. He was weak and weak leadership never survived long. The Boralian people deserved the strength the Rhiis had always provided them. Miri and Xander aside, the Rhiis were a strong people, unfaltering in their determination and drive. Not easily shoved aside no matter what people thought.

"Manaen!"

His majordomo appeared quickly, datapad in hand. "Yes, my Lord."

"I want all the information on the investigation of the attempt on the High Lord Councilor's life. As soon as it's available."

"Of course, my Lord." Manaen turned away, already typing into his datapad.

Xalivar watched him. *Good old faithful, Manaen. Thank the gods Andorians are as lazy as they are stupid.* At least they were trainable. Xalivar had spent years cultivating Manaen's usefulness. "Use every resource, Manaen. If Orson Sterling gets it first, I'll hold you responsible."

Manaen nodded. "Yes, my Lord."

Xalivar rewound the broadcast again as his aide hurried out. It had been a while since the networks had provided him with such quality entertainment. The looks on the Council members' faces as they fled for their lives made him laugh. They were all weak. *Your shepherd is returning, my sheep.*

"Turn that off. It's depressing." Davi turned back to watch the cityscape out the window as he paced. The images flashed through his mind again: explosions, Tarkanius falling, the platform collapsing, panicked people running, and, somewhere in the midst of it, he could swear he'd seen Tela. Farien's running the broadcast over and over again for the past hour hadn't helped either. Davi's chest tightened with urgency. He had to get home now. "Where could that kid be?"

"We'd better go find him." Yao sat hunched down on a sofa as Farien turned off the broadcast and leaned against the wall.

"Where do we look, Yao? He could be anywhere." Farien rubbed his hand along the plush, upholstered wall. "I told you it was a bad idea to bring him along."

The accommodations the government had arranged must be amongst the finest in the city, Davi thought. Everything was finery, almost on a scale with the Palace where he'd grown up—gold-encased fittings on reflector pads, doors, window frames, and the cleansing room; Andorian tapestries, Tertullian tile. Even the view itself was the finest, showing the skyline in all its glory. The twin suns' light shone down from high overhead, sending shadows dancing across the faces of the buildings and the street surfaces in between. They'd arrived back at the hotel to find Dru missing. So much for promising to wait for them. Davi wished he was surprised. Dru's impulsiveness had always been his greatest liability.

"I can help," Qajuan said. Davi had almost forgotten the boy was with them. They all turned to look at him. "I know the city. I can ask questions of people who wouldn't talk to you."

"Let's call down to the front desk and ask if the concierge saw him leave," Yao suggested. "He could be somewhere in the hotel."

"If we split up, we can find him faster," Farien said, already moving toward the door with Qajuan.

"Fine. I'll start in the hotel and we can stay in touch by comm." Davi nodded as Yao stood and followed Farien, then picked up the wall comm to call the front desk.

Thirty minutes later, Davi exited for the street. None of the staff had any recollection of Dru leaving the hotel, so Davi went to find Yao, Farien and Qajuan. It took a moment to raise them on the comm. They rendezvoused in a central square near the city market, a cornucopia of chattering voices, bustling bodies and scents. No one paid them any attention as they stood in a circle facing each other.

"This is just a waste of time." Farien sighed, checking his chrono. "It could go on for hours. What if he took an air taxi or something?"

"He knows better than to wander off too far alone," Yao said. He and Davi exchanged a look. In Yao's eyes, Davi saw the same doubts about it that he had.

"I'll find him," Qajuan said. "Let me go alone."

"You don't even know what he looks like." Farien could hardly stand still from irritation.

Yao started punching buttons on his datapad, then held it up for Qajuan to see. A picture of Dru's face filled the screen. "That's him."

Qajuan nodded. "Okay. I'll find him."

"Bring him back to the hotel," Davi said. "We'll be packed and waiting."

Qajuan disappeared around a corner with a nod as Farien frowned. "How do we know we can trust that kid? He's a hustler, probably an orphan, homeless, totally unreliable."

"Who happens to be right," Yao said. "He knows this city and can talk with people we can't. Give him a chance."

"Yao's right," Davi nodded as they started together back toward the hotel. "Besides, he saved our lives at that Black Market and he's made no move against us since. We need to get our things together and get back to the ship. We'll be needed at home now."

"I'm surprised we haven't been recalled already," Yao said as they rounded a bend into the alley Qajuan had shown them as a shortcut between two larger streets.

A Skitter appeared, darting into the alley and parking sideways, blocking their path. The rider grinned, staring right at the three of them.

"This doesn't look good," Yao mumbled.

"Let's just go back the other way," Davi agreed as they turned around.

Two more Skitters appeared at the end of the alley from which they'd just entered. These riders just glared menacingly.

"Any ideas?" Yao asked.

"I don't see any weapons," Farien said, reaching for his blaster.

Davi put a hand on his arm to stop him. "You want us to shoot them? We don't even know what they want."

"Look at their faces. Do you really think this is the time to chat?" Farien kept his hand near his weapon as Davi motioned to the men.

"What do you want?"

The three drivers drew weapons from beneath their jackets with one simultaneous motion, aiming them at Davi and his friends.

"Can we shoot now?" Farien drew his weapon and aimed back, searching for cover as Yao and Davi did the same.

Davi heard the men's laser rifles hum as they warmed up and bolts came flying toward them. He and Yao ducked left, Davi rolling and landing crouched beside a building wall lining the alley as Farien fell to his knees in the opposite direction. The alley floor smelled of urine and decaying trash. All three friends fired back immediately at the riders, who tried to dodge with their Skitters. The grinning man made it, Farien's blast exploding against the building behind him, but Davi's blast hit as the other two riders got in each other's way. Smoke rose from the blackened engine compartment, but the rider maneuvered clear of the alley and ducked around the corner for cover.

The riders fired again, their blasts forcing the three friends to dodge again. Yao ducked and rolled back further along the wall as Davi and Farien dove, ending up switching sides.

"We're dead if we stay here," Farien said as all three crouched again, aiming their weapons.

Other than trash scattered by winds, the alley was clear of anything suitable for providing cover.

"We have to run for it," Yao said with a shrug.

Farien scowled, motioning toward their assailants. "Which way do you want to die?" The three friends fired again, but missed.

"Set your blasters to rapid repeat," Davi said as an idea came into his head. "Three against one's the best odds."

"You're crazy!" Farien shook his head as all three adjusted their weapon's settings.

"We lay down a stream of fire, forcing him to dodge as we rush him. Only chance we have." He motioned to Farien. "You cover the rear to keep them occupied. On three, okay?"

Farien sighed, his eyes indicating resigned agreement as all three readied themselves.

*God protect us.* Davi prayed silently. "One...two...three!"

All three friends fired as they ran, Farien turned partially around to fire toward the two Skitters at the far end of the alley, the barrel of his blaster swinging back and forth to spread his blasts throughout the area behind them. Beams burst from Yao's and Davi's blasters, one after another, the noise deafening. The rider they rushed stopped grinning and fumbled with his controls as he dodged out of the way at the last second. The other two riders were too busy running to fire back. Too preoccupied with protecting themselves from Farien's chaotic fire.

Davi's group reached the end of the alley to find the Skitter waiting. They turned in unison and fired back, forcing the rider to dodge again as they headed away from him down a major street. Pedestrians screamed and scattered. All three simultaneously reset their blasters to normal. There were too many pedestrians to risk it here. Besides, blaster's power packs could only last so long under constant streaming and Davi hadn't brought an extra. He doubted his friends had either.

Rounding a corner into a plaza, they raced to the middle of the crowd before looking back. No Skitters in sight.

"We can't have lost them," Yao said, looking as puzzled as Davi felt.

"They didn't follow us? Why would they stop?" Pedestrians shied away as Farien panned the area with his blaster.

"Farien, lower it. You're scaring people." Davi reached out and pushed Farien's gun arm down.

"I found him!" It sounded like Qajuan. All three looked around for him. After a minute, they saw hands waving from a nearby alley where Dru was waiting with Qajuan.

Davi couldn't believe it. *This kid is good!* He heard the hum of the engines followed by the laser rifles. Blasts landed around them as pedestrians screamed and scattered.

"I knew we didn't lose them," Farien said, raising his gun to fire back as all three took off toward Qajuan.

"What's going on?" Dru asked as they drew near.

"Run! Back to the hotel! Now!" Davi waved his hands to impart urgency as Qajuan and Dru turned and raced up the alley with Davi and the others. As they hit the far end and started down another street, Davi heard the echoing of Skitter engines as the riders entered the alley.

"Who are these guys?" Dru asked, slowing down a bit and forcing Farien to dodge around him.

"Stop and ask if you want," Farien said, annoyed as he picked up his pace again.

Davi grabbed Dru's arm and dragged him along. Lasers exploded on the pavement around them sending chunks of rock and debris flying. Davi felt a sharp pain as one struck his cheek. "We'll never make it on foot."

They were forced to dodge the Skitters, air taxis and air cars which filled the street. An air taxi exploded behind them, its yellow striped body flipping end over end on top of a nearby air car so fast their occupants had no time to react. Woman screamed as pedestrians scattered trying to outrun the flying debris.

"They don't care who gets hurt," Yao observed.

"Follow me!" Qajuan yelled and nodded urgently as he darted to a side toward a set of office buildings.

"There are too many people!"

Qajuan ignored Davi's warning. "Trust me!"

Three more Skitters appeared headed toward them from the opposite direction down the street. The riders were dressed similarly to the others, laser rifles held at the ready.

"Do we have a choice?" Farien asked.

All four of them switched direction to race after Qajuan into pedestrians who started to panic in confusion at what was happening. A few froze; others ran; and others pushed and shoved. Screaming and shouting broke out as a fight erupted.

"Where are we going?" Farien demanded as Qajuan led them twisting and winding through the frightened spectators until he came to a small stairwell and started down.

"We're going where they can't follow."

Shadows covered them as they descended almost into complete darkness, where Qajuan stopped and fumbled a bit in the dark. Then sudden-ly, a door swung wide and light from small reflector pads lining the ceiling of a tunnel pierced the darkness.

Qajuan immediately started running along the tunnel. "Hurry! And close the door before they see."

They followed quickly, Davi glancing up the stairs as he closed the door behind them. No one had followed them...yet. "What is this place?"

"Maintenance tunnels for the cables that power the city and its networks. Few people know about them, but the underground do. We use them more than city workers." Qajuan smiled back at him as he continued running.

"Where do they go?" Farien asked.

"All over the city. We'll be at your hotel in no time."

Davi smiled at Yao, glad their hopes for Qajuan's trustworthiness looked well founded.

"You can relax now. They can't find this easily, and they won't know their way around." Qajuan turned onto a side tunnel as they all followed. "Especially because they won't know which way we went."

Davi looked around as he entered the new tunnel. It was like a maze with tunnels leading off in various directions. He relaxed and holstered his weapon, seeing Yao and Farien do the same.

After meeting with his father, Bordox accompanied his assassins to the hotel in which Rhii and his friends had registered. It wasn't under their names but Alliance delegation, booked by the city government. Since no broadcasts had spoken of any official delegations, it hadn't been too hard to figure out who the delegation must be. Bordox fumed when he saw the hotel. Rhii and his friends were in luxury while Bordox was stuck in diner dives like some low class scum. He would end this today!

They'd waited what seemed like an hour with no sign of their targets. Then six men on Skitters rode up, and Bordox recognized right away from their level of interest and coordination meant that they were professional hit men. They circled the hotel then managed to secret themselves away in various hiding spots from alleys to shadowed doorways. Xalivar's people!

He tensed, cursing. Xalivar would not steal this moment from him! "We need a distraction," he said into his comm. "Those men are here for the same targets."

"L't th'm do th' job for us," an assassin answered.

"No! We're the ones who get to take down Xander Rhii!" Bordox answered through clenched teeth. *Hired assassins telling me to back off? What did I hire them for?* Still, he knew if they all shot at once it would draw local law enforcement and a lot of attention they didn't need. His mind raced for a way to distract the riders and lead them away.

Then it was too late. Rhii and his friends appeared on a corner across from the hotel, from a stairway Bordox never would have noticed which seemed to lead down into the ground. Where had they been?

Their guide, a young blue-skinned Xanthian, led the way across the street. The Skitter riders appeared from their hiding places and moved in, firing laser rifles. Rhii's group drew weapons and immediately scattered, shrinking back into the shadows for cover. Then the guide did something Bordox would have never expected. The Xanthian youth ran straight for a Skitter swinging some kind of primitive elastic band with a metal bar attached. The rider sneered and ignored him racing right toward him, but as he neared, the youth released the bar and it slammed end first into the rider's face, knocking him from the Skitter.

As the rider bounced across the ground and the Skitter slowed to a stop, the youth hopped aboard and gunned it, taking off down the street. Two other Skitters followed, giving chase as Rhii and Brahma fired on the remaining three.

"Th'y'r fight'ng each oth'r," an assassin noted over the comm.

"Ignore the riders and get the targets," Bordox ordered. He couldn't spot Farien and the cadet who'd been with them on the corner. Where were they? Brahma and Rhii continued firing at the Skitter riders as they dodged rifle blasts. Rock debris flew off buildings as walls were struck. A streetlight exploded from a hit. The two officers kept moving.

*Xalivar's men are terrible shots.*

Then he heard the humming of more Skitters and suddenly Farien and the young cadet appeared from behind the hotel, racing toward them. Both fired on the riders from behind, causing them to stop shooting and flee for safety. One rider flew right into Rhii's path and was shot down, flying backwards off his Skitter as a laser blast burned a hole through his chest.

Farien and the cadet pulled up alongside their companions who hopped on behind them, grabbing hold of their driver's waists. Then Farien and the cadet spun the Skitters in an arc and headed back for the hotel. Bordox's men opened fire on them, causing them to fly erratically to avoid being hit.

A yellow flash drew Bordox's attention as a bolt struck one of the Skitters, leaving burn marks on the back panel but not disabling it. *My own men are incompetent. No wonder they have to kill one at a time in close quarters.* Bordox drew his own blaster, prepared to ignore his father's orders to let the hired men do the dirty work. Just as he raised his blaster, the Skitters disappeared behind the hotel to safety.

"Get them!" he screamed into the comm.

As soon as they cleared the building, Farien and Dru took Davi and Yao to the third Skitter.

"How'd you guys make it undetected?" Yao asked as he climbed down and ran for the third Skitter.

"The tunnels," Dru said. "We used Farien's datapad nav system to find one leading under the hotel. Not hard when you know where it is."

Davi and Yao laughed. "Good thinking," Davi said as he motioned to Dru. "Get inside and stay hidden. We need to go help Qajuan."

"And leave me out of all the fun? Come on! I'm great with a Skitter!"

"I don't have time to argue with you."

"Good, then don't." Dru stayed put on the Skitter. The building overhead shook from explosions, rocking back and forth, as they heard the whistle of laser fire overhead.

"There were more firing after the riders fled for cover," Yao said. "More of their friends, I suppose."

"We have no idea how many there are," Farien added.

"What's the plan?" Davi asked.

"They'll be here any minute!" Dru reminded them.

"You two go find Qajuan," Yao said. "We'll do what we can about the people here."

"I have an idea," Davi said. "Don't go inside the hotel. We don't know how many might be in there."

"We can worry about that after we've dealt with these guys," Farien said.

"Here they come!" Dru shouted and accelerated the Skitter as Davi struggled to grab on. Farien and Yao quickly raced toward the oncoming riders as Dru raced into an alley away from the hotel.

"Shoot them!" Bordox screamed.

"Th' rid'rs k'ep g'tting in th' way, boss!" an assassin replied.

"Then shoot them, too! I want Rhii's blood on our hands!" Bordox took aim at one of the riders and fired as streams from his assassin's guns rained down on the five dueling Skitters below.

Farien cursed as the field of fire became thick around them. Were the assassins firing on each other?

He and Yao flew in circles, zipping in and out between the three riders attacking them, dodging fire while firing their own blasters when they could.

Then he heard a yelp as Qajuan appeared on a Skitter and raced toward them with two Skitters tailing. Yao took aim at one of those riders, who hadn't even noticed them yet and blasted him straight in the leg, causing him to veer straight toward Farien. Farien took aim and shot the man off his Skitter with a blast to his face.

"Two down, four to go," Yao said with a laugh.

"But we're badly outnumbered."

Then a blast hit another rider who had just aimed at Farien, knocking him forward over the front of his Skitter, smoke rising from a hole in his back.

Qajuan raced toward another as the rider looked distractedly for who had shot his fallen friend. The youth seemed determined to crash right into him, but the rider finally took notice and fumbled for his joystick. Qajuan jumped off his Skitter at the last minute as the two Skitters crashed and exploded, smashing the rider.

Then Davi and Dru appeared from another alley and raced toward them, both firing simultaneously at the confused riders who'd been chasing Qajuan. One of the Skitter's engines exploded, jostling the rider roughly in his seat. The other rider screamed as a bolt hit his arm, then another shot from overhead struck the back of his head, sending him leaning forward against the joystick. The Skitter took off like a shot, exploding against the side of a nearby building.

"Where'd you learn how to fly a Skitter?" Yao asked as Qajuan climbed on behind him.

"I can fly anything with a little practice. It looked easy and it was."

Yao laughed. "Our people spend months training for it."

"To the starport," Davi said with a wave of his hand.

All three took off down the street as laser blasts rained down from above. Davi aimed at a window above them, firing. Farien saw a shadowed face moving aside.

Bordox ducked as glass exploded, shards flying in all directions, inches from where his face had just been. Rhii had spotted him and fired. Could he have been recognized from so far below?

He watched with frustration as his men's shots failed again and again, striking the Skitters with minimal damage. The cadet swerved as a blast hit his arm, but Rhii reached forward to steady the Skitter and all three disappeared around a corner out of range.

"Follow them! Go! Go!" Bordox waved his fists in the air, feeling helpless. His men would never catch them. *Where would they go?* He cursed over and over. *I can't believe this is happening again!*

# Chapter Eight

An hour after escaping the hotel, Yao landed the transport on a small government landing pad. The Xanthian official who'd greeted them upon first arrival met them with their belongings from the hotel and a doctor to look after Dru's arm. On the ground for only twenty minutes, Yao took off again and rendezvoused with Farien, who was circling above the city, and they set a course for the depot where they'd left Davi's VS28 fighter.

Davi sat in the cockpit beside Yao, while Dru rested in the back. Davi searched the bands for news reports from home. He'd never felt so anxious about anyone as he did after seeing Tela on the broadcasts. What had she been doing there? Security for the event, he guessed. But she was so close to the platform. He took deep breaths as he prayed for her safety and that of everyone else there. Losing Tarkanius would be a huge tragedy for the Alliance right now. It could set back all he and his friends had fought for. Who was trying to kill him? It had to be Xalivar. Tarkanius had always been widely respected. He had no real enemies, only political ones.

An hour after they'd left Xanthian airspace, a message from command came in ordering them to Legallis. All available resources were being called back to quash unrest and ensure the High Lord Councilor's safety. Davi was tempted to ignore the order and head straight for Vertullis, but Farien wouldn't go along with it, and he didn't need to make trouble. Maybe Tela was already back on Legallis as well.

Finally he found a broadcast confirming no deaths and only minor injuries in the attempt on the High Lord Councilor. No official suspects had been named, but some Vertullians were in custody. *Idiots! Why would anyone try to destroy all their people fought for after everything it cost them?* He knew many still held anger towards the Boralians for past treatment, but they'd won their freedom. They were full citizens. The time had come to let it go and move on, for everyone's good. They had a future to build. It was time to leave the past behind. Some people just had no idea how to do that.

Farien had scolded Dru loudly over the comm as they departed, but now the channel was silent with everyone keeping to themselves. Dru hadn't said a word since just after departure. Given the attack on Tarkanius and the expectation that assassins could find them again at any moment, conversations between the others remained brief and to the point. Davi imagined they were as lost in thought as he was. An attack on their leader was an attack on all of them. He and his friends had grown up with respect for the Palace and what it stood for. Being that close to power had both humanized the man and his office and garnered deep respect and love for all it stood for. Davi's heart ached thinking about the societal tensions which led to such an event.

"We have to go in, Davi." Farien broke the silence.

"I know."

"Just in case you were thinking about violating orders, I wanted to say that."

"She might be there waiting," Yao said.

Davi smiled, thankful for the comfort of friends. "I hope so. If not, I can get a message to her when we land."

"I'll drop Dru at the Academy, then I'm coming, too."

"To do what? You're assigned to Presimion," Farien asked.

"Whatever I can. I feel like I was attacked, too. I can't just sit there."

Davi smiled, glad he wasn't alone. "We all feel that way. I'm sure they'll be glad to have you."

"Great. And I just get to go sit in boring classes through all this." Dru yawned as he joined them in the transport cockpit.

"You can skip a day and get some rest first," Yao said. "You need to see to that arm."

Dru smiled, admiring his scar. "My first battle wound. The girls'll love it."

The others laughed and the comm channel fell silent again as they flew onward.

To her surprise, Miri found herself taking to some of the mundane activities of civilian life. In particular, she loved shopping. As a princess, it had always been done for her, but now, she often went with Lura or a friend. It was an opportunity for the women to bond in a unique way, and her favorite stores were supermarkets. She loved the colorful variety of the fruits and meats and other items, the varied smells—from fresh and sweet to sour and earthy, the warmth of spices mixed with the cool smell of raw meat—brought her senses to life.

Today, because of packed shuttles since the attempt on Tarkanius, Lura arrived mid-afternoon, so they had arrived at the market during a busy hour, not Miri's favorite time to go. But she needed items for dinner and Lura happily accompanied her.

They were working their way through the produce aisle when Miri first heard the whispering. She glanced behind them to see two women pointing at them and talking. As princess, she'd gotten used to being gawked at in public, so she blew it off and turned her attention back to Lura and their shopping.

But the whispering followed them. And it grew and grew.

At first, it was one or two people behind or to the side. Then it became several pairs or trios pointing and whispering. Then there were sneers and laughs with the whispers. Soon it seemed everyone in the store was talking about them. Were their food choices so fascinating?

"What's the matter?" Lura asked, her brow furrowed with concern.

"Did you notice the whispers?"

Lura chuckled. "Women gossip in groceries. It's part of the fun." Then she saw Miri's face and her grin faded. "What is it?"

"It's not just the whispers. Some are laughing, pointing. At you and me."

Lura glanced around again and Miri's eyes followed. A couple of women pointed and laughed from a nearby counter. Miri knew it couldn't be good from their expressions. She'd avoided going out much in public since her speeches. She'd been a frequent topic on broadcasts. While some pundits supported her because of the past and her commitment to the Boralian people, other pundits gave the past no regard, calling her a traitor, slave-lover, and more. It was a far cry from the positive press she'd received during the slave's battle for freedom, when she'd helped uncover the Delta V massacre footage and her brother's betrayal of the Council.

Lura frowned. "Do you want to go?"

Miri nodded. "What about dinner?"

"That's what restaurants are for. Come on." Lura took her by the arm, leading her back toward the front of the store. As they passed the cashier, Lura set the basket she carried down. "I'm sorry, we have to go."

The cashier shrugged, obviously unperturbed. They were almost at the door when they heard a voice.

"From princess to traitor—how far some fall."

Lura whirled around, eyes raging. "How dare you!"

Miri turned also, but it was impossible to identify the speaker.

"None of you know anything to say such a thing! This woman has sacrificed so much for you that you don't even know!"

Miri shushed her with a hand on her arm. "Let's go, Lura."

"I won't stand for it." Lura waved a menacing finger around the room at those watching. "Your ignorance disgusts me. You should all be ashamed."

Miri grabbed her arm and dragged Lura from the store. As the doors closed behind them, Lura relaxed and then her face fell. "I'm sorry, Miri. I didn't mean to embarrass you. It just made me so angry hearing that."

Miri smiled. "It's okay, Lura. I feel so lucky to have a friend like you. Truly."

Lura clasped Miri's hand and squeezed it. "That's right. And you just try to be rid of me now."

Lura's glare was so intense it made Miri laugh. Soon Lura joined her as they walked away, hand in hand.

The call to Assembly came with orders for full dress uniforms. Pres arrived to find her soldiers waiting for her, but they weren't alone. Another, equal-sized, group was lining up opposite them in the chamber. Her mind raced to place some of the names, then her breath caught in her throat. Standing near the front was Admiral Dek. She fought the urge to run to him, instead only quickening her pace slightly. It took only a few moments to cross the distance, where she spun on her heels, positioning herself next to him looking back at the assembling troops.

"I didn't expect to see you here," he said, glancing over.

Words almost failed her. "For the good of the Alliance and our people," she managed.

"My respect for you has been well placed, General." He offered a warm smile.

Both turned their backs to the troops as Lucius appeared on a dais before them with Lord Obed.

Each stepped to opposite sides as Xalivar appeared and came forward to the edge of the platform. He stood, hands crossed behind his back, staring, panning them. And then he raised his arms and smiled.

"Honorable friends, welcome to the future. You have made the right choice in joining us—the choice to honor our people and save our Alliance. Events have taken place which we all regret. Our Alliance has become but a shadow of what it once was. The leadership is weak. Values our people treasured for centuries have been compromised. The time has come to restore it to the glory it once held."

He paused as the troops broke into spontaneous applause and cheering. Xalivar savored it, smiling, then resumed as it died down. "You know my leadership. You know my reputation. Forget all the lies my enemies have spread to discredit me. These were said to elevate themselves and you've seen the results. You're here, as I am, and the General and Lord you see with me, because you want what we once had. And you cannot continue to watch your beloved people's history fall to ruin. Join with me and we will restore the Boralian people to greatness. The Vertullians will be enslaved or destroyed. We will tolerate no dissension. Join me, and pride in your work and service will be yours again."

The troops cheered and applauded again, then Admiral Dek stepped forward, joining his fists and raising them in the traditional salute to a High Lord Councilor. Pres followed, and, one by one, so did every other soldier in the room. An awesome display of unity, it was made all the more touching by Dek's presence at her side.

"May it be as you have foretold, my Lord," Lucius said, joining them, with Obed being the last to offer the salute.

Xalivar stood in silence a bit, reveling in the attention, then raised a hand. "You all have duties to attend to. Let there be no more delays." He spun and exited the way he'd entered with Lucius and Obed on his heels.

Their troops broke into excited chatter, shaking hands, joking with one another as Pres turned to Dek. "How long have you known?" Her heart pounded.

"Almost a year. And you?"

"The same."

"I could not risk telling you."

She nodded. "I understand. For me it was the same." She'd never experienced such a mixture of joy, pride and relief.

Dek nodded. "It will be good to continue serving alongside you." He stepped forward and raised his voice. "Officers to the conference room immediately. Enlisted to quarters. Rest while you can. Training begins in two hours. Dismissed."

The troops, who had quieted down to hear him, now began to

disperse. Pres followed Dek into a corridor toward the conference room, excited and nervous about the future which awaited them. If they succeeded, they'd be hailed as heroes. If they failed, labeled traitors. Either way, both had already made the decision which would define the rest of their careers. Pres felt relief knowing they were in it together. She wondered if Dek felt the same.

Xalivar's heart raced as he led Obed and Lucius back to his chambers in the Xanthian caves. To be greeted like a hero by his own soldiers—men and women who'd served under him since their cadet days—after all that had happened, reassured him that victory would soon be his. *How sad it is that honor and loyalty are thicker than blood.* His own sister and the boy he'd raised as close as a son had betrayed him, leading to his downfall. Yet here were total strangers cheering him like he'd risen from the dead. For some, it would soon seem that way indeed. He laughed at the thought. *Oh to see the looks on your faces, Tarkanius, Miri, Kray, Xander.* The fact that his former nephew might have suspicions of his presence did nothing to lessen the glorious visions in his head. All the months of planning, the careful maneuvering, even his suffering would all be worth it soon.

As the door slid shut behind them, Xalivar whirled to face his companions. "Our moment is here, my friends."

"We've not yet won," Obed said. "There's still much to be done."

"Oh ye of little faith, Obed. Can you not already feel the triumph? Our own people recognize me for what I am—their salvation from ruin. These soldiers won't be alone in that sentiment. Haven't you seen the outcry all over the nets? Once we capture the hearts and minds of the people, victory will be swift."

"We'll need a far larger army than these if we hope to claim victory, Xalivar."

Xalivar frowned, shaking his head. He turned his eyes to Lucius who met his gaze. "This is the weakness of which I've warned you, Lucius. Weak leaders make weak Alliances and weak people. Purity is what we need; a cleansing to renew our strength."

"Insult me all you will, Xalivar." Obed stood firm, head held high. "You are far from perfect. You have been defeated before."

Xalivar whirled, fists clenching to face his old rival. "I was betrayed! Lies told. My own family conspired against me. That is not defeat!"

"And who lives in the Palace now, Xalivar?" Obed grunted,

undeterred.

Xalivar bit his tongue, raising his fist in warning. "You push me, Obed. Overstep the lines. Choose your words with care."

"The workers mock you now. And so do many others."

"The workers will soon be back as slaves where they belong, and anyone else who cares to join them can do so freely." Xalivar's eyes bore into Obed, reminding him that he, too, could wind up there. Obed just stood quietly, staring back. Xalivar took two breaths before continuing. "And once we've dealt with them, we'll deal with all the others."

"What others, Xalivar? The workers and anyone disloyal—who's left?"

Xalivar smiled as Manaen brought a tray with a pitcher and three glasses. "Any foreign influences will be removed." Xalivar looked at Manaen as his aide sat the tray on a table and proceeded to fill the three glasses with Talis. "No more tolerance for alien influences. We will purify ourselves and be stronger for it."

"You would eliminate races with whom we've lived in peace for decades?"

"I would eliminate anyone who threatens the sanctity of our people." Xalivar stared at Obed again, the meaning clear.

Manaen finished pouring the glasses as they stood in silence and carefully handed one to each of the three men, then nodded and took his leave.

Xalivar fought the urge to smile as he saw the meaning sink in on Obed's face. Was his old rival actually horrified? Such weakness from a man who actually aspired to Xalivar's position. *You too would be ruin to our people, Obed. And I shall see to it you never have the chance.* Even those who'd served him during his triumphant reclamation of office would have to be purged for purity. No weak links could be allowed to remain—Obed, Manaen, all of them—gone.

Obed sipped his Talis in silence, waiting, as Xalivar turned to Lucius. "Begin the training immediately. I want units training around the clock."

"It shall be done, my Lord."

"And begin the second phase of the recruitment."

Lucius nodded. "At once, my Lord." He saluted then hurried off, leaving his half-finished glass on the table next to the tray.

"We have more allies than you imagine, Obed. Men who are even now working to destabilize the government on our behalf."

"They know nothing of us or our plans. How can you be so confident they'll side with us when the time comes?"

"There will be only two choices. They will go the way of assured victory."

Obed sighed, shaking his head. "Your overconfidence is a true liability, Xalivar."

"As is yours, Obed."

Obed stared at him a moment, then stepped forward, set his glass next to Lucius', and disappeared through the door, leaving Xalivar alone.

Xalivar wondered who the unknown allies were, and more importantly, who was their leader? Could it be someone like Hachim or Niger? The two Lords had sided against him during the workers' rebellion, but perhaps their true sentiments had been against Xalivar, not toward the workers. If such was the case, they too would require elimination at the right time. But for now, they could be very useful to him. And Xalivar intended to use every resource available in achieving his ends.

He hurried to the terminal and sat, logging into his secure band and sending missives to his contacts. He needed an update on the investigation into the events. Surely more clues had been found which would confirm his suspicions about whom he could count on to support his cause. It would only be a matter of time. *Gods, I love the feel of victory.*

Within hours of their arrival back on Legallis, Davi, Yao and Farien reported to command for a debriefing. After taking Dru to the infirmary, Davi sent Qajuan to personnel with a note asking them to make use of his gifts. He'd check on the youth later, as clearly the last thing any of them needed was a bored Xanthian underfoot. There'd been no chance to send a message to Tela. Davi had barely had time to change uniforms.

General Grif, Aron, Uzah, and the High Lord Councilor sat at a large, round table, waiting as the three officers entered the conference room. They stood at attention as the door slid shut behind them.

"At ease, gentlemen," Tarkanius said immediately. "Join us please."

Davi and his friends found seats at the table, facing the leaders.

"The report you sent en route mentioned an incident at the Black Market on Xanthis," Uzah said. No time for pleasantries? Clearly recent events were taking their toll.

Davi nodded. "Yes, sir."

"You confirmed the identity of the Andorian?" Grif asked, his face emotionless as usual.

Farien shook his head. "We tried. He got away."

"But the locals said he's often at the market," Yao added.

"For what purpose?" Grif asked.

"We're told he hired mercenaries, buys supplies, etc. No one will cross him."

Farien jumped in as Yao finished. "He hired Lhamors."

"He has a powerful employer." Davi emphasized the last word, letting it hang as his eyes panned the leaders.

"Xalivar, you believe?" At the sound of his voice, all eyes turned to Tarkanius. "The situation has reached crisis here, gentlemen. The attempt on my life was but part of a larger conspiracy. At the very moment that attack was occurring, Admiral Dek, General Pres, and numerous officers and soldiers left their duty stations and disappeared. Communications sent on various channels were ignored. Several ships left the system, but controllers had no log of their destinations or flight plans. We're still trying to locate them."

Davi couldn't believe it. The conspiracy had reached heights he'd never expected. He knew Xalivar was bold and had his supporters, but to steal warships with full crews? Davi's mouth got dry as he struggled to wrap his mind around it. His throat tightened as waves of sadness poured over him. Yao and Farien looked as shocked as he was. Did so many really want another war? As memories of dead friends flashed through his head, he struggled for words. "Defections of senior staff?"

"The defections stretch throughout the ranks. A total of six hundred so far." Grif's face remained steady, but Davi thought he detected anger in his eyes.

"So it *is* Xalivar! It has to be! Who else would be able to command such loyalty?" Davi looked around, waiting for the leaders to agree.

Tarkanius nodded. "We suspect you're right."

"No one's seen nor heard from Xalivar since he disappeared from Eleni 1," Grif said.

"Disappeared, still alive," Tarkanius said.

Aron's eyes met Davi's with a sadness which matched Davi's own. "We believe Xalivar is alive and involved in efforts to destabilize the populace and government to regain his power," he said.

"Just after the attempt on the High Lord Councilor, a secret meeting of conspirators took place at a café in Iraja," Uzah said. "The entire staff was left dead as those in attendance departed."

"If no one's alive, how do you know of this meeting?" Farien asked.

"Security cameras captured a few images—several men entering, whom we believe to be those responsible."

Davi frowned. "I thought you had people in custody."

Aron nodded. "We don't believe they acted alone. They know too little and all of them claim to have been hired by a major in the Borali military."

"Do you have a name?"

Uzah shook his head. "Only a description. But security footage captured a face you may find familiar." He slid a datapad across the table to Davi.

Davi took it and looked at the image on the screen. A rotund face stared back at him, uniform collar and insignia showing at the bottom of the image. This time he remembered exactly where they'd met. "I know this man. From the corridor after the Generals briefed us." Uzah nodded.

"Who is he?" Farien asked.

Grif punched a button and a screen on the wall filled with the major's picture and accompanying data. "Valenti Broks, a Major in intelligence. Current whereabouts uncertain. Solid service record."

"In other words, your average officer who stayed off the radar?" Davi looked to Uzah for confirmation. The General nodded.

"Off the radar but suddenly gone missing from his duty post?" Farien's scowled. "Let's find him." Despite the troubles he'd faced from honoring orders, Farien's convictions about loyalty duty hadn't changed.

"We're working on leads now," Uzah said, typing into a datapad and pausing a moment to read the screen. "Men were already sent to his residence and current post."

"Hence the 'whereabouts unknown,'" Davi nodded. "He doesn't seem the type to act alone."

"We're sure he didn't," Tarkanius said. "However, he's the perfect type to organize the murder of civilians at a café."

"How many?"

"Five employees, two customers." Aron sighed, his face shadowed with grief.

"How many conspirators do you believe he has?" Yao turned from the screen to look at Tarkanius.

"Four to six from the meeting. Who knows how many could be involved." Tarkanius shook his head. "We believe more than one is on the Council." The High Lord Councilor looked gaunt, his shoulders sinking as he said it.

"But you don't know who?" The answer shone in the leaders' eyes as soon as Davi finished the question. "And you think they're in league with Xalivar?"

Aron shrugged. "We could be dealing with more than one conspiracy."

"My gods! If there's so many, how can we begin to stop them?" Farien leaned back in his chair with dismay.

"I'm prepared to declare a state of martial law, restrict interplanetary travel, whatever it takes," Tarkanius said. "We must restore order while there's still time."

"The outcries are increasing, anti-worker sentiment growing, ever since the attempt on Tarkanius," Aron added. "The Alliance is becoming quickly divided."

"So whatever they're doing, it's working." Farien shook his head.

"We need full reports of everything you encountered and discovered as soon as possible," Uzah said. "Farien and Davi, your investigation will be expanding."

Tarkanius turned and nodded at Yao. "You're still needed at the Academy."

Yao bowed his head. "I'm needed more here. This threatens all of us." Davi had never heard Yao object to an order before but his friend's red eyes almost glowed with determination.

"I'm due leave. I'd like to stay."

Tarkanius smiled. "I thought you might feel that way."

General Grif cleared his throat. "You'll need to escort the cadet first, then you'll be temporarily reassigned to continue assisting with the investigation."

Yao looked up and broke into a grin. "Thank you, sir."

"We must proceed with extra caution. Those responsible for these murderous acts will not allow anyone to deter them." Tarkanius suddenly looked weary and concerned.

"They've made several attempts against us and failed," Davi said, exchanging looks with his friends. "Just keep yourself safe, my Lord." He stood and offered the traditional salute. Yao and Farien joined him, soon followed by the others.

"The gods be with us all," Tarkanius said as they finished.

Niger's aide escorted Hachim into the fellow Lord's study and left him to wait. It seemed an interminable period before Niger appeared, smiling and relaxed in a way unexpected from someone who had the entire planet searching for him.

"Hachim!" Niger extended his hand, shaking Hachim's warmly. "Our plans are proceeding perfectly."

Hachim shook his head. "You've crossed a line, Niger."

"We crossed it together, Hachim."

"You gave me no choice. Those people did not need to die." "They were in our way."

Hachim swallowed a gasp, stunned. Human life had value. Elevating slaves at the expense of their own people was one thing. But this was another. Murder was too far. When had he and Niger grown to be so different? "A year ago, we supported Tarkanius and Miri in removing Xalivar. We allowed the Vertullians to become our equals."

"They can never be our equals!"

"They are human beings, Niger." Hachim turned away, pacing, his chest tightening with worry. "This is not what I wanted."

"What did you expect, Hachim? Their humanness does not make them our equals. We enslaved them through our superiority. And we freed them in weakness. We must be strong again. Sacrifices will be necessary."

"I agreed with you that things went too far. I agreed that we needed a change of leadership. Destabilizing leadership is one thing. I never agreed to murder."

"We're overthrowing a government, Hachim. People often die in such pursuits."

Hachim stopped pacing, spun and pointed his finger in warning. "Not like this, Niger."

Niger stared at him, holding his gaze. "We agreed to do what must be done for the good of our people. And that's what we've done."

"I don't know you. You're not the man I thought."

"Neither are you."

Hachim held the stare a moment then turned away toward the window, moving across the room to stare out at the cityscape under the bright light of the twin suns. Shadows reflected off windows, painting the streets and ground with varied patterns like a puzzle. It reminded him of what his life had become. He'd been a man of integrity once, determined to live honorably in conducting his business and all of his affairs. What had happened to him? He'd been angry. He'd shared reasonable doubts and resentment about the direction of the government. Now he was a party to murder.

He had to stop it, change course somehow, before it was too late. "We've done what we set out to do. Now we can wait and let things unfurl."

Niger shook his head. "We have yet to achieve our goal. We cannot stop until we do."

"We've gone beyond our goal, Niger. We serve the people. With honor. We've done so for many years. Do not forget who you are." His eyes pleaded with his old friend but were met with an icy glaze in return.

Niger leaned forward over the desk so fast he almost flew, his hand waving threateningly. "Do not forget who *you* are, Hachim."

"I do not forget. But I have a choice. We made this plan together, recruited our allies. And now you act as if it yours alone." Hachim prepared to dodge, but Niger stopped just short of him.

"Someone must have the vision and see it through. If you are too weak, I am willing."

"It's a distorted vision, Niger!"

Niger slammed a fist into a pillar beside the door. "If you do not have the stomach for it, do not stand in my way. Or you will become like them."

Hachim gasped. "Are you threatening me?"

"I will do what must be done."

"You go too far. And yet nothing will stop you."

"Never forget it."

"I cannot." Hachim whirled and hurried out the door, rushing past Niger's aide, who came from a room down the hall to attend him, and letting himself out the front door. He hurried up the street as the blinding rays of the suns bore down on his neck and shoulders, adding external heat to match the internal one. He and Niger had been friends since joining the Council at almost the same time. But he no longer recognized his old friend, and he had decisions to make. *A threat on my own life?* The time had come to set aside loyalty and take care of himself.

Davi watched from the observation deck as Tela's Squadron landed. After the briefing, he'd finally tracked down her whereabouts—on a long security patrol around Vertullis. He'd gone to rest, setting an alarm on his datapad to awake him in plenty of time to shower and greet her. The VS28s set down one by one on parallel landing strips, rolling to a stop in a neat row, like the pilots had practiced it for hours, which they had.

Taking the lift to the hangar floor, Davi watched them climb from their fighters. Jorek and Virun were the first to see him and rushed over to shake his hand and ask about his adventures on Xanthis. Then Brie and Nila and a couple of others joined them. Davi kept an eye out for Tela, but she took her time filing a flight report before sidling up with the rest. Their eyes locked on each other as soon as she arrived, despite Davi continuing conversations with the others. It always amazed him how her blue flight suit highlighted her figure. Despite twelve hours in the cockpit, she looked ravishing. Finally the others said their "goodbyes" and started clearing out, leaving Davi and Tela alone.

As soon as the door slid shut behind the last of them, Tela rushed into his arms.

"I've been worried about you." They both said it at the same moment, then turned their heads to kiss, lips locked passionately for what seemed like forever.

"I saw the footage of the attack on Iraja—"

"All we had were rumors—" She stopped as she realized she was talking over him.

"You first," he said, hugging her again.

"Barely a word from you for ten days, Davi Rhii. Rumors of attempts on your life. All kinds of things. You've had us all worried."

"I'm sorry. Other than Dru getting shot, I'm fine, really."

Tela gasped, her hands tightening on his arms. "Dru? Shot?"

"Just in the arm. He'll live."

Tela relaxed and shook her head. "I need to know, Davi. I need to hear from you."

He nodded. "You'll understand better when I explain, but you're right, and I'm sorry."

Tela sighed as they stared into each other's eyes a moment, then kissed him again.

"I caught a glimpse of you in news broadcasts. I didn't know what to think."

"They put me in charge of security," she said. "I'm fine. And thankfully, so is everyone else."

Davi nodded. "I got the briefing while you were on patrol."

"They pulled in anyone they could. Things have really heated up since you left—politicians ranting, news media debating, people protesting. Any underlying tensions are now inflamed and on the surface."

Davi shrugged, not knowing where to begin. "I heard. But an attempt on the High Lord Councilor—"

Tela nodded. "Whoever's behind all this is using violence to incite the tensions, divide the people. It's working." As soon as their eyes met, she knew. "Xalivar's behind this?"

Davi sighed. "Some of it. We're fairly sure. We believe we spotted Manaen on Xanthis but couldn't catch up with him. An Andorian working for a rich, secretive boss has been hiring Lhamors and buying up weapons and resources."

Tela's face turned sad, her eyes telling him she'd reached conclusions similar to his own. "We knew he was alive somewhere."

Davi took her hands in his as their eyes met again. "Which is why I need you to be safe, Tela. No more dangerous security details and such. I need you to come home to."

Tela frowned, pulling her hands away. "Don't you think I feel the same about you?"

"I don't need distractions. I have to focus on my job."

"And I don't need them either." She pulled her hands free of his, frowning.

Davi dropped his hands his sides, wondering how he'd managed to upset her again. "I just want to protect you."

Tela turned away, cheeks reddening with anger. "But I'm not allowed to protect you?"

"I'm not saying that."

"Either we both take the risk or neither of us do. You can't expect me to sit at home and worry while you're out there in danger—"

Davi sighed. "I'll be safer knowing you're not in danger, too."

"Maybe you'd prefer not having to worry about me at all."

Davi reached over and put a hand on her shoulder. "Come on, Tela, I'm just trying to take care of you. I love you."

She shoved his hand away and spun. "Then stop being such a jerk!"

They turned at the whoosh of a door sliding open down the way. A bulky man strolled casually into the hangar. Davi's heartbeat pounded. It was the major! The man glanced over then, perhaps sensing their stares. As soon as he saw Davi, he turned around and bolted back toward the door.

"Wait! I need to talk with you, Major!" Davi started after him as Tela followed.

"Who is he?"

"A man we suspect in the attack on Tarkanius." Davi reached the door, but it didn't open automatically. He punched the button on the wall and got no reaction. "Go back to quarters. I'll catch up with you later."

He punched the button on the door again, several times in rapid succession.

"I'm not letting you go after him alone."

"I can't face him if I have to protect you at the same time."

"I don't need protection. I'm an officer, just like you."

"There's no time to argue. Just stay here!" It came out as order. After another punch, the door slid open and Davi stepped through, turning back to motion. "Please. Just be safe, okay?" His hand went to his blaster and he hurried up the corridor, leaving Tela fuming. He hadn't meant to sound so harsh. How could he be so bad at communicating with the woman he loved?

He searched the hallway for a sign of the major. A few mechanics and techs passed but the man had disappeared. Davi hesitated a moment then went toward the next hangar. His pace increased with every step. The landing bays were always busy. There'd be plenty of witnesses. All Davi wanted to do was talk. He thought about radioing for Yao and Farien but by the time they got there, the major would probably be gone. Then it struck him how stupid it would be to call them, when he'd refused Tela's help and sent her away. Maybe he was being a jerk. He swore he'd make it up to her later.

He reached the next hangar and the door slid open immediately. Stepping inside, Davi nodded to the techs at the flight status station and moved on through, wading along rows of shuttles and passenger craft. If the major was already aboard a ship, he'd never find him. But then if he'd intended to leave by fighter, he might have to steal one. Pulling out his datapad, Davi began typing as he walked, calling up the departure schedules from the military channel. For pilots, both civilian and military schedules were interspersed in separate colors making the flight class easy to distinguish. It was a quiet day for schedule. He remembered flights had dropped since the violence.

Turning right at the end of a row of shuttles, he glanced ahead, looking for any sign of the major. Then he heard running footsteps and turned just as a bulky figure dove out of the shadows and threw him to the ground on his stomach. They wrestled on the floor of the bay as Davi's datapad slid away out of reach. The man's breath was hot and stunk of wine. Davi finally managed to turn on his side and catch a glimpse of his attacker. It was Major Valenti Broks.

"I just want to talk with you, Major."

"Talk? Like you did with my brother?"

"Who? I don't know your brother."

"Oh, yes you do!" The Major's fist slammed into Davi's stomach, knocking the wind from his lungs and forcing him to cough and gasp for breath. In the process, he released his hold on the major's arm, allowing his opponent to attempt flipping him onto his stomach again, but as the major rolled him, Davi pushed, rolling over and over out of reach and landing on his back. The Major hurried toward him, but Davi jumped to his feet, squaring off to face the man.

Both stood there a moment, sweat soaking their clothes as they gasped for breath. Then the Major drew a blaster, pointing it at Davi. "I've waited for this moment for too long, Rhii."

"You're Valenti Broks, right?" Davi hoped the mention of his name might prove a distraction.

Broks frowned. "How do you know that?"

"Put the blaster down and talk to me."

"There'll be no talking. This is vengeance, period."

"Vengeance for what?" Tela's voice came out of nowhere and Broks spun around. Tela stood nearby, blaster aimed at him.

The Major took aim but Davi dove, knocking him from his feet and sending his blaster spinning across the floor and under the shuttle. They wrestled and rolled again as Tela hurried over, trying to get a clear shot. Neither man could get a solid grip on the other's sweaty body, but they continued gasping for breath as they rolled and struck blows at each other.

"Stop right now!" Tela held the blaster steady, aimed at the man as he and Davi jostled for position on top of each other.

Davi heard footsteps pounding toward them on the hangar floor. "I told you to stay out of this," Davi said.

"You should be glad I didn't."

"Drop your weapon!" A voice called as armed security men appeared, weapons raised and pointed at Tela.

"We're on official business," she said.

"Three officers fighting? Have a little too much to drink?" the lead security man asked, looking her over. Tela lowered her gun slightly as she turned to argue.

Broks pushed with both legs, slamming his fists into Davi's stomach from below and sending him flying toward Tela. Tela tried to dodge and aim her blaster again, but Davi had no control and his feet spun and forced her to jump to avoid being knocked off her feet. As her aim faltered, and the security men dodged her fall, the Major jumped to his feet.

"You stop right there!" The security lead ordered.

The Major plowed right through, shoving them aside and disappearing behind the shuttle.

"That man's wanted for murder!" Davi called as he helped Tela up and started after Broks. The security men blocked his way.

"What are you talking about?"

They spent a few minutes explaining, then the security chief called to confirm. Afterwards, they searched for the Major together but found no sign of him. Finally, the security men went back to their posts, leaving Davi and Tela alone.

"Aren't you going to thank me?" Tela asked as she holstered her blaster.

"Thanks. Look, I didn't mean to be so harsh before. You didn't deserve that."

Tela shrugged it off, not meeting his eyes. "Forget it!"

"I can't help wanting to protect the woman I love. I hope you can see that."

She spun back to face him, forcing him to stop inches from her as their eyes met. "What I see is your lack of trust in my abilities as a soldier and pilot and a woman, Davi! You're treating me like I'm less than you are!"

"I'm treating you like my future wife."

"How do you know I'm your future wife? We've never talked about it."

"We've mentioned it."

"Not seriously!"

Davi sighed, his shoulders rising and falling as he caught his breath. "You're amazing. Everything to me."

Tela sighed, too, shaking her head. "I don't know if I want to be anymore."

"What does that mean?"

"I don't want to be treated like some fragile child. I want a man who respects me as an equal partner. You don't seem capable of doing that, no matter how many times I prove my skills."

"Would I have appointed you to lead the Squad in my absence if I felt that way about you?"

Tela shrugged. "I don't know, Davi. I don't know what you'd do. I'm beginning to wonder if I know you at all."

Before he could respond, she spun as the door opened to admit two mechanics, then she raced past them and disappeared around a corner.

Davi started to chase her, then stopped, shocked, as he processed what she'd said. What had happened to them? When had things gotten so hard again? Had he lost her? Did she really believe what she'd just said?

A mechanic appeared, waving his arms at Davi. "You dropped this, Captain." He held out Davi's datapad.

Davi sighed and nodded, retrieving it from the mechanic's hand. "Thanks." The mechanic nodded and hurried off, as Davi headed for the corridor. He had to figure out what to say before he found Tela. Why was he so bad with words?

# Chapter Nine

Miri stood quietly at her apartment window watching the playground below. The preschool stood out as an oddity in her neighborhood of high rises and high prices, but for Miri it was a blessing. With all the changes she'd endured, watching children laugh and play, oblivious to the problems of the world around them, was a reminder of a future filled with possibilities. No one knew who those children might grow up to be, what impact they might make, the decisions they'd face. But maybe one or two of them would actually make a difference; change the world for the better. Imagining that gave Miri hope.

She needed it, too, because her hope for her son's future was clouded with insanity. How could two people once so in love make such a mess of things?

"Should we go to her?" Miri turned as Lura finished refilling her mug of Talis.

Lura shook her head. "Whatever's the matter, she'll tell us when she's ready."

Tela had arrived an hour earlier in tears. Miri and Lura did their best to comfort her but all she'd managed to choke out between sobs was "Davi wants to marry me." Miri was thrilled. Why was Tela in tears?

"It makes no sense. We know they love each other. Why isn't she dancing with joy?"

"Something else must have happened. They haven't seen each other in weeks. You know how touchy she can be and how careless Davi is with his words sometimes."

"But he proposed! My gods! I'm bouncing off the walls for them!"

Lura laughed. "I feel the same, Miri. We just need to give her time."

They heard feet shuffling in the corridor and turned as Tela appeared, sniffling and wiping her eyes on a sleeve. "I'm sorry." Her cheeks were red from constant rubbing and shadows clouded her eyes. The girl was way too stressed for someone with such good news.

Lura smiled. "It's okay, dear. We're just concerned about you." Her eyes glistened with sympathy.

Miri nodded. "Come, sit with us. Can we get you some Talis?"

Tela nodded and walked over, sitting on the sofa beside Lura. Lura tried to get up, but Miri waved her off and went to retrieve another mug herself from the cabinet where they'd left the pitcher on a warmer.

"I seem nuts, right?" Tela sniffled and offered a weak smile.

Lura laughed. "Well, we did expect a bit of a different reaction."

Tela sighed, sinking back on the couch. "It wasn't like he got on his knees. It's just that he referred to me as 'my future wife.'"

Lura nodded as Miri returned, handing Tela a mug of hot Talis and taking a seat on the other sofa across from them. "It's about time he got serious."

Tela sipped her Talis then shook her head. "He's not."

Miri laughed. "I know my son, Tela. If he's mentioning marriage, you can believe me—he's serious!"

Tela stiffened as if she'd been insulted and looked away. Gods, these younger generations were so dramatic! "He treats me like I'm incompetent. Like I'm not a good soldier. Like I need protecting."

"That's instinct. Men protect their women. It's been that way forever, dear; since Adam and Eve you might say. It's best to allow them their illusions. We know who the real strong ones are." Miri chuckled, looking at Lura for affirmation.

Lura smiled, lost in memories for a moment. "Miri's right. Sol still treats me that way. But I've grown to appreciate it. It's men's way of showing they care about us." Miri admired the glint in Lura's eyes as she spoke of it. What must it be like to know a love like that?

"But neither of you are military officers. I've been through training in weapons, flight. I saved his life today." Tela's eyes found Miri's again.

"What?" Miri demanded as she and Lura both stiffened and they leaned forward with alarm.

"He met me at the bay as my squadron landed. We ran into some major whom command suspects in the bombing. Davi tried to talk to him and the man attacked. Davi had told me to stay where I was when he chased the man, but it's a good thing I didn't listen."

Miri and Lura both nodded. Who could argue with that? Miri's biggest mistakes in life had come from listening to men. Especially Xalivar.

"But then, after, he acted so disappointed that I didn't respect his request to stay safe. I'd just saved his life and he was angry at me for being there."

Miri and Lura exchanged a knowing look. All of a sudden, Tela's emotional outburst made sense. When would Davi learn how to talk to this girl? She wasn't like his mothers. She was a different breed. He had to stop treating her like a delicate flower and treat her more like a peer or he'd lose her. Miri felt a sudden tension as anger rose within. She hadn't been mad at her son in ages. If only he were here! "You just let us handle him, okay? We'll set him straight, I promise."

Tela shook her head, relaxing as if their support had relieved her of her burden. She held out her hands and squeezed as theirs joined hers. "No. We have to sort this out ourselves. He'd probably be mad I even told you. I mean, he wants to marry me, right?" Then as if the realization had just hit her, she smiled. "He thinks of me as his future wife!" She looked at them as they nodded and grinned.

Lura hugged Tela as Miri stood and hurried over. "We're so happy for you both!"

Tela stood and Miri hugged her. "And for us, too!"

A low rumble rose from the street. Tela and Miri struggled to stay on their feet. The building started shaking and a huge flash lit the window; then she heard an explosion and saw rising smoke. All three women rushed to the window.

Miri's throat went dry as the breath rushed from her lungs. She couldn't believe her eyes. Debris layered the street outside, clouding the air. A smoking crater was all that remained where the playground and preschool had been moments before. *My gods, the children!* Miri's hand went to her mouth as Lura and Tela gasped beside her.

"Isn't that—" Miri nodded, cutting Tela off.

Miri pushed against a column to steady herself, suddenly feeling faint. Children, teachers, staff—the entire building had been wiped away by the explosion. Pedestrians stumbled out of buildings below, faces frozen in shock as they tried to make sense of the site before their eyes.

Tela hurried to the wall and turned on the flat screen, dialing up the news channels. Vooriflies fluttered in Miri's stomach. *Gods, please let it be some horrible accident.* They'd know as soon as the talking heads did. But even as she thought it, she knew it wouldn't be so.

Tarkanius' aide turned on the broadcasts as soon as the first reports came in. Tarkanius and Aron had been discussing recent events, but the footage of the crater left them in stunned silence. The talking heads were all speculating at this point. Although they made mention of the possibility of a terrible accident, all assumed the bombing was intentional. Just the thought of it had Tarkanius feeling weak in the knees. Boralian children murdered? Who would ever do such a thing? And these children came from elite homes, too. The outrage would be uncontrollable.

Catching his breath, Tarkanius motioned to his aide, who muted the broadcasts as Tarkanius punched in a code on the throne room comm station, motioning for Aron to join him. Soon Joram and Uzah's faces filled the screen. "Good afternoon, my Lord," both said simultaneously.

"Have you seen the broadcasts?"

Joram shook his head. "Something's coming up now."

"My God!" Uzah exclaimed as they stared at a screen off camera.

"I need to know as soon as anyone claims responsibility. Things are about to get a lot worse." Tarkanius winced as images of protestors carrying 'Vertullian babykillers' signs appeared on the broadcasts. Months of attacks had built up a certain numbness in him but this...the nature of this attack shredded that inner wall in an instant. Children's body parts were scattered for blocks.

"I assure you, my Lord, we will make every effort to find out if anyone here's responsible." Joram choked out the words, clearly overcome with emotion at the images he was seeing.

"To kill innocent children..." Aron's voice trailed off as his face darkened.

"It's possible it's an accident," Uzah said.

"Let's hope for all of our sakes that proves to be the case," Tarkanius said. "Gods help us if this crisis has reached such a level."

"You'll hear anything as soon as it comes in," Uzah said with a nod.

"Our prayers are with everyone there through this time," Joram added.

"Thank you," Tarkanius said before the screen went dark.

Aron sank onto a step, looking gaunt and pale, similar to how Tarkanius felt. "I can't believe this. Has the world gone insane? A year ago, we had such hope."

Tarkanius sighed. "Long simmering differences were ignored too long. We grew complacent as things went our way. We should have addressed them all along. Now we're paying a price." Tarkanius blamed himself. How could he have been so short-sighted? What kind of leadership had he shown in ignoring the issues? He'd been tired of the conflict and drama; caught up in the excitement of hope for change. As a result, he'd failed to lead well. Now even children were paying for it with their lives. He'd never forgive himself.

"You're not responsible, Tarkanius. No one could have predicted this." Aron looked up at Tarkanius, his sadness replaced by concern.

Tarkanius shook his head. He couldn't even meet Aron's eyes. "I should have. It's not like the tensions weren't there before. We just ignored them, as if they'd disappear. Instead they've blown up like a nuclear wave, radiation tainting everything it touches."

"The Council must unite to push through this crisis and be an example for the people."

"The Council members can't even agree amongst themselves, Aron. Until we can, a united front is impossible." Tarkanius saw, as their eyes finally met, that he and Aron both shared the fear that unity might never be achieved. "If Council members are part of the conspiracies, we have no hope of coming together."

"All we can do is pray," Aron said sadly, his eyes lifting toward the ceiling.

"I'm afraid you'd be better with that than I would. I'm quite out of practice." Tarkanius' mind raced with possibilities. He had so much to consider, so many choices and decisions to face.

Aron smiled. "Would you like to pray together?"

Tarkanius hesitated. Two men of different religious views praying together? Would it even be possible when they didn't share the same gods? Aron was a good man and had become a close friend. *It can't hurt anything, Tarkanius. If you want to unite the people, the willingness must start with you.* Tarkanius nodded and moved toward Aron, who stood. "Please lead us."

"Of course." Tarkanius regretted it the moment he said it. He'd never been religious. His participation in rituals had come from honoring tradition, not belief. Internally, he'd never put much stock in faith or gods, but Aron really seemed to believe and somehow he couldn't refuse.

They bowed their heads together as Tarkanius closed his eyes, hoping that somehow the powers of the universe might hear and intercede. At that moment, he longed to be proven wrong.

The two freighters were already exchanging fire by the time Davi and his Squadron arrived. Splitting his pilots into two groups, one lined up on Farien, the other on him, Davi headed for the Boralian freighter and keyed the comm. "This is Captain Davi Rhii of the Boralian Alliance, Squadron One Alpha. Cease fire immediately and identify yourselves."

The Boralian freighter was almost twice the size of the Vertullian one. It reminded him of a bully picking on a runt, and Davi had always hated that scenario. The Vertullian ship's markings identified it as an agro supply ship, while the Boralian freighter was designated for deep-space shipping of larger cargo. Whereas both appeared clean and well maintained from the outside, the Boralian freighter had ten years on its Vert-ullian counterpart and the modern weapons to prove it. The Vertullian ship's hull already showed significant damage. Davi's Squadron had arrived just in time.

Neither freighter responded, the larger Boralian continuing to fire on its smaller counterpart.

"Okay, I want warning shots fired off the bridge of both freighters on my mark," Davi ordered. "No damage. Just a warning."

"Ah gees, Captain, sir, that's no fun," Brie said in a mock whine. Davi could picture her grinning ear-to-ear.

"Lined up and ready on your mark," Farien confirmed.

Davi looked around to confirm that his group was ready as well then keyed the comm. "Fire!"

Nine fighters simultaneously sent lasers to the same point just outside the bridge windows of each freighter—Davi's group the Vertullian and Farien's the Borallian. The lasers exploded harmlessly, vibrating the bridges. Suddenly, Davi heard other voices on the comm.

"Wait! Alpha One Leader, this is Captain Jel Cain of the Agro Freighter *Eden One*. We're delivering a shipment of grain to Xanthis when this guy comes out of nowhere and starts blasting us."

"Your people declared war on us today by murdering innocent children! This is Captain Vrel Dagan of the Freighter *Dragon Dancer*, Captain Rhii. We're just defending our citizens from further attacks by these terrorists. Doing our civic duty, you might say."

The attack on the preschool was two hours' old. *This is just what we need, overzealous mercenary captains taking the law into their own hands!* "Last I heard, Captain Dagan, no one had yet claimed responsibility for that attack nor had any suspects been named."

"We all know who did it, Captain! They're all animals, these people!"

"We weren't even aware of the incident ourselves until this madman attacked us!" Captain Cain responded.

"Regardless, civilian commercial vessels are not authorized to attack each other in official shipping lanes," Davi said. "Your vehicles are permitted weapons for defensive purposes only, per regulations."

He could almost hear the Boralian Captain frown. "Don't quote regulations to me! This is a time of war! Exceptions must be made!" The Boralian freighter fired two more cannon blasts at the *Eden One*.

"This guy has a hearing problem," Virun muttered into the comm.

"Another failed cadet wannabe living his fantasies at any excuse," Jorek agreed.

Davi laughed. The two men could have been describing themselves as new recruits a year before.

"We had nothing to do with those children's deaths! We regret it as much as anyone!"

"Captain Dagan, one more blast from your freighter and I'll shoot out your weapons myself." Davi allowed the irritation he felt to come through clearly over the comm.

Dagan's voice changed pitch as he stuttered for words. "We're on your side, Captain!"

"This is a Vertullian unit, Captain Dagan," Davi said, smiling as he imagined the man's reaction. "But my duty is to protect all civilian and commercial interests regardless of their origination."

"We don't take orders from slaves!"

"Then take them from me!" Farien yelled. "This is Captain Farien Noa of the Borali military. Cease fire as ordered or I'll personally make sure you're enjoying the comfortable vacuum of space in the next thirty seconds!"

The Borali freighter's cannons relaxed to their resting position as the ship's Captain cleared his throat. "A Borali officer serving with slaves?"

"These men and women are free citizens just like you, Captain! And I use the term loosely. You clearly lack the character deserving of such a title!" For once, Davi found Farien's temper useful on a mission. He watched as Farien fired a shot toward the Dragon Dancer. It exploded just off the wing outside the bridge window.

"Stop! Please. We'll comply with your instructions." Captain Dagan pleaded.

"Order all crew members away from weapons and prepare for boarding," Davi said, relaxing a bit as the confrontation ended. The last thing they needed was every civilian in the system taking up arms and choosing sides. "I'm sending someone aboard to supervise as we escort you back to Legallis."

"I have a deadline to meet!"

"You won't be meeting it," Farien said.

Davi debated for a moment whether it should be Farien who boarded then decided he'd rather send the Captain a message and keep Farien handy in case the man made trouble. "Nila, land in their bay and get to that bridge to await my orders."

"Me?" Nila sounded as confused as Davi expected the freighter captain was.

"We're sending a message, Nila. You're the perfect choice."

Brie chuckled. "Oh, he'll love taking orders from a woman."

"Trust me. She loves bossing men around." Virun's voice dripped with mock suffering as Jorek and the others' laughter filled the comm.

Davi saw Nila swing her ship around and head toward the Borali freighter. "Eden One, damage report."

"We've got some scratches and bruises, but we can still make Xanthis," Captain Cain replied.

"Do you want an escort?"

"Negative. We'll keep to distance shipping lanes and we should be okay."

"Affirmative. You're cleared to leave."

As Davi and his Squadron formed up around the Boralian freighter, the Vertullian ship began to turn and head off away from them.

"I wonder how many more heroes like this we'll be dealing with," Jorek muttered.

"They'll likely be hundreds. Tensions will spin out of control after today." Yao sounded sad. He'd been assigned to Davi's Squadron as part of his temporary reassignment.

"Jorek and Virun, you pair with Brie and Yao on those weapons, in case the Captain decides to be difficult. Farien and I will take the lead, the rest of you cover the engines." Davi formed with Farien and headed for the front of the freighter as the rest peeled off to their various assignments. He hoped Yao's prediction was an exaggeration but feared it wouldn't be. The preschool incident would send things to the next level and that meant this incident was only the beginning.

*Manaen should be meeting with the first of them by now*, Xalivar thought. He'd sent his majordomo off with recorded messages to the leadership of various alien species in the system. It was time to implement phase two of his plan. If they joined his cause as expected, his army would triple in size in a few hours. With most of the alien species on his side—he had doubts about the Tertullians who were fiercely loyal to the government and the Idolians who were fiercely independent—victory would be his all the faster. He'd always treated the aliens with indifference, but they hadn't been persecuted, not any more than would be typical of systems where various species lived in close proximity. After all, his grandfather had stopped terraforming on planets like Xanthis when intelligent life was discovered there. They'd been allowed to maintain their lifestyles and home planets under his family's rule. Most of them still lived as they had for generations. The fact that Xalivar planned to destroy them once he regained power would go unmentioned, until they helped get him there. *Even an idiot like Manaen can't screw this up. Just play the recording and let me do the talking.*

He wished he could go himself. Undoubtedly his presence would be more convincing, but with the government suspicious of his involvement, he couldn't risk stumbling into a patrol or having video footage confirming his presence make its way onto the nets. No, he'd continue to maintain a low profile for now. The time for glory would be soon enough.

Watching Generals Lucius and Pres and Admiral Dek take their recruits through training was thrilling. Xalivar hadn't been on a battlefield since the Delta V incident thirty years before. He'd seen a few training exercises visiting his former nephew at the Academy, but now he felt like a real military leader—strategizing with his commanders, watching the troops train to implement those plans. He leaned his head back and laughed with delight at the images flooding his mind. Was there any sweeter sensation than that of victory?

A younger officer stumbled as he jumped from the Floater. Despite the wide opening behind the long benches where troops rode, he managed to get his boots caught as he leapt off the ledge to the ground and fell flat on his face. Why did he suddenly miss Xander? So many times as a child, he'd watched his nephew and designated heir keep at such exercises until he had them down perfectly. Xander had been awkward and clumsy until his mid-teens. To see him successful now as a pilot and officer ought to be a source of pride, but instead it stung with betrayal. Xalivar cursed his sister again for raising her son to be weak. He cursed her for adopting a slave behind his back, contaminating his household and manipulating Xalivar to care about him. *Damn you, Miri! I hope your new life is so much less than you want!*

He turned and motioned to an aide. The aide hurried forward with a pitcher and cup. Xalivar took the cup and held it as the aide poured cold Talis. Xalivar drank slowly, allowing the energy inherent in the brewed beverage to calm him as it flowed down his throat. Not only had Miri and Xander both betrayed him, they'd stolen his rightful power and left him with no heir. That was another issue Xalivar would have to resolve. He might even have to take a mistress to bear him an heir personally. He scowled at the thought. Women were such an encumbrance—so emotional, demanding, weak. He hoped another alternative would present itself, but knew he couldn't risk another embarrassment like Miri had caused. Perhaps adoption would be the best course. He'd have to run any cand-idate through rigorous genetic testing first, of course.

He thought of Manaen again. At least his Andorian servant was too stupid to betray him. No ambition whatsoever, these Andorians! He laughed. The perfect aide. He reached for his datapad to check for incoming messages. No word yet on alien leadership responses. He supposed he'd have to be patient, but patience had never been one of his strengths. He'd already wasted enough time waiting for what was his to be restored.

He heard footsteps on the stairs and turned as General Lucius joined him on the balcony, smiling. "They're doing quite well, wouldn't you say?"

Xalivar nodded. "Who is that young one?"

"The one who stumbled dismounting from the Floater?" Lucius read the answer on Xalivar's face and continued: "I don't know. Do you want him removed?"

"No. He reminds me of someone is all, Lucius. See that he gets some extra attention. It won't do to have our troop's entrance marred by such accidents."

"Of course, my Lord," Lucius said. They turned back to watch the troops continue their training.

Normally Xalivar had a very low tolerance for failure, but, for some reason, he felt charitable toward the young soldier. He supposed it wouldn't hurt to extend some leeway to his recruits. After all, he wanted and needed their loyalty. His reputation had been scarred enough. For now, they respected him. He wouldn't want to damage that over something so minor. At least for now.

"Our plans are succeeding, General. It's only a matter of time." Xalivar's eyes met the General's as Lucius beamed with pride. Xalivar finished his Talis then turned, handing the cup back to his aide, and marched back into the building toward his new office. It was time to turn on the networks and see if his latest surprise for Miri was having the expected impact. He hoped she was home to see the explosion. By now, he imagined the Boralians would be close to declaring war on the Vert-ullians over it. His head went back as he laughed and disappeared inside.

LSP Major Isak Zylo paced inches from the other side of the one way glass as Tarkanius and Aron watched with General Grif. Lord Kretzu sat calmly, erect in his usual dignified manner, so far unperturbed. Even when confronted with the camera images which revealed his presence at the café, he watched impassively, looking like he was fighting a yawn.

An experienced veteran, Zylo had aligned himself with Xalivar during the war with the WFR but survived because he had followed orders and had an outstanding record prior to that. Tarkanius had been in a bind. If he'd eliminated every officer who'd obeyed Xalivar, he'd have no officers left to lead the military. And since the WFR's victory, Zylo had served with distinction. Mid-forties, Zylo had short, blonde hair and a muscular frame for a man his age, although signs of his age appeared around his growing midriff and in the gray spotting his mustache.

"Come on, Kretzu, this is your chance to tell your side of it," Zylo said, his voice menacing. "You won't get another one. We know you were there."

Kretzu frowned as his head spun so their eyes met. "It's 'my Lord,' Major. No matter what you accuse me of, do not forget your place."

"My apologies, *my* Lord. Perhaps your title won't be an issue much longer."

Kretzu slammed a fist down on the metal table. "Do not threaten me, Major. Lord Elul is a personal friend of mine. He'll hear of any mistreatment or disrespect!"

*Lord Elul won't know this yet*, Tarkanius thought. *You two are too close. He's under suspicion as well.* The thought that his trusted security chief, head of the Lord's Special Police, might be involved in attempting to assassinate him had been giving Tarkanius nightmares. He'd handpicked the Major for his experience, hoping that once the circumstances had been explained, he could rely on the man's complete discretion.

"Ner Zebah, my Lord, have you heard the name?" Zylo's tone hadn't changed, despite his interrogation subject's anger.

At the very least, Tarkanius had hoped the images would shake the older man. Cameras had been secretly installed in the area surrounding the metro center prior to the High Lord Councilor's speech—added security measures. The conspirators wouldn't have expected them, but Kretzu held up well.

"Who else was with you? Who else shall I be charging with murder?!" Zylo slammed his palms down on the table, leaning across it to look Kretzu in the eye as he emphasized the last word. It came out almost like spit.

"Murder?! How dare you! I have served this Council and Alliance since before you were born!"

Tarkanius exchanged a look with Aron. "This isn't working."

Aron's shoulder sagged. "He doesn't believe we have enough to charge him."

General Grif cleared his throat and the two Lords turned toward him. "Perhaps an alternate tactic might be more effective." He continued staring through the one-way glass even as he spoke.

"Alternate tactic?" Tarkanius looked at Aron again, worried. "What are you suggesting, General?"

Grif smiled. "The battlefield here is Lord Kretzu's mind. He believes he has the upper hand, that he's in control. We need to remove that confidence."

"How?" Aron asked then watched the General as he stepped back from the window and turned to face them.

"Lord Aron, will you accompany me? And follow my lead?"

"Of course, General."

Grif turned and opened the door, stepping into the corridor. Aron followed, leaving Tarkanius alone in the observation room. Moments later, they entered the room with Major Zylo and Lord Kretzu.

"Ah, General," Kretzu sighed, "here to put an end to this spectacle, I hope. Please instruct the Lieutenant to release me at once."

Grif offered a forced smile. "Of course, my Lord. You're released."

Kretzu shot Zylo a look of hatred as he immediately stood.

"Into the custody of Lord Aron."

"Excuse me?!"

"Yes. You're to be temporarily assigned to help Lord Aron and the Vertullian leadership with the crisis," Grif continued. Tarkanius smiled, grasping the General's tactic. *It just might work.*

"I have business of my own to deal with. I have no time—"

"We must all make sacrifices at times like these," Grif continued, cutting him off. "Wouldn't you agree, Lord Aron?"

Aron smiled and nodded. "Of course, General. We're all in this together."

Kretzu frowned. "Custody? I am under arrest?"

"Not exactly," Grif said. "But, unfortunately, word of your detainment leaked. It's already been on the broadcasts. And we are worried for your safety."

*Brilliant!* Tarkanius chuckled to himself.

Kretzu's eyes widened and he stiffened. "So you're sending me to the planet of those who might harm me?"

"Your presence there shall be low profile," Aron said, "and the military will provide a protective detail."

Grif smiled. "Of course. Your generous dedication to helping the Vertullians through this can only serve to endear you to them and change the minds of any who might oppose you."

Kretzu shook his head, arms crossed over his chest. "I refuse. I want no part of this."

"You have no choice," Grif said.

"I most certainly do!"

Grif crossed his own arms over his chest and leaned back against a wall. He waited in silence as Kretzu's eyes continually darted toward the door, as if gauging whether it was unlocked, so he could bolt. "The High Lord Councilor has evoked the Emergency Powers Clause and, as such, has requested your compliance. As you know, in times of Emergency Powers, even Council members are expected to serve as needed by the High Lord Councilor. Your refusal gives the military power to take other necessary actions, which include detaining you further. Major, please check the status of open cells at Centauri Two."

Zylo pulled the datapad from his belt and began typing. "Of course, General."

Tarkanius noticed Kretzu's robe darkening with sweat at the mention of the Alliance's most secure prison. "I know nothing of a café. I am a loyal citizen!"

"The warden confirms availability," Zylo said, with a casual glance at Grif.

Kretzu's legs seemed to collapse from under him as he fell against the wall. Aron hurried over and took his arm, helping him to a chair. Grif sat in a chair across the table, the Major taking another beside him. Tarkanius almost felt sorry for the old man.

"Okay, Lord Kretzu. Tell us about Ner Zebah." Grif's stare was so intense, even Tarkanius felt a tinge of nerves on the other side of the glass. And then Kretzu leaned back and began to talk.

The group gathered in Simeon's apartment, the same one once occupied by Tarkanius when he headed the Council. Owned by the Alliance, it was one of the perks of office for the Council's elected leader. With a 360-degree view of the city center through its windows, the round, revolving penthouse sat atop a highrise near the Palace and government complex was the envy of all who visited and Simeon knew many of those present dreamed of a day they could call it "home."

Lords Kray and Qai sat together on a lush sofa made of Krikatru leather from Eleni 1. Dark, almost shiny, it had a tendency to mold to the skin such that anyone sitting on or wearing it almost didn't notice the separation between the leather and his or her own skin.

On an identical sofa across from them sat Pharah Brahma, Yao's father, and Lords Buj and Amie. Younger than Pharah, they had joined the Council together two years before but had quickly risen in influence due to their strong values and work ethic. As a Tertullian, Pharah could not serve on the Council, but his red eyes were famous for their warmth, and, with his smile, won him much admiration from all he knew. He'd long been a respected citizen and worked his way comfortably into the upper class elite, so many on the Council knew him socially. But Simeon had asked him there for other reasons.

Shiny, gold-encrusted lamps and handwoven Tertullian tapestries and carpets complemented the Idolian woodwork on the walls and furniture. Even most of the Lords' lifestyles were severely lacking compared to this. Usually it made Simeon embarrassed, but today it aided his cause.

"Thank you all for coming," he said as he sat in a plush, white lounge chair made from Gungor fur which sat at the head of the two sofas. "As you all know, the Alliance faces a great crisis, one which threatens to tear it apart. And plans are being put in place to protect it, but today I would ask your help."

"The entire Council must be willing to help," Lord Qai said.

Simeon's sleeve rustled as he raised a hand in agreement. "Of course, Qai. But this meeting is to be kept private until I grant permission for you to speak of it. We have matters to discuss of a very sensitive nature. And you're each here because I respect your judgment, covet your advice and need your support—unofficially for now."

Pharah looked around at the others, shifting on the sofa as if he felt out of place. "Of course, Lord Simeon. Whatever we can do."

Qai frowned. "Mister Brahma is not on the Council. Why is he here?"

"His presence is the most important of all." Simeon glanced reassuringly at Pharah. The Tertullian had smartly worn a robe to the gathering; despite its different coloring, it helped him blend in with the others, though he was the only nonhuman present. "He represents citizens for whom we cannot speak." Simeon made a wide arc with his outstretched arms. "Not just the Tertullians but all the alien races. They are citizens of our Alliance, too, and it is time we started treating them as such."

"You have always been most gracious to us," Pharah said, smiling as if embarrassed at being singled out.

"No, my friend, we have not. And that must change." He couldn't bring himself to match Pharah's smile. A generous man like his son, the Tertullian was far more forgiving than Simeon himself would be in his place.

"He has no official authority," Lord Amie noted, looking down from his towering height at Pharah with an apologetic look. Pharah waved it off.

"That's why this meeting is unofficial," Simeon said. "And must remain our secret for now. Our friend, Pharah, is needed to deliver a message to the alien citizens of this Alliance."

Pharah nodded, leaning forward with interest. "I will, of course, do what I can. I'm not an ambassador."

"But you are a diplomat," Kray said, "a very talented one." She smiled as Pharah's purple skin lightened with embarrassment.

"Thank you, my Lord. Your faith in me is most humbling."

"This message is from the High Lord Councilor," Simeon said, his discussion with Tarkanius flashing through his mind. "It is time for all our citizens to be equals and have equal voice in this government." Qai and the other Lords exchanged surprised looks. "If you nonhumans will help us fight off the threat that menaces us all, we will work with you to re-invent a government that's inclusive of all our peoples."

Pharah's purple eyes lightened as they widened, staring at Simeon and then panning the others, his lips opening and then closing again as he sought words. "It is a message which will surprise many, but one which some of us have been waiting generations to hear."

"Will the majority be receptive?" Kray's eyes met his with eagerness.

"Some will be fearful of a trap. Others encouraged. But I will do all I can to get the dialogue open."

Simeon smiled. "Good."

Lord Buj, shorter and stockier than his counterpart Amie, nodded but looked to Pharah as well. "Will they fight with us?"

"Many of us are not belligerent peoples. We have no history of warfare like you do. But there are many ways to support your needs, wouldn't you agree?" Pharah's eyes moved between them, seeking agreement.

"Of course," Kray was the first to say.

"Dialogue is the first step," Simeon said, encouraged as he took a moment to meet each of their eyes in turn. "Once that begins, many details will come into focus. All we ask at the moment is a commitment to work together. The rest will come in time."

The others exchanged looks then mumbled in agreement, smiling back at him.

He had them! It was in their posture and faces. He'd chosen his group wisely, it seemed. Now for the hard part. "But first, we must discuss some recent events and discoveries involving members of the Council. Sadly, not all of us appear to be on the same side."

"That explains why you're handling this outside the Council," Lord Amie said with a sigh.

"You have evidence of treason?" Lord Buj asked.

"Let me show you what we've uncovered so far," Simeon said and clicked a button on the arm of his chair and a black flat screen lowered from the ceiling at the opposite end of the couches. Everyone turned to watch as images began to appear. He observed them carefully, offering a prayer to the gods that their passion would soon match his own.

The Idolian landscape shifted from gold to gray as the twin suns slid further down the horizon under the encroachment of night. Manaen felt a small quake under foot, the result of orbital interference from Charlis, the system's smaller sun. With Idolis currently at its nearest orbit to Charlis, quakes were a daily occurrence, along with hotter days and shorter nights. He hadn't felt one in years. Legallis' orbital pattern brought different effects.

He sighed as he stood there, watching the suns, basking in the warmth of the humid air, the sweet scent of Andolian berries in the nearby trees. Their purple shells still glistened in the remaining light. How fortunate he was that Xalivar sent him here this time of year. It had been decades since he'd had the opportunity to experience these smells, and tonight he would taste fresh Andolian berry pie for the first time since he was a teenager. A smile forced its way to his lips despite worried thoughts.

He heard the shuffling of feet on the sandy path and turned as his younger sister, Vibryd, stopped beside him. "A smile, my brother? How long it's been since I've seen such on your face."

Manaen laughed. "It's good to be home."

"It's good to have you here." She smiled as she reached over to gently stroke his arm. "Why do you stay?"

"It is my sworn duty to serve."

"But you're unhappy."

"Andolian oaths are not modified by emotions. It's a sacred trust."

Vibryd sighed, rolling her red eyes. They stood out starkly from her dark-blue skin. The extra time she spent in the sun had given her a tone Manaen's body never matched. "You're still young enough to find a promisemate and build a life here."

"It's too late for me, Viby."

"He's not the High Lord Councilor anymore!"

"Perhaps he will be again."

Vibryd scowled, exhaling deeply. "I hope not for all of us. I could never serve such a man as you do."

"There is more to Xalivar than his reputation, my sister." But Manaen found her words echoing in his mind.

Why did he stay? Xalivar was not kind to him—insulting, condescending. Manaen was like a piece of furniture or a walking datapad to him. The purpose of his mission came back to his mind then. He'd chosen a course of action, almost immediately, when told the assignment. His whole life, Manaen had never made such a decision. The consequences could bring harm to him and his family. He was willing to bear whatever came to him, but he longed to protect Vibyrd and her children. The alien leadership deserved his honesty. He could have just delivered Xalivar's pretaped messages and let them speak for themselves. But then the leaders always had questions and would turn to him, and Manaen found himself wanting to be honest with them. It came easier to him than he'd imagined, a fact which made him question himself all the more. *What does the oath mean to you, Manaen?*

Vibryd yawned, reaching up with a delicate hand to cover her mouth. Manaen's nose crinkled at the smell wafting from the kitchen window of the domed, mud-brick house behind them. "Mmmmmmm. Andolian berry pie."

Vibryd laughed. "Mother's recipe. I made two, so you can have extra."

Manaen shook his head, shooting her a stern look. "Mother wouldn't approve."

She rolled her eyes as she punched his arm. "Mother's not here. I'm the only one left to spoil you now so prepare yourself. You might even need your extra stomach tonight!" Laughing, she turned and headed back toward the house, disappearing inside.

Manaen laughed as he thought of their childhood. Their father worked hard, long hours and was rarely home. It was he who had taught his children the meaning of honor and service. Their mother raised all four children with stern discipline, yet much love. In truth, she'd snuck him a few extra slices herself from time to time—when he'd had a bad dream or a bad day at school or for his birthday. Vibryd looked so much like her; laughed like her. And he knew in that moment he'd made the right choice. He just hoped he had the strength to see it through and protect his family and all who might share their fate.

The noise of the open air market crowded their senses—vendors of all species yelling in competition with bleating Qiwi, roaring Gungor, grunting Krikatrus and screeching birds of all shapes and sizes. The earthy smell of manure and dried feed mixed with sweat, the nectar of flowers, the sweet scent of fruits. The market was cleaner than any Sol had visited in a long while, catering to the Borali capital's elite. He and Telanus had jumped to comply when Lura asked them to go for some ingredients she'd need at dinner. Tela offered to accompany them, but they'd waved her off, allowing her only to drop them off while she ran another errand, so they could enjoy "man time for a bit."

Weaving their way through crowded aisles, the rush hour, Telanus read off items from the list as Sol kept his eye peeled. "Tertullian turnips."

Sol spotted the long, bulbous brown taproots to their right. "How many?"

"Three."

Sol forced his way to the table and picked up a very large, conical vegetable with the pointed brown taproot converging into a round, greenish, tomato-like top. "This one's big enough; it might suffice."

"Get three just in case. We don't want to run short."

Sol snickered. "We'd never hear the end of that!" Telanus laughed, too. Sol grabbed the roots and turned on his heels, bumping into another man and knocking a handful of Gixi to the ground. "I'm sorry—" The man shrugged as he bent to retrieve the purple fruit and Sol recognized him. "Joram?!!"

Joram looked up as he retrieved the last Gixi and smiled. "Hello, Sol."

Sol shook his hand vigorously as Joram juggled his left arm, trying to keep the Gixi from falling again.

"You do your own shopping?" Telanus smiled quizzically as Joram shook his hand more gently.

"My wife said just three things, and here I am."

The men laughed at the familiar scenario. "We're here escaping, too." Telanus sighed. "Tela's sad. Miri and Lura are bossy. We haven't gotten away in three days."

Joram laughed. "A trip to the market was sounding good, I'll bet." Sol and Telanus joined his laughter, nodding.

"Why are you shopping in Legon?" Sol asked.

"We're at a hotel around the block. A meeting with Aron and Telanus today." Joram shifted as he almost dropped his fruit again. His body twisted as he juggled them, trying to find his balance again.

"Can I help?" Telanus reached for the Gixi, but Joram waved him off.

"We just have a couple more things," Sol said.

"I'll walk with you."

Sol and Telanus smiled. "Great."

They pushed through a crowded intersection of aisles into a section with meat on the left and breads to the right. The smell of fresh, uncooked fish filled Sol's nostrils, mixing with the earthiness of the leaf vegetables across the aisle. Sol noticed a few people staring. They must have recognized Joram. The Governor ignored them and walked on, searching for the next item on the list.

"Why's Tela so down?" Joram asked.

Telanus rolled his eyes. "A fight with Davi. Something silly they'll get over soon."

Joram chuckled. "Sounds like my teenage daughter."

Telanus slapped him on the back as he guffawed. "Do they ever outgrow it?"

Sol stopped as three husky men blocked the path. Looking up, he found their eyes watching him—full of hate. He smiled. "Excuse me."

As soon as he moved to push through, a man growled and grabbed him. "Don't touch me, slave!"

Joram stepped forward, frowning as Sol shook free of the man's grasp. "There are no slaves in the Alliance now. All are free."

"A mistake!" Another of the men said—gray-haired but just as bulky, with muscles bulging from his shirt and every exposed piece of skin covered in thick hair.

"Not your decision." Joram didn't meet their stares, instead attempted to pass. The gray-haired man threw him to the ground, Gixi scattering, bruised, across the aisle. The first man caught one and smashed it with his foot.

Sol hurried to help Joram up. "Do you know who this is?"

"A slave who knows his place before us—on the ground, kneeling," the first man said and guffawed with his friends.

Sol grabbed Joram's arm and helped him up as Telanus went to retrieve the fruit. "Leave it. I'll get more."

All three turned to go back up the aisle the way they'd come and found three lanky men there, blocking the way. "Where you going?" one of them asked.

"We're just picking up items for dinner." Telanus stood relaxed, his shoulders slumped, not meeting their eyes.

"Not anymore, slave!" The lanky man's fist slammed into Telanus' jaw, knocking him back into Sol and Joram. Then the six men were upon them, fists punching, feet kicking, grunting, groaning as Sol, Telanus and Joram struggled to defend themselves.

"Why are you doing this?" Joram pleaded. He was silenced as one of their attackers smashed a Gixi against his face.

Sol heard others mocking laughter around them, as he lost his footing and fell to his knees. The pounding and hitting increased. He ducked his head down beneath his arms for protection. He heard a grunt. Then Telanus cried out. He turned and saw a man beating his friend with a wooden crate, which shattered and disintegrated a bit at each strike.

Joram was pleading next to him, but also was forced to his knees by the gray-haired hulk. A boot to his ribs knocked the wind from him and he gasped, tears rolling down his cheeks, as his eyes pleaded with Sol.

Two men smashed crates over their heads now. A splinter dug into Sol's shoulder, adding to the throbbing already coming from dozens of other places and causing him cry out.

"Stop! You're hurting them!" A woman's voice. *Tela?*

Sol couldn't see through the men, but then he heard a blaster bolt and the men started to scatter.

"Leave them be!" *It was Tela!*

The men ran past, kicking them again as they passed. Some dropped fists down for one last shot as well. Tela fired again, kicking up dust with her boots as she pounded up the dirt aisle toward her father and his friends. Laser bolts struck an attacker, who screamed and grabbed his shoulder as his buddies pulled him to safety around a corner, and they all scattered into the crowd.

Telanus was lying face down, blood pouring from his scalp.

"Daddy!" Tela ran to him, holstering her blaster, looking to Sol and then Joram.

"I'm fine," Sol said, but his ankle throbbed and his arm was numb.

"Someone call help, please!" Joram said.

People moved around them—shoppers fleeing the scene, vendors retrieving smashed or scattered merchandise, and others approaching with offers of help. Sol brushed them off, but sweat and tears clouded his vision. Then his head began to ache and he felt weak, his eyes hazing over as he fell to the ground.

"Sol!" Tela's concerned yell was the last thing he heard before the world went dark.

# Chapter Ten

Obed denied he needed security, but Bordox insisted. He held anything and everyone suspect. His father was taking a great risk even going to Legallis, but the meeting had been arranged for a café in Estrela, a small city on the far side of the planet, away from the capital. Since Council members travelled frequently, Obed thought no one would question Niger and Elul's trip, even though Estrela was far from a popular destination. At least this café wasn't a dive. The booths were well lit and clean with sparkling, waxed tabletops and smooth Gungor leather benches. The waitress greeted them as they entered and took their drink orders as they settled in at a booth.

By the time she delivered their order, Niger and Elul had slipped into the booth to join them. Bordox glanced around. The café was almost empty at this early hour—a good thing. The last thing they wanted was for their conversation to be overheard.

"You look well, Obed," Elul said with a grin. "Life as an outcast agrees with you." The Lord's rotund belly jiggled as he laughed.

Bordox shot him a cold stare as Obed smiled back. "Exiled by choice, my friend. We are not fugitives."

"Indeed." Niger hadn't smiled once since arriving, even when shaking their hands in greeting. Bordox wondered what had him preoccupied. "You said you had information which might be of use to us?"

Obed nodded, looking pensive. "Perhaps. If I can trust you."

"How do we know we can trust you?"

Obed chuckled. "Touché, my friend. I understand not everyone shares Tarkanius' views on the success of the slaves' integration as citizens."

"Surely that comes as no surprise to you," Elul said.

Bordox wondered how long it would take for the constant grin to permanently warp his fat facial muscles. Bordox's fist balled involuntarily from his desire to wipe it off the man's smug face.

"Like many of us, your reservations are well known," Elul continued.

Obed looked at Niger. "Yet some were supportive of Tarkanius at first."

"I objected to Xalivar's attempts to control and deceive the Council. Plus the citizenry seemed in favor of the idea. But the citizenry's optimism has led to economic disaster for many. Tarkanius is an honorable man but utterly unprepared for the realities of leadership, I'm afraid." Niger's eyes met Obed's as each tried to read the other for several moments.

"What do you want in exchange for this...information?" Elul's grin finally went away as he sized up Obed.

"I want what we all want—the glory of our Alliance restored. The strength of our people assured."

All three men stared at each other a moment, as Bordox watched, his eyes darting back and forth. How could his father stomach working with men who so clearly held him in contempt? Politics was insane.

"I ask only for your support, when the time comes, and I wish to have a voice in affairs again," Obed said.

At last Niger smiled. "I believe the Council has greatly missed your voice, Obed. Although I fear restoration to your former status is unlikely."

Obed nodded. "I don't expect it to be easy. Although I will happily play whatever part I can. For now, it must be behind the scenes, as they say."

"What's the source of your information?" Elul's face dripped with suspicion. Bordox tensed and fought the urge to slap the man. His father had more honor in one finger than Elul had in his entire paunch.

"I cannot reveal my sources at this time, except to say, you will find the information proves quite reliable." Obed clearly saw the Lord's doubts but never faltered.

"You may count on our support, friend. I'm sure your information is as reliable as you say." Niger looked at Elul. "The former head of the LSP is a highly qualified source, I'd say."

Elul shrugged, relaxing a bit on the leather seat.

"Good. Shall we discuss this over provisions, then?" Obed leaned back and smiled at Bordox. The waitress appeared again, anxiously holding her datapad ready. Bordox could see his father remained determined to plunge ahead. He hoped the trust would not prove misplaced. He'd do whatever it took to protect Obed. Especially from men like these.

Pharah Brahma began his meetings with the leadership on his home world of Tertullis. It was where he had the most contacts and having an ally already on board would strengthen his case when meeting with alien leaders from other planets. Major Isak Zylo kept his opinions to himself. He'd been assigned as security for Brahma on the tour, not as a participant. In fact, he wasn't even allowed in the room for the discussions so he had no idea, beyond hints Brahma himself let slip, what was actually being said. Zylo felt lucky to even have a career. After the debacle of the loss to the Vertullians in their rebellion, during which his ground troops on Vertullis had born huge casualties, he was grateful to have been allowed to remain in the military, let alone trusted with security detail on an important diplomatic quest. Despite being out of the official discussions, Zylo was listening carefully and the information he'd gathered would be of great interest to certain highly-placed friends. One, in particular, would be excited to learn of the discussions. He decided to wait until the journey was a few days in and gauge the leaders' reactions before sending his report.

To no one's surprise, the Tertullians jumped aboard almost before Pharah Brahma finished asking them. The Xanthians were more hesitant, although, given their planet's black market activities and their interest in maintaining a level of low interference from the government that was hardly surprising. Now they were meeting with the leaders on Italis. A sparsely populated, terraformed planet, colonized by human outcasts from a variety of backgrounds, it had always been surprising Italis didn't draw more interest. From what Zylo could see, the terraforming was a complete success. The vegetation was lush, the landscapes beautiful, the land plentiful. There were plenty of natural resources from water to food to various minerals and gasses easily available for use by settlers. He'd have expected a lot more migration, but for unknown reasons it had stalled. Zylo's guess was the location. Except the great recreation hub of Regalis, another terraforming success, the planets further out were barely habitable and highly undesirable. That made Italis the edge of the universe as far as most people were concerned and populations seemed to gravitate toward the centers in solar systems.

Pharah Brahma emerged from the meeting with a broad smile on his face. "Well, that was easier than dealing with the Xanthians."

"The Italites are mostly human. Why are they being treated like an alien race?"

"Because the majority of them never bothered to apply for official citizenship. Strengthening our ties and unity is the goal of this mission, so we need to bring them on board."

"Bet they don't take too kindly to being lumped in as aliens."

Brahma smiled. "They refer to themselves that way. They claim they have more in common with the alien races than regular human Boralians. I believe I just convinced them they were wrong about that."

*Was it the purple eyes or the orange skin I wonder?*

"In any case, they've signed on tentatively. It's enough to mention them to the other leaders at least."

Zylo nodded. "Any change to the agenda?" Maintaining his casual tone and manner kept him on edge whenever the Tertullian was around.

Brahma shook his head. "No. We'll proceed on to Kronis as planned. The Italites offered to throw a reception this evening, but I declined on the basis of urgency. The High Lord Councilor really needs this alliance solidified as soon as possible."

Zylo sighed as the tension he'd felt dissipated. The sooner this was over, the better. "Whatever you say, sir. I'll alert the flight crew."

"Thank you. Let me just grab refreshment at the spaceport for an hour and I'll be ready to go."

Zylo finished adding to the notes in his datapad and pulled the comm from his belt. "We'll be waiting for you." Brahma was so old fashioned when it came to technology that he hadn't noticed Zylo never communicated with the pilots by datapad but always used the comm. Just a mention of the pilots and Zylo could freely take notes right in front of his subject. *So much for diplomats being smarter than the rest of us.*

Brahma smiled as he hurried off to find a restaurant while Zylo keyed the comm channel and hailed the pilots.

Davi gasped for breath when he reached the top of the stairs. The hospital was busy today, and he hadn't felt like fighting for an elevator. He raced down the slick, newly waxed floor, his boots slipping with each step, searching the walls for the room number. He rushed past startled nurses and burst inside. Tela was crying as she sat beside the bed, holding Telanus' hand. Telanus looked white as a cloud and thinner than ever, dark bruises circled his eyes and spotted his face. If his eyes had been closed, Davi would have thought he was dead. Davi saw Lura just past Miri, holding the hand he knew must be Sol's but he couldn't see his father yet. Miri stepped back when she spotted her son and turned to embrace him. As she did, Davi caught a glimpse of his father.

"My God! What happened to them?" Davi's eyes flickered from Miri to Lura and then Tela. Of the three, Tela was the most distraught.

He heard a moan and saw Sol's eyes open. A smile formed on his lips as he looked up at his son. A hand raised slowly, as if with great effort, reaching out. Davi hurried over and grasped it. "Don't move, father. I'm here."

Lura smiled. "He's okay. The surgery was successful." Davi nodded as her warm eyes met his, then frowned, nodding toward Tela. Lura gave a slight shake of her head. Davi squeezed his father's lukewarm hand before releasing it and hurrying to Tela.

"Don't touch me!" She shoved away his outstretched arm.

"It'll be okay, babe."

"Okay? My father's dying! Those bastards murdered my father!" She spoke loudly, almost a scream, her eyes biting into his as they met, like blades. Davi didn't know what to do or say.

"What happened?" His patrol had been tied up with incidents and run long. He'd gotten word of the attack but hadn't been able to break free for twenty-four hours—the longest day of his life.

"We just needed a few items for dinner," Miri said. "They went alone to get them. Tela dropped them off and ran an errand. When she came back..." Miri's voice faded as her face sunk into sadness.

"Who did this?"

"Animals!" Tela shrieked, her voice almost unrecognizable to Davi. "Boralian monsters!"

The hospital was a government facility. Nurses and an orderly glanced in through the doorway as they walked past. Miri hurried over and shut the door.

"This is not all Boralians, Tela. You know that."

Tela scowled at him. "Just the true ones. The ones who don't bother to hide who they are!"

"We've lived and worked among them, Tela," Davi said, shaking his head. "You know better." She'd never looked so lost and distant. The eyes that met his were like a stranger's, with a coldness that made him shiver.

"I know nothing! They're our enemies! Our persecutors! Killers!"

"Your father's still alive, dear," Lura said softly.

"Barely." Tela continued staring at Davi, even though her voice softened in response.

"They'll find who did this. Put them on trial."

"They'd better put them under *protection*!"

Davi forced himself to hold her glare, narrowing his eyes in sympathy, as he struggled against his own emotions. "Don't make threats, Tela. I know you're upset—"

"All those years, Davi! I missed him! Wondered if he was alive! Longed for a father!"

Davi choked back tears, wanting to take her in his arms, but unable to move. Instead, he stayed still, feeling impotent. "I know, Baby."

Tela released her father's hand and stood, hurrying over to clasp his hands. "Names, Davi. Get me their names. Find out who did this."

"The authorities will handle it."

She shook her head. "If you ever loved me, you'll do this." Davi didn't know what to say, he squeezed her hands and pulled her to him in an embrace as she cried on his shoulder.

A brutal attack on the eve of The Returning—the first time the holiday would be shared by all citizens. Aron couldn't imagine a worse scenario. He'd ridden the shuttle back with Joram from the hospital. Of the three men, his injuries had been the least somehow. Joram barely spoke to him, then stayed secluded in his home the next two days. Aron was meeting with Uzah and Matheu when he appeared, taking them by surprise, joining them around the table in the conference room at Borali command near the starport in Iraja.

"How are you feeling?" Matheu asked.

Joram brushed it off with a wave. "Fine."

"We're so sorry about what happened," Uzah said as the others continued staring at Joram.

"Telanus may not live. There's a deep sickness in people these days." Joram's eyes were hollow and his skin paler than ever.

Aron nodded. "Hatred is a powerful motive to wrong thinking and bad decisions."

"Bad decisions? Is that all this is to you? They attacked us like wild animals, Aron. All we did was walk around. That's it!"

Aron closed his eyes and leaned back. "I know. It's horrible."

"They can't take it back, Aron. They can't do anything to change it. It's permanent. We'll carry it with us all our days, the three of us, if Telanus even survives." Joram's fist pounded the table in emphasis with his words.

"Take some time off, whatever you need," Uzah said, putting a hand atop Joram's wrist. "We all understand."

Joram shook his head, pulling free of Uzah's touch. "No. The Returning is in two days. I must be a part of it. It's important for our people."

"I've already discussed it with Tarkanius," Aron said. "He's making a speech this afternoon, but we agreed the ceremonies will be low key. We don't need to aggravate tensions at this point."

"Aggravate tensions? By what? Celebrating our religion? How dare us!" Fury filled Joram's eyes as his cheeks reddened with anger.

"We agreed to downplay the religious aspects publicly and promote unity." Aron had never seen his friend like this. He shifted in his chair, tense with worry.

"Maybe we were wrong? If anyone needs the power of salvation, the understanding of grace, it's the Boralians!"

"They can't get it being beat over the head with it," Aron said, his eyes locked on Joram's.

Joram refused to meet Aron's gaze. "Maybe they can't get it at all. Maybe they don't have the intellectual capacity. Have you asked yourself that? I used to hope, like you do. Now, after this, after so many failures, I have to ask a different question."

"If you're right, unity is doomed."

Joram laughed, turning side to side in his chair. "Unity is fiction, Aron. And I think we've all known that all along." He looked at Matheu, as if expecting agreement, but the old General kept a straight face, waiting. "So how are the plans coming?"

"We can handle it, Joram," Uzah said. "I think rest is a better idea for you."

Joram shook his head. "No. I want to be a part of this."

"We will make you a part, I promise." Uzah smiled, reaching over to pat Joram's shoulder, but Joram pulled away again.

"All we want is for you to recover quickly," Matheu said. "We'll get the plans in order and let you sign off later today. But you don't need to sit here for this part."

Joram scoffed, panning the three men. Their faces showed agreement. "Fine. If I'm not wanted, I can leave." Joram shoved back in his chair, sending it across the carpet with a tearing sound as he stood. "But I am elected the leader of this planet. I will have my say, I promise you." Not waiting for a response, he turned and stormed out.

Uzah frowned, watching him go. "I hope his anger subsides quickly."

"Can you blame him for his feelings?" Matheu asked.

Uzah shook his head as Aron nodded. "Leaders have to lead with reason and forethought, not emotion at such times. Uzah's right. If Joram doesn't gather his senses, he could make things worse for all of us."

"Let's pray for God's peace then and hope it's enough." Uzah bowed his head. Matheu and Aron followed. Aron's mind raced for words of comfort he could offer his friend but none came. He himself had been attacked, his life in danger. But he'd never carried the anger Joram had just evidenced. His attackers had been Lhamors, however. And they had not beaten two others in front of his face. They did not have the history of enmity the Boralians and Vertullians did either. At such a moment, he supposed, those things mattered more than they might at other times.

As Uzah began the prayer, Aron added his own internal voice to the chorus, calling their God, the God of Israel and Jacob, to work a miracle in the hearts of the men and women of the Alliance. If He didn't, Aron feared, the Alliance's future history would be all too short.

"You'd think I'd be used to this by now," Tarkanius said as aides finished preparing his hair and makeup for the broadcast. Inside a tent, just off the edge of the very market where people he admired had been violently attacked three days before, Tarkanius found himself as nervous as a little boy. He'd botched everything as leader of his people. He already knew his reign would go down in history as a troubled one. All he could do now was to try and fix things so that his legacy spoke better of him than his term in office did.

Simeon and his allies on the Council had stepped up and become a great support to him. They'd already seen to spreading false data around the Council in an attempt to flush out leaks and betrayers. They'd chosen the time, date and location of Tarkanius' planned meeting with alien leaders. Even Simeon didn't know the real information, so when the press reports came in, those Councilors whose unique information had been leaked would be suspect. Some might, of course, discuss it amongst themselves first and discover the trap, but even then, many would arrogantly assume their own information must be correct, that they were trusted. Still, Tarkanius feared a scenario requiring him to incarcerate half the Council. He'd spent the prior afternoon making libations to the gods and meditating at the Temple. What could it hurt? Aron's faith inspired him to hope, and he needed all the help he could get.

Simeon appeared in the door of the tent, smiling. "It's almost time, my Lord."

Tarkanius nodded. "Tell me this is not a big mistake, Simeon."

Simeon's smile faded as both their thoughts turned serious. "The people need to hear from you, my Lord. It's vital during such a crisis."

"When I think on all that's happened, I can hardly speak. I have no words."

Simeon sighed. "Me too, Tarkanius. But we must try. The others and I will stand beside you, lend you our strength."

"Please forgive me for saying, I hope you are all very strong."

Simeon chuckled. "We share that hope, my Lord."

They walked outside together, their aides trailing behind, and found Kray, Qai and Aron waiting for them. Aron's report from his visit to Vertullis the day before was deeply disturbing. If the planetary Governor was no longer on their side, so much could result from it, none of it good. He vowed to go there himself soon and offer what comfort he could. If the man would even see him.

The crowd itself was small, less than expected. Security almost outnumbered them, with palace guards and military officers well in sight at each sidewalk and beside each tent or building. He saw snipers on rooftops, and Floaters of soldiers in nearby clearings waiting armed and ready. Their presence was a regret he'd not been allowed to reject. It would not add to the ambiance he wanted to project. Those present might even be more afraid instead of less, but it couldn't be helped. He knew his own death could be the catalyst for disaster. So protection was unavoidably necessary. He just wished his men knew how to be more discreet about it.

He stepped to the microphone, cameras and lights aiming in his direction, and felt like a first timer rather than a veteran politician of decades. The heat assaulted his body, causing him to sweat as the lights themselves blinded his eyes. The air was surprisingly clear of the ash which had grayed it since the explosion. He took a deep breath, savoring it as the cool rush relaxed his body. He looked down at the datascreen on the podium. The speech was there, waiting. He'd memorized most of it, but still, it was a comfort to have the prompt available. Licking his lips, he took several deep breaths then waited for the broadcast people to signal their readiness. The signal came, and with one final breath, he began:

"My dear fellow citizens, I stand today on the very spot where a great tragedy occurred. Three of our fine citizens, shopping quietly, were brutally attacked. Now two are in the hospital, and one's life hangs in the balance. The attackers were fellow citizens—Boralian men, every day people, with good jobs and families. What hatred drove them to such desperate measures? It's hard for most of us to understand why anyone would commit such violence. How could someone be so brutal and cold? It almost seems inhuman."

"But make no mistake, these attacks were perpetuated by men just like us. Men with emotions and five senses, capable of feeling pain and empathy. Yet men who shut such things off. How? It's a question asked for centuries, as long as there have been criminals. And these men are criminals, mind you. Despite declaring themselves heroes, they are the worst of us, not the best, and we must not allow their actions to go unpunished. My administration will do everything in our power to bring them to justice. We will not let this crime go without proper response. It's an incident I, for one, can never erase from my mind. And I truly believe many of you feel the same."

"For years our own government allowed violence against the Vertullians for ancient crimes by their ancestors against our own. The time has come to join together and stop blaming each other for the actions of our forefathers. In two days, we will celebrate together, a new holiday for many of us, The Returning—one our new allies have long celebrated as their own. Yes, it bears religious significance for them, but we don't ask you to worship. Instead, for Boralians, The Returning symbolizes a return to civility, to common recognition of our mutual value, to living and working in peace together, to no longer spreading blame and hatred to divide us over perceived wrongs of a dark past. It's a returning to the right way, not the wrong way symbolized by that disgusting attack. I humbly ask you: return with me to a new era of the Alliance we all love—an era of peaceful coexistence and mutual respect like we all desire. Do not allow the recent incidents to cloud your focus on what really matters, to stop you from pushing for the future we all desire for ourselves and our children."

"I urge you, my friends, my fellow citizens, to unite with determination to not allow such evil to win. We are better than that. We are stronger than that. We are wiser than that. And if we come together, such wisdom, strength and superiority will prevail. Will you join me?"

He stopped, eyes panning the multi-colored faces in the crowd before him. They stared back a moment, clearly moved by his words. Then he heard clapping from behind him—Simeon and the other Councilors. Gradually the crowd joined in and along with it a chant began, their voices uniting to cry out: "We will do it!" over and over again. Myriad emotions overwhelmed him like waves at the sight of his people, their faces spark-ling with determination and pride, tears gleaming in the corners of their eyes as their voices rose as one. Tarkanius stood there and listened and watched, hoping they truly meant it.

Xalivar laughed several times during Tarkanius' speech. Emotion had been rife on his old friend's face, a weakness leaders could ill afford. You led with wisdom, power, assurance that you knew best. Emotion could only encourage doubts, regrets, weakness. It just proved all the more Tarkanius' failure at leading their people. He was unfit, illogical, and totally incompetent. Xalivar's people needed him. The attacks on workers were a cry for help. Even the attack Xalivar himself had arranged on the preschool wasn't necessary. The people were taking charge of their own destiny and demanding change. Xalivar loved every minute of it.

"What they demand, Tarkanius, is a return to the old ways of recognition of our superiority, our strength, and our deserved place above the Vertullians and anyone else in the Universe. You have cost us much with your foolishness. Humiliated and embarrassed our people. But the time is upon us for change, Tarkanius. Your failures have only served to remind our people how great my leadership was; how successful they were with me showing the way." Xalivar giggled as he watched the pathetic applause and chanting from the ridiculously small crowd in attendance at the High Lord Councilor's speech. "I never made a speech in the presence of under a thousand people. You speak to hundreds. What does that tell you, Tarkanius?"

Xalivar reached forward and clicked off the monitor, whirling to where his military leaders were watching. All three stood in silence, waiting. For a moment, Xalivar wondered where Obed and his fool son had run off to. "Family business," they'd claimed. Xalivar had sent spies to discover the truth of it. But they'd been gone a week already. It was too long. Their focus needed to remain here until the right time. He would be ready to deal with them if they dared to return.

Manaen had yet to report in as well. But one of Xalivar's informants had sent word of Pharah Brahma travelling on a diplomatic mission to the alien leadership on Tarkanius' behalf. The informant was travelling with him in the security detail. He had limited access to discussions, but Xalivar already knew the purpose of the mission matched his own goals. Tarkanius wanted the alien leaders on his side as well. But Tarkanius offered them only weakness. Xalivar felt sure they'd recognize where the strength lay and align themselves appropriately. They all knew how he'd respond if they didn't, and fear would keep them in line.

"Do they really believe such drivel?" he asked as he faced Generals Lucius and Pres and Admiral Dek. The military leaders shook their heads in amazement. "How could our people have fallen so far from the greatness they once knew? I ask you? What reputation and future do you want for our people?"

"A superior one, my Lord," Lucius said. "The one the gods have called us to."

"Yes! Anointed by the gods we are! And who can restore that?"

All three military leaders spoke in unison this time: "Only you, my Lord!"

Xalivar laughed. "How can so many of our people be fooled? We must reexamine our sense of values, our educational system. We cannot raise our children in such weakness and disbelief. The ignorance of it disgusts me!"

"And us as well, my Lord," Dek responded.

Xalivar smiled at them. "Your valiant service and dedication will be rewarded, my friends. I promise you. You have stood by me through so much adversity. It will not be forgotten."

"Thank you, my Lord," all three said, their eyes lowering to the floor in humility Xalivar wondered if they really felt. Men and women of such discipline rarely let emotions rule them. What were they thinking? Not that it mattered as long as they continued to obey his orders. They were a means to an end. Xalivar trusted no one. He'd learned his lesson when his own family turned against him. Trust was for fools and weak men. Xalivar Rhii was not weak, and he would never be a fool!

The door slid open and Manaen appeared, hurrying toward him.

"You're late!"

Manaen bowed his head, his red eyes fading to pink with embarrassment. "I'm sorry, my Lord. I worked as fast as I could in delivering your messages."

"And what was their response, Manaen? Did our new allies embrace their future?"

Manaen nodded. "The meeting is arranged. Some had doubts, of course, but I believe they recognized the importance of the decision and they will be there."

"Do none accept me at my word? They all insist on a meeting?"

"The Andorians and Lhamors are ready, my Lord. We join with you willingly to embrace the future you alone can provide. A few are less certain. They need reassurances."

"I can assure them their failure to align themselves will lead to their destruction."

Manaen sighed. "As did I, my Lord. I followed your instructions exactly."

Xalivar smiled. "Of course you did, Manaen. Why wouldn't you? You've served me most of your life. Haven't I always been kind to you? What reason would you have to do anything but accede to my wishes?"

"None, my Lord. Of course." Manaen bowed, eyes focused on the floor at his feet.

Xalivar watched his aide carefully. He detected nothing to alarm him. Manaen had done just as he reported. His loyalty remained intact. Xalivar took several breaths as he turned back toward the window to ponder what was coming. Andorians were weak. They had no backbone. But they would never betray him. Their years of service to his family had brought them many benefits no other species had. They couldn't afford to choose otherwise. It was a comforting thought. Xalivar rarely let kindnesses dictate his policies. Occasionally, it did serve his purposes to be merciful. The thought of it made his stomach roll. At the moment, he needed allies. Tossing them aside later would be all too easy. But for the moment, he needed them, and it appeared his preparedness throughout his reign would pay off, after all. A warm rush coursed through his veins. Loyalty had that effect on him. At least some people knew their place.

Ignoring Manaen, he turned back to the military leaders. "I'll call a meeting with the local leadership. We must find out if a delegation from Tarkanius was here."

"We've had no word of it, my Lord," Lucius said.

Xalivar brushed it off with a sweep of his arm. "You've been preoccupied with training, my dear General. But we will soon know the truth. I want armed soldiers in the meeting, standing close and ready. The leadership will know what to expect if they try to deceive me."

"I thought they didn't know we were here," Pres said.

"They don't, my dear. But the time to reveal ourselves has come. We have need of information they alone can provide. And my presence should be enough to extract it easily."

The Generals and Admiral nodded. "Fear is a great weapon, my Lord," Dek said.

Xalivar chuckled. "My favorite one, Admiral. The time is fast approaching. Increase your efforts. Train around the clock if necessary. Our soldiers will not have to wait much longer for their victory."

All three leaders quickly formed the salute with their hands. "Yes, my Lord." Then whirled on their heels in unison and marched out under Xalivar's silent scrutiny.

The Vertullian's official ceremonies for The Returning were well attended. A crowd of regular citizens joined the dignitaries at their new capital in the heart of the government center in central Iraja. Aron arrived early, hoping to catch Joram before the official activities started in order to gauge his frame of mind. Uzah had already arrived and was waiting along with the two religious leaders who would lead prayers and offer a brief message. Several low-level government people who'd been involved in the planning surrounded them.

It was fifteen minutes until the start of the ceremony when Joram finally arrived. Matheu had barely beat him and stood there chatting with Uzah and Aron as they all waited. Their wives were behind them chatting as well, and a large crowd was well in place, conversing, laughing, etc. The electricity in the air surpassed what Aron had experienced during Tarkanius' visit. Their people had never celebrated The Returning with such public fanfare since leaving Old Earth for the stars, and so, although the standard celebratory expectations were in place, everyone also anticipated something special for the occasion. Aron hoped he and the others wouldn't let them down.

As soon as Joram stepped from the air car, Aron moved to intercept him. Joram extended his hand as if he were on a campaign tour. "Aron! Good morning! Good to see you." His smile was as plastic as his enthusiasm.

"How are you feeling?" Joram's grip was firm and confident, but Aron searched his eyes trying to see if it was how he really felt.

"I'm fine, my friend. It's a special day for our people. Very exciting."

"Yes, it is. We're glad you're safe and able to celebrate with us."

The smile stayed frozen on Joram's face as he released Aron's hand, but Aron caught a flicker of sadness in his eyes. "I only wish Telanus could do the same."

With that Joram was gone, moving into the crowd of dignitaries to offer similar greetings and handshakes. Aron watched him go, sadly, as Calla joined him and they returned to their seats together. "He seems fine."

Aron sighed and nodded. "That's what worries me."

A few minutes later, the ceremonies opened with an Invocation by the pastor of the Cathedral of Iraja, a newly built, modern structure of sharp edges and spires which had quickly come to define the downtown skyline of the capital of free Vertullis. The pastor spoke of God's faithfulness, of the history of deliverance of His people from oppression—first from the Egyptians, now from the Boralians. He noted the significance of the fact that the Israelites fled and started over elsewhere, but their own people had instead befriended and worked alongside their captors to build a new, united nation and forge a new way. This was the way of love, the way of the Gospels, he said. "And it is a path which will carry us throughout our lifetimes and which requires diligence and con-stant dedication but of which course we can be very proud."

Although Aron agreed with the words, he kept glancing over and wondering what Joram might be thinking, especially after the part about the Israelites fleeing Egypt. Joram had been making statements about leading their people to the stars to make a fresh start. None of the leaders took it seriously. They all considered him to be blowing off steam, residual anger from the attack he'd suffered. But still, if the idea went public and caught fire, it could lead to disaster.

The Invocation was followed by remarks from Uzah about the security of their people and God Himself as their protector who deserved their trust even in times of uncertainty and opposition. It was quite moving considering it came from a military leader and not a pastor. This was followed by a sermon from the pastor of the planet's second Cathedral, newly built in the past three months in Vertullis' other major city, Pam-pulha. The pastor was young and nervous, but the sermon was concise and well written.

As the sermon drew to an end, Aron saw commotion near where Joram was sitting. An aide hurried up the aisle, a comm attached to his ear, and bent over from behind the row of chairs to whisper in Joram's ear. Joram frowned, looking concerned, then nodded as his eyes went to his feet. Bad news, it appeared. Aron tried to get the attention of the aide, but was ignored. He looked at Uzah, who had also seen the commotion, but the General shrugged. Then the pastor finished praying, and Joram headed for the podium to great applause.

"Good morning, fine people of God. It is good to be here among you. It is good to know my words will also be broadcast to our brethren throughout the system, for this is indeed a monumental day. The pastors and General spoke of the significance of our history—the returning of our Lord; the constant presence of God amongst us, His people. God is good!"

The people echoed back in unison: "He is good indeed!"

Joram smiled and nodded as they quieted back down. "But God's goodness is not always enough. Sometimes we have to rely on His Spirit to give us wisdom to make tough decisions in times of great difficulty. Unfortunately, this is one of those times. And the pastors' and General's goodwill is duly noted, but I believe their generosity is misplaced."

Aron glanced at Uzah, as both men tensed in their chairs, trying not to panic. *Please, God, guide His words,* Aron prayed.

Then Joram dropped the bombshell.

"I was just informed that an old, dear friend of many of ours has died from his injuries. Telanus Sarwa was hard working, loyal, a good man, a dear friend, brutally attacked by men who hated us for no reason other than our genetic origins and our religious beliefs. Sol and Telanus have been in a hospital on Legallis for almost a week now. Today, Telanus lost that battle."

A murmur rose from the crowd, a mixture of sadness, anger and confusion, as Joram watched. Aron's heart sank under the weight of sadness for the loss Tela and Davi must be feeling. He would go to them as soon as he could. Then Joram spoke again.

"The time has come to do as our forefathers, the Israelites did. They sought deliverance from God who sent a great leader, a former prince, to guide them out of Egypt to freedom. Our great prince, Davi Rhii, already helped us win that battle. But the fight is not over. We are not truly free. And the time has come to change that—to claim the freedom we believe is the right of all men and women! To pack up our families, take to the stars, and find a new home for our people; to make our own exodus. I will go. Who will join me?"

Several shouts of agreement came from the crowd and Joram raised his arms in the V of triumph. Hands raised and the crowd began to chant. "We will! We will!"

Uzah appeared ready to leap for the podium. Aron reached over and squeezed his arm, shaking his head as their eyes met. On a system-wide broadcast, they could do little except wait.

Joram reveled in the crowd's response, waving his fists in the air for several minutes before speaking again. "I have a message for you, High Lord Councilor; the same message Moses gave to Ramses. Hear me now: Let my people go!"

"Let us go!" Joram led the crowd in the new chant as the fervor seemed to catch fire until the majority had joined in. Aron, Uzah, Matheu and a few others remained silent, forcing smiles but shifting anxiously. Aron felt like a helpless animal frozen under a hunting party's spotlight. The can had been opened before the eyes of the whole world, and Aron had no idea what they could do to close it again, or if they even could.

"Let us go! Let us go! Let us go!" The words echoed around him as Aron's heart sank deeper and deeper with every passing minute.

# Chapter Eleven

The doctors and nurses moved around Telanus like ants on a picnic. Tela just stood there stunned, clasping her father's hand as they moved around her. She'd been chatting with her father moments before. He was telling her how proud he was of her and how happy he'd been to have her back, when he just stopped mid-sentence, his breathing became a rasp, and then his head collapsed on the pillow, and his chest stopped moving. Davi knew right away he was gone, but Tela refused to accept it, yelling for the doctors and nurses to do their job and save her father.

Then the doctor turned, shaking his head as his staff whisked past and out the door. "I'm sorry. We did all we could."

Davi felt as if he'd had the wind knocked out of him. Tela just sank down on the chair beside the hospital bed, head against her father's chest as she sobbed and held tightly to his cold hand. Davi caressed her back and hugged her from behind, but she pushed him away. Sol, Lura and Miri watched in silent vigil from nearby, but none of them knew what to say. Then the news alerts flashed on the monitor overhead, broadcasts of ceremonies on Vertullis and Legallis and around the system for The Returning. The fact that Telanus was returning to his God on that day didn't escape Davi. It gave the words a whole new significance. But all that was still lost on Tela.

Finally, she took a deep breath and looked up at Davi's parents. "I can't believe he's gone."

Their faces creased with pain as they nodded. "We know, dear. We're so sorry." Lura's voice cracked as tears rolled down her cheeks.

"He's been a lifelong friend," Sol added. Davi knew they'd come to think of Tela as a daughter, and he turned his eyes away from them as he fought back tears.

"I just got him back," Tela rasped, her voice almost a whisper.

"Oh, Tela, if there was something I could do..." Miri's voice cracked as she said it.

Tela stiffened, her face reddening with rage. "Well, you can't. None of you can. And no false solaces either. They murdered him in cold blood. Those bastards stole my father from me twice! And I can't forgive it. Ever."

Davi winced as blades sheared his heart with her every word. "Tela, at least we know he's at peace with our Lord."

Tela whirled, scowling at him. "Peace? You talk of peace? There can be no peace as long as men are monsters! I'm sick of the Boralians! Sick of being treated like I have no value. Sick of always having to be honorable and forgiving and kind to a people who have hated us for generations and done all they can to bring us harm, to destroy our people!"

"They've made an honest effort at peace, living side by side, Tela—"

"You grew up on the inside, the highest echelons of their society. I can understand how it would be difficult for you to accept things; to see things as they are. But I didn't, Davi. I grew up at the bottom and had to claw my way. And half of that, I had no parents to help me. No one to love me through."

Davi winced at the reminder, but he couldn't deny the truth. His life had always been much easier than that of most Vertullians.

"You have us now. We all love you." Lura stepped forward hesitantly but stopped at Tela's stare.

"You love me. And it's wonderful. And I love you. But it's not enough. I am done. Done following their orders. Done treating them like equals. Done being civilized. I hate every one of them! They are not equals! They are animals! They are criminals! And I swear to you, I'll do all I can to make them suffer as I have!"

Miri's lips pursed as she hurried over to close the door to the hallway. "Tela, I don't blame you for feeling this way. If I were in your shoes, I would, too. And I tell you, I've seen a lot that's disappointed me in my own people of late. But remember where you are. Getting arrested for treasonous threats will not bring your father back."

"Yes, Princess Miri! Forgive me, your royalness!"

Davi spun, his breaths catching in his throat as he sought to control his temper. "Don't treat her like that! She's right. She's trying to protect you."

"I don't want protection—from her or anyone else! Especially no Boralian!"

"She didn't do this!"

"Her family led the oppression of my people for generations! That's historical fact! And no matter how kind Miri has been, she can't erase that!" Davi cringed at Tela's every word. There was no point arguing. What she'd stated were facts. And even though Davi and Miri had dedicated themselves to reversing that legacy with every day they had left, they'd never be able to do enough to erase it.

Sol reached over to clasp Davi's shoulder, his eyes brimming with sympathy. "If it weren't for Miri, our people wouldn't have the freedom we have now," Sol said. "I wouldn't have my family! You wouldn't have seen your father again."

"And I'm grateful for her part in that. Really, I am. But my father's dead at their hands. And I just can't act like I don't see them for who they are any more."

Davi took deep breaths, waiting for his heart to stop beating against his ribs. "If you need us, we're here. Take the time necessary to go do what you need to. I know you don't mean all that."

Tela jumped to her feet, her fists balled as she pounded them into Davi's chest. "Don't tell me what I need! You don't give me orders in our private lives, Davi Rhii!"

"I didn't mean it like that. I thought we were partners."

Tela scoffed. "Partners? Me, your stay-at-home little missus while you go out and fight to protect, risking your life for the people who killed my father?" She sighed and frowned, her nose and mouth crinkling with disdain. "That sounds really equal. No thanks!"

Davi wanted to snap back. He'd never thought of her that way. Her piloting abilities had been part of what attracted him to her in the first place. But instead of arguing, he threw up his hands. "What do you want then? A personal war against an entire system?"

"I want my father back!" Then Tela sank to her knees in sobs as Miri and Lura hurried toward her. Sol watched from his hospital bed as Davi stepped back, knowing nothing he could say or do right now would make a difference. He hoped he was right—that she truly didn't mean what she'd just said. He couldn't bear the thought of losing her. Time would lessen her pain and make her regret her words. She had to. He needed her.

---

Manaen cringed as Xalivar entered his chamber and slammed his datapad down on the desk, then whirled around, his fists clenching at his side. His master scanned the small room, comparable to a closet in Xalivar's own chambers. It was adorned simply with only a desk, bed and chair and old military-issue crates for storage of Manaen's few belongings. A single terminal occupied the desk, allowing Manaen to be proactive in seeing to his duties and Xalivar's every need. A single reflector pad hung overhead from loose wires, casting shadows along the walls as it swung back and forth.

"I trusted you and you failed me!"

"I delivered the message as you sent it, my Lord."

Xalivar's eyes tightened as he searched Manaen's eyes for any sign of betrayal. Manaen simply relaxed and stared back. "Xanthis and Italis alone sent actual leaders. The Andorians and the Plutonians sent mere 'representatives.'"

"The Lhamors came."

"Representing themselves! And they alone accepted my offer. Do they forget who I am?"

Manaen held back a smile and shook his head. "It's not that, my Lord. But they expressed doubts." *They know exactly what you think of them. They are not the fools you assume them to be. Do you really expect to fool them with your rhetoric?*

Xalivar's scowl deepened. "About what?"

"Whether you can be trusted."

Xalivar scowled, his fists clenching and unclenching as Manaen waited for the explosion. "Trusted, you idiot?! They are in little position to doubt me! None of them have known the power or borne the responsibility I have!"

With that, Manaen knew he'd chosen the right course. He'd tolerated years of abuse. And Vibryd was right. It had to stop. He lowered his eyes in pretend humility. "Of course, my Lord, but you are no longer High Lord Councilor."

Xalivar spun, causing Manaen to step back for fear of being struck. Xalivar had never physically harmed him, but he wouldn't assume anything when his boss was in this agitated state. His master instead just stared out the window at the desert beyond. "It is *I* who needs fear trusting *them*, not them me! Without me, they will lose everything!"

"I tried to convince them, my Lord. Perhaps Tarkanius' offer came first."

"Tarkanius made an offer?" Xalivar turned back to face him. "I never heard of it."

Was Xalivar really unaware? The story dominated the nets. Did he really depend on Manaen to tell him? This could be useful. "It's been on the broadcasts today. There seems to be some confusion regarding the location, however."

Xalivar had reached the desk before Manaen finished speaking and was already turning on the terminal to one of the major nets. The announcers rambled on with speculation about the High Lord Councilor's major meeting the following week. "Xanthis? Eleni 1? Idolis? Where's it being held?"

Manaen shrugged. "I learned of it as you are, my Lord."

Xalivar cursed. "What good are informants if none of them keep me informed?" He slammed his butt down into the chair and began fiddling with the terminal on his desk, sending e-posts to various sources, Manaen assumed.

He stood still, watching Xalivar unravel. So many feared his power and unrelenting confidence. If only they could see him for the weak man he really was.

"Don't disappoint me again. Dismissed!" Xalivar's eyes never left the terminal.

Manaen wondered how long it would be before his master realized he was in the majordomo's chambers. It didn't matter. He preferred to go elsewhere when his master was in such a mood. He turned and smiled as he hurried toward the door. Betraying his master had inspired great fear. But no more. He'd done what he must. And so far, it was working.

Tarkanius sat with Simeon, Kray and Qai in his study, watching the broadcasts with growing amusement. Their plan had worked perfectly. The networks were going mad speculating about all the different locations leaked for Tarkanius' meeting with alien leaders. None had the real story, and yet their reports revealed everything to Tarkanius and his friends. Of the thirty-seven members of the Council, twelve were now under suspicion, including the several Tarkanius and Simeon had most suspected. "Elal, Hachim, Niger—they're no surprise."

Despite his prior suspicions, Tarkanius felt relief at having further proof. While Kretzu's testimony would have been sufficient at a trial, it was reassuring to know the Lord hadn't just passed blame off as revenge or other ulterior motives. Still, the joy and pride he'd experience when he'd first joined the Council were all but erased. Now his service had become just work. He wondered if it would ever be the former again?

Simeon nodded. "But a few others are. The Council will be weakened by this for decades, I fear."

"We must arrest them, for the good of the Alliance," Kray said.

Simeon and Tarkanius nodded. "Of course. And we will. But it will make us all look bad in the process." Tarkanius sighed. "Once our service was honorable, prestigious."

"It's still got the prestige," Qai said. "It's the honor that needs restoring."

"If we replace them with good people, it will all be forgotten in five years," Kray said.

"Yes. Provided the Alliance survives," Simeon added. They all exchanged worried looks and Tarkanius sank back in his chair, resting his face in his hands. Five years was forever in politics, and, with all that faced them, the burden weighed on his heart.

"Do we have enough men we can trust to execute the warrants?" Kray asked.

Tarkanius nodded. "Let's hope the corruption hasn't spread that far. The military are still sworn to serve at my command." Those officers who stayed, at least. The defections left them all tainted and suspect.

"With the rest of the Alliance torn at the seams, one has to wonder." Kray shrugged.

"I'll send Rhii, Brahma and Noa. They can be trusted." Tarkanius looked at each of them for agreement, his eyes meeting theirs. One by one they nodded. "I know of a few others as well."

"Use a mix of Boralians and Vertullians. We don't want just Vertullians on this." Simeon stared out the window as he said it. He and Tarkanius shared a sadness in all that was happening. They had tried to discuss it earlier but found it hard to explain. It was not the Alliance they'd hoped for in their youth, nor the one they'd imagined when joining the Council. And neither had confidence he knew how to fix it.

"Who first?" Qai asked.

Simeon and Tarkanius exchanged a look. Simeon clearly deferred to his friend's office. "Niger and Elal. Hachim will be so afraid, he might surrender on his own. The others can be gathered after they are secured."

Simeon's face showed resolve. "I agree. Niger and Elal are the most dangerous."

"Perhaps it would be wise to send more than three men," Qai said.

Tarkanius shook his head. "We'll allow them the dignity of a quiet arrest until they force us to change plans. We're not out to humiliate them. Publicity of the arrests will come soon enough and will harm us as much as them." The press would elevate it on their own, and Tarkanius refused to do anything to further stain the legacy of his reign.

"Might it help for one of us to accompany the officers?" Kray looked back and forth between the two leaders, but both shook their heads.

"They'll know soon enough who we are," Simeon said. "Let's not tip them off while there's risk of endangering ourselves further."

Tarkanius sighed. "It's a sad day for our people. Perhaps tonight prayers and libations would be in order." He'd been praying a lot lately, and, to his surprise, it had helped calm him and give him focus if nothing else. Were there really gods or a God up there?

"With Joram calling for an exodus, we may already be too late to repair the damage," Kray said, shaking her head.

"We have to try," Tarkanius said. "Even those who wish to enslave again recognize the Vertullians as vital members of this community. Our agricultural industry would fall apart without them. We'd have few mechanics for our star ships." The thought of it terrified him. The loss would be devastating on levels most couldn't comprehend, including Tarkanius. Just trying to imagine all the scenarios it would affect sent his mind spinning. It had to be averted at all costs. Having one-third of the human population of the entire system depart for good seemed impossible just from logistics, but gods help the Boralians if it happened somehow. His eyes met Simeon's and he saw that his friend shared his alarm.

"The ramifications are frightening for us all," Simeon agreed.

"Where could they go? It would require an enormous fleet." Qai clearly thought the idea was ridiculous.

"More importantly," Simeon said, "many lost their lives bringing us together. We cannot give up without a fight."

The others nodded. "Agreed."

"May the gods protect us and give us wisdom." Tarkanius raised both hands, palms upward, as he said it, as if in prayer. The others nodded. "Send the warrants."

Kray nodded. "I'll issue them at once in the name of the Council." She and Qai hurried off as Tarkanius and Simeon stared at each other again.

"If we are wrong about them, we cannot change course," Tarkanius said.

"Why have you any doubts? It's clear they've broken our trust." Simeon looked resolved. Tarkanius envied his confidence.

He closed his eyes and turned away again. "That doesn't lessen the heartbreak."

Neither spoke again, both lost in sadness that their years of work and dedication had now come to this.

"It's getting out of hand." Uzah shook his head as he paced the control room. "I understand his anger. A lot of people share it. But this is turning serious."

Aron nodded as Matheu watched from a desk nearby. "We can talk to him again. Maybe he's had time to cool down." His own emotions were hard enough to control. Seeing Uzah lose it, he realized how on edge they'd all become. Joram was inciting the people daily, and, with every passing hour, the effects multiplied. People protested by skipping work, boycotting Boralian businesses and goods, even pulling their children from schools or Boralian-funded community programs. All it would take is one incident of Boralians striking back to fan the embers into a full-on flame, and Aron feared the outcome.

"Cool down?! Look!" Uzah motioned to the monitor which showed the third rally in as many days, a crowd of thousands, with Joram raising his arms in triumph.

"He's always been a reasonable man. Surely he can see the difficulties his proposal creates." But the new Joram was anything but reasonable. Talking with him was like conversing with an iron wall. It went nowhere.

Matheu cleared his throat. "He's a politician. Logistics are someone else's concern. He's all about ideals."

"The best ideal I can imagine is living here in peace with the Boralians," Aron said.

"I wonder if that's even possible now," Matheu said.

The entire room grew silent as Joram appeared in the doorway, smiling, surrounded by his entourage of aides and supporters. He saw them and waved, moving across the room, shaking technicians' hands and greeting them as he passed their stations. Some looked wary, while others looked thrilled to see him. His movement would soon threaten government order more directly, Aron feared.

"Oh, great," Uzah muttered, "he brought friends."

Just watching him, Aron marveled at the transformation. Joram's selection as planetary Governor had empowered him, but since the attack and growth in number of his supporters, Joram had become a different man. His posture, even his smile and eyes had changed.

"Uzah! Aron! Matheu! How are you my friends?" Joram quickly

pumped their hands, beaming at them as he joined their circle. Matheu stepped from behind the desk to shake. "You asked to see me?" The Governor scanned their faces, each in turn.

Aron and Uzah exchanged a look, then Aron nodded. "Yes. Can we speak alone in the conference room?"

Joram shrugged. "I have nothing to hide from my team."

"Private government business. They don't have clearance." Matheu's voice was firm.

Joram sighed and nodded. Matheu led the way with Joram, Uzah and Aron following. Joram remained casual, as if he had no suspicion they were about to confront him, but Aron knew he was smarter than that. When they were inside the conference room, Matheu keyed the lock behind them, waiting as the door closed.

"What's this about?" Joram asked as they took seats around the table.

"You've created quite a movement," Matheu said.

Joram laughed. "Just like-minded people coming together around a common cause."

"And what is that cause, Joram? To destroy our people?" Uzah offered Joram a cold stare. The Governor blustered and looked surprised.

"Let's all keep our heads, please," Aron said, raising a palm to gesture for calm. "We're old friends. We know how to work together."

"This old friend is doing his best to undo all we've fought so hard for," Uzah said as he shot Aron a look.

"Undo what? Years of abuse? Suppression? Betrayal? Come now, Uzah. The Boralians have proven they can't be trusted." Joram leaned back in his chair, his eyes full of confidence.

"Do you honestly believe we can relocate one-third of all humans in this system? The number of ships alone is monstrous to consider!"

"God is on our side, Uzah. Where's your faith?"

Uzah's fist slammed the table as he stood and began pacing. "Where's yours?" Joram just held Uzah's stare, the smile locked on his face.

Aron raised a hand, drawing their attention. "Let's all take a deep breath, okay?" He felt himself tensing even as he said it. Even he was struggling to keep his emotions in check. "Faith in God doesn't mean we can just stand by and not take appropriate action."

"Exactly." Joram nodded as if he'd meant that all along.

Matheu sighed. "Bankrupting ourselves to take our people on a foolhardy quest to the stars hardly sounds like appropriate action." Even the General's own emotions were apparent now.

"You'd prefer we stay and continue to enjoy our host's abuse? Let them kill us off one by one?"

Aron took a deep breath and reminded himself this was a new Joram. The old one of polite reason had been replaced. Reasoning with a herd of Gungors might be easier. "Joram, even you can recognize the difficulties your proposal creates. You've been in leadership long enough to understand logistics."

Joram shrugged. "There are always ways, Aron." Aron and Matheu stared at him, waiting, while Uzah continued to pace. "We'll get a meeting with the High Lord Councilor and negotiate." He said it as if it were the simplest concept in the world.

"Negotiate with what?" Uzah said, whirling to meet Joram's eyes. "We lack the resources to pay for ships and fuel, let alone provisions. You're talking about a journey which could potentially last years."

"And save thousands, if not millions, of our people's lives."

"We could die of starvation, face unknown enemies, pirates. What makes you think this journey is any safer?"

"God delivered the Israelites. I believe He'll deliver us." Joram spoke with the fervor of an evangelist, not an experienced politician.

Uzah looked aghast. "Our people aren't even united around the idea. All you're doing is creating further division and increasing the security risk in the process!"

"Security's your job, Uzah. Mine is to lead the government. Let's not forget our places."

Uzah growled and began pacing again.

"We all have to work together, and always have," Aron said, his voice cracking as his own frustration showed. "Be reasonable, Joram. We're having this discussion out of concern for the best interest of our people."

"You mean to tell me you honestly believe the best interest of our people is to continue living with a people who hate us?" Joram leaned forward as his eyes met Aron's. His smile faded and his eyes looked sad. "I expected you of all people to understand, Aron. Your whole adult life you fought to free us from their tyranny."

Aron nodded. "Not to exchange tyranny for exile and foolhardy decisions."

Joram scowled and scooted back his chair. "I am not a fool."

"No, you never have been. But your emotions have gotten the best of your reason. Please. You must stop and think through the full implications here."

Joram scooted back his chair and stood. "I've heard enough."

"We're on the same side," Matheu said.

"Really? You stood there as they beat you, killing your friend, for nothing but just your presence, did you?"

"We've all lost friends to their hands over the years, Joram," Aron said.

Joram raised his hands in dismay. "And when shall we demand that it stops, Aron? When?"

The others watched him in silence. After a moment, Joram turned and marched to the door, pressing the lock and disappearing as soon as the door cracked enough to let him through.

Uzah sighed and leaned against the wall in a corner of the room.

"We need to pray for him," Aron said. "And for ourselves. We handled that badly." Aron put his face in his hands.

"It's past the point of prayer, Aron! Go talk with Tarkanius. Get him to refuse to meet with Joram." Uzah's eyes were locked on Aron.

"I'll do what I can, but in the end, I fear it's a confrontation that can't be avoided." Aron took another deep breath then scooted back from the table and headed for the door. The world was going crazy around him, spinning out of control more each day. And he'd never felt so hopeless.

The Squadron briefing room rippled with tension as Davi arrived from the officer's briefing. The pilots had split into opposing groups. Davi spotted Dru, newly called back from the Academy, with Brie, Nila, Virun and Jorek. Command had called back anyone with flight experience to aid with the extra defense.

Dru smiled and waved. "Has the world gone mad while I was gone?"

"The only ones who are mad are the ones who think we should continue being pacificist against Boralian aggression!" Jorek said, angrily.

"You're standing in a Boralian military base!" Farien growled.

"What're you gonna do, bring us up on charges, sir?" Virun almost spat the words, staring at Farien as he said them.

"I'd have every right!" Farien looked ready to charge, but Davi stepped between them and shot him a look, pleading for calm.

"We're all on the same side here," Davi said, frowning. The last thing he needed was broken morale. They had enough to handle with civilian pilots fighting each other, protestors, and increased duty hours already adding stress.

"Oh sure, take his side, Prince! We all know you both used to supervise our slavery!" Jorek yelled back.

Davi took deep breaths to control his anger as Nila punched Jorek in the arm. "Hey! That's Davi, okay? He has nothing to prove about loyalty."

Brie nodded. "He's helped all of us."

"So has Farien. He's served with us for six months." Davi's eyes panned them one at a time, offering his best stern look. "This bickering is pointless. Do you really want us to fight each other? Don't we already have enough to deal with?" The others' eyes went to the floor with embarrassment. "We're all in a tough enough spot. Let's not forget who our friends are."

"How's Tela?" Brie asked.

Davi sighed. "She's angry, heartbroken. She'll be on leave 'til all this is over."

"You can't blame her; the way those bastards murdered her father!" Jorek growled.

"We should make them all pay!" Virun added. The two looked pleased with themselves.

"Enough!" Davi stared at Jorek and Virun, taking several breaths to calm his rising anger. "I understand your anger. I even share it. But there's a time and place and this is not it!"

Both looked down at the floor.

"Is there anything we can do?" Nila looked up, her tanned face filled with grief.

Davi shook his head. "Stay rested, stay focused and stop fighting. Each of us has the right to make our own choices when the time comes. If you can't do your duty, I want your resignation immediately. Otherwise, shut up!"

"Captain!"

Davi turned to see Qajuan standing in the doorway, grinning widely. The young Xanthian's jumpsuit matched his blue skin. "I got those radios installed as requested."

Davi nodded. "Thanks. Just the two cockpits?"

Qajuan shrugged. "I can do them all if you want."

Davi waved dismissively. "No, no. It's not official. Just a little extra initiative, I thought would be helpful. Thanks for hooking it up so fast."

Qajuan chuckled. "Hey! It's my job, Captain!" Davi smiled back. Quajuan had really taken to his new duties, especially proud to be on the legitimate side of things for once. "Be safe out there!" And the Xanthian was gone. Davi had secured him a job helping the mechanics, who'd found the youth's ability to acquire hard-to-find parts quickly at fair prices came in handy, even when government requisitions were involved.

"What's he talking about? Radios?" Yao shot Davi a puzzled look.

"I had two civilian radios installed so we can monitor broadcasts and other traffic. We don't always get the latest when we're on long patrols and these days it seemed prudent to have more information."

Yao smiled. "Your cockpit and who else's?"

"Mine and Farien's. Should be enough." Davi turned to the Squad-ron. "We're on eighteen and off six for sleep cycle for the next week. That means no time off, people. So get your heads in order and get your ships prepped. We leave in three hours."

Groans filled the room. "A whole week?!" Virun shook his head.

"So much for escaping the Academy. At least they gave us time off!" Dru caught sympathetic looks from the others.

"Don't tell us the Academy's made you a pansy," Virun teased, ruffling Dru's hair.

"And Farien's still second in command, don't forget it," Davi reminded them, scanning their eyes for objections. They all nodded somberly as Farien smiled. "Dismissed."

"Who's a pansy?" Dru hurried to catch the others as they filed from the room.

As the others broke into chatter and cleared the room, Davi grabbed Farien's arm. "Take it easy. Everyone's confused and scared right now."

"I'm not the enemy!"

"I know that, and so does Yao. We've got your back. But antagonizing them won't help."

Yao patted Farien on the back. "You antagonize us enough already."

Farien rolled his eyes. "I was just trying to remind them of their duty. If a senior officer had overheard—"

Davi sighed. "I know. But you come across unfriendly."

"Unfriendly? Please. Just because I'm serious about my work..." Farien looked insulted.

Yao laughed. "You love to argue more than anyone we know, man."

"Only when I'm right." His eyes twinkled.

Davi chuckled, rolling his eyes back. "When have you ever thought you were wrong?"

"It's rare, yes. But when it happens, I apologize."

Davi and Yao slapped him on the back as they exchanged amused looks. "Just do your best to stay professional and not rile them up, ok? We have to work together no matter what's going on between our peoples."

"Do you think the Vertullians will actually leave?" Yao asked.

Davi shrugged. "It seems impossible, but people are angry. I hope the politicans can find a more sensible course."

"Want me to go knock some sense into them?" Farien scrunched his face up like a street fighter.

"Gods, no!" Yao said as he and Davi grabbed Farien's arms and yanked them back behind his back. "We're protecting society from everyone else, but who'll protect them from him?"

Farien grinned. "I was only kidding!"

Davi and Yao exchanged a look and laughed, letting him go. Farien pulled free, rubbing his arms as Davi said: "Now come with me. We have an arrest order to execute."

"An arrest order?" Yao raised an eyebrow, but Farien looked eager.

"Straight from the Palace. I'll explain on the way." Davi turned and headed for the door as his friends hurried after him.

Xalivar had kept to himself since the failed conference with alien leaders, strategizing, trying to devise a plan that would remind everyone with whom they were dealing. A plan finally came into shape the night before, his mind waking him as it came into focus. He immediately began composing the briefing he was about to deliver to his leaders. He smiled as he entered and saw Dek, Lucius and Pres sat around the table with Obed, waiting. Things were finally going to move to the next level. Xalivar would declare himself again as a power in the Borali system in a way history would long remember and no citizen would ever forget.

"Gentlemen and Lady," he nodded to them as he moved around the table to take his seat at its head. "A monumental moment is upon us. We are about to make history in a way that will change our people's destiny ...forever!" He watched them a moment as their eyes met his, calm yet determined, anxious to follow where he'd lead. Even Obed's face held anticipation. "As you know, Tarkanius has called a conference with alien leadership at which we suspect he will enlist their partnership in his plans for defense. Great effort has been made to conceal its location. But my sources have confirmed the true destination. That conference is our target. We will take out the High Lord Councilor himself and as many others as we can in the process. Cut off from leadership, the Alliance will fall into chaos, and I will move in to provide the leadership they need to reunite."

"Reports are flying in of destinations all over the system. How can your source be so certain?" Dek's questioning eyes met Xalivar's.

Xalivar smiled, raising his datapad and typing the code to send his brief to the leaders' own datapads. After a few moments, datapads beeped in unison as it arrived and Xalivar watched their faces as they started reading.

"Tertullis?" Surprise registered on Lucius' face. "Would Tarkanius risk straying so far from the safety of his military command knowing a threat exists?"

Xalivar smiled. "It's Tarkanius who's behind the false reports, no doubt. He's so confident he's got us fooled, he hasn't even bothered to worry about safety."

"It could be a trap or a decoy," Pres suggested.

Xalivar shook his head. "My source is on the security team. His loyalty to me goes back to before the slave rebellion. Both he and his father owe me their careers."

"They'll have defensive forces there," Dek said.

"And it will be all too easy to destroy them," Xalivar said. "They don't expect to be found and won't be diligently awaiting us. That gives us the element of surprise." He had it all sorted out and nothing could sway his confidence now.

"Without knowing the numbers and make up of that defense, it's impossible to prepare a plan of attack," Dek said.

*Trust, Admiral. Is your faith in me so weak?* "The plan is to take out all defensive forces and execute the High Lord Councilor and anyone else present at the conference. As the Alliance falls into disarray, we move in."

"And if the Council opposes you?" Obed asked.

Xalivar chortled. "Tarkanius is sure to invite key allies to attend the conference. Anyone remaining who dares to object will be executed." He shot Obed a look to assure his rival he truly meant anyone.

"Even if the force defending the High Lord Councilor is not significant, we'll be greatly outnumbered," Pres looked to Dek and Lucius for support.

Dek nodded.

"Tarkanius will employ worker forces for his defense, to send a message to the Vertullians," Xalivar said. "The others who remain, after those forces have been destroyed, are loyal to you and the Admiral, General. And you will command them."

"When they discover where we've disappeared to, they may not follow." Pres' doubt was starting to get on Xalivar's nerves. She'd been so strong of late. Had her former weakness returned?

"You will make them obey, General. You do know how to command your men, yes?" Xalivar stared at her, unrelenting, until she sighed and nodded, ashamed. Xalivar grinned. "Diagrams of the attack plan have been provided. Study them well and come to me with any questions or suggestions. Double the training and make sure your people are ready. Failure will not be tolerated."

The Generals and Admiral stood as their fists formed in salute. "Yes, my Lord."

Xalivar smirked as they turned and hurried for the door. He felt Obed's cold stare on the back of his neck and ignored him. Let the man grow impatient. *This is my moment!* When the door slid shut behind the military leaders, he slowly turned. "You have doubts?"

"What if it's a trap?"

"I already told you—"

"I heard, and, nonetheless, you're trusting an officer who still serves the High Lord Councilor with the safety of our army, Xalivar."

"My people are loyal! And the army is mine, Obed! Not yours! Never forget that. You may feel free to stay here and cower, if you wish."

Obed shook his head. "I will serve as commanded, my Lord."

Xalivar stared at him in silence for a moment, then: "Good. You disappeared, Obed. Were you off beating discipline into your problem-child son?"

"Bordox will obey," Obed said, his face tensing with anger.

"Then have him report to me. I want to be sure those instructions are understood this time. No more mercenary activities."

Obed looked ready to protest, but then his face relaxed. "As you wish."

Xalivar waved an arm dismissively and turned to look out the window. He heard the door slide open and footsteps as Obed departed. He was alone again. *You would betray me, old rival. I can sense it in you. But you are the one who will be betrayed.* Memories of their past conflicts flashed through his mind and he laughed at the reminder of so many victories. *No one can defeat me. This is my destiny.* The Vertullian rebellion was a fluke, a mistake. If his people had supported him, it would have been put down. They needed to see the consequences to recognize their need for Xalivar's leadership. When he was back in control, they'd be thankful and more loyal than before.

"All right, what's the plan?" Farien turned and joined Yao, looking at Davi as they rang the bell at the tower where Lord Niger kept a ground floor apartment. Amidst an elite grouping of residential high rises near the city center, the twin suns glinted off its shiny exterior, lending it a glow. "Home to the rich and mighty," it seemed to say. Today one of their number would fall.

"He's not gonna like this," Yao said.

"He should have considered that before he betrayed our people," Davi said as the door slid open to reveal a dark-skinned woman with her hair up. Her eyebrows rose in a question mark as she stared at them with concern.

"We're here to see Lord Niger," Yao said.

"My Niger's in his study and can't be disturbed right now," the woman replied, Davi searched his mind for her name—Abena, if he remembered right.

"I'm afraid he'll have to be," Davi said, extending his datapad.

Abena's expression changed to confusion. "What's this? A warrant?"

"It's from the Palace, ma'am," Yao said. "I'm afraid we really need to speak with your husband right away."

She scowled, shaking her head and stepping back inside, ripping the datapad from Davi's hand as she did. The door slid shut.

"Great! That was perfect!" Farien rolled his eyes.

"You would've done better?" Davi shot him a look.

Farien guffawed. "I always do better, Rhii. I think you've forgotten some of your diplomatic skills since you got demoted from Princehood."

Yao chuckled as Davi made a face. Then the wall beside them exploded in a shower of crumpled steel, broken glass and smoky dust. All three ducked and reached for their blasters, spinning around as their eyes panned for the cause of the blast. Six men approached up the street on Skitters, blaster rifles recharging with a whine. Davi recognized one of them as Major Valenti Broks.

"They're after me!" Davi called. Diving into a roll, he came up on his feet again; firing in the middle of the street. As soon as the blasts left his pistol, he took off running toward the corner. He caught a glimpse of the Skitters dodging to avoid his blasts and those Yao and Farien fired after him; then he was around the corner, searching the street for a place to hide. The smell of sulfur and melting metal filled the air amidst clouds of dust and debris.

"What do we do now? They outnumber us and we're sitting Gungors on foot." Yao said as they joined Davi, running up the street as fast as their feet could go. They heard lasers whining and a pole next to them exploded as a blast landed. Two more singed the sidewalk to either side of where they ran.

"Does this remind you of Xanthis?" Farien asked as Davi reached an intersection and scanned the traffic for an air taxi.

"There!" he said, pointing as a taxi rounded a bend a block down and headed in their direction.

"A taxi?" Farien asked as they followed him, running toward it.

"Yeah, it's empty. Taxi!" Davi waved his arm and jumped into the street as the tires squealed from the cab-bot's hurried efforts to bring the vehicle to a stop.

As soon as it stopped, Davi raced for the door, pulled it open as servos squealed in protest, and jumped aboard.

"Good evening, sir. Need a cab?" The cab-bot inquired.

"Yes, thank you," Davi said and ripped the cab-bot free of the wheel, disengaging the autopilot as his friends joined him.

A klaxon sounded as a computer voice scolded: "Violation! Violation!" The sound of the Skitters drowned it out as more rifle blasts landed outside.

"Where'd those guys learn how to shoot?" Farien's face crinkled with disdain.

Yao laughed. "Why are we taking a taxi? Skitters are faster."

"With cab-bots driving, yeah. I outraced Bordox, remember?" Davi accelerated as he said it, throwing his friends toward the rear seats. Recovering, they quickly strapped themselves in and slid down the seats, seeking shelter from the lasers. "Don't just relax. Lay down some cover."

"What?" Farien looked confused as Davi reached over and flicked three buttons on the dash. The side windows whined and slid down. His friends took the hint and aimed their blasters as they passed the Skitters, firing repeatedly and forcing the men to duck and dodge as Davi spun around a corner and headed onto an on-ramp for the airoad overhead.

In moments, they'd merged into heavy traffic.

"I'd rather be on patrol," Farien grumbled.

"Are you kidding?" Yao teased. "All through graduation you complained about your boring assignment. Finally, you get some action and you want a boring patrol?"

"Haven't we had our fill of action lately?" Farien said as the Skitters appeared behind them, closing fast. "Here they come!"

Davi had spotted them in the mirrors. "Keep 'em busy for me."

Yao and Farien began firing back the way they'd come, doing their best to target the Skitters and miss the civilian traffic. The Skitter riders returned fire, despite civilian vehicles and pedestrians moving between them.

"There are too many civilians," Yao said.

"Just scare 'em for now. I'm hoping it slows them down."

"It's not working," Farien said as another explosion rocked the air taxi.

Just then, two civilian air cars shook from explosions at their rear and swerved into each other. Davi cursed to himself and swerved off onto a ramp, cutting off an intracity shuttle. The driver shot them a stern look as

Davi accelerated onto the ramp, waving apologetically. They had to get out of this traffic before innocent people died.

Davi hugged the wall of the ramp and zipped past cars lined up at a flashing red signal. "Hang on!" He waited just long enough for his friends to grab on, then slid out and did a ninety-degree turn onto the tail of a large, slow-moving delivery barge. The rough jostling of the taxi was sure to leave them all bruises, but he braked just in time to avoid the barge, then glanced back and forth between the mirror and the road ahead, waiting for an opening.

The air taxi rocked with explosions again as the Skitter riders closed in and began firing their rifles. The back window exploded inward as more bolts singed the sides and top.

"This isn't working!" Farien yelled as he fired several blasts toward the Skitters over the tops of civilian cars waiting behind them.

Davi saw the civilian drivers' terrified faces in the mirror. Then the next lane was open. He accelerated and slid over, racing forward and around the delivery vehicle. He heard explosions and cursing as the Skitter riders found themselves blocked, then he ducked around the next corner, hoping to lose them.

"Well, Niger's seeming pretty guilty to me now," Farien said.

"You think?" Yao teased.

The Skitters were back on their tail in moments, firing at them from both sides as Yao and Farien ducked and then stuck their heads back up and fired back.

"You said you could outfly them, Rhii! We're about to die in here!" Farien cursed as a blast tore up the seat beside him.

Davi rounded another corner and zig-zagged the air taxi in and out of traffic toward a large freight yard with huge metal containers, lifts, and other equipment scattered around. Entering the yard, he scooted past the obstacles and ducked the air taxi in between two shipping containers.

"Maybe we can get lost in here," Yao suggested.

Davi shook his head. "The Major's been after me for a while. He won't be taking any chances."

Suddenly, an explosion flashed behind them and a chunk fell off a building back toward the street they'd entered from. Davi spotted Skitters zigzagging in and out of the obstacle course as he navigated.

"What now?" Yao asked.

Two Skitters moved to flank him, so Davi began swerving the air taxi left and right, forcing them to drop back. "Perhaps a change in tactics." Then he slammed on the brake and let the Skitters shoot past. "Pick them off!"

Farien and Yao fired at the startled riders as they peeled off to the side, but a blast from Farien's blaster damaged one of their engines. The rider limped away, smoke curling up from the back of his Skitter.

Three other riders opened fire to their rear as yet another shot out from the alley where he'd hidden and raced up alongside again. Davi swerved toward him, and they began switching positions as they dodged around other vehicles and obstacles, entering a new street from the shipping yard.

"I have an idea!" Farien called to Yao. "Duck!"

He and Yao ducked as the fourth rider dodged around another taxi and slid in next to the window just in time to pass a public transport. The rider sneered as Davi snuck a peek back at him, then Farien popped up, leaned out the window and grabbed the rider, pulling him into the taxi. The Skitter skidded out from under him as he lost control and Farien released him, letting the man fall away right in front of the public transport at full speed. His limp body fell to the pavement below.

"Gods, Farien, where'd you learn that?" Yao asked, looking at him with amazement.

Farien shrugged. "Improvising. Here they come!"

Four Skitters raised up, one carrying the rider whose Skitter Farien had disabled.

"Okay, Yao, your turn. Don't leave this all to me."

Yao scoffed, shooting Farien a look as Davi laughed. "Told you, you were having a good time."

Farien grinned.

The four riders began firing their rifles. They'd clearly changed settings because the bursts were a constant stream, raking across the roadway in front of them, tearing into everything they touched. The public transport swerved to the side, smoke rising from its engines. Two private air cars burst into flame and swerved off to wreck into vehicles on either side. A civilian on a Skitter screamed as he fell sideways and crashed into the transport. Then the blasts were raking the air taxi.

"They'll tear us apart!" Yao warned.

"Hold on and get those blasters ready!" Davi called back, then glanced in the mirror to ensure that his friends had secured themselves handholds and put the air taxi into a one-eighty turn and headed straight for the Skitters. The Skitter riders kept up a raking fire across the front of the air taxi, dodging out of the way at the last second.

As they came alongside the taxi, Yao and Farien fired dead on, sending two riders to the pavement.

"Three down!" Yao called.

Davi chuckled. "I think we're getting good at this." Davi raced around another transport and took the next corner in a sharp arc, moving through skyscrapers. Only Valenti Broks and one other rider remained.

"You have a plan, don't you?" Yao asked.

Davi nodded. "Just follow my lead." It was rough, but he was making it up as he went.

Yao hollered as a blast shot through the window and struck him in the arm. He dropped his blaster and sank down in his seat.

"You okay, Yao?" Davi called, glancing back to check on him.

"He's fine. Keep your eyes on the road!" Farien fired randomly out the back at the approaching Skitters as Davi said a prayer for his friend then slowed the air taxi.

"What are you doing?" Farien asked.

"Part of the plan," Davi said.

The Skitters raced up again, the riders firing streams from their rifles again.

"Get ready to jump," Davi called.

"Jump? Where?" Farien looked confused and startled.

"You go right, I'm going left," Davi said. "Now!" He slammed the air taxi's brakes on and locked them with a button, then drew his blaster and dove out the window, rolling and firing. Moments later, he heard Farien firing from the other side. The riders skidded to a stop, aiming their rifles as the blasts missed them. A laser beam shot out the back of the stopped air taxi which looked a total mess. It hit the Major's companion dead in the chest, causing him to fire his rifle. Major Broks jumped clear as the rifle beam tore his Skitter to bits.

Davi landed on his feet and raced toward the Major, Farien close behind. The Major struggled to raise his rifle, but a blast from Farien hit him in the arm. He moaned.

Davi stuck his blaster in the man's face. "Why me?"

"Gods curse you, Rhii!" the Major spat.

Farien slammed him in the face with the butt of his blaster, leaving blood streaming from a smashed nose. "He asked you a question."

"He killed my brother!"

"Your brother?" Davi and Farien exchanged a look. "In the Battle of Vertullis?" Davi stared at the man, trying to recognize any soldier he'd battled. Too many had been unknown pilots in distant ships though.

"In an alley on Vertullis. Executed him!"

The Sergeant?! "It was an accident. He was attacking an innocent girl."

"A dirty slave whore!" The Major's feet flew up kicking at them, forcing Farien and Davi to dodge to the side. The Major reached for his rifle again, rolling over and aiming for Davi. Davi and Farien fired at the same time, hitting the man square in the chest. His rifle fired, but the beam shot over their heads.

Then the Major fell back, rasping for breath. "You'll pay!" he gasped and fell still. Davi struggled to refill his lungs, winded, as Farien kept his blaster tight on the Major. Was he really dead? After a few minutes, they both relaxed and turned back to find Yao.

# Chapter Twelve

"Why am I here?" Hachim choked out as light from the large reflector pads overhead glistened off his skin, blinding Aron through the one-way glass. Sweat dripped off the arms of the chair as it soaked through Hachim's robe. After twenty minutes alone in the interrogation room, he looked like he'd fallen into a lake. Tarkanius and Aron shook their heads, and Aron was thankful the glass covered the odor. They watched through the one way glass as Major Zylo stopped across the table from the sweaty Lord, staring at him.

"You know why," Zylo said.

Hachim coughed. "I've done nothing wrong."

"So you always sweat this much when you're innocent?"

Hachim grabbed the towel Zylo tossed across the table at him and began wiping the exposed flesh of his face, brow, neck and arms. "It's hot in here."

"I'm perfectly comfortable." Zylo sat in the seat across from him and leaned back, watching as the Lord cleaned himself. "You're gonna need a new robe."

"What is this about? You have no right to detain me without cause!"

Zylo nodded, then slid a datapad across the table, watching as Hachim set down the towel and began to read.

"Conspiracy? Assassination?" Hachim's eyes darted up from the screen. "I had nothing to do with it."

"You knew about it."

Hachim shook his head. "If you could prove it, you'd have already arrested me." He smiled smugly.

Zylo laughed. "You're in an LSP interrogation room and you think you're not under arrest?"

Hachim's eyes darted around. "I've done nothing to warrant it."

Zylo didn't react. "The Alien Leadership Summit."

Hachim's eyes raced down the screen to finish the charges. "What about it?" Hachim slid the datapad back across the table and shot him a confused look that wasn't very convincing.

"What's the location?"

"That's classified for the Council."

"I have clearance, trust me. I'm on the security team."

Hachim hesitated, then melted under Zylo's stare. "Idolis."

Zylo shook his head. "Buzz! Wrong answer. And it was all over the news."

"So? I am not the only person privy to that." Hachim leaned back in his chair, attempting to appear bored, but Aron saw the fear in his eyes. And Zylo saw it, too.

Zylo chuckled. "Yes, you were."

Hachim looked at him again, startled. "What?"

Zylo nodded, smirking. "Each Lord was given a different location."

Hachim frowned. "A different location? They can't hold the Summit in more than one place…" His voice trailed off as the implications sank in. Zylo raised a brow as their eyes met. "Lies? A trap?"

"A security precaution. How many people did you tell?"

Hachim shook his head. "No, I'm innocent. I'm not going to tolerate this abuse." Slowly, he stood from his chair and took a step toward the door.

Zylo leapt up and shoved Hachim back into the chair. "Sit down and start answering." Hachim winced, grabbing his shoulder and looking offended at the treatment. Zylo casually returned to his chair. Aron was amazed by his performance. "Now!"

Aron looked at Tarkanius, wondering if it were time for them to join the interrogation. Tarkanius shook his head. "No. Let him suffer."

"Then their fate will be yours." Zylo shrugged and turned to casually stroll toward the door. Hachim's eyes widened.

"It was Niger's idea," Hachim began. Zylo turned back as Hachim's shoulders sank with his weight in the chair.

---

The days after Telanus' funeral were hard for everyone but, for Davi, in particular, it was a living nightmare. On his first break from the round-the-clock patrols, he'd come back to Miri's apartment to check on Tela. At least she was talking now. Before, she'd just stayed alone in a room, crying or silent. But she was civil to the others. With Davi, she became as electric as a thunderstorm.

"I understand that you're hurting. I understand you hate those men for what they did. But it's not all Boralians."

Tela spun around and slapped him hard across the face. "Don't justify them to me!"

Lura started toward Davi but, Sol held her back, shaking his head.

"It's not me, either!" Davi rubbed his cheek where it was red and tender from her attack.

"You're the one still defending them—both here and in your cockpit. Serving those monsters as an officer! I'll file my resignation this afternoon!"

Did she mean that or was it a bluff? Davi couldn't read her well anymore. "You can do that, if you wish. Throw away your military career. I still hope for a peaceful solution to be found."

"Peace?! With those monsters?! Our abusers?! Murderers!" Tela raised an arm like she meant to slap him again, but he stepped back. "I don't know who you are anymore!" She whirled and ran down the hallway toward the room again as Lura rushed to Davi, caressing his cheek.

"Are you okay?"

Davi nodded. "What's wrong with her? We used to be in love."

"You still are," Sol insisted. "Grieving does strange things to people."

Davi shook his head. "It's hard to love someone who keeps offering such abuse."

"Can you blame her for being angry?" Miri asked. Davi turned to face her. Miri looked more weary and older than Davi ever remembered seeing her, like she'd aged overnight. "I've seen a lot of things that disgusted me over the years done by my people, but now...this is the end for me. I can no longer defend them. If this is who they are, I'm ashamed to be Boralian. I can no longer respect or defend them."

"But it's not everyone, Mother! It's a few idiots on the street! The majority of Boralians are good, decent people. You know that! They supported our fight for freedom. It's a big factor in why Xalivar was overthrown!"

Miri shook her head with unusual fervor, her lips tight and thin as she raised her hands in protest. "The last few months I've seen hatred on a level I'd never imagined." She blushed a bit as she noticed Lura and Sol watching. "I'm sure your people have seen far worse, but I'd never seen it firsthand. Even when I was in prison, they treated me differently. Now there's no respect. No honor. It's unacceptable! I can't stay here with them!"

Davi groaned. Had all the women on this planet gone crazy? "What? You're leaving now too? What—joining Joram's circus? The star act—Princess Miri, Boralian convert? As if people will even accept you!"

"If they won't, I can go somewhere alone. Either way, I won't be here. Won't be a part of a people so depraved." She'd always been emotional, but the words stung. Despite his own anger at the Boralian's behavior, the change in Miri startled him.

"This is our home, Mother! For generations now! Where would we go? Where would you go?"

Miri shrugged. "There are many star systems. Many planets with human populations. The borders of our galaxy are far beyond the two suns that grace our sky, Davi."

"I've seen that, Mother. I've been to the edge of the system and back. The number of ships it would take to transport a third of the human population...the amount of supplies, food...and, speaking of food, Vertullis is the main agricultural supplier in the system...it would cause a mass crisis. Maybe starvation!" The implications sunk in even as he listed them and Davi felt flush with emotion.

"That will be Tarkanius' problem and that of the Council, Davi. The Vertullians must do what's best for them."

"We can live here in peace. I know we can." Davi looked at Lura and Sol for support. Sol didn't react but Lura nodded, hopeful. "I'm not leaving yet."

"That's your choice. It will sadden me if you choose to stay, but I know I must go." Miri said, with a firmness Davi had never heard from her.

Davi's shoulders sank as he lowered himself onto a couch. "And you two? Are you leaving also?" He looked at Lura and Sol.

"We don't know yet," Sol said. "But it'll be hard to stay."

Davi put his face in his hands. He'd never felt so defeated. Despite all the people who'd chased him and threatened his life, this was worse. His family was falling apart before his eyes, and he felt helpless to interfere. "If we leave, Xalivar has won. Do you realize that? We'd be letting him win."

"If he wants it so bad, let him have this place," Sol said, his eyes sad. "It hasn't been good to us." A moment before, Sol had claimed they were still undecided, but now he sounded convinced. Even gentle, kind Lura had a hardness on her face he'd never seen.

"We've never really known peace here," Lura agreed.

"Mother, not you, too," Davi said as his eyes met hers. "I need you."

Tears flowed from Lura's eyes as she nodded. "We need you, too, Son. But we can't force you to accompany us."

"We won't even try," Sol added.

Davi raced through the arguments in his head, searching for something convincing to make them change their minds. "Joram has no plan... limited resources. The other leaders aren't with him. It may not happen."

Sol nodded. "We're prepared for that."

"So you'll go anyway?"

Sol shrugged. "We haven't decided yet."

"It's just something we're thinking about," Lura said, looking at Miri. "And discussing."

Davi frowned, looking at Miri. "You let those two get to you, huh? Miri and Tela? I love you all, but I don't understand this!" His chest grew tight, and he needed fresh air. He stood, brushing off Lura's arm as she reached for his hand.

"Please, Davi. Don't go." Miri's eyes pleaded as he reached the door.

Davi just shook his head and pushed the button, stepping through as the door slid out of the way and marching down the hall toward the lifts. He needed to get away; needed time to think. It was all overwhelming, and he'd had no rest. He glanced at his chrono. He had a security meeting about the peace summit in less than an hour. Great! No time to rest yet. *God, please let this meeting be short!* He entered the lift and rode down to the street, hoping to at least get some Talis before the meeting started.

Xalivar watched his men assembling from a balcony high above. His face was a mask, yet inside he swelled with pride. To lead an army again—he reveled in the power. The Fist of Xalivar, he'd taken to calling them in private. Soon, they would demonstrate his might for the whole system. The has-been, deposed leader would be ruler again.

As Lucius and the other leaders finished the roll call, Xalivar turned and made his way down the stairs from the balcony to the dais, where they awaited him. The troops stood at attention, uniforms pressed and polished, not even a hair out of place. The only movement he observed from them was that of their eyes following his every motion. As he stepped onto the platform, he nodded to each of the leaders, then turned and stepped to the microphone at the front.

"Gentlemen and Ladies, our finest hour is approaching; the moment when we will together stake our claim that our people must be restored to their former greatness. I led you well for years, my family for generations. And now, once again, I will lead you to victory. We fight together for the restoration of the Alliance we hold dear. Generations of our ancestors gave their lives to defend it, to preserve it. And now we must do the same. A terrible disease has infected our populace and the leadership. They have been led astray, and like doctors, we must wipe out the virus and restore them to health. Our weapons are the medicine, their rebellion the infection. We will tear them down and sew them up again, reuniting us in the process of destroying this menace. You've already proved your honor and dedication. You've worked hard for this moment. And finally, it is here. I commend you, I thank you on behalf of future generations, and I commit you into the hands of the gods!" He smiled as he raised his hands in the V of victory. The troops erupted into cheering and applause, the Generals and Admiral joining them.

It was then Xalivar realized Obed and Bordox were missing. Where had they gone? He had ordered that everyone be there. And where was Manaen? Up to some miniscule task which could wait, as usual, no doubt. Anyone with any recognition would not miss such an important moment. Oh well. Manaen was expendable as all aliens and slaves were. Soon enough, he'd be rid of them all. Not even Manaen's usefulness would protect him when the time came.

"Get good rest, my friends," he continued as he lowered his arms. "Tomorrow we have a meeting with destiny. We must be well prepared." He smiled, panning the assembly, then turned and nodded to the leaders. As they stepped forward to dismiss their troops, Xalivar started up the stairs again. He would find Obed and Bordox and make sure he reminded them of their place in this. He didn't trust them, all the more for their recent mysterious activities. But they might still be useful. And when they weren't, they too would meet tragic accidental deaths. He thought of Miri and Xander. *I hope they send you, Nephew. It would be good to face you again and watch you die!* He chuckled as he walked, seeing Manaen at the top of the stairs.

"Have you no sense of history, Manaen? This is a great moment for all our peoples!"

Manaen bowed, eyes focused on the floor. "I'm sorry, my Lord. I was attending to the dinner you requested."

"Very well then, I hope it meets all my specifications. I want to remember this night well."

"Of course, my Lord," Manaen said as Xalivar reached the top of the stairs. There was something off about his majordomo these days, something in the eyes Xalivar couldn't quite place. He had been watching him closely but still uncovered nothing. *What is it, my old friend? Will you betray me? Have you already?* He knew that one way or another he would find out. He always did.

Pres stood next to Admiral Dek as they watched their troops break formation to return to their quarters. Dek looked so handsome in his dress uniform. It would be odd to fight others in the same colors. They'd add ribbons to the shoulders to allow them to distinguish their own people, and their fighters and ships had special transmitters to emit a beacon as well. But where face-to-face combat was required, her troops would feel as if they were fighting their own. It would be hard, but she'd done all she could to prepare them. Now she wondered if she'd prepared herself.

As the last of the soldiers filed out, Dek turned to her and nodded. "The moment has come."

She smiled. "Yes, Admiral, we go to war again together."

"You've done well, General. You should be very proud. I am very proud of you."

For a moment, Pres couldn't form the words to respond. He was proud of her? She struggled to come up with what to say. "Thank you, Admiral."

He smiled back. "I've watched you triumph over great difficulties for many years, and I want to express my admiration and gratitude for your service to us all."

She couldn't bring herself to meet his eyes. "I've only done what any loyal citizen soldier would do, Admiral."

He shook his head. "You've distinguished yourself. There is no need for modesty, among friends. It is an honor to serve with you, Pres." He turned and extended his hand.

Pres hesitated a moment, then extended her own and took his firmly, shaking it. His warm, firm grip on her hand sent shivers through her. She had to focus just to breathe and then force words out. "I'm honored to serve with you as well, Dek."

"When this is over, I hope you will finally have a chance to return to a normal life."

She did her best to hide her shock at the suggestion. "Retire?"

"Do you not want more than this, Pres? A family perhaps? A normal life?" He glanced at her with a tenderness she'd never seen from him.

She steeled herself, repressing the tears forming at the corners of her eyes, and shrugged. She hadn't ever given it much thought. In truth, she'd never found a suitable mate, not until Dek. "I am happy with my career."

He released her hand and smiled again. "Of course. But don't make the mistake I have and live your life only for the Alliance. There's more out there. You should take the opportunity to discover it."

"You don't think Xalivar will have need of us once he's restored to power?"

"Perhaps, but arrangements can always be made."

"I cannot imagine a life not in service." She stopped herself before she admitted she meant a life without him by her side. What would she do if she couldn't see him every day? Did he ever think about her the way she thought about him?

"The Alliance is not all there is for someone like you. You can make your own piece of history. You deserve it. I want that for you. It's something I never had."

*You could have it, my dear Dek...with me.* For a moment, she almost confessed; almost told him everything on her heart, but then Lucius approached. "Well, we have a dinner to attend. I believe our Lord is waiting."

Dek and Pres both nodded. "We are honored, of course," Dek said. He looked at her, offering his arm in a gentlemanly manner. Another thing he'd never done before. Maybe he did have feelings for her.

But then he started walking, pulling her gently along and the moment passed. They followed Lucius up the stairs to the balcony, where Manaen greeted them with a nod and led them inward toward Xalivar's chamber. Would she ever get a moment to express how she felt to him? Maybe she'd find one, once this was all over.

Obed and Bordox ate dinner in a small clearing just outside the compound. It was their last dinner as father and son before the fighting began and Obed said he wanted their time together to be fruitful without distractions. As they sipped Idolian wine, Obed smiled. "Bordox, I'm proud of you."

Bordox coughed, struggling to avoid spitting out his mouthful of wine. "Father?"

Obed nodded. "I know I'm hard on you. But you've distinguished yourself as a fine, dedicated officer. And I know you'll only go farther in the future."

"Me?" *Who are you and where's my real father?*

Obed frowned. "Don't act so modest, my son. We are alone here. You have as much pride as I had at your age. I see that. That's why I'm hard on you. You cannot let pride control you. You have to rise above it or it will become your downfall."

For a moment, Bordox recalled an article he'd read about scientists developing bots with human skins. Could they have cloned his father somehow?

"This is an important moment, not just for Xalivar, but for our family, Bordox. We have an opportunity at last to set things right."

"Of course, father." Bordox watched him warily. His father looked more at peace than he'd seen him in years.

Obed reached over and put a hand on Bordox's wrist. "You must control your anger and focus on our goal."

"The destruction of the Rhii family is always on my mind." Bordox swallowed another sip of wine. Starting with his insolent rival, of course.

Obed shook his head. "This is bigger than the Rhii family. Your obsession with revenge cannot interfere with what must be done."

"If Xander Rhii is there, he's mine, Father. He will not live to stand in my way again."

Obed sat his glass down and reached for some fresh bread and Gixi jam. He spread the purple paste on the brown crust with a knife and watched his son. "The time will come. But this moment is about so much more. We have the chance to finally correct the history of our family and change its future."

Bordox sighed. This was a clone or his father had lost it. "We have no support, Father. Do you honestly believe they will elect you in Xalivar's absence?"

Obed's eyes widened and Bordox could tell he was struggling with rage. "Watch your tongue with me."

"I speak only the truth. I mean no disrespect. But for my whole life, it's all you've thought about. Sometimes we have to set realistic goals; focus on things we know we can do."

Obed chuckled. "A son lecturing his father?"

"I am no fool, Father."

"You act like one!" Obed slammed the bread down on the small table, angrily.

*So much for being proud of me.* "Why? Because I dare to question you?"

"Because you fail to consider anyone but yourself!"

Bordox jumped to his feet and began pacing as his own rage swelled. His father had always treated him like a burden, brushed him aside. Yet Obed called him selfish? *You have no idea, Old Man!*

"The world does not revolve around you, Bordox!"

"Nor does it revolve around you, Obed!"

Obed's mouth dropped open at the use of his name. "How dare you use that tone with me?"

"I'm surprised you even remember my name! My whole life you've treated me like a weed to be plucked and thrown aside; like a pack you were forced to carry, instead of a blessing given you by the gods! How many times did you humiliate me? Mock me? Put me down?" Bordox fought the sudden urge to strike his father. It would be so easy to pound him into ground at this very moment.

"I told you. That was to humble you. Keep your pride under control." Obed's eyes never left his son's.

"What about your pride, Lord Obed? If I have pride, I never got it from listening to you! You treat me like nothing!"

Obed stood and faced him, brushing dirt off his legs. He remained eerily calm, despite his anger. "I have done everything I can to give you the best. I worked hard to provide your food, clothes, education. You have no appreciation!"

"Neither do you! I don't follow your orders! And I won't follow Xalivar's either! He has humiliated us enough! Starting with allowing that slave to live in the castle that should have been ours!"

"That slave was raised there against my knowledge!" Xalivar's voice boomed from the shadows, and both Bordox and Obed whirled with surprise in the direction from which it came.

Xalivar stepped forward, the light hitting his face as he smiled. "Plotting against me. That explains your failure to accept my dinner invitation. I suppose it also explains your recent absence, your secret trip to Estrela." He stood smiling as he watched their faces. "Did you really think I would not know? I have many friends, many sources. And I always knew I needed to watch you."

Obed shook a finger at Xalivar. "No. That was a business trip. I still have properties, my family's future to secure."

"If it was legitimate, why hide it from me?"

Bordox watched his father, but Obed said nothing and Bordox could see Xalivar knew the answer. Now Xalivar turned his eyes on him. "You wish my nephew dead? Fine! Kill him! But if your quest stands in the way of mine, you'll die too!" Xalivar pointed a finger in warning and waved it at Obed. "Your family has no legitimate claim to the throne. Your grandfather gambled it away to mine like it was nothing!"

"My grandfather was drunk! Yours took advantage!" Obed slammed his hands against his side in anger. It hadn't been as easy as Xalivar said. The throne couldn't be gifted in such a manner, but when the Council learned of Obed's grandfather's behavior, they deposed him and a vote awarded it to the Rhiis. Disrespect for the office and his duties, they'd said. Dishonor toward the Alliance. Bordox fumed just hearing of it. Given Xalivar's family's behavior, it was a mockery!

Xalivar laughed. "Utilizing weakness is how the strong prevail. Survival of the fittest, I believe our Old Earth ancestors labeled it. If your family is weaker, it is not the Rhiis who bear the blame!"

"We will see who's weaker!" Obed looked ready to commit violence himself now. The eerie calm of before had disappeared.

Bordox couldn't help himself. He started to laugh. Both Lords turned to glare at him. "You sound like children. It's amusing."

"You dare speak to me like that?" Xalivar's fists clenched at his side.

"Who? A deposed Lord? Thrown out by his own family? You speak of strength as if you have any. You've mocked my father all my life. And what have you done to prove yourself better? Our family's support helped make you strong! How easily you forget!" Bordox smirked, enjoying the anger his remarks prompted.

Obed stared at Bordox, and, for a moment, Bordox actually caught a glimpse of what might be real pride in his eyes.

"Leave! I want you both off this planet and out of my sight immediately! If you value your lives!" Xalivar pointed at Bordox. "And there will be no place for you in the new Borali Alliance. All your property will be claimed by the state. If I allow her, your mother may fly to meet you."

"You've not heard the end of it," Obed warned, shaking his finger again.

"Next we meet, one of us will die!" Xalivar shook a fist at them. Obed grabbed Bordox's arm before he could respond and rushed him away through a door leading back inside the compound.

The assembly took place in a park near the Iraja starport, the largest such clearing in the entire city. It had not been a park when the Boralians ruled, but the area's buildings were decimated during the fighting between the Worker's Freedom Resistance and the Alliance, and the new Vertullian government had moved quickly to relocate affected Boralian proprietors. They'd been given their choice of prime locations elsewhere and had been assisted while they settled in, while the old area had been converted for use as Iraja's largest park, a central gathering place with gazebos and an outdoor amphitheatre which was being used for the assembly. The crowd was several thousand. As word had spread of Joram's movement through broadcasts and conversations in bars and restaurants, interest had grown, and, today, Joram had promised some surprise announcements.

Miri could feel the anticipation of those around her as she waited backstage. Would they boo her as so many had in the past few months? Or would they accept what she was about to do and applaud her? The rejections by her own people still stung but not as much as the anger and bitterness of the bombing at the preschool or Telanus' death. Still, excitement filled the air around her as the crowd chattered amongst themselves. They were of many races and backgrounds, united in common belief. They looked just like so many Boralian crowds she'd faced over her lifetime. The commonalities were so evident that she couldn't fathom any longer how anyone could fail to see it. In a mixed crowd of the two peoples, it would be a challenge to tell them apart.

She watched stage hands going about their business as she scanned past them for Tela. She was out there somewhere amongst the crowd. How would she feel about Miri's presence? It was too late to ask her and too late to turn back. She hoped Tela could accept her. Miri treasured Tela's opinion more than anyone else's. Tela was like the daughter she'd never had. Had she really meant the hateful words she'd said to Miri or was it all in anger?

"All ready?" Joram asked as he appeared beside her.

She'd been so focused on the crowd, Miri hadn't heard him approach. She nodded and smiled. "Yes, of course."

He laughed, smiling and patting her forearm. "Don't be nervous. They may have bad associations with your name from the past, but you also raised our great hero and having a Boralian support our cause only lends strength to it."

"I'm just worried about Tela."

Joram's eyes searched the crowd. "Where is she? Out there? Why's she not here with you?"

"She's still dealing with her father's death. She doesn't want anyone Boralian near her. It's been most painful, as I'm sure you understand."

Joram nodded, and, for a moment, looked sad. "That anger serves us now, but the time will come to let it go and move on. She'll come around, I promise you." He grinned at her.

"I'm sorry for what they did to you."

"It was not you. I know your heart and your honor well, Miri. I do not hold you responsible." He reached over and clasped her hand, squeezing it gently with his own.

"Thank you."

He took a deep breath, releasing her hand. "But we must begin. Just relax while I introduce you." He offered a reassuring look, then headed up the stairs to the platform as the crowd's chatter turned to applause. Raising his arms in the V of victory, he greeted them with a broad smile and waved.

"Hello, my friends," Joram said and motioned for them to quiet down, then waited before continuing: "Twenty-seven years ago today, a great tragedy was perpetuated against our people, only a few miles from here. Barbaric forces from our age-old enemies, those who had long oppressed us, brutally attacked our brothers and sisters who sought to improve working conditions in a revolt against mistreatment. Let these memories serve as yet another reminder that the time has come for us to bid the Boralians 'goodbye.'" He stepped back as the lights faded and screens overhead lit up.

Miri's eyes turned toward the screen, but the images flashed through her mind instead. After all, it was she who had released these images to the world after discovering them hidden in her family's vault, concealed by her brother for over two decades. Leaking them to the media had helped bring Xalivar's downfall. The images and accompanying sound had haunted her ever since.

On the video, people yelled and screamed as lasers fired all around them. Alliance soldiers, led by Xalivar in full military uniform, mowed them down again and again in lines, bodies falling into piles in large pits dug in the earth. As the first row fell, the next stepped forward to the same position until they fell on top of the others. The numbers of slaves shown were endless. It was shocking, gruesome, unforgettable!

Miri clamped her eyes shut, trying to shut out the images, to end the suffering. She heard gasps and grumbles from the crowd as those assembled watched and became engraged. The noise rose in volume to a loud buzz by the end. Joram just stood on the stage, in the shadows, waiting. When the video finished, the lights faded back up, spotlighting him.

"Today, we are fortunate to have the woman responsible for finally ensuring that footage became public. She might have been the last one you'd have expected to release such damning evidence, but Miri Rhii is anything but predictable." The crowd mumbled at the mention of her name. "Raised in the Royal Boralian family, she risked everything because she believed we were being wronged and the time had come to set things right. The release of the Delta V evidence helped inspire a movement, even amongst Boralian citizens, in support of our freedom and greatly aided our fight. Please welcome with me, Miri Rhii."

With that he applauded and the crowd joined in, some reluctantly, as Joram turned toward Miri, motioning for her to join him on the stage. As soon as Miri stepped into the lights, the tenor of the crowd's reaction changed. She heard shouts of protest and even booing as the applause faded. Joram made jagged cutting motions beside her and the lights faded again as videos filled the screens overhead.

Miri glanced over at a stage-side monitor and saw herself surveying the banquet room where Danae had taken her to speak that horrible day. There she was being applauded, and then she spoke, her smile projecting such warmth. When was the last time she'd smiled like that?

"Good afternoon, my friends, it's so good to be here with you today and share with you about some new friends who are now part of us." On the video, she saw herself pan the crowd as she began with her speech. A few moments later, her onscreen self paused as new applause broke out around her from most of the tables. The bored onlookers toward the back remained indifferent.

Then, on the video, that deep voice came from the shadows in the back: "Not hard enough, and not long enough, I'd say."

Miri watched herself struggle to maintain her composure as her eyes sought the speaker. As the taunting continued, she saw herself glance over at Danae for reassurance, but Danae looked lost. Then Miri stepped back from the podium, her face filled with shock and sadness. The Miri on screen winced at every word, pained, and Miri relived it all over again. As her host rushed forward and Danae comforted her, the video disappeared and the lights faded up again.

Miri felt relief as Joram took to the podium again. "She has suffered on our behalf, my friends," Joram said, his voice filled with emotion. "Whatever you think of the past and her family's leadership of the Alliance, Miri Rhii has proven herself our ally and friend. And let's not forget the man she raised her son Davi to be. We all remember him as a hero in our fight for freedom. Please. Let's honor him now by hearing what she has to say."

The crowd remained silent this time as Joram watched them. After a moment, he smiled and motioned for Miri to step to the microphone. She did.

Her voice cracked as she tried to speak. Clearing her throat, she took a deep breath and tried again. "No words would be enough to tell you how sorry I am for the past; the way you were treated at the hands of my ancestors and my people. I make no excuses for that now. But know that I recognize it for the wrong that it is. And I did take action to help end it. Unfortunately, there are many who refuse to let it end. The time has come for you to seek the life you deserve in a new place. And I'm here to tell you today, that if you will let me, I'd like to come with you and start a new life for myself there, too, with my son and his family."

The crowd stared at her. She could see their uncertainty. Then a woman near the front spoke: "How do we know you don't come as a spy; to help the Boralians track us, so they can conquer us again?" Several grunted in agreement.

Miri saw a jostling in the crowd and stepped back from the microphone, fearing violence. She saw that someone was making his way to the front, then Tela appeared and came to the front of the stage. The young woman stared up at Miri for a moment, then pulled herself onto the platform and came to stand beside Miri.

"I vouch for her," Tela said.

"Who are you?" the woman hollered.

"Tela Tabansi. My father was Telanus, murdered by our oppressors in the attack on Joram in Legon." The crowd silenced, staring at her with respect and awe. "I've known this woman for eighteen months. She's been like a mother to me. She is no spy. And she's not a liar. You can trust her. Her honor is as great as that of her son. If she asks to join us, I assure you, she means what she says." Tela turned to Miri and smiled, then walked over and embraced her. Miri sniffled as tears formed in her eyes. Hugging back, they both cried for a moment, tears flowing onto each other's robes. She saw on Tela's face that she'd meant every word. It was better than an apology. They were family again and Miri knew that it would take a lot more to separate them again.

And even as they embraced, Miri felt the whole energy around her change. Glancing over Tela's shoulder, she saw a warmth in the eyes of those assembled which hadn't been there moments before. All of a sudden, she not only had their attention, but, with Tela and Joram's endorsements, she had the beginnings of respect. For the first time in months, Miri felt like there might be some place where she could belong. She squeezed Tela's hand, then wiped her tears on her sleeve and turned back toward the microphone. She had many words to say. It appeared they would listen.

Davi discovered Zylo's involvement with Tarkanius' plans at the final pre-summit leadership meeting. Zylo greeted him like they were old friends, but from the moment he saw him, Davi had a bad feeling. He'd not forgotten the tour Zylo took him on, when he'd first arrived to his station on Vertullis, nor Zylo's attitude toward the workers, or his involvement leading troops on the ground against the Worker's Freedom Resistance. Having him involved in a top secret summit so vital to restoring peace put Davi on edge, and he made a mental note to investigate. But first he had to get back to his room for a quick power nap before the next patrol.

As he exited the tunnel connecting the civilian starport with the military one, he spotted a familiar face at a terminal in the military comm center. Zylo sat alone in a cube, looking intently at the terminal as he typed. Coming so close after final discussions about the secret summit, Davi's spine tingled.

"What's the matter, Captain?"

Davi turned to see Qajuan smiling at him. "Hi, Q. Nothing. Just off to catch a nap."

Qajuan turned, following Davi's eyes to Zylo. "Old friend or old enemy? You don't look pleased to see him?"

"He's not a pilot." Davi said, turning his eyes back to Zylo.

Qajuan nodded then pulled a datapad from the pocket of his jumpsuit and walked to a terminal on the wall. He fiddled with some cables for a moment and then his fingers raced across the keypad. After a moment, he handed the datapad to Davi.

"What's this?"

Qajuan smirked. "What your friend there is seeing."

Davi shook his head, worried. "You tapped into a military comm center?"

Qajuan shrugged. "I have all kinds of skills. Do you want to know what he's doing or not?"

Davi sighed and took the datapad. The message appeared incomplete but Davi recognized the coordinates and time of the planned summit. Scanning it over, he couldn't figure out who the recipient was. "He's revealing the location of a top-secret meeting."

Qajuan shrugged, taking the datapad back. "He hasn't sent it yet. Hold on." His fingers danced across the keys again as his face took on a satisfied grin. "There."

Inside the comm center, Davi saw Zylo's face turn to frustration. He grumbled at the terminal, then slammed a fist against it before logging out and yelling at the attendant. Davi drew his blaster and stood ready.

"Going somewhere, Major?" he said as Zylo stepped into the corridor.

Zylo turned, surprised. "Rhii. Why are you pointing that at me?"

"You're under arrest. Suspicion of treason."

Zylo scoffed. "For what?"

"That little missive you just tried to send."

Zylo's face took on a confused expression, but Davi saw the fear in his eyes. "I don't know what you're talking about." Zylo tried to remain casual, but stiffened in spite of himself.

Qajuan cleared his throat and waved the datapad he'd now disconnected from the terminal on the wall. Davi and Zylo looked at him questioningly. "I transferred it here."

"Transferred what?" Zylo frowned, growing annoyed.

Davi kept his eyes locked on Zylo as he answered. "Your message. The High Lord Councilor might find it very interesting."

Zylo spun and ran. Davi spun with him, disabling the safety on his blaster as he did. Zylo stopped as he heard the hum. "It's not what you think."

Zylo turned back, looking defeated. Davi hurried toward him. "You can explain that to Tarkanius."

Zylo's shoulders sank as Davi grabbed his arm. "Thanks, Q."

Qajuan nodded, amused as Davi keyed the comm and requested an LSP air car to take them to the Palace. He hoped it wasn't too late to undo whatever damage Zylo had already done.

As soon as they arrived, Tarkanius' majordomo escorted them into the throne room.

"What's this about?" Tarkanius said, his face filled with concern as soon as he saw whom Davi was escorting. Davi quickly pulled the e-post up and handed Tarkanius the datapad. Both he and Zylo stood silently as the High Lord Councilor read the screen. His shoulders sunk and his brow creased as his eyes took in the words.

"Is this what I think it is?" Tarkanius looked shocked. Davi nodded. "Can you explain this, Major?" Tarkanius turned to Zylo.

Zylo shrugged, cool and relaxed. "I was sending information to one of the men on the security team."

"The time and coordinates? Wouldn't he already know?" Tarkanius stared at Zylo, but the Major refused to meet his eyes.

Tarkanius looked at Davi. "Who's the recipient?"

Davi shook his head. "I haven't traced it yet sir."

Tarkanius turned back to Zylo, frowning. Davi saw his eyes darken with emotion. Tarkanius motioned to Davi. "Your blaster, Captain."

"Sir?" Davi looked at him. Was Tarkanius asking him to draw?

Tarkanius wiggled his fingers. "Give me your blaster, please, so I can execute the Major for treason."

Davi drew the blaster, choking back a laugh as he handed it to the High Lord Councilor. Zylo leaned back in his chair, curious but still calm.

"I'm tired of people suggesting I'm weak. Perhaps this will change their minds." Tarkanius pointed the blaster at Zylo as the Major's eyes widened in surprise.

"My Lord, this is a misunderstanding—"

"The misunderstanding was my notion that you could be trusted, Major," Tarkanius said, his voice full of anger. "Shall I tell your wife the truth?" His intensity surprised Davi.

Zylo scoffed. "You won't shoot me."

Tarkanius swung around like a lightning bolt and slammed the blaster up under Zylo's chin, knocking his head back. Zylo looked as shocked as Davi was. Then Tarkanius shoved the blaster hard against Zylo's forehead, holding him in place. "Try me."

Zylo wobbled as his legs failed him, and he toppled off the chair to his knees. "Please, my Lord..."

"I need a better answer," Tarkanius said as he stiffened his arm and held the blaster to Zylo's forehead. "Lord Hachim has been effusive in providing information. You can join him and earn leniency, or I can find out what it's like to kill."

Zylo remained silent. Tarkanius shoved the blaster harder against his head, leaving a mark. As he did, his eyes met Davi's. For a moment, Davi thought he might have to interfere, but then the High Lord Councilor winked. Davi saw Tarkanius' majordomo's shocked expression and coughed to stifle a smile.

Then Zylo began filling them in on Xalivar's plans.

Miri arrived home from the rally, feeling exhilarated. After Tela's endorsement, the Vertullians had been rapt at her every word, applauding her like one of their own. Several rushed to greet and shake her hand afterwards. For the first time in a long while, Miri felt like she mattered. Knowing Tela still respected her just made it better.

A light flashed on her living room terminal. Message waiting. After pouring herself a cup of Talis, she sank, exhausted, into a chair beside the terminal and logged on.

To: MRhii@Federal.emp
From: Unknown

My dearest sister,

My long-awaited reunion with dear nephew Davi appears imminent. As you can imagine, I await it with bated breath. I only wish you could be there to join us. Perhaps our reunion will come at his funeral. Something to look forward to, no doubt!

Your loving brother,
Xalivar

Miri's throat tightened as her elation turned to fear. Davi was a strong warrior but for Xalivar to be so confident, she knew her brother had a plan. She had to find Davi and convince him not to go. She couldn't bear to lose him or anyone else at the hands of Xalivar or his ilk. It wasn't their fight anymore. Why couldn't Davi see that? Joram had convinced her: an exodus was the only option. The Vertullians had no chance but to cut ties and start over somewhere else. She had to convince Davi some-how. Sipping her Talis, she typed in commands for a comm line to his quarters.

# Chapter Thirteen

"What's going on?" Davi asked, confused as he and Farien forced their way through the crowd at the military hangar. Crews and mech-bots scrambled to prepare the fighters for launch as people circled around them waving signs and chanting. "Not our fight!" one sign said. "You are free!" said another.

Yao appeared beside them in a brand-new blue flight suit, carrying his helmet. "Protestors. Vertullians. Guess who's in charge."

Farien pushed through the protestors with a shove, drawing angry stares. Davi and Yao followed, hurrying to catch up. Before Davi could say anything, they turned a corner and spotted Miri and Tela at the head of the column. As soon as they spotted him, the women smiled and rushed to meet him.

"Davi!"

He fought the urge to hide. "What are you doing here?" He did his best to look pleased to see them but inside he felt anger rising.

"You don't have to go. It's not our fight." Tela put a hand on his arm.

*Not our fight? Who are you? What happened to make you forget all we fought for?* He resisted the urge to shove her hand away. "I have a duty to all citizens," Davi said.

"They're not your people anymore," she said.

"They'll always be my people." His eyes met hers, and he saw a flash of anger at his words. He'd grown up amongst the Boralians. They'd been good to him much of his life. He'd always have friends and family amongst them. How could she expect him to just turn his back and throw that away?

"Don't go, Davi," Miri added. "Don't risk your life for people who wouldn't risk theirs for you." Both women's eyes pleaded with him as he brushed off their hands and moved past.

Hearing that from Miri stung. Unlike him, she'd always be Boralian by birth. She was one of the reasons he felt so attached to them. "They've risked their lives for me dozens of times. Many are my friends. I made an oath, and I'll honor it."

"Don't you understand?" Tela pushed him gently, then stepped into his path. "They don't consider us their equals. They've murdered so many of our people. We have to stand up to them." There was something in her eyes, a haunted look that diminished their usual sparkle, almost like looking at a stranger.

"If we don't stop Xalivar a lot of innocent people who had nothing to do with the murders will be hurt." Davi gently pushed past her.

"Don't do this, Davi. Please." Miri begged. "If we lose you—"

"Mother, you of all people should understand why I have to go," Davi turned back as Miri shook her head, tears rolling down her cheek. "He's done you enough harm. Don't let him destroy you."

"So you've already decided he's going to win?" Davi turned to where Farien, Yao and the rest of his Squadron stood waiting, helmets under their arms. "Pilots to your fighters. We have a mission to complete." They nodded and pushed through the protestors, hurrying for their crafts.

"So we don't matter then?" Tela's arms went to her hips as she frowned at him in anger.

He cursed inwardly, wishing their emotions had no effect on him. But his heartbeat boomed in his ears. Why couldn't they listen to reason? "I care about you both very much. You're why I'm doing this."

Tela shook her head. "Ignoring us is not showing us you care."

Davi sighed and gave them each a quick kiss on the cheek. "You're not yourselves right now. I'll be back and we can talk then."

"Don't bother!" Tela whirled and stormed off as Miri stared at him sadly.

As Davi climbed the ladder to his cockpit, he glanced back at them and smiled. "I love you, Mother. Take care of her for a bit."

Miri just stepped back toward her group then pumped a fist in the air. "It's not your fight! It's not your fight!" They began chanting with her as he turned his attention back to his ship and slipped inside.

In moments, the fighters launched.

Xalivar watched from the bridge of his command ship, *Tarragon*, General Lucius at his side, as the armada formed up around them. It was a ragtag group, for sure, not the usual sight one would expect from a Boralian armada, but then, they'd put it together piecemeal, and strength was all that mattered. The combined firepower would be more than enough. Just a few hours. He could already taste the victory. The whole bridge smelled of it. Oh, how Tarkanius would be surprised. He chuckled at the thought. This was just the beginning; still, a day long awaited had arrived.

Admiral Dek issued orders as technicians chattered around them. Consoles beeped and lights flashed. Data flashed across the screens of monitors and scanners. The various ships' captains acknowledged their orders as Dek coordinated everything with ease. Pres and her men were aboard several ships prepared to land on the planet's surface as soon as they arrived at Tertullis.

Xalivar hadn't gone to war in decades. Adrenaline rushed through his veins as he took deep breaths and smiled. He looked around him. Manaen waited a few feet away from his Lord, ready at a moment's notice. Xalivar remembered standing beside his father and grandfather on the bridge of an old battleship as they conquered the slaves; the pride he'd felt at being with them. How proud they'd be seeing him today! The family honor would soon be restored. "It's a beautiful day for a battle, isn't it, Lucius?" Xalivar asked.

Lucius nodded somberly. Always so serious when it came to his duty. "Yes, my Lord."

Dek strolled toward them, nodding as he stopped a few feet away. "All ships are in position and awaiting your orders, my Lord."

Xalivar cleared his throat as Dek motioned to a comm tech nearby. The tech hit a button and a panel lit up, indicating the fleet channel was open. "My friends, thank you for joining me in this moment of triumph. Victory will soon be ours. You have shown great honor in your loyalty. And I honor you in my thoughts as we go forward into battle. Fight well. Our people's future depends on it. May the gods be with you."

He glanced around again as all those on the bridge watched him closely. Slowly, he raised his fist over his head. "Fleet, away!"

One by one the ships launched into FTL on a path to Tertullis. Xalivar's heart raced and he cackled with delight.

"Lord Niger, in the name of the High Lord Councilor and the Council of

Lords, you are hereby placed under arrest for treason and murder," Simeon continued, reading the charges.

Lord Simeon himself led the LSP in the arrests. The first took place at a residential tower where Niger kept an apartment. He knew Davi and his friends had been attacked there earlier and took extra security in case. But Niger answered the door alone and, despite his wife's protests, was taken into custody with little fuss. To Simeon, it seemed almost like he'd been resigned to it. His name had already been leaked to the news as a suspect. And the man looked tired and defeated. Simeon found himself a little disappointed.

Lord Elul drew a blaster as soon as Simeon and the LSP officers entered the restaurant where he was dining.

"Lord Elul, you must stop this right now. We're here under the full authority of the Council and the Palace." Simeon's eyes met Elul's in a cold stare.

For a moment, Simeon feared innocent civilians might get caught in the crossfire, but then restaurant staffers interfered—two men tackling Elul from behind and pinning his yelling form to the floor as the LSP men moved in and restrained him. Elul cursed, his voice booming, but at the moment he resembled more of a bratty child.

"You can't do this! I've done nothing! You have no proof!"

"We have sworn statements," Simeon answered as he bent to retrieve the fallen blaster.

Altogether, it was quite humiliating, made all the more so when some of the innocent civilians snapped photos which later turned up on the news. Simeon chuckled at that. Elul's pride would be permanently scarred, but given his likely sentence of life in prison for treason, it wouldn't matter much.

Simeon was relieved when it was over. LSP squads all over the planet were making similar arrests. He'd made it a point to be present at the arrests of the two Lords lest they try any political power moves with the LSP. Simeon witnessed both arrests in their entirety, so there could be no false claims or charges made by either suspect.

As he arrived back at his apartment, he wondered how Kray and Tarkanius were faring with their own responsibilities in the mission. Attack was imminent. He hoped their forces would prevail. If not, perhaps he would be the one to wind up with the life sentence. Ironically, he already felt like he had one.

Xalivar returned to the *Tarragon's* bridge after a brief meditation period to watch his fleet's arrival at Tertullis. He'd hardly relaxed at all, despite his best intentions, because his mind raced with the anticipation of his return to power. Images of the throne room and his triumphant return to the Palace filled his head. A glorious restoration of the honor of the Boralian Alliance would follow. *Ah, the satisfaction which shall be mine in avenging myself!* The thought of his enemies' suffering made him laugh. They should have known better than to oppose someone of his caliber. Men like Xalivar didn't lose.

Admiral Dek approached, interrupting Xalivar's thoughts. "My Lord, we're arriving at the planet now."

Xalivar smiled and nodded as they both turned and watched the star field normalize as the ships slipped out of FTL one by one and into formation again.

"Jamming on. Shields on full," Dek ordered as techs rushed to comply.

Tertullis glowed with a purple hue as they approached, and Xalivar saw a familiar gray shape. The High Lord Councilor's flagship, *Alcazar*, orbited the planet surrounded by her usual escort—two Borali destroyers, three squadrons of fighters, and two light cruisers. There was no sign of reinforcements, no indication that they expected anything but a routine visit. The Boralians still thought their conference was secret. Xalivar chuckled. He'd already won.

As he watched, Admiral Dek and General Lucius issued orders and the fleet dispersed into attack formations; the ships hauling ground troops slipping off toward the planet's surface. The Boralian ships began realigning as fighters abandoned the fleet and hurried to intercept Xalivar's force.

"Shall we offer them a chance to surrender, my Lord?" Lucius asked from his station between the scanners and comm stations.

Xalivar chuckled. "We'll show them the same mercy they showed me, General. Launch the attack."

"All ships, fire at will," Dek announced over the fleet comm channel.

Fighters burst from their mother ships, hurrying to intercept their incoming enemy counterparts. The larger ships began laying down a barrage of fire. Three VS28s exploded within a few seconds as the lasers found their marks. In moments, they'd be in range of the larger Boralian ships.

Xalivar turned to a panel on the rail nearby and punched a button. General Pres appeared on a small monitor. "Yes, my Lord."

"General, our victory is at hand. Securing the location is your priority. Except for the High Lord Councilor, eliminate anyone who gets in your way."

"By your command."

Xalivar chuckled as Pres turned and the screen went blank. Who'd have thought he'd be relying on a woman to command ground forces in his lifetime. Pres was capable. He'd never have allowed her to take command if she weren't, but still, Xalivar had instructed Lucius to stay in constant contact with her and ensure nothing went wrong. Women were weak. His own sister had demonstrated it clearly. They were too emotional to be trusted fully in such situations. But Pres had more than proven herself so far, and he expected she'd do well. If not, her time of service would be over along with her life. He could almost smell the adrenaline as men and women raced around him, performing their duties. Those seated sat on the edge of their seats, their eyes locked to screens and consoles, their brows furrowed with extreme concentration.

A blaring klaxon rose above the din. Xalivar whirled and looked at Dek and Lucius for answers.

"Incoming ships, my Lord," Dek offered as he stared puzzled at the scanners. He glanced over at a nearby tech.

"Boralian, Admiral. Four light cruisers, five destroyers and a flagship just slipped out of FTL behind us," the tech said with alarm as he punched commands into his console.

"What?! They had no idea we were coming!" Xalivar scowled at his commanders, demanding answers with his glare, but they were too busy assessing the situation to reply.

Davi shifted in his seat and loosened the strap on his helmet. His head was already starting to sweat. His Squadron had circled the High Lord Councilor's escort for an hour by the time Xalivar's armada appeared. Immediately, he issued the order and the fighter groups sped toward the incoming craft. "Shields on full. Battle ready. Fire at will."

"They're not even reacting," Virun remarked.

"They don't know what we have planned for them," Jorek said with a laugh.

"Focus," Farien said, all business. "There's still enough of them to do real damage."

"Oh yes, master Boralian," Jorek replied, voice dripping venom.

"That'll be enough! We're on the same side here and we all have to work together!" Davi took a deep breath, lowering his voice as he realized he'd been yelling into the comm. Tensions remained rife and he'd been struggling to keep his Squadron unified and morale high.

"This is our chance to take out all that resentment on Xalivar. He caused all this." Yao was one of the few who'd stayed above the tension. The Squadron members enjoyed his company, especially his tales about Farien and Davi in their wild younger days. Yao seemed to enjoy the attention. And since he and Dru were add-ons, he'd insisted on them working together as wingmen, despite Davi's reservations. Neither had spent much time in a fighter cockpit in the past year. Still, both were skilled pilots and Davi needed them. With the tensions already raised, he was reluctant to rattle things further by breaking up existing teams, so he acquiesced.

Dru laughed. "I wish he'd come out in a fighter and give us a fair shot."

Davi heard the smile in Nila's voice. "Xalivar's always preferred to let others do his dirty work."

Davi's scanner beeped and he saw blips appear behind the oncoming armada. Help had arrived. He wished he could see the look on Xalivar's face now.

Aron stepped off the freighter *Cordelia* with the rest of the High Lord Councilor's entourage at the starport on Idolis, where the alien leadership waited to meet with them. Idolis was a bold choice. Known for their loyalty and dedication to serving others, many Idolians served high officials, including Xalivar, so having a meeting on their planet would be public knowledge quickly. However, with the precautions of no advanced notice of the meeting's purpose and Tarkanius' surreptitious arrival on a freighter, the High Lord Councilor still hoped to keep things low key as long as possible.

Tarkanius strode confidently into the large hangar the advance LSP team had cleared for their meeting and greeted each leader in turn. Pharah walked beside him as interpreter, as much for appearances' sake as practicality. It had been Pharah's idea, since he'd been the ambassador to recruit leaders for the conference. Aron was grateful to have such a smart, kind man helping them.

The humid hangar smelled like the depot on Vertullis where he and

Sol used to work—sweat mixed with chemicals and industrial cleaners. Effort had been made to make it presentable, and Aron knew it looked nothing like this on a normal working day. Any starships and mech-bots had been cleared out, along with most of the equipment and supplies. It was an amazing feat for a few hours' notice, but the LSP men were that good. As a result, the site lent the conference a more official, pristine air.

The building vibrated under foot, one of the small tremors Idolis was known for this time of year, influence from Charlis as the smaller sun was at its nearest. A sweet scent filled his nostrils as Idolian servants arrived with pitchers of water, juice, Talis and other beverages and a selection of sweet rolls, pastries, cookies and other delights. They distributed these evenly around the table where the leaders sat, serving any who asked, then quietly slipped away.

Tarkanius raised a hand, and the chatter died down. "Friends, welcome. It's good to be with you." He smiled warmly. The aliens smiled back, at least their approximations of it. Despite being on the Council, Aron had yet to venture so far outside the radius of the inner system. The only aliens he'd encountered were those who came to official functions or served the government. Amongst the twenty or so in attendance, there were a few races represented whom he had never seen outside of datapad histories. His senses delighted in it. *Ah, the diversity of your creation, Father. How wonderful you are!*

Various aides sat in a ring a few feet behind them, circling the table, ready at a moment's notice to assist those they were there to serve. Takanius motioned and his majordomo punched codes into a datapad. Datapads around the table beeped as the leaders each received a copy.

"Friends, today will be a great day in the history of the Boralis system, I assure you. I'm here to tell you that the time has come for us to become one people—joint citizens—with joint determination reflecting our joint interests. I'm here to invite you to participate fully in government. And to assure you that we will work with you to create a unity few of us would have every dreamed possible before."

Aron watched the leaders' faces as they took in Aron's words, some listening through electronic translators; others relying on aides. When the High Lord Councilor finished, most of them looked delighted, at least in their eyes. Would they accept his sincerity after years of being ignored, mistreated, used by other High Lord Councilors? Aron felt a burst of hope rising within. For the first time, it looked possible.

Uzah coordinated ground troops from his armored Floater as the battle unfolded, in constant communication via monitor with Lord Kray and General Matheu on the bridge of the Borali flagship *Reliance*. She had arrived just after Xalivar with a fleet of ships and quickly engaged the enemy from behind, but Uzah and his troops had been waiting on the surface since before Xalivar's armada arrived. General Grif and his Boralian forces accompanied the High Lord Councilor to his rendezvous, leav-ing Uzah, Matheu and Kray to coordinate this ambush.

Platoons of men surrounded the starport in Cree, the Tertullian's industrial port, the leaked location of Tarkanius' summit. When the enemy landed outside the city and moved in, his men had attacked from their positions as soon as they'd come in range. Explosions dotted the horizon now, punctuated by clouds of smoke and the whirr of lasers. He'd already spotted General Pres, who was leading the attack. Uzah had always admired her intelligence and dedication to duty. It was unfortunate to have to face off against her now. Her soldiers seemed highly skilled and numerous. Uzah wished he'd brought a dozen additional platoons. But if Matheu and the air forces were successful, he wouldn't need them. He just had to hold out long enough.

"Can you hold your position?" Lord Kray asked.

"For a little while, yes," Uzah replied. "They're strong and they outnumber us, but if you are successful, it won't matter."

"We'll be successful," Kray replied. "All else depends on it." She and Uzah glanced toward Matheu, who remained his stoic self, his face giving away nothing.

He offered a curt nod. "We took them by surprise. I'm expecting reinforcements soon. They should be enough to assure victory. He had greater numbers than any of us anticipated."

"Perhaps we all relied too much on military discipline and our own sense of loyalty," Kray said.

Uzah sighed. "Clearly times are changing and so must we."

"If enemies were predictable, there'd be no wars," Matheu answered. "Military cannot function without discipline and loyalty. Fortunately, enough still believe in those things to join our cause."

Explosions rocked the Floater and Uzah grabbed a rail to hang on as men jostled around him. "I have incoming fire. I'll be in touch again." As the screen went blank, he glanced back to the battle and spotted Pres' troops with artillery on the rooftops. He opened a comm channel to his field commanders: "Get men to take out those artillery banks. We need to hold the high ground at all costs!"

After the WFR's fight, Uzah had hoped he'd never have to face battle again. He'd had enough of it in his lifetime, including the disastrous Delta V incident. *War is a game at which no one wins.* Already, sulfur mixed with human sweat tinged the air. He softly offered a prayer and then called out orders changing the coordinates of his column to avoid the artillery.

General Pres appeared poised and confident in the monitor even as explosions rocked her Floater and flashed in bright yellow and orange smoke behind her. Xalivar, Dek and Lucius convened with her from *Taragon's* bridge, keeping up to date on the battle.

"Have you made it to the conference location?" Xalivar asked, looking for any sign of weakness. Their success depended on her troops on the ground.

"We're getting closer, but their resistance is concentrated in the surrounding area, so we're still fighting our way through," she said, eyes confident.

"Your men outnumber theirs and our ships outgun them," Dek said. "It's a matter of time."

The *Alcazar* and its accompanying cruisers were lightly armed. They'd been designed to evade attack with great speed, not enter into battle. So that left only the eight destroyers, four light cruisers and a flagship against Xalivar's twenty ships plus fighters. In sheer firepower, he'd already won. "Indeed. A great day we can savor." Xalivar smiled. "I can't wait to see Tarkanius in his defeat. Prepare my shuttle for the surface."

"My Lord, it's not safe," Lucius protested. "It would be better to wait until we've secured the planet."

Xalivar whirled to face him. "I decide when and where I go, General. Prepare my shuttle. It's obvious we're going to triumph and I want to savor the look on Tarkanius' face." He relished it even as he said it. Once Dek moved the *Tarragon* closer to the planet, the shuttle could hide behind its mass. The fighters would be too preoccupied with each other to respond in time.

"We'll take him alive and hold him for you, my Lord," Pres said.

"I plan to be there to watch," Xalivar said. He motioned, and Dek hurried off to issue the orders for the shuttle preparations.

"Shall I accompany you, my Lord," Lucius asked.

Xalivar shook his head. "You're needed here to wrap things up securely. You have my complete trust. I know you won't disappoint me."

Xalivar nodded toward the monitor, and Pres then turned away to converse with Lucius.

"He's taking an awful risk," Pres said.

Lucius sighed. "It's our job to protect him, and we shall do what must be done."

Davi raced his VS28 in between and back out of the mass of fighting ships. Explosions jostled him in his seat and sweat soaked his flight suit. The past ninety minutes had been some of the most intense fighting he'd ever seen. Pilots were being shot down left and right. So far, he hadn't lost anyone from his Squadron, but, with the firepower they were up against, he feared that wouldn't last. Brie kept tight on his wing, with Nila and Farien, Virun and Jorek, Yao and Dru and two other pairs working as coordinated teams in their attacks.

"We can't even break free to attack the larger ships," Brie groused. "The air's too thick with fighters."

The larger ships had moved into close contact, Borali and rebels fighting side by side against each other. "They'll have to fend for themselves for now," Davi replied. "We have to concentrate on staying alive."

"So many lost already," Nila said, her voice soft.

He hoped his people could hold their emotions in check. As experienced as they were, the losses were devastating. Another Squadron had lost half its members. At the present rate, Davi knew they couldn't hold out for long.

"Are we actually losing this?" Virun sounded dismayed. "We need those reinforcements."

Lasers exploded in a blinding flash of oranges and reds outside his blastshield. Davi spun his ship into a dive as he keyed the comm. "The General sent the call. They'll be here." He glanced at his scanner to see Brie diving alongside him. Both spun in an arc and came back around straight at the enemy ships, firing a barrage of blasts straight at them as they came in range. Brie's blasts decimated a fighter's wings and sent it spinning off into space. Davi's shot out another's engine and it limped hurriedly away to safety.

Davi switched off the Squadron channel and sent a call to *Reliance*. Lord Kray and General Matheu appeared on the screen. "We need some help out here."

Kray nodded. "Hang in there, Captain. More ships are coming."

"We need to eliminate those fighters, so you can help Uzah on the surface," Matheu said.

"We're losing men like Gungors at a shooting range," Davi said, gritting his teeth as he fired at another enemy fighter passing into range. "Uzah will have to fend for himself a while longer."

Matheu nodded. "He's holding out for now."

Stoic even in battle, Davi envied the General for once. He spun his ship again to evade an enemy fighter attempting to get on his tail. "Can your ships do anything to help with these fighters?" He saw Brie shoot up from underneath and blast the enemy's underside, startling the pilot, who dove up and away.

"We fire on them whenever they come in range," Matheu said, eyes dropping to check a monitor as he spoke. "But they're as preoccupied with you as you are with them for the moment."

"Perhaps you can distract them." Davi glanced over as Brie slid up alongside and gave him a thumbs up and a big grin.

Matheu nodded. "We'll see what we can do, but mines and torpedoes would damage as many of your ships as theirs. Do your best, Captain."

"And be careful," Kray added. Then the screen went blank.

Davi sighed, switching back to the Squadron channel as another explosion flashed off to his right. "We're on our own a while longer. Use guerilla tactics if you have to. Just don't get shot."

"I think we're all on the same page on that one," Dru said with a laugh.

"Good to have you back with us, Dru," Nila said.

"I wouldn't have missed this for anything." He let off a rebel yell over the comm. Davi cringed as he turned down the volume then lined up another enemy fighter in his sights and fired.

Miri circled in front of Iraja's Starport with the other protestors as Joram stood at the center, cheering them on. Many carried signs bearing phrases like: "Let my people go," "We quit," "Not our fight," and "We're Free." Joram wanted those Vertullians still cooperating with the Alliance to see that their people didn't support their dedication to the oppressors. The location was perfect, just outside the military hangars near the depot where Sol and Aron had worked for decades before Davi was born. The protestors were a hodgepodge of men, women and youths of all ages, shapes and sizes. They were dressed from casual to formal, some having come directly from work or on a lunch break. If Joram had his wish, they would have quit their jobs to join the movement full time, but people had to eat and not everyone had the same resources.

"Let us go! Let us go!" The chant continued like a mantra around her, a cacophony of voices, who'd been saying it so long it had become a mishmash rather than a unified call.

Miri saw Tela across the circle with her placard reading "Not Our Fight." They'd had no news of the battle, despite Miri's regular checks of her datapad. Tarkanius had enforced a news silence to protect the secrecy of his ruse. Still, she knew someone was getting reports. If she could sneak away long enough, she might be able to find a friend in the military and get the status. She said a silent prayer to the gods to keep Davi safe.

A cold wind tousled her hair. A mass of clouds had settled overhead, only adding to her somber move. The planet was moving into fall now and with the changing colors of the foliage came changing weather. It wasn't an ideal day for a protest. Joram didn't even seem to have noticed.

As she turned to circle back to the other side, following the woman ahead of her, Miri spotted two familiar faces approaching. Lura waved as she and Sol stopped outside the line. They stared at Joram, who hadn't noticed them yet. Miri waved back, questioning them with her eyes. Both looked tired and worried. Miri made a decision and slid out of line, moving toward them.

Lura embraced her as she drew near. "Miri! We're worried about Davi. There's no news."

Miri nodded. "I haven't gotten any either. There's a blackout at Tarkanius' orders." She turned to hug Sol.

"We thought maybe Joram could help," Sol said, nodding toward the marchers as he hugged her back.

Miri glanced over at the protestors. Joram was patting people on the back and offering words of encouragement. A man slipped through the line and approached the Governor—some kind of messenger. She'd seen him cross the lines several times that morning. From his business attire, close-cropped blonde hair and tanned skin, Miri assumed he must be one of Joram's aides. The two men conversed silently a moment as Joram scanned a datapad the messenger handed to him. Then Joram smiled, nodded, and the messenger hurried away again. As he did, Joram noticed Miri, Sol and Lura. Smiling, he stepped through the line and hurried toward them.

"Sol! Lura! So glad you've finally decided to join us." He shook their hands with fervor, smiling. "It's a great day for our people."

Sol and Lura nodded, not sharing his elation, but Joram didn't even notice. "We came hoping you could help us, Joram." Sol's eyes met the Governor's.

"I'm helping all of us by leading this movement." Joram's jolliness didn't miss a beat.

"We've heard nothing on the fighting," Lura burst out. "Just a little news. Surely with your connections—"

"It's not our fight." Joram waved dismissively. "We serve our oppressors no more."

"Our own people are fighting with them in this," Sol said. "If Xalivar wins, it will mean great danger for us."

"Which is why we must leave and make our home elsewhere," Joram said, still unsympathetic to their concerns.

"Please, Joram, we've known you so long," Lura pleaded, placing a hand on Joram's arm. "It's our son out there!"

His eyes glowed with fervor. "A grown man who made his choice. What will yours be?" Despite her agreement, Miri wanted to slap him.

The messenger returned and motioned to Joram. "Excuse me," Joram said when he saw him. "The blackout applies to all of us I'm afraid. I have important matters to attend to."

*More important than the feelings of your friends?* Miri fought to control her anger. She believed in Joram, but his coldness toward her friends had her temperature rising. She started toward him, listening intently as she drew near.

"How long until we know for sure?" Joram asked.

"It's imminent from the military reports," the messenger answered, then clamped his mouth shut as he saw her watching them.

Miri's fury exploded as she rushed toward them. "Not our fight? Yet you've been getting regular reports all morning." She grabbed for the datapad, but the messenger yanked it out of reach and stuffed it inside his coat.

"This is government business," Joram said with a frown. "Not civilian, Miss Rhii."

"Don't talk to me like that," Miri scolded. "My security clearance is still as high as or higher than yours. I have knowledge of things you don't."

Joram motioned toward the circling protestors as the messenger hurried off. "Your duty is with the others. Please. We must get back to work here."

"Not until you tell us what news you have of the fighting," Miri said as Sol and Lura reacted to her words and hurried over.

"You have news?" Lura looked hopeful for the first time since she'd arrived.

"I told you, the blackout is for all of us," Joram turned to walk back toward the protestors, but Miri grabbed his arm.

"I heard what your messenger said about military reports," Miri said, squeezing his arm until he winced. "Tell us right now. What do you know?" She moved forward, her face inches from his.

Joram yanked his arm free of her grasp and stepped back, looking ready to snap at her. But then, seeing their faces, he sighed, hesitating a moment before: "We're losing men left and right. I have no word of specific personnel. But the battle is all but lost." Then he spun and hurried back to join the circling protestors.

Lura's shoulders sank at the news and Miri felt her own panic rising. Her heart thundered in her chest. Sol put an arm around his wife to comfort her, but both couldn't even manage to meet Miri's eyes. "I'm sure he's fine," Miri said. "He has to be." She said it as much to reassure herself as Sol and Lura.

Lura nodded. "We'll be praying in the chapel." Sol reached out and grabbed Miri's hand, and they walked off together toward the Starport. Miri didn't know what to do. She didn't share their religion. But yet, she was consumed with worry. How dare Joram keep this from them! She stood there watching the protestors as she offered her own silent pleas to the gods to protect her son.

The Tertullian Ambassador, Adoo Kwase, was the first to ask: "What happens if we align ourselves with you and you lose?"

Tarkanius handled the issue with poise. "We can't lose. That's why we need your help. The future of our entire system and all of us with it depends on victory." Aron resisted the urge to shout "amen."

The High Lord Councilor scanned the faces around the table—Italites, Regalians, Xanthians, Idolians—every planet in the system was represented. Red, purple, green—eyes of every shade, skin tones too. Some appeared almost human, like the Xanthians and Tertullians; others were more clearly alien. All spoke Common well, but most had accents. None used a translator—as diplomats all went through years of language training. It was a necessity given the ruling race's past refusal to compromise in dealing with them. Electronic translators could malfunction or be accused of being inaccurate or even get it wrong. Direct communication avoided issues and the rulers of the Boralians had a long history of deliberate mistakes against other races. No one could afford to take chances.

"I know you've been mistreated, marginalized, ignored. It's time for that to change. We changed it for the Vertullians, now we extend the same invitation to you. Come alongside, work with us, help us make this system strong and united. It can't survive unless we do. Help us defeat Xalivar and leave a past riddled with misrule behind." Tarkanius' eyes made it clear he meant every word.

A fruity Idolian incense floated past Aron's nose. Famous for its calming effects, the incense was clearly intended to aid the civility of the present proceedings, but, although their voices remained business-like, the leaders themselves dripped with tension.

The Xanthian ambassador, Quatol, spoke next. "You seem to be a different man than the type we are used to. Yet you cannot live forever. What assurance would we have that the one who follows you won't go back to the old ways?"

"The assurance that history and tradition rule the hearts of men as strong as love and fear. If we start now and integrate completely, by the time a replacement comes you will be able to help in selecting him. And you will have the power to stop him from taking back your rights."

"It's an awful lot to promise," Quatol said, clearly doubtful of Tarkanius' ability to pull it off. The Xanthians had tentative relations with the government, which is why their planet had such successful black markets. They had long flaunted their rebelliousness before the system but always paid their taxes and otherwise followed the laws, cooperating when needed. So the government hadn't bothered to crack down on them. Quatol was one of the older ambassadors here, so Aron suspected his personal feelings were stronger than most of the others.

"If we don't try, it will never happen," Tarkanius leaned back in his chair. "This system is home to all of us. Don't you want the same rights as everyone else?"

"We serve the same rights as every other race," the Idolian ambassador, Kanaan, said. "You came here, took over our planets, called us 'aliens,' despite the fact that we were born here. And now you talk about rights? We were born with such rights, but that didn't stop you."

Tarkanius nodded. "And I'm sorry for it. Sincerely. Which is why I want to change it."

The alien ambassadors kept their eyes on Pharah and Aron throughout the meeting, as if trying to read their minds. It made Aron self-conscious about every gesture or reaction he made, but Pharah seemed at ease. He cleared his throat from the seat beside Aron and smiled, panning the faces around the table. "We have an opportunity here, an opportunity unlike any we've had before. Some, like me, have been given extraordinary chances and worked closely with the Boralians. I can assure you there are good people among them. Most of them, in fact, are good. You can build a relationship of mutual respect and trust, but it takes all of us to do it, and we all face risks in doing so."

"We trust you, Pharah, but you have lived among these people so long, you have a soft place for them," Adoo said. "We have to keep perspective here."

Pharah nodded. "Ask Lord Aron. His people were more mistreated than any of us, and yet he is willing to work with them." Pharah turned and smiled at Aron, a sparkle in his purple eyes.

Aron well understood their concerns, because he'd shared them once himself, but Tarkanius had earned his trust and leaders like Simeon and Kray inspired hope as well. He nodded. "The majority have been very supportive. Until the efforts of Xalivar and his agents inflamed old anger, we were living peacefully and quietly together. Hatred is taught, and a hard thing to unlearn, but we can do it if we work together. Combined, we'll equal their numbers. And if we're all united, we'll be a force to reckon with."

"What of the movement amongst your people to leave?" Kanaan asked.

Meeting the eyes of each ambassador in turn, Aron spoke slowly, choosing each word. "Political movements of all sorts arise. I'd rather see us stay. But to stay, we need support. And having you on our side would make a big difference." Aron truly believed it, even if he doubted Joram and his followers would ever change their minds.

"You're giving us much to think about," Adoo said, sitting back and rubbing his chin as he thought. Several aides leaned in to whisper to their Ambassadors, reading off datapads. Aron had heard no reports of the battle, but he hoped it was going well. The last thing they needed was negative reports to influence the ambassador's decisions.

Uzah sat in his Floater atop a rise looking down at the devastation his troops were enduring. Explosions launched men into the air before his eyes, their screams mixing with the rumbling as debris, blood, flesh and foliage flew around them. If help didn't arrive, and soon, he'd have no choice but to withdraw.

He typed a code into the comm and watched the monitor flicker as Kray and Matheu appeared. "We're running out of time. I need air support or it's over down here." An explosion boomed in the valley behind him, punctuating his words.

"We don't have anyone we can send you," Matheu said, shaking his head.

"Free up three or four, or I'm calling for a retreat," Uzah answered, firm in his resolve. He knew Matheu wouldn't refuse help if he could spare it, but still, this was an emergency, and he needed to impart the urgency to the others in command.

"We'll find someone," Kray replied. "Hang in there!"

Uzah nodded as he heard a whistling overhead and quickly dove out of his Floater to the ground. The Floater exploded into flames behind him. Dirt clods slapped his head as he felt grass ricochet off his bare neck. He motioned to his driver and aides, who'd also made it out in time: "Let's hope they send those ships!"

Davi circled around and blasted two fighters as they stayed locked on Farien's and Nila's tails. Brie fired off her own lasers and the ships finally exploded into fireballs of orange, yellow and red.

"Thanks, Cousin!" Nila called.

"That was way too close," Farien added.

Davi saw streaks of black on the fuselages of both fighters. No one in his Squadron had gone undamaged at this point, not even himself. In a couple cases, pilots were lucky to still be flying. He'd have sent them back for repairs if he had anyone to replace them.

Davi signaled Farien as he came alongside and they switched to a private channel. "We can't hold out like this much longer. Suggestions?"

"Do you have a white flag?"

Davi chuckled. "Think Xalivar would honor it?"

"Oh yeah, he's always seemed really merciful to me."

Davi smiled. "At least Yao and Dru are holding up better than I thought."

"We need relief, or we're done for. All of us." Farien sounded as exhausted as Davi felt.

Davi nodded. "Matheu promises they're coming."

Farien sighed. "Maybe you should ask that God of yours to speed them up. Too many already dead."

Davi sighed and said a quick prayer silently as Farien slid off to rejoin Nila, and Brie closed up in formation on his own wing. His comm beeped. "Hang on. Command's calling." He switched channels, and Matheu and Kray appeared on the monitor.

"We need some ships to provide air support on the ground," Matheu said right away.

"We're not exactly rolling in extras."

"Can you spare two or three?" Kray asked, her eyes pleading.

Davi's ship rocked as an enemy's lasers exploded just right of his blastshield window. "Sure. Why not? We're already dying out here." He sighed. "Sorry. I'll find somebody." Clicking off the comm, he glanced down at his combat computer. Its calculations dutifully warned him they were outgunned and outnumbered badly with no chance to win. He spun in an arc to chase down the enemy who'd engaged him, while mentally running through his Squadron to decide whom he could spare.

"Is my shuttle ready?" Xalivar stepped out of the lift onto the *Tarragon's* bridge and strode toward Admiral Dek and General Lucius as they watched the scanners.

The officers exchanged a look of concern then turned to face him. "My Lord, it's still very dangerous," Lucius said.

"Great men gain through great risk," Xalivar said. "Pull out so we can get through to the planet."

Dek nodded. "Of course, my Lord. Still, perhaps you could wait a few more—"

"I've waited a year, Admiral! I will wait no longer! My victory is now! I want Tarkanius' surrender delivered in person. Tell them to be ready to depart in five minutes." Xalivar turned and marched back toward the lift, headed for his quarters, and then the landing bay. He heard Dek and Lucius issuing orders behind him and smiled. At least, they knew when to shut up and obey. He needed more men like that.

The protestors' lines were thinning. It was obvious and Joram looked annoyed. Miri kept marching, but even she was tempted to leave as she watched another couple headed for the Starport.

"Where does everyone keep disappearing to?" Tela asked, slipping up beside Miri.

"The Chapel, I think. Lura and Sol are leading prayer for those fighting."

"I thought we were protesting this fight?"

Miri turned and searched Tela's eyes. "You don't mean that. You have friends out there, including Davi."

Tela stared back a moment then her shoulders sank as she sighed. "I know. But this has kept my mind off of it."

"I appreciate the loyalty of those who remain," Joram said through a loudspeaker, as he launched into another speech intended to inspire and motivate them. As he rambled on, Miri realized the words that had once lit a fire in her now left her numb.

She halted and held a hand out to stop Tela. "I can't keep doing this. I want to go pray too." She didn't know who she'd pray to. She didn't share their faith, but being with them would comfort her. And she wanted to comfort them as well.

Their eyes met, and Miri saw the worry Tela was trying so hard to hide. Reaching out, she clasped the young woman's hand and squeezed. Tela's eyes softened and she nodded. The two women slipped from the line together, ignoring Joram's angry stares, and hurried toward the Starport after the others.

With Jorek and Virun providing air cover for Uzah's troops, Davi found his Squadron stretched thin. Another pair had been sent back to *Reliance* for repairs after suffering unsustainable damages, leaving Davi and Brie, Farien and Nila, Yao and Dru and the remains of two other squadrons to fight. Being spread out over a large area made covering for each other increasingly difficult, if not impossible, requiring them each to face twice as many targets as they'd faced before.

Farien's rebel yell came over the comm, followed by Nila's. "That's two more, Captain!" Davi could sense his friend grinning from ear-to-ear.

"Never thought we'd be shooting down VS28s with our own," Nila commented. "Still feels good when they're the enemy."

"Yes, it does," Farien laughed.

"Try and stay focused despite your enjoyment, okay?" Davi teased. He noticed a blip moving away on his scanner and turned to look. The *Tarragon* was moving out of range and pulling away from the fighting.

"Where's *Tarragon* going?" Brie wondered.

"I don't know," Davi said.

"Just let me finish cleaning up these fighters and I'll give them the attention they deserve," Farien said as he and Nila swooped in for another run against oncoming enemy fighters.

A flash from the *Tarragon* caught Davi's attention, and he turned again to see a shuttle launching. *They're launching a shuttle in the middle of battle?* It was the kind of small shuttle used by dignitaries and important businessmen. Now he knew why the flagship had withdrawn. Someone was trying to get down to the planet's surface.

"Do we intercept that shuttle?" Yao's voice came back over the comm.

Davi glanced up and saw Yao and Dru circling back. They were between him and the *Tarragon*, easily within range of the shuttle.

"It's got to be someone important," Dru commented. "Xalivar?"

"Xalivar's too scared to put himself at risk like that," Yao said.

"Unless he thinks he's already won," Brie suggested.

"Whoever it is, they're on the wrong side, and last I checked we were still fighting," Farien said.

Davi hesitated, wanting to go himself, but his computer put him too far out of range to catch it. Then an explosion rocked his fighter again and his eyes searched for the source. Two black stealth ships, like they'd encountered off Eleni 1 a month past, appeared against the starfield, cannons blazing. He fired back and knew he'd never make it. "Take them out, but keep clear of the *Tarragon's* weapons."

"We'll be careful," Dru said.

"Dru, stay with me," Yao answered, already focused on the mission.

As he and Brie exchanged fire with the stealth fighters, the two wingmen peeled off and headed for the departing shuttle. The *Tarragon* was between it and the fighters as the shuttle arced toward the planet below.

Bordox and his assassins snuck almost to the edge of the battlefield unnoticed, their small, dark fighter-sized craft blending in with the starfield. There were so many other ships, the scanners would confuse them and he fired off decoys to add to the confusion as they drew near. It didn't take him long to locate Xander's squadron, and then it was just a matter of watching behavior before he spotted Rhii himself. Xalivar could try to keep them out of this fight, but it wouldn't happen. Obed had sent them to sabotage Xalivar's ship and give him an in with the Council as an ally again, but Bordox had a debt to settle first.

He almost couldn't sit still as they moved around the edge of the battlefield toward the *Tarragon* together. Adrenaline had his heart racing and his head felt light, almost as if he were floating inside the cockpit. As they drew near to Xalivar's ship, he spotted a shuttle heading for the planet and two VS28s racing to intercept. The perfect distraction!

"Go after that shuttle!" he ordered his men. "It must be someone important."

As the assassins turned off to comply with his instructions, Bordox veered off and headed for Rhii.

"W'ere 're you going?" his wingman called into the radio.

"To deal with an old friend, just hold position and follow my lead."

"Our ord'rs—"

"I know what the orders are! I'm in charge! Now shut up and follow me!"

Stupid Lhamors! They'd served a purpose, but he couldn't wait to be rid of them. They refused to just shut up and follow orders! They didn't respect him any more than anyone else, but he'd show them all! This was it! His moment of triumph. And no one could spoil it for him now.

Circling in, he brought Rhii's VS28 into his sights and let loose a barrage of fire.

Yao let Dru lead the way, keeping a close eye on their proximity to the *Tarragon*. The larger ship's cannons could blast them to bits if they got in range, and Dru seemed to be cutting it close.

"Watch it, Dru! Change your angle, or you'll have those cannons on you!"

Dru adjusted course. "Fear not, Prof, I'm on this shuttle." Dru sounded as tired as Yao felt, but Yao was determined. He hadn't ever been in battle. He'd seen lots of friends die, even shot down a couple classmates. War was as horrible as he'd expected but they had to win. Everything depended on it.

The shuttle spotted them and shifted course, arcing back upward slightly. Dru and Yao stayed on its tail.

"Fire and get out! They're headed back toward their—"

Dru and the *Tarragon* both fired simultaneously. Dru's lasers singed the shuttle, but then the cannon blasts struck his engines. In moments, he was spinning out of control toward the planet.

"Dru!" Yao spun his fighter but saw there was nothing he could do. The young cadet's fighter disappeared into the planet's atmosphere and turned back to the shuttle. "I lost Dru!" He fumed in silence, rage building as he hoped the young cadet could land safely on the surface.

Tensing in his seat as he focused, he aimed himself for the shuttle, hoping to come upon it at an angle that kept him out of range of the cannons.

"Forget it, Yao, it's a trap!" he heard Davi warn over the radio.

Then his scanner flashed as it locked on target and Yao fired. He immediately arced his trajectory to head back out. Moments later, his own ship rocked with explosions. The cannons had gotten his right engine. He felt his ship lose power.

The shuttle arced back, clearly deciding Yao was no longer a threat. It was headed for the planet again.

"Pull out, Yao!" Davi ordered.

Yao made a decision. "Negative. I'm taking this guy out."

He turned his fighter and put his remaining engines to full, racing after it.

"Hang on, Yao, we're coming!" Farien called.

But Yao knew help couldn't get there in time. Then his ship rocked again. Another blast from the flagship. He hadn't realized he'd flown back in range when he turned after the shuttle. His ship slowed as he lost another engine, but he was still faster than the shuttle. The *Tarragon* was turning in pursuit. Whoever was on the shuttle was that important. And no matter what, Yao was going to make him pay. His fingers clamped tighter around his controls.

Davi and Brie swooped and dove, exchanging fire with the stealth fighters, while also dealing with whatever VS28s paid them any mind. The fighting was pure chaos. It took intense focus just to fly, let alone lining up targets and firing off the cannons.

"Who are these guys?" Brie wondered aloud.

"Xalivar must have done more than rely on stolen Boralian ships," Davi replied as he dodged oncoming fire from the lead stealth ship.

Davi's hands tensed on his controls as he spotted Farien and Nila racing to assist Yao, enemy fighters hot in pursuit. It wasn't like Yao to be so aggressive. Maybe the loss of Dru and so many others had him on edge. The *Tarragon* turned in pursuit. "The *Tarragon's* chasing a fighter? Who's on that shuttle?"

"Whoever it is, I'm on them," Yao said. His voice sounded oddly cold. The exhaustion must be getting to him.

"No! Pull out and get to safety!" Davi ordered.

"Just one more shot, first."

Davi fought the urge to race over and protect his friend. He couldn't get there in time. Explosions rocked his right wing and he turned his attention back to evading and led Brie in an arc onto the tails of the fighters chasing Farien and Nila instead.

A stealth ship stayed tight on Davi's tail.

"These guys are starting to piss me off now," he said.

"You get ours, we'll take care of yours," Farien said as Davi lined up on the fighter giving his friend a run for his money. Glancing quickly over, he saw Brie lined up on the other. Just a few seconds and they could take off to help Yao and let Farien and Nila knock the stealth fighters off their tails.

Davi and Brie fired just as the *Tarragon's* gunners took out Yao's last engine.

Yao fired at the shuttle and missed.

"Yao!" Davi cringed as sweat dripped down and stung his eyes. He blinked it away as he heard:

"It's too late. One option." Yao sounded resigned.

"What do you mean? Just eject." Davi accelerated, desperate to help his friend.

Instead, Yao turned sharply and angled at the shuttle. The shuttle tried to evade, but Davi saw the angle was too sharp. They were going to crash. And then he realized it was intentional.

"No, Yao! Wait!"

Both ships went up as they collided, disintegrating into minute particles in a flash of orange and yellow light. The shuttle and Yao's fighter both gone in seconds.

"Yao!" Davi heard himself scream, but it was like he was somewhere else. He blinked, hoping the sweat fogging his eyes had created an illusion. But Yao's fighter and the shuttle were nowhere to be found.

Davi tried to shake off his numbness, but he couldn't grasp it. Yao was really gone.

Alarms sounded in his cockpit and he checked his scanner—a huge mass of incoming craft. In moments, the computer identified them. The Borali fleet was here. The tide of the battle had just turned.

"All squadrons return to base," Matheu's voice ordered over the comm. "All squadrons return to base."

Davi saw Farien and Nila turn and head back for the *Reliance*. Then Brie did the same. Davi froze, still trying to come to grips with what had happened. It couldn't be true. Yao couldn't be gone.

Bordox watched the fighters explode and saw Xander's VS28 wobble. He had him lined up almost perfectly, then two other VS28s circled back and tried to get on his tail.

"Fall back and deal with those two while I handle these," he ordered his wingman.

"Your fath'r instruct'd—"

"Stop quoting my damn father to me!" Bordox fired but missed as Rhii's fighter suddenly dove. Then the VS28s behind him were firing as his wingman obeyed and fell back. Bordox had his hands full and lost track of Rhii while he responded. He launched into a steep climb, firing decoys to confuse the battle scanners. Decoys hadn't been employed in decades, but that made them all the better, since modern combat equipment wasn't designed to handle them. The two VS28s shots went wide, following the decoys.

Bordox whooped and turned back to look for Rhii when a shot came from his right and exploded one of his engines. He cursed and turned to see one of his own stealth fighters firing on him.

"What are you doing?!" he screamed. "It's me, you idiot!"

"Your fath'r instruct'd us to disabl' you if you deviat'd from orders," one of the Lhamors answered. The stealth ship fired again, narrowly missing Bordox's other engine. He swerved right into an arc.

"Stop! Damn you!" He was cut off as his other engine failed, and his ship was floating under no power.

"Orders." The Lhamor replied. His wingman appeared on his right side and the other stealth fighter on the left. They used the fighter's tractor beams to lock on and led him off toward the planet away from Rhii. Bordox spotted the other stealth fighters lining up around them for cover.

Pres heard a whistling overhead. Turning in her Floater seat, she saw a damaged VS28 spinning toward them. "Get us moving! Now!"

Her driver reacted with surprise but slid the Floater into gear.

"Hurry!" She motioned toward the incoming fighter.

Her driver's eyes widened with panic, and she was pushed back in her seat as the Floater shot forward. Just in time. The VS28 exploded behind them, leaving a crater in the ground.

"Get us out of here!" She ordered as the comm beeped.

"Code seventy-seven!" Lucius said as he appeared on the monitor, looking shaken and disheveled. "ASAP!"

"Full retreat? Why?" Pres couldn't believe her ears, but she'd never seen Lucius looking so frazzled.

"No time to argue. A whole Boralian fleet is here. Pull out and get back now! We're leaving!"

The monitor went dead as her mind raced. She didn't have time to save all of her men. How could she abandon them? Her driver was already turning back toward their ships.

Pres' fingers raced to send codes through the computer to her men.

He'd had to push his engines to get there, but Davi reached the spot where Yao's fighter had been and slowed his ship, stunned. The enemy fighters paid him no mind as they responded to the arrival of the Boralian fleet. He ran his scanners through the paces searching for any sign of his friend. But it came up clear for VS28s. Just the *Tarragon* and her cruiser escorts remained there. He couldn't believe his friend Yao was gone. It couldn't be. Tears streamed down his face so fast he could barely see his controls. He felt numb and struggled to breathe. Who was on that fighter? Who was responsible? The family necklace weighed heavy against his chest. He thought of the images on it: laborers, soldiers, farmers and priests—those were the people he was fighting for. And they were more than just his flesh and blood. Yao was family, too. In pure rage, he screamed and accelerated straight for the *Tarragon*, targeting her engines.

Ignoring his computer this time, he made mental calculations. "This is for Yao!"

Then the big ship accelerated, her FTL engines lighting up as she took off like a streak and disappeared.

"Nooooo!" Hands clenched around the controls, Davi unleashed his weapons at her as he raced through her exhaust trail, but there was nothing he could do. Both Yao and the *Tarragon* had disappeared.

# Epilogue

The footsteps echoed across the hangar as the aide ran toward the table. Aron wasn't the only one who looked up and took notice, despite the intensity of the ongoing conversation. An Idolian aide approached Kanaan, leaning over to whisper in his ear. Aron watched the ambassador's face for a reaction. His face went from disbelief to amazement to shock in a matter of seconds. Then the aide stood, waiting for a response, but the ambassador only waved him away.

"If we had some sort of guarantee," Quatol was saying. "Good faith only goes so far, Lord Tarkanius."

"The whole world has changed," Kanaan said, as if he could bear the secret no more, the news burst from him.

Everyone at the table turned, puzzled. "You have something to add?" Adoo asked.

Kanaan gave only a slight nod, still in shock. The news must be something very serious. "Xalivar is dead."

"What?" Tarkanius looked stunned. The others appeared uncertain. What was he talking about?

"Killed in a shuttle near Tertullis, during the battle. His troops have fled. Many pilots died. One gave his life to destroy the shuttle."

Xalivar dead?! Could it really be true? Everyone reached for their datapads, typing as furiously as Aron did, searching for information.

"How do we know Xalivar was aboard?" Quatol asked the question hanging unanswered in most of their minds.

"A shuttle from the *Tarragon* headed to the planet in the midst of a battle where Xalivar believed this conference was being held. Who else would be aboard?" Kanaan's voice was more confident.

"We must know for certain," Adoo said.

"Preliminary battle reports are frequently inaccurate," Pharah said, nodding.

"Xalivar's troops have fled in fear," Quatol said with a pleased smile as he confirmed the news. "They are defeated."

"It is a glorious day!" Kanaan exclaimed, smiling now too as he transitioned from shock to glee.

"News we've hoped for many years," Adoo nodded.

"We must know for sure," Tarkanius cautioned. He still looked stunned as his aides buzzed behind him, working to obtain fuller reports.

"If this is true, we are in," Quatol said.

Kanaan's head bobbed vigorously. "And we as well."

Adoo watched them as several other representatives joined the chorus. Finally, he cleared his throat. "We echo their sentiments. Let us hope the news proves true."

Tarkanius glanced at Aron, amazed by the turn of events. "We will gather the data and ascertain its truthfulness as soon as possible, of course." He sat back in his chair as an aide handed him a cup of hot Talis. Tarkanius sipped slowly. Aron knew exactly how he felt. Xalivar's death would ensure a new beginning, a new age of certainty for everyone. Much of the chaos might end just from the news. Protestors would lose their will. Their hopes would be dashed, while, for those on the other side, hopes would be renewed. It was a remarkable moment.

Aron closed his eyes and offered a prayer for peace.

Word had reached them at the chapel within two hours. The flagship *Tarragon* had fled. The Boralians had won. A few other ships had been captured, but several got away along with part of the forces on the ground. Still, there'd be a lot of courtmartials for treason in the near future.

The news of Dru and Yao's deaths was a shock. Dru had come through training with Tela, helped with the Resistance. It was like losing a brother, and Yao, he'd become beloved quickly. She could only imagine how Davi must feel. But had Yao really taken out Xalivar? If it was true, it made him a certified hero. He'd saved them all!

She thought back on all of the tension between Davi and her over the past few months. She'd really been hard on him, and, reflecting now, she wasn't sure why she'd been so emotional. Certainly the reunion with her father had reignited old fears of abandonment and loss and feelings of protectiveness as well. That Davi wanted to protect her, given their relationship and his own recent reunion with his parents—especially his own father—now made some of her reactions seem inconsiderate and selfish. Most of it, they could have talked through, if she'd just made more effort.

She said a joyful prayer of thanks to God for the news of Davi's safety and the victory of the Boralian forces. But with Yao, Dru and other friends lost, Davi would now face the very feelings Tela herself had been wrestling with. She promised herself she'd help him through it. They could help each other. The relief and happiness which flooded her heart upon hearing he was alive reminded her how much she loved him; how much she still wanted the future they'd dreamed of together. Yet her throat tightened and her heart ached for the pain she knew he was experiencing now.

That night, she gathered with Davi's family and other families as the first wave of troops returned to Legallis' starport. Davi and Farien couldn't even meet her eyes. Nila and Brie hugged and cried as they stepped off the shuttle. Everyone who'd fought looked devastated from more than mere exhaustion.

Tela's eyes met Davi's and he fell against her, weeping. She wrapped her arms around him and wept with him. Lura and Sol and Miri moved in to lend support, whispering words of encouragement. Each embraced Davi in turn as he cried. It dawned her that she was no longer alone. For years, she'd grown used to depending on no one but herself yet here she was surrounded by family, even after Telanus' death.

"I'll miss them, too, Davi," Tela managed to say. It had been so long since she held him that she'd forgotten how comforting it was. She pulled him closer, knowing he needed her right now as much as she needed him.

Sol hesitated a moment, glancing at Miri. "Is it true about Xalivar?"

Davi's eyes grew sadder. "We think so. Unconfirmed but the flagship left right after." He glanced at Miri. Tela knew both still cared about Xalivar despite all that had happened.

Miri nodded and forced a smile. "Then they're heroes and they've saved us all! Long live the memory of Yao and Dru!"

"Yao and Dru!" Others around them heard and picked up the call. Soon everyone in the hangar was shouting it out like a mantra. Tears dried forgotten on cheeks as frowns became smiles and pride filled the eyes of everyone present. Except Davi.

"I ordered him to pull out. He wouldn't listen."

Tela pulled Davi's head against her shoulder again. "People do what they have to in battle. He wanted Xalivar."

Davi nodded. "I just can't believe he's gone."

"Thank God for your victory," Sol said, and reached out to squeeze Davi's arm.

As the news of Xalivar's death spread around them, some cheered, others laughed, everyone's moods brightened. Tela hoped the official confirmations proved it to be true.

She focused her concern on Davi.

"Thank God you're safe," she said as she held him.

"Amen." Lura caressed Davi's back and shoulders.

There'd be time to sort it all out tomorrow. It was a day they'd never forget, but they'd find a way through. And for the first time in weeks, Tela felt hopeful.

# THE EXODUS

## The Saga Of Davi Rhii Book 3

# Prologue

Xalivar's elation lasted until the moment he stood before his father and grandfather in the Palace Throne Room on Legallis. Elder Xonas stood by his son, who sat on the throne his father had once held before him. Standing there together, the family resemblance had never been stronger. Both had graying hair, but Xerxes' was only starting at the temples and a few highlights, whereas Xonas' head resembled a mountain peak with its white snowcap. Both wore the gold ceremonial robes of leadership, with white collars and cuffs. Their robes bore the family crest but Xerxes' also bore the crest of his office, a change that, even ten years after his grandfather's abdication, Xalivar still hadn't gotten used to. His father also wore the Lord's Eye around his neck. A purple gem with gold highlights, it had been a symbol of the High Lord Councilor's office for generations. And both were scowling, their faces scrunched, eyes narrowed with displeasure.

Xalivar moved toward them, stepping down off the raised floor ringing the room. He followed the red carpet, his bootsteps still echoing from his confident footfalls as he approached. Xalivar smiled and raised his hands in victory. For a moment, Xalivar wondered what had them in a foul mood on such a great day for the Boralian Alliance. His triumph over the Vertullian uprising should make them proud, so he ignored their looks and pressed on. "The rebellion at Delta V has been put down as ordered, my Lords. The perpetrators have been stopped and punished. It's a glorious day."

Xalivar's father, Xerxes, stared at him as if Xalivar had spoken a strange tongue. "A glorious day for whom?" He turned and punched a button on the throne, activating the vidscreen on the wall. Xalivar recognized the news feed as coverage of his troops squelching the rebelling slaves.

Floaters bearing the military crest discharged armed troops who opened fire on the rebels. Laser fire and smoke filled the screen as people ran and screamed. The smells and sensations of the day came back, flooding over him. Xalivar's skin tingled, warming as adrenaline filled his veins again. It was clear on the video that the Boralians had outgunned and outnumbered the Vertullians, and there was Xalivar in their midst: firing his weapon, shouting orders, riding triumphantly on his command Floater in full uniform, his royal crest and golden shoulder emblems glistening under the light of the twin suns.

The battle went on for a few moments before the footage skipped in time to later that day, when Xalivar and his troops had rounded up the instigators and lined them up for execution. Row by row, they fell into large pits as Xalivar's men strafed them with blaster fire. New bodies fell atop the previous ones into the earthen pits. The footage seemed to go on forever, and Xalivar saw himself there, observing, the same smile of triumph on his face he knew was there now. A couple of times he even joined his men and fired off shots, executing the slave leaders. Xalivar's men adored him for his strong leadership, and the fact he wasn't afraid to fight beside them and issue orders he was more than willing to execute himself.

As the footage ended, Xalivar turned to see Xerxes and his grandfather, Xonas, watching him with dismay.

"You delight in the dishonor and humiliation of our family, Xalivar?" Xonas asked. Xalivar had never seen his grandfather looking so angry, and the old man had never once in his life leveled such anger at Xalivar. It caught him totally by surprise.

"Humiliation? Dishonor? They rebelled against our authority. Denied our rights as leaders. Disobeyed us. That's dishonor. I restored our honor, our glory."

Xerxes silenced his son with a stare. "It's all over the nets, Xalivar. It wasn't enough to issue the orders. You had to be there personally and allow them to film it."

"Leading by example is why men adore me, father," Xalivar replied, amazed at their reaction. "If I'm willing to do it, none would dare question the orders I give."

"A leader has to know when to act, Xalivar, and when to put the responsibility on others," Xonas said. "A member of the royal family executing slaves …" He shook his head. "Those images will be replayed for decades, encouraging resentment, and sympathy to the detriment of our family's reputation and power."

"You sent me to handle the situation," Xalivar said, struggling to control his temper. His fists ached with the urge to clench but he couldn't allow his father and grandfather to see his anger. "It had dragged on for weeks, so I put a stop to it quickly and efficiently. It sent a message to any others with such ambitions as to the nature of our response to acts of rebellion."

"Gods, Xalivar," Xerxes shook his head. "Your pride will be your downfall. You must learn discretion and common sense. Tough decisions must be made, but if the people don't respect us, honor us ..."

Xalivar sighed, fighting the urge to roll his eyes. "You wanted a show of strength. I demonstrated our family's strength. Now, no one will question we have the will to do what it takes." He waved a hand dismissively toward the bay windows which looked out upon the starport and darkening night sky beyond. "They mocked us for weeks, called us indecisive. They questioned your fitness, father."

Xerxes frowned. "Politics is a game, Xalivar, in which one man elevates himself by lowering another. But it's false elevation. I am the High Lord Councilor, and no one has taken that away, nor can they."

"Our family has ruled now for seventy years, Xalivar," Xonas added. "And a big part of that success has been the respect and reputation we've maintained by not letting ourselves be seen as ruthless and uncaring. People respect and admire passion. They thrive on leaders who hurt with them, cheer for them, who live to see their people succeed. Senseless killing is not success."

"Shall I send the surgeons and see if any can be revived then?" Xalivar surrendered to his disgust, fists clenching and unclenching at his side.

"Do not mock us," Xerxes warned.

"You mock me!"

"Don't speak to us as if we are soldiers under your command," Xerxes answered. "We are your elders, and *we* are the ones in positions of power. Your future lies in our hands."

"Don't speak to me as if I am not your son and heir!" Xalivar spun and marched toward the formidable, rectangular entry door, carved with the royal crest, his hands shaking with rage as he went.

"Your heritage should inspire respect, son. Everything you have comes from all we've done before you!" Xerxes scolded, his voice rising after his son.

Xalivar stopped by the door and turned to face them again. "And when will I get recognition for what I have done? For my years of dedicated service to you both—following your orders, enduring your lectures, the endless lessons? I have proven my honor and dedication to this family!"

"You have undone much of that today with that foolishness at Delta V, and your attitude toward us!" Xonas yelled.

Again, Xalivar was too shocked by his grandfather's outburst to offer much response. After a few moments more enduring their castigating stares, he regrouped and asked: "Shall I issue an apology then?"

Xerxes responded by pushing buttons to rewind the footage on the vidscreen and freeze on an image of Xalivar, his teeth clenched, his eyes glistening with pride, his weapon raised and firing. "Does that look like someone anyone would believe feels remorse?"

Xalivar just stood there, teeth grinding, refusing to give his father the satisfaction of a response.

Xerxes continued: "Every time I task you, you push the boundaries, Xalivar. It's as if you can't just complete a mission, you have to elevate it somehow into something far more than was asked. I'll never understand it. It's dangerous and reckless."

"Am I dismissed?" Xalivar said, attempting to choke back his disgust.

"Dismissed and relieved of duty. Your military career is over."

Xalivar spun again and waited for the door to open. After a few minutes, he heard his father click the button on the arm of the throne and the door lifted. Standing there waiting, he felt their eyes boring into his back and swore: *I will be the greatest leader the Boralian people have ever known. I will make them rue this day! They mock everything I stand for, but it's they who have failed. Not me!*

As the door slipped upward over his head, Xalivar strode out into the corridor never looking back.

"*What* did you say, General?" Xalivar cursed his father and grandfather again as he shook off the memory and turned from the vidscreen. He'd been watching the stars streak by as the *Tarragon* continued speeding away from Tertullis in hyperspace. The folds of his robe swirled around him as he spotted General Pres a few feet away on the raised dais of the *Tarragon*'s bridge, staring angrily, General Lucius beside her.

"I said—"

Lucius cut her off. "General Pres was just remarking that Admiral Dek's actions saved your life, my Lord."

"And cost his own," Pres added, still raging.

Xalivar saw blame in her eyes. And despite Lucius' attempt, he had heard her words of accusation: *Senseless killing is not success.* The very words his grandfather had said to him on the day Xerxes and Xonas showed their true colors and Xalivar forever changed. No longer would he invest himself in impressing others or caring what they thought. He was on his own, and he would live and act accordingly. Pres blamed him for her mentor's death but what did people like *that* know of duty and honor? Xalivar had always had one mission: to set the world right. And he had no respect for any who allowed weakness to distract them from that goal.

Shaking off his reverie, he took a deep breath to control his anger. "Admiral Dek knew his duty well, Generals. He gave his life in dedication to it. I hope you would do so as well."

"Of course, my Lord," Lucius muttered. Pres just continued staring out the vidscreen.

Xalivar turned back to the streaking stars. They were in retreat. Lucius had pulled them out on the apex of triumph. Once again, someone else had stolen Xalivar's moment. "Retreat?" Xalivar spat the word. "You've evacuated in our moment of triumph."

"We are outnumbered, my Lord," Lucius replied, meeting Xalivar's eyes. "I have a responsibility to protect your life, just as Dek did."

"At the cost of victory?"

"We would not have been victorious," Pres said bitterly, turning away in an attempt to hide her disgust.

"General, your tone disturbs me. Perhaps you'd prefer a reassignment?" Xalivar watched the Generals as he said it, knowing full well they knew he'd never allow anyone to leave his service alive, at least not as long as he was still seeking to restore his rightful place as High Lord Councilor.

Lucius flinched. Pres ignored him.

"I want the officers assembled as soon as we reach the base," Xalivar continued. "We have plans to discuss and very little time. I suggest, General Pres, that you get control of your emotions before then."

"Of course, my Lord," Lucius said with a nod. Pres remained silent.

Xalivar turned and strode out of the bridge into the corridor which led to his quarters.

As the servos whined and the door slid shut behind him, he flipped on a vidscreen and stood in the center of his quarters. Gray walls, standard military issue furniture—the place had none of the luxuries he'd grown used to during his reign, but Xalivar had made no attempt to correct it, wanting both funds and focus to be on his mission. There'd be time to resume his lifestyle later.

Flipping channels, he stopped on one of the nets as his image filled the screen, a profile shot from one of his appearances before the Council. Curious, he hit a button on the wall panel, turning on the sound.

The announcer's booming baritone filled his ears: "… It is believed that Xalivar Rhii, deposed High Lord Councilor, was aboard the shuttle when it was destroyed …"

*They think I'm dead?* Xalivar flipped to another news channel.

"… the death of deposed High Lord Councilor Xalivar Rhii has sparked mixed reactions from all over the system …"

Images appeared showing celebrations by various groups from human to alien on places as remote as Regalis, Idolis, and, unsurprisingly, Vertullis and Legallis.

Xalivar smiled as he flipped channels again.

"… Xalivar Rhii's death marks the end of an era. Authorities at the Palace said they have strong suspicions the deposed leader was behind many of the assassinations targeting Vertullian citizens throughout the Alliance …"

Xalivar had never been more tempted to dance with elation. *They think I'm dead!*

Despite Dek's disobedience, once again, the gods had shown their favorable light on Xalivar. He smiled. Once again, he had the advantage. *Yes, fools, consider me dead. That way, you'll never see me coming!*

His laughter bounced off the walls of his quarters as he relaxed for the first time since leaving the battle, enjoying the warmth flooding over his body like waves of triumph. Xerxes and Xonas had been the first of many to underestimate Xalivar. But he hadn't gotten where he was by letting weak fools affect his confidence. His former people had declared him dead, yet here he was, alive and well, and that gave him an advantage. Let them think him dead as long as they liked. It just gave him more time to plan and execute his return. They'd all realize their mistake the day they knelt in allegiance before him!

He tipped his head back and laughed, truly enjoying the sensation for the first time in years.

# Chapter One

The Xanthian's fist struck Farien's jaw like a hammer, twisting his head back and to the right as he shifted his body to cushion the blow, then launched a strike of his own. The Xanthian merely chortled at the weak effort, and Farien wondered how his team had gotten off mission so fast.

"I don't think this is what Lord Aron had in mind when he sent us to locate supplies," Tela muttered from beside him as she ducked the swinging arm of the Xanthian's companion, a Tertullian pilot who looked alarmingly like a steroid-enhanced version of Farien's old friend, Yao.

Farien winced at the memory, but he knew she was right. It was the first combat any of them had seen since the engagement off Tertullis six months before. At least then they'd been in fighters, not face to face with their enemy. "Let's just wrap this up before Matheu gets back, all right?" he replied.

He spotted his pilots—Virun, Jorek, Os and Ria—squaring off against other bar patrons nearby and wondered why he'd been so quick to jump in and try to save their asses. After all, they'd started this foolishness.

"He insulted Ria," Os had claimed, when Farien and Tela came running at the sound of the commotion.

"I can take care of myself," Ria had growled back, sending a Xanthian flying with a punch from her fist. Her foe flew across the bar top, shattering glass as various liquors splattered then pooled out in her path from their broken containers. Patrons scattered.

The two young pilots had just joined them, and to Tela they looked like kids. Inseparable, Os was blond, bulky, chubby, and short, while Ria was tall and thin, with dark red hair stretching halfway down her back making her appear far more feminine and frail than anyone who dared tangle with her would discover. Their flying skills rivaled anyone else in the squadron and their fierce loyalty to and competitiveness with each other drove them to excel far more than Farien's orders ever would.

The dimly lit bar was crowded and the raging techno music had cut off mid-chorus when the fight broke out. Now groups of patrons lined the bland, wooden walls, making bets as they cheered on various participants, like gamblers choosing their champions at an Old Earth cockfight. The bartender and waitresses also stood in a group, watching with dismay as their workplace became a shambles. Other than smashed tables and chairs, broken glass and spilled drinks, Farien barely noticed a difference. With its creaky worn floor and unpainted, undecorated wood-slate walls, the bar had been nothing to brag about from the beginning, but still, shack or not, some people did come to consider their workplaces like second homes.

"Do you think they'll make us pay for this?" Farien wondered again to Tela, as they stood back to back, preparing to repel yet another attack from the Xanthian brute and his Tertullian sidekick.

"They started it," Tela answered as she planted a foot and reared back with her fist, launching it toward the Tertullian.

Farien echoed the move and both struck their opponents at the same moment to little effect. "If we don't find a way to finish it, none of that will matter. What are these guys made of?"

"Your nightmares," the Tertullian said with a laugh as he and the Xanthian swung their own fists, and Tela and Farien bowed and ducked, trying to avoid them. Pain shot through Farien's right shoulder as the Xanthian's fist grazed him, but Tela swung clear, untouched yet again.

"For a woman, you're way too good at this," Farien muttered.

"What? Women can't fight?" Tela laughed. "You're starting to sound like Davi."

Actually, it had been a misunderstanding that caused a deep tension between Tela and her fiancé for several months, but they'd worked it out. "I thought you'd settled that," Farien replied as the Xanthian rushed forward and got him in a choke hold. The brute dragged Farien backwards on his feet as he punched him in the lower back from behind.

"Feel free to prove it on this big guy," Farien choked out as he struggled to free himself.

"You'd rather fight the one that looks like Yao then?" Tela asked as she and the Tertullian circled, each trying to anticipate the other's next move.

"I was trying to take it easy on you," Farien said again as his hands pulled at the Xanthian's sweaty bluish-gray skinned arm and his back raged with pain from the continuing blows. "These guys don't fight fair."

"We fight to win!" The Xanthian's scratchy voice boomed in the familiar slurred accent.

"Ah, right, maybe we should try that," Farien muttered and threw his left foot back to land on the brute's toes then raised his right foot between the Xanthian's legs and kicked upward. The Xanthian's grip released slightly as Farien made contact with the tender patches on the alien's inner thighs and he emitted a gasping groan. Farien imagined the feeling of blinding pain human males experienced when their genitals were assaulted and took advantage of his opponent's wavering grip to pull free, spin, and then kick him again in the same spot, slamming fists up into his face as the alien bent over in agony.

"Nice move," Tela said with a laugh as she battered the Tertullian in the face with a fist and sent him reeling backward, then threw her own feet up to kick his chest with such force that he went airborne and crashed to a landing atop what had once been a drinking table. With a satisfied look, she stood upright, brushing her hands against each other with dramatic flair. "Next?"

"We could use a little help over here," Virun called from where he and his best friend, Jorek, were engaged with six pirates, all big enough to give Farien's Xanthian a run for his money. All were hairy and dirty enough that Tela couldn't immediately identify their species. A couple looked human but two others could be humanoids of other roots.

Like Os and Ria, Virun and Jorek were inseparable. Short, bulky and brunette, Jorek was the Farien to Virun's Yao. Virun was dark-skinned, with short dark hair and light blue eyes, lanky and tall. Both were as skilled on Skitters and in VS28 cockpits as they were with blasters and hand-to-hand combat. Watching them hold off six attackers was an impressive sight. Farien almost preferred to stand back and appreciate their skills, but instead he rushed in, leaping on the back of a pirate who had just struck Virun from behind.

"You realize none of these people are likely to want to trade with us now, right?" Tela called. One of the pirates spun to square off with her as she approached, and she launched herself at him without missing a beat.

The ten of them became a cornucopia of flying fists, kicking legs, grunting, groaning, sweaty bodies for several minutes before Farien saw a flash and heard a blaster shot then coughed dust as splintered wood and metal pieces rained down from the ceiling above.

Everyone ceased fighting and turned toward the door. The smell of singed wood mixed with the charming ambiance of sweaty bodies and spilled alcohol.

General Matheu stood in the doorway, blaster raised, his face as hard and expressionless as his blue uniform and gold medals were shiny and sparkly. He glared at them all like an instructor who'd caught cadets after curfew violating regulations. "Enough!"

Farien glanced around. Even the pirates and Xanthians looked intimidated by Matheu.

"What happened?" Matheu said, pronouncing each word like a curse.

Tela and Farien stepped forward as the rest of the pilots straightened their uniforms. All of them were disheveled with dirt splotches, wrinkles, and a couple torn or stained with liquor or some other liquid, including his own—a sharp contrast with that of the General.

"Just a misunderstanding, sir," Tela said.

"We're here to requisition supplies, not teach the locals our customs and manners," Matheu replied, his face unchanged. "This is *not* the way officers are to comport themselves—on duty or off. Unacceptable!"

Farien and Tela exchanged a look, each searching his or her mind for a good excuse. Finally, Farien looked away and motioned toward the pirates. "They started it, General."

Matheu scowled like Farien had questioned his authority. "As far as I'm concerned, you were in command so you're responsible, Noa! And it's you who will be disciplined, not some civilian drunkards and hoodlums." The General turned to the rest of the pilots and the crowd. "Why are you still standing there?"

In an instant, everyone rushed for the door—pilots, pirates, Xanthians and other patrons scurrying and stumbling over each other in a race for the exit.

Matheu just stood there with Farien and Tela, watching them go. "I expect you to compensate the proprietor for damages, and apologize."

Farien cursed to himself. Another week's wages down the tubes. The bartender and waitress had begun inspecting the damage. Farien and Tela sighed and located the bartender, moving toward him as they each pulled credit sticks from their pockets.

The bartender frowned as they approached.

"We're sorry for the mess, sir," Tela said.

Farien nodded. "Please allow us to compensate you for damages."

The bartender stared at the proffered credit sticks for a moment, before taking them and inserting them into two slots on the counter. Farien heard beeps and saw lights flash as the bar's computer transferred the funds. Then the sticks went dark and the bartender retrieved them and handed them back to the pilots.

Farien cursed as he accepted his stick and examined it. "There were four thousand credits on there!"

The bartender waved a hand around at the chaos of his bar and glared. "Please find another place to entertain yourselves if you ever return to Xanthis," he said, his slurred accent far more intelligible than those of the brutes with whom they'd been fighting.

"We don't expect to be back any time soon," Tela said.

In the six months since Xalivar's death and defeat at the Battle of Tertullis, the Vertullians had set into motion their plans to leave Boralis behind and find a new home elsewhere. If things worked out, they'd never be back.

The Vertullian fleet had launched a week earlier from Iraja and was headed now for the edge of the system along the same route Matheu and the scouts had taken to prepare the way. The fleet had made plans to stop for supplies and passengers at various points along the way. With Vertullians scattered throughout the system, they wanted to be sure no one who desired to join them got left behind.

Matheu continued to glare as Farien and Tela turned back toward the door. He motioned sharply with a flick of his hand and the two officers continued past him in silence, following their fellow pilots out the door.

The pirates dragged Bordox out into a dark, dirty alley as he struggled to free himself, finally stopping and slamming him back first against a wall.

"What's your damage, pond scum?" The leader demanded. Etan, a human raised by colonists on Idolis, was only inches taller than Bordox's shorter ex-classmate, Farien, whom he'd just seen among those fighting in the bar. But in sheer mass, even Bordox feared him. Solid muscle, a born fighter, Etan had the missing front teeth to prove it and he took pride in the gap. The others had told him Etan refused to see a dentist because he liked how it looked. With a brown, bushy beard grown down six inches off his chin and fanning out like a lion's mane from his face, the teeth and his ragged clothes and dirty face combined to add an air of threat that intimidated most everyone he encountered.

"I knew one of those people," Bordox said, feigning a relaxed look as he leaned back against the wall and hoped to avoid any more manhandling.

"Enemy or friend?" Etan's second, Jurgen asked. Blond, blue-eyed, and tanned, he was tall and thin and hailed from one of the small settlements on the far side of Legallis from the capital, Legon, where Farien had grown up.

"Both," Bordox replied and the pirates guffawed like the half-drunken ruffians they were.

"Those are the best kind," Jurgen joked as the others nodded.

"Doesn't matter," Etan said, his face serious again. "We can't take on the whole fleet."

"Besides, you wasn't exactly jumping in to help," said Rufa, who made even Etan look small, from the leader's right. An even rougher looking human from places undisclosed, he spoke in a gravely bass with the grammar of one who'd turned his back on education at an early age.

"I was weighing my options," Bordox said. It was true. He had stayed out of sight in a dark corner, watching and waiting. He'd hoped to get Tela alone so he could pull her outside and use her in his plan for revenge against her fiancé, Xander "Davi" Rhii.

The pirates laughed. "You think too much, pond scum," Etan said, shaking his head. "You want to be one of us, as you claim, you'll learn to participate."

Jurgen nodded. "We're a team and that means we fight, you fight."

"Or you're next," Rufa said, stepping forward threateningly, a couple of his silent companions also jostling toward Bordox.

Bordox raised his palms in surrender, his heart racing at the thought of what their fists would feel like on his already bruised body. "I'm sorry. I'm learning as fast as I can."

Rufa sneered. "Learn this: we do it, you do it. That's how ya stays out of trouble, boy." His companions snorted and chuckled around him, nodding in agreement.

"Okay," Bordox said, and they backed off again.

"A few drunk pilots in a brawl, that's fun," Etan said. "When the brass show up that means reinforcements are nearby. Not worth the risk."

Jurgen nodded again. "Until we're ready."

Etan grinned. "Exactly. Come!" He started swaggering down the alley and turned right on the next street as Bordox and the others rushed to catch up.

He'd found them on RB7, a small moon of Idolis long abandoned by anyone but thieves, outcasts and those people not wanting to be found. Explored and tapped for mining by the famed Boralian geologist Rober Bailes, its rocky surface formations had yielded a third of the resources anticipated by Bailes' study, at ten times the cost, so the mining companies had closed down within eight months and left RB7 for good. But, in doing so, they'd left behind perfectly good accommodations and facilities built from scratch and these had now been claimed and modified by various bands to suit their own purposes, the pirates amongst them.

When he'd left the battle at Tertullis, disowned by his father, Obed, humiliated once again by Xander Rhii and his rebel friends, Bordox had wandered looking for options. He'd encountered a few of the pirates at a port on Xanthis and followed them, hoping a man with his skills and experience might find a place with them. But while he'd expected them to be cautious, he'd never realized the lengths to which that might take them. After five months, he'd never seen their real leader. He was only allowed to participate with Etan's squad. All leadership and official meetings were off limits, as was any facility outside Etan's squad's quarters. On RB7, Bordox was a nonperson. He couldn't even go to local bars for a drink. At least when they were out on missions, he got included at bars like the one they'd just left. When they were on RB7, he got one of the others to bring him back beer and other spirits and stayed in their quarters, drinking by himself. Except when the others invited him to play cards or some other amusement.

Bordox didn't care. He needed no one but himself. The pirates were just a means to an end. Only a fool thought he could survive without contacts out here. And the pirates had access to anything and everything Bordox needed to execute his plans and bring down Xander Rhii once and for all. The best part of it all: Rhii would be coming right to him on a fleet with all the loved ones he held dear, providing ample targets for Bordox to inflict maximum suffering on his enemy before he sent him to his death.

He smiled, getting a spring in his step as he pictured Rhii's bloodied body. It was the one triumph he'd waited for years to see, and soon enough, he was sure, he would finally get to see it.

"How many of these barges are there again?" Nila's sarcasm barely masked the irritation they all felt walking through their sixth DB7 Barge on an inspection tour.

Brie chuckled. "Twelve, last I heard, and then there're the transports, the Agra-ships, the …"

Nila cupped her forehead with a hand and sighed. "Okay already, I get the picture."

Davi and Brie exchanged a smile. The Captain reached out to rub his young cousin's shoulders. "I know it's not the most thrilling duty assignment we've had—"

"Ha!" Nila snorted. "Virun, Jorek, Tela, and Farien are the lucky ones. At least they get to visit exotic ports, unusual places, see the system."

Davi fought the urge to laugh. He'd seen far more places in the Borali system than either of his companions and although unusual certainly fit his experience, exotic wasn't a word that he'd have used to describe most of them. "With a fleet this big and a journey this long, we'll have all kinds of interesting experiences, I promise. We just have to get safely out of our own system first."

The mishmash of ships making up the Vertullian fleet would have been laughable if Davi wasn't one of those in charge of leading and protecting it. The leadership had negotiated for months to purchase and lease as many available ships as they could find. Some had been located abandoned in space and repaired. Others had been found grounded by owners short on funds who were more than willing to allow the Vertullians to borrow them if they paid for overhauling and brought them back up to regs. The result was a fleet of mostly civilian vessels—a large percentage of which had never been intended for long distance, extra-system passenger travel—being escorted by a few select military vessels on a quest for a new home and a fresh start.

The DB7s in particular, were the dregs of the group. The smallest of barge-class vessels available, they were designed for hauling resources between planets within a solar system. With a small bridge at the front and a dozen small crew cabins just aft, followed by one dining-gathering area, the bulk of each ship consisted of a long cargo bay, lined in the center by a corridor and on each side by small compartments for carrying the various cargo. These small compartments had been modified, the doors removed and replaced by curtains, with hammocks and cots installed for passenger travel. Some were occupied by up to five people—two adults and three children—while others held only three adults. Either way, the occupants were forced to cram in shoulder-to-shoulder to fit, making these the least desirable accommodations in the fleet, but also the most affordable. The few crew cabins had been refitted and rented to a few higher paying passengers, with only a minimum number set aside for the skeleton crew manning the barge itself.

Davi and his squadron had been sent throughout the fleet inspecting ships one by one to make sure they met the minimum fleet regulations for safety and hygiene—and while they hadn't failed any yet, they'd also realized their own expectations and standards far exceeded those accepted by the new Vertullian leadership.

As they sidled past two particularly crowded compartments, Davi and the women exchanged looks of dismay but remained silent. Two kids appeared, running down the aisle making engine and laser noises as they played with toy fighters, pretending to attack each other.

"I shot you."

"You did not!"

"Did, too. You lost an engine!"

They were so intent on their play that they failed to notice the pilots. Nila and Brie stepped to the side, allowing them to pass, but the second boy ran right into Davi as he dodged to the side to avoid the first. Davi grunted as they impacted, reaching down to steady the boy so he wouldn't fall.

"I'm sorry, Captain!" A woman cried out and came running toward them. She grabbed the boys by their arms and scolded them. "Apologize! I've told you to be careful."

"Sorry," the boys mumbled, looking down, their enthusiasm gone now.

Davi waved it off. "No harm done. It's fine." He smiled, ignoring the chuckles and jeering looks offered by Brie and Nila. Then he heard voices shouting and a murmuring drone ahead.

"What's going on?" Brie wondered.

"Fight!" Someone yelled as passengers surged forward seeking a look. Davi and his companions were forced to push and pull their way through to reach where the incident was taking place.

"This is perfect," Nila muttered.

"You're the one who wanted more excitement," Davi teased as they worked their way forward. He wondered how much of the ladies' envy was as much about loneliness as jealousy. Viron and Jorek had been dating Nila and Brie for over a year now and, when they were off call, the four were almost inseparable. Being assigned to separate duties was a hardship he knew well being separated from Tela, and he imagined the ladies and their beaus would be experiencing similar emotions.

The circling crowd grew denser and Davi and the ladies had to actually push people aside to get through. "Official business!" They all called, over and over, receiving irritated stares and growled rebukes.

"Sir, you can let me through or I can arrest you right here," Nila snapped at a particularly obstinate older man, who'd continually ignored her taps on his shoulder.

Finally, he scowled and stepped aside and Davi, Brie, and Nila found themselves facing a rotund bald man in a white robe wrestling with two skinny blondes in the midst of the aisle.

"It's not yours!" One of the women screamed, looking at the other, then reached out and slammed the other girl's head to the deck using a fist full of her yellow hair.

"You see how she is?" The beaten girl responded to the man, who now looked like he was doing his best to pull them apart.

"What's going on here?" Davi demanded as he stepped forward.

"It's a private family matter, sir," the bald man replied. "We'll settle it once they've calmed down."

"You're not in a private place, sir, and you're disturbing the other passengers."

"It's not our fault they won't *mind* their own business!" The first woman snapped, reaching for the other's hair again.

The second blonde jerked her head away, accidentally slamming it into the jaw of the bald man, who cried out in agony. "What do you know about minding your own business…? Oh, sorry, baby." She turned and gently rubbed the bald man's jaw, looking apologetic and worried at the same time.

Davi motioned to Brie and Nila and they all three moved in, prepared to pull the three apart. "What's your relationship to these women, sir?" Davi asked, ignoring the women for now. The man sounded far more reasonable at the moment.

"I'm his wife!" The first blonde shouted, staring daggers at her counterpart.

"And I'm gonna be!" replied the second blonde. The two women began flailing and struggling again to get at each other as the bald man once again fought to keep them apart.

Of all the things the women could have said, the second girl's comment was the last thing Davi had expected. He had enough trouble handling one woman. How could any man actually think he could handle two? Plus, this guy wasn't exactly the kind women typically fought over either. What was his secret?

Pushing aside his thoughts, Davi motioned to Nila and Brie. They each grabbed one of the three and pulled, separating them. Davi had the hardest time, since the bald man outweighed him by double at least. The blondes both cursed, fighting against the female pilot's efforts, while the bald man used his feet to push himself up and to his feet, balancing as Davi released him and offering a smile of thanks.

"Whatever the issue is, you need to settle it quietly or keep it to yourselves," Nila scolded.

"How are we supposed to do that when we're all shoved in here like Gungors?" the first blonde demanded, finally ceasing her struggle and pulling free of Nila's grip, then straightening her hair and clothes as she stared daggers at the other blonde.

"Figure it out!" Brie said as she released the other blonde, making sure to slide around so she and Nila were both between them.

"We're gonna be stuck here for months," the first blonde complained.

"All the more reason not to embarrass yourselves in front of everyone," Brie answered.

"I'm sorry," the bald man said, looking at Davi. "I tried to reason with them, but they just can't get along."

"Sir, it's none of my affair, but the laws of our people don't permit bigamy. . . ."

"We're not your people," the second blonde snapped, sounding almost disgusted.

"You're in the Vertullian fleet, ma'am," Nila said.

The second blonde nodded. "We paid for passage like everyone else."

"Rigel!" the bald man scolded, then turned to Davi again. "I'm a merchant. I've lived on Vertullis my whole life, working at the market in Iraja. When my customers all decided to leave, I thought starting over wherever they landed made sense."

"Not if you three kill each other on the way," Davi said.

The bald man chuckled. "Rigel and Cassie just have their moments, Captain. Most of the time, we're a loving family, I assure you."

Davi just raised his hands and nodded. "I'm sure they're lovely. But if we get called in for trouble like this again, your assurances won't be enough."

The bald man nodded and placed a gentle hand on Davi's arm. "Of course, Captain. We're very sorry. It won't happen again." Then he shot the two women a dark frown and began herding them into the nearest compartment. To Davi's amazement, both women turned humble and looked like scolded dogs sulking at their master's feet.

Nila and Brie turned back to the crowd. "Show's over," Brie called. "Go back to your own compartments please!"

All three of the pilots began directing the onlookers as they slowly dispersed back to where they'd come from.

"We're military, not police," Brie muttered.

"Not for the moment," Davi replied, quietly. "And that's not likely to change until we're settled on a new planet."

Nila sighed. "I can't wait to do the paperwork on this one."

Davi and Brie laughed as Davi spun once more to be sure all of those watching had gone back to their own business, then turned and led them forward again along the aisle.

"Let's just get out of here before they start up again," Brie urged.

Davi shared their laughter but worried how, if the citizens were so wound up already, the Vertullians could ever survive such a long journey. This was far from the only such domestic incident military personnel had been required to address in the week since they'd launched, and it would only get worse. He made a note to discuss with Aron, Sol, and the rest of the Council the ramifications for security if they didn't find a way to increase the morale on ships like these.

Tarkanius finished the libation and closed his eyes in a final prayer. His encounters with Aron had led to his initiating daily morning visits to the small Palace temple for meditation and communion with the gods. In the six months he'd resumed practicing his people's traditional religion, he'd come to consider that time indispensable for any successful day. Besides the comfort he found in communing with beings higher than himself, the time helped him start each day focused, relaxed, and at peace with himself and the world. Given the first appointment on his daily schedule, he figured today he'd need that more than ever.

Taking a deep breath, he offered the traditional four fingered salute to the pantheon and stood, adjusting his robe before turning and starting down the side aisle for the secret passage to the throne room. Until he'd taken office, he'd had no idea the Palace had so many secret passages, but even now he only made use of a few like this one and never as a means of sneaking around behind the backs of staff or others. In this case, the only other route to the Palace temple was to leave the building and walk outside and, if the group awaiting him contained the expected members, getting there sooner rather than later would be to his advantage.

Lords Simeon and Kray had set the appointment on their behalf, but Tarkanius knew that others like Lords Qai, Amie, Buj, Pharah Brahma, Kanaan, and Quatol had been behind it. His decision to include representatives of all the planets' native peoples on the Council had been a hard sell, yet Tarkanius pushed it through because he knew the future of the Alliance depended on it. The new members had all been involved in the peace meetings on Idolis, and, in the month since they'd officially joined in Council deliberations, he'd found them invaluable additions to the leadership. The segment of the Council who'd been resistant had quieted a lot in that short time because the new voices had brought with them ideas and solutions, which successfully addressed a number of crises resulting from the Vertullians' decision to abandon their planet and leave the system.

Tarkanius sighed. The relief had been temporary. With the actual departure, all sorts of new problems had arisen which hadn't been anticipated, and once again, everyone was stressed and on edge, and, of course, they all looked to Tarkanius for quick solutions. He'd asked the gods for wisdom and strength and patience, and he knew he'd need all three to face the days ahead.

He'd never been overly religious as a youth, but like everyone, he'd studied the traditions of his people in school and heard about it from family, especially his grandmother who was the most pious person he knew. There were gods for every occasion and need, from water and sustenance to business and sports. He'd never lost his sense of irony at how peoples of such divergent belief systems had come together to combine them as a pantheon in the name of tolerance and peace.

The Old Earth groups who'd melded into the Boralian system included former mainstream Protestants, Episcopalians, some Catholics, Hindus, Muslims, and others. After years of fighting over theological differences and public policies, a group of leaders had bound together in ecumenism and started the movement which resulted in a new combined religion. And after decades, it had evolved into the system the Boralians used today. The gods existed to serve man and man honored them for their blessings and interference. Along the way, the disagreements, which had once divided and defined the groups, faded away into aspects tied to particular gods.

And now people were free to follow the god or gods they wished without offense to followers of others. Each believer lived in confidence that his or her gods guarded, guided and assisted him in daily living and allowed and encouraged others to seek peace wherever their own paths might lead them.

Tarkanius had modeled the changes he'd brought to the Council on ideas he'd learned from that history. If men and women of such diverse cultures, ideologies, etc., could peacefully coexist and come to consider themselves one people as the Boralians had, then he believed the time had come to do the same with the entire Borali System. One day the Tertullians, Idolians, and Boralians would all consider themselves one people, united. No matter what else he accomplished during his time as High Lord Councilor, Tarkanius believed that if he could foster such a bond, it would be his greatest legacy.

As he reached the outer corridor leading to the throne room, he stopped and offered a quick prayer again. *Oh gods, hear my prayers and manifest in me.* Then he stepped forward, triggering the sensors to slide the large throne room door upward toward the ceiling and stepped inside to face his fellow Lords.

Simeon and Kray stood at the foot of the steps leading to the throne itself with the other Lords lined up around them. All turned as Tarkanius strode in, his gold robe with white cuffs and collar a contrast to their own white Council robes with gold trim. The alien Lords looked surprisingly natural in their robes. Several were unaccustomed to human clothing but all had adapted well, with the Council's official tailors' assistance to modify the standard robes for better fit and comfort.

"Welcome, my friends," Tarkanius said, spreading his arms in symbolic welcome as he moved amongst them, shaking the hands of any who offered.

Simeon and Kray smiled back warmly, delighted to see him as only dear friends could be. Unlike Tarkanius, whose belly had expanded with his age, Simeon remained tall and thin and wore his graying hair like a crown of achievement. Soft spoken when he needed to be but also stern and focused when his job as Head of Council required it, he'd been a longtime friend and ally of Tarkanius.

Kray, the first female elected to the Council, was also graying now but still two decades younger than either of them. She was highly educated and had grown up around the Palace where her best friend, Miri Rhii, lived as princess of the Rhii dynasty. Kray was strong-willed yet compassionate and levelheaded and had been a key supporter of the Vertullians' quest for freedom and full citizenship.

"We're sorry to have disturbed you so early, my Lord," Simeon said.

Tarkanius chuckled. "These days my sleep comes second to the demands of my office, I'm afraid."

The rest of the group looked a bit less friendly. The other human Lords were younger and new. Qai was yellow-skinned and thin, hailing from ancestors amongst the Eastern continents of Old Earth. After barely two years on the Council, he'd taken a key leadership role recently along with Kray, Buj, and Amie. The younger pair had risen to leadership because of dedication and a strong work ethic. Unlike legacy Lords who'd inherited their positions, Amie and Buj had earned their way onto the Council the hard way and appreciated the opportunities it provided them. Both were physically fit but Buj was slightly taller than the bigger boned Amie.

Pharah Brahma hadn't been his jovial self since the death of his son, Yao, at the battle over Tertullis. Yao had sacrificed himself to save others and brought down Xalivar himself in the process, and Tarkanius knew the diplomat was deservedly proud of his accomplished son, despite reeling from the loss. With dark orange-tinted skin and purple eyes, the humanoid Tertullian was tall and thin like his son but his hair was streaked with white from stress and age. His robe and dress were impeccable. Of the alien Lords, he was the one most used to human attire after years spent amongst them. He clasped Tarkanius' hand warmly and forced a smile. "It's our honor to meet with you, my Lord."

"Of course," Lord Quatol, the Xanthian representative said with a nod, "but the crisis at hand concerns all of us, and quick action is required to avoid it becoming worse." Older like Tarkanius and Simeon, Quatol was not one to waste words, especially when the topic was one he felt passionate about.

"Which crisis are we speaking of?" Tarkanius asked, ignoring the rudeness.

"There are several, actually," Kray started to say, when Lord Kanaan interrupted.

"The one which we're primarily concerned with is the complete collapse of the agricultural sector." Unlike Quatol, the Idolian ambassador was taller and thinner, his lighter blue skin and red eyes contrasting with the Xanthian's blue-gray skin and rounder form. Quatol wore the decorative jewelry and piercings signifying his cultural status while Kanaan remained more simply appointed. "Adoo informs us people are on the verge of rioting."

Pharah bristled at the mention of his chief rival's name. Adoo had been the peace representative at the talks with Tarkanius, but the High Lord Councilor preferred the more laid-back style of Brahma and had lobbied for him when the Council positions came up. Adoo continued to resent the slight and made his voice heard by staying in touch with any Lords who would listen. He'd become a thorn in everyone's side, especially Pharah's.

"I'm sure Adoo was very open about his concerns," Simeon jumped in to say, "but as he's not on the Council, let's do our best to focus on our own firsthand knowledge not speculation."

Both Tarkanius and Pharah shot Simeon looks of thankful relief as Tarkanius directed the conversation again. "Collapse is a strong word, Lord Kanaan. What news have you that I might not be aware of?"

The Idolian's boldness came out when he was partnered with Quatol but on his own, he faltered into the typical humbleness of his people, and struggled for words. "Unproductive or abandoned farms, workers without proper knowledge or training assuming responsibility, agricultural transports grossly in violation of safety regulations or grounded in need of repairs …"

"Everyone's doing their best to get up to speed," Tarkanius answered. "With the loss of our Vertullian citizens, we've had to find people to fill in gaps who are unfamiliar with them. But those desperate for jobs should be grateful for the work, and we'll do our best to provide them with government support and training."

"We already have a committee in place to formulate plans," Simeon added.

Tarkanius nodded his thanks for the assist.

"In the meantime, our markets are suffering without proper shipments to sell," Quatol jumped in. "Black Market competition is raising inflation, not to mention health concerns from their lack of proper … inspection."

"People buy from Black Markets at their own risk, Lord Quatol," Kray replied. "Unless your government wants to shut them down…."

Quatol bristled, as expected. The Black Market on Xanthis was known to be a huge unofficial boost to the planet's economy, which is why officials there looked the other way. If Tarkanius had his way, he'd send his own men to shut it down, but they were too occupied elsewhere to be bothered at the moment.

"When we can't provide what's needed through legitimate channels, people have a right to look elsewhere," Kanaan said, defending his friend.

"And we wouldn't expect them not to," Lord Buj said. "But if those alternate sources spread disease or other issues—"

"Our Black Market is not responsible for spreading disease!" Quatol objected, his face reddening as his body tensed. "You find me one factual case—"

Tarkanius raised a hand to silence him. "It was not an accusation, Quatol. Merely a statement of our mutual desire to avoid complicating the problems."

Quatol scowled at Buj and backed down with a nod.

Tarkanius continued: "I will have the military send mechanics from our depots to oversee the problems with the agricultural ships. In the meantime, if you know of anyone with expertise who might help these new farmers and producers come up to speed, please don't hesitate to make suggestions."

"We can certainly improve the situation by speeding up settlement permits for Vertullis," Lord Qai suggested.

Quatol and Kanaan nodded vigorously.

"They virtually abandoned an entire planet already fit for agriculture and we have people dying for land who are ready to move in and take over."

"You can't complain about unqualified people on the one hand and demand that we just open the gates to anyone on the other," Kray said, shaking her head. "We're trying to be sure we get qualified people who can utilize the existing infrastructure appropriately, not refit or destroy it."

"And the process is taking months. We need people now to keep our food supply viable," Qai replied.

Tarkanius wasn't surprised to see Qai taking the opposite side in this. Despite his helpfulness, the young Lord had always been unafraid to stand up for his convictions, wherever they led him. "Lord Qai, if you'd like to work with Lords Kray, Kanaan, and Quatol to come up with a way to speed the process, we'd welcome it. In the meantime, those already there need to double their efforts and pick up the slack."

"So, applicants from elsewhere wind up with poorer choice in land while those already there get double and top pick?" Quatol sounded ready to roll his eyes but managed to avoid it. "That will certainly engender good feelings amongst any future settlers."

"Land taken to assist with the crisis can be reexamined and redistributed later," Simeon said. "We'll make it clear, but solving the immediate problems has to be top priority."

"Agreed," Lords Amie, Buj, and Kray said together.

"We have to be patient and give it time," Pharah added. He nodded to Tarkanius. "The government is doing the best it can from everything I see. It's extremely difficult, and many issues have arisen which couldn't have been anticipated."

Tarkanius nodded, relieved that at least some of them understood his position. "I am as frustrated as all of you, I promise. I think of little else these days. But big changes require careful solutions, not rash action."

"There's talk of layoffs at some of the plants," Qai said then. "With the farms not producing up to expectations, the workers have nothing to do. The owners don't want to continue paying them."

Tarkanius felt his heart sink. Every problem compounded another. It was like endlessly treading on a stormy sea with no land in sight.

"They cannot strike," Amie said, shaking his head. "The repercussions would be staggering."

"They don't see that as their concern," Qai said.

Tarkanius raised a hand again for silence, then paused a moment, scanning them, his eyes meeting theirs each in turn. He'd been criticized in the past for being indecisive, and he knew he couldn't afford to be so now. "I suggest we all work together to find a solution to this crisis and the many others. I cannot lead in isolation. Our peoples must join as one to create a future that will sustain us."

One by one he watched them as the words sank in. Then, together, Kray and Simeon nodded. The others followed, some individually, others in pairs.

Tarkanius smiled, motioning them toward his conference room as he recalled his earlier libation and prayers. *Peace, my gods, peace.* He hoped he'd feel it again very soon.

# Chapter Two

Pres stopped in the corridor outside Xalivar's *Tarragon* quarters and took a deep breath. Her comfort level around her leader was far better now than it had been after her outburst six months before; still, internally she raged over the loss of the only man she'd ever loved. The fact that she'd never told him, that Dek had never returned her passion, didn't matter. He'd died for Xalivar and everyone knew it. And she struggled to believe it had been worth it.

The gray corridor's walls shined as light from the reflector pads overhead invaded the shadows. Xalivar liked it dark, perhaps for the ambiance. He enjoyed intimidating those around him. It was all a game, one she was tired of playing.

She reached out and pressed the button notifying Xalivar of her presence then listened as the door beeped and whooshed upward into the ceiling. She raised her datapad, calling up the battle reports and stepped inside.

Xalivar waited for her in a small dining area off his meeting room, as he finished a breakfast of Qiwi fruit salad: a mix of the native Plutonis animal's meat with Jax, Gixi, and other fruits. It was a favorite of many of the upper crust, sweet and tart combined with the salty, juicy meat.

She paused across the table as Xalivar wiped his chin on a napkin and then nodded to his majordomo, Manaen, who took the napkin and the plate and disappeared into another room.

Pres watched the tall, blue-skinned alien retreat and wondered what he thought of his own employer. The Idolians were known for their loyalty and self-sacrificial service to others, but surely the majordomo had seen enough to realize he served a man who was hardly worthy of honor and sacrifice.

Xalivar cleared his throat, interrupting her thoughts. "You have news for me?"

Pres nodded and glanced at the datapad. "Yes, my Lord. Our raids on Idolis were a success. The planet was taken entirely by surprise. Ruxan was hit at sunrise and the government buildings are in shambles. Major damage was also done to the infrastructure throughout the city. It will take them years to recover. We also shut down the starport for the near future, including the particular target of most interest." By the last, she meant the building in which Tarkanius' leadership summit with alien leaders had taken place. It had been false leads about the location of the conference which lead to the attack off Tertullis and Pres felt no sorrow at seeing the real location destroyed, in part, as revenge for the deception.

*At least, for now, it's something in your honor, Dek.* Pres had plans for more.

Xalivar chuckled, pleased at the report. "The Idolians deserve to pay for their role in the deception. And soon enough we will make that fool Tarkanius and the others pay as well. We had no trouble with the planetary shields?"

Pres shook her head. "The command codes gave our techs full access to download the viruses that disabled the shields. But if they catch on and start changing them—"

Xalivar dismissed it with a wave. "Then we have other ways. What news is there of the slave fleet?"

Pres found Xalivar's refusal to refer to the Vertullians as anything but "the slaves" indicative of his one-sided worldview. The whole world revolved around his vision, as far as he was concerned. While Pres had once embraced his vision and what she thought it would mean for their people, she now realized she'd aligned herself with the wrong side, but it was too late to matter. "The fleet is moving slowly, my Lord, as they gather resources and prepare some of the less distance-worthy ships for the journey. They have scouts out seeking supplies as well as transporting other Vertullians from further out in the system who wish to join them."

"A perfect opportunity for us to engage in more disruptions," Xalivar replied, nodding. "I want continual raids disrupting that fleet. Target fuel ships, agri-ships, anything vital that will slow them down. If we destroy a few passenger vessels in the process, that's fine, but I want them to suffer and live in fear for the moment."

"My Lord, we did suffer losses in the attack on Idolis, and we're still recovering the losses from the battle at Tertullis. If we stretch too thin—"

Xalivar's brow furrowed. "I'll decide when we attack, where, and how. Your job is to execute the plans and make sure the force is adequate for the mission, General."

Pres fought the anger rising inside her like acid burning her throat. "Yes, my Lord."

"We will no longer tolerate the weak and impure controlling what we do. The Boralians are the rightful leaders of this system, and we shall reclaim it. Anyone who cowers under the demands of these usurpers will pay as the Idolians did this morning. That was only the beginning. We will retake the system by force and cower at nothing until we do. And we'll leave them all with searing memories of the suffering we inflicted because of their failure to recognize destiny." Xalivar's eyes drifted to the vidscreen showing the stars outside as he spoke. For a moment, he looked almost like a child lost in daydreams, but he finished by pounding his fist on the table and jumping to his feet; a move that was anything but childlike coming from a tall man with such a booming voice.

He stared at her then, waiting for her agreement. But Pres' eyes were drawn to the doorway where Manaen stood, listening, his red eyes slit with concern at the mention of the suffering of his own Idolian people. *Will you remain loyal, Manaen, or will you rise with me to stop this madman?* she wondered.

Then Xalivar's cold, dark eyes bore into her, demanding a response and she turned back. "May the gods bless our victory, my Lord."

Xalivar laughed, leaning back smugly in his chair. "Like the gods, they will fear me, General."

Pres nodded as she caught Manaen slipping back into the shadows and pushed a button to transmit the battle reports to Xalivar before returning to the bridge.

Sol gathered in the conference room of the Vertullian fleet's command ship, *Reliance*. One of two flagships of the Borali Alliance fleet, the battle cruiser had been gifted to the Vertullians by order of the High Lord Councilor. A new flagship was already being built in the Boralian space docks above Legallis and due to be delivered in a matter of months, so Tarkanius took the political hit, fearing the danger to the Vertullians without sufficient military escort for their ragtag ships as they left the system.

Despite years spent working as a mechanic in the depot on Vertullis, repairing Boralian ships of all shapes and sizes, Sol had never been aboard any ship as grand and majestic as *Reliance* before. White and sleek, despite her thick armored shielding and the massive cannon and weapons emplacements on her hull, the *Reliance* was an awe-inspiring sight as he and Lura arrived aboard a shuttle in the days before the fleet's departure. The quarters he shared with his wife on board dwarfed both their meager home on Vertullis before the battle that won their freedom and the quarters they'd been granted afterwards by a repentant government. It was luxurious to a point that Sol and Lura felt embarrassed, knowing that there were so many others living in subpar conditions on barges and other ships never intended for civilian passengers.

But Sol had been chosen as a member of the first Vertullian Council and the Councilors all had been given quarters suitable to their status aboard *Reliance*, where they would hold their sessions. His election caught him totally by surprise, yet he supposed it inevitable due to the heroic status awarded to both his son and himself as symbols of their people's cause. The fact that his oldest friend Aron was amongst the leadership certainly didn't hurt either. Still, Sol was not a man accustomed to the etiquette and protocols of the halls of power, and while he wore the blue robes chosen officially by the Vertullian Council, dressing the part didn't change the heart and mind inside the man or resolve his struggle to feel adequate or at home in the position.

Sol took his place at the large table, which was clearly meant to seat a lot more than the ten leaders and five advisors present at the meeting. Being dwarfed by the environment just added to his tension, but watching the Council divide themselves over loyalties between Aron and Joram was even worse.

The former planetary leader and his entourage made a stir as they entered. Tall and thin, like Sol, Joram's height gave him a visual advantage over the shorter and stockier Aron. Joram's former clean cut look had been replaced by that of a long-haired visionary after Joram started the exodus movement in response to a vicious attack in the Legallis marketplace. The incident had left Sol and Joram fighting to survive and resulted in the death of their friend Telanus, father to Tela, Sol's son's fiancée.

Head held high as it always was these days, Joram promptly placed himself near the head of the table where Aron and Uzah would lead this gathering. Uzah was the appointed military leader on the Council and Aron, having been the only Vertullian to serve, however briefly, on the Boralian Alliance Council of Lords, was a natural choice as well. But one of the items on the agenda was to decide who would lead the Council for the near future, and Aron and Joram were the top contenders.

Joram was joined by newly chosen Lords Tamora and Hula, female leaders who'd risen to influence fairly recently with progressive ideas closely matching Joram's own. Filling out their side was Lord Chad, who represented people from settlements on the far side of Vertullis from the capital, Iraja, where Sol had spent his life. Dark-skinned with wavy, braided hair and a long, thick beard, he was stocky in build but not particularly tall. Lord Klima followed them in and took a seat opposite the door. Almost as round as he was tall, Klima only spoke when necessary, rarely engaging in debate and often only raising his voice during votes. It made Sol wonder why he'd even bothered with joining the Council. But at least he, like Chad, remained an independent voice.

Aron and Uzah arrived shortly after with Miri and Davi, followed by Lords Nachor, Coz, and Zarah, the third female elected to the Council. All three were merchant and civil leaders dating back to the Boralian rule, where their smart business and diplomatic skills had elevated them to positions of importance despite their status as slaves.

In short order, Aron called the meeting to order with a smile. "Thank you, my Lords, for coming today. It's an important time for our people, and I'm grateful to have so many wise and experienced minds to help lead us to our new future."

Short and bulky like Aron but more from muscle than years, General Uzah nodded beside him. "We have, indeed, made great strides. As of this afternoon, all ships have been certified travel worthy and all immediate repair needs are being addressed. There are a few other matters which we will be addressing in the near future, but we feel confident the journey may proceed on the planned schedule."

"Yes, yes," Joram said, offering a smile closer in sincerity to that of a net salesman or news anchor than those of Aron and Uzah, "our journey has begun, as appropriate. But far more important is the decision about how we will decide upon our new home and what form leadership and government will take once we arrive there." He glanced down the table at his supporters who were nodding like disciples at a rally with their guru.

"The form of government has been generally agreed on, a Council overseeing elected planetary leadership," Aron countered. "But yes, one of the matters before us is the election of someone to lead this Council, and that person will certainly play a major role in shaping things to come."

Joram looked at Aron like he was the lone chick in a Daken formation, making Sol wish he could literally reach out and pluck the cocky leader's feathers. Joram was not the same man Sol had known for so many years, and Sol found the changes both disturbing and disappointing. "And what we need in that person is someone of unquestioned loyalty to the best interests of our people and their history."

Sol took a deep breath, struggling to control his tone as he spoke: "Loyalties can lead us in many directions, even with the best of intentions. We need someone with knowledge of the issues we must face and a plan to work through as many as we can before we even arrive and settle on a new home. Someone whose political interests come after his concern for the well-being of our people, including their need to start over in peace and unity." It was a direct jab at Joram, even though Sol had spoken no names. Since his shift, Joram had risen to be one of the most divisive leaders in the history of their people and his political aspirations were always at the top of his agenda above everything else. Aron, on the other hand, fit Sol's description exactly, and all of them knew it.

Joram turned, staring daggers at Sol. "The well-being of our people includes their right to know that those who have hated and dehumanized them, enslaved them, cannot be trusted and counted as friends no matter what they claim or attempt to do to assuage themselves of their guilt."

"The present Boralian leadership's support has directly resulted in not only our achievement of full citizenship, but our ability to assemble this fleet and depart the system," Sol argued, his temper flaring.

"They have been most supportive, as indicated by the presence of a few key Boralian military escorts who are helping to ensure our safety even now," Uzah added.

"Safety from whom?" Joram snapped. "Those among their own people who continue to insist we are less human and less deserving of the freedoms they enjoy?"

"What about those in our own numbers who would gladly reciprocate in kind against them if given the chance?" Sol countered, placing his palms down on the table's surface and scooting forward in his chair for emphasis.

"None of this will matter if we wind up settling in a populated system and must share governance with existing people or work to integrate ourselves into the existing societies," Lord Hula interjected.

Lord Tamora and Joram both scowled as their supporters shook their heads.

"I'm not saying any of us want that," Hula said, raising a palm before they could interject, "but will we have any choice? We don't know yet."

"If we find an occupied system, we will keep moving and find what we're looking for," Lord Tamora snapped, glaring at Hula.

"As I said, we may not have a choice," Hula replied.

"We always have a choice," Tamora insisted, eyes locked in battle with Hula.

Aron cleared his throat and leaned forward in his chair. "So much remains to be discovered as we undertake our journey. We must be prepared for whatever we find. It's true that we cannot succeed if we waste our energies on revenge rather than progress," Aron said with a nod to Joram. "That's why we've chosen to leave rather than stay and continue our struggle here."

"A struggle which you mock by coming to this meeting alongside one of the very people whose family orchestrated our suffering!" Joram said, turning his eyes to Miri, who was seated away from the table against the wall behind Aron with her and Sol's son, Davi, out of obvious deference to her status as visitor.

"Miri Rhii is a friend to our people as you well know!" Sol said, standing now and glaring at Joram. Whatever attempts he'd made to control his emotions fell by the wayside. Miri was like family to Sol and Lura and her behavior had been honorable and generous toward their cause. She'd even spoken in support at Joram's rallies and joined his protests.

"She has certainly lent her support to your cause on numerous occasions," Lord Chad said, looking puzzled. Even Joram's allies Tamora and Hula looked aghast at his bold disrespect toward their guest.

Miri, on the other hand, sat quietly, her eyes closed in meditation or prayer.

Sol could tell Davi was ready to leap from his chair and defend his adoptive mother. Father and son shared a passionate nature but Davi was also a guest and had no status officially here, so Sol knew any outburst from him would do more harm than help. He closed his eyes for a quick prayer to ask God to give him strength and guide his words, then spoke again: "Everyone in this room has joined your call to leave Boralis and start over, Joram. But don't mistake that for an endorsement of your tactics, especially the willingness to ignore common decency and politeness in your remarks."

Aron raised a hand. "Please, we must not devolve into insults and personal attacks. It will only divide and prevent us from doing what we've been elected to do—represent our people."

"We will not allow others to determine our future any longer," Joram demanded. "We need leadership dedicated to putting our people first in every decision and action we take from now on."

Multiple grunts of agreement came from around the table—not exclusively from Joram's own supporters.

"No one here has anything in mind but putting our people first, Joram," Lord Zarah, a gray-haired woman who looked like a mix between a grandmotherly librarian and a stern school administrator, said. "Why else would we dedicate our time to this Council?"

"Why else indeed?" Joram replied, looking accusingly at Sol and Aron. "Sabotage most often comes from within, history shows us."

He nodded to an aide, who punched buttons beside a vidscreen on the wall. Immediately, images appeared on vidscreens around the room of Davi, Nila, and Brie yanking two blondes and a fat bald man to their feet on one of the barges as a jeering crowd looked on. Several of the Councilors appeared shocked as Joram continued: "When our own military treat their people this way, how can we expect more from our former captors and their friends?"

"Wait a minute!" Davi jumped to his feet, fists clenched. "You're taking things completely out of context! We were breaking up a fight as the dialogue would show if you allowed us to hear it."

Miri grabbed his arm and pulled him back down onto the chair beside her as those present mumbled to themselves.

Then the video switched to a scene of several pilots, including Farien and Tela, fighting in a bar.

Sol watched the distaste spreading to faces around the room.

Joram smiled smugly. "These incidents are fairly recent, I am told."

"The second incident was a misunderstanding and is being dealt with appropriately by military command," Uzah insisted.

"Images speak louder than words, as they say," Joram replied with a dismissive wave. "Regardless of circumstances, our people have been through enough. They don't deserve to be treated in this manner."

"That man we confronted is a merchant from Iraja," Davi replied. "He himself says he is not 'one of our people'—"

"And you have nothing to gain by claiming that?" Joram replied, smiling as if he knew he'd won.

"You're the one using this for gain—" Davi said, his face knotted with fury.

Miri rose now and put a hand on Davi's arm, silencing him as Uzah stood. "We've had full reports of both incidents. Both are regrettable but I can assure you that Captain Rhii and his companions acted fully in compliance with orders as keepers of the peace. The people involved were having an altercation, as he stated, and they merely jumped in to restore order."

"Methods no doubt modeled after the fine ways of our age-old captors," Joram said, shaking his head. "Such barbarism must be left behind for us to achieve real progress."

"You can't really expect to never have people behave inappropriately—" Davi objected again, but Aron rose, blocking him from view.

"Perhaps it's time to decide whose vision for leadership we feel suits the best interests of our people then," Aron said. "Joram has made a strong case for his own approach, and you all know mine very well. You're here because the people look to you as those who would most consider their interests and represent them. So, let's do that now and vote for our leader."

Joram, Uzah, Sol, and Davi all sat now as others of the Council mumbled and nodded in agreement with Aron's proposal.

"Aron and I, of course, will not participate in any vote," Joram said.

"Who will make the quorum should a tie occur?" Lord Tamora asked. Everyone looked around the table for a moment, their faces indicating none had a good answer for the question.

"Perhaps a tie would best be resolved by putting the matter before the people for a quick vote?" Lord Chad said then. "If we are truly representing them, allowing them to participate would be demonstrative."

Sol knew the challenge of organizing an effect vote would be daunting. The condition of the fleet alone would require someone to go around and take many votes by hand, which required finding someone all factions would trust. Plus, Joram's popularity was at its height at the moment, with his own exodus having spearheaded the movement favoring their present course. He bristled at the idea for fear of how it might bias the decision, but then saw that those around the table had already deemed it a viable plan.

"Very well, then," Aron said with a nod. "Joram, let's step outside now and allow the Council to vote."

"If they can't speak their minds in our presence, how can we hope to get the input we'll need as their leader?" Joram replied.

Lord Nachor, who feared no one in Sol's experience, nodded. "I have no fear of my vote being known."

Sol watched as the others slowly nodded in agreement, Joram leading the way. In the end, he himself reluctantly nodded too. Only Aron and

Uzah gave no indication of their preference one way or another.

"All right," Aron said, looking resigned. "Since that's been decided, let your votes be made known."

One-by-one, the Council raised their voices as Uzah tallied results on a datapad, sending them to the vidscreens around the room as he did. When they'd finished, as Sol had feared, the Council was evenly divided: five votes for Joram and five for Aron.

"We'll announce the election this evening and plan it for two weeks from today," Aron said then. "Does anyone object to Uzah and I continuing to lead meetings until that time?"

Joram raised his hands in resignation, his face smug as others around the table mumbled and nodded their assent.

"So it shall be," Aron said and watched as Joram and his supporters stood and left the meeting before Miri and Davi's reports could even be presented.

"So much for your leading the meeting," Sol mumbled.

"We'll call another tomorrow mid-day to complete today's business," Aron replied, his smile weak but clearly an attempt at reassurance. But Sol needed more than a smile to calm his fear that things had just taken a tragic turn for the worse.

Tela hadn't checked her e-posts in weeks when she sat down at the terminal on Italis' largest moon, Forbeck 7. Named for the astronomer who'd identified and catalogued it ages ago, it was much smaller than any of Legallis' or Vertullis' moons. It had been terraformed early on and developed as a waystation for pilots, housing both a small military refueling outpost and similar stops for both civilian and merchant ships. As Vertullians, the scouts couldn't use the military stop, so they were instead classified as merchants, which at least kept them away from the civilian craziness but also exposed them to shady and questionable mercenaries and others the merchant fleets employed.

Still, the comm center was relatively private, with separated cubes for those willing to pay extra and rows of general terminals for those who would not. Tela had paid extra and ensconced herself with lunch in a back-corner cube, closing the door so she could neither be seen nor overheard by other customers. There, she logged into her official and unofficial accounts and began sorting through messages. Most of it was the usual drab military updates and news feeds with a few spam and trash items mixed in. Thankfully, no lovely images of drugs for sexual enhancement or weight reduction filled the screen as she flipped through. But she did have a nice stack to sort.

Then she came upon a vidmail from Lura labelled "wedding thoughts."

Davi's two mothers, Lura and Miri, had been pushing them to get married for a while, mostly with gentle teasing. They'd had some rough spots surrounding Tela's frustrations with her military assignments and the death of Tela's father, along with disagreements over the Vertullian exodus, but after Davi's old friend Yao's death, Tela had dedicated herself to helping them both heal, taking leave from the military and dedicating her time to being with Davi as much as she could. They'd had better conversations and more relaxing and fun time together than they'd ever had in the course of their relationship. Although Tela knew Davi would never get over the loss of Yao, just as she would never get over the loss of her father, Telanus, the time really helped heal the rift that had developed between them and reaffirm their love and desire to spend the rest of their lives together. They still had things to work through, as all couples did, but when the Vertullian fleet assignments came in and Tela went back to piloting, she'd also let Davi's mothers know the time had come to start thinking about a wedding.

Of course, getting Davi to buckle down and propose had also taken a conspiracy. It wasn't that he didn't want to marry her. He just wasn't in a rush. And he had been worried she wouldn't be ready after all they'd been through. Still, after months of continuing hints from his three parents and ribbing from her, Davi had finally made a genuine, old-fashioned proposal on his knees at the Legon Botanical Garden, one of their favorite places. And Tela had been thrilled.

Flipping on the speakers, she clicked the link to let the video play. Lura's soft eyes appeared, her thin lips forming a warm smile. Her long brown hair had streaks of gray now but Davi's mother was still startlingly beautiful. Her skin was silky smooth with a nice, light tan and, after all this time, Tela saw so much of Davi in her that looking at his mother was almost like looking at Davi.

"So … Tela, I hope you're being safe out there," Lura said in her lilting voice. "We miss you, but Miri and I are getting everything organized as we discussed. Uzah assures us that we can use the Botanical ship for the event. He'll even order one of the docking bays cleared that day for hosting the reception. I've never been to a wedding in space. It's quite exciting!"

Tela knew that Lura had never flown on anything larger than a shuttle, so the whole experience of being aboard a battle cruiser like the *Reliance* must be overwhelming for her. Still, it made her smile and laugh hearing Lura sound as excited as the bride was supposed to be. Despite the loss of both of her parents, Tela knew that Davi's family counted her as their own now and they meant the world to her.

As the message ended, she tapped a button to quickly send a reply, and the screen filled with her own image. Tela was startled by how tired she looked. Her blue eyes were gray with dark circles surrounding them, her brown hair was shiny from oil and sweat, the result of hours spent in cockpits wearing her flight helmet. She sighed and prayed Davi would never see her looking so awful, then forced a smile. "I'm better than I look, Lura, I promise. I don't have much time but thank you for your vidmail, and for reminding me that everything is in good hands. We're definitely keeping busy and having a few adventures out here, but nothing to worry about. I'll see you soon, I hope. Kisses to Sol and Miri. And don't let Davi see me like this, okay?" She laughed and closed the video. Typing in a code, she hit the button to send it along.

She glanced at the chrono on her wrist and sighed. She was late to dinner with Farien and her squad. They had agreed to debrief over Qiwi steak, the first real meal they'd had in weeks. As his second in command, she shouldn't be late. She scanned the emails quickly looking for one from Davi, but none stood out. Closing the terminal and logging out of both accounts, she headed for the tavern they'd agreed upon.

The rest of the scouts were already on their second round of beer and appetizers by the time she joined them at a corner booth. Music blasted from a speaker just outside the kitchen near the entrance, and customers of all shapes and sizes chattered happily as the smell of popular Boralian cuisine filled her nostrils. The environmental controls and lighting had been set to create a warm, cozy feel contrasting the rest of the fuel depot, almost enough so Tela could pretend they were back home and not far away on a planet she'd never seen.

Everyone was jovial except Farien, whom she could tell right away was in one of his dark moods again.

"So, way to show leadership there, junior boss," Jorek teased. "It took you that long to fix your hair and makeup?"

Tela had done neither and shot him a scolding look as Virun, Os, and Farien chuckled.

Ria, however, looked irritated. "What's your excuse, Jorek? Just got up from a nap or is your hair plastered to your head like that because you thought it was the style?"

As the rest of them laughed, Jorek nervously began fiddling with his hair, shooting Virun a questioning look. Instead of letting him off the hook though, his best friend merely shrugged and took another sip of his beer.

"Apparently, we're famous now," Os said, changing the subject as he motioned to a waitress to bring Tela a drink.

"Famous?" Tela frowned. It didn't sound good.

Virun scowled. "Some jackwad filmed the little incident at the bar the other night, and it's all over the nets."

Jorek smiled. "Along with footage of our significant others dragging some fat slob civilian away from two blonde women who were fighting over him on a barge."

"Davi, Brie, and Nila?" Tela felt confused.

Ria nodded. "They edited it to make us all look criminal, of course. Apparently Joram is using it in his bid to win leadership of the Council—out of control military using barbaric Boralian tactics and all that."

"What?!" Tela growled, grabbing the beer from the waitress's hand before she could even set it on the table and swigging it down in long draw. "Thanks," she said, nodding to the waitress then turned back to her friends. "I helped him campaign for the exodus. Nice way to thank me."

"He's a politician," Jorek said as the waitress distributed baskets with more fried, breaded Daken strips and other appetizers around the table.

Tela looked at Farien as the waitress disappeared. "What's your take on this?"

Farien continued brooding as if he hadn't heard her. He'd been prone to frequent dark moods ever since Tertullis and the deaths of his old friend, Yao, and the cadet, Dru.

"Farien?"

He cursed, swirling his beer in its glass. "It's a Vertullian matter. I'm just here as an advisor and to help make sure you get safely to wherever you're going."

Tela exchanged a look with the others, all of them as accustomed as she was to his moods. But at her nod, they still made the effort to help shake him out of it.

"You're one of us, Farien," Os said as the others mumbled agreement.

Farien shrugged. "You know I hate politics."

"Yeah, but you also never liked being made to look a fool," Tela said. "Doesn't sound like that footage was complimentary."

Farien munched on a Daken strip and nodded. "No, but we're leaving soon, and who knows when and if any of us will be back."

His dreary energy bothered her. Of all of them, Farien had taken his friend Yao's death the hardest, blaming himself, despite the fact that everyone knew Yao had deliberately put himself in harm's way to save his friends. Tela's old friend and training mate, Dru, had also died there, along with a few other pilot friends she'd flown with for over a year. But while she, Davi, and the others had been working through their grief, Farien didn't seem to have made any progress at all. It was almost like he'd stopped trying—to care, to live, to heal.

It made her sad for him. He was still Davi's closest friend and supposed to be best man at their wedding. She put a hand on his shoulder, searching for words to ease his pain. "If these fools hadn't started that argument—" she shot a look at Os and Ria then.

The two friends sputtered, making excuses. "It was Os really …"

"I was defending a lady's honor!"

"You insult me all the time!"

"That's different. I'm supposed to."

Tela rolled her eyes. "We can't afford to be fighting with civilians. We're still military. Besides, you can't tell me any of you enjoyed the butt chewing Matheu gave us."

All of them, except Farien, laughed.

"The General gets way too serious about stuff," Virun said.

"He's a General, that's what they do," Ria teased.

"I think yelling makes him happy," Os added.

"Come on, boss, loosen up," Jorek said then, noting Tela's concerned looks at Farien, who remained unaffected by their ribbing.

Farien forced a pained smile. "I'm perfectly happy, see?"

"You looked happier when that Xanthian was kicking your butt," Ria said.

The others nodded, fighting smiles.

"Well, every once in a while I need a good butt kicking," Farien said.

They all laughed in spite of themselves.

"That one guy did look a lot like Yao," Jorek noted.

Tela shot him an irritated look as Ria elbowed him in the ribs.

He grimaced and mouthed an apology but Farien was too busy tipping back his beer to notice.

"If Yao had been there, he would have stopped it before it got fun," Farien said and chuckled.

"He always was stuck on regs," Tela added.

Jorek chuckled. "Dru would have been in there trying to take on one of the big ones."

Virun and Tela laughed.

"And he was scrawny and weak, a total wimp," Virun said, shaking his head.

"Yao was a genius," Farien said. "None of us will ever be half the soldier he was." He reached for the pitcher and refilled his glass as they all watched in silence, then raised it in a toast. "To Yao!"

Tela winced, her chest tightening as he said Yao's name, but then they all clinked their glasses to his, despite the sad looks filling their eyes, and drank in toast.

Then Virun raised his glass again. "To Dru!"

As they raised their glasses, echoing the sentiment, Tela added, "And to Telanus!"

Echoing her words, they all drank again.

Obed made his way from the starport at Legon to the Chez Aleks in the city center for the first time in eighteen months. The city that had been his home since birth now felt like a stranger. It wasn't that it had changed so much. The familiar buildings and landmarks stood where they'd always been. But Obed had definitely changed, and he wasn't at all sure he'd be welcomed back.

He'd had to do a lot of convincing to set up the meeting with Simeon and Kray. Simeon, because he headed the Council, and Kray because she had confronted him on Eleni 1 during Xalivar's plot to capture the Vertullians at the peace conference with the rebellion. She'd had him arrested, and, although he knew she'd be skeptical, he needed to plant seeds of doubt in her about her opinions before he could ever hope to resurrect his old life. Both Councilors had insisted on meeting in Chez Aleks, a restaurant frequented by those in power, a very public place. Obed had no objection. He understood their desire to protect themselves from any accusations of conspiring or sneaking around. He desired to come back and serve his people, if they'd allow it. What form it would take remained to be seen.

Chez Aleks sat on the edge of a park across from the government center. Exclusive, yet large enough to hold banquets for their important clientele, the restaurant practically sparkled, its architecture and interior design as elite as its clientele.

The Councilors waited for him at a corner table along the transparent west wall of the main dining room. Providing a floor to ceiling view of the city, the mixed transparent aluminum windows allowed diners to see out while preventing passersby from looking in. Simeon and Kray looked as refined as he'd expected, although both showed signs of age from the stress they'd been under, not only in their tired eyes, but the gray dominating their hair. They wore the traditional white, flowing Council robes, while Obed was dressed more simply in black pants and a button down black shirt. The dark colors highlighted his light yellow skin and dark beard. Obed knew both the beard and his hair were streaked with gray like Kray's own, but at least he hadn't reached the state of Simeon's all gray.

They stood and extended their hands, smiling reservedly as he joined them.

"It's been a long time, Obed," Simeon said as the men shook hands.

Obed nodded. "Yes, it has, my friends. I hope the time has treated you well."

"We're still standing," Kray said, examining him as if she expected tricks. Her handshake was as cold as the look in her eyes.

"Well, I appreciate the both of you making time to meet with me," Obed said.

"Of course," Simeon said, but Kray's eyes demanded an explanation.

Obed smiled. "I've been away since. And I've had time to consider many things."

A waitress interrupted briefly, pouring red wine from a bottle they'd ordered before he arrived, then left. The wine was warm and fruity, a sweet contrast to the bittersweet humility Obed felt at crawling back to his former colleagues. Obed had fought so hard to maintain the family's honor despite deep losses against their longtime rivals, the Rhiis. The Palace had been stolen from his grandfather. A trick by Xonas Rhii. But years of resentment and scheming to get it back had destroyed all of his hard work. They'd lost almost everything, and Obed had decided the best course of action was to accept the inevitable and align himself with people he could trust, rather than Xalivar, a man responsible for so much of his suffering. His rebellious son, Bordox, remained obsessed over his rivalry with Xalivar's nephew, Xander "Davi" Rhii, and refused to respect his father's wishes, culminating in a particular recklessness during the battle at Tertullis, so Obed had disowned him. Any grief he felt failed to match his joy at returning to a place where he knew he belonged. He sighed and glanced around the room, spotting many old familiar faces.

Several smiled warmly and nodded in greeting. He nodded and smiled back.

"Exactly what have you considered?" Kray asked, interrupting his thoughts.

"I was wrong to defy the Council," Obed said, meeting her gaze. "I was wrong to side with Xalivar on anything. Our families' long rivalry is well known. But also well-known is our dedication to leadership and serving the people of this Alliance."

"When it suits your own ambitions," Kray said with a shrug.

"Come now, Kray, let's not be hasty to judge," Simeon said, offering Obed a sympathetic look. "Many among us have made poor choices at times. But few are willing to take responsibility and offer apologies."

Obed smiled thankfully at Simeon. The man was shrewd and strong but still possessed a kindness that few younger politicians bothered with these days. "I'm sorry, to you both. And if I could go back and undo it, I would. But I cannot." It hurt less to say it than he'd imagined. In fact, it almost felt good.

Simeon's eyes sparkled, pleased, but Kray remained cold and distant.

"Your removal from the Council is irreversible," she said. "And simple words are far from enough to erase the memory of all that's occurred."

"I ask only for the opportunity to try," Obed said. Smart politicians knew when they'd lost. They also knew there was a time to accept things they disagreed with and serve while they awaited a time when the winds of favor allowed them to restore things to their proper place. Obed was smart, and, if he'd learned anything, it was patience. The only thing he wanted back was the hereditary estate of his family. Business property and other lands he was willing to let go, but he did want compensation. And he'd already been in contact with lawyers who assured him that, with no criminal conviction, the courts would support it.

"I can't believe this!" Someone shouted from the lounge behind the bar and they turned with the other patrons to see what was the matter. A man rushed in pointing to the vidscreens behind the bar. "Turn on the High Lord Councilor's speech!"

The bartender started to object but the man shook his head. "All citizens need to hear this. Come on!"

A manager motioned and the bartender turned on the screens, flipping on the nets to show the High Lord Councilor standing before a microphone. Unlike most speeches, where dignitaries would have lined the platform behind him, Tarkanius was alone. Obed thought he recognized the Palace conference room. While others muttered around them, Simeon, Kray, and Obed simply watched in silence.

"... With difficult times come difficult tasks and we face one now together. With the drop in production at agricultural providers, many agricultural plants face issues of productivity as well. To avoid compounding this crisis with plant layoffs of agricultural workers, all available workers will be temporarily reassigned to agricultural plantations to assist in restoring them to full productivity. Training and assistance will be provided, and the government will supplement your wages as needed to make up for any shortfall based on your current positions."

People throughout the room gasped and chattered. Forcing people who didn't like manual labor and had avoided it to engage in it was going to create all kinds of negative sentiments. Did Tarkanius realize what he was risking? Again, Obed fought back an amused smile at watching his former leader blunder so massively.

"We're all in this together," Tarkanius continued. "So, we must all do our part, even if it means sacrifices for a time in order to find our way back to the place of success and strength we once took for granted. I and your leaders will also be making sacrifices ..."

"I think a man of your talents could be a great help during this present crisis," Simeon interjected as Tarkanius continued. "There will be unique opportunities, if you're willing to do your part—"

"Of course," Obed answered immediately, nodding with enthusiasm.

As the speech continued on the vidscreens, Obed was too lost in his thoughts to listen. Kray might be a skeptic but Simeon was reacting exactly as Obed hoped. He expected the unique opportunities wouldn't involve him engaging in actual physical labor. He doubted Simeon would have the heart to ask it of someone who had once shared his own status as a member of the Council. Instead, Obed suspected, Simeon had something more in line with Obed's experience and skills in mind, and Obed looked forward to discovering what that might be and figuring out how he could use it to restore himself to his proper place amidst the Boralian elite and powerful.

By the time Davi, Sol, and Miri arrived back at his parents' quarters from the Council meeting, Davi could barely contain his fury. Joram's manipulation of video footage showing Davi, Brie, and Nila aboard the DB7 Barge to support his claims of misconduct by Vertullian military and the leadership crossed a line that left Davi dismayed. And then footage of Tela and Farien in a bar fight! What was going on? Was she safe? He swallowed those concerns and instead growled, "After all we've done, the sacrifices, the loss—he made a mockery of all of it!"

"People know you, Davi," Miri said, still calm, despite the fact that Joram had accused her by name. "They know you don't go around bullying people."

Sol nodded, patting Davi's back as the cabin door whooshed shut behind them. "Listen to your mother, Davi. If she can control her temper after what Joram said about her—"

Davi whirled to face them. "That's another thing. What he said about you, mother, he had no right!"

"Why, Davi?" Miri asked, shaking her head as her eyes met his. "What he said was true. The Rhii family caused a lot of suffering for your people."

"But you had nothing to do with that!"

"I enjoyed the benefits of it as much as anyone," Miri replied, "and so did you once."

The reminder stung, leaving Davi stumbling for words as emotions churned inside him.

Then Miri reached out and caressed his shoulder. "I don't accuse, dear. I'm just pointing out that getting angry about what our ancestors have done is appropriate even when it's others pointing a finger at us. As long as we bear the name, we will always share that history."

"You stood beside him, spoke on his behalf—" Miri nodded with agreement at everything Davi said, and he turned to Sol. "You called him friend. You were there alongside him during that attack at the market."

Sol sighed. "Something changed in him that day, Davi. He's not the same man he once was."

Lura appeared from the kitchen, smiling warmly, an apron spotted with spills reminding them all of her labors in the kitchen. "Food's almost ready. How was the meeting? I just heard from Tela about the wedding," she cooed, then kissed Sol on the lips then looked at each of them and frowned. "What happened?"

"There was footage of Tela in a fight," Davi said, fumbling for words but not ready to discuss the details in his present mood.

Lura looked worried. "A fight? I just got vidmail from her." Her eyes turned to Miri. "She looked tired but fine, and excited about the progress we've made on the wedding plans."

"Apparently, they had an altercation on Xanthis," Sol added, reaching for her shoulders and smiling as he rubbed them. "It was taken out of context. Another of Joram's schemes."

Lura frowned. "That man has changed so much. He used to be kind and caring."

Davi grunted, distracting himself with thoughts of Tela. They'd had a lot of time together the past six months to heal a rift that had almost torn them apart. Her gentle care had helped him deal with his grief at the loss of Yao. His mind flashed back to the footage of her fighting alongside Farien. He felt a sudden urge to run to his VS28 and find her, protect her.

A hand touched his, shaking him from his reverie and Miri's eyes met his. "She can take care of herself, Davi. She's a trained warrior, too."

Davi sighed. Tela had complained he was too protective, but he found it hard to stop. It was not because he didn't trust her, but if anything happened to her, he didn't know what he'd do. "Does that mean I shouldn't want to protect her?" He closed his eyes as warm fuzziness came over him. He'd never imagined loving another person the way he loved her. He needed her like he needed air to breathe.

"Of course you do," Lura said, smiling and tousling his hair. "But sometimes you have to let her ask before you jump in."

Sol sighed. "Don't bother trying to figure out how they're thinking, Davi. I have no clue after all these years."

"We do it with our brains, Sol," Lura teased, winking at him.

"That wasn't what I meant—"

Lura grabbed his arm and dragged him toward the kitchen. "Just shut up and come help me finish dinner, okay?"

Miri remained behind, her worried eyes locked on Davi. "Is that all that's bothering you? Joram? Tela?"

Davi sighed. "You'd prefer there were more?"

Miri chuckled, gently punching his shoulder with her fist. "You know what I meant."

Davi grinned. "Other than the fact that she's having all the fun and I'm stuck here dealing with silly domestic arguments and politicians?"

Miri nodded. "Yes okay, other than that."

Davi turned again and moved toward the living room area, collapsing on a white, Gungor skin couch. "No, that's pretty much it."

"You're getting a taste of her frustrations then," Miri said as she took a seat beside him, her back straight as she turned to watch him.

"What are you talking about?"

"The less thrilling assignments, stuck at home worried … she used to feel that way a lot when you were off chasing down assassins or leading patrols."

"It wasn't my fault she drew those assignments. Who knows what Uzah and Matheu are thinking?"

Miri shrugged. "Did you ask them about it?"

Davi felt a headache coming on and searched for the right way to change the subject, but his mother kept staring at him. "Eventually …"

Miri laughed. "Maybe she'll eventually speak up for you, then."

Davi groaned. "I liked it better when we never discussed anything serious." Those days were long gone; the days of his youth at the Palace with private tutors, fun with his friends, and hours spent talking about music, the arts, history, philosophy—anything and everything except emotions, relationships and politics. But he knew she was right. He hadn't taken care of Tela where those things were concerned. He'd been plenty ready to protect her physically but when it came to her career and frustration …

The sound of Tarkanius' voice came from the kitchen, interrupting. They both turned, listening.

"… With difficult times come difficult tasks, and we face one now together. With the drop in production at agricultural providers, many agricultural plants face issues of productivity as well. To avoid compounding this crisis with plant layoffs of agricultural workers …"

They both stood and walked over to the door where they could see the vidscreen. Lura and Sol watched the screen with surprise as Sol stirred a pot on the stove and Lura held a knife over partially cut fruit and vegetable stalks.

"We're all in this together," Tarkanius continued. "So, we must all do our part, even if it means sacrifices for a time in order to find our way back to the place of success and strength we once took for granted. I and your leaders will also be making sacrifices …"

"My gods, they'll rise up and riot," Miri said, shaking her head with disbelief.

"Is the whole system falling apart?" Davi wondered.

Sol shrugged. "And you thought our Council meeting was a nightmare. Imagine what he's facing."

With that, Lura punched a button to shut off the vidscreen. "And that ends our discussion of politics for the evening. Surely we can find something more pleasant to discuss during a family dinner."

Sol, Miri, and Davi exchanged looks but offered no suggestions.

Lura rolled her eyes. "You three are just awful." She motioned to the table. "Davi, set the table. Miri, start slicing. If you're hungry enough, maybe that'll keep your minds off of it." She offered Miri the knife.

Sol, Miri, and Davi chuckled as Miri took the knife and resumed cutting where Lura had left off.

Davi walked to a cupboard and pulled out plates and cups, happily distracted for the moment by some semblance of normal life.

As soon as Tarkanius finished the speech, he grabbed the datapad on the table next to him and reviewed the latest reports from Idolis.

"When word breaks, it will only increase the pressure, my Lord," General Grif said, standing at military rest nearby.

Tarkanius shook his head. "I want your best people on this investigation. Identify those ships and find out where they came from before another planet is attacked."

Grif nodded. "Many of my best people either betrayed us or left with the Vertullians, sir, but the rest are working on it, my Lord." He shook his head. "Xalivar had a hand in it, no doubt."

Tarkanius frowned, his eyes rising to meet the General's. "Xalivar is dead."

"Perhaps his legacy of revenge and terror didn't die with him."

Tarkanius hoped that wasn't the case. The Borali System had been plagued more and more by pirates of late, and if enough of them banded together, they could have mounted such an attack. With all the problems he faced, the last thing he needed was another coup by Xalivar loyalists. He cursed to himself then immediately closed his eyes in a silent prayer for peace. *Gods, grant me serenity.* His mind grasped the concept but his body remained tense as his heartbeat echoed through him like a pounding tribal drum.

"The speech was good, my Lord," Grif said, attempting to offer encouragement.

Tarkanius nodded. "The speech was necessary, but it will bring troubles."

Grif simply nodded again.

Tarkanius longed to go back to the days when heading the Council was his sole providence. He'd never aspired to be High Lord Councilor. Others had always had the ambition but Tarkanius had been content to serve quietly. Even his election as head of the Council had come at others' hands. Still, he'd always embraced whatever task he was given and served faithfully, dedicated to helping his people. He was doing so now, but the stress was quickly turning him into a tired old man. *Who are you kidding, Tarkanius. You were old before you came to the Palace.* He chuckled to himself.

"My Lord?" Grif's eyes questioned him, having heard the chuckles.

Tarkanius smiled. "Just remembering the days when my life was simpler, General."

Grif offered a rare smile. "I think most of us do that from time to time."

Tarkanius nodded, intrigued. "Even a career officer like you, General?"

Grif relaxed, releasing his arms to his sides. "I started with the hopes and dreams of most of us—making a better world for our people, my Lord."

Tarkanius grunted to signify his understanding.

"But in the process, the leaders' lives become far more complicated."

Tarkanius laughed. "And filled with stress and complications."

"Aye, my Lord," Grif agreed, "and more than just those of our own."

Tarkanius chuckled, enjoying the moment. He couldn't recall every having such a candid discussion with Grif before and wondered if he ever would again. Sometimes you caught people at just the right moment. "Come, General," he motioned as he stood, taking the datapad with him. "Join me for lunch before we allow others' troubles to swallow the rest of our day."

Grif grinned. "My father always said: 'Troubles are best faced on a satisfied stomach.'"

Tarkanius sighed. "Your father was a very wise man, General."

"And my mother was a very good cook, my Lord."

They both laughed together. Then Tarkanius patted him on the back and led the way.

He wondered how the Council would react to his speech. He had no doubt it was being played over and over across the nets. Would Aron and the Vertullians see it and realize the difficulties they'd left behind? Would it satisfy the thirst for revenge some of them carried? Not that he could blame them. For years, his people had subjected them to dehumanizing slavery and revenge resulting from conflicts started on Old Earth by their ancestors. Few today could remember the original cause of the disputes. The conflict had continued like many because of focus on differences rather than similarities.

Why was it so difficult for humans to tolerate differences and live in peace? For most, it seemed, the only acceptable solution was to prove anyone who disagreed with them wrong first before they could be satisfied. And ideological wars rarely ended with such clarity. All too often they just died out for a time, only to rear their ugly heads again days or years later. So much energy, suffering, loss, and pain wasted on problems that had no real, clear conclusion.

His realization of that had led to his support of the Vertullian's quest for freedom, a movement which had changed the Alliance forever, Tarkanius would always believe, for the better. But still so many of his people, even the educated and so-called enlightened, refused to accept it; sought to revert to the old ways. If people far brighter and saner than Xalivar couldn't live in tolerant peace, what hope was there for anyone else?

General Grif walked a step behind him in deferential silence, appearing to recognize his leader was lost in thought. Tarkanius led him to the Palace kitchen. He'd bucked the custom of eating in the High Lord Councilor's private dining room, instead preferring to dine in a common room off the kitchen with staff. Contact with regular people kept him grounded, reminding him what all the hard work and dedication was for. Servant or master, at heart, he believed, all people were equal and alike. All people wanted the same things. And all deserved the same happiness and peace.

Tarkanius had no simple answers. But he knew to the end of his days, he'd be seeking them.

"... With difficult times come difficult tasks and we face one now together ... the government will supplement your wages as needed to make up for any shortfall ... We're all in this together, so we must all do our part ..."

Xalivar laughed again and again as he replayed Tarkanius' speech over and over. Such a delightful performance from a man in ruin!

Manaen hadn't shared Xalivar's glee, standing silently and nodding with a "Yes, my Lord" this and that when forced to comment, so Xalivar sent him to find General Lucius instead. He needed someone to share the moment with, further evidence of their victory already at hand.

Lucius entered and offered the traditional salute reserved for the High Lord Councilor.

Xalivar nodded in appreciation and grinned. "We may win this without any further effort on our part, Lucius, my friend."

Lucius' eyes sparkled with agreement. "The speech did demonstrate desperation, my Lord."

"Desperation caused by total incompetence!"

Lucius grunted in affirmation as Xalivar continued.

"He actually put aliens on the Council, Lucius. The man is so desperate for friends, he's embracing the dregs of society!"

Lucius nodded. "The replacement ships will soon be ready, my Lord. And the damage reports from Idolis continue to pour in."

Xalivar's brow furrowed. "There's been nothing on the nets about that attack. How that fool Tarkanius has managed to keep word of it suppressed, I don't know …"

"The footage and eyewitness interviews you requested have been forwarded to Orson Sterling and others, my Lord," Lucius replied.

Xalivar chuckled. "Good. Public outrage will only manifest in more troubles for Tarkanius. And the more distracted he is, the better."

"They have increased patrols around some of the planets," Lucius said, his voice taking on an edge of worry. "And serious inquiries are being made about the origin of the attacking ships."

Xalivar brushed off Lucius' concern with a wave. "They will find nothing because there's nothing to find. You used only ships modified by our people, correct?"

"VS fighters refit with modified bodies and other customized adjustments, my Lord. Nothing that would reveal their origins."

"Then we have nothing to worry about."

Lucius bowed his head slightly in agreement.

Xalivar continued: "But what does disturb me is Pres' attitude of late."

"She's performing her duties with the usual efficiency," Lucius replied.

Xalivar raised an eyebrow questioningly. "Efficiency can mask much emotional turmoil, General. Her attitude toward me since Dek's death has not been favorable."

"They were close, and she took his death hard, my Lord, but Pres knows her duties."

Xalivar's eyes met Lucius' for a moment and he stared, trying to read the General's thoughts. Lucius was a smart one, one of his most valuable advisors, but the man's softness to his own people betrayed him. He might trust Pres, but Xalivar had given up. "One who has betrayed trust and switched loyalties can always switch again, General. I did not get where I am by lightly dismissing discontent amongst my staff. Watch her closely. And monitor any external communications she makes from now on."

Lucius grunted. "Yes, my Lord."

Xalivar's eyes stayed locked on his General's for a moment more, then he nodded with approval.

"If you'd prefer, my Lord, she could be reassigned."

"Reassigned to where? I keep my enemies close, as I kept Obed, General. There is nowhere else in our organization she can be trusted." Xalivar knew the General was fond of Pres and protected her like a father, but he hoped Lucius' sense of duty and mission would override those feelings or he'd have to watch Lucius as well. He made a note to have his spies keep tabs on them both. "The plans for further raids?"

Lucius straightened to attention again. "We will have them to you by oh-twenty tonight, my Lord, and I've set a strategy meeting for first thing in the morning."

Xalivar turned his attention back to the vidscreens. "Good, good. We shall launch the next raids imminently, General. We must help ensure the reign of chaos plaguing Tarkanius is constant. I have other tricks pending as well."

"My Lord?" Lucius looked at him as if hoping for an explanation.

*You should know by now, General, that I always have many things going that even you are not aware of.* He was surprised Lucius had the courage to ask. "Our loyal friends have been quite busy, General."

Lucius nodded with understanding, his eyes indicating he knew to expect no further details. "Very good, my Lord."

"Shall we enjoy Tarkanius' comedy again then?" Without waiting, Xalivar turned and hit a button to replay highlights from the High Lord Councilor's speech.

Lucius stepped forward on his right for a better view of the vidscreen and, as the speech replayed again, they both laughed together.

# Chapter Three

Etan, Jurgen, and Rufa escorted a blindfolded Bordox from their squad's quarters through the larger complex on RB7. Although Bordox couldn't see it, the air felt thick around him, wrapping him like a blanket of warmth and humidity that had him soaked with sweat after only walking a few yards. With the starport connected to the barracks, Bordox had never actually stepped onto the moon's surface before now. He wasn't sure that, if given a choice, he'd want to do it again.

His companions treated him as kindly as pirates could, not shoving him or hollering insults or otherwise abusing him. For once, they were all three quiet and reserved, a symptom, he suspected, of their nervousness at introducing a new man to their reclusive leader. Bordox didn't even know the man's name, and Etan had already instructed him to keep his answers brief, punctuated by, "my Lord," if he wanted to avoid trouble. Bordox had internally scoffed at the idea of calling any such criminal "Lord," but if his survival depended on it, he'd ignore his reservations for now. He no longer had anyone to watch his back, at least not against the pirates themselves, so he'd swallowed his pride and nodded to Etan, keeping his mouth shut.

A sliding door whooshed open and cool air assaulted his skin as they continued into a new building. The echoes of their footsteps and breathing indicated a far bigger space than the quarters and starport corridors and bays. Quiet chattering came from various points around them, but no one spoke to him, so he followed his escorts in silence.

Then a hand rested on his shoulder and they stopped, waiting. After several minutes that dragged on like hours, even the chatter ceased. All he heard now were footsteps as someone slowly, deliberately made their way past in front of them, then turned.

A throat cleared and a growling baritone asked: "Is this him?"

Etan moved beside him. "Yes, my Lord."

Bordox's nose caught the scent of sweat and cologne as someone circled them, pacing slow. Examining him, he supposed. The person stopped so close he could feel breath on his cheeks and neck. It reeked of beer and fish.

"Looks like a spoiled rich boy to me," the growly baritone commented.

Etan and the others laughed, joined by echoing guffaws from many others around the room.

"Basically," Etan said, then added, "my Lord," almost as an afterthought.

"What's your plan, rich boy, to come here and rebel against daddy for a little while? Maybe burn up some inheritance all in the name of proving he can't control you?" The baritone asked.

The pirates responded with another round of laughter.

Rufa took pity on him. "They disowned him, my Lord," he said quietly.

"Disowned?!" the baritone chuckled. "What did you do to piss off daddy so badly, boy?"

Bordox bristled at the mocking tone, stiffening. "I attacked a Boralian fleet and hired some assassins."

A couple of pirates whistled as if impressed while the others jittered around him.

"What's the matter? No courage to kill anyone yourself?" the pirate lord asked snidely.

Bordox scowled. "Would you like to find out?"

Etan and Rufa elbowed him hard in the ribs then, knocking the breath from his lungs.

Bordox bent and gasped for breath as the pirates chortled again.

"'Would you like to find out, my Lord,' you mean," the baritone said, "and yes, I do very much intend to find out." It was matter-of-fact with no change in emotion. Apparently Bordox's boldness had bothered his companions more than their leader. "Can he fight?" The voice faded slightly and Bordox realized the question was directed at Etan.

"He holds his own from what I've seen, my Lord," Etan replied. "Seen more of his flying than his fighting so far."

"So he can fly, then?"

"He's one of my most skilled pilots, my Lord."

Bordox could sense the leader's smile. "I see, Etan! Pilots we need!" The voice grew stronger again as it turned back toward Bordox. "Rebellious, cocky rich kids—we don't."

"I have access to all kinds of useful data, my Lord," Bordox said then, careful pronouncing the last in an effort to make it sound sincere.

The baritone laughed. "That was painful, wasn't it?"

Bordox took a deep breath to refresh his lungs and help him relax. "My Lord?"

"Calling me that."

The fresh air tingled in his lungs as Bordox closed his eyes and allowed his legs and arms to loosen, his shoulders drooping slightly as he shifted his body to a more comfortable stance. "No, my Lord."

The baritone roared and stepped back. "If he's half as good a pilot as he is a liar, he could indeed be useful, Etan."

The other pirates joined in the laughter again around him.

"The information's good, my Lord," Bordox continued. "Please allow me to demonstrate."

The baritone spoke again, this time from further away: "I don't doubt your information … yet. Only your sincerity at calling me by my title."

Bordox cringed and cursed himself for not being better at hiding his emotions. He'd have to work on that to survive here, he suspected. "Forgive me, my Lord."

"What's this information?"

"I have access to channels," Bordox said, not wanting to reveal everything just yet. "I can get you information on military placements, shipments, planetary shields, the location of the Vertullian fleet …"

"The Vertullians?" The baritone asked as the room returned to silence. "What makes you think I'd have interest in slaves, boy?"

"It's Bordox, my Lord. The fleet is preparing to leave the system and will be passing right by here with years' worth of food, supplies, weapons … resources I thought might benefit a man like you."

The room remained silent, except for a few whispers, but Bordox felt the baritone leader's eyes scanning him again. Then footsteps approached again and he felt a hand near his face. Light blinded him as the blindfold was ripped away, forcing him to squint and lower his head.

It took several moments of blinking for his eyes to focus but then Bordox made out the baritone through a haze. He was Bordox's height but rail thin, yet with well-toned muscles on his arms. Tattoos covered his chest, neck, and arms, and he wore no shirt, only a Gungor-skin vest and dark fabric pants with thick, studded boots. His brown hair was long, stretching halfway down his back and his face covered with stubble, but his dark blue eyes were piercing as they stared at Bordox. He looked about a decade older than Bordox, closer to Etan's age.

"How do you know where the fleet is?" The pirate leader continued.

Bordox blinked again, allowing his tears to wash away the haze as his vision cleared. "I've been tracking them, my Lord," Bordox answered. The Pirate Lord's only response was a raised eyebrow, so Bordox added, "I have business with an old friend among them, my Lord."

"Revenge?" The pirate leader grinned. "My favorite kind of business." Then the grin disappeared as his brow furrowed and his mouth creased sternly. "As long as your revenge doesn't put us at risk."

Bordox shook his head, clearing his throat of the phlegm which had suddenly risen there. "No, my Lord." His muscles tensed with excitement as he thought of Rhii but he fought to keep it from showing, adrenaline warming his veins. "It won't."

The leader watched him, cockeyed for a moment, then a slow rumbling came from him, rising quickly to a full-on laugh. The other pirates joined him.

Bordox scanned the room now, making out various groups. Some were dressed similarly to his escorts. In fact, he spotted a few more of their companions there, leaning against the wall in a corner. Others appeared far different, one group even looking more like cadets or college kids than pirates. The room itself was a dark, industrial space with walls at least a meter or two away from the center where Bordox stood, facing the leader.

"See that it doesn't," the leader warned then, his laughter fading to a cold tone.

"You have my word, my Lord."

After a moment, the leader stepped forward and extended his hand. "It remains to be seen what your word is worth, Bordox."

Bordox reached out and gripped the man's hand, a firm clasp revealing great strength despite the man's thin frame.

"But welcome to the Raiders."

As they shook, the pirates around them broke into cheers. Etan, Rufa and Jurgen grinned and reached out to clap him on the back. He'd passed.

"Now," the leader said, putting an arm around Bordox and steering him toward a nearby exit. "Let's discuss the location of this fleet, and how we can use it to our advantage."

"Can you explain that again, Captain?" Davi stood in the cargo bay of the Agro Freighter *Eden One*, trying to control his temper, but what Captain Jel Cain was saying made no sense. He caught looks from Nila and Brie, urging him to calm down, and brushed them off. Theft of food staples in the fleet was no minor problem. It could be the beginning of huge troubles for them all.

"I know it sounds unbelievable," Cain said, raising his palms with dismay. "I made my Lieutenant explain twice when he told me. We spent two days investigating before I called you, but when it happened the second time, I knew there was no mistake."

Davi dragged a palm across his forehead for the dual purpose of emphasizing his frustration and removing the clammy sweat that was building up there. "Two days is too long, Captain. We can't afford to have people taking provisions whenever they see fit, and with no record? You should have notified command before you even started investigating."

Cain sighed. "Come on, Captain, you understand how it is with these officers. Any sign of incompetence and they jump all down your throat, start making assumptions …"

"The only assumption you should be worried about is the one I'm drawing right now. Your story stinks and *that* has me wondering if you're involved."

Cain scoffed. "I'm an honorable man, Captain—"

The odd thing was, Davi believed him. It wasn't his first encounter with Captain Cain. He and his squadron had rescued the man from attacks by a Boralian freighter ten years its junior several months earlier, when tensions between the Boralians and Vertullians had reached their height. Since then, he'd encountered the man a few times, mostly at fleet briefings, and both his own impressions and Cain's reputation convinced him the Captain was a hardworking, honest man. But with enough grain, flour, fruit, and bread gone from his hold to feed several families for a week, reputation and honesty wouldn't be enough if word of the theft spread.

Davi took a deep breath and offered the man a stern look of warning. "Your honor has never been in doubt, Captain, but when word of it gets out, my routine questions are going to seem like the least of your worries, believe me."

Cain understood immediately and sighed, nodding with frustration as he looked at the ground.

"That many provisions can't be easy to hide," Nila said. "If we conduct a search—"

"Whoever took it has *A*, hidden it, and *B*, knows we might come looking," Davi said. "It's probably for some sort of celebration or gathering and won't be around long, but my concern is, if they can pull this off, what happens when they decide to make it regular?"

"So we just ignore that someone stole it?" Brie asked, shooting him a puzzled look.

Davi frowned at her. "No, we're going to have fleet install better locks on the agro ships to try and prevent further incidents, and we'll rotate guards through here to regularly check them and discourage anyone sniffing around."

"But no one lives on this ship but crew, so if they had to come from outside—" Nila thought aloud.

"That's why we'll search the ship now, just to be sure," Davi said. "Then we'll run security checks on the Captain's crew and call them all in for interrogation."

"Won't that take hours?" Brie asked, looking as if she dreaded the prospect.

"You have something better to do? Something more exciting?"

Brie sighed. "No."

"My crew are good men," Cain said, shaking his head. "I can't believe they'd do this."

"Well, this is how we investigate—eliminate suspects one at a time," Davi replied.

Cain nodded. "I know. I'll set you up in the conference room."

"Brie, head up to the bridge and check the logs tracking all hull breaches, airlock doors, entrances, etc. Also, check all communications bands and find out if anything odd turned up during the nights when this occurred."

Brie nodded and hurried off.

"Nila, round up the men assigned to cargo duty that night and get them to the conference room. The Captain and I will meet you there."

Nila saluted and hurried after Brie.

"Is there any way we could keep this quiet," Cain said, "just for now?"

"To preserve your reputation or to avoid a panic?" Davi eyed the Captain, assessing his reaction.

"Both," Cain said.

Again, Davi believed him. He relaxed his stance and looked at his fellow Captain. "I have nothing against you personally, Jel. I'm just doing a very hard job right now, and this kind of thing could become a major problem if we don't put a stop to it quickly."

Cain's eyes met his. "I should have reported it, I know. But I didn't want to believe anyone could be so selfish."

Davi chuckled. "Spent too much time in space and not enough with people, have you?"

Cain grinned. "Yeah, for some reason I prefer that."

Davi felt the tension drain from his body as they chuckled together. The next few hours were going to drag like days anyway. It was good to know the Captain wouldn't stand in his way.

Miri gathered with the Vertullian Council in the conference room aboard the *Reliance* to await election results on the Council leadership. Uzah stood at the head of the table near the door as Sol, Nachor, Coz, and Zarah occupied their usual places to his left. Facing them sat Tamora, Hula, and Chad. Lord Klima came in late, mumbling apologies and took his usual place at the far end of the table as aides circulated with pitchers of Gixi juice, Talis, and coffee. Once everyone was settled, Uzah raised his hands to call the meeting to order and the chatter died out.

Despite Davi's frustration with her silence, Miri knew exactly what she was doing. She had no official voice in the Council's matters. As it was, she knew Aron had pushed hard to have her brought in as a consultant and the Council had accepted, only because of her insight on Boralian politics and government. She'd had no personal conflicts with any of the Council's members and worked hard to keep it that way. Her silence was not the result of lack of emotion over Joram's accusations or guilt over her family's past, but a realization that for her voice to be heard even a little, she had to maintain her composure and not alienate the Council members. This was her last opportunity to participate, as she once had, in determining the future for herself and her son. If she had to bear silly insults and politicking like a pawn to have that, it didn't bother her at all. Someday Davi would understand.

Besides, no one was more ashamed and angry about her family's past than she was. Redeeming the Rhii name was forever on her mind, especially as long as Davi chose to retain it even after discovering he'd been adopted from the Vertullians. She knew his decision still raised eyebrows, but not amongst those who knew him well—and knew her. She could do nothing to erase the past, but she could do much to redeem the future and she'd dedicate her life to that purpose.

"All right, let's call the meeting to order," Uzah said. "Sol, will you lead us in prayer please?"

As Sol and the others stood and prayed, Miri took her usual place behind Uzah on a chair in the corner. Davi was not present, probably as much because of her and Sol's urging as his duties, but Joram remained unpredictable and they'd feared his anger might get the best of him. She wondered if Joram and Aron had anything to say to each other as they waited outside. She imagined this room was a far more comfortable place to be right now.

"Father, we pray for wisdom and decisiveness in our decisions today," Sol said as he finished his prayer. "Let us come to a speedy decision so that we may move forward together for the best interests of our people, to your glory and in your will. Amen."

The others echoed Sol's "Amen" as they returned to their seats.

Uzah nodded. "Results are being tallied at this moment overseen by Lords Aron and Joram and their staffs. Does anyone have any further questions about this process at this point?"Lord Zarah chuckled. "I believe Lord Sol has made his known already."

She winked at Sol, who laughed and nodded. "So I have."

"If you have such little faith in our people and process, it's surprising you'd want to serve," Lord Hula groused, furrowing her brow at Sol.

"Faith in the process, yes," Sol said. "Faith in the populace? At this moment, they are far from focused and not well rested—conditions not generally conducive to considerate thought—so I confess to being a bit nervous, yes."

Lord Tamora rolled her eyes. "The privilege of voting is too new for them to take it lightly. They will rise to the occasion as they always do."

Lord Chad nodded. "Just as have all of us here."

Lord Nachor chortled. "Our people are poorly educated cattle, most with little or no education and only the skills that were required of them in their duties as slaves. If it's deep thought you crave, we can't count on them to provide it."

Lord Hula looked ready to burst, her face reddening with anger. "Have you so little respect for your own, Nachor?! It's hardly their fault they were denied education and the opportunity to learn."

Nachor shook his head. "No one said who's to blame. I merely pointed out the problem, and it's one this Council must be prepared to address if we hope to survive as a people."

Lord Coz nodded. "Nachor's right. We should begin organizing classes for those interested even while this fleet journeys to wherever we're going. By the time we settle on a new home, we can raise the education and skill levels considerably."

"These are hardly matters we can decide without Aron and Joram," Lord Zarah said.

"Yes," Sol agreed. "I thought we were here to await election results, not hold a formal meeting."

Lord Coz smiled. "We're only bringing the Council's attention to appropriate concerns." One of the younger members of the Council, he was in the best physical shape of any of them—a man dedicated to running regularly, even on board the *Reliance*. He had passed Miri many times in the corridors as she made her way around the ship.

"When do we expect results?" Miri asked, hoping to distract them and change the topic.

"Momentarily," Uzah replied as he typed furiously into his datapad to confirm it.

Lord Tamora finished sipping her Talis and sighed. "Is there any more news of the tragic raids on Idolis? And can we be certain whomever's responsible won't send his or her forces to attack our fleet?"

Lord Hula sat forward nodding. "Yes, my constituents have been barraging me with that very question."

"The nets have given no indication of the identity of the attackers or the make and origin of their ships," Uzah said, "and no further word has come in from Boralian command."

"We have separated ourselves from them," Lord Chad replied. "Can we really rely on them as a source of information?"

"We are not leaving on foul terms, Chad," Zarah said with a smile. "They've sent pilots to assist us."

"And who assisted the raiders with codes for Idolis' planetary shields?" Lord Tamora added. "The leak is either in our military or theirs. They couldn't get through without them."

All eyes went to Uzah, who barely seemed to contain his frustration. "We're both looking into that. I have no reason to suspect either side just yet. And we continue to exchange information quite freely." He spun then and punched buttons into a wall screen, activating the vidscreens around the room. Miri saw numbers and charts filling the screen as election result tallies were finalized.

It took a few moments but there was collective chatter—some in excited congratulations—others in reticence, then the doors opened and Aron and Joram strode in, accompanied by their aides.

"The results are final," Joram said triumphantly.

Aron nodded, looking resigned, and Miri stopped watching the screen in fear. "Congratulations, Lord Joram," Aron said then, extending his hand. They shook as Joram beamed.

Miri's heart fell. She hoped the decision didn't spell doom for them all.

"Good. Now can we get back to more important matters?" Lord Tamora said, as if she'd expected it all along and was annoyed by the time they'd wasted waiting.

Joram laughed. "The Council will meet in the morning. Tonight, we celebrate!"

His aides cheered and Tamora and Hula joined them as Joram made his way around the room to shake everyone's hands.

Aron met Miri's and Sol's eyes briefly before turning and disappearing back out into the corridor.

After shaking Joram's hand, Sol slid over to stand beside Miri.

"Poor Aron," Miri whispered.

"Poor all of us, I fear," Sol said, but they dared not insult Joram by leaving and stayed there, watching with the others.

Obed and Kray took an official shuttle to the surface, having instructed the pilot to deposit them outside the starport near the civilian transport rental booths. Obed hadn't set foot on Vertullis in over a decade, and he was surprised by how much had changed. Kray pointed out a few things the Vertullians had undertaken after winning self-rule, but there were many others the Boralians themselves had made to bring Iraja and Vertullis up to a much more contemporary state than he remembered.

Their first few stops were uneventful with factory managers and foremen accepting Obed's new role without objection but when they reached the first plantation, there was tension in the air from the moment they stepped off the shuttle.

"You're in charge of this mess?" The foreman asked, after Kray made introductions. "Well, the High Lord Councilor sure knows how to pass the buck, doesn't he?" He sneered. "So then I'm gonna let you explain to those people why they're out working fields instead of assembly lines in plants." He motioned to a crowd of angry looking civilians chattering over beside a fence behind his office.

Obed sighed. "You're the foreman. Morale and discipline is your responsibility. The High Lord Councilor made it clear in his speech why people have been reassigned. My job is to make sure you get back up to efficiency as quickly as possible."

The foreman laughed. "I can't get to efficiency without willing workers and those people refuse to listen and do the job. So, if efficiency's your job, then so are they. I've wasted two days arguing, and I have other things pressing at this point." With that, he turned and marched back into his office.

Obed looked at Kray.

"We can at least talk with them," Kray suggested.

"They don't look particularly open to input," Obed replied.

Kray shrugged. "Maybe seeing a member of the Council in person will help."

Obed had doubts but nodded and followed her over toward the protesting group.

"What seems to be the trouble?" Kray asked, pushing gently through to stand in the midst of the gathering.

"You are!" the man who'd been the center of attention said. Kray's height, but shorter than Obed, he had the soft hands and skin of an office worker, despite wearing clothes common to field workers. His skin was pale, his hair neatly combed. And his demeanor suggested a refinement that better fit administrators and government officials than a farmhand.

"We've only just arrived," Kray said, smiling warmly. "But we're happy to help if we can."

"You can help by knocking Tarkanius upside his stupid head and getting us back to our real jobs," an angry woman shouted from their right. They turned to see a rotund woman with a similar out of place look shaking her fist in their direction.

"You'll all be back there as soon as we get these plantations back up and running at full capacity," Obed said.

The man shook his head. "We aren't trained for this. And it's not the job we were hired to do."

Grumbled assent came from those gathered around.

"Well, we're in a crisis that requires all of us to band together to create a solution," Kray said.

"At least those who want to eat," Obed added.

Kray shot him a warning look, her eyes urging caution.

"You obviously like food, so you do it!" The angry woman shouted, clearly referring to Obed's round belly.

Others around her echoed the sentiment.

Obed bristled, but Kray spoke up before he could respond, "We're here to help you, so you don't have to be here very long."

"We're leaving right now," the man said.

The crowd surged, heading for the official shuttle.

Obed glared at the sweaty, angry workers bustling around them, bumping him and Kray in their fervor to reach the shuttle. He slid his hand inside his pocket and wrapped his fingers tightly around the small blaster he'd carried with him, withdrawing it and raising it to point up in the air.

The loud explosive flash of the laser stopped the workers in their tracks and silenced their shouting as they all spun around, looking for the source. The shuttle rocked back and forth, its door closed, the pilot shooting a worried and confused look out the window at them.

Obed stepped forward, holding the blaster where everyone could see it.

"What are you doing?" Kray whispered. "Put that away."

"The next person who touches that shuttle will learn what a blaster bolt can do to a human limb," Obed warned, scowling at the workers as he ignored Kray.

"First, you force us into jobs that are beneath our skills and training, then you threaten to shoot us when we complain?" The man leading the workers was exasperated.

"I don't want to shoot you, but I will if I have to."

Kray rushed forward, putting herself between Obed and the protestors. "No one's shooting anyone."

Obed ignored her again. "You all need to stop complaining and do the jobs you're assigned. Now! That's the only way you can get this over with quickly, I guarantee."

Obed's body tensed as he stared at them, meeting each protestor's eyes in turn with a warning look. Fear floated off of them like waves. Despite their anger, it was clear none of them had expected to face a show of force.

Finally, a few on the edges started drifting away and soon only the man, woman, and a couple of supporters remained.

"You can't assassinate people for objecting to government policies," the man said, his voice rising again to an angry pitch.

"What else would we expect from the man who used to run Xalivar's

Secret Police?!" a woman shouted.

"A blast to the leg would merely facilitate arrest and is acceptable tactics for dealing with protestors and others disturbing the peace," Obed repeated words from the Lord's Special Police Policy Book. He'd run the High Lord Councilor's private security force for more than a decade during Xalivar's rule.

The crowd grumbled and shouted in anger again now, and a couple more supporters drifted off as Kray looked at Obed with exasperation.

"We understand your concerns, and we realize this is not an ideal situation," she said, raising her voice to be heard.

"We thought the days of such vile threats against lawful citizens ended with Xalivar," the woman said, her face twisted with a mix of fear and disgust. "At least now we know that Tarkanius and this Council are as cruel as ever!" With that, she and the man and their supporters hurried off, headed for the nearby buildings.

Kray spun and pointed a finger at Obed's chest. "That was unacceptable! What are you doing carrying a weapon on civilian matters?"

"I carry it for protection," Obed said, unperturbed by her outburst. "I've had death threats ever since I led the LSP, and I find it wise to be prepared. My hunch proved correct." He slid the blaster back in his pocket and offered her a satisfied smile.

"You just compounded the issue in so many ways, Obed! You had no right to escalate it like that!" Kray fumbled just to get the words out, her body tense with frustration and anger.

"Fear is a motivator, Kray," Obed said. "It keeps people in line. Those people wouldn't listen to reason. You were wasting your breath."

"You work for the Council now, not for the Lord's Special Police," Kray said, poking his chest again. "It demands a different comportment, and you'd better get that straight now!"

She spun and marched for the foreman's office then, leaving Obed wishing he'd come alone. Having the humility to crawl back and plead for a second chance was hard enough. Having to deal with overseers who were weak and ignorant of how to solve problems added wrinkles he'd hoped to avoid. Still, he had a job to do, and he intended to do what it took to turn things around. He was here to prove he still belonged in leadership. If Kray and the rest of the Council couldn't handle the tough decisions required, Obed would show them how it needed to be done, and, in the end, his success would override their objections.

"We wouldn't be where we are right now if it weren't for you! Instead they choose that … maniac!" Davi fumed after Sol and Miri told him about Council election results.

"Politics is a popularity contest, Davi," Sol said as he and Lura did their best to calm him.

"He'll be the official, public head, Davi," Aron said, smiling. "I'll still be here doing what I've always done. It's fine."

Sol and Lura had invited Aron and Calla over, hoping Aron's presence would help ease Davi's frustration but Davi was still wound up over Joram's treatment of them all during the last Council meeting, and, even Aron's kind, humble words had little effect on his mood.

As they gathered around the dining table in Sol and Lura's quarters, Sol raised his glass of wine in salute. "To Aron, a lifelong friend and hero of our people."

"To Aron!" The others called out, as they raised their own glasses and clinked them to his.

Aron looked embarrassed, shaking his head. "Nothing I've done is heroic. Davi's a hero. I'm just a humble man trying to do what's right."

Sol grinned at his old friend. "From someone else that would be the height of arrogance and false pride, but when you say it, we believe you, which is why you're such a hero."

"Hear, hear!" Davi and Lura echoed as everyone clinked their glasses again.

Aron's wife, Calla, sat quietly beside him. Short and thin, she looked frailer than when Sol had last seen her and her hair had grayed, almost as if it had been she who'd borne the stress of office and not her husband.

Sol glanced at Lura and wondered if she worried about him as much as Aron's wife obviously did about her husband. It was so easy for a man to take his wife's concern for granted, as long as he thought he had things under control. It was the man's job to worry, he told himself. But, in truth, women worried in ways men couldn't begin to grasp, and the sight of Calla reminded him. He leaned over to Lura and gently kissed her cheek, rubbing his own next to hers.

"Mmmmm, Sol, we have guests," Lura teased.

"They can close their eyes if they'd rather not see," Sol replied, "but I'm going to keep being affectionate with my wife." He kissed her again, and she gently reached out to caress his face with her palm.

Lura's sister, Rena, and Nila, her daughter, chuckled across the table. "You two never stop," Rena said.

Nila smiled. "You and daddy were the same way, Mama."

Rena smiled softly at the memory. Her husband, Res, had passed away of heart trouble just after the battle at Tertullis, after being sick on and off for years. Her face turned sad then and Nila looked guilty.

"I'm sorry."

Rena took her daughter's hand and shook her head, raising her own head with pride as two tears blazed winding trails down each cheek. "Don't you dare apologize. You're right. He was the love of my life, and I was lucky to have him."

"We all were lucky to have him," Lura echoed.

And they all raised their glasses in toast again.

"You come from strong stock, Davi," Aron said then, "A people who rise above trouble and persevere."

Miri patted Davi on the shoulders. "Indeed. The Rhiis are no different."

"Some of them," Davi added, and Miri's smile faded a bit as both of them thought of the family's history.

"This is a happy occasion, son, stop ruining the mood!" Sol teased.

"With Joram leading, it won't be long 'til you won't need me to spoil it," Davi replied, as he tipped his head back and gulped down the last of his wine.

"No more for him," Miri said, waving Nila off from refilling Davi's glass.

Davi balked. "I'm not drunk … yet."

Miri nodded. "And we want to keep it that way."

"Now who's the spoiler?" Davi replied, rolling his eyes.

"We had a rough day," Nila added.

"More than the usual excitement?" Sol asked, hopeful because he knew how bored and frustrated his son had been.

Davi shook his head. "Someone broke in and stole provisions off one of the agro ships, twice."

The others looked worried and Davi appeared to regret having mentioned it.

"What kind of provisions?" Calla asked.

"Four bags of grain, three of flour, five loaves of bread, and two baskets of fruit," Nila said. "Each time."

Davi shot her a look that warned she'd said too much. "The agro ship Captain wasted two days trying to investigate before he reported it."

"That's a lot of provisions," Aron said. "There must still be some around even after a few days."

Davi shrugged. "Good luck finding it. We interviewed the crew, searched their quarters. Whoever took it is hiding it well."

"We think they already moved it off of their ship," Nila said.

"Or divided it up with co-conspirators," Davi added.

Aron sighed. "People stealing provisions is just what we need. If that becomes a habit—"

Davi nodded. "We've kept it quiet so far, but word will eventually leak out. By then, we'll have new locks and upgraded warning systems on all the agro ships as well as regular rotations by military guards."

"If they're stealing now, imagine what will happen when there's a real shortage," Calla said sadly.

Aron took her hand in his and caressed it. "I think this calls for a visit from the Council. We need to see for ourselves what's going on aboard the ships, speak with the citizens, let them know we're aware of them, and trying to make sure their needs are met."

"You want to go shake hands with them?" Davi said, his tone skeptical, his eyes making it clear he considered that a waste of effort.

Aron nodded. "Yes. Tomorrow, in fact. Sol, why don't you and Miri come as well. Calla can come, too, and I'll invite others from the Council."

"Won't you need the Council leader's permission?" Davi cracked.

"I'm still the official Council liaison to the fleet, no matter what the results of the election, Davi," Aron said and smiled. "I believe a handshake tour is just what we need to build morale and community, to remind the people that leaders they know and trust are looking out for their interests."

Sol chuckled. "I have been wanting to see the fleet. Lura?"

His wife shook her head. "Oh no. I'm sure it's dirty, crowded, noisy. I'd just be in the way. Besides, I've never been one for politics."

Calla nodded. "Me either."

"But it will be good for you to see it, dear, and for us to be seen together," Aron said, squeezing her hand. Their eyes met.

Sol saw Calla surrender as she always did. Although she preferred life behind the scenes, when her husband asked it of her, she was always willing to stand beside him publicly. Aron was thoughtful enough to make such requests sparingly though. So, when he actually asked, Calla knew it was important to him.

"And you and Nila and Brie can escort us," Aron said then, looking at Davi.

"It sounds way better than twelve hours of inspections if you ask me," Nila said, raising her own glass to toast the idea.

"You think you need bodyguards to see the fleet?" Lura asked, surprised and worried.

Aron chuckled. "Not bodyguards. Official military presence. To remind them that the leaders and military work hand in hand. Besides, I can't fly a shuttle, can you, Sol?"

Sol laughed. "No. Where's Tela when we need her?"

Davi grinned at the ribbing. "I don't have a choice, do I?"

Sol and Aron both raised their glasses again and clinked them together like they'd pulled off a coup.

Davi shook his head as the others laughed.

"Just like the games we used to pull on Tran at the depot, Sol, remember?" Aron said, referring to their old Lhamori supervisor when they'd been mechanics for the Boralian military years ago; before Sol went to prison. Before he and Lura had sent Davi away to save him from Xalivar's orders that all firstborn Vertullian slave children be slain.

Sol nodded and they both chuckled at the memory of Tran. Sol flashed back to the Lhamori supervisor's disproportionately large orange eyes peering at them as he'd watched the courier pod carry his infant son away to the stars. He and Lura had thought they'd never see their precious son again, but twenty years later he'd returned to save their people. He glanced over at Davi's wrinkled uniform and still felt a burst of pride. Davi's eyes met his and Sol felt tears welling up.

Then Lura squeezed his hand and rubbed his arm, distracting him, and Davi turned back to his meal.

The alarm woke Farien at dawn and he groaned as he rolled over and heard Joram, Virun, and Os stirring nearby. *Where am I?* He'd been so many places lately and put in such long hours, even the little sleep he'd managed never left him feeling refreshed. He dragged his feet over the side of the cot and sat up, yawning.

"It's too damn early," Os whined.

"Early Daken gets the flower," Jorek said, grinning.

It was an old cliché and irritating even when not directed at him. "Stick to intelligent banter this morning, okay?" Farien replied, stretching as he tried to stand and shake off the sleep.

"Well, you woke in a great mood, I see," Virun said, smiling too much for someone who'd just woken up. He was always so annoyingly cheerful in the mornings.

Farien grabbed a towel off the bedpost and headed for the cleansing room. "We launch in thirty. Less chatter, more prep." He thought of Tela and Ria. They were lucky having only two of them. The biggest lesson Farien had learned so far this mission was to be first in the shower or cold water might be his only option.

As he entered the cleansing room, Os was ahead of him.

"Ah, ah, Captain first."

Os turned and rolled his eyes. "There ought to be some situations where rank has no privilege. I haven't had a warm shower all week."

"I'm next," Jorek called, poking his head in the door.

Os groaned. "Not if I get there first, and I'm staying right here."

Farien chuckled and slid past him, hanging his towel on a hook and stepping into the bathing cube.

Thirty minutes later, the three pilots arrived at the launch bay of Kronis' sole moon, K1, the last survivor of a meteor shower that had pockmarked the planet a hundred years before and decimated two other moons. The facilities here were spartan, even more so than most military outposts, but at least they had cleansing rooms and clean sheets. Farien knew their future destinations might offer far less.

Tela and Ria were chipper like his companions and the mech-bot was just rolling away from refueling the VS28s as they approached.

"All ready, sirs," it chirped as it passed.

"Thank you," they all mumbled.

Then Farien spotted a wire hanging from one of the cockpits. "What's that?"

"What?" Ria asked.

Farien heard curses as they all spotted it.

Virun rushed forward, recognizing it was his fighter and took the ladder two steps at a time as the others hurried for their own fighters.

"Someone's been in here," Virun called, cursing again.

"Mine, too," Os said.

"They got all of them," Tela said.

Farien cursed at seeing his own cockpit in tatters. He stood and rotated in a circle, eyes searching the bay. "Who did this?!" he demanded to no one in particular. A couple of maintenance men were working off in the shadows across the way but the only other movement came from his pilots and more mech-bots, which ignored him.

Farien cursed and punched buttons to initiate a systems check.

"Systems check's turning up nothing, Major," Ria called.

"Same here," Virun said.

"Then what the hell are these wires?" Jorek asked and disappeared to fiddle under his control panel.

Farien jumped down to the bay floor and marched off toward the nearest maintenance worker. The man looked up with surprise as Farien stomped toward him. His gray jumpsuit was stained with oil and dirt, his brow sweaty and hair a mess. He was human, tall and thin, but not muscular and very pale. "What's going on?" he muttered, seeing Farien's anger.

"Someone's been in our fighters," Farien replied, wondering if he should radio Matheu's shuttle. The General had gone down to Italis alone to communicate with a small Vertullian colony there overnight. The local authorities refused to grant Vertullian fighters permission to land, instead directing them to K1. They were to rendezvous with him in an hour.

The maintenance man looked puzzled, shaking his head. "I don't know nothin' 'bout it, sir."

Farien sighed. "Do you know who would?"

Then Farien heard chatter and shouting from a nearby corridor.

"Everything's in order," Tela said as she caught up with him. "Your systems check read clear. Just a few wires to reconnect but nothing broken. Someone was either looking for something or just trying to intimidate us."

Farien nodded, reaching for the blaster at his hip. "Well, they failed."

Tela put her hand over his, shaking her head. "Who are you planning to shoot? We don't know who's responsible."

Farien growled, knowing she was right, and left the blaster where it was. Then a small mob of angry humans, Italisans, and other aliens marched in, headed right for them. Hands waved in the air as voices shouted: "Unwelcome here!" "Go away!" "Back to the fields where you belong!" and a few epithets.

Tela slid her own hand down near her blaster now, too, as the rest of the pilots rushed up and surrounded them, tensing, their feet snapping automatically to ready positions as their eyes narrowed in focus. They had their blasters at the ready as well.

Farien nodded to his squadron and stepped forward to confront the mob. "What's the meaning of this?"

"You're not welcome here!" shouted the leader, a tall Italisan with bushy hair, three small antennae sticking out atop his head, the greenish-gray skin of his arms sparkling with the decorative glitter their species wore to signify status. The glitter circled his arms three times, marking him as upper class. Several others wore two or three bands—middle and upper class as well. Most of the humans looked lower middle class like the maintenance man, and a couple of four-armed Lhamors stared at him with their oversized, bulbous orange eyes. All of them had angry faces.

"We're leaving now," Farien said.

"As soon as we repair our ships," Virun added.

"Where are your provisions?" the leader demanded.

"What provisions?" Tela asked, looking at Farien with shared confusion.

"Your food, agricultural products," the leader continued. "You must eat. Leave them with us!"

Farien shook his head, feeling both adrenaline and anger rising in equal measure inside of him. "No. We need them for our long journey."

"We don't carry much," Tela added. Her face like those of the other pilots was tense and worried now.

"We don't care! They say it's a shortage and our children need food," the leader said.

A short, bulky human male pumped his fist. "It's you people's fault if there's a shortage anyway!"

"We're pilots, not farmers," Farien replied, his cheeks reddening as he fought to remain calm, despite feeling ready to explode at any moment.

"Vertullian slaves are farmers," the leader replied, shaking his head. "Go back to your farms and do your jobs!"

The crowd rallied, joining this cry with: "Slaves do your jobs! Slaves do your jobs!"

"We are free, not slaves!" Tela shouted, trying to be heard over them.

"We're not even all Vertullian," Ria added. "Three of us are Boralian."

Farien motioned sharply. "Go back to your homes and jobs. We don't want trouble. We'll be gone shortly."

The crowd didn't budge. They glanced around, shifting anxiously on their feet, grumbling, some with hands clenching, others tensing further as if preparing to attack. Farien had seen enough mobs to know they were awaiting a signal. He drew his blaster and the rest of the pilots followed suit, waving them at the mob.

"I said, go away," Farien said, raising his voice. "This is your last warning."

"We've done nothing to you!" the human shouted.

Pilots shuffled and shifted behind him, flight suits swishing with each movement.

"You're interfering with our duties," Farien said.

"Your duties are back on Vertullis!" the leader answered, rallying the crowd again, who jostled as they chanted and jeered.

"Go!" Tela ordered, whirling and pointing to Os, Ria, Virun, and Jorek. Then she grabbed Farien by his sleeve and pulled him back with her.

"We're not running away!" he yelled, fuming.

"We're not going to fight them either," she said. "No one wins, Farien."

The four pilots climbed the ladders to their ships seconds later, the crowd holding where they were but looking ready to rush.

"Fix what's essential and leave the rest for later," Tela said.

"Just a couple cables and we're good," Os called.

Farien kept his eyes fixed on the mob, blaster raised as the pilots fiddled in their cockpits behind him and Tela. Tela had her blaster out but pointed at the ground.

"I had it under control, damn it!" Farien said to her, but he knew he probably hadn't. He'd just been in the mood to fight. Plus, he didn't like being bullied, never had.

"Someone get ours," she called over her shoulder, ignoring him.

Farien heard rustling, then saw Ria and Virun climbing into Tela's and his cockpits and fiddling for a bit. The crowd shuffled and chanted, pushing closer.

"Done!" Virun called.

"Here, too!" Ria echoed.

Tela holstered her blaster. "Let's go."

Farien stayed where he was, body tense, finger itching to fire a shot as his anger pulsed. He wouldn't hurt anyone, just scare them.

Tela pushed him toward the ladder of his fighter. "Go, Farien! Now!"

Farien heard the hum of fighter engines starting behind him. Finally, he growled and slid his blaster back into its holster, turning and racing toward his ship's ladder.

Tela stayed put for a minute until she heard the whine of the engines warming up on Farien's VS28, then, when the mob came no closer, she turned and raced for her own fighter.

Servos whined as blast shields lowered and everyone donned their helmets.

Then his ship was vibrating and Farien saw a flash as the others launched one by one.

Tela waited beside him, shooting him a look.

Farien took one last look back at the crowd, who stood where they'd left them, then pulled back the joystick, hitting the button, and was thrust back against his leather seat as the fighter launched.

Despite having spent most of the past two weeks touring the fleet, Davi found himself enjoying the day more than he'd expected. For one thing, the official visit took them to places he'd never had time to explore—like the botanical ships, where literal food gardens thrived indoors. Plants of all shapes, sizes, colors, and types grew in neat rows on artificial fields, lovingly tended and harvested by trained agro workers. The Vertullians might be headed off to strange planets and systems, but they were taking their old diet with them.

They stood now beside a row of tall, slender Gixi trees with their dense cluster of leaves at the top and hanging sacks containing the purple, sweet fruit. Paired with each was a smaller, stubbier Jax plant, the tallest only reaching to Davi's shoulders. Its stem and leaves were dotted with the same blue as the skin of the fruit itself, which grew two to a plant near the top of the stalk. The sweet smell of cedar rows behind them filled his nose as he turned. He'd asked the guide why non-edible plants had been included, and the guide had said a few transplants from old Earth were taken with the hopes that they could be repopulated wherever they settled, reminders of their former home. In addition to the cedars, there were palm and coconut trees, along with bananas, apples, oranges, and so on. The plants were just as numerous and varied from berry bushes to tomato plants, corn stalks, and grape vines. If they kept them alive, they could feed the fleet indefinitely. Although other staples were likely to dwindle down to short supply if they didn't find traders and planets to buy replacements from.

Davi savored the pulpy, tender sweetness of a freshly picked Gixi handed to him by one of the workers, then chased it with a few Tertullian blue cherries. He found himself humming with delight as he licked the remaining juice off his fingers.

"Not the boring waste of time you'd feared?" Aron's wife Calla smiled at him from a few feet away. The rest of the group had already moved on with the guide and they'd have to hurry to catch up.

"Not when I get to savor this, no." Davi grinned back, then offered her his arm.

Calla nodded as she took it and they hurried after the others. "Sometimes it amazes me what technology can accomplish. To imagine all this growing in space as we move."

Davi had to admit he was impressed as well. "It's not something you think about when you're firmly rooted to a planet, is it?"

Calla laughed. "One of many such things we'll all be discovering, I imagine."

"Or fearing perhaps?" Davi teased.

Calla grinned. "That too."

Ever since he'd met them at their home on Vertullis, Calla and Aron had treated him like the son they never had. In those days, he was running from murder charges over the accidental death of a Borali sergeant who'd accosted him, when Davi interfered in the attempted rape of a worker. That worker tuned out to be Nila, his cousin, and the sight of her necklace, identical to the one Davi still wore daily under his uniform, which bore the family crest, had led him to find Lura and discover the truth about his past.

Nila joined them now, finishing her own Gixi with a similar look of delight to Davi's own. "I think we should inspect this place more often."

Calla and Davi laughed.

"I wonder if we could arrange it," Davi replied, pondering it with a smile. Being here in the gardens, he realized he'd hardly thought of the fleet, his duties, the theft, and other worries. It took him back to his weekly strolls of the botanical gardens in Accra, back home. He'd started the practice as a child and continued it as an adult, the only difference being royal security no longer accompanied him once he'd joined the military academy. He wondered if he'd ever stroll those magnificent gardens again and figured he'd seen their last, a thought which made him momentarily sad. Then he thought of the journey, the Council, and all his problems came back. "Of course, with Joram in charge, I'm not as well connected as I once was."

Calla elbowed his ribs as she and Nila laughed. "I'm sure you'll be just fine."

Brie found them then, offering a curious look at their happy demeanor. "Don't tell me you're actually enjoying a tour?"

"Enjoying the spoils at least," Nila answered.

Davi nodded in affirmation.

"I wonder how our significant others are enjoying the spoils of theirs?" Brie wondered, bringing Tela to Davi's mind.

"From what I've seen, they're too busy starting bar fights," Davi said.

The ladies laughed as Davi heard the tour guide explaining a particular preservation process to Aron, Zarah, and Sol. Miri stood nearby smelling some beautiful red flowers.

"Smell good?" Davi asked as he joined her.

Miri nodded. "I've never seen them before."

"They're Vertullian Roses," Davi explained. "They grow in the forests around Vertullis. I forget the scientific name. I'm surprised we never had them on Legallis."

Miri laughed. "Yes, what kind of Palace staff didn't make sure I saw everything? Especially flowers this beautiful!"

"Perhaps you should warn Tarkanius of their negligence," Davi teased.

Miri laughed. "Probably Xalivar trying to deprive me," she teased and Davi joined her laughter.

Then the ship vibrated as a rumbling boom sounded from the distance. The smiles disappeared from everyone's faces as they glanced around, alarmed.

"What was that?" Calla asked.

The guide furrowed his brow, looking uncertain. "I don't know. Are we passing through the outer belt yet?"

"Not for another day, I'm told," Aron replied.

The ship vibrated again, this time more violently, and they heard an explosion.

Davi, Brie, and Nila looked around, slipping back into warrior mode.

"Were we hit?" Brie wondered aloud.

"Get to the comm and call the bridge," Davi ordered and Brie hurried off.

"Perhaps we'd better move away from the roses," the guide said then. "Their thorns would not be a good place to land if this continues." He motioned up the aisle then led the way as they followed.

They'd only gone a few feet when the ship rocked again and they heard another rumble, followed by an explosion that lit the transparent aluminum view bays overhead and sent dust and leaves flying around them. This time, the vibrating continued, forcing them all to stop moving and struggle for balance. Calla nearly fell, but both Davi and Miri reached out to grasp her arms and steady her.

"Are we under attack?" Miri wondered then.

"Who would attack us here?" Sol asked.

Miri, Calla, and Zarah screamed as an explosion sent beams and shattered aluminum raining down on them, and Davi heard the loud whoosh as the hull was breached and atmosphere sucked out into space.

They held onto each other, running together toward an exit.

"My gods! Who could it be?!" Zarah shouted, speaking for all of them. Faces reddened and breaths shortened as bodies tensed.

Davi saw Brie running back toward them.

"The hull's breached. We've got to get out of here!" she called.

"We're trying!" Davi called back, their voices almost drowned out by the whooshing atmosphere whistling through tears in the hull.

They reached the exit now, shadowed by a slight overhang as the guide reached for the door.

"We should be safe through here," he said.

Then they were thrown to the floor by another explosion.

Davi reached out to grab onto anything he could find as the ladies screamed, and Sol shouted. The overhang rocked as more debris fell down atop it. And then it gave way and came down on them.

# Chapter Four

Although Etan led the attack, coordinating with several other pirate squads, Bordox directed strategy. He knew the pirates still didn't trust him entirely, but it felt good to be given a chance again to fulfill his destiny and fly, leading men into battle. Being in a cockpit using his training again was something Bordox hadn't gotten to do enough of since his father banished him. The idea of being kept from what he knew he was born to do enraged him, but he took a deep breath and focused. He had to prove himself to the pirates first, if he wanted to keep doing it.

The Vertullian fleet stretched out over several miles in space, a collection of ships of every shape and size imaginable. Despite the ragtag appearance, they'd all been declared intrastellar worthy and appointed to the fleet. It was risky, but then desperation led to less caution, and less caution made them better targets.

The pirates themselves flew a collection of modified ships from small freighters to refit fighters, even a couple of destroyers. All had been given aesthetic overhauls to remove any traceable markings and modify the hulls enough to confuse combat computers seeking to identify them or their capabilities. Bordox's own ship was a VS15 fighter formerly but with a brand new body and souped-up engine capabilities; old but reborn, with maneuverability and power he wouldn't have expected.

At Bordox's suggestion, the pirates attacked in coordinated groups. Etan's squad created a distraction by first attacking agro and botanical ships, with the hopes of focusing the fleets defenses there before the other groups attacked the supply ships grouped on the opposite edge of the fleet.

They'd monitored the comm channels as they headed in, and Bordox had actually heard Xander Rhii's voice at one point. The great Davi Rhii was escorting Vertullian leaders on a botanical ship. The timing couldn't have been more perfect. Bordox grinned as he fired the first shots and concentrated his efforts on doing as much damage as he could. If he got lucky, he might even win the pirates' trust and execute his revenge along with it, a bonus.

The attack went on for almost half an hour before Vertullian fighters appeared, which was puzzling.

Etan asked the question on all of their minds over the pirates' private channel. "What took them so long? Are they seriously travelling with this many ships and no defenses?"

"I don't think they expected to be attacked here in our own system," Jurgen said.

"Easy prey like grazing Krikes's what they are," Rufa said with a laugh. Bordox had spotted the bovines, native to Legallis' moon, Eleni 1, during his efforts to spy on Rhii several months past when assassins struck a student at the prestigious Presimion Military Academy.

"They trust the Boralians," Bordox said. "The slave leader, Aron, is buddy-buddy with Tarkanius." Bordox crinkled his face, refraining from spitting as he said both names.

"Aron? Isn't that one 'er the names we heard on the comm visiting these ships?" Rufa asked.

Bordox smiled. "Indeed. Along with old friends I hope are personally enjoying our little show."

"Rufa and Jurgen, you, Cley, Stevens, and Staggs go shut down those fighters, while we make another run here," Etan ordered them.

The pirates acknowledged the order, echoing each other as their fighters turned off and circled back.

"Let's go say 'hello' again to your friends, eh, Bordox?" Etan said.

Bordox could hear the ear-to-ear grin in his voice and laughed as he followed the leader on another attack run.

A rebel yell filled his cockpit as his fighter dove.

"Davi? Miri?"

Davi heard his father calling and rustling around in the debris nearby and blinked to clear his eyes. The ship vibrated from distant explosions and rumbles as he sat up, extricating himself from a piece of ceiling tile which had fallen on him.

Davi stood and saw Nila and Brie brushing off their own haze as they examined themselves for injuries and did the same for himself before starting toward his father.

Sol was in a panic, looking a bit delusional as he shuffled and turned his head erratically, searching the rubble for Miri, Aron, Calla, the guide, and Zarah.

"Where are they?" Sol almost shouted, his voice cracking as Davi reached his side.

Davi put a hand on his father's shoulder. "We'll find them, Dad. Why don't you go sit down and catch your breath?" He pointed to a bench along the wall nearby, just outside the debris field.

Sol shook his head. "We have to help them!"

*We will, Dad*, Davi thought, *I just don't think you're in any condition to do it.*

Davi went to work clearing debris a piece at a time, focusing on the largest pieces and piling them off to the side along the walkway. His heart pounded in his chest and his breaths sounded deafening, but he knew it was only adrenaline.

Nila and Brie worked around him, echoing his efforts as Sol continued calling out the names, while listening for any answer. None came.

Then Davi lifted a piece of the overhang and saw a foot. It looked like Calla's pant leg. He started digging more rapidly, throwing debris aside.

"I found Aron!" Nila called as she helped the Councilor to rise from the rubble and dust himself off. "Are you injured?"

Aron shook his head. "No. I just need a cleansing."

Nila smiled as Sol hurried to his friend.

"Where's Miri? Calla? Zarah?" he demanded.

"They're buried still, along with the guide," Brie said as she continued digging with Nila.

"I have someone here," Davi called as he uncovered the leg. Then he heard moaning and dug faster, but the moaning was coming from his right. "And there're more over here."

Nila and Brie hurried to help him as Davi continued to work at uncovering the first person he'd found. He heard more explosions in the distance, then the botanical ship vibrated and shook again from another hit.

"Here we go again!" Sol called out, frightened.

Davi glanced up to see Aron comforting his father as both moved closer to a wall for safety from falling debris. Davi, Nila, and Brie stayed put and continued digging.

Davi heard coughing then and the girls helped someone up. It was

Miri. Her face was brown with dirt, her hair disheveled, but her eyes found Davi and asked the same question Aron had.

"We're still looking," Davi called to her. "Are you okay?"

"Let me help you," Brie said as she and Nila grabbed Miri by the underarms and helped her to stand.

Davi pulled off the last piece of debris and saw Calla's face. Her eyes were closed, blood ran in streams from both corners of her mouth. She wasn't moving, and there was no sign of breathing.

"It's Calla," he called out. "She needs help. Someone call Sickbay."

Brie rushed off to find the wall comm again as Aron and Sol rushed over to Calla and Miri.

As Aron knelt beside his wife, Sol embraced Miri. "Are you okay?"

"I'm fine, thank the gods," she replied.

"She's not breathing," Aron confirmed as he examined his wife.

Davi and Nila scrambled to remove more debris as Sol and Miri joined Aron beside Calla.

Davi found a leg and threw aside debris. He uncovered the guide, his head smashed by part of the overhang. He was definitely dead. He caught a glimpse of multi-colored fabric next to him. Zarah? "She's over here!"

Brie returned, hurriedly, pausing briefly to catch her breath before reporting, "They're sending the doctor, and a medical shuttle from command is being prepped, but they can't come while the attack is ongoing."

Davi and Nila kept digging and uncovered the Councilor. Her face had cuts and abrasions. A large bruise showed on her neck. She showed no sign of breathing either.

"Damn it!" Davi said, feeling helpless. Tears flowed down Davi's cheeks as Aron, Miri, and Sol sobbed beside him. He spun toward Brie. "Did they say who's attacking us?"

"Unknown ships," Brie replied. "They think they're pirates."

Davi wanted to run to his fighter and launch an attack, but his fighter was on the *Reliance* and he couldn't get there in time. They'd kept light defenses, not expecting trouble while they remained in the system. Half of their fighters were off on scouting duty. Many of those left behind were new pilots with no combat experience. And they'd sent him, Nila, and Brie, three of their most experienced, on political escort detail? Rage built inside him as he raised his hands to the heavens and fought the urge to scream.

*If you're up there, God, do something!* He was tired of people he cared about dying.

And then two medical personnel from the *Eden One* showed up and moved in to examine Calla, Zarah, and the guide. Aron just knelt beside his wife, tears flowing and squeezed her hand, his eyes closed in prayer, while Davi stood there, raging and helpless.

The *Tarragon* remained locked in orbit around the moon, hovering forever on the dark side of Ohm from her mother planet, Plutonis. It was a dreary, dreadful rock as close to the edge of nowhere as Xalivar had ever imagined he'd be, but it was also the perfect hiding place for planning a coup to restore himself to his rightful place of power.

He chuckled with glee as he reviewed the reports Lucius had routed to his leader's datapad about the pirate attacks on the Vertullian fleet. It was as if the pirate leader was cheering him on. Xalivar couldn't have planned it any better, and what's more, the attack provided an ideal opportunity.

The door buzzed and Xalivar spoke the command to allow Lucius and Pres to enter. As the door whooshed into the ceiling and they stepped inside, he wondered if they shared his delight at the course of events. Lucius, stoic and soldierly as always, still had a glint in his eyes Xalivar recognized as pleasure. Pres, on the other hand, remained distant and cold. Too bad she'd decided to question her loyalties. She would have been useful in the new Boralian Alliance. Now she'd have to be executed for the treasonous thoughts he knew were filling her head. His spies continued monitoring her every move to prevent her taking any actions without Xalivar's approval.

Manaen appeared with a carafe of wine and poured a glass for Xalivar, offering others to the Generals. "Regalian Sauvignon?" the majordomo asked.

"We're on duty, no thank you," Pres said, stiffly.

Lucius sighed. "Ah yes, I'm afraid General Pres has gotten it right. I do sorely hope I can partake another time, however. Regalian wines are my favorite."

Xalivar bowed his head slightly in affirmation as Manaen turned and left the room.

"These pirates have presented us with a unique opportunity," Xalivar said, smiling. "Did we confirm the codes for the planetary shields?"

Pres had used personal contacts in the Boralian military still loyal to her for confirmation, because they all knew the codes were regularly changed for security. Pres nodded. "Yes, my Lord. We have them."

Xalivar nodded. "Launch attacks as planned on Xanthis and Italis. The other half of our force should attack the Vertullian fleet at once."

Lucius reacted with surprise. "I'd thought we were waiting until we'd regained full strength, my Lord?"

"And miss this opportunity the gods have just laid at our feet?" Xalivar chortled. "We must not let this gift go to waste." Xalivar took a long sip of his wine, allowing it to roll around in his mouth a bit as he savored the sweet berry taste. Then he continued: "Order the pilots to inflict as much damage as possible, even destruction. They should approach like pirates but attack like executioners."

Lucius nodded. "Of course, my Lord."

"If we decrease the forces sent to Italis and Xanthis, we'll have to restructure our attack plans," Pres said, still masking any emotions about what Xalivar had said.

Xalivar smiled at her, his eyes locked on her own. "Of course, General Pres. Focus both attacks on the infrastructure in the planets' capital cities. Forget about the outlying cities for now."

Pres nodded. "As you wish, my Lord."

Xalivar savored another long sip. The wine was of a rare vintage his aide had discovered quite by accident at the Black Market on Xanthis. Xalivar had sent him back twice now to retrieve more, the last time purchasing a dozen cases and cleaning the vendor out. "When we regain control, the aid we send to rebuild all these planets will endear them to us in ways that cement loyalty for the future," Xalivar said. "Of course, delivering such aid will require increased access on a level we haven't needed in years, and once that access is granted, it will never be revoked."

Lucius chuckled. "A good plan, my Lord."

"Be sure and patch the pilots' feeds to my vidscreen so I can witness the attacks," Xalivar said. "I do enjoy these little victories." With that, he called over his shoulder. "Manaen!"

As the aide appeared, Xalivar waved his almost empty wine glass and smiled. The Idolian hurried over and tipped the carafe. Wine sloshed over the side and ran down Xalivar's hand—Manaen cringed but regained focus and continued filling the glass.

Xalivar frowned as he watched a drop fall from his pinky finger toward the floor. Then he spun and glared at his majordomo. "Manaen!"

"I'm sorry, my Lord," Manaen replied, bowing his head, eyes on his feet.

"We have limited supply, and you waste precious drops with your incompetence? Why do I tolerate you, Manaen?"

"You are most merciful, my Lord," Manaen said, kneeling as he withdrew a cloth from the pocket of his robe and wiped at the spilled wine.

Xalivar watched him, enjoying the servitude. Manaen could teach Pres a thing or two about knowing her place.

When he was finished, Manaen stood, head bowed, turned and left the room quietly.

"Don't stand there, Generals! Launch the attacks! There's no time to waste." Xalivar punctuated his words with a grin, waving towards the door.

Both Generals bent slightly, moving their hands in unison—crossed fingers with their right hands lying atop their left fists as they formed the traditional salute for the High Lord Councilor. Xalivar had allowed them to forgo it for a period, but now they needed to get used to the idea of it whenever they were in his presence, so he'd ordered it resumed.

The Generals turned, in formation, and walked to the door.

Xalivar sipped his wine as the door whooshed into the ceiling and the commanders exited into the ship's corridor outside.

"Soon, my friends. Soon," he whispered.

"Let me get this straight," Davi said, pacing on the bridge of the *Reliance* as Joram, Uzah, and several Council members looked on, "they just boarded the ships and walked away with no response?"

Behind them consoles beeped and technicians chattered, checked readings, monitored ship's systems, and issued orders. Warning lights flashed on a wall screen identifying various fleet ships damaged in the attack. Several officers gathered around it discussing the damage with the fleet's chief engineer. The bridge remained as busy as if the battle were still occurring.

"We launched fighters to engage, and all ships with weapons capabilities responded," Uzah said, "but their ships were too fast and the fleet was unprepared."

"And three people died as a result!" Davi snapped.

The Councilors watched him, shocked by his brazenness, but Davi and Uzah went back a long way, and he was still reeling from the loss of both Calla and Zarah, not to mention the guide. The Councilors looked haggard, considering they'd all rushed in from various ships after the attack. Davi had first piloted a shuttle to take the injured to the *Reliance* for treatment and then come straight to the bridge, his uniform and face still dirty and dusty from the debris.

Uzah sighed. "I understand your anger, Captain. I share it. We've recalled the scouts to make sure the fleet is better protected."

"Or protected at all," Joram said, shooting them a cocksure look.

Davi turned back to Uzah, ignoring Joram and the Council members. "I should have been in my fighter, not escorting politicians!"

"You were assigned where we needed you, Captain," Uzah's tone shifted to one Davi recognized as growing irritation. "You couldn't have stopped them alone."

"I had two of our most experienced pilots with me," Davi replied.

"This second guessing gets us nowhere," Lord Chad said, interrupting.

Davi fought the urge to snap at the man, realizing his issue was more with himself and frustrations over his current duties than with anyone else. He turned with Uzah to look at the Councilors again.

"We can't fix what happened," Chad continued. "But we need to prepare ourselves for future attacks. How long will it take to repair the damage?"

Uzah consulted a datapad. "We're still assessing that, but the botanical ships will require a few weeks to restore full hull integrity. If their cargo even stays alive that long."

"We assume you have a plan for that?" Tamora asked.

Uzah nodded. "Temporary hull seals are already in place. But they'd be worthless in another attack."

"We need to split the botanical ships up and surround them with strong ships to act as decoys in case of another attack," Davi said.

Uzah nodded. "We're making plans to shift the fleet already. Plus, the fighters will be on round-the-clock rotations for a while."

"Have we notified the Boralians?" Nachor asked.

Joram scoffed. "And have them interfering in our matters again? We've finally gotten them to let us be. You've got to be joking."

"We're in their system," Coz said, nodding at Nachor. "I'd say it makes sense, especially given the attack on Idolis from unmarked ships."

"Unmarked ships not necessarily matching the description of the ones that attacked us," Joram pointed out.

"So we should automatically discount any connection?" Coz asked, clearly irritated by Joram's sarcasm.

"I notified them, yes," Uzah said. "They're sending over footage from the Idolis attack and I from ours. If we can help each other, we will."

Joram shook his head. "We can't trust them. Give them a little, they'll take over the fleet."

"They're letting us leave, loaning us ships, giving us supplies, assigning pilots to escort us," Lord Nachor looked at Joram as if he'd lost his mind, which Davi considered a fair assessment, "and that little has not come with any push for control."

"How do we know the Boralians didn't send these pirates themselves?" Joram asked. "After the assassins sent to kill us, the attack on myself, Sol and poor Telanus at the market in their own capital …"

"Joram's right," Lord Hula echoed. "The raids on Idolis involved knowing codes for the planetary shields. Who else could provide those but the Boralians or ourselves? Caution in dealing with them is well advised."

"These pirates are the least of our worries. What if the Boralians decided to take advantage of our weakened state and reconquer us?" Tamora asked.

Davi laughed. Had these people learned nothing from what they'd all been through together? "What's next? Monsters in your storage unit trying to eat you? Tarkanius is an ally, and he still controls the government. They locked up several members of the Council for conspiring against us. Xalivar's dead. Why would they attack when their own people are with our fleet?"

"Their own people who are off with our best pilots gallivanting around when we needed them here!" Joram replied, raising his arms in dismay for emphasis.

Davi tensed, warmth rising as he struggled to control his fury. "Is it so hard to believe they would actually let us leave in peace? Have they not demonstrated that?" He was incredulous at their paranoia.

"If we believed that, we wouldn't be leaving," Tamora replied.

Davi sighed. She did have a point. "Look. Some of the Boralians refuse to accept us as equals. That's far different from viciously attacking us and killing us. The ones responsible for that were arrested and tried."

"And you refuse to believe more such people might arise amongst your beloved people?" Joram said, sneering.

It had been a while since Davi had actually wanted to punch someone, but Joram was pushing all the right buttons.

Uzah stepped between them, sensing his mood. "This is a military matter, which means I am in charge. For the record, the Boralians have given us codes to the planetary shields of Regalis, Kronis, and Plutonis in case we wish to shield our ships inside the atmospheres while we undertake repairs. That doesn't sound like the act of those who wish to betray us."

"A trap!" Joram snorted.

Uzah cut him off before he could say more, "And Lord Aron is Council liaison to the military. You can run any further concerns through him. But for now, I must ask you to clear the bridge."

"He's mourning the death of his wife," Joram said. "I'll appoint a replacement."

"You'll do no such thing," Lord Nachor said.

Coz nodded. "Aron is the only one among us who's qualified and knows the military well. The last thing the Generals need are amateurs telling them how to do their jobs."

Davi smiled, liking Coz more by the minute. "Thank you."

Coz smiled back and nodded.

Joram postured like a preening Daken. "Well, that's too bad because we're going to be making changes. As head of the Council, I refuse to be banished from such decisions. Besides, I have past experience working alongside the military as planetary governor during the fight for freedom. I'm not entirely ignorant of such matters."

Nachor shot Joram a stern look as Coz crossed his arms over his chest.

"You can bring all of that to a vote, we'll be happy to veto it," Nachor said. "We prefer things the way they are right now. We were only invited here for a briefing. The General's made it clear we're now interfering with his duties during a crisis." He pointed toward the door and began ushering the others in that direction.

"This isn't over," Joram said, shooting Davi and Uzah a warning look, his face red, eyes narrow and threatening.

Both ignored him.

"Are you done venting your anger at me?" Uzah asked as soon as the Councilors were out of earshot.

"Calla was like a second mother to me, General," Davi said, his voice cracking as his shoulders sank with grief, and he exhaled loudly.

Uzah put a hand on his shoulder, nodding. "I know. And they're dear friends to me as well."

"They'll be back." Their eyes met and Davi silently communicated that he meant both the Council and the pirates.

Uzah nodded. "And we've got to be prepared. I'm open to your ideas as always, but you need to get your emotions under control."

"Would you rather deal with me or that nutjob Joram?"

Uzah shuddered. "You know the answer to that. On the other hand, part of what drove him over the edge are his emotions. Don't let it happen to you."

"Is that a threat or a warning?" Davi teased. They both laughed as the tension between them eased.

"Come with me to check on Aron," Uzah said. "We can discuss flight rotations and other precautions."

Davi sighed as some of the tension left his body.

Uzah punched a button on the comm in his ear and led the way toward a nearby lift. "Commander heading to Sickbay. Colonel Cardno's in charge until I return."

"Did you get a count on the pirates?" Davi asked.

Uzah pulled up a screen on his datapad and handed it to Davi. As they stopped at the lift doors to wait, the numbers came up, and Davi found himself hoping his inexperienced pilots would be enough.

The echoey, industrial space where the pirate Lord held court was brighter today, and the surrounding factions stood in formation around them, as Etan and the others from the raid accepted their leader's praise.

"Executed like experts," the Pirate Lord continued, twirling to take in all the spoils of the raid piled around them. "It's like we struck an untapped goldmine, isn't it?"

The pirates guffawed and mumbled in affirmation, enjoying the moment.

"And it was our new friend here, who paved the way." The Pirate Lord smiled at Bordox, patting his shoulder. "We can do great things together, Pirate Bordox."

"Not much of a pirate name, is it?" Rufa teased.

The rest of them laughed.

"As opposed to Rufa?" Jurgen teased.

Even the Pirate Lord and Bordox joined the laughter this time.

"Come! Let's celebrate!" The Pirate Lord did a little dance and led them toward a buffet set out in the corner—tables with wine, trays of food, the lushest meal Bordox had seen since the night Xalivar caught Bordox and his father conspiring against him on Xanthis. That moment had sealed their fate and led to their rift and Bordox's shunning. He soured thinking on it, but then Etan and his crew slapped him on the back as they passed, chuckling and jiggling excitedly. Their enthusiasm was contagious, so he brushed it off, forced a smile and hurried to join the revelry.

He was given a seat of honor at the table opposite the Pirate Lord. Later, when the meal was but carcasses and scraps, the Lord himself chatted with Bordox. "I assume we can continue the attacks indefinitely?"

Bordox nodded. "They will call back scouts to reinforce, realign ships, make repairs, but yes, we can enjoy ourselves, my Lord."

The Pirate Lord grinned. "Avenging ourselves on those who have victimized our people by abandoning them and who murdered our ancestors, all while availing ourselves of their supplies … how sweet it is, eh?"

Bordox joined in the pirates' laughter. "It is sweet, indeed, my Lord."

"Tell me, Pirate Bordox, you know the strategies they will use, the way they think," the Pirate Lord continued. "Can you ensure we minimize losses and maximize gains?"

"I believe so, my Lord," Bordox said. "There are always variables."

The Pirate Lord smiled and clapped him on the back again. "You'll anticipate them and have a contingency, of course?"

Bordox shifted on the hard bench, hoping to hide the irritation he was feeling and offered a nod. "Of course, my Lord."

"Good. And when the time comes, can you provide us with codes for the planetary shields?" The Pirate Lord asked, locking eyes with Bordox.

Bordox hesitated, wondering if he could still manage that. He'd left the military, had few friends left, and surely his own computer access had been shut off for good after his role in the battle at Tertullis. The Pirate Lord's eyes bore into him.

Bordox cleared his throat. "I will try, my Lord. They change them frequently. It will not be easy."

The Pirate Lord laughed, a hearty baritone rumble. "Life is never easy for pirates, my friend. You will do your best?"

Bordox nodded and took another sip of ale. The Pirate Lord clapped him on the back and returned to his own meal as Bordox gritted his teeth.

The food was surprisingly good and the ale and wine excellent. The pirates definitely knew how to celebrate with class and clearly raided the finest places, too. Compared to their usual provisions, it was definitely a step up, although Bordox assumed the Pirate Lord allowed himself access to their finer acquisitions.

His mind raced through Boralian military strategy and fleet protocols. He expected the damaged ships would be repaired, but that would take time. Meanwhile, the most likely strategy would be to recall any scouting parties to ensure a full fighter contingent and move the other ships to surround those damaged in the first attack so that they could provide cover and run interference against future attacks. The sooner the pirates launched another strike, the better. Allowing the Vertullians time would only enable them to strengthen defenses. Keeping up a constant drain would be far more effective. Bordox determined to devise several plans and strategies and have them ready to present whenever he might be called upon. The more capably he handled himself, the greater the pirates' trust in him would be.

He did bristle at the Pirate leader's insistence on being called "my Lord." Bordox had had more than enough of that garbage his whole life on Legallis. But he'd have to make do for now. Still, he vowed that if the leadership ever changed, he'd be sure and make his voice heard for a few changes. Of course, he had to be fully accepted first.

Tipping back his glass, he downed the rest of his ale and let out a loud belch, smiling proudly and rubbing his stomach. "Ahhhhhhh, a meal for the gods, my Lord," he said, glancing toward the Pirate Lord who had drifted into conversation with others nearby.

The pirates laughed and called out their support, a few patting him on the shoulders and back.

"Aye, Pirate Bordox!" The Pirate Lord answered. "And as far as the Vertullians are concerned, we'll be godlike in our ruthlessness, too!" He cackled as his men joined him and then raised his glass for a toast. "To the five foundations: Health! Life! Food! Money! Victory!" he called off the list then took a swallow.

The pirates echoed each word and followed suit with Bordox joining in. They were the things most men longed for, and Bordox had no problem toasting to them. He intended to have them all, many times over, for years to come.

"They were disturbing the peace," Obed said again for the third time as Tarkanius paced, fuming, in front of the throne.

"And that justified firing your blaster on civilian agricultural workers?" Tarkanius considered physical fighting to be beneath him, but, at the moment, his fists clenched from a desire to fly out and connect with Obed's nose.

Kray and Simeon shook their heads, looking as dismayed as Tarkanius as they watched from nearby.

"I was shocked by his actions, my Lord," Kray said again, shooting Obed an angry look. "And I didn't mince words....

"She scolded me like a school teacher," Obed snapped. "I may not be on the Council anymore, but I am not a child, and she is *not* my mother."

"Then don't act as if you need one!" Kray replied, her eyebrows furrowed as her face crinkled with fury.

"You cannot fire a weapon on innocent civilians, Obed," Simeon agreed. "There's no room for LSP tactics when you're representing the Council."

"I wasn't aware that I had any association with the Council whatsoever," Obed said, and to Tarkanius' surprise he appeared sincere.

"We assigned you. The Council is overseeing the transition since the Vertullians' departure," Simeon said. "Lord Kray even accompanied you. And still you did not see the connection?"

Tarkanius sighed, raising a hand to silence them all. He stopped pacing and turned to face Obed, their eyes meeting as the High Lord Councilor examined his old peer, trying to understand his motives and thinking. "Your actions have created questions about the Council and this government that we don't need right now, Obed. Your intentions may have been right ..."

Kray turned, starting to object but Tarkanius' raised palm cut her off.

"... but the result is not. You are not to go armed in your capacity as Council negotiator and overseer of the agricultural crisis, is that understood?"

"Are you ordering this as High Lord Councilor? Your role is as representative and member, not supervisor of the Council."

Simeon sighed. "Then I second the command as head of the Council, Obed. Tarkanius is speaking as your friend and former peer, but if you want it officially, there you have it."

Tarkanius nodded his thanks to Simeon and was surprised to see Obed looking smug and satisfied. He would not have trusted Obed with such a sensitive assignment after so long an absence, but he knew Simeon had been under pressure and was trying to be kind. None of them would have expected the man to draw a weapon while doing his duties. But then again, given his background, perhaps they should have. "We have not seen each other in a long time, nor worked together. You were firm and tough in times past, but you were fair and reasonable. We need you to be that man now, no matter what has passed between us. One more incident like this, and you will be removed from your position and not allowed to serve in any role of public trust."

Obed's smugness faded, replaced by frustration as his body tensed and he stood taller and straighter. "We cannot allow them to control the situation. We have a crisis. They were refusing to do as requested for reasons solely of personal pride … Of all people, we understand the dangers of pride well after serving with Xalivar." Obed turned and met each of their eyes in turn.

Tarkanius saw that even Kray had to concede this point.

"I was only trying to ensure compliance with an implied threat, to be taken seriously," Obed said. "The safety of our pilot was at issue, not to mention the shuttle itself."

Tarkanius and Simeon nodded together. "Decisive action was called for, but an unarmed warning would have been just as effective," Simeon said.

"Yes," Tarkanius agreed.

"And should that have failed?" Obed asked, raising an eyebrow for emphasis.

"It should have been tried first," Kray said. "Given an opportunity to work."

"And if they refused?" Obed pressed his point.

"We never got the chance to find out," Kray snapped.

Tarkanius sighed, relaxing himself and leaning against a pillar to encourage the others to do the same. "I thank the gods there were no cameras to get pictures. The sight of a Council member and armed escort threatening workers is the last thing we need."

"What authority do I have to deal with such situations in the future?" Obed asked.

Tarkanius nodded. "You may dock their wages, fine them, have them hauled in for questioning or arrest, but no violence. If the Police must be called, let them take any physical action and only as a last resort."

Obed held up his palms facing Tarkanius in surrender. "As you wish, my Lord."

It was the first time in the meeting Obed had shown Tarkanius such deference, a fact the High Lord Councilor took note of. Despite the humble approach he'd shown in meeting with Simeon and Kray, as Simeon had described it, Obed's present attitude and actions warned of inner conflict and struggles that required caution and a watchful eye. He could be of great help to them, Tarkanius had no doubt, but he could also bring great trouble.

"I'd like your weapon," Tarkanius said.

Obed balked, his hand instinctively reaching for his side where the holster normally sat.

"We must investigate fully," Simeon said. "It will be returned … eventually."

Tarkanius extended his hand.

"You know weapons are not allowed in here except for official guards or military officers," Obed said. "It is aboard my shuttle."

"Then you shall accompany me there and surrender it after we've finished," Simeon said sternly.

Obed tensed, his lips pursing as if he planned to respond, then his eyes softened and he sighed and nodded.

Tarkanius offered the man a grateful smile, relieved. "Now, come, let us talk of strategy and plans, and share a drink, shall we?"

They mumbled with agreement and followed him to the sitting area as Tarkanius pressed a button to summon his majordomo and settled onto a couch.

Pres found Manaen alone in Xalivar's quarters, cleaning. Xalivar had gone to the bridge to oversee the initiation of the three attacks, and Pres had quietly slipped away, making excuses to one of the Lieutenants that she needed to retrieve something from her own quarters. She'd hesitated to risk being caught alone with Manaen in Xalivar's quarters, but with the leader on the bridge, she knew it was the one place she could be certain wouldn't be bugged. Anywhere else aboard was suspect.

As she stepped inside and the door whooshed shut behind her, Manaen reacted with surprise. "My Lord has gone to the bridge."

"Yes, I know, Manaen. I've come to speak with you."

He shot her a puzzled look and went back to cleaning the kitchen.

Pres swallowed and took the plunge. "Why do you allow him to treat you as he does?"

"How do you mean? I am his aide, and he is our leader."

Pres knew about the oaths Idolians took toward those they served. It was a matter of great pride and honor for the Idolian people that they were so valued for their loyal service. She'd only heard of two cases where an Idolian had violated an honor oath. Getting Manaen to open up would be difficult, but she had to try. If anyone aboard would understand her feelings, it had to be him.

"He leads using fear to manipulate us," Pres said, choosing her words carefully. "He is cruel and deliberately vengeful. It puts all of us at risk."

"We should not be having this conversation," Manaen said, not even daring to meet her eyes. He finished cleaning the counter and switched to another cloth to polish the cupboards overhead.

Pres knew the majordomo had served his master for decades and pressed. "Xalivar is not here, and he would never allow listening devices in his own quarters," she continued. "He attacked your home, destroyed the capital, killed many of your people."

"People die in war," Manaen said.

Pres fought to control her irritation. "Don't you have family? Surely someone you care about lives there."

Manaen stopped a moment and stared at her. He was the one looking irritated now. "I love my planet, as all Idolians do. And my family is there. But I am also a man of honor. And I have sworn myself to the house of Rhii. I have served my whole life there."

"And if he asked you to watch him kill your family, your oath would supersede even your love for them?"

Manaen frowned and went back to polishing. "He has asked no such thing."

"His cruelty knows no bounds. If you gave him reason to doubt you—"

"Which is why this conversation must end."

Pres sighed, looking away to release Manaen from her demanding stare. "All right. Forgive me for making you uncomfortable. I only thought that you, of all people, would understand my feelings about the cost we have all paid in his service." She turned toward the door.

Manaen exhaled loudly. "The cost is high, yes, but my sister and her family were safely away from the areas of the attacks," Manaen said. "And my people are nothing if not resilient. They will recover."

Pres spun back toward him. "You speak so matter-of-factly about it. As if you have no emotions—"

"I have feelings about it, yes," Manaen said, his voice measured but his eyes glistening with emotion. Was it sadness? Anger? He appeared conflicted. "I am a man of peace and service, not war and killing."

"Then I ask you to do something to help me stop the madness," Pres blurted out. Immediately she wondered if she'd made a mistake as Manaen stiffened.

"You should go. Quickly." He whirled back toward the cabinets.

Pres took a deep breath and activated the door, peering out

cautiously. The corridor was clear. Then she exited, hearing the door whoosh as it shut behind her and headed for the bridge, offering prayers to the gods that Manaen would not betray her.

Davi was overseeing the installation of the security locks on *Eden One*'s cargo lockers when the klaxons blared. Brie and Nila rushed to his side in moments, and all three headed for the landing bay and their fighters.

"Good thinking on using the fighters for our duties," Brie said as they entered the lift, and she pressed a button for the landing bay.

Davi nodded. "Not everyone agreed, since it limits which ships we can board."

"They'll be less adamant after this, I'd hope," Nila answered.

Davi chuckled. "Never underestimate the eagerness of politicians to complain."

All three laughed as the lift vibrated to a halt and the doors opened again, depositing them in the landing bay. They raced for their VS28s and started pre-flight checks as mech-bots hurriedly detached hoses and equipment from the three fighters. Maintenance checks weren't routine aboard ships like this but Davi had wanted their fighters in constant readiness so he'd requested it of the bots upon landing. As the computers and bots did their work, Davi and the others slid quickly into their flight suits, then climbed up and settled into their cockpits.

"Greedy, aren't they?" Brie asked over the squadron comm channel as Davi donned his helmet.

Davi keyed his mic. "Ever heard of non-greedy pirates?"

"Good point," she replied.

The fighter vibrated as Davi started the engines and heard the servos whining up to full speed. "Weapons and shields on full as soon as we launch," he ordered.

"I hope the other pilots were just as ready," Nila said.

"Let's find out," Davi said, finishing his preflight check. He flipped the controls on his dash and typed commands into the computer, then leaned back in his seat and pushed the joystick to full. The revving engines thrust him back against the seat with great force as the fighter vibrated then shot forward, accelerating straight for the launch door.

It surprised him sometimes how much just the act of launching set his adrenaline to pumping, but he felt the usual surge of engines and gravity pressure and reveled in it. From the first time he'd sat in a cockpit, Davi had always felt like he was born to fly, and his skills had more than proved to be a match for that aspiration. When he was flying, he and the ship became one in a special way. It was almost like an out of body experience, one he'd never been able to explain well to those who hadn't experienced it, especially his mothers and Sol. At least Tela, being a fellow pilot, understood. Her skills matched his own in many ways, and he knew she was well familiar with the rush of every launch.

As his blast shield switched from streaking blur to starfield, and he piloted the VS28 away from the agro ship, Davi ran scans for enemy fighters and visually searched the stars around him.

"Do you see the targets?" Brie asked.

"Negative. Searching."

"There!" Nila called. "Oh-four-hundred behind the DB7s."

Davi's eyes followed her directions and spotted explosions and spinning ships.

"Why are they attacking passengers this time?" Brie asked, sounding puzzled.

The previous attacks had centered on supply, agro, and botanical ships, not those carrying passengers in mass, but she was right. This time the attacks centered on the barges they'd been inspecting a week before.

"It's probably a distraction from their real target," Nila said.

Davi cursed, keying the comm. "A distraction that will cost a lot more than three lives if we don't stop it! Shields and targeting to full, weapons armed! Let's go get 'em, Alpha!"

He heard the women's whoops through the comm as he checked his shields and scanners and then led the way, the others forming up around him as they raced to engage their attackers.

Uzah stood on *Reliance*'s bridge as klaxons blared and warning lights flashed around him.

"They're targeting the civilian barges, General," Colonel Cardno confirmed from his chair at the command console nearby. All around him, techs controlled the engines and vital systems—weapons, and launch control as well as communications with the fleet.

Uzah turned to the younger man and nodded. Cardno was a fast-rising star, having joined the military only two years before they'd declared their intention to leave. His life and business successes combined with his education had made him an officer candidate, and he'd started as

Captain and risen fast. Around Davi Rhii's age, he was skinny and tall, but strong of will and body. Uzah had never met a man more stubborn which proved to be both an asset and a liability at times. Still, Cardno had his back and Uzah was grateful. "Status of fighters?"

"All launching, sir," the launch control tech, Arora, replied. "Including Captain Rhii."

Despite his hesitations and Cardno's objections, Davi's decision to take VS28s along on his duties today was clearly a wise one. The fleet was on full alert, all ships with full shields; now they had to hope they could do enough damage to chase off the pirates before they reciprocated. "All ships' weapons fire at will," he ordered.

"Fleet commanders fire at will," the fleet comm tech, Katra, repeated, sending it out over the fleet channel.

"And order those barges to shift position and lead their attackers toward those cruisers and the other armed ships," Uzah said. "They can't fight them off alone."

"Aye, sir," Katra replied, turning back and sending the order out over the fleet channel.

If the barges could lure the enemy ships into range of the battle ship's cannons, between those and the fighters, they'd have a real threat to deal with. He just hoped the DB7 captains could pull it off before one of their own wound up destroyed.

"Incoming communication from Captain Rhii, sir," Arora said.

"Put it on the bridge comm," Uzah said.

Davi's voice filled the bridge, coming from speakers overhead. "… repeat, they appear to be different make than the pirate ships from before, sir."

"Captain, this is General Uzah, can you repeat, please?"

"Yes, sir. We're engaging with the enemy now. They're flying primarily modified VS28s according to our computers with a few odds and ends thrown in."

Uzah and Cardno exchanged a look. The Pirate ships' engines had left similar signatures to VS28s in some cases but they'd used a lot more varied craft in their attack.

"Could it be an allied band, taking advantage?" Uzah wondered aloud.

"Possibly, sir," Davi agreed. "But it honestly looks a lot more like the ships Xalivar sent against us at Tertullis."

"Xalivar?" Cardno asked, echoing everyone's surprise.

Xalivar was dead. They'd confirmed the destruction of his shuttle. His ships had fled quickly under threat from the larger Boralian fleet. Had they reassembled under a new leader?

"I know it doesn't seem possible, sir," Davi said, filling the silence. "And I doubt General Lucius would be so bold on his own, but perhaps a group has gone rogue."

"That's a sizable group for rogues," Uzah said.

"Yes, sir, just a guess."

Uzah turned to the scan techs at a console below. "Deep scans, full power on those ships. Find anything you can to identify and have the computers compare them with the ships we fought at Tertullis. Every possible comparison."

The scan techs nodded, speaking their affirmations as they went to work.

"Do you think it's them, General?" Cardno asked.

"If it is, we have a lot more to worry about than we did from those pirates," Uzah said.

When Davi and the girls first arrived to engage the enemy, there had been two dozen fighters, but shortly after he'd called in to Uzah, three Destroyers had arrived and their blazing cannons were creating the equivalent of a laser minefield in space. Davi and the Vertullian pilots had no choice but to stay clear and work around it as they tried to take out enemy fighters and guns, one-by-one.

The barges had begun shifting position as soon as Davi disconnected with Uzah, splitting up and moving toward nearby cruisers and armed transports, their attackers following. Davi grasped the plan immediately. *Smart thinking, General.* The transports' and cruisers' heavy guns would give the attackers much more cause for concern than just his three fighters.

Within fifteen minutes, the first cannons came into range and opened fire. And, as a couple of enemy ships exploded, more Vertullian fighters arrived.

"We late for the party, Captain?" Ace Biggs of Beta Squadron called over the comm.

Cocky, young, but unnaturally skilled and he knew it, Biggs was one of three other squadron leaders at present. He'd come to fighters from flying shuttles and freighters for shipping firms, and Davi had put him in Tela's squadron until she was assigned to the scouts. Reluctantly, because no one else was more skilled, Ace had been given command of the squadron in Tela's absence. If the scouts returned soon, he'd be back to second and Farien, Virun, and Jorek would each lead squadrons. Davi would feel a lot more comfortable with familiar hands in those roles.

"We left a few of 'em for ya, Ace," Brie teased.

Cocky and unpredictable as a pilot, Ace was also a whiz with the ladies, and they all loved to flirt with him, whether they had mates or not.

"Oh good," Ace replied, and Davi could almost hear him sneer. "Otherwise I'd have to file a complaint about you Alpha types taking all the fun."

"Like to see the reaction to that one," Nila said, chuckling.

"If you all are done with social hour, how about we focus on taking out more of these fighters," Davi said.

"Whew, Captain, relax," Ace teased. "I can do more than one thing at a time."

With that, Davi spotted Ace's fighter in a steep, swooping turn as it came up behind a cluster of enemy ships and let loose with all cannons and guns on full, ripping into their wings and fuselages as the startled pilots scrambled to evade. In seconds, all that was left of them was one badly damaged fighter and floating bits of two others.

"Now ladies, where were we?" Ace asked, jeering.

"Lucky shot," Davi mumbled and spun his fighter into a steep dive, Brie tight on his tail, as he targeted two more enemy ships.

"Jealous?" Brie teased.

"I can make you his wingman, if you're so confident in him," Davi replied.

"No, no, no, let me fly behind her," Ace said. "I like the view."

Brie and Nila laughed as Davi rolled his eyes and lit up his cannons, the vibrations traveling from the joystick up his arms as trails of laser bolts tore into the enemy.

Brie followed suit and the engines on one of the targets exploded, sending it veering off in a spin while the other limped away to regroup.

"Just one, Captain?" Ace asked. "You're losing your touch."

Davi muted his comm and vented his thoughts in the privacy of his cockpit. Then his blast shield lit up as one of the enemy cannons took out the engines on a barge.

"Damn! Now they're just sitting there, waiting for their deaths," Nila said, thinking aloud.

Davi spun his fighter into a sharp dive and headed back to protect the barge. "Not yet. I want a formation around this barge."

"We can't protect them all that way," Nila said.

"Let's hope it doesn't come to that," Davi replied as the ladies followed along with several of Ace's squadron.

Just then, the rest of Alpha Squadron appeared and formed around them. "Nice of you guys to show up," Brie teased.

"Sorry," the young female, Dami, replied. She and her wingman, Pree, were an odd match. Both farm kids who'd grown up together, he was awkward and big boned, short and chubby while she was tall, thin, and looked like a model, not a pilot. The moment they'd showed up at the squadron's quarters, Dami had drawn lots of attention from the pilots, while Pree won them all over with his humor and smarts. His ability to constantly take their money at cards didn't hurt either. Still, they were only six months out of training, and Davi watched over them like any rookies. They'd been doing inspections in other parts of the fleet and Uzah had praised their work, but their combat experience was nil, so this would be a real test.

"Watch yourselves, okay? Don't take unnecessary chances, but get those fighters out of commission," Davi instructed.

"Really? We thought we'd just watch all the pretty lights they're making with those laser-thingees, Captain," Pree teased.

Dami chuckled. "Don't worry about us, Captain. We've got this."

"You just tell us if you need any of them alive, sir," Pree replied as they swooped in together and opened fire.

Davi prayed their bravado wouldn't get either or both of them killed.

As soon as the DB7's engines failed, their urgent cries for assistance elevated to frantic, and Uzah couldn't blame them.

"Get those cruisers in closer, now!" He ordered, knowing full well his staff was already doing everything they could to speed the process. They all knew the inexperience of some of the captains and crews was the issue. They couldn't respond as quickly as needed nor maneuver their ships with the skill required to maximize their capabilities when they were too busy remembering how to do everything. But saying it still made the General feel better.

*Reliance* vibrated from an explosion off her hull, forcing him to grab a nearby rail as he walked. He stopped behind Cardno and put a hand on his aide's shoulder, shaking his head as the Colonel looked up at him.

"How are we to survive another week, let alone potential years as a fleet without better qualified people," Uzah whispered.

Cardno shrugged, his eyes making it clear he was wondering the same thing.

In this case, having someone agree with him didn't make Uzah feel better at all. "Take us over there," he said, deciding on the coordinates and motioning. The few fighters engaging *Reliance* were just a distraction to keep them out of the fight, but Uzah knew better. They could do little harm alone.

"General, the other ships in our path—"

"Will move clear or we'll fly over the top of them," Uzah snapped. "Just get us there." He had not time to argue or explain. *Reliance* was the most powerful ship in the fleet. The attacking destroyers wouldn't survive a head-on attack by her guns, and the command ship might be the only chance for the endangered barge and her civilian passengers and crew.

Cardno nodded and typed the coordinates into the command computer.

Arora began issuing the commands to the ships involved, and the helmsmen discussed the safest route.

Uzah nodded with approval then had another thought. "And Colonel, monitor all communications going out of this bridge. No one is to release information on the attackers until we have identified them properly." The last thing they needed was rumors of Xalivar's return fueling people's paranoia, especially Joram's.

Even as he thought the man's name—an old, formerly dear friend—his comm beeped with an indicator that he had an incoming call from Joram's quarters. Uzah sighed and made the connection. "Councilor."

"What's this I hear about remnants of Xalivar's fleet attacking our civilian transports?"

"We haven't finished identifying them yet," Uzah replied. "Nothing's been confirmed."

"But it's possible?"

Uzah sighed. "I repeat. We don't know for sure who they are yet."

"So it could be the Boralians then?" Joram asked.

Uzah tensed, feeling relieved the comm was audio only and not a telecall. Then *Reliance* vibrated again. "Look, Joram, I'm a little busy right now. I'll let you know as soon as we have more information. But I can assure you these are not Boralian forces. That much we know."

Joram cleared his throat before continuing. "You know, General, we're on the same side. It would be a lot easier for us both if we could work together."

"If you want to set up a meeting to discuss our working relationship, do it later. For now, it'll have to wait," Uzah replied. "I'm trying to save civilian lives, Councilor." Uzah closed the connection, certain even then that somehow Joram would find a way to use his words against him.

Uzah turned back to the giant bridge vidscreen and the *Reliance*'s engines surged as the ship accelerated toward the fighting. Smaller ships were already moving slowly out of their path, but Uzah saw that Cardno and the helmsmen had decided not to wait and charted a path up and over the top of them. The mere sight of the battleship looming down on them should be enough to give the destroyers' crews pause. Moving a ship its size was no minor effort and Uzah prayed silently that *Reliance* would arrive in time to save the barge.

Davi hated being forced to look at the barge, but he had to as he spun around trying to defend it. It was kind of like watching an animal struck on a roadway waiting to die, but the attacking fighters had centered on it now, and the third Destroyer would soon come in range of the barge with its cannons.

Davi and his squadron sped in and zigzagged in and out, firing at any enemy that drew near, even though their blasts had minimal impact on the Destroyers. Davi couldn't bear the idea of watching those civilians die. He kept thinking of the two boys he'd seen playing on the barge, when they'd inspected it. Other passengers' faces flooded his memory.

He spotted one of the Destroyers turning now to bring its cannons into better range of the barge. In moments, it would be all over if they couldn't find a way to stop them. He targeted the Destroyer's center cannons and raced in for a strafing run.

As he turned, he saw *Reliance* arcing over the top of several slower ships to make her way toward the battle. He wondered if the Destroyer crews had noticed and what effect on them facing the battleship would have. Even combined, they were outmatched.

The combat system beeped at him as the Destroyer's cannons came into range and he released every weapon he had, firing on them at full. He peeled off, watching his lasers' and torpedoes' progress on his scanners as he went. Explosions rocked the cannon placement and pricked at the Destroyer's hull, but he knew it would take several runs to weaken the deflectors enough to break through. And there wouldn't be time.

Then he saw flashes as Brie and Nila followed in his wake, hitting the same cannons he'd just targeted.

"We need bigger guns," Brie muttered.

"It's not the size, ladies, it's what you do with it," Ace teased.

"Hmmm, let's see how you feel about it if I use them on you," Nila replied, irritated more at their lack of progress than Ace, Davi imagined.

"We can't just stand here and watch them die," Brie said.

"Who's standing? Let's go again!" Nila said.

Their chatter died out as they each circled back, Ace, Pree, and Dami joining in to attack the Destroyer's cannons. They also managed to fire at oncoming fighters afterwards as they pulled out and circled around again.

Then Davi saw explosions rocking the barge's hull. He heard the captain calling *Reliance* to report: "Hull integrity at forty percent, shields failing." And he knew time had run out. One more hit like that and the barge was done for. The battleship wouldn't make it in time, and neither would their cannon runs.

"Get back and keep blocking incoming fire and ships from hitting that barge," Davi ordered. "We've got to give them more time." Then he killed the comm and turned on his flight suit's internal life support, disconnecting the hose from his fighter and making sure his laser weapons were within easy reach. He hated to do what he was about to do, but it might be the barge's only chance to last long enough for more help to arrive.

He reached down under his seat and unlocked the release lever for ejection, hoping his plan would work, and aimed his fighter's nose right at the Destroyer's cannon emplacement.

"Davi, what are you doing?" Nila called, sounding concerned.

"What has to be done," Davi replied. "Hang on."

With that he punched the button and his VS28 shot forward like a rocket toward the cannons, forcing his body back hard against the seat. He fired as he went, locking the ship's navigations system on course and engaging automatic defensive weapons. He had seconds to put everything in place, and then, as the nose of his ship was about to make contact, he pulled the lever and ejected, seat and all, grabbing his weapons as the bolts exploded beneath him and the blast shield servos whined and lifted it away.

He shot up into space and used the seat's boosters to navigate himself away from the Destroyer toward clear space as the fighter exploded on impact, taking out the cannons and making a serious breach in the Destroyer's hull.

He smiled, pleased at his success before noticing enemy fighters turning to target him now.

"That was crazy!" Brie called.

"They're coming for you, Davi!" Nila warned.

"I'm a small target," Davi said, aiming his rifle and firing a blast at the nearest enemy. "Let's see how well these chairs can move." He fired up the boosters to full and faced into the oncoming fighters' path, firing his rifle again.

"You're insane!" Brie called.

"I'm coming for you!" Nila said as Davi saw her fighter turn and barrel back toward him.

Davi hadn't realized until that moment the choice he'd made—his life for the others. And even as it sunk in, he knew he'd be fine with it as long as the barge wasn't destroyed, and there was little certainty of that. He wondered what more he could do to increase their odds, then a laser blast struck and exploded a few feet away, and he spun, maneuvering the boosters again to see enemy pilots sneering as they headed for him.

"If they don't kill you, I'm going to do it for them!" a familiar female voice groused.

Then the enemy fighters exploded as an influx of new fighters arrived—VS28s with Vertullian and Boralian markings.

"Sorry we're late for the party, all, but you should have sent the invitation much earlier," Jorek teased as Davi realized the scouting ships had returned.

Suddenly, the enemy fighters were outnumbered as sixty more VS28s filled the skies, doubling his people's numbers. More than that, the new arrivals were flown by more experienced pilots and their combat readiness showed immediate results. A dozen enemy fighters fell under their cannons and even the Destroyers became occupied defending themselves from the new arrivals.

Ace's voice deafened him as the pilot let out a victory yell and started yet another run against a Destroyer.

And then Davi saw the enemy had realized they'd lost the advantage and their strategy changed from offensive to defensive. He felt the tug of a tractor beam and saw a VS28 pulling up underneath, Tela's angry glare coming through the blast shield. It had been her voice he'd heard, before Jorek. She looked worried as she tractored his chair in close and then opened her cockpit to allow him inside. Although they rarely used them, each VS28 had a jumpsuit behind the pilot for emergencies.

Davi unstrapped his seat and slid over to squeeze in behind her as Tela hit a button, servos whining as the blast shield slid closed over them.

He grinned, relieved to see her. "I missed you."

Her angry lecturing response was not quite what he'd hoped for.

# Chapter Five

"Did I raise you to be an idiot?!"

Miri's voice cut through the din of beeping monitors, whirring med-bots, jingling trays and tubes, and chattering doctors and nurses as she marched across the *Reliance*'s Sickbay toward her son. Located on the same level as the bridge, it was relatively quiet at the moment, so Davi and a few other pilots had come in to be "checked out." Davi hadn't had a choice. Tela had dragged him there. And now, apparently, she'd told his mothers.

Lura followed hurriedly in Miri's wake. "Your father had to go to an emergency Council session, but we came as soon as we could." She put her hand on Davi's forehead as he lay on an exam table.

"I'm fine, mothers, really," Davi said, hiding his annoyance at all the fawning. Between Tela and his mothers, he felt like a child again, and the racing thoughts in his mind made it hard to sit here and be nice. He started to stand but Tela pushed him back down.

"You stay!" She ordered as Miri and Lura each hugged her in turn.

"So good to see you!" Lura trilled, smiling with joy.

"Welcome back, Tela, maybe you can knock some sense into this boy's head," Miri said.

Tela shook her head. "He's lost his sense, apparently."

Miri spun back around, tense, to glare at Davi. "Ejecting in the middle of a battle? You could have been killed! Whatever possessed you?"

"The lives of two hundred civilians, mother," Davi replied, ignoring her stare. "Should I have just let them die?"

"Committing suicide is not a solution!"

Lura put a hand softly on Miri's arm. "We're just relieved that you're okay."

Davi sighed and smiled at her. "I'm fine. The med-bots confirmed it. Right, Tela?"

He looked at his fiancée, who held out stubbornly a moment and then nodded, her face still crinkled with disapproval.

Davi raised his palms in a question.

The three women just stared at him, but their bodies relaxed a bit.

"It was the only way to take out that cannon. If I'd have known the scouts were so close, I might have waited, but it bought them the time they needed."

"And destroyed your fighter," Tela said.

"There are other fighters."

Tela chuckled. "I hope I'm there to hear you tell Uzah and Cardno that. They talk as if you threw away a goldmine."

"The General knows I did what I had to," Davi replied.

"The General knows you were out of your mind!" Miri said, arms crossing over her chest. "He's been so out of sorts with you gone, Tela. Bored. Jealous of all the adventures you've been having."

Tela cocked an eyebrow and Davi could tell she was fighting to hold back a smile. "Oh really? I figured you'd have plenty to keep you busy here."

"Inspections, maintenance, crowd control, policing," Miri continued. "Nothing as exciting as your encounters with aliens in bars."

Tela blushed a bit. "The Nets really exaggerated that stuff; took it out of context."

Lura patted her arm. "Of course they did, dear."

Davi turned his head to the nearest med-bot. "Can I go now?"

The med-bot stopped, tray of vials jangling, and rotated its head so the LEDs that served as its eyes and mouth were facing him. "We are waiting for clearance from command, Captain. It should be momentarily."

"You said that half an hour ago," Davi grumbled as the med-bot turned back to its path and scooted onward.

"Maybe I can call and have them hold you for a few days," Miri threatened.

Across the way, a patient moaned loudly and metal trays rattled as he thrashed around. A med-bot and two nurses moved in to calm him.

Davi jumped to his feet, pulling off the sensors taped to his arms and chest with a wince as he did.

"Davi!" Lura stepped toward him, worried.

Davi smiled at her. "They said I have to wait for clearance. They didn't say I had to do it sitting there." Davi turned and found his uniform shirt draped over a nearby exam table and picked it up, raising it over his head.

As he did, Lura and Miri reached out to inspect some scratches and bruises on his chest and back.

He jumped a bit at the feel of their cold fingers. "Ah! What did you do, soak those in ice before you came?"

"A mother's blood runs cold when her child's in danger," Lura joked.

"Or being stupid," Miri added.

Tela laughed, watching them with amusement.

"And I thought your lecture was unpleasant." Davi shot her a look as he pulled the shirt down over his head and neck, then moved his hands across it to straighten and smooth it out.

Tela shrugged. "It's terrible to be so loved, huh?"

Davi sighed and raised his hands in surrender. "I give up, okay? I'm sorry. I reacted quickly. I didn't know what I was doing."

Tela and Lura softened, smiling with appreciation.

"Admitting you have a problem is the first step, they say," Miri said, her eyes still hard.

"How many casualties?" Davi asked Tela.

"Ten pilots, six minor injuries, two admitted for a few days of treatment, broken bones sustained during battle."

The cockpits were comfortable but with the right amount of turbulence or an erratic flight to escape an enemy's guns, one could get knocked around.

Davi relaxed, leaning against the exam table. "It could have been a lot worse."

Miri started to speak but Lura interrupted her by leaning forward to kiss Davi's cheek. "For all of us." Her eyes filled with relief.

He hugged her as she drew near, wrapping her warm body with his own and kissing her forehead. "I wouldn't do that to you."

"Don't even come close," Lura said, her voice calm but her eyes pleading as she leaned back to meet his gaze. He felt tears threatening to form in the corners of his own eyes and just nodded, shaking it off as he hugged her again.

"The Boralian Government is not responsible for this attack!" Aron insisted.

"If Boralians fly the ships, issue the commands, and execute them, they should be!" Joram insisted again.

Tension dripped from the walls of *Reliance*'s conference room. Sol expected the Council to come to blows at any moment. If it had been divided before, the divide had only deepened now; even those who'd been formerly neutral choosing sides with either Aron or Joram. Sol watched with amazement, a sadness welling up within. How had a people who were once so united in their common fight against oppression, suffering, and slavery come to this? Had they forgotten who they were, where they came from, and the price they'd paid for their freedom? And how could he bring them together?

"We don't know for sure what the connection is to Xalivar or anyone else," Uzah said, his military discipline clearly aiding him in maintaining a calm tone and demeanor. But emotions flared in his eyes.

"I know!" Joram said, leaning forward in the chair to emphasize each word. "I don't need some investigation to tell me. And they targeted civilians specifically! It's just like the old days of oppressing us, slaughtering us!"

"We're going to talk with the High Lord Councilor," Aron said, "find out what he knows."

"Oh yes, because we can trust him to tell the truth," Joram scoffed. Beside him Lords Tamora, Hula, Chad, and Klima nodded and mumbled their support.

Lord Nachor rolled his eyes and leaned back in his chair. "The truth? You've been manipulating people for months! Ever since the attack by a bunch of hoodlums!"

"An attack which cost a man's life and nearly mine!" Joram countered, fist pounding the table.

"And Sol's as well," Coz said, waving to Sol, "but you don't see him losing his head."

"If we don't take this seriously, we may all lose our heads!" Lord Hula said.

Uzah raised a hand and took a deep breath. "We were unprepared for an attack inside the Borali System, I admit that. But we have our scouts back and we're increasing defenses. We're also hoping to trade barges for some larger, more appropriate ships for the rest of the journey, to accommodate the citizens and protect them better."

"For which you intend to ask Tarkanius' help?" Joram sneered.

"The High Lord Councilor will be made aware of our needs," Uzah nodded. "We do not expect him to take responsibility for solving them."

"It's their system," Sol said. "They need to be aware of the aggressive attacks given their own experiences with attacks on planets."

"Yes!" Aron motioned to a vidscreen as a system map appeared with red flashing indicators for the locations of each attack. "It's possible the same people are involved, and by sharing information, we can better protect ourselves and determine who's responsible."

Sol was tempted to add: "Aron's already lost his wife," but thought better of it. Aron had been forced to return to his responsibilities despite his grief at the loss of Calla. How his friend could function so well and appear so strong, Sol didn't know. Sol knew he would have been incapacitated. Though everyone knew of Calla's death, somehow it seemed cruel to mention it, if Aron hadn't. Instead he said: "Rash action will only put us in more danger."

"Right," Aron agreed. "We've got to work quickly, but with care and forethought."

"They could strike again at any time!" Joram said.

"Which is why making the Boralian forces aware of the issue is vital," Uzah said. "They might provide assistance or at least an early warning next time."

Sol winced at the choice of words. Joram's reaction was no surprise.

"Assistance?!" Joram almost shouted. "We washed our hands of them. Keep them out of our affairs!"

"This situation affects all of us," Aron said.

"Our responsibility is to our own," Lord Tamora said.

Aron nodded. "Yes. And that means doing everything possible to protect them, including gathering what information we can from all sources. And making sure that the authorities know our intent to respond aggressively to attacks and defend ourselves."

"The last thing we want," Uzah added, panning their eyes and meeting each in turn, "is Boralians interfering or accusing us of unwarranted aggression."

"Unwarranted aggression?" Lord Chad laughed, shaking his head. "They defined the term!"

Joram and his friends grunted vigorously in support.

"And our people have paid for it for centuries," Joram added.

"We will let you know as soon as we have more information," Uzah said, turning toward the door as Aron followed.

Joram looked affronted, but then Nachor and Coz turned as well and Sol decided to join them.

"I head this Council," Joram reminded them. "I am elected by the people! I expect to be involved in any discussions with other governments."

Uzah stopped at the door and turned back. This time his calm, professional demeanor cracked along with his voice, "When the time comes that your involvement is needed, you will be." His eyes locked on Joram, an intense stare somewhere between a warning and a plea.

The two men held each other's gaze for several minutes, then Joram sighed and looked away. "I appreciate your recognition of my role," he said, turning back to his supporters as Uzah and Aron led theirs out the door.

Everything about the meeting was unusual. Instead of speaking by vidcomm, Xalivar had ordered the pilots and captains to assemble on the *Tarragon*'s bridge. Pres lined up with the rest. Only the most essential techs and officers remained at their duty stations.

The attacks on the Vertullian fleet, Italis, and Xanthis had all been successful. Pres had watched with Lucius from the bridge, while Xalivar watched from his quarters. The leader spent more and more time alone, she'd noticed. She'd assumed it was paranoia, frustration, meditation. There had been many setbacks. Xalivar's record had been an almost unbroken string of successes until the Council intervened and removed him from power. He'd been trying to recapture that greatness ever since. And Pres knew the continued failures had to wear on him. Xalivar was larger than life, but he was human, even if he himself rarely acknowledged it.

He arrived from his quarters after they'd been standing at assembly for five minutes, awaiting him. He marched in, a stern look on his face, wearing a military uniform she'd never seen him wear and hadn't even been aware he possessed. According to tradition, the High Lord Councilor was the default head of the Boralian military, but Xalivar's field service had ended during the Delta V incident decades before. Lucius had served alongside him then. No one since had seen him in uniform. Clearly their leader wanted to make a lasting impression.

Ignoring the *Tarragon*'s command staff, Xalivar instead focused on the commanders of his destroyers and their pilots. He strode in front of them like a General inspecting his troops, which no doubt he was. He stopped a few times, examining their uniforms, checking their stance, locking eyes with an individual or two. Most, she knew, had rarely been in his presence and certainly never so close. Pres was sure it made them nervous, but Xalivar no doubt enjoyed it. He took his time, gliding past row by row, giving each the same examination and interaction. When he finished, he strode to the front again, face forward, not even making eye contact with anyone, until he whirled on his heels to face them.

"The attacks today on Xanthis and Italis were triumphant," Xalivar said. "Great successes, for which you are all to be commended." He nodded at the commanders involved.

They saluted, looking pleased, and Pres saw smiles crack the faces of several pilots in the lines behind them.

"The attack on the Vertullian fleet, however," Xalivar continued, "was not as successful. How do you explain this, Captains?" He watched the three commanders carefully, his face a shadow of doubt, unwavering.

Finally, the senior Captain, Captain Pruett, as Pres recalled, stepped forward. "They were reinforced at the last minute, taking us by surprise, my Lord."

Xalivar turned his eyes on the Captain, a man of dignity, his hair graying and his belly swelling from age and stress, but his posture still straight and firm from years of practice in military service.

The Captain met Xalivar's gaze, but unlike their leader, his eyes glistened with emotion: a mixture of regret, apology, fear, and even conviction filling them.

"By surprise, you say? Did you not expect resistance?" Xalivar's intensity made him sound louder than his actual voice.

Pruett nodded. "Of course, my Lord, but we met so little resistance. The battle was well underway, and we'd almost destroyed a civilian carrier when they arrived."

"Yet you failed to destroy this ship, to annihilate those rebel civilians."

*Boralian citizens*, Pres wanted to say. Despite her shared frustration at the changes Tarkanius had wrought, despite her belief the Vertullians should never have been granted equal status, once they had been granted freedom and citizenship, she believed they had the full rights of Boralian citizens and that meant that treating them as rebels worthy of annihilation was a crime. It was a crime she'd been complicit in attempting, she knew, but something about Xalivar's inability to recognize the real stakes involved irritated her.

"A ship crashed into our hull, destroying our cannons and forcing us to evade them and make repairs," Pruett explained. "*Reliance* herself was closing—"

"You ran," Xalivar cut him off. "You fled in fear for your lives."

"We retreated to regroup so that we could attack again and do further damage," the Captain corrected, the fear and apology now fading from his eyes, replaced by a spark of defiance.

"Your orders were to finish, not to regroup for another day," Xalivar said, enunciating each word as if it were poisonous to him.

"General Lucius ordered us to use appropriate strategy, my Lord," Pruett replied, glancing at Lucius, who stood beside Pres, his face frozen in formal rest as he stood at attention.

Xalivar didn't even give his General a look. A blaster appeared in his hand. She heard it whine as it warmed up, then the barrel flared and exploded with a flash as a laser bolt tore into Captain Pruett's chest and his body collapsed to the floor at Xalivar's feet.

The blaster disappeared as fast as it had appeared. "Would anyone else like to make excuses?" Xalivar asked, panning the room as he slowly rotated.

Pres saw the shock radiating through her body reflected on the faces of the officers, techs, and pilots around her. Even Lucius appeared stunned by Xalivar's actions. She panned the room and saw Manaen, frozen in the doorway, back to the wall, a wince on his face as their eyes locked. He wore a pained look she'd never seen on him, and somehow she knew he'd never expected this either.

Only the beeping of control panels and chatter from comms broke the silence as everyone waited, stiffened at attention, a few daring to even breathe.

Then Xalivar nodded, turned, and strode from the room, moving right past Manaen, who turned and followed in his wake, ever the dutiful aide.

The unspoken message hung clearly in the air for all who'd witnessed: failure was no longer acceptable.

Farien arrived at Aron's quarters last to find Davi, Uzah, Aron, and Sol awaiting him. All four looked as somber as Farien felt. He was glad his squadron had returned in time to deflect the attackers, whoever they were, but the divisions he now found amongst the Vertullians gave him pause. He wondered how he and his fellow Boralian escort pilots would be treated if the anti-Boralian sentiment continued to rise. Farien had dedicated himself to helping them start over for a long while now, and the death of his friend Yao had only strengthened his resolve. But if they decided he was an enemy spy, he could wind up in a world of trouble, and he and his few fellow escorts would be far from home and very outnumbered.

"Welcome," Aron said, smiling and nodding as Farien strode in.

Farien walked to where they sat, around a vidscreen, and took an open chair beside Davi. His old classmate looked overjoyed to see him.

"What time is the High Lord Councilor coming on the call?" Farien asked.

"Any minute now," General Uzah replied.

Davi reached over to squeeze Farien's shoulder. "I hear you kept my fiancée busy out there."

"We had a little bit of action, yeah," Farien said with a nod.

"Well, she came back with plenty of fire," Davi agreed. "In fact, if you could put in a good word …"

Davi's father Sol chuckled and shrugged.

"After that stunt you pulled, we should all be on her side," Farien teased. "What were you thinking, Rhii?"

Davi grimaced. "Not you, too, after all we've been through."

"Hey, if you're suicidal, don't come to me to be your second, okay?" Farien replied, forcing a smile to hide the resentment he really felt. He'd already lost Yao. Did Davi really need to be so careless?

"I saved that barge, didn't I?"

"Hopefully it'll never come to such drastic measures again," Aron said as the vidscreen flickered.

Tarkanius appeared from his private quarters at the Palace on Legallis. Farien could see the room hadn't changed much since Xalivar inhabited it, although the curtains and linens were less posh and bookshelves filled a wall where Xalivar had once hung portraits of his forefathers.

"Gentlemen," Tarkanius said. "It's been too long."

Aron smiled politely and nodded, skipping the traditional salute given by those entering the High Lord Councilor's presence. Davi and Farien did it automatically, their hands moving unbidden as they crossed fingers over their opposite fists. Tarkanius gave no sign he'd noticed or cared. "We wish the circumstances were better."

Tarkanius looked sad. "Aron, I don't know where to begin. I'm so sorry about Calla."

Aron's eyes misted a bit as he replied, "Thank you, my friend. It's a terrible price to pay, but she believed in our cause as much as I do."

Tarkanius sighed. "And so do I when I hear of troubles like this. Although the consequences you've left me with your departure involve some frustration and chaos." He chuckled.

"And we regret that more than you know," Aron said.

Farien knew the Vertullian leader meant that but doubted any of his compatriots would agree.

"We've analyzed the attack data you sent," Tarkanius said. "The forces appear similar to those who have attacked Xanthis, Italis, and Idolis in recent days. And they are not at all like the pirate ships you encountered before."

"So Xalivar lives?" Uzah asked, speaking the question all of them were wondering.

Tarkanius shrugged. "We don't think so. We saw the same footage of the Tertullian Battle that you did. But with his supporters still out there, we do agree it appears they've taken matters into their own hands."

"What can they possibly hope to accomplish?" Sol asked.

"Revenge is a great motivator, even if the end goal is undefined," Tarkanius suggested.

"They caught us unprepared, I'm afraid," Aron said. "And Joram is using it to build anti-Boralian sentiment. He believes you've betrayed us."

"I hope you know that's not the case," Tarkanius said sadly.

Uzah nodded. "We don't believe it, no, but we cannot continue safely with the barges being so vulnerable. And we find ourselves with no good solution to the problem."

Knowing what he'd heard of the troubles the High Lord Councilor was facing back at home, Farien didn't expect him to be much more than sympathetic, but Tarkanius' answer surprised him. "I have someone in mind whom I believe can be of help."

Lord Hachim's image filled the screen. The chubby, dark-skinned former Councilor had fallen into disgrace after he'd joined a plot to kill Tarkanius himself and reverse the leader's decision to grant the Vertullians full citizenship. But when caught, Hachim had confessed and testified against his co-conspirators, sparing himself the prison time they now served. Still, Farien wondered why Tarkanius would even suggest him at this meeting.

"Hachim is no longer on the Council, but his shipping company is still very viable here," Tarkanius continued as he came back on screen.

"The very man who sought to assassinate you and re-enslave us?" Uzah said, bristling as he shook his head. "Joram and his supporters would have a field day."

"Well, it's my hope they'll never know of his assistance," Tarkanius said. "If I offer Hachim a chance to provide loaner ships to aid in his redemption and raise his status, I believe he'll jump at it. I won't do so without conditions, of course."

"And you trust him?" Sol asked, his tone softer than his scowl.

Tarkanius sighed. "I trust more in his driving desperation to restore his influence and status. That gives me an edge I can use to negotiate."

Aron and Uzah exchanged a look.

"What conditions will you require?" Aron asked.

"Full access to inspection of all ships, Boralian crews chosen by me to man them, a few of whom may stay on to advise your own crews as you continue your journey, and full fighter escorts to the edge of the system or beyond if desired, so we can react as needed if he were to attempt a deception. Plus, he will donate the ships for your use until your journey ends."

"Free?" Davi chuckled. "He's not going to like that."

Tarkanius smiled. "I'm going to send one of our refueling ships to ensure that you have the fuel you need, at our government's expense, and we will defend you against any further attacks, at least until you've reached the edge of the system."

Sol shrugged. "Are there other options?"

"It's an incredibly generous offer," Aron said.

"But we have a responsibility to consider all possibilities, don't we?" Sol replied.

Uzah nodded. "Lord Sol's right. And we have to be prepared to deflect Joram's questions and complaints."

"If I recall correctly, the transports Hachim owns would hold the passengers of three barges, correct?" Davi asked.

"That should be the case," Tarkanius agreed.

"So we'll need four of them," Davi said, calculating figures in his mind.

"And his full complement is fifteen or twenty," Farien added.

Tarkanius nodded. "He's got the largest shipping fleet in the system."

"Can the crews be trusted?" Uzah asked.

"I will provide most of the crew members myself, with handpicked helmsmen from his own employees," Tarkanius said. "I have people I trust."

"The barge crews should be able to shift over, once they dock the barges," Davi said.

Farien nodded. "Are most of them willing to continue on?"

"Their plan was to stay with us wherever we settled," Aron said and turned to the High Lord Councilor again. "Have you approached Hachim?"

Tarkanius shook his head. "No. I wanted to be sure you were even open to it first."

Aron met each of their eyes, evaluating their responses before answering. No one raised a question but Farien knew he was not alone in his skepticism.

"I think we have no choice but to explore all options," Aron said.

Tarkanius smiled. "I will approach him immediately and get back in touch then."

Aron offered a warm smile of his own.

Farien knew the two leaders had grown quite close in the previous year while working together on the Boralian Council, where Aron had served as the first Vertullian member. It had always appeared they genuinely liked each other and despite circumstances that clearly hadn't changed.

"Very good, my friend, thank you," Aron replied.

"And if you have trouble finding a buyer for the barges," Tarkanius said, "I may have a solution for that as well."

Uzah nodded. "Any help would be most appreciated. We have so many other concerns at the moment."

"We'll speak in a few days," Tarkanius said. "The gods' blessings upon you and peace, my friends."

Farien couldn't recall the High Lord Councilor offering the traditional Boralian blessing at any time in the past and wondered, as the vidscreen faded to black, what changes the last few months had wrought at the Palace. Could the man have embraced the old religion again? Had his contact with Aron had influence on that? Farien had never imagined anyone finding peace in religion of any form, but the High Lord Councilor's countenance had shone with calm despite the stress they all knew he must be under. He found himself curious about the source of that peace.

The others stood around him.

"We'll want to meet with the pilots soon," General Uzah said.

Farien and Davi nodded.

"Of course," Davi agreed and put an arm around Farien's shoulders. "But not tonight. Tonight, these two old friends are getting drunk."

Uzah frowned. "Not while the fleet is under alert."

"Oh, did I say that out loud?" Davi said, shooting him a coy look. "I meant drunk on reminiscing and good food."

Farien smiled, amused. "Of course, we need something warm to wash it down."

"Of course," Davi said with a wink and steered him toward the door as the three older men chuckled behind them.

As he meditated in his quarters aboard the *Tarragon*, alone, Xalivar wondered how he'd ever forgotten the thrill of the power to take a life. Issuing orders and military strategies just wasn't the same. No. Leading by example was something Xalivar had never stopped believing in, and so he would provide it, over and over if needed. And one day, they'd all remember that Xalivar came back to power, not just by the work of others' hands, but by the work of his own.

For hours after the assembly on the bridge, Xalivar's mind flashed back to that day in the Palace, when his father and grandfather had watched the Delta V footage over and over, then ended his military career. They'd treated Xalivar as if he had shamed the family. This from the very people who'd worked hardest to maintain Vertullian slavery and all that it meant. Xalivar had restored the very system that allowed the Borali Alliance to thrive under their rule, and they'd thanked him by discrediting and disgracing him. Xalivar would never forget.

Today, he knew he'd restored credit and honor, or at least made a leap further down that road. Xalivar was tired of failure, tired of disappointment. He'd tolerated the weakness and incompetence of his own people for far too long. If they needed a reminder of who he was and how seriously he took his mission, he'd been more than happy to provide one. And the shocked looks on their faces was all the reward he needed.

Captain Pruett was an example of the kind of officers Xalivar's new Alliance could do without. Death was more honorable than fear and surrender. Retreat was unacceptable. It never led to victory. If it cost Xalivar every last soldier, the price still wasn't too high. He experienced no emotion over the man's death. He could always find more. All that mattered was his return to his rightful rule, and anyone who doubted or failed to grasp that was expendable.

"You delight in the dishonor and humiliation of our family, Xalivar?" his grandfather had asked. "Senseless killing is not success," he'd later said.

Well, the killing was not senseless if it served a greater purpose, and Captain Pruett's execution was a memory which would remain with Xalivar's officers as long as they lived, a reminder of their place and his;

who he was and what awaited them if they ever forgot.

Xalivar hadn't dirtied his hands directly since Delta V, but now that he had, he realized that had been a mistake.

Again, he thought of his grandfather, Xonas' words: "People respect and admire passion."

*Let them see my passion then. Let it remind them of what's at stake. We're all fighting for our lives. And if one man's death is what it takes to revive their passion and focus, then fine. Let them remember it.*

He imagined himself in the throne room on Legallis again, wearing ceremonial robes as he once again donned the Lord's Eye around his neck. And this time, his former nephew, Xander Davi Rhii would be nowhere nearby to stop him. Let him flee with his inferior race. If Xalivar couldn't destroy them before they left the system, there'd be plenty of time later to hunt them down and set history right.

And once he'd settled in at the Palace again, he'd do what he'd never thought he had to: find a wife and make an heir. This time, there would be no doubt about the purity of the offspring's heritage. The boy would be raised by Xalivar, and Xalivar alone. The woman would be sent away, for the safety of her son, of course. Xalivar could not risk the temptation that came from women's weakness of mind, their emotional overruling of common sense. With that, his future and that of his beloved Alliance would be secured.

His head tipped back at the thought of it, a smile broadening his face, and for the first time in months, Xalivar laughed loudly, adrenaline causing his body to tingle as it raced through his veins, a celebration of his pure delight.

When Lura woke her, Tela couldn't believe she'd slept for ten hours straight. And in a normal, soft bed, too. It had been ages since she'd had that luxury. In fact, after dinner with Davi's parents the night before, she'd never made it back to her quarters, instead falling asleep in their spare room aboard the *Reliance*. And she felt the most rested she had in over a month.

As Lura served her warm Talis, prepared eggs and Daken sausage for breakfast, Tela wiped the crust from the corners of her eyes and yawned for the fifth time. "I can't believe they didn't call me with orders yet."

Lura smiled. "Oh, they sent them over this morning. I told them you'd report when you'd had a good rest, and the Yeoman knew better than to argue with a mother."

Tela chuckled as Lura approached, handing Tela her military-issue datapad. "The Yeoman came in person?" She called up her messages and flipped to the folder where official orders would be routed.

Lura shook her head. "When you failed to report, he did. But when I called Uzah on the vidscreen, neither of them tried very hard to argue with me."

The orders had instructed Tela to report for maintenance duties to the shuttle bay at 0900 that morning. Instead, here she was at 1100 and not even dressed for duty, let alone showered and fed. The Daken strips sizzled on the stove, their salty scent teased her nostrils. "Mmmmm, thank you," she muttered, closing her eyes to savor the thought of real food. They'd been limited to military rations since leaving K1, off Kronis.

"Uzah said you could report in the morning," Lura said as she stirred the meat and glanced at the eggs. "So I thought maybe we could find some time for wedding planning, if you're up for it."

Tela nodded through a yawn. She'd been surprised and pleased that neither Lura nor Miri had brought it up the night before. Then again, they'd known she was exhausted and the conversation had been more about the political situation and Davi's crazy risk taking than personal matters. Tela had been thankful for the reprieve, but now, it felt like she could barely remember what a normal day felt like, and she knew it would be good to experience one for a change. "Sure, I'd like that."

She'd been hard on Davi, as had they all, but after that stunt he pulled, despite its worthy consequences, he'd needed a reminder of how much he meant to them all. He'd worried about them enough the past few years, it was time he remembered they worried, too. Part of her was mad as hell at him for putting her through that. What if she and the scouts hadn't arrived to send the enemy running? In truth, her awareness of the jeopardy he was in had lasted less than five minutes, still, the mere thought of losing him …

Tela closed her eyes, choking back a sob, and fought to contain the tears welling in her eyes. She thought then of her father, Telanus. She couldn't bear another loss like those she'd already suffered. It had been her love for Davi and his own grief that had pulled her out of her angry wallowing and helped her find her way back to functioning again. She'd focused on taking care of him, being there for him. Somehow, despite all the arguments and stress between them, nothing mattered but finding a way to keep him from pain, stop the hurting they both shared.

She'd mourned Yao, too. She still did. And that fact that Davi had lost not just Yao but Farien, at least mentally, in that tragedy weighed on him heavily, she knew. But the night before, Davi had called to skip dinner just so he and Farien could hang out and catch up. She hoped they'd found a way to close the distance. Farien and Davi both needed each other, even if they wouldn't admit it.

Typical men.

She still found herself amazed by Davi's courage and humbled by God's faithfulness in keeping him safe. When they'd finally found the courage to talk about what had happened between them, he'd apologized again and again, holding onto her like bark on a tree, tears in his eyes. Telanus had told her that the most anger and frustration you'll ever experience will come from those you love, and Tela had discovered he was right. But the love, the joy, the comfort of their presence, when returned, overcame everything else as if none of it mattered.

Lura slid a plate in front of her and the warm steam and delicious scent of spiced eggs and Daken strips filled her nose, snapping her back to reality. "Ready for some real food again?" Lura joked.

Tela's answer was to cut a bite of each with her fork and lift them to her mouth, closing her eyes as the taste delighted her tongue. "Mmmmm, you are wonderful."

Lura laughed. "Thanks. You'd think I was a chef the way you compliment my cooking."

Tela took a sip of the Talis and prepped another bite, smiling at her. "You could be."

"Well, eat up, dear," Lura said, taking a seat across the table as she enjoyed watching Tela's appreciation of her efforts. "Then we have so much fun planning to do!"

For just a moment, she thought of Telanus again and fought back tears by stuffing more food into her mouth and focusing on the salty, warm tenderness of it. She knew he'd been proud of her, and how much he approved of her choice in Davi. She told herself the price he'd paid for so many years, even his death, would prove worth the effort, when they started fresh on a new planet with no more oppression and hatred to contend with. A fresh start, like she'd gotten this morning, that would be life changing.

And Tela was more than ready for the change.

Their second raid on the Vertullian fleet came as the fleet left the outer belt between Plutonis and Regalis. Why they were stopping there, Bordox had no idea. One last fling before they sailed out of the system for unknown space, perhaps? He chuckled. With the barges limping, they'd been unable to use FTL for days. Perhaps they'd made arrangements for repairs or something more. Either way, the fleet's emergence from the asteroid belt left them vulnerable again, and Bordox, Etan, and the other pirates had laid in wait, allowing the asteroids to confuse scanners about their numbers and ship types until it was too late.

He'd heard vague reports via the Nets of another attack by unknown forces. He wondered if it was Xalivar's crew. Who led them now with the dark lord dead? Could it be his father? For just a moment, Bordox felt sadness and a longing to reconcile. Then he growled and shook it off, focusing himself for the attack.

"They'll be emerging in seconds," Etan announced over the radio. "Get ready."

Rufa cackled. "Born ready."

"Give the word, chief," Jurgen agreed.

And then the first ships emerged, and they launched their attack.

"Remember, if we can isolate a supply ship, we'll go in, but the goal is destruction they can feel," Etan reminded them.

"Damage they can feel, eh?" Rufa laughed again. "I wonder how it feels to incinerate."

"Not that far, Rufa," Jurgen warned. "For now, we want them afraid, not dead."

The goal this time was to take advantage of the Vertullians' fear. Inflict damage, slow them down, cause internal division—anything to keep them around longer, allowing more time for raids. Bordox knew the people would be rattled from their previous encounters, but surely they'd called back scout ships, which would mean more fighters, and he had no doubt they'd increased other defenses as well, however they could.

"Keep your eyes open for those extra fighters," he reminded them, eyes flipping back and forth between his fighter's sensor screen and the blast shield. Electronics might rule the age, but Bordox had never forgotten the value of using his human senses just as often.

"The more the merrier," Etan said.

"Ain't a real party without crashers," Rufa said.

Bordox shook his head. Despite their bluster, they all knew the danger those fighters posed and that they would be flown by the most experienced pilots the fleet had, including several Boralian escorts. Caution was the watchword. And the Pirate Lord had emphasized the need to not take needless risks.

"The day for reckoning is another day," he'd said. "Today is for a little reminder that we'll be waiting wherever they go."

The philosophy behind it, Jurgen had later explained, was that if the pirates seemed as interested in damaging the fleet as stealing from it, it made them less predictable and more threatening. Supplies could be replaced easily. People and ships could not. If each attack had unpredictable goals, the Vertullians would be less prepared for counterattacks and less confident as well. It reminded Bordox of Xalivar's tactics—always keeping others on edge. At least these pirates rewarded those who aided in their victory.

The fighters were upon them in moments, pouring from *Reliance* and two Destroyers as soon as the pirates cleared the belt. They raked the pirate craft with fire, engaging, countering in an attempt to lure them away from the fleet.

"Make them come to us," Etan reminded them.

And come they did. Three squadrons swooped in from different directions, letting loose with their cannons, and Bordox knew the pirates were in trouble. Used to the element of surprise, they found themselves not prepared instead and forced to take the defensive just to survive.

Two fighters, in particular, stuck to Bordox's tail like magnets to steel, following his every twist, turn, and jerky evasive maneuver. Sweat stung his eyes as lasers exploded off his wings with flashes of yellow and orange. He smelled smoke in his cockpit—had he been hit? The computer indicated some kind of instrument short, but fortunately his flight controls weren't affected.

"Someone get them off me!" Jurgen cried out, his voice rising in pitch with his panic.

"I'm coming, Jurgen!" Etan replied. "Hang on!"

As he turned, barely dodging another volley from the pursuing fighters, Bordox spotted Jurgen with two fighters on his tail, smoke and flames coming from his ship's engines as Etan swooped in and fired, strafing a VS28 along the side of its fuselage.

As the Vertullian pilot reacted, however, his wingman took aim and fired. Jurgen's ship disintegrated before their eyes.

"Pull out! I say again, pull out!" Etan called out.

The pirates abandoned their plans and fled from the fleet, with VS28s following in pursuit.

Bordox's targeting computer beeped, and he fired torpedoes at a fighter on Etan's tail while another pirate spun his ship and fired at the

VS28 trailing Bordox.

The VS28 chasing Etan shuddered as its right engines exploded and arced sharply down, leaving the fight. Bordox's ship rocked with explosions from behind, and as he climbed and circled back, he saw the VS28s that had been pursuing him turn back, one's left wing in shambles.

"We lost Jurgen," Rufa said, choking on the words.

"They were ready for us," Bordox spat, anger and adrenaline filling him now as he shifted in his seat to keep blood circulating in his lower body.

"Their defenses are at a new level with those new pilots," Etan said. "We'll need a different strategy."

As pirate squadrons radioed in their status, Bordox learned that two Vertullian VS28s had been destroyed and six damaged, with four pirates dead and ten ships damaged. On the other hand, a squadron had done significant damage to three more Vertullian barges. The fleet would have to stop and regroup, and that gave them time to strategize about seeking their revenge.

Bordox was ready. The next opportunity that presented itself, he'd find a way to hurt Davi Rhii and the Vertullians—for Jurgen and the other pilots and for all the humiliation he had suffered for years.

# Chapter Six

Despite its status as a resort planet, Regalis' spaceport was every bit as big and well-equipped as those of Italis and Accra, the two capitals where Tela had spent the most time. Ships of all shapes and sizes rested in various states of loading, unloading, refueling and repair as mech-bots whizzed and whirled around them, the smell of fuel cells, sweat and anti-contaminant sprays filling the air as clanging, rattling, and voices chattering filled Tela's ears.

She found Davi just where she'd expected to: supervising the preparation of several large transports for the transfer of passengers from damaged ships. The transports were large shipping barges, temporarily converted into basic housing—their large holds modified with temporary walls and doors to create cubes in various sizes, including gathering spaces, play areas, dining halls, a chapel and exercise areas. She knew all this from the reports she'd read. It was tempting to go inside and see it for herself, but given the length of the journey ahead, she imagined she'd have plenty of chances for that later.

Her fiancé was presently scrolling through a datapad as Brie, Nila, and several yeomen scurried around him or waited for instructions.

He looked up as she stopped, facing him, and smiled. "Ah, there you are," he said, leaning forward to kiss her cheek.

She mock scowled, shaking her head. "Not on duty, mister!"

They both laughed.

Davi offered her the datapad. "Just in time to jump in. I need you and Ace to go requisition supplies for the fleet. A full accounting is here. Fleet Supply is supposedly on level B of the Trade Complex."

Tela grunted. "Such exciting duties for us, Captain."

Davi shrugged. "It's all that glorious stuff we trained for, right?"

Tela laughed and turned to leave as a commotion broke out nearby—men yelling.

"Where is he?!" a familiar voice demanded.

"Our supporters reported seeing him here," added another voice.

Joram approached with Lords Chad and Klima and several aides and supporters as Davi, Tela, Brie, and Nila turned to confront them.

"What's going on?" Davi demanded, irritation coloring his voice.

Joram frowned and waved his fist. "We have reason to believe a traitor is aboard those ships!"

"I have no idea what you're talking about," Davi said.

"Hmmph. You're on their side, so of course you deny it," Joram said.

Davi stiffened, his jaw clenching as he gave Joram a harsh stare.

Tela jumped in, setting a gentle hand on his arm as she asked, "Who are you talking about?"

"Hachim!" Lord Chad said, almost spitting the name. The former Boralian Councilor had been part of a conspiracy to murder Vertullians and other leadership a year before.

"Hachim? Why would he be here?" Davi asked, shooting Tela a confused look.

Tela shrugged. "It's a resort. He could be on vacation. He's a private citizen now."

Davi locked eyes with Joram again, motioning a hand. "Nila, go find out."

He waited until Nila nodded and hurried off before continuing, "If he's here, it has nothing to do with the Vertullian fleet and these transports."

"What about the rumors that these ships come from Hachim's own fleet?" Joram said icily.

"They come from the High Lord Councilor," Davi insisted. "That's all I know, and they are manned by people personally vetted by him and overseen by our people. They are safe, I promise you." His shoulders had slackened and his face relaxed, showing he'd regained control again.

So Tela relaxed, too, beside him. Her mind flashed back to what Davi had told her about Hachim's fleet being requisitioned by the Boralians to use as transports and wondered how he kept such a straight face. He was a better liar than she'd realized. She hoped she knew him well enough that it would never work on her. Joram and his companions clearly didn't believe him.

"He was spotted in this very bay an hour ago," Joram insisted. "We demand that you find him immediately!"

"We just told you we don't even know for sure he's here," Davi said, standing firm.

"Our lives could be at risk if you're wrong," Lord Chad said.

"Rumors are not reliable," Davi said. "You of all people should know that."

"Are you calling us liars?!" Joram said, almost screaming now.

Around them, both crew and passengers and local maintenance had taken notice and stopped to watch the scene. The last thing they needed were rumors starting a full-on panic.

Tela reached out to gently touch Joram's arm. "You need to calm down, Councilor," Tela said.

He shook her hand away like she was a leper, his fierce stare leaving her uncertain whether he might attack her at any moment. "Don't patronize me, Tela! I have a responsibility to our citizens."

"We all do," Davi said, stepping between Joram and Tela protectively. "And that includes keeping unnecessary personnel out of this bay while we load the transports. Your presence here is disrupting our duties, so you need to leave. Now!"

"You can't just order us about like we have no status," Lord Klima objected.

Davi drew his blaster, his body stiff, his glare a warning. Reluctantly, Tela and Brie followed, along with several other pilots, backing up their leader.

"I can and I will!" Davi yelled back. "It's my job. Or I can arrest you and have you detained in cells aboard *Reliance*, if you prefer."

The three Councilors stared angrily at Davi in silence as the pilots moved into a defensive semi-circle facing them. Her fiancé could be risking a lot drawing weapons on them, but it was the type of tactic she'd seen him use before with bullies, and if anyone deserved it, Joram certainly did.

After a few moments of staring down the nose of several blasters, Joram's face started to redden. "We are just trying to protect the fleet," he muttered, shifting his stance and relaxing a bit as he took a deep breath.

"So are we, Councilor," Davi said, calmer but firmly.

Joram sighed and gave a slight nod, then turned to his supporters. "I'm sure Captain Rhii and his staff will do full inspections to ensure the safety of the transports and keep any traitors or other riffraff from interfering." Turning back to Davi, he added, "We will report this to the Council and Generals Matheu and Uzah."

Davi smiled. "I'm sure you will." Davi holstered his blaster and the other pilots followed suit. He nodded to Brie. "Organize teams and take a look for Hachim. Don't mention his name. The last thing we need are false rumors causing mass panic. Just see if you can find anything."

Chad and Klima relaxed, then, and some of their aides and supporters began following suite.

Brie grunted. "Yes, sir." And hurried away.

"Please keep your concerns to yourselves for now," Davi said, turning back to the Councilors. "We will keep you informed. Further concerns can be brought to our attention via Colonel Cardno on *Reliance*'s bridge. As you can imagine, we have a lot of work to do."

Joram sighed and nodded. "Thank you, Captain." And with that, he and his supporters turned and marched back across the bay the way they'd come.

"That was fun," Tela said. "I can't believe you drew your blaster."

"So did you," Davi said.

"You always get me in trouble," she teased.

Davi's face took on a look of mock irritation. "What are you still doing here? I believe I gave you orders, Lieutenant."

She snapped to attention, firing off a snappy salute. "Yes, Captain, my love." Then spun, laughing, and headed off to find Ace.

"You had no right to offer assistance without the approval of the Council!" Lord Kanaan shouted, standing at the Council table and frowning as he looked around the Chamber for support.

"Kindly keep your demeanor civil, Lord Kanaan," Simeon said from his seat beside Tarkanius on the dais.

They looked down on a slanted floor where rows of tables occupied by the Council members faced them. Modeled after the Chambers of the U.S. Senate on Old Earth, the large Chamber was a centerpiece of the Council Building, across the government complex from the Palace on Legallis.

"They abandoned us to our fates," Kanaan said, his blue skin paler, almost pink, with emotion. "Our planets are being attacked and our people struggling. Our job is take care of ourselves! They wanted independence, so let them have it."

Several Councilors shouted in support of the idea.

Tarkanius took a deep breath, choosing each word with care. "My responsibility to lead our people includes the power to make decisions about military matters without consulting with the Council. I cannot declare war without your approval, but I can send forces where I believe they are needed to best defend this system. And I believe assisting the Vertullians is in our best interests."

"Would they rush to our aid if we'd asked?" Lord Quatol said then, jumping up in support of the Idolian ambassador.

"Gentlemen, please," Lord Kray said from a table two rows ahead, turning back to meet their stares, "sit down and let's discuss this honorably as we've always done."

"Yes, as in always allowing High Lord Councilors to override this Council," Kanaan snapped, but he and Quatol took their seats, glaring at her.

"The last High Lord Councilor who tried to override us was removed," Simeon corrected, his voice tense. Tarkanius could see his friend lean forward in his chair, palms planted on the dais, struggling to control his anger. "Lord Tarkanius knows his place and the role of the Council well. And you shall refer to him properly from now on."

"Oh yes, my Lord," Kanaan muttered, crinkling his face with disgust.

"We do have need to focus on our own people at this moment," Lord Qai said, in measured, calmer tones. "We have many crises to resolve without the added burden of once again protecting a group that has insisted upon leaving us."

"The very choice which has resulted in many of the crises of which you speak," Lord Adoo added.

Several others grunted in agreement around them.

"We have made great strides recently with the shift of agricultural workers from plants to the plantations," Lord Kray said.

"Thanks to Obed's diligence," Lord Buj agreed.

"His methods are disturbing," Lord Adoo said, scrunching his face with displeasure.

"He has been warned, and since then he's complied with our restrictions," Lord Simeon said.

"Nonetheless, we've seen significant progress in the past few weeks under his guidance," Lord Brahma said, smiling at the others. His was a voice of calm Tarkanius had always been grateful for.

"And we will continue to see it, but there are other problems," Lord Amie said, shrugging. "We must not consider progress on one issue an excuse to ignore the rest."

Tarkanius nodded. Amie had always been a helpful support but he was always focused on the practical and he was right. "The aid I have sent to the Vertullian Fleet is not a distraction. A few key officers will cooperate to exchange and analyze data and determine if the forces attacking them are the same as the ones who attacked Idolis and the other planets. We need more information to counter these attacks."

"What of the ships it's rumored you sent them?" Lord Quatol asked, calmer now.

Tarkanius smiled. "I made arrangements with an old friend who is forever in our debt. His company provided the ships on loan to the Vertullians. There was no expense or sacrifice from Alliance coffers."

"Old friend?" Kanaan asked as he and Quatol exchanged puzzled looks.

"A former member of this Council, in fact," Tarkanius said with a nod.

Lords Qai, Adoo, and Buj reacted with realization then Buj and a few others laughed. Adoo and Qai shook their heads.

"Will they even trust him?" Adoo wondered.

"Hachim is here running his enterprise," Tarkanius answered. "And I made sure the crews selected were reliable people."

"What of the health concerns, the agricultural ships, inflation?" Adoo ticked off the list on his hand.

Simeon cleared his throat and nodded, his eyes meeting Adoo's. "Repairs to the agricultural fleet have resulted in increased shipments and the markets are responding. Inflation has decreased."

"Far too slowly," Lord Amie said.

"Yes, but we see that as a result of greedy merchants taking advantage of public fear and anxiety, not from the previous supply problems," Lord Kray said.

"Government personnel have been dispatched to address the issue," Simeon added.

"Address greed?" Lord Buj chuckled. "Pray tell, how will they do that?"

Tarkanius and Simeon exchanged a look. The plan had been Simeon's idea and had an element of risk. If it backfired, they could have a whole new set of issues, but the taxes they'd decided upon were designed to fluctuate with the market, and it had seemed the best alternative to affect the price wars and regain control.

"Taxes will be based on market values," Simeon explained. "Anyone selling items at more than twenty percent markup will pay higher penalties."

Buj scoffed, clearing his throat as he stooped in his chair. "The merchants will be up in arms! Forty percent is fairly standard in many cases."

Tarkanius smiled. "Our agents have discretion to pardon certain legitimate merchants from the increases, and certain goods and services are exempt."

Simeon nodded. "Much depends on supply and demand. And it will need to be monitored carefully, of course. We do not want to cripple anyone."

Kray turned to look at Buj. She'd learned of the plan that morning and had been quite impressed with their attention to detail. "It's meant to target specifically those who attempt to manipulate prices and keep them high."

"Which is why we have involved a larger number of agents than normal," Simeon added.

"So this plan distracts government agents from their regular duties?" Lord Adoo asked.

"It required some shifting, yes," Tarkanius agreed. "But many of these people are also monitoring the health issues and have to be on site regularly to do so, it made sense to add to their duties rather than reassign others to assist us in matters here."

"It's temporary," Simon said. "And we hope it will sting enough to resolve the problem in short order."

"You appear to have thought this through quite well," Lord Amie said, chuckling.

The look he gave Tarkanius assured him the younger Lord would make no further objections on the matter. In fact, he looked impressed.

Many groups broke into chatter around him as they discussed the plan and other concerns amongst themselves.

"What plans does General Grif have to counter these attacks on our planets?" Lord Quatol asked then.

The chattering faded off as the Council members tuned in again to hear the answer.

"We are assembling forces and prepping our ships," Tarkanius said. "And patrols have been increased in volume and frequency around all planets, except Plutonis, Kronis, and the inner four."

Glendaris, Endolis, Jonis, and Andaris—closest to the system's larger sun, Boralis—were the least habitable and only Glendaris had a significant settlement, consisting mainly of a trading post and a few mining facilities with units to house workers. None of them were suitable for humans, although a few brave souls ventured to Glendaris on business from time to time, usually departing a few hours after arriving. Even then, most of the complex there was buried underground, a necessity for residents to survive the intense daytime heat. At night, the temperatures only dropped two dozen degrees at most, creating a constant summer time that was only aggravated during the two periods when Endolis' orbit brought it near the smaller sun Charlis as well. Tarkanius had never been there but every story he'd heard was such that he had no idea why anyone would want to go, not to mention how anyone tolerated it for more than a day.

"Dear God, the Qiwi are at risk!" Lord Buj joked, eyebrows raised in alarm, referring to the prized antelope-like creatures the ice planet was known for. Their meat was a popular mainstay of diets throughout the system.

"Don't worry, they still have their antlers," Amie fired back. Buj noticeably relaxed, winking at Amie.

Tarkanius joined in as several present laughed. He felt thankful for the lightening mood. "The damage of the last three attacks was significantly less than the attack on Idolis."

"They sent less concentrated forces and spent less time," Lord Quatol replied.

"Yes, but patrols did engage them," Simeon said.

"Their attack against the Vertullians was quite a bit more focused, I hear," Kanaan said.

"Which is why we are working together to identify these forces and launch a counter offensive that's in the best interests of all of us," Tarkanius said.

Simeon looked around the room, assessing, and Tarkanius did the same. "If that's all the questions we have, perhaps we can finish the rest of our business so some of us can actually focus as promised on the crises at hand," Simeon suggested.

Mumbled agreement and nods came from around the room and Tarkanius relaxed at last. The confrontation was over for now.

Tela and her second, Ace Biggs, left the spaceport, per Davi's orders, to supervise roundup and delivery of supplies for the fleet. Neither had ever been to Regalis before, the most famous resort in the system, and seeing it for the first time, it did not disappoint. With sparkle and shine on everything from floor to ceiling, every fixture, handle, pattern, etc., smacked of luxury and wealth. Despite the abundance of civilians in every combination of dress from casual to formal, the place itself shimmered with class in every way. It might as well have been paved in gold. Even the cleansing rooms where they'd stopped to freshen up looked like something right out of the Palace on Legallis, at least as Tela imagined it. She'd never actually been there, and Davi wasn't with her to confirm.

"That was like using the High Lord Councilor's private cleansing room," Ace commented, as he met her in the corridor. "This place is amazing!"

Tela laughed. "I was thinking the same thing."

"From fighting pirates to a shishi resort in the same day?" Ace joked, wobbling his legs with each step like a clown. "What a life we have!"

"Too bad we can't hang out long enough to enjoy it, right?"

He grunted, back to his normal walk. "Hope the civilians don't wander off and see this. After all the complaining we've heard about their accommodations, this would just rile them up again."

"No doubt," Tela agreed as they turned a corner and headed toward the Trade Complex to the north of the starport. Because it was the furthest planet from the sun, the entire planet was either domed or connected from building to building with enclosed walkways and corridors. It made them run together almost like one from the inside, but from the outside, each building was very distinctive.

Ace's eyes sparkled, his voice filled with amusement. "Bet those pirates had their tails between their legs all the way home. Wish we hadn't had to let them go."

"We have a long journey ahead," Tela replied, fighting the urge to roll her eyes. Ace was fortunate to have the talent to back up his talk, but that didn't make her less tired of hearing it. "We need our fighters in top condition. They took out your engine. Better to regroup and fight another day, per the General's orders."

Ace sighed. "Oh, I get that it makes sense from that perspective. It's just a whole lot less fun."

"Trust me, the fun doesn't last long, when you get used to fighting," she said. "In the end, if your enemy runs, you count it a victory, and thank God you're alive to face them again."

Ace raised his hands in surrender. "Okay, okay, boss. Enjoying the win, okay?"

Tela chuckled. "Just don't let that enjoyment make you careless."

"Done."

They reached a door marked "Fleet Supply," and Tela pushed a button, waiting as it whooshed, servos whining, and slid up into the ceiling. Then she led the way inside.

"What are we doin' here, Bordox?" Rufa whined as they stalked the shadows in the Trade Complex on Regalis. "I thought we came down here to have some fun?" He raised his eyebrows suggestively.

"We're about to. Just hang on," Bordox said. He'd talked the other pirate into accompanying him to gather intel on the Vertullian fleet. With pilots from Alpha Base on Plutonis running regular patrols, the pirates had to be careful about when and where they tried another attack. Etan and the Pirate Lord wanted intel first, and Bordox promised he could get it for them, so they'd sent him and Rufa ahead to scout.

It had been Bordox's idea to actually land at the resort. He'd been there once as a child with his family, many years before, but he knew it mostly by reputation. People of all races and backgrounds showed up out here. He'd made sure he and Rufa dressed like merchants before they left the pirate's base. As long as Rufa let Bordox do most of the talking, they'd blend in just fine. But Rufa had a problem not running his mouth. Bordox began wondering if he'd have been better off coming alone.

"What do you want with those two anyway?"

"They're Vertullian pilots," Bordox said. "Part of the group that killed Jurgen. Didn't you hear the guy bragging about sending us home with our tails between our legs?"

Rufa brightened, hand going to his blaster. "Well, yeah, I remember that. Let's get in there and take 'em out then."

Bordox shook his head. "Wait! We're going to take out the guy. The girl has other uses, trust me."

Rufa frowned. "We don't do kidnapping, Bordox. Does Etan know 'bout this?"

Bordox shushed him. "Trust me. I know what I'm doing."

The plan to go after Xander Rhii's fiancée, Tela, whom Bordox had first encountered during a spy mission to Vertullis several months past, had come about on the fly. He just happened to spot her and another pilot heading off alone from the starport and followed them. Having her for leverage would present all kinds of advantages, and now it provided the perfect opportunity to inflict the kind of pain on his old rival that he'd suffered at the imbecile's hands.

Tela and her companion had been inside the "Fleet Supply" office for over half an hour already, so Bordox shared Rufa's anxiousness. But he might never get another such opportunity, and he intended to take full advantage of it.

Then the two emerged, Tela examining something on her datapad. They were casual and relaxed, clearly not expecting any trouble.

"So we don't have to wait for them, right?" the male pilot asked, clearly distracted by other ideas.

"Not necessarily," Tela replied. "They'll send us a notification when they've prepared the load so we can sign off. What did you have in mind?"

The male pilot chuckled. "I hear they've got great places to drink and dance here."

"We're on duty, Ace," Tela said, lips pursed. She didn't like the guy much.

Bordox and Rufa slunk back into the shadows, unnoticed, and watched them pass.

"Besides, I thought you had a thing for that Yeoman from Rec."

Ace shrugged. "Doesn't mean I can't enjoy flirting with new faces from time to time."

Tela scowled with clear disapproval.

"If you flirt with me, I might have to shoot you," Bordox said as he stepped out, blaster leveled at the pair and strode toward them.

They spun around, hands going automatically for their own weapons, but Rufa and Bordox closed the distance fast.

"Try it and we will shoot," Bordox warned.

Ace looked like he was still flirting with the idea.

Bordox shook his head. "Trust me. You're not that fast."

The two pilots' hands relaxed then as Rufa closed in behind them.

"What do you want?" Tela asked.

"You'll find out in time," Bordox said.

"Can we shoot 'em now?" Rufa asked, looking eager.

Ace shot him a threatening look.

"Now come on, let's be civilized about this," Bordox joked. "We wouldn't want to leave these folks with any bad feelings about the finest resort in the Alliance."

Bordox watched as Rufa reluctantly changed his blaster's setting to stun. The pirate moved in closer, preparing to fire, when Ace spun around and the two struggled for the blaster.

"Hey! You better watch it!" Rufa shouted.

Tela rushed Bordox.

Bordox smiled. "Big mistake." He fired straight into Ace's back, then turned his weapon back on Tela as Ace stiffened, groaned, and slid to the floor. "Don't ruin your fiancé's day, Tela."

"How do you know who I am?" she demanded.

"Let's just say Xander Rhii and I have a long history," he replied and whirled, as she stopped, slamming his blaster—handle first—into the back of her head. He reached out and caught her unconscious form before she crashed to the floor.

Obed and the two Council members arrived at the field by Floater just in time to see the supervisor swinging his fist at two workers as others watched nearby.

"Damn lies!" the supervisor shouted.

"So you say," the larger of the two workers replied as he ducked another blow.

"So I know!" the supervisor answered and swung again.

Obed considered drawing his blaster as he raced toward them from the parked Floater, Lords Buj and Amie close on his heels. But he changed his mind. That move had led to his current probation. Best to try and resolve this first without it. The smell of grain and pollen filled Obed's nose as birds and insects chirped all around and harvesters' engines hummed in the distance from the surrounding fields.

"What is the meaning of this?!" he demanded.

The three men turned angrily, as if prepared to confront some new threat but stopped as they saw it was their boss.

The supervisor stuttered. "These two won't obey orders."

"He's cheating us," the smaller of the workers complained.

"We caught him red handed," the larger worker added.

All three were humans, the workers dark-skinned and the supervisor white. All three had the muscles of men who'd spent many years at hard labor, but the two workers had the dust and grime in their hair and skin to prove who'd worked the hardest.

"Cheated you how?" Lord Buj asked.

Obed bristled again as Lord Buj and Amie watched over his shoulder. They'd been with him all day, alternating with other representatives of the Council, ever since the incident with his blaster, watching him like some cadet on probation. Luckily, his years in politics had left him ideally suited for such circumstances, as he was well used to hiding his emotions—anger, disgust, and more—at the intrusion. He'd had to restrain his usual impulses and put on a good front, but so far, it seemed to be working, and the effort had bought him more and more periods of their absence in which to put his own plans and schemes into place.

"They've shorted every load today," the supervisor insisted.

"He modified the scales," the bigger worked responded, motioning to a nearby terminal beside a metal measuring platform which held an open bag of grain. Sealed bags of grain were stacked beside it.

Obed strolled over to the terminal and examined the settings.

The supervisor stuttered. "I did no such thing. If it's off, the equipment is faulty."

Obed noted the scale zeroed out at negative five. "It's off," he said, adjusting the measurements. "Weigh it all again. Now."

The supervisor cursed. "I weighed it twice already!"

"Every load they brought today," Obed insisted.

The two workers grunted, eyes alight with smug satisfaction.

The supervisor threw up his hand with a heavy sigh. "I've had loads from twenty different teams. How am I supposed to tell them apart?"

"Guess," Obed said.

The supervisor pounded a fist on the terminal. "They're no good! I know it."

"Do it or you'll be replaced tomorrow," Obed said. With that he turned and led the two Lords back to the Floater, planning to return to the office.

"Aren't you going to stay and watch him?" Lord Amie asked.

Obed shook his head. "He knows what to expect if he tries it again."

"Fear of being shot?" Buj commented.

Obed shrugged. "My methods work. No matter how distasteful you find them."

Amie grunted, his eyes wary. "We can say you've done nothing to further alarm us since the incident, but we still prefer a gentler approach."

"I have respected the Council's wishes, and I'll continue to," Obed said, and he started up the Floater and drove the Councilors back toward the office and their waiting shuttle.

"We'll report as much when we return," Lord Amie agreed.

Obed smiled, turned away so they couldn't see his face. It was working.

Five minutes later, he brought the Floater to a stop beside their shuttle.

"Have a safe journey," he said as they all disembarked.

The two Councilors shook his hand firmly, each in turn, then hurried toward their shuttle.

Buj turned back in the doorway. "Go back and double-check on him, please. To be sure. We must be seen as treating our workers fairly."

Obed forced a smile. "Of course." Then watched as the two Lords boarded the shuttle and its engines hummed to life. In two minutes, they were gone, as the shuttle soared overhead onto one of the skyways overhead.

As had been his intention all along, Obed immediately went back to the Floater and headed for the field again. He found the supervisor and two workers there arguing again as the grain was remeasured.

"You two," he motioned to the workers as he hurried toward them, "get back to work. I'll see that you're paid fairly."

They eyed him suspiciously.

"But we don't trust him," the shorter one said.

"You've established that," Obed said, his tone filled with menace. "Go!"

The two workers turned without further argument and left, muttering to themselves.

When they were well out of range, Obed turned to face the supervisor. "Don't ever argue with me in front of the Council, Nan!"

"I did what you told me," the supervisor said, frustration wrinkling his face. "I don't know how they caught on. The others haven't."

"They won't be here tomorrow to argue," Obed said. "I'll see to it. You just do what I say and you'll be taken care of."

The supervisor nodded. "We almost have a load ready."

Obed grinned. Good. The extra profits he was earning from selling grain on the side would fund everything he planned. And no one would be the wiser. As long as nosy workers kept their minds on their jobs and didn't get suspicious. The two today would have to be eliminated. He'd do it himself as soon as he was done with the supervisor.

"Leave room for two packages," he said, knowing the supervisor knew he meant bodies. They'd done it before.

"If they catch us—"

"They won't catch us as long as you stay the course, Nan," Obed said coldly. "You do intend to follow the plan, don't you?" The menace in his voice caused the supervisor to shudder.

He stumbled for words. "Y-y-y-yes, my Lord. Of course. I was only thinking . . ." His voice trailed off as he wilted under Obed's stare.

Obed just whirled and marched back for the Floater. He had business to attend to in the fields. The supervisor had witnessed the earlier incident with his blaster and knew of Obed's reputation when he'd headed the Lord's Special Police, enforcers for the High Lord Councilors in prior days. Fear would keep him in line, and that's all that mattered. Once Obed got what he wanted, the man would be as disposable as everyone else who got in his way.

Starting up the Floater, he raced out into the fields.

The Trade Complex on Regalis was like a multi-level warehouse, the top level made up of a few cavernous rooms storing large ship parts, fuel tanks and more, with the lower levels featuring offices, workshops, and other support rooms. After Tela and Ace failed to report and let several comm calls go unanswered, Farien decided to drop by Fleet Supply himself and check on them.

The Fleet Supply office was rather crowded, especially considering its size. It mainly consisted of a long counter behind which four employees worked at terminals serving customers both in person and remotely, issuing orders by comm to techs and other workers who fulfilled the various demands, preparing loads, loading ships, etc.

Given that Regalis was a small, resort spaceport, it rarely dealt with multiple fleets at one time, especially any the size of the Vertullian fleet, but it seemed plenty of other commercial fleets had sent representatives or ships there at the same time. Currently, there were long lines at every station, but Ace and Tela were not among those waiting, so Farien moved up an aisle between two rows, ignoring the angry stares of the other customers and headed straight for the counter.

"Excuse me, we're in line!" snarled an angry Tertullian captain who looked ready to jump the human for his insolence.

"Sir, please wait your turn," the nearest Fleet Supply clerk said, not even glancing up from the counter to see who'd caused the disturbance.

"I need to know if you've seen two Vertullian pilots," Farien said, ignoring the objections. "They should have been here and gone two hours ago."

The clerk, also human but scruffy and unshaven with scraggly hair, despite his relatively clean official issue jumpsuit, stopped typing and looked up from his terminal to meet Farien's gaze. "We have all kinds of people in here daily. How am I supposed to remember …"

Farien pulled up images of the two pilots on his datapad and shoved it in front of the clerk. "These two."

The clerk took a quick glance and shook his head, turning back to the terminal. "No recollection."

Farien shoved his way past the burly Xanthian pilot currently talking with the human clerk and moved to the next clerk, shoving the datapad with Tela and Ace's pictures on it at the next clerk, then the next, and the next. Three hadn't seen them, but the third hesitated.

"They may have been here a while back," the clerk said. "We've had lots of customers. But they left and I don't know where they went."

Farien cursed to himself. The clerks were clearly not interested in his problem and could be of little help. What would he do now? Realizing the thick walls of the Trade Complex might interfere with comm signals, he stepped outside and opened his comm.

"Lieutenants Tabansi and Biggs, report," he said and waited for a response.

His call was met with silence, but he began looking around the halls of the Trade Complex as he waited, calling up the list of supplies Davi had given Tela on his datapad as he did. If he had to, he'd check every single place they might have gone. He might have expected Ace to get distracted by some fun adventure instead of finishing his duty, but Tela was too responsible. It wasn't like her at all to disappear, especially not when the entire fleet and Davi were counting on her.

He keyed the comm again. "Lieutenants Tabansi and Biggs, report. Tela, are you there? Come in."

Again, no answer, and there was no sign of either of them in the corridors on the current level.

"We'll just have to use a process of elimination," he muttered to himself as he decided it would be best to start on the top level and work his way down, since the top level held most of the supply storage and fewer rooms. It was more likely they'd have gone there than anywhere else, and starting with the least rooms would be more efficient.

He made his way for the lift and pushed a button to call it. The double doors whooshed open in front of him immediately and he stepped on, pushing a button for the upper level. A few seconds later, the doors opened again to deposit him in a corridor outside the cavernous storage rooms and he began his search.

The first two storage rooms took half an hour each to search but there was no sign of the two missing pilots. Then, as he stepped outside into the corridor to move on to the next two storage rooms, he heard shouting coming from somewhere nearby. He glanced around, trying to figure out what direction it was coming from. Didn't he recognize those voices?

Taking off at a run, he headed the way he'd come to reach the complex and rounded a bend, hearing the shouting grow louder up ahead.

"Who shot him?" a familiar voice demanded.

"Was there a girl with him?" another familiar voice added.

The reply was soft and shaky, as if whomever they were confronting was intimidated.

Then it clicked, the voices were Virun and Jorek!

Farien ran faster now, turning another bend in the winding outer corridors that connected the Trade Complex with the rest of the starport. His body tensed as he ran, his footfalls echoing through the corridor behind him. Bright light from large glowpads overhead bounced off white painted metal walls, creating the effect of a bright sunny day despite the dread filling his mind and heart as his thoughts raced with images of what harm might have befallen his friends.

The voices became clearer now.

"We just found them ourselves," a man said. "We're with security here. Someone reported blaster shots and we came to investigate."

Another man, also sounding intimidated replied, "We found him like this."

Farien rounded a corner, blaster drawn, and found Virun and Jorek aiming their blasters at two local security men, Ace Biggs' fallen body lying in a heap on the floor between them. The minute he saw the security men's faces, Farien knew they were as puzzled as the Vertullians.

"Ace!" he called automatically and they all turned to watch him approach.

Farien knelt beside the fallen pilot, feeling for a pulse.

"He's alive, but wounded," Jorek said.

"Shot in the back," Virun said.

Farien holstered his blaster and motioned to the four men. "Pick him up," he commanded. "We've got to get him back to Sickbay." His eyes met that of one of the security men. "You saw no companion? A woman?" He held up Tela's image on his datapad.

The security man shook his head. "As we told your friends, we came to investigate a report. He was already fallen when we arrived. No sign of anyone else."

Farien had known the answer before he asked but he cursed anyway. "Let's get him back to *Reliance* and warn Davi. Then we'll split up and search."

As Virun, Jorek and the two security men carried the unconscious Ace between them, Farien followed them through the winding corridors toward the landing bay where Davi was supervising preparation of the transports. He thought about calling ahead on the comm, but this was news he wanted to deliver in person.

Regalis was a resort. Who could possibly want to attack and harm Vertullian pilots? Some angry Boralian? Pirates? Was it deliberate or just random? His mind raced for answers as his heart pounded in his chest. If someone hurt Tela, Davi wouldn't be the only one they'd answer, too. Farien had come to love her like a sister. He cursed again. *She'd better be all right.*

# Chapter Seven

"What do you mean they shot him?"

Davi whirled to face Farien as Jorek and Virun stumbled into the landing bay with two local security men, carrying Ace's unconscious body on a stretcher. Davi saw tears in the back of his shirt then scorch marks and a laser burn as they laid him gently face down on the floor of the bay.

"These guys found him in the Trade Complex just outside Fleet Supply," Farien explained as he knelt to examine Ace's wounds and scanned him with a medpad.

"Thirty minutes ago," Jorek added as Virun hollered for medics.

"Where's Tela?" Davi asked, glancing around as he suddenly remembered who had been with Ace. Adrenaline surge through him as his body tensed at the possibilities racing through his mind.

Virun shook his head. "We didn't find her."

Two medtechs appeared and raced toward Ace's body as Farien and Virun stood and jumped clear. The medtechs went to work, asking Virun and Jorek questions as they performed an exam on the fallen pilot.

Davi turned to the security men. "You called this in?"

The taller guard nodded as his shorter companion shifted nervously.

"When we discovered they hadn't shown up at Fleet Supply, we went looking and found these men examining Ace's body," Jorek explained.

Davi cursed, shoulders tightening, as he spun and motioned to every soldier he could see, "Spread out and search everywhere. I want everyone on this!"

"What about the transports?" Brie asked from nearby, her face filled with concern.

"They're loaded. I'll ask Uzah to send some Yeomen to continue coordinating the housing and head counts, but go find Tela."

They all grunted and mumbled in agreement, but despite their sympathetic looks, Davi felt little comfort. He had sudden chills, his stomach rolling, and he steadied himself to hide it from all the eyes staring at him.

"We need to get him to Sickbay stat!" One of the medics announced as his partner took up position at the opposite end of the stretcher.

"I'll get Os and Ria," Brie said, dashing off toward the three transports looming over them like beached whales. Technicians and mech-bots circled and crawled over their fuselages like scavengers on a carcass.

Farien put a hand on Davi's arm. "I'm sure she'll be okay."

Davi silenced him, swallowing deeply even as a dizziness came over him. He couldn't recall the last time he'd been this scared. Changing to the command channel, he keyed his comm. "Code Seven-six, we have a pilot missing. Initiating a search. I'll need personnel down here to help finish the coordination and counting."

"What's going on?" Uzah replied, after a few moments.

"Ace has been shot and Tela's unaccounted for." It was terse and direct, but it was all Davi could do to keep from bolting for the door to search himself. He had to stay here until Uzah sent replacements and all was under control.

"Want me to stay with you?" Farien offered as the medtechs moved away behind him carrying Ace on the stretcher.

Davi shook his head and motioned brusquely. "What are you all still doing here? Go find her!"

"Yes, sir," they said in unison as Virun and Jorek dashed back out the door with the two security men and Farien hurried off to find Nila.

Colonel Cardno appeared from behind the first transport, marching toward him. "Seven-six?" he called.

Davi sighed, knowing he'd have to explain again. He couldn't believe he was standing here talking when Tela was God knows where in God knows what danger.

Then Jorek and Brie appeared with Os, Ria, Pree, Dami, and several other pilots.

"We'll find her, boss!" Jorek called.

Seeing the couples together salted the wound and Davi cringed, turning away quickly as they raced off.

"Wait!" Cardno called. "Who's seeing to the count and—"

"The General's sending replacements," Davi replied, not waiting for him to finish. "Tela's missing and Ace has been shot."

The Colonel just stared at him, fumbling for words as Farien appeared and raced toward him.

"They're splitting up," his old friend said. "We'll find her."

Davi raised a hand to shush him and keyed the comm again. "Where are those personnel, General?" his voice cracked with stress, and he regretted it immediately. Uzah had always given him a lot of leeway but he was still a senior officer.

The comm cracked as a harsh voice responded. "Watch your tone when addressing senior officers, Captain!" Matheu scolded as Davi grimaced. "The General is coming himself with the replacements. ETA five minutes."

"Thank you, sir," Davi replied, knowing better than to say any more. "Perhaps there's footage from security cameras?"

"We'll handle it. Just go," Cardno said, motioning. "But we want regular updates."

Davi nodded, his eyes offering the best thanks he could as he choked up.

Cardno's eyes sparkled with sympathy as Farien put a hand on Davi's shoulder again.

Davi took a breath then whirled and hurried off after the others with Farien right beside him.

He probably should have let Cardno deal with it but the Colonel already had his hands full and Uzah figured he and Aron could handle this situation. The Yeoman who'd called it in claimed someone confiscated a large suite aboard one of the transports and refused to surrender it to those assigned on the list.

"Some bigshot Boralian," the Yeoman had said, which raised all kinds of red flags since no Vertullian would call themselves Boralian.

They arrived via lift in the lead transport's crew quarters just off the top deck behind the cockpit and flight control areas via lift and followed the raised voices to the corridor outside the suite.

"You have no right to confiscate anything or move me, Yeoman!" a booming male voice insisted.

"Sir, we have assigned all of the available space as fairly as we can," the Yeoman explained. "We can't just have people choosing their favorites. There's just too many factors to consider."

"Not when the person owns the ship," the man insisted.

Uzah could hear the Yeoman's eyes roll without even seeing her face as they approached from behind her. "Sir, none of us own this ship. It's on loan. Perhaps you'd like to come with me to Sickbay for an evaluation." Her voice grew more patronizing with every word.

"I am not crazy!" the man shouted. He was dressed like a businessman in dark slacks and an expensive pullover, his hair neatly groomed, beard trimmed.

Then Uzah recognized him: Hachim, disgraced former member of the Boralian Council of Lords. He'd been caught conspiring against the Vertullians and only escaped punishment by turning on his compatriots and testifying. He also owned the largest shipping fleet in the Alliance, which was why Tarkanius had asked him to loan transports to the fleet, but Hachim wasn't supposed to come along personally.

When Davi had reported Joram, Klima, and Chad's claims, Uzah had been as skeptical as the Captain. But it turned out they were right. And Hachim's presence here could stir up all kinds of resentments.

"We'll take it from here, Yeoman," Uzah said as he stepped up beside her. "Why don't you continue with your duties."

"Are you sure, General? I was about to call security," the Yeoman hesitated, her eyes questioning despite her obvious recognition as she saw who'd spoken.

Uzah smiled. "If I need them, I can call. Thanks."

The Yeoman stiffened, saluted, and marched off, shooting Hachim a cold glare over her shoulder.

"Aron! Old friend! So good to see you!" Hachim grinned warmly and extended his hand.

Aron shook it and smiled back, his eyes narrowing even as his face remained steady, unemotional. "What are you doing here, Hachim?"

Hachim scoffed. "Is that any way to greet a former colleague?"

"A colleague who tried to have him assassinated and conspired to re-enslave his people?" Uzah accused with a cold stare, neither impressed nor amused by the politician's attempts at charm.

Hachim blustered as the grin disappeared. "General, the attack on Aron was not part of …" His voice trailed off as he considered his next words. "You've clearly confused the facts, General."

Aron shot Uzah a look and continued: "Regardless, Hachim, if our people find out you're here, it will cause great problems for us. We already had several on our Council demanding a search when the mere rumor of it arose."

Hachim raised his palms, questioning. "Did you really expect me to just allow you to take valuable property off to gods know where for free without my wanting to keep tabs on it?"

"Your crewmen were hand chosen by the High Lord Councilor," Uzah replied. "Your ships will be returned."

Hachim nodded. "There can be no doubt if I'm there to see to it."

Aron bristled, taking a deep breath. Uzah could tell even his usual calmness was changing fast into irritation with their unexpected guest. He hoped the Councilor had a good idea what to do with him because anything to incite more headaches, especially with Joram, was the last thing they needed.

"Hachim," Aron said, "I bear you no ill will. But we bear serious responsibility for the safety of our fleet and people and your presence could endanger that."

Uzah nodded with fervor. "Absolutely. Allowing you to stay could put your own life at risk."

"Then that's my responsibility, isn't it? Besides, someone has to open trade wherever you're going, and no one is more expert at that than me," Hachim replied.

"We could be gone for a long time, Hachim," Aron said.

"And I've made the arrangements for people to manage my company and affairs if that's the case," Hachim said, still calm and undisturbed by their obvious doubts. "You both speak as if you have a choice," he continued, meeting their eyes each in turn. "If you want my ships, I come with them. If not, unload immediately, and we'll be on our way."

Aron and Uzah exchanged a look of frustrated dismay. Uzah had no idea what to do and clearly Aron felt the same. Hachim was serious. His eyes and tone made it clear, but he was putting them in a terrible position. So many ramifications could come from his presence, yet he didn't seem to care. While they, in turn, couldn't afford to refuse his offer and lose the transports.

"We have to consider this carefully," Aron said. "Please stay in your quarters and try not to make a spectacle for now. If you need something, the crew will be instructed to deliver until we make a decision. As an 'old friend,' please do me this favor."

Hachim's eyes met Aron's and then Uzah's in turn and he nodded in acceptance. "But don't take too long please. I don't want to have to come find you."

Aron raised a hand signaling Hachim to wait. "I promise. It will be a top priority."

Hachim smiled, "Good to see you again, Aron."

Aron merely nodded, waiting until Hachim disappeared back into the suite and sealed the door. "We'd better notify personnel. If Joram hears of it, he'll be furious."

Uzah sighed. "They'll be told it's Top Secret and not to be discussed with anyone." But Aron's look told him they both knew a secret like this could only be contained for so long. Trouble would come eventually. They had to be prepared.

With that, they both turned and hurried back for the lifts. A tense silence hung like a cloud around them. With a little time and pressure, Hachim might change his mind, but Uzah wasn't hopeful. The man had never shown much common sense.

"This is getting us nowhere," Davi groaned, turning and wringing his hands as his face flushed. He spun back to the departure control supervisor again. "Look, we just need to know about any ships that left here in that time frame. My fiancée is missing. Please."

"We don't just hand out that information to anyone who asks," the supervisor said again. "I understand you're upset—"

"I'm a Boralian officer and he used to be," Farien said, furrowing his brow and feeling his own irritation growing to match Davi's. "In fact, he was the damn Prince of the entire Alliance!"

"Used to be," the supervisor said, meeting Farien's gaze. "So he has no authority to help me when I get questioned about violating protocols, laws—"

Farien's hand flew across the desk so fast, he didn't realize what he'd done until he'd pulled the man back toward him and their faces were inches apart. "Who's going to protect you from me?!"

Davi sighed and grabbed Farien's arm. "What are you doing? Let him go."

"We need this information, and he's going to provide it," Farien insisted.

"Not like this. Is violence the only answer for you?" Davi said, shaking his head in exasperation.

Farien growled and opened his hand, letting go.

The supervisor slid back, landing on his feet and brushing at his collar to straighten his shirt. He glared back. "Not at all. Have a nice day."

Farien cursed and started to reach for him again, but Davi yanked him by the arm and dragged him out the door. "Davi, come on! That idiot is just being difficult!"

"So you assault him? How is that helpful?!" Davi shot Farien a disgusted look.

Farien shrunk back, biting a retort. "I'm trying to help you."

Davi glared. "How? By assaulting people? He's right. We don't have any authority."

"Tela's life could be in danger," Farien replied.

"I know that!" Davi winced at the reminder, turning away. His shoulders lifted as he took a deep breath, gathering himself, then turned back. "What did the others say?"

Farien had taken reports from the other teams when they'd arrived as Davi started talking with the supervisor. "Nothing so far."

Davi cursed, a thing Farien rarely ever heard him do these days. "I cannot believe this is happening."

"Let's go back to the *Reliance* and get Matheu, Uzah, Aron—someone to call Tarkanius. He'll get us the information. The Boralians can help search."

Davi shook his head. "Asking for his help already put strain on both of them. They're concerned with the entire population's issues right now, not one man and his missing fiancée."

"It's you, Davi!" Farien had never felt so helpless. Watching Davi suffer like this was tearing him apart. It was bad enough he'd lost Yao, Tela's father, and his whole place in the universe, but Farien hadn't even backed him up, too afraid for his own career and family. In the end, he'd helped Miri prove Xalivar's intentions to the Council, leading to the interference that shut down Xalivar's plot and sent him into exile, saving Davi, Yao, Tela, Aron and the others. But Farien had never been able to forgive himself for that breach of trust. They'd been buddies all of their lives almost—Davi and Farien first until Yao joined them a couple of years later. After that, the three were inseparable, and now, once again, Xalivar had torn them apart, this time, permanently, with Yao's death. Farien had to fix this. He had to get Tela back safe, no matter what it took.

Davi swallowed. "We've been through a lot together, Farien," he said softly.

Farien nodded, forcing a smile. "She's going to be fine, Davi. We'll find her."

Davi showed no emotion as he led the way back through the winding corridors of the Regalian resort toward the starport, but Farien noticed his every step was deliberate, measured—almost as if he was afraid he might lose his balance any moment.

Civilians and employees weaved around them chattering, laughing, talking, bustling as if the world was its usual place—life went on. But for Farien, life had stopped when Yao died, and again when he'd heard about Tela. He was tired of his friends suffering and not being able to help them. It was not what he'd signed up for when he went to the Academy and accepted the military commission. They'd all three told themselves they'd change the world and make it better. So why was it so hard to do that for his friends then?

*I should have protected her*, Farien thought. He could have gone for the supplies himself. He could have gone with her. A thousand possibilities played out in his mind. So what if Davi had issued the order. He had no obligation to check with Farien, of course. Farien had let his lifelong best friend down.

"Is there anywhere we haven't looked?" Davi asked, breaking Farien's train of thought.

"What?"

"You know, wondering if we thought of every possibility, where else we should look …"

Farien tensed, his voice pained, "I can't think of any either. I'm so sorry."

They turned a corner and moved through the booming music and flashing lights of a restaurant district just off the starport. More people celebrated and enjoyed life, while Farien wanted to shout at them all for being so insensitive to his best friend's pain, for not caring, for not knowing. Irrational, he knew, but the urge to strike out somehow was overwhelming him. And then the command channel beeped and Davi moved to answer his comm, drawing their focus back to their task.

Tela awoke on a cot amidst the shadows of some sort of makeshift cell, her head sore from being hit with the blaster, her shoulders aching from being dragged. She could smell the laser burns where several metal bars had been melted together over one end of a large shipping crate. Blinking, her eyes adjusted and she could make out the opening now down toward her feet. Outside was a very large, dark room with walls stretching off to disappear into the darkness. Above her head and to each side were the metal walls of the shipping crate with a single door to her right, bolted, no doubt, from outside. Arguing voices came from the other side, muffled a bit by both the walls and the merging of the muffled sound waves with clearer ones traveling through the opening to inside the crate.

She turned her head, listening.

"Your instructions were clear—information, not a prisoner!" an angry male was saying.

"We know, my Lord, but she'll be of great value," another, younger male argued.

"To whom? You? Or to us?"

"To both!" The younger male insisted.

"Who is she, Pirate Bordox?"

*Bordox?!* Her eyes widened as her mind searched for the memory. Davi's old rival from childhood, the one who had stalked him through the forests of Vertullis during pilot training when they'd met. His family's rivalry with the Rhiis had led to years of resentment and scheming in attempts to get back the throne, and Bordox had been involved with Xalivar in trying to capture them on Eleni 1, too, until Lord Kray and the Council intervened. Bordox had taken her? Her adrenaline spiked as her heart pounded in her chest. Dizziness gave way to fear.

"She's the fiancée of Xander Rhii," the young male, Bordox, replied.

"Xander who?"

"Davi Rhii, Xander Rhii, Xalivar's former nephew, born a slave, exiled in disgrace," Bordox explained. "Helped lead the slave rebellion. He's also largely responsible for ruining my military career."

"So this is about personal revenge then?!" another voice said, with rising dismay.

"That's a side benefit, Etan," Bordox said. "I promise you, she can be quite useful to us."

Tela felt faint then realized she'd been holding her breath. Slowly, with care, she took a breath, controlling the speed to be sure it couldn't be heard outside. Of all the people to capture her … and who were these others?

"We deal with stolen property, Pirate Bordox, not human trafficking," the first, older male said. "You've jeopardized our entire operation just bringing her here."

"They'll search for her, and the fleet will have to wait," Bordox explained. "Plus, Rhii is their best pilot. Top people will be involved. It'll weaken their defenses, giving us more opportunity—"

"We did fine already!" the second older male, Etan as she recalled, said.

"Tell that to Jurgen then," Bordox snapped.

"I've known him half my life!" Etan shouted. "I don't need you—"

"Shush!" the first, older male said and all three got quiet, listening.

Tela held her breath again, praying they wouldn't come and check on her. She closed her eyes, letting her head lull to the side, pretending to sleep in case.

But, after a few moments, the first, older male continued: "You'll wake the prisoner. That attack was only a failure because they expected trouble, Bordox. The opportunity for surprise will arise again."

"And they'll be less prepared with Rhii off searching for her," Bordox insisted. "She knows the fleet's defenses, strategies, personnel—all kinds of useful information. Even locations of supplies, what they have …"

She heard a sigh, then the first, older man spoke again. "What will we do with her, even if your plan works?"

"Kill her for all I care," Bordox said. "It would be the least I could do to Rhii after all he and his family have done to me and mine."

"Your personal vendettas are not to interfere with our business, Pirate Bordox," the older man said. "We kill for defense and to take what we need, not for vengeance."

"It's too late now," Etan said and she heard a groan.

Tela's heart raced, her body tensing as she struggled to keep her breathing from increasing with it. Her mind filled with one thought after another—how to escape? She had to either find a way out or get a message. She felt around, searching herself. Blaster and comm were gone, as expected. Datapad, too. Still, if they came to interrogate her, maybe an opportunity would arise. She wouldn't know until she had time to scope things out more.

She smiled then, at the absurdity of this. One minute she was holding her breath trying to stay unnoticed and the next found her longing for them to come and get her? The insanity of captivity sure set in fast. She could only imagine what her father and Sol had been through in all their years of captivity by the Alliance.

"Whatever's done will be done far from here," the older man said. "Etan will help you get the information, but at the first sign of anyone following you here or tracking her, you'll both leave and disappear."

"And I'm in charge of her until then," Etan added.

She heard Bordox scoffing. "I'm the one who knows what to ask, knows the system—"

"I've lived in this system my whole life, Bordox," Etan scolded. "My lack of military experience doesn't mean I don't know how to get the right information from a prisoner."

"I didn't mean—"

"You'd better damn well learn some respect if you expect to stay around here as one of us!" Etan continued. "Know your place, Bordox, or she won't be the only one learning how much I know about Alliance techniques!"

Bordox remained silent and she heard them shuffle and breathe for a minute.

"Enough," the older man said, "it's decided. Let her sleep a few more hours while you prepare, then get to work. I want regular reports, Etan. On *both* of them."

"Yes, my Lord," Etan replied.

Then she heard shuffling again as they all stood and footsteps walked across the floor headed away. In a few moments, servos whined and a door whooshed open, then closed again. She was alone. *God, please, lead someone here to find me,* she prayed silently. And then she thanked him for all the training Davi and others had given her since she'd joined the military. She'd need it more than ever very soon.

Whatever his crew thought of Captain Pruett's termination, their resulting focus and dedication pleased Xalivar to no end. Fear energized him like sunlight to solar panels. He hadn't been this focused in months. At last, everything was coming together perfectly, according to his plan.

He entered the bridge taking long strides, face focused ahead, even as his eyes panned out of their corners. The crew stiffened upon seeing him, chatter quieting as they grew more attentive to their stations.

Lucius nodded, saluting as Xalivar approached. "My Lord, the replacement ships have been delivered early. Repairs to the others are finished. And recruitment numbers have never been higher. It seems the economic crisis resulting from the Vertullians' departure has benefitted us well."

Xalivar emitted a rolling laugh, savoring the feeling. "When they discover the glory of their future under my new reign, they'll all wish they'd joined us." He smiled. Lucius nodded as Xalivar lowered his voice. "You've continued to monitor General Pres' activities."

"Yes, my Lord," Lucius answered quietly. "No suspicious communications or comments. She's come back in line perfectly. I suspect her grief is fading."

"Good," Xalivar replied. "I'd hate to lose her on the eve of battle."

"She's always been exceptional when called upon, my Lord."

"As have you, Lucius. As have you."

Lucius bowed slightly, looking humbled but said nothing further.

They'd spent hours together in Xalivar's quarters and the command conference room devising a plan of attack. Invigorated by the new ambiance since Pruett's death, Xalivar had gotten more involved in the details than he had in years, and it felt good. Despite his father's and grandfather's reactions, Xalivar's own memories of his time in combat and military service were of victorious glory. It had been his first taste of power, commanding men, bringing life or death as he chose to their enemies. It had shaped his vision for the future of the Alliance he would one day lead and informed his beliefs about the Vertullians' proper place in the universe and his own calling to rule.

From what he could tell, he hadn't lost his touch. Of course, even Lucius was too afraid to contradict him, but the General was also good at diplomatically examining decisions from every angle aloud, allowing his fellow officers and leader to modify suggestions without feeling corrected or reprimanded. Xalivar complied, of course, because he wanted to win and Lucius' leadership was vital to his success. He couldn't ask the General to lead a plan he didn't believe in without losing the key passions and drive which had gotten him to that rank in the first place. And out of all his allies, Lucius had been the most loyal throughout the past two humiliating years. One day, Xalivar intended to reward him greatly for it, but first, they had to achieve the victory of which they'd long dreamed.

"Great days lie ahead of us, Lucius," Xalivar said, smiling at the General. "Your loyalty and service will not be forgotten. One day you will have your choice of positions in government, on the Council."

As was typical, Lucius bowed and offered a salute again. "You're too generous, my Lord."

"You're the only one I can trust," Xalivar said, wondering if it was true. He trusted no one as a matter of course, but then Lucius had never misled him or failed in his responsibilities. They'd both been victims of cursed circumstances, jealous gods perhaps, but their losses had never come from lack of wisdom or from incompetence. "All our years of labor will be rewarded, my friend. I promise you."

Lucius' eyes were tired but still sparkled as they met Xalivar's. "I anticipate it with eagerness, my Lord."

Just a few more days and it all would come together. They'd wait until the Vertullian Fleet was near the edge of the system and isolated, far away from any chance of Alliance military assistance arriving in time. With his fleet restored to full strength, even increased, and his forces swelling,

Xalivar intended to give them one choice. Return to their proper position of service to the superior Boralian people or die. He'd order his people to save the warships if possible, but not at the cost of victory. This time the Vertullians would suffer more than ever at his hands—a reminder of their betrayal and humiliation of a greater man.

Xalivar laughed. "As do I, General. As do I."

The General laughed too then, but Xalivar knew the older man could never truly appreciate the childlike glee filling his leader's heart. Defeating the Vertullians, Tarkanius, and Xander Rhii would be fantastic enough but, with this victory, he'd also send a message to Xonas and Xerxes about the true meaning of honor, glory, and success.

Several hundred people gathered in one of *Reliance*'s two landing bays for Calla's funeral. They'd delayed plans, distracted by the attacks, but at Regalis, Aron had finally managed to make arrangements, and the leaders thought it best to perform the ceremony there before they left orbit.

The past two days had been spent on the transports. They'd departed Regalis with no difficulties and joined the Fleet, but then time had to be spent determining the best flight order for maximum safety, resolving continuing disputes over assigned quarters and rations, and generally preparing everyone for the rigors of the journey. Davi had heard nothing from Tela or her captors during that time, and although he'd made inquiries and a few scout patrols had as well, no new information had come in. He hadn't slept from worry, and Matheu's and Uzah's continuing refusal to release him to search on his own left him angry and despairing.

"It'll be okay," Miri tried to reassure him as she stood outside his quarters inspecting his dress uniform. "I promise you we'll find her." Her own eyes were shadowed, tired from worry. She loved Tela, too.

"With no one looking that doesn't seem likely," Davi replied, irritated.

"There's too many places to look, son," she answered. "We need something to go on."

Davi sighed. He knew she was desperate, too, and on his side, but her calmness didn't offer him any comfort.

"We need to do this for Aron," Miri continued. "For all he and Calla have done for us."

Davi nodded. "I can't believe she's gone." He meant Calla but the double meaning of it wasn't lost on either of them.

"Things happen for a reason, Davi," Miri said. "It's often hard for us to understand what that reason might be, but we have to trust that there's a purpose to everything."

"I know you're trying to help, but you're just making me feel worse," Davi said. "Let's go."

That had been an hour before, and now, standing with his family at the ceremony, Davi found the conversation replayed over and over again. He couldn't get Tela out of his mind.

He closed his eyes and turned back toward the platform where a preacher spoke about the cycles of time: "… a time for everything, and a season for every activity under the heavens: a time to be born and a time to die, a time to plant and a time to uproot, a time to kill and a time to heal …"

Davi wondered why it was that when one experienced such "times," they often came with stress and doubting and never felt right. *If God has a plan and everything is so ordered then why is it so hard to live in those moments, to accept them?*

The preacher continued: "… a time to weep and a time to laugh, a time to mourn and a time to dance …"

Davi glanced at Aron, standing solemnly to one side behind the preacher, his cheeks red and face puffed from tears, his posture attentive, yet his eyes distant as if he were somewhere else. What would it be like to have spent over forty years with someone and then have them gone, just like that? If Davi felt this lost over Tela after barely two years, he couldn't imagine how Aron must be feeling.

The preacher's words snapped him back to focus again: "… a time to search and a time to give up, a time to keep and a time to throw away …"

*A time to give up? That cannot be the message I'm to take from all this!* His lips pursed and his body stiffened as he fought the rage rising within him. Someone had taken the love of his life, the woman he wanted to spend the rest of his life with, the partner he'd dreamed of since he was a boy. She could be out there being beaten, raped, or even dead, yet he was supposed to stand here and do his job like none of that mattered? Maybe a better man could do that but not Davi. He had to find her, and, in that moment, he knew, whatever the cost, he couldn't help the fleet or anyone else until he helped Tela. He had to try!

The rest of the service went by in a blur. He thought he'd managed to maintain his composure and respond as expected to anyone who looked at him. At least, no one had let on as if he hadn't. Afterwards, he followed Miri, Sol, and Lura as they paid their respects to Aron—embracing him, whispering promises of prayer and support and Davi did the same.

But then, as they headed for the lifts, Miri stopped him, stepping in front to face him as their eyes met. "You're going after her, aren't you?"

Davi frowned, shaking his head. "You know my orders, mother."

Miri chuckled. "Yes, and I know you, son."

Davi went to step around her but she shuffled to the side, staying in his path. "Talk to them first, Davi. Make them understand. Don't throw everything away."

"Tela is everything, mother." He slammed his lips together then, choking back tears and looked away but felt Miri's arms around him then, hugging him tightly. Her hand reached up to caress his hair.

"I love you both, Davi, no matter what. May the gods go with you!"

"I love you, too, mother," he said and sighed as he relaxed enough to hug her back. He spotted Lura and Sol whispering near the lift and glancing back toward them with worry.

"I'll talk to them, Davi," Miri said, having followed his eyes and seeing the looks on his parents' faces. "You just do what you have to do. But please … be careful!"

Davi nodded. "You know I will."

"I know you're as lucky as you are foolish sometimes, and you've never listened when I said it before," Miri teased. "Be *careful*!" She squeezed his arms.

He hugged her again and smiled. "I promise."

Then she let him go as he spotted Uzah and Matheu getting onto a lift. While Miri went to join Lura and Sol, Davi raced after the Generals.

"Generals, I need to speak with you," he called, raising his voice slightly to cross the distance as he ran. His heart pounded in his chest as adrenaline surged through him like it did when he flew his fighter. He wondered if they'd agree to let him take the VS28 along.

"It was a beautiful service," Uzah said as he joined them on the lift.

Davi nodded. "A sad day."

The Generals both grunted as three people behind them chattered and the lift rose on whining servos.

"Have you heard any more word?"

Uzah shook his head. "The latest scouts returned two hours before this ceremony and none of the inquiries have led anywhere. I also got a message from General Grif. The Boralians have heard nothing as well."

Davi closed his eyes and took a deep breath, steeling himself. "I have to go after her."

"We've had this conversation," General Matheu growled, stiffening.

"Yes. You asked me to focus on my duties in the fleet and I have, but it's been a constant struggle," Davi said. "Maybe you've never been in love, but watching Aron today, after all those years, I don't know how he managed to keep himself together but I can't sleep, I can barely eat, and it's all I think about."

Uzah put a hand on his arm. "We understand it's extremely difficult. But with nothing to go on, we fear you'd be wasting your time. The system is so large and they could be anywhere. Surely if they intend to ransom her, contact will be made."

"We just have to wait," Matheu added with a nod.

Davi exhaled, choosing his words. "For how long? And how good do you think I'll continue to be with little sleep and focus?"

"Perhaps the med team can offer you sedatives—"

Davi cut Matheu off. "Are you really this cold, General? Is there no one you've ever really cared about?"

Matheu bristled. "We've all lost people, Captain—"

Uzah raised a hand to stop his compatriot and turned to Davi as the lift opened and people filed out around them. The General's eyes were soft, filled with compassion. "What will you do, Davi? Fly off alone prepared to take on the whole universe? What if the pirates took her or some other group? If they're organized, with large numbers—"

"I'm well aware of the risks, sirs," Davi said, nodding. The floor vibrated as the lift doors whooshed shut again and it continued moving upward toward the next level. "But if something happens to her and I never tried … I can't live with that."

"So you'll go regardless of our orders, then?" Matheu asked as the lift stopped again, the doors opening onto a corridor leading to the bridge.

The Generals stepped off together as Davi followed and then they stopped, facing him.

"I *have* to do this," Davi said.

"We can't spare a fighter," Matheu said, still stiff and stern, though his voice had softened. "And you can't go officially, in uniform."

Davi almost couldn't believe it. Had the old battle-axe changed his mind?

"We can't spare anyone to go with you either," Uzah added. "Losing you and Tela is already a major loss for our defenses."

Davi nodded, fighting the urge to smile. "I understand that. And I promise I'll come back as soon as possible."

"We leave tomorrow for the edge of the system," Matheu said. "That puts us there in four days. We'll continue at normal speed the rest of the week to make sure the rest of the ships are running smoothly. After that, it would be difficult to catch us."

So he had nine days. "She won't be alive if I don't find her before that," Davi said, then as his mind filled with worst case scenarios, he cringed.

Uzah's hand squeezed his arm again. "Officially our story will be that you left on your own. Otherwise, Joram or someone else might raise issues with us."

"Mutineer Rhii understands, sirs," Davi said and saluted, grinning.

"Be careful, son," Uzah said then, sounding a lot like a father.

Davi reached up and grabbed the hand on his arm, squeezing it. "Thank you. For everything." He let go as Uzah pulled his hand back to his side and nodded.

Davi looked at Matheu but neither words nor any gesture seemed appropriate. He extended his hand.

"You want me to shake the hand of an officer who's announced his own mutiny?" Matheu asked wryly, his face as emotionless as ever.

Davi hesitated, trying to decide if he should pull back his hand, but then Matheu shook it, his grip as irony hard as his demeanor. "I'll order some supplies and materials put aboard an old VS20."

"We have VS20s around?" Davi asked as the General released his grip as his hand returned to his side. The old model fighters were long out of service and rarely in running condition.

"We have two," Matheu said then. "In excellent condition. They're aboard the *Ferrar*, in storage." It was one of the Destroyers.

Davi had a million questions but Matheu raised his hand. "We have duties to attend to. The crew chief on the *Ferrar* will have one ready for you." With that, he turned and strode toward the bridge.

Uzah remained a moment, meeting Davi's eyes one more time, as if he had something to say. But after a long silence, he finally nodded, then turned and followed Matheu. Davi whirled and raced for the lift. He had to pack.

## Chapter Eight

G'morning, Captain," a familiar voice said as Davi stepped off the shuttle onto the landing bay of the Destroyer *Ferrar.*

Davi turned in the direction of the sound and spotted a smiling youth with blue-green skin and rainbow-striped hair waving from beside two VS20 fighters. The Xanthian had met Davi, Farien, and their lifelong friend Yao when an investigation into the murder of a young Presimion Academy cadet led them to his planet. He'd saved them from assassins, putting his own life on the line, and they'd brought him back to the Alliance, saving him from the Xanthian Market's famed underbelly. Qajuan had turned out to be great with his hands—anything mechanical from ships to computers—and Davi had quickly found him an apprenticeship under a Vertullian mechanic.

Davi smiled back and extended his hand as they met halfway. Qajuan shook vigorously. "It's good to see you again, Captain."

"It's good to see you, too," Davi said. "I wasn't aware that you'd decided to join us."

Qajuan grinned and shrugged. "Well, Vertullians are the ones I've trained with and lived with. They're my family now. Where else would I go?"

Davi chuckled. It was a solid point.

Qajuan turned and led the way back toward the two classic fighters as he continued. "Besides, you need me. These old junkers took some work." They shone like brand new, just off the line models—like they'd never been used.

"They look vintage," Davi commented.

Qajuan raised his palms in the air and bowed. "Thank you."

The youth was good but also prone to a bit of exaggeration at times. "You did this?"

"Well, yeah, they needed some modifications to be sure you two would be able to handle whatever you might encounter out there," the mechanic said. He cupped his mouth with a hand and whispered, "Don't tell the General. They're from his private collection. I can put them back later, and he'll never know."

"He might notice the shine," another familiar voice said as Farien stepped out from between the fighters and moved toward them. He was wearing his full flight suit, helmet tucked under one arm.

"What are you doing here?" Davi had told no one of his plans as requested by the Generals. Qajuan had been contacted by Matheu himself. Davi had left a vidmail for his parents timed to arrive after he'd gone. So seeing his old friend there immediately raised alarms.

"You didn't actually think I'd let you do this alone, did you?" Farien smiled. "She's my friend, too, and squadron-mate. You'll need help."

Davi glared at Qajuan, who blanched. "I didn't say a word. He came to me," the mechanic objected.

Tense, Davi took a deep breath, fighting to control his temper as he turned back to Farien. "You're not going," he snapped. "You have orders."

"Which include keeping Vertullians like you safe," Farien replied.

No way was he taking Farien along. He still outranked him. "I'm your superior officer," Davi replied, "and I order you to stay here. I don't want you with me." The last thing he needed was a half-cocked companion getting into the wrong kind of trouble on this mission.

Farien flinched like he'd been wounded. "Stop me."

Davi growled, then remembered who he was dealing with and softened his eyes as he made an appeal. "There's no need for both of us to get in trouble. This is not an official mission. I'm AWOL as far as command is concerned."

Farien nodded. "Yeah, well, I don't work for them. I'm one of those shady Boralians, remember?"

Davi shook his head, moving toward the nearest fighter and climbing the ladder to the cockpit. *Don't make me force the issue, damn you.* "I appreciate what you're trying to do, Farien, but you're needed with the fleet."

"So are you."

Davi climbed into the cockpit and examined the controls.

Qajuan popped up onto the ladder after him and looked in. "I upgraded the weapons to state of the art. Put an extra launcher in the nose cone. You push this red button here." He pointed to a button atop the dash, which was clearly an add-on. "Targeting system does the rest.

And there's four days' worth of provisions, a jetpack, a case of charged blaster cartridges and two scope rifles tucked in the back seat, along with a few other gadgets and such that might come in handy."

Davi stared at the youth, fumbling for words. "You thought of everything, didn't you?"

Qajuan shrugged. "Like the other Captain said, we need you here."

Davi spotted Farien climbing into the cockpit of the other fighter. "You're not coming!" he called.

Farien ignored him, flipping switches as the engines whined to life and the beeps of the computer going through preflight checks echoed across the space between them.

"I can't ask you to risk this," Davi called. "Don't make me call fleet security." His comm beeped. Davi slid into his helmet and keyed the mic.

"I volunteered," Farien's voice said over the comm. "I already lost one best friend. I can't chance losing another."

Images of Yao flooding his head, Davi's heart stung as he started protesting, fumbling for words. "Qajuan, I order you to disable that fighter. Use the manual override."

The mechanic hesitated and shot him a puzzled look, glancing back and forth between them.

"Let me help you, damn it! You need me. Besides, Matheu insisted," Farien replied, grinning.

Davi cursed. After all the coldness to his exterior, the old General actually had a heart? Davi extended his hand again to Qajuan who shook it with enthusiastic pride. "Thank you, Qajuan."

"You be careful, Captain," and with that, the Xanthian youth disappeared down the ladder as Davi started his preflight checks.

His engines whined to life and the ship vibrated. It wasn't all that different a feeling than the VS28's they flew now, despite its age. The controls were fairly similar, along with the feel, and the seat fit surprisingly well.

"Qajuan even swapped out our molded seats," Farien said over the comm, chuckling. "Kid's amazing."

Farien was going and there was nothing he could do about it. "You'd better not screw this up," Davi warned but instead it sounded almost like a plea. "I'm in charge."

"Yes, sir, Captain," Farien mock saluted as he grinned over through his cockpit shield, then his voice changed to a more serious tone. "Whatever it takes, Davi. We'll get her back."

With a sigh, Davi bowed his head and offered a quick prayer for safety and success for themselves and Tela. Then he gave the word and, as Qajuan watched and waved from a safe distance across the bay, both fighters launched into space.

Etan, Bordox, and Rufa had been questioning Tela for hours, all they'd gotten from her so far was confirmation of the things they already knew. But then, Bordox hadn't even begun using the techniques he knew about to make her talk. They'd only stopped the first round when one of the pirates arrived with food and water for the prisoner, orders of the Pirate Lord. Bordox would have gladly let her wait a bit longer to wear her down, but the Lord's warning about not letting his vendetta interfere made him hold his tongue. So, he, Etan, and Rufa had left her alone to eat.

When he returned, he found her sleeping, head lolled down on the table, her feet and legs still securely fastened to the chair. He smiled as an idea came into his head. Neither Etan nor Rufa had come back yet. Nodding to the pirate standing guard duty, he watched as the man unlocked the door then brushed past him and burst inside, racing toward the table, where he pounded both fists down on its surface on either side of Tela's resting head as hard as he could.

The prisoner came alert almost instantly, her hands fumbling for the weapon she was used to carrying at her side, even as she attempted to stand. She came crashing right back down against the table as the restraints on her lower body refused to budge. Her forehead hit the table with a crack and she moaned, then sat back again, looking at him as blood trickled down her cheek from a cut on her temple.

"After dinner nap?" Bordox asked, smiling.

"What do you want?" she snapped, glaring at him as she realized who it was.

"If I were you, I'd show more manners and less attitude, considering the position you're in."

"Based on what I've heard about your sense of fairness and civility, I figured it would be a waste of time," she replied, holding his stare. The blood stream thickened and her nose twitched. Bordox guessed it had started to itch, but Tela made no effort to wipe it away and Bordox offered no assistance.

"You have guts for a woman who's facing death," Bordox said then.

"Death like that of my parents at the hands of scum like you?" she asked.

Bordox laughed. “I can see why Rhii likes you. Fiery. Give even better than you get. Of course, that would never have been tolerated at the Palace. But then he’s had to lower his standards, hasn’t he?”

“Not really. He still can’t stand you.”

She was good, Bordox had to give her that. “I could hardly feel jealous of a man who so readily accepts his place amongst slaves.”

“Yet even as a slave, he’s twice the man you’ll ever be,” she sneered.

His arm flew out almost before he realized it and slammed her hard across the face, sending her head back hard and to the left. “Oh, look, I wiped some of that blood off for you. You’re welcome.”

Tela snapped her face back forward to resume staring at him. “So much for not being jealous, huh? Where are your bosses?”

“Who said they’re my bosses?”

“It’s pretty obvious at least one of them has you on a leash.”

Bordox growled as his anger flared and he leaned forward, palms down on the table so his face was inches from hers. “No one’s the boss of me. I’m here by my choice. And you’re here by my choice, slave! At my mercy!” He slapped her again, this time with his left hand, sending her head flying back to the right.

Once again, she turned back immediately to stare at him. “Did I have blood on that side, too?”

“You’re going to tell us what we want to know.”

“Or what? You’ll hit me again?”

He returned to leaning on the table, their noses inches apart. “Worse.”

“Your breath is worse,” she turned away with disgust.

“You’re going to die, wench.” He balled a fist, leaning back to strike her again.

“Stop!” Etan’s voice startled them both.

Bordox hadn’t even heard the door open but he turned around to find Etan and Rufa hurrying toward him as the pirate guard looked on with disapproval.

“Strike her again and it’ll be you in that chair next,” Etan said.

Bordox scoffed, glancing back to see Tela grinning. She was enjoying this.

“She provoked me!” he whirled back to Etan.

“She’s not to be harmed.”

“I’ll decide what happens to my own prisoner!” Bordox shouted.

“Not as long as you’re living here with us!” Etan insisted.

Rufa moved around the table, leaning in to examine Tela's wounds. "It's jus' a surface cut, Etan."

"I'm fine," Tela agreed.

"Get her cleaned up," Etan ordered and Rufa nodded, hurrying over to a bucket in the corner and running water into it as Etan squared off with Bordox. "The Pirate Lord ordered us to work together. You should have waited outside."

"I want that information!" Bordox said, still fuming but taking breaths and lowering his voice as he struggled for control. He relaxed his posture, though his body remained tense.

"Well, you seem to have been so successful in getting it," Etan snapped.

Bordox glared at Etan, struggling with the urge to strike him. He knew if he did, the pirates would kill him and he'd never get what he wanted—revenge on Xander Rhii.

"We're going to clean her up now and make a video for whoever might be willing to offer something to get her back," Etan continued, not waiting for a response. "You can either help us or get out." He stared at Bordox coldly, his eyes glistening as if daring the younger man to challenge him again.

Bordox stood there, returning the stare as he took deep breaths, then, without further word, he spun and marched toward the door. "I'll be back."

Etan said nothing but Bordox heard Rufa whispering to Tela as he cleaned her wounds, water splashing softly. He forced open the door and marched out past the startled guard, letting it slam behind him.

It had taken Obed weeks of acting like a trained stooge before the Council stopped watching him constantly. At present, they were more preoccupied with the attacks and other issues, so the plans he'd been formulating had come into shape. Obed had chosen his aides with great care. He'd learned from the first incident: this was a new regime, one that celebrated weakness. The old tactics he knew worked well had to be performed out of sight and with discretion. The kind of freedoms the Boralian people now knew had only deepened the problems. No one made them work so why value their jobs? Laziness was bred from lack of motivation, and fear motivated people better than any force he knew. Xalivar may have been intolerable and selfish, but, until recently, he had exploited it to great success, and Obed saw no reason why he shouldn't do the same. In his rise back to the power and influence he deserved, he needed men in whom he could trust. So his agents began quietly buying up extra farming and agricultural equipment, land, and resources. So many disgusted Boralian owners were more than glad to sell out and go back to other, more profitable interests.

When he'd acquired enough to start his own operation, Obed had hired select workers, offering them pay much higher than the Alliance government had, to go to work for him. By controlling the food supply, he'd have tremendous power. By leaving the government run facilities with their least productive employees, he'd ensured that it was just a matter of time before his own operations became the foundation upon which the whole system had to depend. Biding his time wasn't easy, of course, especially no longer hiding, working out in the open, in familiar surroundings. But at least he was no longer under a tyrant's thumb. Tarkanius, the weak, and his Council minions wouldn't know what hit them. And Obed's family name would be restored to greatness where it belonged.

Not having to start any of the enterprise from scratch had been a huge boon. He'd bought up existing, productive farms and equipment. His own lack of knowledge had been a bit of a liability at first, but he'd hired the best advisors and managers his money could buy and let them carry the bulk of the work while he educated himself. Obed was a fast learner and he was good at leading men. Even if they were ambitious, his reputation from leading the LSP in the past was enough to squelch any thoughts of personal ambition they might entertain.

The only downside was he had no one to share the glory with. His wife had been gone a decade and his son … Obed cursed when he thought of him. Bordox?! An embarrassing incompetent. How Obed had tried to lift the boy above his own natural inclination for trouble! He'd lost count of how many times the father had saved the son's day. And now the imbecile was off who knows where, doing who knows what? As long as he could no longer embarrass the family, Obed would put him out of mind. Bordox had chosen his path, and it no longer coincided with his father's plans.

He thought all of this as he made his third pass around the fields at the government run complex where Lord Kray had first brought him to get the workers back on track. Some of them still eyed him warily. Others, whose success had brought them to trust him, had been hired and diverted to his own operations. Obed had used exercise for two purposes. To be seen by workers as he circled their workspaces, and to plan his interests. A third benefit he hadn't given much thought to at first now became as important: staying in shape. After all, with no heir, he'd need time to secure the family legacy before passing it down to one of his cousin's children or, perhaps, even his sister's oldest, if the boy could somehow be wrested from her overprotective hand and trained. The boy had always been more book smart than street smart, unlike Bordox, but he'd risen to success in his father's company and now branched out on his own into a small technology development firm. If Obed could just convince him there was more money over the long term in agriculture, he might be perfect.

"My Lord." Obed slowed as his chief aide, Rikan, stepped onto the path from a field and joined him, jogging alongside. "We just acquired them."

Obed nodded, waiting for more.

Finally, the man continued. "Three are in perfect condition. The other needs minor repairs."

"Hachim finally surrendered his obstinacy?"

"Hachim is away, with the Vertullians and his ships," Rikan said, taking Obed by surprise. "But his aide was more than happy to make a side profit. He's got months or years to think up answers to defuse his boss' anger by the time he returns, *if* he returns."

Obed laughed. Hachim was a fool as always. He put too much trust in his own people and too little distrust in his competitors and fellow Lords. Sure, he'd sided with Niger in their poorly planned scheme to undercut Tarkanius' government with guerilla attacks, but it had been Hachim himself who'd caved under questioning and brought the whole thing down around them. His cohorts, including Niger, were now living out their days in prison, while Hachim continued to scheme and smooth talk his way to second chances. But this time, Obed would show him a thing or two.

"Get them painted and prepped as instructed," Obed replied to Rikan.

His aide nodded. "Repairs commence in the morning. The parts are already in route."

Now *that* was a man in whom one could place some trust. Not enough to leave an entire enterprise to his care, of course, but at least enough to know he'd make sure things got done when they needed to be. The four transports might be older models, but they were larger than their faster, more modern counterparts, and with them, Obed could ship when and where he wanted to, creating demand, shortages, and whatever else solidifying his power might require.

In no time, he'd be able to demand a seat on the Council. How could the most powerful man in agriculture possibly be denied? Banned for life? Obed laughed. *We'll see about that.*

Sol, Uzah, and Aron arrived via shuttle in Regalis' starport near the transports. Jorek and Virun were waiting for them.

"Where is he?" Uzah asked.

"Right this way," Jorek said with a wave and led them up the corridor.

"I hope you have better luck with him than we did," Virun said. "He keeps ranting about how civilian matters are Council purview, not military."

"Not when it involves my ships!" Uzah replied, fuming. His whole body tensed as he strode forward. His companion's footsteps echoed off the walls as they hurried up the passageway after him.

Jorek led them through the common areas shared by crew and passengers—a mess hall, small Sickbay, entertainment cubes—and down a flight of stairs to the door which led to the converted cargo hold which held most of the passengers.

"How many are with him?" Uzah asked, his eyes meeting Jorek's.

"Everyone on board except a few of the crew," the pilot replied, his scowl indicating his own frustration with the situation. "He's trying to make them more comfortable, put them with their 'own kind.' Why should they complain?"

"We're one people here," Sol said, frowning.

"Not anymore," Uzah said, lips tight as he fought the urge to yell, and swung back the door, slamming it against the wall, then storming into the long bay with Jorek and the others tight on his heels.

Uzah heard Joram's voice as soon as he entered. "Yes, yes, gather your things. You'll be much more comfortable amongst your own, those who share your wisdom and vision for the future."

"We have no future without each other!" Uzah said, raising his voice to just below a yell.

The tension of it made everyone present whirl to face him. People parted like the Red Sea along the crowded aisle as the General marched into their midst. Some looked at him with defiance, others with fear. Some just looked confused. Sol had always admired the General's ability to take command of any room he entered, but he'd never seen him do it with so many non-military personnel.

Joram stood twenty feet ahead now, six aides fanned out in a circle around him, with Lords Tamora, Chad, and Hula in similar groups down the aisle behind him. All of them stared toward Uzah, and, as he continued his approach, broke away from their aides to stand together and confront him.

"Ah, General, what brings you here amongst the scattered hordes, we little people, today?" Joram said, his voice warm but his eyes defiant.

"What's going on here?" Uzah demanded.

"It's a civilian matter," Joram replied. "Nothing the military need concern itself with."

Aron stepped forward. "Then I'll ask on behalf of the Council. What's going on here?"

"Almost half of the Council is here, Lord Aron," Tamora said, her eyes as defiant as Joram's as she stopped at his side. Chad and Hula quickly positioned themselves at Joram's other side.

"Why are these people packing?" Aron said again, ignoring the others as he stared at Joram.

Joram hesitated a moment, staring at Aron, then finally shrugged. "They are being relocated to more suitable quarters."

Glancing around him at the small cubes, every one overcrowded with people and belongings, Uzah understood their frustration. But there was nowhere else for them to go. Still, the old transports had been even smaller.

"Based on what criteria?" Sol asked, stepping up beside Aron in a show of solidarity.

"Based on their needs," Joram said dismissively.

"Which needs have made these accommodations unsuitable?" Uzah asked, his eyes locked on Joram's, daring him to argue.

"These accommodations are unsuitable generally for decent human beings," Lord Chad said now, disgusted. "How can you expect people to survive like this for months, even years?"

"They are far from the only ones," Aron said, looking at the citizens around him with sympathy. "We've tried to do what we can. The new ships are better than the cramped older barges, are they not?"

"Why don't you move in and find out?" An angry older woman with disheveled hair and a stained robe shouted from just behind Joram, shaking her fist. "You with your cushy quarters on board *Reliance*." Her face shifted to mock horror. "Oh, how you suffer there!"

"How many hours do you spend caring for this fleet's needs?" Uzah demanded, stepping forward to face her. "How much sleep do you lose from the stressful burden of responsibility for your fellow citizens—keeping them, safe, fed, and civil with each other?"

The woman laughed, waving it off with a raised palm. "That's not my job, but then, you try sleeping in one of these cubes, an entire family huddled together. Why do you need a bed of your own when we're suffering here?"

"Have you ever seen military officers' quarters?" Uzah replied, his hands reddening as his internal temperature rose. "You shouldn't believe every rumor—"

"If your job is to keep us civil, why are you here creating tension?" an old man said, his voice scratchy, as he stepped out of a nearby cube. He walked with a limp, frail in appearance but the strength of the challenge in his eyes and voice spoke otherwise.

Uzah sighed and took a deep breath as Aron put a hand on his arm and stepped up beside him. "If you have specific complaints and concerns, the Council will gladly convene to hear representatives—"

The old man laughed much as the woman had. Uzah noticed she'd shrunk back into the crowd now. He could no longer spot her over Joram's shoulder. "Why should we go to the *Reliance* with our complaints? Half the Council is here. They heard us and are making changes to address the problems."

"They don't have that authority!" The words burst from Uzah's throat, and, from the look in Joram's and the passenger's eyes, the General realized he should have chosen them with more care. Uzah shifted, relaxing his stance to look less threatening as Aron continued.

"The General's right," Aron, ever calm, said with a nod. "Fleet arrangements are handled by the military. The Council advises them and advocates for the people, but—"

A young mother stepped forward, a baby clutched to her chest as she led her toddler son with her. Their faces were smeared with dirt or dust, their clothes looking as if they hadn't been washed in days.

Uzah detected an odor and realized it was coming from them.

"We don't want to stay here!" the young mother said, her eyes glistening as if she stood on the verge of tears. "Fighting for cleansing rooms, food, clothing. There's nothing to do. People fighting over silly things. We want to be with those like us. It will be easier. We'll help each other."

"I understand it's hard," Aron said, meeting her eyes, his voice that of one who truly cared. "But there's nowhere to go. If you move, someone else must come here and they won't like it any better than you do. How can you expect us to choose?"

"That's exactly the point!" Joram said, stepping forward to put his arm around the woman. Remarkably, he showed no sign of being bothered by the smell. "We are no longer slaves. We have a choice. We fought hard to get out from a government and people who dictated our every move. Why should we allow you to force us into that life again?"

Uzah admired Aron's restraint. He didn't even tense at the implied accusations in the fellow Councilor's words. "No one's trying to force anyone. Everyone who joined this voyage chose to do so of their own free will."

Joram ignored Aron's explanations and continued: "That may be how you ran the Council, but you are no longer in charge of it. The people have chosen a better way." He nodded.

Lords Tamora, Hula, and Chad nodded, too, and the crowd began mumbling in support around them.

Uzah realized then what this was: Joram was attempting to win loyalty and decrease Aron's and Uzah's power and respect among the people. Joram and the others knew the nightmare moving people would create but, in a power play, such concerns were trivial. Let someone else deal with the consequences.

"I hereby close the docks of this ship," Uzah said loudly in a matter-of-fact tone. "No further departures are authorized without my express permission."

"You can't do that!" Hula protested.

"I can and I have," Uzah said. "Move these people however you want within this transport, but none of them will be allowed to leave."

"How are we to return to our own quarters?" Chad asked, his voice shaking as he struggled to control his own anger.

"You'll be allowed aboard a shuttle, when you're ready," Uzah said. "Thoroughly searched. But you won't be returning here until I allow it. And that goes for all transports."

"You can't ban us from talking with the people we represent!" Hula said, flabbergasted, as she shook her head.

"You can use fleet communications channels dedicated to the Council as you see fit," Uzah said, stiffening to his command stance, "but you will not endanger my personnel and ships by inciting mutiny!"

"Mutiny?!" Joram's voice rose to almost a yell as he stepped toward Uzah.

Jorek and Virun stepped forward, hands on their blasters, but Aron and Sol rushed between the two men.

"Enough!" Aron shouted. "We can discuss your desire to make people more comfortable as a Council and then coordinate with the military on appropriate changes, if any are possible. But you cannot take it upon yourself to relocate people."

Sol turned to the pilots, his eyes pleading with them. *Hold your fire, please.*

"We'll see about that!" Joram said, his face twisting and reddening as he stared at Aron and Sol then back at Uzah and the pilots. Then he spun and marched back down the aisle. The other Councilors stared a moment more, then turned to follow, the various aides hurrying after them.

Aron sighed and relaxed.

"That went well," Sol mumbled.

"As well as expected," Uzah said quietly. "Thanks for your support." He turned to the pilots as they headed back the way they'd entered. "Get me a list of their specific complaints if you can. Make sure that woman and her children get access to a cleansing room and clean clothes and do the same for any others like them if you can."

"Yes, sir," they replied in unison, exchanging looks of confusion about how to accomplish it.

"Just do the best you can," Uzah added as the bay door closed, and they climbed the stairs to the common rooms again.

At the top, he turned to them again. "When Joram's group wants to leave, feel free to make them wait." He smiled as they chuckled and headed back for his shuttle with Aron and Sol at his side as Jorek and Virun turned back toward the bay again.

Inside, Uzah feared things would only get worse.

He'd returned to the starport on Legallis in a daze, barely remembering to breathe, let alone walk or move. Those gathered, civilian and military, had cheered them as heroes, slapping them on the back, shaking hands, offering words of congratulations, but Davi had heard only muffled sounds. Then Tela appeared there, rushing toward him, screaming his name. Her eyes filled with relief, joy, and sadness. She'd wrapped him in her arms and they'd cried together.

Later, somehow, he found himself back in his quarters alone with her. She'd brought him there and held him again as they cried. When he awoke hours later, wrapped in her arms, he took a deep breath, trying to get his emotions under control. Yao was gone—his best friend since childhood, his wisest councilor and staunchest supporter, dead. He'd never see him again. Davi blinked as tears welled at the corners of his eyes again. Yao had died a hero. He supposed that should comfort him. Instead, he heard voices inside blaming him. If he'd been a better friend, a better squadron leader, Yao would never have been in such danger. The fact that Yao had gone willingly didn't matter. Yao and Dru, Davi's charges, were both dead because Davi had failed them.

"I can't believe he's gone," he finally muttered.

Tela kissed his shoulder then raised her head, pressing her forehead to his as she nodded and their eyes met. "I know. I'll miss him, too."

"I should have …"

"Shhhh," she said, putting a finger to his lips. "Don't do that to yourself. It was a battle. He went bravely to do what needed to be done."

Davi shook his head, pulling away but she matched his movement, eyes locked on his. "If I'd been a better leader … a better friend …" But he knew Yao had been the only pilot in close enough range to intercept the enemy command shuttle when it appeared.

"No, Davi," she'd said. "That's not true."

Davi had choked back more tears then as she continued, "I'm sorry I've been so terrible to you lately. I've been struggling with so many emotions since my father came back, and then, after he died—"

"You had a right to be angry, Tela," Davi said. "I wasn't supporting you like I should have. So distracted—"

"I shouldn't have been relying on you," Tela said. "I can take care of myself. I could have confronted it more readily. Instead, I blamed you. It was easier, I guess. But it wasn't fair. And it wasn't right to do to someone I love." She'd pulled him to her then again in a firm embrace. "I do love you, Davi. I promise I'll do better at showing it from now on."

Davi sighed. He vaguely remembered embracing Miri, Sol, and Lura at the starport before heading off with Tela. They must be worried about him. "I suppose I should go to see them."

Tela smiled. "We can go together, when you're ready. They went to see Pharah Brahma."

The mention of Yao's father had brought tears welling to Davi's eyes again. "He was like a brother to me," he choked out.

"To me, too, Davi," Tela had agreed as she laid her head on his shoulder again and embraced him.

He'd pulled her back to face him again and then they'd kissed with a kind of passion missing from their romance for months. "We have to do better, Tela."

"I know we do," she'd agreed, a tear rolling down her own cheek.

Davi had reached up to wipe it away. "I don't want to lose you."

"I don't want to lose you either," she'd echoed, sniffling.

He'd smiled then. "You are cute when you get all emotional."

She'd softly punched his shoulder. "Stop that."

"What happened to being nicer to me?" he'd teased.

She'd grinned. "Better. I didn't say anything about being nicer."

"We'll see about that." He'd launched into tickling her and they'd rolled around, tickling, struggling on the bed, giggling like they had in the beginning, when they'd first fallen in love.

Davi shook off the memories as Farien's voice came over the comm. "Let me do the talking when we get there, okay? I've been to this place before."

Davi remembered the broadcasts he'd seen of bar fighting on Farien's last mission and scoffed. "Yeah, I saw it on the news. Everyone did. I'll take the lead."

"Damn reporters!" Farien muttered as he followed. "I didn't start that," Farien countered. "Os and Ria did."

Going back to the Xanthian bar had been Farien's idea, but Davi knew it was a hangout for mercenaries and criminals, making it a logical place to go when they needed to track down whoever was holding Tela.

"We have to be very careful. If anything happens to her—" he said for the third time.

"I know, Davi, I know," Farien's voice trailed off as he choked up.

Farien was taking Tela's abduction far more personally than Davi had expected. It wasn't just sympathy for his best friend either. Obviously, the time Farien and Tela had spent together scouting had created a close bond between them, and the fury in Farien's eyes reflected Davi's own. "If they harm one hair on her head, I swear, I'll kill every one of them."

"Let's hope it doesn't come to that. Enough people have died already." Davi thought of Yao, Dru and many others then, taking a deep breath. He'd do whatever it took to get Tela back safely. But killing had consumed so much of his life since he'd rescued Nila from the Boralian Sergeant attempting to rape her in a Vertullis alley two years before. He'd wound up on the run, then joined the WFR to fight for freedom. Now he was a warrior and they'd fought again against Xalivar's forces. He'd killed men and women he'd once trained with as they faced off in the rebellion, then watched pilots he'd trained, like Dru, die in battles. Telanus, Tela's father, had been beaten to death in a market on Legallis. And now Yao, too. Would the killing ever end? Would the fighting ever be over? It was far from what he'd dreamed his life would be.

He keyed the radio, gathering his words. "We get her back, whatever it takes, Farien. But we do it with honor, okay? Both Tela and Yao would want that."

Farien didn't answer for a moment, and Davi wondered if the mention of Yao had choked him up, too. When he did speak, his voice was measured and cold. "They may choose this path, not us. We can't let them succeed, Davi. We have to make them pay."

In his heart, Davi understood the sentiments, because he felt the same, but unlike Farien, he was fighting hard to resist them. Tela's life could depend on them staying calm, focused. Farien had been on edge ever since Yao died. He needed a companion in control, not ready to explode without warning like a hair trigger. "They'll pay. Believe me. But we do this the right way."

Again, silence answered him for a moment.

"We'll do what's necessary, Davi. Tela's life is all that matters."

Despite their agreement, the tone in which his friend said the words didn't offer Davi much comfort.

Like many, Pres had blindly followed Xalivar for decades. For one, his family had long proven their rightful place at the Palace, and they'd led the Boralian people to heights of glory and success never achieved before, despite the fact that their methods could be cruel and ruthless. Xalivar had struggled to ably fill his father's and grandfather's shoes. In the Delta V era, he'd been admired by his men for his singular passion. That's when he'd won Lucius' undying support. And in the decade that followed, young officers like Pres had come through the Academy regaled by stories of Xalivar's singular strength, invincibility, and passion for Boralian greatness. It was hard not to admire someone who wanted his people to be the best they could be and focused his whole life on that goal. It was what any people wanted for their culture, wasn't it? Even Old Earth history had proved that time and again as one group conquered another until they, in turn, were conquered by someone else.

Admiration and belief in Xalivar and that the Council had deposed him in error had led Pres to join Xalivar's rebellion, breaking her lifelong military vows of loyalty to the Palace. She'd become a mutineer, an outcast, a traitor, in some eyes at least. But she'd done it all for the same reasons she'd enlisted as a young woman—to protect and lead her people to further strength and greatness. Who wouldn't follow a man who'd successfully brought that for decades? Ruthless and cold, yes, but Xalivar was cunning and relentless, too, never wavering no matter what obstacles he faced.

She'd sacrificed her dreams of family to serve. Military officers rarely had time for personal lives, and, given the traditions of male leadership that she had struggled to overcome, prospects for a strong female officer had been even slimmer as a result. Then she'd met Dek. Widowed, his determination matched her own. He was loyal, yet kind and compassionate toward his people. He served fearlessly yet his passion for the men and women who served under him equaled his loyalty and dedication to obey his commanders.

It was that which had made her fall in love with him, yearn to be with him. She'd been fortunate to serve alongside him more often than not, calling in favors on occasion, but mostly by the grace of the gods. In the last few months, she'd come close to confessing her feelings to him, but then they'd been called by Xalivar to launch his revolt, and Dek had died saving Xalivar from his own foolishness.

That's right. The man she'd followed and believed to be invincible and a genius had turned out to be nothing but a fool. How many had died blindly following his incompetent schemes? How many had been fooled by his charisma, his ruthless strength, and his history of success? Far too many. Including Dek and Pres. But Pres could no longer remain blind. She'd seen Xalivar for what he was, and the time had come to make him pay.

She'd left the bridge that day under Lucius' instructions to inspect the fighter squadrons. Keeping their people ship shape and ready at a moment's notice required attention to detail: surprise inspections, constant questions, continued pushing. It was the only way military personnel could be reminded of their place in the equation, their oath to serve and be ready. It had long ago become so part of her routine that Pres could almost walk through it without thinking about it. But she'd focused enough to respond as expected to the pilots, mechanics and officers she inspected.

And then she'd left the landing bays and started back for the bridge. She'd remembered Xalivar was on the bridge. Manaen wasn't. That meant Manaen was likely alone in his Lord's quarters. After their previous encounter, there was risk involved, yes. The Idolians' legendary loyalty to those they served was almost impossible to overcome. Still, she'd seen something there, something in his eyes the past few months. Since he'd returned from meeting with the alien diplomats, and even more so since the attack on Idolis. Could Manaen have his doubts, too?

She stopped at the outer door to Xalivar's chambers and took a deep breath as her comm beeped. "Pres."

"Lord Xalivar wants a report on the status of our forces, General," Lucius replied.

"Is he waiting on the bridge?" she asked.

"In his conference room, yes."

She nodded to herself, pleased at confirming Xalivar's absence for the moment. "I'm on my way there, General."

"Very good," Lucius said as the comm switched off.

Pres stepped forward and pressed the door alert to notify Manaen she was waiting outside.

"Come in, General," the alien's voice said through the comm panel beside the door.

The doors slid aside with a whoosh and she stepped forward, entering Xalivar's chambers.

Manaen stood waiting for her just inside, arms crossed behind his back. "I watched you approaching on the monitor. Lord Xalivar is absent at this time."

He'd been watching her? She wasn't certain how to react. "Yes, he's waiting for me on the bridge." She hesitated, but his expression looked merely curious, showed no other emotion, and the urge inside was too strong, so she continued. "Spying on the corridors, Manaen?"

"I was checking the calibration of our vidscreens," the majordomo replied with a thin smile, his yellow teeth still hidden beneath his blue lips and skin.

"Ah, we can't have our Lord receiving less than top quality vids, can we?" Pres smiled back.

"I think we both know you hardly care anymore about our Lord's needs," Manaen said, watching her, his face revealing nothing.

Pres froze a moment, alarmed by his directness. Did he intend to turn her in? What was his motive for confronting her so plainly? "I've not been myself since Dek's passing."

Manaen watched her a moment, then nodded. "Did he know of your love for him?"

Once again, Pres blanched at the Idolian's boldness. She hadn't discussed her feelings with anyone, let alone Dek himself. Manaen was a casual acquaintance. She gathered her emotions with a deep breath and said, "Our relationship was complicated."

Manaen smiled again. "It's a human tendency to make things far more complicated than they need to be, I've found. It's something we Idolians shun greatly. You humans find us odd for our loyalty, for example, but honoring an oath of service has nothing to do with our opinions of those we serve but with our opinions of ourselves. To dishonor an oath shows weakness in our character and brings shame to our people. Even when the master, as you may call him, is unworthy. We make such oaths based on our own character not the character of those whom we serve."

It was the most words Pres had ever heard Manaen speak at one time, and the deepest insight into his people's culture she'd ever encountered. Did that mean she'd be wasting her time in approaching him? Still, he was being uncharacteristically open with her and she wondered why. "Your loyalty has earned you undying respect throughout the Alliance."

Manaen seemed satisfied and nodded. "It's a source of great pride to my people. Which is why it's so hard for me to do what I must do now."

Pres' eyes widened as his red eyes sparkled and met hers.

"Let me help you, General, to right some wrongs. I know you have a plan in mind, and I offer you my oath of loyalty if you'll accept it."

Pres was stunned. She had come expecting she'd have to win him over to her way of thinking, but instead, he was offering himself in the highest manner of his people to her. She nodded, reminding herself to breathe before she spoke. "The honor is mine, Manaen." She slowly extended her hand.

His blue fingers clasped hers with surprising strength as his yellow teeth appeared in a broad smile.

Crowded, dimly lit, with raging techno music, the Xanthian bar hadn't changed a whit in the past two months. Patrons gathered in pairs and small groups, scattered around the room between bland, wooden walls. Bartenders and waitresses, including Xanthians, Tertullians, and humans waited upon the crowd at both the bar and tables as Farien and Davi made their way to a corner table and sat down. They'd both changed out of their uniforms and concealed their blasters inside dark coats. The heat of the overcrowded small room had Farien sweating already and smoke, sweat, and alien scents filled his nostrils.

"Stop looking so nervous," Davi teased. "We need them to think we do this all the time."

Farien scowled. "That illusion will last until somebody recognizes me, okay? Let's just stay in the shadows until we find the right people."

Davi shrugged, seemingly satisfied as a short, cute, blonde Tertullian waitress with a curvy form stopped at their table, smiling. Strobe lights from the bar sparkled off her orangish-hued skin and her purple eyes blended into the shadows. "What can I get you?"

Farien's eyes scanned her with approval. "Mmmmm. Well, I can think of a few things."

"Only if they're on the menu, hotshot," she said but her grin widened as her eyes examined him now, too.

Farien frowned with mock disappointment. "Too bad. I can think of a few specials I'd like to take advantage of."

The waitress giggled as Davi rolled his eyes. "Two beers, please."

She winked at Farien then headed off toward the bar to get their drinks.

"Making eyes at the waitress isn't exactly helping us stay off the radar."

Farien sighed. "Relax, Rhii. Just playing the part. Cocky humans are no serious concern to most around here, trust me." He shifted position, trying to get comfortable on the bench and glanced back over to where the waitress was chatting animatedly with a bartender. She *was* sorta cute.

"Because trusting you has brought me all sorts of luck so far?" Davi snapped.

The words hit Farien like a dagger. He'd blamed himself for Yao's death since the day it happened and suspected Davi blamed him, too. Now he had confirmation. Farien's chest tightened and he felt a thickness in the back of his throat. "I've been working these dives for months," he choked out, "I know what I'm doing."

Davi's gaze told him no doubts had been assuaged. Then his eyes turned to the door.

Farien's eyes turned in the same direction to see two scruffy humans making their way from the door toward a shadowy corner near the bar. Both wore blasters at their hips and patches showing strange insignia. Their clothes and weapons were a mishmash, which reminded Farien of pirates he'd seen in the past.

The waitress returned with her tray and swung her hips in a tantalizing way as she looked at Farien. "Two beers it is, gents." She set one in front of Davi and then slowly moved the other toward Farien, holding it as if it were something sensual in and of itself.

Farien shoved his guilt away and grinned, playing along. "Mmmm, foamy, cold, just the way I like it."

She giggled then winked. "Into aliens, are ya? You better be careful. Some around here don't appreciate humans flirting with locals."

"Like who? Your boyfriend?" Farien winked.

Davi just shot him an annoyed look.

"Nah, I'm single, baby," she replied, winking back. "So maybe if you keep sweet talking me—"

A bulky fist slammed against the table as someone grabbed the waitress and whirled her around. Farien hadn't even seen the bulky Tertullian approach, but recognizing him as the pilot he'd fought here before, he shrank back into the shadows. "Flirting with humans, Wena? Don't humiliate yourself."

The waitress yanked her arm free of his grasp and snarled at him. "He's cute. I can take care of myself."

"Bringing shame on our family is taking care of yourself?" The Tertullian sneered at Davi and Farien, squinting in an attempt to make out Farien's face. His speech was slurred and his movements erratic.

Farien shrank further back on the bench, his hand automatically settling nearer to his blaster. He noted Davi did the same. *Great, a drunk alien. Even better.*

"You know what father would say if he saw you flirting with the likes of these."

"A girl's allowed to have fun, Abel," the waitress whined, pouting as her brother stepped closer to the table.

"I know you!" he almost shouted as his eyes widened in recognition at Farien's face.

"I don't think so," Farien said, shaking his head.

Heads turned around them as other patrons took notice of the commotion.

Abel sneered. "Yeah, I do." He glanced around. "And I don't see no General here to save your ass this time."

Farien cursed to himself but forced his best innocent look to his face. "You're making a mistake," Farien protested, but the Tertullian's huge fist was already swinging across the table.

He and Davi ducked as the waitress groaned.

"Abel, why do you always have to make trouble in here?" she wailed.

"A boy's allowed to have fun, Wena," he snapped as he lunged forward onto the table, trying to grab at Farien.

Davi was already sliding around the bench and Farien followed right behind him.

"Great job keeping a low profile—" Davi growled as they both dodged the alien's swinging fists. "Trust me, I know what I'm doing," Davi mocked as he launched himself off the bench and rolled away from the table.

"He came to us—" Farien replied, as he copied Davi's move. The Tertullian hulk was already struggling to get back to his feet and off the table. Farien's temple ached with the memory of Abel's fists connecting there the last time they'd met.

"Run away, weak humans! There's nowhere to hide!" The alien's fists came down hard, splitting the table down the sides. Glasses clinked and shattered, beer seeping out into puddles and legs scraped the floor loudly as their attacker shoved the pieces aside and rushed them.

Davi and Farien were back on their feet in a flash. Farien's hand went instinctively for his blaster, but Davi's hand on his arm and firm headshake stopped him. "Not in here."

"You have a better idea?" Farien asked as the hulk rushed them.

They dodged aside, and Farien felt thankful the alien had been drinking.

"Hold still, human scum!" He swung his fists, wildly. Both pilots ducked in turn, circling around as the drunk hulk struggled to turn too and keep them in sight.

Davi shook his head. "You had to flirt with his sister."

"Can I help it if she's cute?"

"Can you focus on the mission for once?" Davi snapped as they both turned and charged the Tertullian, tackling him like players in one of the many Old Earth sporting games they'd played a few times in their Academy days. Again, the alien's inebriation worked to their advantage as his knees faltered and he went down with them on top of him. Both pilots swung their fists.

"You're going to die," the alien growled.

For a moment, they rolled around, fists flying. Grunts, groans, the smell of sweat and obnoxious alien breath. *What in the gods did he eat last?* Farien scowled as his fist connected with the hulk's thigh and the alien groaned. He felt his circulation cut off as a large hand wrapped around his forearm, dragging him back onto his opponent. He saw flashes as Davi punched and rolled, then the brute had him, too.

The Tertullian stood and dragged them to their feet with him.

"She flirted with me, too," Farien said weakly, but that only made the hulk scowl and spit.

"She won't do it again," Abel said and growled, pulling on their arms to swing them together. Their feet dragged across the floor and Farien flinched, bracing himself for a head butt with his best friend.

"Gods damn it, Abel!" Another voice shouted as footsteps pounded the floor and their attacker looked down with sudden fright.

Hands pulled them at them, lifting Davi and Farien and dragging them apart again, then pulling the Tertullian away as he shook his head. "They started it. I was protecting my sister."

The waitress rushed over to examine Farien and Davi for wounds. "I'm so sorry about that."

Farien brushed it off, tension seeping from his body. "We're fine. It's not your fault." He motioned to the shattered beer glasses mixed with the remains of the table on the floor nearby. "We wouldn't mind those drinks now, though."

She smiled, winking at him. "Coming right up, cutie!"

"You've got to be kidding!" Davi muttered as their eyes panned the bar around them.

Surrounding them now were armed men in simple vests and loose-fitting pants Farien recognized from his scouting as common amongst mercenary types. Their weapons were a hodgepodge of older issue models, many former military. Probably purchased at the Xanthian black market Farien and his friends had visited, where they'd met Qajuan. Most of the men were Xanthian, but a couple were humans.

An older human with graying temples and beard and a rounding belly stared at them as Abel's voice faded in the distance behind him. "Sorry about that. The brute is bad for business."

Farien examined himself for injuries. Other than scuffed and dirt stained sleeves he was fine. Davi finished checking himself and nodded. "I think we're okay. Thanks for the assist," Davi said.

Farien glanced toward the bar where Wena was chattering with a bartender.

The older man nodded. "That hulk's been tearing up my place for almost a year. Until a couple months ago when he and his friends engaged military men, the wrong group. After the cost of repairs from that incident, he was warned he'd be banished if he started any more trouble."

Farien smiled. "Probably a good idea with those types."

Hadrian chuckled. "I appreciate your understanding. Perhaps it would be best if you also left."

Farien glanced at Davi, who shrugged. Both glanced over toward the bar to see the pirates had disappeared. How had they gotten past without them noticing? Must have been during the fight. "Sure. We're sorry for the trouble."

The man eyed him suspiciously, his men frowning around them. "You're welcome back, but your little incident has spoiled the mood, you might say."

Davi bit his tongue and forced a smile, controlling his tone even as he glared at his friend. "We understand."

The old man nodded, satisfied, and stepped back, watching them head for the door.

"Did you see them leave?" Davi whispered as he reached for the handle.

Farien shook his head. "Must have been during the fight, I guess."

They stepped outside onto a dimly lit street, a cool breeze caressing their skin. As the door slid shut behind them, the sounds of the bar fading with every inch, Farien detected voices from somewhere nearby.

"Those two are as incompetent as that idiot Bordox," one man said and guffawed, a companion joining him.

Farien and Davi both stiffened at the mention of their old nemesis' name.

"The Lord doesn't trust him, despite the help he's given with raids on the Vertullians," the companion said then.

Farien motioned for Davi to move carefully as both sidled in the direction of the voices.

"Taking that woman was the final straw," the second man continued. "He's going to bring the kind of attention we don't need. As long as we take what we can and leave, the authorities don't have time to bother with us, but live hostages can't be ignored."

The first man grunted.

Farien and Davi reached the outlet of an alley at the bar's north end. Davi stopped and Farien went to step up even with him but his feet slipped on some loose rocks hidden by the shadow. Rock scraped on pavement and pebbles went scattering toward the alley.

In seconds, two blasters were in their faces and two men dragged them by their shirt collars.

"Are you spying on us?!" one demanded. Farien recognized the voice as that of the first man they'd heard.

"Kill 'em!" His companion said with a sneer. Both were chubby and older. Farien recognized them as the two scruffy, bearded pirate-types he'd seen in the bar.

"I ain't no killer," the first man said, frowning. "You go ahead." He shoved Davi toward his companion who held Farien fiercely with a strong grip.

The second man cursed. "They ain't heard nothing they can use."

Farien heard a thump and Davi collapsed beside him, then a sharp pain rippled through him as something hard struck the back of his head and his eyes went dark as he fell.

His last thought was that he'd failed his best friend all over again.

# Chapter Nine

Tarkanius focused his thoughts and emotions as he finished preparing the libation. The Palace Temple was quiet at this hour, although he knew the priests on duty would take moments to arrive if he called for them. Ornately carved arches and columns stood around him like sentinels, watching as he meditated and communed in spirit with the gods and ancestors. He drew strength from each encounter, and the gentle breezes that jiggled the tapestries and drapes of the outer walls appeared almost like affirming breaths of their spirits acknowledging approval. If not of his actions, at least of his faithfulness, perhaps. The return to worship had centered him like nothing before, and he felt as if the wisdom of the ages passed into him with each encounter, lending him insights and wisdom for each crisis and decision he faced.

The weight of his office burdened him like Atlas holding the Earth in the ancient legends of their ancestors. How had the saying he'd read once gone? "The weight of the world on his shoulders" or some such. Tarkanius experienced every bit of that pressure, and yet, his daily time here lent a peace to his soul that made it easier to bear than he'd anticipated. Pouring the libation into the traditional bowls, he placed each at the corners of the altar. Softly, he muttered the words of his prayer—gratitude, surrender, and need combining in his heart as he did.

If only more on the Council maintained such practice, he suspected their support would be far less shaky than it had been the past few weeks. Surely if more of his peers experienced infusions of such ancient wisdom from the gods, they'd understand better the decision he'd made to assist the Vertullians, even when their own people were in dire need as a result of their old enemies' actions. His friendship with Aron and others as they worked to bring peace and freedom during the WFR rebellion had convinced Tarkanius that only by standing together could the best future be realized for both of their peoples. That Simeon, Kray, and a few others shared that vision was but small comfort amidst the constant accusations of betrayal, dishonor, and more thrown out by those who opposed the idea.

"A step backward," they called it, and yet, going back to ancient enmity was surely no step forward in Tarkanius' mind. When he'd mentioned the Temple, some had even sneered and shown contempt for such "superstitions."

"How can you honor the very ones who brought us into war with the slaves in the first place?" Lord Cale asked with a sneer. "Surely their actions are responsible for the crisis we now face."

Tarkanius didn't believe that their predecessors bore the brunt of blame for results they couldn't have predicted. They may have been wrong about enslaving fellow humans and even the endless fighting, but surely subsequent generations' actions had shaped history beyond the consequences of those early decisions. Surely the present had been shaped as much by recent leaderships' errors as the mistakes of those who came before. History fascinated him and he'd spent many hours reflecting upon it. No. Each generation had to take responsibility for itself. The course of history could be changed, regardless of what came before.

Regaining his focus, he took a breath and finished his prayer, then offered the traditional four fingered salute as he stood and nodded his final thanks toward the altar. Let the spirits of the pantheon and ancestors honor his faith as well as his noble intentions.

Winding his way through arches and pillars, he entered the secret tunnels that would return him to the Palace and headed for the throne room.

His majordomo had sent the usual reports to his datapad, and Tarkanius read them as he walked. The domestic situation had improved as far as citizen morale with the agricultural fields back to near full productivity and shortages declining, but then he got to the military reports and stopped in his tracks. Defections at high levels amongst officers, more pilots, a few battleships and crews? Defections to what? They'd left their posts for destinations unknown, disabling the shipboard trackers? The last time that had happened had been when Xalivar called in his supporters. But Xalivar was dead.

He flipped back and reviewed the numbers. Someone was assembling an armada. With Xalivar dead, who could it be? Someone acting on his behalf? Another traitor? Xalivar had no offspring or heirs to carry on his plans or seek revenge. On a hunch, Tarkanius flipped to legal records verifying the status of Niger, Elul, and others imprisoned for their traitorous attempts to undermine himself and the Council in the past year. None had escaped. Could one of their unidentified co-conspirators be behind this?

Rushing into the alcove, which lead from the tunnel to the larger throne room suite, he punched commands into a terminal on the wall, calling up a coded comm channel and hailing Lord Aron on board the Vertullian flagship *Reliance.*

Aron's eyes squinted at the monitor, his hair disheveled as he answered. His pupils were red and his face flush. Clearly he'd still been resting when the call came. Aron yawned, covering his face with a hand. "My apologies for my grogginess and appearance, my Lord."

"No, forgive me, Lord Aron, for disturbing you at such an hour."

Aron brushed it off with a smile. "I'm available at any time for you, you know that, my friend."

Tarkanius smiled back, nodding. "For which I am truly grateful."

"You're up early yourself."

Tarkanius turned somber, his smile fading as his eyes met his old friend's. "Information just came in about the loss of three battleships and their crews along with two squadron's worth of pilots and officers."

"Another attack by the pirates?"

Tarkanius shook his head. "They left their posts without proper orders, filed no reports to explain and disappeared."

Aron's eyes widened as he processed the implications, likely drawing a similar conclusion to Tarkanius' own. "Has anyone escaped custody?"

Tarkanius shook his head again. "I double-checked."

"With Xalivar dead …"

Tarkanius nodded. "Someone is assembling an armada, and we must be ready for whatever that means."

Aron took a deep breath. "Our forces are already so thin, between the search for Tela Tabansi and the need for protection from further pirate raids. Now Captain Rhii and Farien Noa have run off on a rescue mission, leaving us short of experienced combat leadership. I'm afraid we can offer little assistance."

"It is I who wish to assist you," Tarkanius said. He began outlining his plan to reposition portions of the Boralian fleet so they'd be available to respond wherever an attack might come, throughout the system.

"I've already seen members of the Council condemning you for assisting us on the nets—"

"They don't know but a portion of what I know, and with possible conspirators at loose, I can hardly reveal more now," Tarkanius said. "But my charge remains to do what's best for the Boralian people. You have not yet left our system, nor founded a separate society. Until you do, that makes you Boralian citizens as far as I am concerned. Your safety is my duty. And in the best interests of the Alliance."

Aron yawned again, looking embarrassed. "Forgive me. I wish more men had your wisdom and compassion, my friend."

"I wish more men had friends of your caliber," Tarkanius replied.

"We will send out scouts and put our ships on alert to be ready."

"Please inform me immediately of anything you discover."

"Of course."

"May the gods bless you, my friend."

"God's blessings on you, too," Aron replied, smiling warmly.

With the punch of a button, the terminal went blank and Tarkanius immediately opened a channel to military command.

The response had come fast after Xalivar gave Lucius the signal. The first defectors had arrived within a few hours and coded transmissions confirmed the rest were on the way. That he still had believers after all that had happened encouraged Xalivar. He'd been harsh, he knew, but then life had been harsh to him, and the harshness of his father and grandfather were what had given him the strength to push on no matter what obstacles arose in his path.

The new additions had been carefully recruited by a few key spies after the battle at Tertullis. While the Boralians might claim it as a victory, it was Xalivar who had won by convincing others that the possibility existed to rise up and fight for the honor of their people. Some had attempted contact almost right away, others had to be lured, but the numbers were enough to bring their forces back to a sufficient level to wipe out the Vertullian fleet and conquer the neighboring planets. With Tarkanius and the Council fighting and distracted and Boralian forces already spread thin both protecting and rebuilding planets and searching for pirates, that left most of the planets with the barest defenses. A few well-planned attacks would soon put him in control of half the system.

After that, public and political pressure would assure Tarkanius resigned in disgrace and, while the others fought over who would succeed him, Xalivar would move in and take the rest of the system. There would be casualties, of course, but his Generals had retrained their men in new tactics and approaches designed to confuse Alliance squadrons and platoons used to "the Boralian way." Unprepared for the unexpected, they'd be frustrated and quickly sent into disarray by Xalivar's army, and then it was only a matter of time until they were overcome.

Xalivar laughed, his stomach vibrating with glee at the thought. The son written off by his father and grandfather as a failure, a disgrace, would instead be the one who restored his family's name and rightful place. And no one would ever call him a failure again.

He watched from a balcony overlooking the *Tarragon*'s landing bays as troops arrived and were mustered into existing platoons and squadrons by his Generals. Officers were reassigned to form additional platoons as needed with newer officers taking their old places, so that every division was led by Xalivar's experienced people. A few bristled, at first, at being placed under their old subordinates, but Lucius and Pres masterfully convinced them of the wisdom of the decision. A glance up at their Lord staring down at them and a reminder of the end goal quieted further objections.

Xalivar couldn't wait for the final planning to begin. He and Lucius had been over the strategy and battle plans endlessly. But watching his commanders do their bidding would make it real and bring them that much closer to the realization of his dream. High Lord Councilor again! Maybe he'd change the title? After all, once he regained the office, Xalivar knew he would never give it up again. The Council would be dissolved or filled with puppets under his control. Dissenters would be executed. Xalivar had fought too hard and paid too steep a price to risk another revolt.

"Why do they follow me, Lucius?" Xalivar asked his General at their next meeting, giving voice to the question he'd been pondering since Dek's death at Tertullis. "What holds their loyalty? I am not soft or gentle or kind with them."

"You are strong and you are a survivor," Lucius replied. "You win, my Lord, and they know that what you prophesize you will deliver. History has proven it."

"Even after I lost my power? They would still believe?"

"They believe in what you stand for more than who you are, my Lord. You represent what we all want our people to be."

Xalivar laughed. "Heartless? Ruthless? Feared? That's what some call me."

Lucius tilted his head back, a grim twist to his mouth, as he replied somberly, "They are right to fear you. You can be harsh and ruthless when it's necessary. But you also honor and respect those who are loyal and dedicated. You have always been good to me."

The General dripped with conviction and that made Xalivar very pleased. He grunted. "And I am thankful for your trust and honesty, my friend. Few understand as we do the difficulties of leading. The importance of strength in the face of weakness, of iron determination no matter the cost—we are antiques, I fear."

Lucius grinned. "Perhaps we are, my Lord. But then we'll go out fighting, in glory."

This time Xalivar's whole body shook from the rumbling laughter as Lucius joined him. "How right you are." Then he turned thoughtful again and his mirth faded. "Sometimes I wonder how I came to be where I am. In isolation, alone. It challenges me at times."

Lucius straightened, meeting Xalivar's eyes again. "We all make sacrifices in the name of power and honor, my Lord. Some more than others. And for some that includes family, love, and many things most take for granted. It does not make us lesser men or weak."

"Doesn't it?"

Lucius shook his head. "I think it defines our strength. Few can stand alone in strength without dependence on others. Those who can have a gift with which they can change the world, as you have."

Xalivar growled. "Ruined it, my sister would say."

"She needs others to survive, my Lord. She doesn't understand."

"I want to fulfill my destiny, Lucius. What I was made for, gifted by the gods. If I am cold and harsh, it is because emotion has no place in leadership decisions. Emotions are selfish and self-centered. Reason and logic demand more of a man, don't they?"

Lucius grunted in agreement as his eyes met Xalivar's. "I believe they do, my Lord."

Xalivar wondered why he'd become so pensive that day. *Are you suffering the weakness of your sister and father? Your grandfather?* He shook it off, strengthening his resolve with deep breaths and visions of his return to the Palace. They would all be grateful some day for his sacrifice and single-minded focus. He would set the world right. They would see it with their own eyes soon enough.

"Are the soldiers ready?" he asked.

"We await your command, my Lord," Lucius said, stiffening to attention before him.

"It shall be given soon, General. Our day of victory draws near."

Lucius turned with him to stare out the view screen at the stars as they continued in orbit around Ohm, Plutonis' moon. The farthest reaches of space, where starships rarely ventured. Away from the merchant lanes and passenger channels. So far from the place he'd once called home. He longed to return there, and inside he could feel it, taste it, smell it—the scent of the blooming orchids around the Palace in spring, the taste of the finest cuisine and wine served daily there, the waves of power that emanated from its walls. He'd missed it. Felt lost without it. His return would be far more than a restoration of destiny and a righting of history, it would be a homecoming for himself. Those who called him cold could never understand the warmth and joy he truly felt as he pondered it.

Davi awoke on sheets, his body weighed down as his eyes blinked, struggling to focus. He shifted, attempting to shake off the haze in his mind. The weight was from a blanket, and as he turned his head, he saw Farien similarly situated on a nearby bed, his face bruised, his hair ruffled. They'd been in a fight. Did he look that bad, too?

The last thing he remembered was the pirates jumping them after catching them outside near the alley. *Where am I?* It didn't look at all like he'd expected a pirate hideout to appear.

"If Tela's getting this kind of treatment, she might not appreciate a rescue," Farien mumbled, his eyes opening to stare at Davi.

Rage rose like bile in Davi's throat as he fought to control his tongue. "You're going to get us all killed."

Farien moaned, pulling a hand from beneath the blanket and pressing it to his bruised forehead. "Just minor damage so far. Where are we?"

Davi looked away, avoiding his eyes. It made it easier to focus on the mission and control his rage. "These can't be normal pirates."

Mumbled voices came from behind the walls and they both turned toward a door at the foot of their beds. In moments, the door opened and the Tertullian waitress from the bar appeared.

"They're awake!" she called over her shoulder as she hurried toward them, grabbing a wet rag and bowl of water as she came. She stopped beside Farien and dabbed at his forehead.

Farien winced, his fist clenching but he didn't object. "Wena?"

She giggled. "Hey, cutie. You look about as good as you feel, I'd imagine. Thank goodness Hadrian's people found you in time. You must have really taken a beating."

Farien nodded, wetting his lips with his tongue as she continued cleaning his face. "Pirates."

"Ah yes, I feared you two weren't done making trouble when I asked you to leave," a male voice said.

The old man who owned the bar stepped into the room, but this time no guards were in sight. Instead of anger or disapproval, his eyes sparkled with amusement. "I hope the rest helped."

"How long did we sleep?" Davi asked.

The older man smiled, stepping closer and between the beds where Wena was working. "My name's Hadrian. You're in my home. And you've been out a good twelve hours."

Davi sat up, wincing with pain at the effort. "Twelve hours?! My God, we've got to go!"

Hadrian raised a palm to stop him. "Slow down. What's your hurry?"

"We're searching for someone," Davi said, leaning back against the pillow as he gathered his strength. His body ached like it had been run over by a Floater or a herd of Gungors.

"That's why you were interested in the pirates, then?"

Farien glanced at Davi, who shrugged.

Should they be trusting this stranger? He'd helped them, maybe saved their lives. And they'd lost twelve hours. They had to start somewhere. Davi decided to be as cryptic as he could. "We just overheard them talking. And thought they might know something."

"Very few pirates around here risk the wrath of the Alliance by kidnapping people."

Farien cleared his throat. "Yes, but they mentioned our fleet and the name of the person we suspect."

Davi nodded. "A former acquaintance."

Hadrian's brow furrowed, his lips crinkling in distaste. "Those types know better than to come in my establishment. I might shoot them on sight. We get a few pirates and such, of course, but what you're talking about is a much more ruthless lot."

Farien sat up and interrupted as Wena finished with his face and moved over to start on Davi. "Do you know where they might have gone?"

Hadrian grunted. "Perhaps you could try the places closer around the starport? Depot side, not passenger loading, that's where the shadier types go."

Farien smiled. "Thank you very much, Hadrian. That's very helpful." He took a breath and then threw the blanket off, swinging his legs over the side of the bed and sitting up with a wince and a moan.

"Let me help you!" Wena said, looking concerned as she pulled the wet cloth from Davi's cheek and turned around, standing.

Farien stopped her with a hand. "It's okay. I'm fine."

"We've been in worse spots," Davi mumbled. He pulled back his own blanket and started to sit up.

Wena whirled back around to help him, grabbing his arm.

He let her help pull him upright. "Thanks."

"You'll need that courage," Hadrian said as he stepped back toward the door, making room between the beds for Davi and Farien to stand. "Abel is nothing compared to the types you might encounter where you're going. I'd send a couple of guards but there are political and legal considerations."

Davi spun his legs over the side of the bed and stood up. "It's okay. You've been gracious already."

Hadrian smiled. "May the gods keep you." With that, he turned and headed back out the door.

Wena watched them a moment as if wondering what more she could do to help.

Davi and Farien exchanged concerned looks.

"We should have brought more men," Farien said.

"I should have come alone," Davi muttered.

Farien winced then grinned. "Too bad we don't have Yao to talk some sense into us," he joked. But he alone laughed as they stumbled toward the door.

Sol, Aron, and Uzah hadn't been aboard the transport since the incident with Joram and the other Councilors. They'd stayed away, giving them free reign, so to speak, as long as they didn't interfere on other ships. But a frantic call from the transport's captain ended their exile.

Nila, Jorek, Virun, and Brie met them at the docking port and formed around them as escorts, with Jorek leading the way through the transport to the upper levels.

"It's Hachim," Nila said as they walked.

Uzah looked exasperated. "What about Hachim?"

Sol dreaded the answer. So far, the secret of the traitor's presence had been closely held. They'd even discussed trying to relocate him when Joram and his allies had begun their conspiracy. If they'd gotten word of his location …

"He claims he was being hassled by squatters looking for better quarters," Virun explained.

Jorek uttered a loud sigh. "He went to Joram to negotiate."

Sol cringed as Aron and Uzah exchanged a pained look.

"The fool!" Uzah exclaimed.

They rounded a bend to find the corridors crowded with people. Only a few wore the uniforms of crew or military. The rest were citizens of all social echelons. Several were blatantly pandering.

A woman in a worn red dress grabbed Sol's arm. Nila jumped in to pull her off right away. "Please, my Lord, just a few credits. Anything will help."

Nila frowned at her and growled, "Stay back!"

The harshness of her tone worried Sol. He knew their officers were under tremendous stress and pressure but to have them talking with such harshness to citizens was not going to help fleet morale. From the look on Aron's face, he could tell his old friend shared that concern.

"How long have people been wandering like this?" Aron asked, picking each word with care.

"Since the last incident with Joram," Brie said. "Before that, they were confined to their quarters and the public dining and rec areas, except for a select few."

Nila nodded. "Now Joram lets them have free run of the ship."

Uzah scowled. "We'll put an end to that." He rushed forward, raising his voice. "Everyone not assigned to quarters on this level, return to your own levels at once. You are jeopardizing the safety of this ship and yourselves."

The few people who even chanced a look at him sneered or laughed. The rest just continued about their business, ignoring him.

Uzah cursed. "This has gone far enough."

Virun put a hand on the General's arm. "Save your energy, sir. Trust me."

Sol found himself speeding to keep up with the others, who all suddenly quickened their pace.

They skipped the lift and went for the stairs to the upper level, which held just crew quarters, common areas, and the bridge. Hachim had remained there in one of the larger cabins, at their insistence. But when they entered the corridor, Sol's heart leapt into his throat.

"You have no authority!" Hachim yelled as he stood flanked by the ship's captain and first officer and confronted Joram, Hula, Tamora, Niger, and several angry, well-dressed passengers. Os, Ria, Pree, Dami, Ace Biggs, and a few crew members were trying to work crowd control.

"We have every authority to try you! I am president of the Council!" Joram's voice was filled with rage beyond anything Sol had ever heard from him. "If I could, I'd have you shot on the spot!"

"Step away from him, Lord Joram. I won't warn you again." Ace's voice shook from stress as he pulled at Joram's arm.

"And then I'd have you shot!" Uzah yelled, marching into their midst as the gathered crowd parted to let the group through. "I've had enough of this! Hachim, get back in your quarters now! Joram, get off this ship! And take your—hangers on with you."

Everyone spoke at once:

"Hangers on?!" Lord Tamora sounded outraged, her voice rising to almost a squeal.

"I did as you instructed," Hachim said, "I promise, but these … people wouldn't leave me alone."

"You just try and shoot a member of the Council, General!" Joram threatened. He pushed back toward Uzah but Ace shoved him, eliciting a cold stare.

"You make it so tempting," Os mutter under his breath behind Sol.

"You want us to stun them, General?" Ria asked, looking at Uzah.

"This is getting out of hand," Aron said softly.

Uzah whirled and grabbed the blaster from its holster at Brie's side, raising it in the air and sliding off the safety as he moved. He fired twice into the ceiling. All of the pilots' hands shot to their blasters, ready to draw.

"My ship!" The Captain protested.

"Have you lost your mind?!" Lord Hula scolded.

"Have you lost yours?!" Uzah screamed back at her. Sol thought his eyes might actually pop out of their sockets. "I'm done arguing with you people. I want these people arrested and confined to quarters, right now!"

"Under whose authority?" Joram demanded, hands on his hips.

"Military commander of the fleet," Uzah continued. "I'm declaring a state of emergency. We are already at full alert. Your activities are threatening the safety of this entire fleet, and I won't have it!"

"You already confined me to quarters!" Hachim protested.

"You're leaving with us!" Uzah answered, glaring at him.

Hachim started blustering in muttered protest but Uzah motioned and Nila and Brie hurried to grab him by the arm and drag him back toward his quarters, presumably to pack. Os, Ria, and Dami stepped up to back Uzah.

"Enough of these games!" the General said.

"You are overstepping your authority," Lord Niger said.

"Majorly!" Lord Tamora agreed.

"Not according to military law during war times," Sol said. "The General has the right to confine any and all citizens who threaten civil unrest, at his discretion."

"Boralian law does not apply to us anymore," Joram said.

"It does until we declare our own laws," Aron said. "And Uzah's right. You're threatening the safety of the entire fleet with this craziness."

"Crazy? You let a traitor who conspired to kill our people and reenslave us join this fleet and I'm crazy?" Joram scoffed.

"That's only one of many reasons," Uzah added.

"We won't stand for this!" Lord Hula said, arms crossed over her chest as her face flushed with fury.

"You're welcome to file a protest with the military council, when we elect one," Uzah answered, shooting her a smile like a dagger. His eyes glinted as if he might laugh.

"He can't be trusted!" Joram said and his companions mumbled loud agreement.

"Why do you think we confined him?" Aron said.

"Some confinement," Lord Niger said. "He found us in the common dining hall."

Sol and Aron winced as Uzah continued to fume.

"His actions proved him an idiot before. Does further stupidity surprise you?" the General snapped.

"If you dislike him so much, why are you protecting him?" Lord Tamora demanded.

"We are not barbarians," Aron said. "You cannot just run trials and execute justice as you see fit!"

"After what he's done, who's going to object?" Joram said, looking flabbergasted.

"Get them off this ship!" Uzah said, waving dismissively.

The pilots stepped forward as the captain and first mate made calls on their radio.

"You can come willingly or be taken in chains," Virun said, glaring at the Councilors and their supporters.

"We live here," one man said.

"Then get back to where you come from and don't leave again or I'll take you somewhere even less pleasant," Jorek threatened.

The citizens exchanged looks, mumbling and glancing at Joram before spinning and disappearing down the nearby stairs.

"Move!" Ace said, pushing Joram.

Joram turned, face bunched in rage, but said nothing, hurrying forward as Virun and Jorek's hands massaged the blasters at their sides. Niger and the women followed with Os and the other pilots escorting them.

Uzah turned to the captain. "They are banned from this ship. And no more loitering allowed. Do what you have to to get this situation under control, Captain, or you're next!" With that, he turned and marched after the pilots and protesting Council members.

Sol put a hand on the Captain's shoulders. "Do the best you can. He knows what you're up against."

The Captain relaxed a bit, nodding.

Sol sighed, his eyes meeting Aron's. "Instead of fighting the Boralians, we're fighting ourselves. Is this what they call progress?"

Aron squinted like a wounded quat and took a deep breath. Sol patted his back and they followed the others.

Bordox left the meeting with the Pirate Lord and Etan more disgusted than ever. They had no sense of vision, these pirates, not a one. Rufa was his only real friend at this point, even after a couple months with them, and Rufa couldn't be trusted either. He was a follower. He never thought for himself.

Bordox cursed under his breath as he marched through the winding corridors—an epithet for Xander Rhii, Xalivar, even his father. All of them had betrayed him. None of them had ever appreciated his gifts. This time he would show them all. He had to. He couldn't take any more of serving others, when it was so obvious he'd been born for greatness, born to lead.

The pirates were growing restless about Tela's presence. They didn't want the extra attention the kidnapping would bring from the Alliance and others. Snatch and grab guerrilla raids were their style, and they were perfectly content to keep it that way. They had no sense of the possibilities! Bordox growled as he recalled it.

Both leaders insisted Bordox take Tela elsewhere until this was resolved. They'd decide his "fate" as a new member after that. He knew well what that meant. They were trying to get rid of him. Only Bordox had learned one thing, it was that he couldn't reach his destiny alone. He needed men to follow him. And these pirates were the best chance he had left.

Oh, sure, they were a ragtag group of misfits and outcasts, but many had the right skills to make the switch from outlaws on the fringe to legitimate forces when the time came. They just needed the right leader. Bordox knew he could take them there. But first, he had to get them to share his vision for what they could accomplish. Why was it Rhii had no trouble recruiting people, but for himself it had always been a struggle?

He cursed the gods then. Clearly, they weren't on his side either. They may not have given him the charisma or speaking skills those others thrived on, but Bordox had more determination than all of them combined. That had to count for something. He knew he needed a treasure to whet their appetites. Some nugget of something to make them so driven they'd forget all their stupid doubts.

Remembering where he'd left off with Tela, he headed for her cell. She had to have something he could use. He'd just have to get it out of her, whatever it took.

She was resting on a cot in the corner as he entered the dark, shipping crate cell. He stood in the doorway staring at her as he gathered his words.

"Stop staring at me like that," she snapped, rolling back over toward the wall.

"We need to talk," he replied.

She shrugged but remained on her side facing away from him on the cot. "I'm a good listener."

Bordox clenched his fists, fighting the urge to hurl her across the room. He had to do this right. "It's you who'd better talk, Tela. I need information from you. And the time is now."

He looked around a minute then grabbed a metal chair from the corner and slammed it down a few feet from her cot and sat facing her.

She yawned then, turning her head to look at him. "Aren't you just in the best of moods? Are you ever not angry, Bordox?"

"Not when it comes to you," he growled, frowning.

She rolled her eyes and turned over, still lying down but facing him. "No wonder people won't tell you anything."

"You're making things worse for both of us with this stubbornness," Bordox replied, eyes locked on hers. "If you want to survive this little trip, I'd suggest you change your attitude."

"Oh? I'm making it hard for you?" Tela chuckled. "I'm so sorry about that."

Bordox swung a foot and kicked her cot hard. "I'm not screwing around with you, slave!"

She sat up then, rubbing her thigh. "Kill me, then, you wretch. I'm no one's slave."

Bordox took a deep breath, biting off the words burning to leave his tongue. They stared at each other for a moment, until he relaxed a bit and said, "Give me something I can use."

She laughed, shaking her head.

Bordox stood, leaning toward her. "Don't make me force you."

"Yes, because you're all about supporting my free will here, right?"

"Look. Your best chance is to work with me. These pirates care nothing about you. We have to show them your value. Otherwise, you might as well just go away." His expression made it clear he meant she'd be killed.

Tela stared at him a moment, her eyes boring into his. Her face took on a look as if she were reading him. He turned his eyes away, but she sighed, clearly unconvinced. "Let me guess. They don't like kidnapping. It draws the wrong kind of attention."

Bordox sighed. "They have no vision."

"And so you expect me to help you change their minds?"

"Would you rather be here with them looking over you or off somewhere alone … with me?"

"Do what you will, Bordox. But you can stop acting as if I have anything to benefit from helping you. You want me to believe you're on my side? Let me go."

Bordox growled, his arm flying forward to slap her across the cheek. Her head snapped back to the side in the direction of his swing. "You know I can't do that!"

Tela turned back, rubbing her jaw with fury in her eyes, her mouth crinkled in rage. "You want to hurt Davi? Fine! Hurt me! But I'll die before I tell you anything!"

"I may just grant you that wish!" He slapped her again then kicked the cot, spun and marched toward the door. "I tried being reasonable. Whatever happens now you brought on yourself."

Tela spat blood on the floor at his feet. "Go to hell, Bordox!"

He cursed, starting toward her again. She stood, facing him, as if she were waiting for it. Instead, he whirled again and slipped out the door. Losing control was not going to get him where he needed to be. He'd have to try drugging her. Rufa would know if the pirates had anything available. He'd move her if he had to. Xander Rhii was going to pay once and for all.

Farien and Davi hadn't been barhopping since their Academy days. And their last bar visits before the current mission hadn't exactly been pleasant, from being beat up by the pirates the day before to trying to rekindle their friendship after Yao's death. Yao had been the middleman, like the glue holding the trio together. Without him to mediate the others' passions, hanging with Davi had become an exercise in awkwardness as memories flooded their minds, reminding them not just of the good times but past hardships and clashes as well. Farien knew it was as much his fault as anyone's. Yet talking about it was something they just never did. Yao had been the one to help them sort this emotional stuff out. Without him, it just came out in fighting and pain.

Until Tela's kidnapping had thrust them together again, Farien had concluded the old days had passed with their childhood friend, but Tela had become a friend to Farien, a fellow squadron member and close supporter. And he'd be damned if he was going to let any harm come to her. The fact she meant so much to Davi just made Farien more determined to help.

Now here they were, playing the part of business partners, moving from one shady dive to another on a strange planet and getting nowhere fast as they continued clashing over the best approach.

"Bar number six," Davi mumbled as they approached the well-lit steel door surrounded by shadows.

If the door hadn't been under spotlights, they might have walked right past it. The surrounding tenements and warehouses were dark and quiet this well into the night. Farien wasn't even sure at this point if the men they were looking for would still be awake and out, but neither would give up until they found her, no matter what it took.

"Remember. I'll lead," Davi said, and it sounded like a warning. He took a slow breath, preparing himself for another round of the game.

"What do you want to do? Announce ourselves as military and demand that whoever knows where Tela is give us information or else?"

Davi shot him an exasperated look until Farien grinned, then they both started laughing.

"You always were the dumb musketeer," Davi teased.

"I thought I was the funny one," Farien quipped as they stopped before the door.

Davi shook his head as he reached for the door button. "You're a legend in your own mind, pal."

Davi pushed the button and the door slid into the wall, releasing a bombardment of scents—alcohol, sweat, colognes, smoke, and more—along with a tidal wave of blasting techno music that vibrated their skin and clothes as they stepped inside.

They both stood there, allowing their eyes to adjust to the flashing lights of the dance floor and bar as the door slid shut behind them. The room was humid from the warmth of both bodies and atmosphere controls. Bodies thrashed and writhed on the dance floor, some intertwined in almost unnatural poses. Tertullians, Xanthians, humans, and more all mixed together. Farien even spotted an Idolian and two scruffy-looking Krons, the hairy, primate-like natives of Kronis. No one paid the two pilots any mind, except a barkeep and waitresses, who smiled.

Davi led the way to a table near the dance floor, well positioned in the center where they could survey the whole room and sat.

"Doesn't this make us more conspicuous to the very people we're after?" Farien asked.

Davi shrugged. "I thought you wanted a different approach?"

"I was thinking more of changing our cover or something, not painting targets on our backs."

Davi smiled. "Come on, Noa, live a little," he teased.

Farien sat across from him and rolled his eyes. "Okay, but if it comes to it, don't expect me to save your ass again this time."

Davi guffawed. "I'll probably have to save yours as usual."

Farien chuckled, enjoying the brief respite from the tensions and the return to a comfortable banter as a short Xanthian waitress approached, smacking the sticky Gixi stem pulp her people loved to process and package as small, flavored, rectangular sticks. She took their order, chatting amicably and then went off to get the drinks. That's when Farien spotted a familiar face staring at them from the shadows across the dance floor.

*I know that chin.* But even squinting and leaning forward, he couldn't make out more. There were two figures and they were talking. He nodded toward them when Davi looked at him, but as Davi turned, they disappeared.

"What?" Davi asked, puzzled as he squinted across the dance floor.

"There were two people watching us there a moment ago."

"Did they leave?"

As the waitress appeared and set drinks on their table, winking at him, Farien stood. "Let's go find out."

"Seriously? If we don't know who they are?"

Farien grabbed his drink. "Yeah. Better idea?"

Davi shook his head, grabbed his drink and stood. "Safeties off."

Farien grunted as they both reached under their coats to adjust the settings on their hidden blasters. He led the way, sipping his beer and winding around the edge of the dance floor toward the opposite side.

Hands grabbed them and slammed them to the floor as they rounded the first corner, sending their mugs crashing to the floor as beer spilled out in pools. Farien looked up into a pair of glowing silver eyes.

Davi groaned beside him. "Had to flirt with the waitress."

"It was idle chit chat," he replied as the Kron picked him up and swung him around like he weighed nothing, preparing to throw him as patrons scattered around them. He went flying, struggling to prepare himself for the landing. He landed, crashing through a table as Davi crushed a chair beside him. Both went for their blasters.

The Krons emitted low rumbles, their bellies shaking in what appeared to be their version of laughter.

"Whatever we did, please let us apologize," Davi said.

Farien aimed his blaster at his attacker and Davi did the same. But before his eyes could register the movement, hairy legs kicked out and knocked the weapons from their hands, then hairy arms grabbed them and dragged them to their feet. The Krons were remarkably agile for creatures of such bulk.

"Bring them outside," a scratchy voice instructed.

Farien was swung up over a shoulder like a pack and carried roughly across the room as patrons chattered and stared. Then the door opened and they were outside again in the breezy night air.

Farien struggled for balance as he was set roughly back on his feet and found himself facing four pirates: two scruffy with beards, he recognized from the alley the night before, and the two Krons.

Davi steadied himself beside him and frowned. "What's this about?"

"You didn't get the message last night, eh?" One of the bearded men said, his glare menacing.

"What are you talking about? We just came to get some drinks," Farien said.

The pirates chuckled. "Don't treat us like we're stupid," the other bearded one said. "What d' you want?"

Farien noticed one of the men was holding their blasters. "We're businessmen."

"What's that have to do with us?" The first scruffy pirate asked.

"We're looking for certain kinds of partners," Davi said. "But it's our first time on Xanthis, so we needed to look around a bit."

Farien nodded, admiring Davi's quick thinking.

"Why does your 'looking around' always bring you to where we are?" the first pirate demanded.

"We're not exactly doing the kind of business the Alliance approves of," Farien added.

The pirates chortled. "You expect us to believe you're involved in something like that?" the second bearded one asked, looking amused.

The first bearded pirate shook his head. "They look like military, don't they?"

"Let's not take any chances," his companion replied.

Farien and Davi tried to dodge as the Krons grabbed them from behind and the pirates moved in. Punches landed on his arms, legs and stomach, knocking the wind out of him and causing him to cough and sputter for air.

"We used to be," Davi choked out. "It didn't pay well."

"Just shoot them," the first pirate replied.

The men and Krons roughed them up a bit more and then they were thrown up against the wall of the bar, their backs to it as blasters rose toward them.

"Can we talk about this?" Farien said, raising a hand to signal them to wait.

"Every time I go to a bar with you we wind up in trouble," Davi groused.

The pirates glared and adjusted their aim as the leader fiddled with his blaster.

Farien closed his eyes, preparing for the worst, then heard the whine and shuddered from a sting as he fell into darkness.

# Chapter Ten

As soon as Aron called the meeting to order, the Council room erupted into chaos. Sol was immediately glad that General Matheu had also joined them. The Generals stood together at the head of the table shooting stern looks at Joram and his supporters as they raged and ranted about mistreatment at the hands of the military. Chad, Hula, and Tamora surrounded him with Nachor and Coz in between. Sol sat opposite Aron with Klima and the Generals filling out the end of the table. With no replacement for Zarah chosen yet, a seat would remain empty but Miri had joined them, at Aron's request, and was sitting in it for the moment.

Joram slammed a fist down on the table and glared at Aron. "You don't run these meetings, I do!"

"From what we've seen, the only thing you run is civil disobedience," Uzah replied, sarcasm staining every word.

"You've overstepped your bounds, General!" Lord Tamora said.

Lord Nachor slammed a chubby palm flat on the table. "Wait just a minute! You want to discuss overstepping, what do you call inciting rebellion in the civilian population? We're on a fleet in the middle of space with attack imminent, Lord Tamora!"

"If you want to lead, lead," Aron said, deferring politely to Joram.

"It takes more than a title to make a leader," Lord Coz said, shooting Joram a disgusted look.

Sol just sat there, taking it all in. He exchanged a worried look with Miri. If they didn't stop talking over each other and start listening, nothing would come of this but greater frustration. But Sol had no idea how to make them realize it.

"Enough!" General Matheu's voice boomed through the room like thunder. "Sit! All of you!"

The Councilors stared, startled, but shut their mouths and complied.

Matheu glared at them, meeting the eyes of each one for a moment, before continuing. "Bickering like children, and you want to call yourselves leaders? I was leading men into battle when most of you were still fighting pimples and finishing school. Selfish, that's what you are. Leadership is about serving others, putting their needs before yourselves. There's not a leader amongst you as far as I'm concerned."

"You have no right to talk to us this way, General," Lord Chad said, his voice rising in anger.

"One more word out of you and I'll declare martial law and have you locked up personally, *Councilor*."

Chad's eyes widened with shocked surprise but he held his tongue and turned away.

"Uzah and I are charged with the safety of millions of our people," Matheu continued. "That's not a responsibility we share with any of you. And as such, given we are on a military fleet, traveling in space, we will be taking over decision making until such time as we believe this Council is fit for the task."

Joram raised a hand, starting to protest, but Matheu's head snapped around to face him, interrupting. "No! You and your 'friends' have disrupted and distracted my people enough, putting all of us in danger. What if an attack had come when our pilots were too busy playing playground monitors to your fiascos? You want responsibility? Take responsibility for the risk you are creating for all of us!" He stared at the far end of the table but no one there would meet his eyes.

Sol fought back a smile, impressed. Matheu had always been intimidating, especially for those like Sol and Aron who'd served under him at Delta V, but this was a side of him most had never seen. Sol hadn't seen it in a long time.

"Lord Aron will be leading a committee to report to us on domestic concerns and coordinating with our fleet officers to handle all issues and needs which arise," Matheu continued. "The rest of you can bring any concerns to him, but I warn you, anyone making efforts to thwart or undercut our authority from now on will be sent to cells on the detention levels of our military vessels. And will remain there until the fleet arrives at its final destination, if I have any say about it. Any questions?"

The General's biting stare panned the room and Sol did the same. You could have heard a leaf fall from all the silence. Even General Uzah remained still and waiting beside his compatriot.

"Don't make me try anyone for treason against our people. We've had enough of that already, I think," Matheu added.

"We were elected to positions of responsibility, General," Joram said, and Sol could tell he was riling himself up for a speech.

Matheu dismissed it with a wave. "Elected officials who don't know their place are useless. You have failed to carry forth with the duties they charged you with so you've been removed from that position, at least for the moment."

"You can't do that, General! No one gave you the authority!" Joram said, standing angrily.

"Then I guess you can court martial me after we've settled somewhere, Councilor, but for now, I have all the authority I need under military regulations and if you continue defying me, you'll be the one on trial."

Joram scoffed. But the General's face was a stone wall, his body tense and in command. He didn't give an inch.

"From the information Lord Tarkanius sent me yesterday, an attack is imminent," Aron added. "An unknown force is assembling of what might have been Xalivar's former fleet combined with a new set of defectors from the Alliance. We're going to full alert and must be at the ready with an instant's notice to defend ourselves."

Uzah nodded. "We can't do that with all these distractions, so, until such time as we deem fleet safety is no longer a concern, this is the way it will be."

"As far as we're concerned, you have our full support, Generals," Aron said, looking at Sol, Coz, Nachor, and Klima.

Sol and the others nodded, mumbling their assent.

"Absolutely," Lord Klima said, his voice rising above the others from enthusiasm.

"Meeting adjourned," Uzah said then as he and Matheu turned and marched for the door.

The Councilors remained seated, looking stunned. Sol, Aron, and the three on their side stood, talking softly. Miri rose to join them.

"We've not heard the last from them, I'm sure," Sol whispered to Miri.

"Men and women like that live for arguing," she said with a nod. "But I think they'll pick someone other than Matheu to joust with." She chuckled.

Sol opened the door and they stepped through. "I think you're right."

Tela scraped away the tears clouding her eyes with a sweep of her right forearm and stared at the images on the screen again. She couldn't breathe or speak. Her mind raced as it tried to wrap itself around what she was seeing—Davi and Farien's crumpled forms lying dead on the floor of a bar with two grinning, bulky pirates standing over them.

Bordox chuckled as he watched her. He had burst into her tent and set up the mobile vidscreen fifteen minutes earlier, positively bursting with excitement. She'd known right away that wasn't a good sign. "No one's coming to rescue you now. Your only chance to save yourself is to tell us everything you know."

Tela blinked, shaking her head as she struggled to gather herself enough to respond. "When?"

Bordox's face remained frozen, cold. "Several hours ago on Xanthis."

Tela groaned. "I don't believe you." She knew what her eyes saw, but her heart refused to believe it.

Bordox frowned. "You can see their faces clearly. What more do you want?"

"They're not dead," she insisted, shaking her head as she wrapped both of her arms across her chest and grabbed her shoulders, sitting back. "It's a trick."

Bordox's nostrils flared as his eyes shone with anger. "Tell me about the Vertullian fleet."

She scoffed. "Why? You've gotten your revenge on Davi. That was what you wanted, right? What more is left?"

Bordox cursed and raised a hand to slap her again.

She shrunk back automatically, feeling the pain where he'd knocked out teeth and cracked her lip hours before. Her bottom lip and cheeks had swelled since then and bruises covered her face. She wouldn't give him any more satisfaction than he'd already had seeing her cry. She cursed back and spat at his feet.

Inside, she feared he was telling the truth. Davi would have come after her, and she wasn't surprised that Farien had come along. Xanthis was a rough place. They'd learned that on their prior visit there with Yao and Dru. She'd worried many times, feared Davi would get hurt or killed. But he'd always come soaring through. He'd always made it. She supposed anyone's luck was bound to change when they lived a life of such risks. It had been part of why they'd fought so much. Davi hadn't realized how worried she was after her father got back. Worried about losing either of them again. Worried about more pain. She wanted to have every moment with him and fight alongside him, take the same risks. Frustration had eaten away at her and made her tense and irritable. But to actually see their bodies like this … it was surreal. Something she'd never anticipated, never imagined how it would make her feel.

"I won't ask again," Bordox said.

"Kill me," she whispered.

"What?" he demanded.

"If it's true, if they're dead, just kill me," she replied, more loudly this time. "I have nothing to live for, then."

Bordox laughed. "And miss out on all the information you have with which I could repay the Vertullians for everything they put our people through? You'll die when the time is right, but not before I get what I want. No matter how much you must suffer first."

She nodded. "He always said you were a loser. Clearly, he was right."

"What?!" Bordox's fists clenched as he stepped toward her. "Rhii called me a loser?"

He'd winced. Point scored. Now for the salt. She smiled. "They both did. Laughing about all the times they'd beat you at the Academy, how petty and jealous and stupid you were. And how it all was really your own fault for being arrogant and incompetent and blinded to it."

Bordox swung his fist but Tela ducked and fell onto her side, dragging the chair with her across the floor. Bordox cursed, stomping after her.

"The stories were quite amusing to all of us in flight school," Tela added.

"He told the pilots?"

"He shared it with anyone who wanted to know," she said, locking her eyes on Bordox's as she reached the back of the tent. "You're a popular folk villain, you might say."

Bordox's eyes widened as his cheeks flushed and he stood over her, his breathing loud and coming out with grunts. "Blaster shots were too good for him! He died better than he deserved!"

Tela laughed. "He beat you again really."

Bordox lashed out with a foot, kicking her in the thigh as she twisted in the chair. Pain shot up her body and she choked back more tears, then she heard footsteps and voices and two others burst in, one an older leader he'd argued with when she first awoke there.

"Leave her be!" The older pirate commanded. She searched her memory for his name. Etan, was it?

"Let me finish!" Bordox insisted.

They grabbed him by the arms and pulled him back, then the older man squared off with him as the younger came and bent, examining her, then lifted the chair back up gently so she was sitting upright again.

"The Pirate Lord wants her alive, and you're needed elsewhere," Etan continued.

"Doing what?"

"Obeying orders and not questioning your superiors!" Etan spat, glaring at Bordox.

Bordox turned to stare back at Tela a moment. She could see him raging, his shoulders tense, fists curled tight.

"Now!" Etan almost yelled it.

Then Bordox cursed again, spun on his heels, and left the tent.

"Are you all right?" Etan asked her, eyeing the bruises and swelling on her face.

She chuckled. "I'm alive. You see what he did to me earlier."

Etan scowled. "He'll pay for that. I promise you." He turned to the taller, younger man with him. "Help her clean up and get her water and food. Have Cley come look at her wounds, too. I'll check on her later."

The younger pirate grunted and nodded before Etan turned around and hurried out after Bordox.

After dragging her chair back to its old position at the center of the tent and asking her a long string of questions about her injuries and how she was feeling, the younger pirate finally left her alone. Only then did Tela admit what she was feeling. Her shoulders sagged and tears wet her cheeks again as pain wracked her body and breathing became a struggle. She sobbed like she'd never sobbed before as she let it all out.

Dropping productivity at the government farms caught up with the market faster than Obed had expected, enabling him to raise prices on his own products sooner than planned. After just two weeks, he'd created a huge demand for Gungor meat and Gixi, of which Vertullis had long been the primary supplier. With Obed's plantations and lots producing at much higher rates, he'd started bidding wars for his shipments, with representatives from various cities and planets competing against each other as the shortage increased. The latest shipment had netted him a five-hundred percent profit and that would only increase as time went on.

To increase the odds further, Obed's people had poisoned some stock and plants on government plantations, killing half of two herds and ruining several fields. It would take months for them to recover, of course, and, in the meantime, Obed would become a more and more dominant supplier. He grinned at the thought. Everything was going just as he'd planned. Finally, the gods had handed him a friendly fate.

The best part was that it had all happened right under the government's nose but, so far, no inquiries had been made, no questions asked. His position overseeing agricultural production for the government assured Obed would be among the first to know. *All too easy!*

Staring out the window of his office, he started at the sight of a Council shuttle coming to a rest on the landing pad in the yard. He hadn't been informed of any official visits or inspections. The Council had always done so before. He watched as Lords Simeon and Kray stepped out onto the landing pad looking dire and hurried toward his office. Obed had time only to take a few calming breaths and gather his senses before the door whooshed, sliding into the wall admitting them.

He stood as they stopped before his desk, nodding.

"Lord Obed," Simeon said.

"My old friends, to what do I owe the surprise?"

Kray stepped forward, offering Obed a datapad.

He accepted and began reading the screen. It was a toxicology report.

"We have a problem," Lord Kray said then.

"Poison?" Obed asked as he continued reading, not daring to meet her eyes as he steeled himself to lie.

She nodded. "Gungors, several half herds, and fields of Gixi wiped out."

Simeon's eyes locked on Obed's as he asked, "Do you have any idea who might be responsible?" It was an accusation.

Obed scoffed. "If I knew, do you think I wouldn't have informed you already and put a stop to it?" His eyes met theirs at last, and he saw them relax a bit.

"Of course," Simeon replied. "We meant no disrespect."

Obed dismissed it with a wave. "How did you come to run toxicology reports? I ordered none. I had no such suspicions."

"It's standard procedure where government interests are involved," Kray said. "Your foreman followed the procedures and sent samples to an official lab."

"Why did they inform you and not me?" Obed put his hands on his hips, feigning frustration.

"A coded report should be in your inbox," Kray said just as Obed's personal datapad beeped to inform him of a new message, "but since the High Lord Councilor put me in charge of oversight, the tech felt I should be informed as well. Plus, we feared some kind of leak, so I asked him to delay sending it until close to our arrival."

Obed ignored the datapad, continuing to meet their eyes. Inwardly, he cursed himself for forgetting the regulations. He'd been so busy with his own concerns, he'd neglected to check procedures and instruct his staff accordingly. He tsked through his teeth, offering a sad, concerned look. "Well, obviously, I'll investigate fully."

"We saw several agricultural transports on the ground being loaded at the starport," Simeon said. "Do you know where they're bound?"

"And what is their cargo?" Kray added.

Obed shrugged. "I believe we have no official shipments today. Surely flight control has records, but I have no knowledge of them."

"The logos on the sides and tops identified them as belonging to Xizor Agricultural Corp," Kray said. "Are you familiar with it?"

Obed nodded. "Yes, one of our private competitors with large plantations of Gixi and other fruits, I believe."

Kray smiled. "A bit of record checking shows Xizor has been quite aggressively buying up abandoned agricultural lots and equipment for months. Do you know who owns it? Perhaps they might be suspects in this sabotage."

Obed feigned surprise, shaking his head. "I can't remember his name off the top of my head, but I believe it's a higher echelon citizen with a sterling record. Not the type to engage in such … trickery."

"Nevertheless, we must follow all leads until the responsible parties are found," Simeon said.

"Of course," Obed agreed.

"And we want coded daily reports of all investigative activities, no matter how insignificant you may deem them," Kray said.

Obed forced a compliant smile to hide his inward cursing. He'd have to do a lot of editing if he hoped to keep them from knowing too much, too soon. They'd discovered his shell company, but luckily his ownership of it was well hidden beneath aliases and other shell investors. He couldn't risk his plot being uncovered until the right time. Not while there was still opportunity to interfere and foil his plans. "You'll know everything I do."

Simeon looked pleased, the corners of his mouth lifting as he grinned. "Thank you, Obed. We knew we could count on you." He glanced at Kray who nodded her own agreement, but Obed read doubt in her eyes as Simeon continued. "Now, since we're already here, why don't you show us where the best places to find a good lunch are. If you have the time."

Obed relaxed and stepped out from behind the desk. "Of course! I was getting hungry myself." He led them to the door, which slipped open as he approached.

"Let's take our shuttle," Simeon suggested.

Obed's mind raced with plans for how to manipulate the investigation and keep his secret as he and Simeon followed Kray toward the landing pad.

---

Davi awoke on his back on a hard surface as every nerve in his body throbbed and cried out in pain. He squinted, trying to focus his eyes. *Where am I?* The last thing he remembered was the whine of a blaster and those two Krons hulking over them as he fell.

*Am I dead? Heaven's darker than I expected.*

He looked around him. Farien lay next to him, still unconscious. *Or is he dead?*

Then Farien was stirring, moaning, blinking, his head lolling to one side. He cursed, trying to sit up.

Davi swallowed, wetting his mouth with his tongue. "Take it easy. We were shot, remember?"

"I thought they killed us," Farien said with a nod as he settled back down on his back.

Davi turned. They were lying on some sort of hard floor, painted as dark as the walls Davi could barely spot through the shadows. "Apparently not."

Farien grunted again and sat up, wincing from pain. "How long have you been awake?"

"Minutes. Since just before you."

Farien nodded. "Remember how you and Yao used to scold me for getting us in trouble back at the Academy?"

Davi smiled. "Yeah, you were a mess."

Farien squinted at him. "This one's totally on you."

"Me?" Davi scoffed, trying to determine if his friend was joking. His face was too crinkled, his eyes barely open. Davi couldn't read him at the moment. "You're the one who's been starting all of the fights."

"Yeah, but you're the one who dragged us out in the open, in the middle of the room. Might as well hang targets on our backs."

Irritation rose like bile in his throat but Davi choked it off and snapped, "We were doing perfectly fine until you decided to go check on someone watching us, remember?"

Loud laughter interrupted them, a cackling from the shadows. Both whirled, squinting and straining to see as Davi sat up beside his friend.

"Who's there?" Farien demanded.

"Such touching banter between old friends. Perhaps I can join in as well. You always sounded better with a third wheel, but Brahma's not available."

Davi heard footsteps, his mind racing to identify the voice. It came to him just as Bordox stepped out of the shadows, glaring down at them. "It's going to be my pleasure to personally kill you both."

"Can't be heaven if Bordox is here," Farien muttered.

Davi just stared at his rival. They hadn't been face to face since the confrontation on Eleni 1 when Xalivar had escaped. When Skitter riders attacked them on Xanthis, Bordox had been there, somewhere, pulling the strings. But they hadn't looked each other in the eye for over two years. Bordox appeared ragged and tired. He no longer wore a uniform and his hair was long, his form bulging in new places. He'd gained weight. What had Bordox been through over the last few years? Had he followed them? Had he been there in the battle above Tertullis?

"You son of a—" Farien's voice rose in anger.

"Mind your words, Noa!" Bordox's hand reached for the blaster at his side. Davi had no doubt he'd draw it and fire at the slightest provocation.

"Where are we? What do you want?" Davi demanded, distracting him.

Bordox cackled again. "Where—you don't need to know. Why is a better question. You're here to pay for your sins, Rhii."

"Sins? Oh, so we're in hell." Farien smirked. "Makes sense you'd be here, too."

Bordox's foot swung out so fast neither of them had time to react, connecting with Farien's chin hard and forcing his head back and to the side as it swung on through. "I've waited a long time to do that, Noa."

Farien spat blood, his hand rubbing his jaw as he whirled his head back to glare in fury at Bordox. "Let me stand up so I can do what I've been waiting too long to do."

"Stay where you are!" Bordox drew his blaster, aiming it at Farien's chest. Farien didn't move. "Although I do appreciate you're making this so pleasant, I'm not quite through with you yet."

Davi swallowed, clearing his throat. "What do you want with us Bordox? To fight? To humiliate us?"

"To make you suffer." Bordox held up a datapad, screen aimed toward them.

It took Davi's eyes a moment to focus in the dark. *Tela!* Then the image moved on the screen.

"No one's coming to rescue you now," Bordox's voice said from the screen. "Your only chance to save yourself is to tell us everything you know."

Tela blinked, shaking her head as she gathered herself. "When?"

"Several hours ago on Xanthis."

Tela groaned. "I don't believe you."

Davi saw the mix of confusion and worry clouding her blue eyes, eyes that had lost their sparkle. His heart ached for what she must be feeling.

On screen, Bordox growled: "You can see their faces clearly. What more do you want?"

"They're not dead," Tela insisted, shaking her head as she wrapped both of her arms across her chest and grabbed her shoulders, sitting back. "It's a trick."

Davi sent energy to her mentally, willing her to feel his presence, internally praying to God to give her peace.

Bordox's reply was terse, intense. "Tell me about the Vertullian fleet."

Tela scoffed. "Why? You've gotten your revenge on Davi. That was what you wanted, right? What more is left?"

Shadows fell over her as Bordox stepped forward. Tela shrunk back, drawing her face up and into the light. Davi saw her cracked bottom lip, swelling along with her cheeks. Bruises covered her face. Someone had beaten her. His body tensed, urging him to leap to his feet and go after her. *Bordox had done this to her!*

"Where is she?!" he demanded, fighting to control his anger.

"Mourning you," Bordox replied, his eyes shining as his mouth widened to a grin, reveling in Davi's reaction. He returned the datapad to a holder on his belt.

"We'll make you pay, Bordox!" Farien said through gritted teeth.

Bordox laughed. "The only ones who'll be paying are the three of you. You're going to watch her suffer, and then, you're going to watch her die. And then, you can watch each other suffer and die. Me? I'm going to enjoy all of it!"

Farien sprang at Bordox's feet, forcing their nemesis to take a step back, while struggling to aim the blaster again. His booted foot swung forward as Farien landed near his feet, kicking Davi's friend hard in the ribs.

Farien rolled away, wheezing for air.

"Stop, Bordox!" Davi raised a hand and struggled to his feet as he yelled. "What do you want from us? What did we do to you besides tease you back every time you taunted us?"

It was Bordox's turn to scoff. "Tease me? You humiliated me in front of my father, my classmates, my professors. You walked around like you were so much better than me, laughing, mocking. What do I want?" Bordox stepped forward again, his face hardening like a statue, steely with determination. "Justice!"

"Justice?" Farien spat the word, chuckling until he was overcome with coughing, clutching at his injured ribs. "As if you even know what that is."

"Fine. Kill me, Bordox. Humiliate me. But let them go. This is not between you and Tela, or you and Farien. You want me? Here I am." Davi raised his arms in surrender.

"Stop trying to play the hero, Xander," Bordox said and spit at Farien.

The wet spittle landed on Farien's leg. Farien scowled but didn't move.

"They'll pay as you will. Because their suffering is part of your punishment."

"Fine. Bring it on." Farien struggled to stand again, glaring at Bordox defiantly. "I'm ready, you bastard."

Bordox cackled, his eyes panning between them. He leaned back as his belly shook, then slowly slid his blaster back into the holster. "Soon, Noa. Very soon." With that he spun and disappeared into the shadows. His footsteps faded as he went.

"Come back here and face us like a man, Bordox!" Farien shouted.

Davi just watched him go. He had to find and save Tela—that meant keeping his focus, thinking it through. The time would come. Another time. It was time he dealt with Bordox for good.

"This is an outrage!" Lord Adoo's fist slammed the table where he sat facing Tarkanius and Simeon on the dais at the front of the Council Chamber on Legallis.

"Hear, Hear!" Shouts echoed from around the chamber as even some of Tarkanius' allies sided against him.

"I thought we were entering a new age, one in which the Council and the Palace worked side by side to build a better future for our peoples," Lord Adoo continued. "But this pattern of ignoring the Council's wishes is too reminiscent of Xalivar!"

Tarkanius winced at the insult, feeling Simeon's hand gently touch his shoulder.

"Calm down, Lord Adoo," Simeon said, raising his voice above the clamor and rising from his chair. "The High Lord Councilor is still worthy of our respect."

"He's not treating us with respect," Lord Kanaan replied. "Why should we treat him any differently?"

Lord Kray rose, her nostrils flaring and chin held high. "He has done nothing but try to protect our people as best he can! If he waited to come before the Council for every decision, how could the military act in time?"

Lord Qai snorted. "Please, Kray, even you can't believe that. We're not talking about decisions made in the heat of battle."

Several others grunted in agreement as Qai's eyes met Kray's but she stood staring back as if daring him to continue.

"Why are we protecting people who have abandoned us?" Lord Buj asked. "They chose their own course, so let them go. Our responsibility is to our own."

The other Lords around them mumbled in agreement.

Tarkanius sighed and stood, raising a hand to silence them. "You're right. I have made decisions without consulting you. But that's only because you refuse to recognize the true danger facing us. Recent reports indicate an entire fleet massing somewhere in this system. More officers and pilots defected, taking Boralian warships with them. Investigations have revealed that not all of the attacks are the same. The threat is far larger than we'd first imagined. And the attacks on the Vertullians seem to match those against our own."

"We have no further responsibility to protect them," Lord Buj continued. "They've abandoned homes, jobs, left our agriculture in shambles, our economy a mess, and they've taken Boralian property as if it was theirs …"

"They have been loaned some resources. Others they acquired on their own," Lord Simeon corrected.

Lord Adoo laughed. "Please, Simeon, we know how they acquired them. They were given most of them at a significant discount or free."

"They have a right to determine their own destiny," Lord Kray said. "And after all we've put them through, we owed them at least the opportunity."

"All we've put them through?!" Lord Buj demanded. "What of all of our lost ancestors murdered at their hands?!"

"Are we really going to rehash this again?" Kray rolled her eyes.

Tarkanius raised his voice to speak over them. "Please, Kray, Buj, Adoo, all of you, listen!" He wound up yelling the last.

They stopped shocked. Tarkanius rarely yelled, let alone at the Council. A few grumbled for a bit but then they all turned their attention to him.

"There are reports I receive daily which you are not always privy to, information I have that you don't," he continued. "I am doing the best I can. We must face this together, but I cannot leave the safety of our citizens hanging in the balance. It takes time to move military resources."

"They surrendered their rights as citizens when they decided to abandon us!" Lord Quatol said.

"And if you move them and we disagree, you'll have wasted their efforts when you're forced to order them back," Lord Kanaan interjected.

Pharah Brahma rose from a seat in the observation area nearby. He continued to attend the meetings as a consultant but preferred to remain quiet and observe rather than participate, so many heads turned as if noting his presence for the first time. "It occurs to me that perhaps we all want the same thing: the safety and security we once had as a people. We're conflicting over the approach taken, and with the High Lord Councilor's access to military reports and information, perhaps we should allow that he's in a better position to evaluate things than we are."

Tarkanius waited for one of the long-time Lords to attack the Tertullian, but instead, the Xanthian ambassador, Lord Quatol jumped in, "Please, Brahma. You've always been a Palace stooge, even in Xalivar's day."

Tarkanius was amazed at the Tertullian's self-control. He didn't even bristle. Instead, he smiled warmly. "Quatol, we've been friends a long time. Long enough for you to know not to mistake my quiet nature for blind compliance."

Quatol turned away as Lord Kanaan spoke, "You trust these humans? Despite all the years they looked down on us?"

"These humans also provided stability and protection for us for generations," Pharah answered. "Some may have looked down on us as Xalivar did, but Tarkanius is the reason we're in this Chamber. So yes, I trust him to have our best interests at heart. And so should you."

The Lords grew quiet then, refusing to meet Tarkanius' eyes as he panned the room. Only Pharah acknowledged their leader with a nod as their eyes met.

"I am open to your wisdom and advice, if presented in a manner that welcomes discussion as always," Tarkanius said softly. "I fear we are on the verge of yet another war, and we must be ready. Time wasted fighting each other will only distract us from doing what we must to survive. Please allow me to share with you information I've only just been made aware of."

With that, he pushed a button to lower a vidscreen above his head. And for the next hour, he took them through military reports, visuals, recordings, and other intelligence data which had left him reeling over the past week. Watching their faces, he saw it sink in for the first time how much more there was to the threat than any of them had imagined, even Kray and Simeon.

By the time, he'd finished, Lord Adoo himself met Tarkanius' eyes and asked, "Do we have enough forces left to truly defeat this threat once and for all?"

Tarkanius sighed. "General Grif assures me that we do, but they must be prepared to relocate at a moment's notice once the focus of any attack is revealed. That's why spreading our forces throughout the system seemed prudent. We now have first responders ready near each of our planets, and others who can quickly move to assist them, the moment the enemy force is located. Meanwhile, we have patrols out hunting for the stolen ships and assembled fleet. We will find them. We can only hope that happens before they attack so we can take the initiative."

This time no one showed any signs of objecting.

Simeon stood beside the High Lord Councilor, patting his friend's shoulder. "Clearly there is much we must consider in light of these revelations. I believe rather than anger, you are owed our gratitude and regret for the attitude many of us have taken."

Tarkanius shook his head. "We are men of passion. That has always been the case with the Council. It's a quality which makes us good leaders, but we must also be able to learn from our mistakes and move past them." He panned the room again. "Please, I am weary from the decisions I've had to make. I welcome your support and your help as we face this threat together."

Lord Kray stood. "We will stand with you, my Lord."

One by one, others followed her example. "We are with you, my Lord," Lord Amie echoed, then Lords Buj, Adoo, Qai, and so on, until the entire Council stood facing him, swearing their allegiance. The tension that had filled the room like hot, stale air dissipated in moments, leaving behind it the solemn reverence of determined men and women united.

Tarkanius relaxed, sighing with relief and sank back into his chair.

As Simeon called for them to adjourn and resume the next day, Tarkanius wondered how long it would be before he had to convince them all over again.

Every cell in Xalivar's body ached as he ran, knowing he didn't dare stop and catch his breath or even think, lest the others might overtake him again. He hated running away. If his father knew, he'd pronounce his son a coward, but these boys were bigger than him, despite being the same age, and Xalivar had tasted enough of his own blood for one day. It continued flowing from the cuts on his forehead and cheeks even as he lifted the back of his right hand to wipe clear the streams from his eyes. He should have never allowed them to catch him alone like that. He knew better. When would he learn?

He slowed as the corridor narrowed further and he reached a corner. Bright light broke the shadows as Boralis and Charlis reached their afternoon peaks together. He peered out, struggling to control his desperate lungs for fear his gasps would reveal his location to his foes. The courtyard was clear. If he could just slip through and back into the Palace, they'd never follow him. The risk of being caught there would be too great. Xalivar had never understood his father's insistence that he study with the sons of the other Lords. What business did a Prince have amongst such commoners? Yet his father reminded him sternly that they were once commoners and their power had come at the will of the people.

"It might seem guaranteed, Xalivar, but if you lose touch with the people's wills, it could be your downfall one day," Xerxes had said.

Even at eight years old, Xalivar resented the way his father only talked to him in lectures, never as a father relating to a son. *He treats me like a subject, not his child and heir!* Exposure to the other boys had only served to deepen Xalivar's resentment of what he didn't have. So many of his classmates spoke fondly of their fathers—laughing together, playing, having fun with them. It only reminded Xalivar of his failed relationship with his father. He was nothing but a disappointment, an embarrassment. He wondered sometimes if his father secretly resented even having a son.

Xalivar took one last look around as he stepped out into the courtyard. No servants in sight, not even his sister. He often found her here playing this time of day. Where had she gone to? Maybe she was busy bouncing on their father's knee or enjoying the affection he reserved only for her? Miri adored Xerxes, and it was clearly mutual. Father and daughter had the relationship Xalivar had always wanted. Xerxes was soft and loving with her. Xalivar hated her for it, and yet, Miri was his only true friend. She'd always looked out for him, despite being younger. Some of the few memories he had of his father's kindness had come from her urging Xerxes to support his son. Xalivar appreciated her concern and yet resented his father needing such reminders to express any love for his son.

"There he is!" a familiar voice shouted.

Xalivar's heart raced as his body tensed, his jaw clenched. His pants chafed his skin as he ran and he cursed. Then he heard their running footfalls and saw them bursting from the shadows around him. They'd lain in wait, knowing where he'd go.

Then he was falling, the wind knocked out of him as two of them dove on top of him, pulling him down toward the stone of the walkway. They rolled around as he felt stabs of pain from each punch and kick. The boys laughed, taunting, mocking. Xalivar couldn't break free. He did his best to curl into a ball, give them as little target space as he could.

"Look at him cowering! Some prince we have!" one of them shouted.

"Get off my brother now!" he heard Miri's voice above them all, a booming alto echoing through the courtyard. "Grandfather! Father! Guards!"

The boys stopped punching and pulled themselves free. "He should learn to watch his mouth," one said. Was it Obed? Niger? Buj? Xalivar was too stunned with pain to think clearly.

"And you need to respect this house!" Xonas' voice, his grandfather. *Oh no! He'll tell father!*

Xalivar struggled to get to his feet so he could run away. Maybe if Xonas didn't see him like this.

Then he heard yells and thumps. "Stop hitting me!" a boy cried.

"That's for my brother!" Miri shouted.

"Miri! Leave them be," Xonas ordered.

Xalivar heard them approaching, even as his attackers ran away. And he lay there, weak, helpless, defeated.

Xalivar cursed the memory as he shook it off and refocused his attention out the vidscreen of the *Tarragon* as an armada assembled before him. On the lower deck, below where he stood, officers were filing into place at attention, prepared for an inspection, a word from their leader. None of them regarded him as weak, helpless, or a target for ridicule. They knew him only as fearless, ruthless, and formidable! And this time his sister wouldn't be rushing to his rescue either!

Everything he had, Xalivar had made happen by force of will and determination. He'd learned early on that emotions were weak, the province of fools and losers. He'd had some setbacks lately but only because he'd faltered. He had allowed Davi Rhii into his household without proper investigations. His weakness had allowed Miri's betrayal and going behind his back with the Council, media and others. And that had enabled the Council to throw him from power. Xalivar couldn't depend on anyone but himself. His family had betrayed him, even Miri. And, as he had as a child, Xalivar learned from his mistakes. Miri and Davi were not around to distract him. And his father and grandfather were long dead. No emotional connections or family ties would detract from his focus this time.

"The men are ready, my Lord," Lucius reported as he spun on his heels and stood at attention beside his leader.

Xalivar smiled. "Very good, General." The light sparkling off medals and emblems on the uniforms of the ranks assembled below sent waves of pride through Xalivar. This was the meaning of power, to have such forces ready at one's every command. Xalivar reveled in it for several minutes, taking deep breaths and enjoying the feeling as his lungs expanded and then exhaled.

"We await your words, my Lord," Lucius added finally, shifting as his eyes darted to examine Xalivar's face.

Xalivar nodded and stepped forward, raising his hand. The officers' heads turned as one to face him, their bodies frozen at attention. "My friends, we stand at the cusp of another historic day," Xalivar began. What would that eight-year-old think of him now? Obed was outcast. Buj a Council member with insignificant influence. Xalivar was a legend. As the men and women stared at him with rapt attention, he knew he'd already won.

"Okay," Farien whispered as he stepped away from the door and turned to Davi, "hit me hard, and make it look good!"

"My pleasure," Davi teased, but Farien looked like he thought Davi was serious. They clasped hands firmly and their eyes met. Neither spoke but Davi read the meaning clearly on his friend's face: *Gods, I hope this works!*

And then they were sparring, yelling, and punching each other like rowdy cadets.

Davi had forgotten how much strength Farien carried despite his shorter height. Of course, Farien was bulkier and always had been, but he quickly discovered Farien kept himself in really good shape.

"Ow." Davi grimaced, rubbing his jaw after a particularly sharp right hook from Farien's fist. "I thought we were faking," he whispered.

Farien grinned and whispered back, "Gotta look real." Then he raised his voice, taunting, "Have you really forgotten how I used to kick your ass in the school yard?"

"You didn't hit as hard then," Davi groused.

Farien chuckled. "You're just old, Rhii."

Davi growled and leapt at his friend.

"Hey, I was just kid—"

Davi's own fist silenced the remark as it landed in the soft center of Farien's stomach, causing him to hunch over, gasping for breath, his mouth open and his eyes watering as they locked on Davi.

It was Davi's turn to grin. He shrugged. "'Make it look good,' you said." He had to admit feeling a certain satisfaction as the tension between them dissipated with each punch.

Farien rushed at Davi, slamming him back hard against the cell wall. The dark surface gave with the force, making a loud popping sound. Was it metal? The paint and shadows had concealed it, and Davi hadn't taken the time to examine its makeup.

"Guards, get me away from this bastard!" Farien called out, winking as Davi landed on weak knees and bent to gather his own breath. Farien stumbled back a step as if fleeing.

"It was my dinner! You had no right!" Davi managed to call out after his lungs had recovered.

"You weren't eating it. Why should I starve?"

"Because it wasn't *yours*." On the last word, Davi threw himself at Farien again and both swung their fists, deliberately whirling and banging their bodies against the wall and door. Davi sensed Farien was feeling release from their fight as well, like a therapy to work out all their issues the only way they could.

Between his own grunts and groans and Farien's growls and shouts, he heard voices and footsteps in the corridor. Then the lock rattled and the door swung open. Two of the four pirates who'd attacked them at the Xanthian bar with the Krons stared at them, breaking into wide grins.

"Told you we should have shot them, Staggs," the taller, rounder one said.

Davi smelled the stench of sweat and ale on them and crinkled his nose.

"We did shoot them," Staggs replied. "But we should have set the blasters on kill, not stun."

Both chuckled, watching Davi and Farien continue to struggle.

"Who knew they'd fight over that mess Carlyle calls grub, eh?" Stevens said, sneering.

Farien's eyes met Davi's and he leaned forward toward the oncoming fist, just as they'd planned. Davi increased the strength behind the punch, and as it connected with Farien's chin, his friend flinched and snapped his head back harder than the force would have, falling on his back and curling into a moaning ball.

"Are you gonna stand there and watch him kill me?" he croaked.

Davi growled and ran toward Farien.

"Freeze!"

Davi looked up to see both pirates aiming blasters right at him. "He stole my meal!"

"He pushed it away and fell asleep," Farien protested.

"That grub ain't worth all this drama," Staggs said, shaking his head. "You leave him be."

"Come over here!" the taller pirate ordered, motioning with his blaster to Davi. He nodded to Staggs. "Check the other one."

Staggs hurried to kneel beside Farien as Davi slid sideways across the wall toward his taller companion, the big pirate's blaster panning and locked on his chest the entire time.

Farien moaned.

"Hold still there," Staggs instructed, examining the fallen pilot. "Couple scratches and bruises, Stevens. He shouldn't even be down." He scoffed and looked up at his friend. "What kind of wussies do they hire as pilots up there?"

At the same moment, Farien's foot swung up and connected with the underside of Stagg's chin, popping his head up and back hard with a loud crack as Davi threw himself on the other pirate's back.

The big one, Stevens, cursed, spinning and pounding at Davi with a closed fist on one side and the butt of the blaster in the other. Pain shot through Davi's shoulders, arms and back as the brute's fists found random targets. Davi squirmed and pulled, trying to get his arms in place around the pirate's neck but failing.

Farien rolled over on top of his opponent, pounding with his fists as Davi heard the smaller pirate moan and wheeze.

"Gods damn it, you leave him be!" Stevens yelled, continuing to twirl and pound at Davi.

Davi resorted to kicking the back of the man's legs to try and throw of his balance, still unable to get his interlocked fingers in place as a choke hold.

"You're both gonna die for this!" Stevens added with a deep growl, swinging and charging toward Farien as he did.

Davi winced and cried out as his legs swung hard against the door frame and back to slam against the brute's waist and legs again. Then Davi heard a laser blast and smelled burnt flesh as the big pirate's knees gave out and he tumbled to the floor, Davi clinging to his back.

Davi looked up to see Farien holding a smoky blaster with crossed arms and smiling. "What took you so long?"

Davi grabbed Stevens' blaster and jumped to his feet, motioning toward the door. "Shut up and hurry. With all the noise, there may be reinforcements coming."

Farien rolled his eyes. "You're welcome for saving your butt again."

"I had him under control," Davi replied as he followed his friend out into a dimly lit, narrow corridor. Doors lined the walls in both directions similar to the one they'd just passed through. "Which way?"

"I thought you were making the decisions," Farien said, looking at Davi.

Davi chuckled, motioning back to the left. "Tela must be in a cell like we were. Let's try down here."

They moved quickly, not quite at a run, stopping at each door and pressing the button. Door after door slid open, revealing small rooms with cots, a simple chair and desk, and closet. They looked like the private rooms awarded upper classmen at the Academy. Yet room after room turned up empty.

At the end of the hall, they turned back to head the other way, doing the same with the doors on that side until they reached the corner and stopped, peering around before continuing on. The corridor wound a bit in a snake-like pattern. Their footsteps echoed off the walls around them as they ran, causing Davi to slow his pace for fear the sound would draw more pirates to them. He felt the moistness as sweat formed on his skin and his chest tightened from drawing in air. He shifted his palm on the grip of the blaster, making sure he held it firmly.

They stopped and checked every door they came to with similar results, until they reached another long stretch comparable to the one into which they'd emerged from their cell.

"This is going to take forever," Farien muttered. He motioned with the tip of his blaster. "You take that side. I'll get these."

They tried the doors on opposite sides simultaneously, with Davi working the right and Farien on the left. Again, similar cots, chairs and desks but empty.

"Not even a cleansing room?" Davi wondered aloud. "And where is everybody?"

"Maybe they're out on a raid," Farien suggested.

Farien stopped at the next corner and motioned as Davi slowed to a stop beside him. Davi raised the blaster, ready to cover them, as Farien bent and stuck his head around the corner, low. "Clear."

Davi was around the corner fast as Farien stood and followed. "This place is like a maze."

Farien sighed. "We can try back the other way."

"No wait!" Davi hurried ahead toward the door he'd just spotted. Dark blue, unlike the others, it was thicker and wider and set back into the wall further. He pressed his ear up against it and listened as Farien turned back to cover their rear.

"Anything?" Farien asked.

Davi shook his head. "All clear."

"Here's hoping God's on our side, huh?" Farien said. Holding his blaster at the ready, he nodded for Davi to open the door.

Davi grabbed the handle and pushed. The door slid back into the wall as both friends aimed their blasters and moved side-by-side through the door frame, blasters aimed. No one was in sight. The room beyond was dark but clearly big as shadows to the left deepened. Davi caught glimpses of a wall running straight ahead from the door and a door on the far end.

Farien stopped. "Got a light?"

"Just head for that door," Davi said, indicating the opening directly across the room.

Farien nodded and moved on with Davi following.

As soon as they were through, the door slid shut behind them. "Help me find a switch for the reflector pads," Davi said as he searched the walls around them.

"She'd be in a cell not a room like this," Farien said.

"What if she's not and we miss her?"

Farien sighed. "Hello? Anybody there?" His voice echoed off the walls.

"As a matter of fact, 'yes,'" a baritone voice responded.

Then the reflector pads came on, illuminating the room in brightness and Farien and Davi found themselves staring at a rail thin man with well-toned arms and a body covered in tattoos, wearing only a Gungor-skin vest and dark fabric pants. Long, brown hair stretched down his back and thick, studded boots covered his feet. He looked at them with piercing blue eyes through a stubbly face. He looked about a decade older than them.

Davi and Farien aimed their blasters at him. "Who are you?" Farien demanded.

"You shall address me as 'my Lord,' while you're in my domain, thank you, and I'd drop the weapons, if I were you," the man replied, grinning.

Both the door through which they'd entered and the one opposite it opened as armed pirates poured through, blasters aimed, faces locked in angry glares.

Davi let the blaster slip from his hand as Farien spun to take in the new arrivals, slowly lowering his.

They were surrounded.

# Chapter Eleven

Klaxons blared and the bridge of *Reliance* erupted in chaos.

Uzah turned to see the targeting screens light up with blips representing large groups of ships closing toward the fleet from two directions.

"General!" Colonel Cardno called. "Multiple ships closing."

"I can see that," Uzah snapped. "Where'd they come from?"

It was unusual for a fleet so big to go unreported until they'd drawn so near. Clearly, the ships had come out of FTL very close to the fleet, but outer Vertullian pickets should have had it on radar several minutes earlier.

"Identification shows Boralian craft, sir," a radar tech nearby replied.

"Several picket ships are under fire, sir," a comm tech added, her face filled with panic as more and more faces around her began showing distress.

"Attack confirmed, sir!" Cardno reported.

Uzah frowned. All ships had transponders and the Boralians were using a specific code for their official ships. Why were Boralians attacking? "Launch fighters!" General Matheu ordered from nearby. "All civilian ships to the center and combat craft to intercept! And get us over there!"

Chatter filled the air combined with beeps from consoles and the whine of *Reliance*'s engines as she accelerated and moved out of position amidst the fleet to intercept the oncoming attackers.

Then the vidscreens flashed and colored bars appeared.

"Are we having a malfunction? In the middle of battle?!" Uzah almost yelled the words as he clenched his fists with growing frustration.

Then a familiar face appeared. The last face any of them expected, and chills spread throughout Uzah's body as the bridge went deathly silent.

"My dear friends," Xalivar said, his dark beard neatly trimmed, his hair as impeccably combed as always, and his smug smile as ominous as the tone of his voice. "You are under attack by forces of the Boralian Restoration. You have only minutes left to surrender or face annihilation. Order in this system has been disrupted by your rebellion for three years but the time has come to return to your proper place or face the consequences." Xalivar's face turned almost pensive, but Uzah knew it was all an act. "I do hope you make the right decision. Lord Xalivar out."

The comms lit up with cries of alarm as ships throughout the fleet called out in fright, reporting the message. The crew around him stuttered in silence a moment, appearing stunned then resumed their duties.

"How can that bastard still be alive?" Matheu muttered under his breath nearby.

"Contact the High Lord Councilor," Uzah ordered with deliberate calm. "Send the message, coordinates of our location, identification of attacking ships, and request immediate support from Boralian ships."

The comm techs went to work immediately as Uzah, Cardno, and Matheu gathered atop the dais.

"When Tarkanius warned us that ships had been stolen, I never expected anything like this," Matheu said.

"I don't think he realized how many defected," Uzah said.

"It must be half their forces," Cardno muttered.

"God be with us if it is," Uzah said and turned away. Half the Boralian fleet defected? Had they really made so little progress? Had all the High Lord Councilor's work failed so completely? There had seemed to be growing acceptance. But Xalivar was back with staggering support.

Uzah closed his eyes and did the only thing he could: he prayed.

Davi and Farien were immediately surrounded by pirates, growling, punching, kicking, and searching every inch of them, confiscating their weapons, and carrying on until Davi feared he'd be nothing but a giant walking bruise.

"Stop!" a powerful voice commanded.

When the pirates finally pulled away, they found themselves in a dark industrial space with walls about a meter from the center. In the actual center stood the rail thin man about Bordox's height with long, dark hair and well-toned arm muscles, tattoos covering much of his body. As hands pushed them forward toward him, Davi caught the scent of cologne and sweat emanating from him. The man looked every inch the pirate, except for his eyes which seemed softer than Davi would expect.

Davi and Farien stepped into the well-lit center to face the pirate leader, Bordox stepping up beside them. Pirates of all shapes and sizes surrounded them on every side, standing with arms crossed or leaning against the wall beams, eyes on them at all times.

"Going somewhere?" the leader asked in a menacing baritone.

"We got hungry," Farien snapped. "Your men haven't fed us in hours."

"We just fed—!" one of the pirates whined but was cut off by a raised palm from the leader.

"Who are these men?" the leader demanded.

"They're supposed to be our prisoners," Bordox growled.

"We found them nosing into our business on Xanthis outside a bar," a gruff voice said. Davi recognized it as one the men from the alley. The pirate had scruffy facial hair and a bald head, with tattoos covering every exposed bit of skin poking out from his ragged clothes. Muscular and menacing, his eyes seemed stuck in a permanent squint.

"Why are they still alive?" the leader said, cutting off any response with a raised palm as he stared at Davi and Farien.

"What do you want with us? Our people?" Davi demanded, keeping his tone calm but firm. "You've raided our fleet, killed our people, but kidnapping one of our pilots? That seems unusual, especially when you've made no effort to communicate demands."

The pirate leader's gut shook as he laughed, then he glanced at Bordox. "I can see why this one hates you. Eh, Pirate Bordox?"

Bordox grunted. "They have a long history of abuse against my people … and murder."

"Murder?" Farien scoffed. "You've got to be … you've killed as many or more of our people as we have of yours, and you've enslaved us for decades!"

Bordox backhanded Farien before he could even prepare, slapping his head as Bordox spat and scowled. "Mind your place, inmate!"

The pirate leader frowned, but not at Davi and Farien this time, at Bordox. "Pirate Bordox! What have I told you about how we treat prisoners?"

"They are spies, not prisoners," Bordox insisted. "Here to infiltrate and harm us, steal what's ours …"

The pirate leader silenced him with a raised palm, too. "I will decide what they are and why they came. Not you."

"This is about your long time personal vengeance against Davi and his family, Bordox," Farien said. "And you know it!"

"Where is she?" Davi demanded, glaring at Bordox.

The pirate lord stared at Bordox, his blue eyes narrowing. "Pirate Bordox?" Davi noticed the leader's voice soured each time he said Bordox's name. Perhaps the pirates didn't like him any better than anyone else.

"It's about opportunity," Bordox said. "That fleet is just waiting for us to raid and steal supplies, fuel, everything we need. Their presence is merely a conven—"

The pirate leader swung an arm harshly across his body dismissively. "Leave us!" he said loudly.

The other pirates began shuffling from the room as quietly as they could manage. Once they left, a sole pirate shut the door behind them and stood inside it, as if on guard as Bordox was left otherwise alone with the leader, Davi, and Farien.

Davi eyed the guard. About Farien's height, solid muscle, with missing front teeth, a bushy dark beard fanning out like a lion's mane, ragged clothes, and dirty hair, he looked every inch of the fairy tale menacing pirate badass.

The pirate leader cocked his head to one side as he looked Davi over, reading him. "You're here about the woman?"

"Where is she?" Davi said, failing to keep the urgency from his voice. "Can we see her?"

The pirate leader raised an eyebrow. "She means something to you, this woman, doesn't she? Who is she? Sister? Lover? Friend?"

"My fiancée," Davi said.

The pirate leader nodded. "Xander Rhii. He's spoken of you, you know." He nodded toward Bordox. "He doesn't like you."

Farien snorted as Davi nodded and replied, "I don't like him either, sir."

The pirate leader laughed and the pirate near the door joined him. "You make enemies wherever you go, don't you, Pirate Bordox?"

Bordox's face crinkled with frustration. "No, I have a lot of friends. I was very influential. My family is powerful."

Farien laughed. "Was once, not anymore. Fallen in disgrace, for the same deceit and scurrilous activities you see Bordox engaging in."

Bordox's face turned red as he stiffened and made to slap Farien again. "You can't believe these people! They lie, cheat, steal, live like animals …"

Farien spun and grabbed Bordox by the arm. The pirate guarding the door was on him in seconds, blaster held at Farien's temple, finger itching near the trigger.

"Never raise your hand against my people!" the pirate leader said with a narrow-eyed, menacing glare at Farien.

Davi felt helpless, with no idea of how to interfere or help his friend.

Farien released his grip on Bordox and stepped slowly backward, the menacing pirate moving with him, blaster tight against the pilot's temple. "I'm sorry," Farien muttered at almost a whisper.

The pirate lord clicked his teeth and nodded, and immediately his eyes widened, softer again and the guard's blaster was holstered as the man headed back for the door.

They all stood in silence for a moment, watching each other.

"I believe you," the pirate leader said, locking eyes with Farien then Davi.

Bordox looked ready to explode. "They deserve what they get. They're not even human—!"

"Do not raise your voice at me!" the pirate leader rushed forward, grabbing Bordox by the lapel and raising him a foot off the floor.

Bordox whitened with a look of fear like Davi had never seen on his face.

"Do not make me tell you again," the leader added, staring at Bordox with the same narrow-eyed glare, their faces inches apart. In seconds, he suddenly released him to fall back to the floor, stunned, as the leader turned and returned to his central place to face Davi and Farien again.

"They follow orders better than you do, Pirate Bordox," the pirate leader snapped. "I've warned you time and time again about how we treat prisoners—told you we don't kidnap. You brought this on us yourself. Men here looking for her. For all we know, the whole fleet will follow."

Bordox sputtered, starting to protest.

"Enough of this insolence. We've gotten none of the things you promised. No information from the woman. No chance to raid the fleet. Instead, we've had people track us and spread the word we traffic in humans, kidnapping—things which can hurt us, bring us more official interest than ever before, the kind we don't need. No, Bordox, I think it's you who lied. You who are cheating, costing men's lives. Enough!"

The last word cut off Bordox as he began protesting again.

"Bring the woman!" the leader ordered as he glanced over their heads toward the man guarding the door. "And find out how they escaped."

The man nodded and turned, opening the door a crack. "Bring the woman immediately," he ordered someone outside, then added, "And find their guards and check the cell. Report to me." After grunted affirmations from outside, he closed the door and turned to resume his position once more.

"What measures might your fleet take to recover you?" the pirate leader asked.

"They'll be here in an hour," Farien boasted. "Fighters, destroyers—"

"We're here on our own," Davi interrupted, shooting Farien a look before his friend could protest. "They have other concerns. Your raids have killed people, damaged ships, and set us back from our journey. We were on our way out of the system."

"You're leaving?" the pirate leader asked, an eyebrow curling upward to punctuate the question.

Davi nodded. "We need a new home." He glared at Bordox. "We are not welcome here."

The pirate leader smiled, almost sympathetically. "Then I could kill you all and no one would attack us?"

"We knew the risk when we came," Davi admitted.

There was a knock at the door and the menacing guard turned back to answer. He engaged in whispered conversation for a few minutes before stepping back. The door opened and Tela was shoved into the room. Her hair was disheveled, her eyes drained, but she looked a lot better than Davi had feared.

As their eyes met, she cried out his name and rushed toward him.

The menacing pirate started after her, but the leader waved him off.

Tela rushed into Davi's arm and he held her as she cried with joy. Farien grinned as Bordox glared from the opposite side.

"The two guards were found unconscious in their cell, but fine, my Lord," the door guard reported. "The weapons they had were theirs."

The pirate leader nodded, his face crinkling when the guard didn't step back into position. "There's more?"

The man nodded. "We've had a report of Boralian forces attacking the Vertullian fleet, my Lord. In great mass."

Davi and Tela parted and exchanged looks with Farien, but Davi motioned for them to remain calm. If the Boralians were attacking, there had to be an explanation. Could it be rogue forces again? This was no time to panic, despite the way his mind was racing at the news.

The pirate lord nodded. "Monitor and report anything essential," he said.

The guard turned back to the door and hurried out.

"It appears your welcome is over for good," the pirate leader said. "What assurance can you give me that your fleet will not come back here for vengeance if they should survive?"

"We're being attacked by the local forces," Davi said, trying to keep his own puzzlement from showing. "If they survive, they'll leave. We can't afford to stay."

The pirate lord locked eyes with them. "If I see you again, I will kill you." He held their gaze in glaring silence a few moments as a warning, then he coughed and looked to the door again. "Etan!"

The menacing pirate rushed into the room again. "My lord?"

"Have these three taken back to Xanthis and dropped there," the pirate lord said.

"What?!" Bordox's fists clenched in outrage. "You can't possibly let them go—!"

"Blindfold them so they cannot identify our location," the pirate lord continued, ignoring Bordox. "And leave Bordox to me." He glared now at Bordox with such menace that his protests were silenced.

Etan nodded and hurried forward, motioning for Tela, Davi, and Farien to go with him.

"Thank you for your mercy, my Lord," Davi said and nodded at the leader before turning to follow the others toward the door.

"This is insanity! Have you lost your mind?!"

The last thing Davi heard before they stepped out into a corridor packed with pirates and the door shut behind them was Bordox's whining protests. Then Etan led them away.

As soon as word of the attack on the Vertullian fleet reached the Palace, Tarkanius headed for the military complex by royal Floater, heading straight for the command center where he found General Grif under siege. He was surrounded by Tarkanius' most vocal opponents on the Council, led by Lords Quatol, Kanaan, and Adoo. Beeping consoles, chattering techs, and the smell of sweat, colognes, dust, and more filled his senses as Tarkanius strode up to the command dais to confront them.

"General, send all reinforcements we can spare to assist the Vertullian fleet," Tarkanius ordered, knowing the General would likely have already taken such action but wanting to add his endorsement.

"Belay that order, General!" Lord Quatol snapped immediately, glaring at Tarkanius.

"You have no power to overrule my direct orders," Tarkanius replied, glaring back. "What's the situation?" he asked, turning back to the General and ignoring the Councilors.

"They are outnumbered on both sides, mostly Boralian ships with a few others mixed in," the General reported. "The defections were worse than we feared. The total numbers equal over a third of our fleet."

Tarkanius' heart stopped. They'd known there were men and ships missing but this many? "They'll be slaughtered."

"That is not our problem," Lord Kanaan insisted. "And you will obey our instructions. We have a resolution from the Council giving us authority over military matters involving the Vertullians."

"What?!" Tarkanius turned, struggling to control his temper as he faced the Idolian Lord. "We held no such vote!"

"You were not in attendance," Lord Adoo said smugly, waving a datapad. "but we did vote. A quorum, in fact."

Tarkanius yanked the datapad from the other Lord's chubby fingers and quickly scanned its screen. "A quorum by two votes. And none of my supporters were represented in the vote. This is mutiny!"

"We did what we feel is in the best interests of our peoples," Lord Quatol said.

General Grif continued issuing orders behind him as Tarkanius faced off with the rebel Councilors.

"This is outrageous! Those people will die without our help!"

Several Lords shrugged as Kanaan said, "They abandoned us. It is not our concern."

Tarkanius took deep breaths, trying to collect himself as emotions raged within him. He felt heat rising and his fists clenched, but he struggled to relax and project calm, reasoned command. It was the only way to defeat them. "If we let them die, their blood is on our hands. And I won't stand for it!"

"You have no choice," Lord Adoo said, unflustered by Tarkanius' rage.

"General," Tarkanius turned back to Grif, about to utter words he'd sworn he'd never use while serving as High Lord Councilor, "Execute Code A136b. Immediately, please."

The General locked eyes with the High Lord Councilor. "Are you certain?" The look on his face was grave.

Tarkanius took another deep breath and nodded. "I have no choice."

General Grif nodded then and hurried to his console, typing in a code. Within minutes, armed security men appeared and surrounded the Councilors on the command dais.

"Gentlemen," the General commanded, "arrest these Councilors and hold them until further notice."

"What?!" the Councilors protested as the security men began gathering them and leading them away.

"You can't do this!" Lord Quatol protested.

"You're through, Tarkanius!" Lord Kanaan added.

Tarkanius ignored their further protests and turned back to the General. "Send everything we can spare to support the Vertullians, General. This is on me, not you. And send a message to Councilors Simeon, Qui, and Kray to join me here immediately."

The General grunted. "Yes, my Lord." Then spun and began firing off orders as Tarkanius pondered what had just occurred.

Code A136b had been part of a secret, a code established during Xalivar's reign as a precaution allowing him to take over various aspects of the military and government as needed. Code A136b, in particular, ordered arrest of the Council without cause should the High Lord Councilor overrule them. As far as Tarkanius knew, it had never been used, and although General Grif and his command staff were well aware of it, Tarkanius had sworn to himself he'd never use Xalivar's illegal code system. He'd spent his entire reign trying to erase all vestiges of Xalivar's illegal codes and activities and restore honor to the Palace and his office. But then nothing could have prepared him for this—a quorum held without his knowledge to deliberately overrule him in military command.

Traditionally, the High Lord Councilor had always been the commander-in-chief of the Boralian military. The Council served as advisors, of course, even voting on important decisions, but actual command was supposed to be left to whomever held the High Lord Councilor's office. These new Lords had been fighting him tooth and nail since the Vertullians declared their intention to leave, and it had been frustrating for sure. He knew their concerns, even shared some of them, but he would not stand by and watch the Vertullians die.

"My Lord?" the General's voice broke him out of his reverie.

"Yes, General?" Tarkanius turned to face his military commander.

General Grif motioned to a nearby monitor. "There's something you should see, a transmission that accompanied the Vertullian fleet's SOS call."

Tarkanius sighed even as his curiosity blossomed. His breathing had eased as tension left his body and he moved toward the General to join him at the monitor. "Show me, please."

Moments later, Tarkanius' heart stopped all over again when Xalivar's face filled the screen. He barely heard the rogue leader's threats, the voice evoking so many memories from when Tarkanius had led the Council and faced off against Xalivar.

*My gods, he's alive!*

Tarkanius knew then he'd done what had to be done. There was no other choice.

"What's that agro ship doing?" General Matheu demanded, disgusted. "Get him moving out of there!"

"Latest report from the fighters," Uzah said to a comm tech across the dais.

"Fifteen kills, eight losses," the tech replied.

*Reliance*'s bridge filled with the usual chaos of battle. Uzah shook his head. Despite the fact they were killing almost twice their losses, his fighters were losing and would be eliminated all too soon. Besides, the strength of the enemy's outnumbering ships lay in the larger ships anyway. With *Reliance* being one of only six major combat ready ships the Vertullians had, they were in big trouble.

"Any response yet from the Boralians?" he asked.

The tech shook her head. "Just acknowledgement of our message."

"Send it again," Uzah said, hoping the delay this time was due to communications issues, not betrayal. He trusted Tarkanius. The High Lord Councilor had always been supportive, but he also knew well the flack the leader had been taking from others on his Council and some in the media. Resentment due to problems caused by the Vertullian's departure was high. But still, Tarkanius had promised to help. What was taking him so long?

He turned and crossed the dais to the combat screens and watched the fighters, coming into range of the flight control comms.

"Ace, Nila, two on your tail," Jorek warned from his cockpit.

"We see them," Davi's cousin replied.

"We just lost Warren," Virun said sadly.

"We're getting our asses kicked," Jorek said. "Where are those Boralians?"

It was a rhetorical question, Uzah knew, but he still had to fight the urge to respond. Telling them he had the same question would not help morale. Right now, they needed to be strong and focused, and letting them believe help was imminent was the best encouragement he could give.

He smelled Matheu's cologne as the General came to his side. "Where are they?"

Uzah shook his head. "We resent the message."

"We can't hold out much longer," Matheu said. "Besides the fighters, we've lost two agro ships and three transports."

Uzah winced. Those numbers meant several thousand of their people—men, women and children—had just died in the past two hours. It horrified him to think about it, no matter how many battles he'd endured. This time civilians were directly in the line of fire like never before, and there was nothing either of them could do to prevent losses. Not without the Boralians.

"Start the ships moving," Uzah ordered, turning on a comm tech. "Close formation but toward sector 308."

Matheu and the tech both shot him puzzled looks.

"There are enemy ships there," the tech mumbled.

"You heard me," Uzah said and turned to lock eyes with the flight control techs. "Order all ships to concentrate fire on sector 308 as much as possible. We need to clear a path." He made sure his expression made it clear there would be no more argument.

"Yes, sir," the techs all replied in unison as they began sending their messages.

Uzah lowered his voice and turned to Matheu. "It's the weakest spot in their lines so far. We have to try something."

Matheu nodded. "I just hope it works."

"Me too," Uzah agreed. *Oh Lord, hear my prayer and grant your people victory today*, he pleaded internally and turned back to watch the vidscreens.

*The Tarragon*'s bridge had an energy of anticipation that had Xalivar's skin tingling and hot blood pumping through his veins. At last the Vertullians would pay for their deceit and betrayal! He had to stop himself from bouncing on his tiptoes.

As consoles humming with alarms and techs calling out reports and orders filled the air around him, Xalivar stood beside General Lucius on the upper level, watching the battle unfold.

"Our losses are minor so far, my Lord," Lucius said. "They've lost two agro ships and three transports."

"Aron's bleeding heart must be weeping by now," Xalivar said. He wished he could have seen their faces when his message took over their screens. "I knew they'd never surrender," he muttered then uttered a throaty laugh, feeling almost as gleeful as a child at play. He'd waited a long time for this day. The energy of the crew's bodies, the smell of their sweat and adrenaline, and the excitement in their voices combined to make him high.

"Any sign of my nephew?" Xalivar's fists opened and closed at his sides as he tried not to fidget.

"We've not picked up his voice on any comm channels so far," Lucius said. "He doesn't seem to be amongst those in the fighters."

Xalivar frowned. Xander was one of their best pilots. Why would they hold him back? Surely he was aboard one of the ships. Was he injured? Xalivar sorely wanted the satisfaction of watching him die.

"Stay on it," Xalivar ordered. "General Pres, are the men ready to board at the first opportunity?"

When he got no response, both Xalivar and Lucius began looking around. Where was the General? She should have been by their side or at a nearby station.

"Lieutenant, where's General Pres?" Lucius asked of a nearby deck officer.

The officer spun, nervous as always at drawing the attention of his superiors, especially Xalivar. "She left the bridge a few minutes ago. Something about checking her troops."

"She's inspecting her troops now? In the middle of battle?" Xalivar scoffed. General Pres had clearly lost her focus since Admiral Dek's death. Xalivar had thought of replacing her so many times, now he regretted not going through with it. "Find her!"

The Lieutenant winced at the vitriol in his Lord's voice. "Yes, my Lord!" He turned and hurried to a nearby comm station as Xalivar faced Lucius.

"This negligence has gone too far, General!"

"There must be an explanation," Lucius said. Despite Pres' recent failings, the General had always held her in high regard.

"It doesn't matter this time," Xalivar said. "Find her and have her brought here, by force if necessary. I've had enough of her unreliability."

Lucius grunted in affirmation. "Yes, my Lord."

As the General hurried off to launch the search, Xalivar turned back to the vidscreens, enjoying the explosions as another Vertullian fighter pilot met his fate and several fleet ships took more damage. He'd almost felt relief at their refusal to accept his terms of surrender. Inside, he'd known they would. The Vertullians were nothing if not a stubborn people. Insolent to the last. Stupid to a fault. It didn't matter. Xalivar was tired of their interference with the Boralians' rule and rightful place as their superiors. He'd rather kill them all anyway.

No more failures. No more waiting. This time, he had the forces he needed to make it happen. It would be a matter of hours. And once he had them, he'd take on the Boralians, certain that once they saw the size of the force they were facing and confirmed it was filled with their own, many Boralian commanders and soldiers would refuse to attack. Anti-Vertullian sentiment was on his side this time. They'd dug their own grave with the problems they'd caused in abandoning their former masters and hosts.

No. Xalivar's moment was ensured. All the frustrations and setbacks didn't matter. Soon, he'd be living in the Palace again, and those responsible would all pay with their lives.

As the rest of the pirates cleaned up the prisoners and prepared a ship to transport them back to Xanthis and freedom, Bordox fumed and slipped back toward the Pirate Lord's gathering chamber. The bastard had put everything Bordox had worked for to an end; he'd finally had Rhii! And yet Bordox had to hold his tongue and cower like a servant, a mere underling! He spat at the thought, his nostrils flaring. No. Not this time.

He slipped back inside the chamber quietly through a side door well hidden in shadows and waited. Etan and the Pirate Lord were having a discussion … *about him*!

"I say we end this and be done with the fool," Etan cringed, his lip curling as he wrinkled his nose.

The Pirate Lord stroked his throat with a palm and grimaced. "If he can learn his place …"

"This one never knew his place," Etan spat. "He couldn't find it with a map."

Both leaders guffawed and Bordox flushed, throat clenching, his body tensed, as he fought the urge to spring.

"I'll handle it, my Lord," Etan offered.

The Pirate Lord thought a moment then sighed, leaning back in his chair and offering a dismissive wave with the back on one hand. "Fine. But take him away from here first."

"Yes—!" Etan's response was silenced by the blaster beam that cut him in two.

Bordox hadn't even realized he'd drawn the weapon, but he quickly spun and aimed it at the Pirate Lord, hoping the rest of the pirates were too distracted elsewhere to hear the laser fire.

"What are you doing?!" the Pirate Lord demanded.

"Repaying my debts," Bordox growled.

"If you do this, you'll never make it out of here alive," the Pirate Lord growled. As usual, he was unarmed in his chambers, but his eyes darted down to Etan's corpse and the weapon holstered at his former aide's side.

"No!" Bordox snapped, rushing forward, waving the blaster. "I had them in my grasp, you stupid imbecile. Years of work undone by your ignorant fear."

"I fear nothing and no one," the Pirate Lord said defiantly.

Bordox cackled. "Fear me." And he pulled the trigger. Again and again and again.

Laser beams flew toward the Pirate Lord, severing an arm, a leg at the knee, cutting into his belly and then disintegrating his head. Bordox pulled on the guard's blasters he'd retrieved from a table outside, one Farien had been carrying when they captured him. He threw it on the ground at his feet and yelled, rushing for the door like a madman.

He burst through the door, deliberately staggering, to find several pirates, including Rufa, Stevens, and Staggs, rushing toward their Lord's chamber.

"What happened?" Rufa asked, his voice cracking with concern.

"Another Vertullian spy, one we hadn't uncovered," Bordox said through forced breaths. "He shot our Lord and Etan!"

"What?!" Staggs replied as all three drew their weapons and rushed into the chamber.

"My God!" he heard Stevens exclaim even as the alarm began ringing throughout the complex and other pirates rushed to respond.

Bordox bided his time. If he slipped away too fast, he'd risk raising their suspicions. As much as he longed to chase down the ship carrying Rhii and his friends, he knew one of the fighters could easily overtake it. First, he had to sell his story.

He turned back to join the pirates, rushing into the chamber, just another grieving pirate, mourning the loss of a great man. "We've got to find the murderer before he escapes!"

Inside, he smiled brighter than the twin suns.

# Chapter Twelve

Davi watched the pirate ship lift off and depart as he stood with Farien and Tela in one of the Xanthis starport's bays. "Let's get to our fighters," he said, hurrying toward a nearby corridor. After the artificial gravity on the pirate's base, it took them all a moment to get their feet under them and move smoothly. As soon as they entered the corridor, laser blasts exploded against the walls around them.

All three ducked, rolled, and pulled a blaster, looking for cover, even as they ducked low and turned to see who was firing at them.

"Who is it?" Tela asked.

Smoke from charred walls obscured their view. "I can't see them," Davi replied, squinting to protect his eyes and aiming his blaster to fire several bolts back through the smoke.

"Do you think there's more than one?" Farien asked as he and Tela also fired in the same direction.

Bordox glared through the smoke at his old rival and enemies. He'd almost caught them before they landed, then decided an ambush on the ground would be more effective. Besides, attacking the pirates seemed unwise, in case he needed them later. His heart drowned almost everything: pounding, his body tense, and his anger so sharp it hurt. But that hurt was nothing compared to what he'd feel if these three escaped him yet again.

As the trio's laser blasts struck the floor and ceiling around him, he fired off three quick blasts straight toward where each shot had come from and then dashed forward, hugging the wall to find a new position.

*You're mine, Xander Rhii, at last!*

Davi and his friends had to dodge the return blasts that headed right for them, then turned and raced down the corridor in the opposite direction. The smooth, white walls offered nowhere to hide or shield themselves. Their best move was to get away, if they could, while the smoke concealed their movements. Random laser blasts followed them as they ran.

Then Davi heard footsteps pounding after them through the smoke and turned back as they rounded a corner, signaling for the others to hold fire as he poked his head around to spot their attacker.

Moments later, Bordox cleared the smoke, spotted Davi, and began blasting away, chipping pieces out of the wall as Farien and Tela fired quickly, then all three went back to running along the next corridor.

"Bordox," Farien said as they went. "We should have known."

"I thought they'd have taken care of him," Tela said.

"The bastard has nine lives," Farien said. "Like a quat."

Davi cursed to himself as they came to an intersection and split, concealing themselves partially behind the walls on each side and readying their blasters to fire the minute Bordox came into view. Davi could almost smell his old classmate's rage. It emanated off him like radiation, his face twisted, his mouth a vicious scowl.

"He never gives up," Davi muttered. He himself felt varied emotions from anger to sadness to resignation. Bordox would never stop. They would have to stop him, maybe kill him. Despite their history of rivalry, Davi had never wanted it to come to that, but Bordox was leaving them no choice.

"Sore loser," Farien snapped. The corridors were growing hotter from the blasting. Local security might appear at any moment, or so Davi hoped. He wiped his brow a moment as his eyes stayed locked on the corridor the way they'd come.

Then Bordox appeared in another opening to their right and they opened fire, singeing his shoulder as their nemesis slid to a stop and reversed course back the way he'd come, cursing all the while.

"Where is everyone?" Tela asked, looking around them. The corridors were surprisingly empty.

"We must be in one of the older sections," Davi said as he pointed behind him and aimed his blaster again, letting off covering fire as Tela and Farien jumped across to join him. Then they all raced up the corridor again away from Bordox.

Bordox cursed as his shoulder burned with pain. Entering the smoke again, he leaned tight against a wall and examined the wound. His shirt had been burned away and his upper arm was bleeding but it was a flesh wound. He was fine. The irony smell of his own blood and the sourness of burned flesh filled his nose as he growled.

Angrily, he fired blindly back toward his attackers and cursed. When no return fire came, he slowly moved forward again in pursuit, thinking about the layout of the starport, something the pirates had taught him well. If he could get around in front of them …

He grinned as he got an idea, then turned and darted back out into the nearest bay at full speed.

"We don't want to take him on in crowded areas," Tela said, thinking aloud as they moved through another landing bay. Mech-bots worked busily around them, servicing ships, beeping and whirring as they communicated with each other and their controllers elsewhere in the starport. "He won't care about shooting civilians."

Davi nodded as they stopped briefly beside several exits, choosing a route. His eyes met hers. "Are you okay? When I think about what he did to you—"

Her hand caressed his cheek as her eyes sparkled with love. "I'm fine, babe. You saved me."

"You two wanna kiss already before he catches up?" Farien teased.

Tela punched his arm as Davi laughed.

Davi nodded toward the middle corridor in front of them. "This way."

"Do you know where you're going?" Tela asked as she and Farien followed him.

"Oh sure," Farien snapped. "Davi and I are right regulars around here."

This corridor appeared like all the others, only there were a few mechanics and service people moving about. Something looked familiar and Davi realized he and Farien had been here before.

"Isn't this—?" Farien started to say.

Davi gave a nod and a grunt in affirmation. "This way!" He raced on with the others close on his heels.

Bordox arrived at the main intersection and waited for his prey, the civilians and workers moving around him, ignored.

He had one single focus: final revenge on Xander Rhii.

The plaza-like area was filled with shops and ticket terminals, the sound of vendors bargaining and calling out to passerby mixing with the smells of their wares—perfumes, meats, spices, grains, and more—all of it of barely noticed by Bordox.

But then Xander and his companions didn't show. After glancing at his chrono, he cursed. It had been too long. Clearly they'd taken a detour. Now he had to backtrack.

He raced toward the corridor where they should have emerged, pushing pedestrians aside as he went, then had a thought and stopped quickly at a nearby terminal. The pirates had also taught him a few hacking skills during his time with them.

His fingers raced across the keys as he pounded in commands, pulling up records of ships parked there and their various locations. He scrolled through several screens before finding what he was after: two VS20 fighters in a private bay just off the main landing zone. *VS20s? Those are relics.*

He searched again for other VS fighters but found nothing. Surely the Vertullians were using newer models. Had they come by shuttle?

The computer found no record of Boralian shuttles landing in the past few days. The VS20s had to be it.

Bordox slammed a button to pull up a map of the route to the small, private bay, then raced on into the corridor, knocking aside more passersby but ignoring their protests. He had to get there before his prey.

Davi, Farien, and Tela entered the small private bay in the starport's busiest zone and began inspecting the two VS20s—right where Davi and

Farien had left them. Davi and Farien typed codes into their datapads to lower the security force fields so they could approach. While Davi did walk around inspections, Tela and Farien hopped into the cockpits to run preflight checks.

"Fueled and ready," Tela called.

"Here, too," Farien echoed.

Tela stood and began removing panels to uncover the rarely used jump seat behind Davi's own, storing the extra panels in the small cargo spaces beneath the cockpit.

"Contact control and let them know we're leaving," Davi said to Farien as he finished his inspections of the ship's exteriors.

The smell of dust and fuel mixed with that of their own sweat as they worked, and the tension eased from Davi's body in relief that they'd managed to elude Bordox.

Davi found nothing wrong with the ships externally. The mech-bots and maintenance personnel had clearly let them be except for the refueling. The force fields had been designed so mech-bots could penetrate but not living beings. This protected ships left for long periods unattended in non-military bays while still allowing routine maintenance. Even so, the bots could have been corrupted or reprogrammed to reveal codes or lower the fields. In a place with as active a black market as Xanthis, neither pilot had been sure when they left them that they'd ever see them in one piece again.

As Davi reached the base of the ladder and saw Tela settled into the jumpseat, he smiled, glad to be taking her home safe and sound. Then as his foot touched the first rung, the air exploded.

Whirling and reaching for his blaster as he ducked for cover, Davi heard Farien and Tela calling out as he saw Bordox, firing from the doorway.

Davi returned fire as Bordox darted around, firing up at the cockpits and then at Davi from various angles, seeking to hurt anyone he could.

Tela fired from the jump seat, using the cockpit shield for cover as best as possible and Farien returned fire as well from his own fighter.

Blaster fire singed the wing of Davi's fighter and ricocheted off Farien's cockpit shield, forcing Farien to duck, cursing.

Davi heard the hum of Farien's engines starting up and the whine of servos as his cockpit shield closed. Surely Farien wasn't abandoning them. What was his plan?

As Davi and Bordox exchanged fire, Tela darted forward over the back of Davi's seat and flipped a switch to start his ship's engines, then ducked back down in the jumpseat just as a blast from Bordox's blaster struck the fuselage just below the cockpit opening.

"You're outnumbered, Bordox," Davi called, looking to distract his nemesis so he could climb up to the cockpit.

"And you're trapped, Rhii!" Bordox yelled back, grinning as he ducked behind maintenance drums and kept firing rapid blasts in Davi's direction. Bolts singed the fighter's undercarriage and then exploded against the floor and walls of the bay nearby.

"You're still a lousy shot," Davi taunted as he fired back twice.

"I only need one good one," Bordox replied and fired again even as Davi's blasts exploded one of the barrels he was using for cover.

Then the whining of Farien's engines grew and his VS20 was lifting into the air as the door overhead rolled back, revealing the sky overhead. Farien was actually leaving?

Farien opened fire at Bordox's hiding place with his front cannons, obliterating the barrels and cutting into the bay floor and walls as Bordox dove, rolled, and ran to escape, diving back out through the door into the corridor.

Davi shook his head. It was extremely risky to fire inside a bay, especially one so small, but Farien looked down as his fighter continued to lift and winked as his friend climbed the ladder and settled into his own cockpit.

"Is he crazy?" Davi muttered as he donned his helmet.

"You're just now noticing?" Tela cracked over the private comm.

Bordox leaned in and fired again from the corridor as armed starport security men appeared around him, trying to determine what was happening. Soon, they were pointing their weapons at him and grabbing his blaster as Bordox cursed and struggled.

Davi punched the controls and the cockpit shield began lowering with the whine and hiss of servos as he lifted off into the air to follow Farien.

The last sight he and Tela saw from the cockpit was Bordox shaking his fist skyward and struggling against ten starport security men, who were trying to apply restraints. Davi half-expected Bordox's eyes to explode from fury.

Then Davi's ship cleared the walls and entered clear air and he followed in Farien's wake, accelerating toward the planet's atmosphere and space beyond.

"These codes existed the entire time Xalivar held the Palace?" Lord Kray repeated, her voice loudening with anger at every word. "It's an outrage!"

"Gods know how many times he used them against us," Lord Qui agreed.

They'd gathered with Tarkanius, Lord Simeon, and Pharah Brahma in a small, private conference room just off military command as soon as they'd arrived, following General Grif's summons.

Tarkanius leaned back in his chair at the head of the table, his eyes sad. "Some of them date back to the time of his father's and grandfather's reign. And I imagine they used them more often than we'd like to think."

"How'd you discover them?" Simeon asked.

"The codes were in a book found amongst things in his private vault," Tarkanius explained. "I've been going over them with my secretaries as time allowed. I was planning to destroy them, as soon as I figured out how to negate their use by any military or civilian leaders privy to them. Naturally, it's not something we'd want made public."

Pharah nodded. "Especially with confidence in the Council presently at an all-time low."

The others looked at Tarkanius with sympathy despite their anger, settling back in their seats to think.

"And now Xalivar has gathered traitors en masse and launched attacks," Lord Qui said. "He must not be allowed to succeed."

The others offered mumbled agreement.

"Where are Lord Adoo and the others being held?" Simeon asked.

"In high security, secret cells below us for now," Tarkanius said. "But that can't last forever."

"You did the right thing, my Lord," Kray said, locking eyes with his. "We can't let them go around undermining your command any time they please."

"Others on the Council may not agree," Tarkanius said, wishing he shared her confidence.

"Hold them until we've had a chance to talk with them or at least until we've dealt with Xalivar," Simeon said. "My gods, the man has more lives than a quat!"

Tarkanius simply nodded. He knew he'd done the right thing locking up the mutinying Lords, but he also knew that in the end, they'd succeed in undercutting his power and confidence in him with the Council. Once word got out of their detainment, he'd have a lot of work to do to restore their faith in his leadership, and the press would go to town on him and the rest of them—making a mockery of the Council, questioning everything they'd done since Xalivar was removed, and lending further fire to the flames of discontent already burning amongst their people.

Lord Kray's datapad beeped, breaking them out of their reverie. The Lord touched the screen and navigated to an incoming message, then read quickly. Her eyes scanned and rescanned the message several times as she sat forward with alarm.

"My gods!" she exclaimed, looking up to meet their curious stares. "I've just confirmed who owns the mysterious Xizor Agricultural Corp."

The other Lords sat forward with interest. "Who?" Pharah Brahma asked.

"Well, it's buried under several shell investment firms and shell corporations, but they all lead to Obed," she said, sighing deeply as her anger grew again.

"Obed?" Tarkanius muttered, as shocked as the rest.

Kray nodded. "When our inquiries through proper channels turned up nothing, I kept digging. Obed's not the only one with connections, and ours like us better and trust us more. He hid it well, but not well enough."

"He's outmaneuvered us again," Simeon snapped.

Kray nodded. "He controls prices and shipments, and he's creating demand, benefitting himself, giving him power. He's managed it despite our close supervision."

"Arrest him! Now!" Tarkanius snapped forward in his chair, letting anger fill his voice again for the second time in a few months before the Council. He'd always considered calm, collected leadership the best route to success and the confidence of others and rarely showed his emotions before his staff or the Council. But this time fury radiated off him like the rays of the twin suns.

"You have our complete confidence, Tarkanius," Simeon assured him. "None of this is your fault. We all thought Xalivar dead and Obed neutered. They will be stopped."

Tarkanius scooted back his chair and quickly stood. "You stay here and coordinate with the General, Simeon and Pharah," Tarkanius commanded. "Kray, Qui, and I have an appointment with Obed."

He whirled and raced from the room without waiting for further comment. The others present exchanged urgent looks then stood and followed.

Pres met Manaen on the *Tarragon*'s war bridge, a smaller, more compact command center at the ship's center, more heavily shielded and protected by outer layers of hull and multiple decks than the huge, standard bridge from which Lucius and Xalivar were operating.

Pres' heart raced as she awaited the majordomo's arrival for several moments. Their moment was at hand: a great risk, a great betrayal. She'd long ago decided she had no choice, but that didn't make it any easier. The cost would be many fewer lives than if they let Xalivar continue with his madness. That he'd not detected them or shown suspicion surprised her, particularly given her absences from the bridge, but she supposed her gender and the fact she was mourning Dek made him write it all off as weakness. Fine by her. For once, being looked down on for her gender didn't bother her. She was about to evoke justice for decades of wrongs.

Manaen arrived, datapad in hand, and handed it to her, a list of codes pulled up on the screen. "Here they are, Xalivar's private override codes. If he gets on the comm personally, we may fail, but until then, these will get it done."

Their plan was to isolate the *Tarragon* by ordering all other ships away from her. Then, jam their fleet's internal communications. Finally, if the Vertullian fleet and their Boralian allies didn't destroy her, Pres and Manaen would enter a self-destruct sequence and destroy the ship and all aboard. With the *Tarragon* gone, the rebel fleet would be cut off at the head and fall into chaos and disarray, allowing the Vertullians and their allies an advantage that just might be enough to overcome them.

Pres had searched and searched for options which would isolate Xalivar himself and punish him alone. But in the end, they decided he'd never leave in the middle of a battle, putting himself in more jeopardy, not without taking his ship along. So, the only way to defeat Xalivar was to destroy this ship.

"Gods help us all," Manaen muttered as he read the screen over her shoulder.

Pres rushed around logging on two command consoles and preparing them for code entry, then motioned for Manaen to sit in front of one. He looked far more relaxed than she'd expect from someone unfamiliar with such systems as he did so. Pres herself was stiff as a board with tension. It seemed as if her heartbeat was loud enough to be heard several planets away.

Motioning to the keyboard, she said, "You enter each code here followed by a comma then the ship command code. Then send it and start the next."

Manaen nodded. "The prompt will return each time?"

Pres nodded. "Until you switch modes, yes." She took her place at the other console then passed Manaen another datapad with a separate list. "You work on these ships, I'll take these."

"Certainly."

"If you have any trouble, ask me before you send," Pres warned him. "One mistake will raise suspicions. We have to get this right the first time."

Manaen smiled. "Fear not, General. I've been working for Xalivar a very long time." Meaning mistakes weren't tolerated and he'd long ago learned not to make them.

Pres grunted in affirmation. "Gods bless us all indeed."

With that their fingers began dancing across the keyboards.

Xalivar had a spring in his steps unlike anything he'd experienced in years as he watched, through the *Tarragon*'s bridge vidscreen, his forces decimating their Vertullian enemies. All but two Vertullian ships had taken damage under Xalivar's fleet's onslaught, and they'd already lost a third of their fighters as well. He glanced around him, feeling waves of success and satisfaction emanating off the *Tarragon*'s crew and officers. *Yes, my friends, whatever doubts you had, welcome to the winning side!* Now, he hoped they wouldn't let him down.

"Concentrate fire on *Reliance*, General," he instructed Lucius who stood on the dais nearby. "If we conquer her, the rest will fall." Tension mixed with excitement and the smell of sweat and adrenaline as every crew member hustled, chattering, operating controls and consoles, all dedicated and focused on one task: restoring Xalivar to his rightful place.

General Lucius grunted and issued the orders. "We have men moving into position now, ready to board at the first breach."

Xalivar's palms rested flatly against his thighs. He'd never experienced such calm, such a sense of ease. It was finally happening. Success was certain. "I want them flooding her," Xalivar added. "And open multiple breaches as soon as we can."

"Of course, my Lord," Lucius said. They both knew the plan—take *Reliance* out or under control and the rest would fall apart or flee, making them easy pickings for his forces.

Xalivar frowned again as he looked around for his other General, the one responsible for ground forces. "Where is General Pres, Lucius? Why has she not returned?"

Lucius' eyes were nervous but he managed to meet his lord's gaze, even as he lowered his voice to respond, "I have men searching for her. She was inspecting troops and transports, but she should have returned long ago."

Xalivar cursed, a foul taste on his tongue as his confidence changed to worry. "I knew she wasn't ready. Find her *now* and bring her to me!"

Lucius nodded and began issuing curt orders over the comm to his ship's security detail.

Wherever she was, whatever she was doing, Xalivar wanted her found immediately. He hadn't really trusted her since Dek's death and if she were up to something nefarious, he'd put a stop to it. Even if he had to find her himself.

"Scan our ship if you have to, General," Xalivar said. "I'm tired of waiting. She hasn't responded to pages or queries for a reason. I want to know why."

Lucius saluted. "Yes, my Lord."

Xalivar fought the urge to say more. Grousing at his commander would only distract the man from his other duties, the important job of coordinating the attack to destroy the Vertullians. If Pres didn't turn up soon, Xalivar would go look for her himself. For her sake, he hoped that wasn't necessary. He was beginning to think her usefulness had run its course. Perhaps it was time to eliminate her.

The mood on *Reliance*'s bridge was somber. With damage afflicting every ship in the fleet, with a couple of minor exceptions, and the loss of a third of their fighters and pilots, the Vertullians were losing and they all knew it. Distress calls were coming in from all over the fleet—panicked crews and civilians crying out, pleading for rescue. But Uzah had none to offer. His own ship was in trouble itself.

To make matters worse, Joram and his supporters had commandeered a shuttle and were demanding to be taken to civilian ships to offer support for the population. No matter how many times Uzah told them they'd be shot out of the sky if they tried, the Councilor wouldn't give up.

"We have an obligation to protect these people," Joram insisted again, his face filling a small vidscreen on the command console, urgency in his eyes.

"We're trying to protect them, but we can't do that when we're trying to protect suicidal Council members off on some harebrained mission of comfort!" Uzah finally snapped, yelling at the screen and eliciting concerned looks from techs and officers around him, including General Matheu.

"Watch your tone with me, General!" Joram replied, scowling.

"Then stop wasting my time with this," Uzah snapped. "You have my answer!" He punched a button on the console next to the vidscreen and it went dark. He cursed to himself and took a deep breath as he turned his attention back to his other duties.

"He'll make you pay for that," Matheu said, amusement in his voice.

"He's been making me pay for it ever since he joined the Council," Uzah said. "If we survive this, I may just retire."

"Oh, I have seniority on that dream, General," Matheu teased.

"Order the most damaged transports in closer so we can provide cover fire," Uzah spun and said to Colonel Cardno, who waited nearby. "And under no circumstances is that shuttle to be allowed to leave this ship!"

Cardno nodded. "Yes, sir!"

"Where are those Boralians?" Uzah groused.

"We just got word that their fleet is in route," Cardno said, turning back from issuing the orders to the technicians nearby.

"How soon will they arrive?" Uzah demanded, his heart threatening to beat its way free of his chest. He was soaked in sweat, despite mostly standing still for the past several hours. His hair was disheveled and his eyes surrounded by dark circles. He imagined he'd aged several years as well. Those around him didn't look much better either.

"Within the hour is the best estimate we have," General Matheu said.

"God help us, I hope we can survive that long," Uzah said, lowering his voice so only his fellow leaders could hear.

Lights flashed on a nearby screen as the deck vibrated violently and several people called out; others fell. *Reliance* had taken another direct hit.

In the aftermath, the bridge returned to chaotic activity all around the dais.

"Fire in landing bay Alpha," a Lieutenant called out.

"We have hull breaches in sections Alpha, Beta, and Gamma, sirs," another tech reported.

"Alpha? Isn't that where the Councilors are boarding that shuttle?" Matheu asked.

Uzah pursed his lips. "I hope they're still alive. I'd better go evacuate personally. They won't obey anyone else."

Matheu offered no reaction, simply saying, "They don't obey you."

"They will if I have to drag them out by their toes," Uzah mumbled.

Matheu chuckled at the image. "Good luck."

Uzah grunted and rushed for the stairs. "I'll be in the landing bay. Colonel, you have joint command until I return."

"Yes, sir," Colonel Cardno called after him as Uzah headed for the nearest lift.

Sol and Aron continued doing their best to convince Joram and his supporters to give up their foolhardy quest even as the launch bay rocked with explosions. They'd been volunteering their skills as mechanics when the Councilors arrived to cause trouble and they overheard Uzah's continual refusals to accommodate them. Personally, Sol was surprised Matheu hadn't just stepped in and thrown Joram et al in the brig. The commander was even less tolerant of politics and civilian interference than his counterpart, a major reason why Uzah served as primary military contact with the Council. But given the circumstances, Sol figured both men must be fed up.

Sol struggled to stay on his feet as another explosion struck *Reliance*'s hull, even closer to the landing bay. The deck rumbled beneath them, and Aron grasped Sol's shoulder to steady himself even as a few of Joram's companions fell to their knees. Dust and debris floated down from the ceiling high above, and then klaxons blared around them as emergency lights flashed.

"Hull breach!" someone shouted, another mechanic or worker.

More thundering vibrations and a few distant explosions followed leading to a high pitched, slow metal creaking sound, almost as if the hull were tearing apart around them.

Sol cringed and exchanged a glance with Aron.

"What's happening?" Joram demanded, far more boldly than circumstances should inspire.

"We need to get to safety," Aron replied, grabbing Joram's arm and shoving him toward the nearest lift. "Go, now! The hull has been breached. It's not safe here!"

Joram yanked his arm free and motioned to his supporters. "We'll wait on our shuttle. All the more reason we should be taking off, not arguing against an insolent General!"

"He's trying to save your lives!" Sol exclaimed, finally overcome with his exasperation.

Joram ignored them both and ushered his supporters onto the shuttle as the decks continued trembling beneath their feet, making their every step perilous and difficult.

Sol shook his head as his eyes met Aron's. Neither had seen combat for decades and Sol could tell from the look in his best friend's eyes that both realized it had been far different when they were younger. "Let's go," Sol said, pulling Aron toward the lift. Mech-bots whirled around their feet, continuing with their duties, oblivious to any concerns borne by their human counterparts, but Sol saw other mechanics and workers headed for lifts throughout the bay.

Then they heard screams, more explosions and blaster fire and smoke began clogging their throats and noses, causing them to cough and sputter as they ran.

"Who's firing weapons on board?" Aron muttered.

Sol realized immediately *Reliance* had been boarded, and rushed Aron more quickly toward the lifts. "They've found a way aboard."

"What?!" Aron's voice cracked as he turned back toward the shuttle. "We've got to get the others."

"There's no time!" Sol insisted.

As they stepped on the lift, blaster fire exploded against a nearby wall. Both men turned to see armed men in dark uniforms storming into the bay, shooting at anyone in their path and a few mech-bots to boot. A few crewmen and pilots exchanged fire but they were badly outgunned, as no one came prepared for hand-to-hand fighting in the landing bay.

Sol changed course, his breathing slow and deliberate, and went for the nearest weapons locker, retrieving two blasters and handing one to Aron. "Do you remember how to use these?"

Aron shook his head. "We can't hold them off alone."

"We have to try something to slow them down," Sol said and took cover behind the edge of the lift platform and began firing at the enemy soldiers. Two fell immediately as Aron took a place nearby, then several other soldiers turned their fire toward the new threat. The blaster handle felt at home in his hand, unexpected given he hadn't held one in so long—his blasts were at least hitting targets.

Sol heard the whine of servos and the smell of engine fumes as he continued firing, spotting Uzah and several officers arriving on another lift across the way. He considered calling out a warning but then their eyes widened and they drew weapons as enemy soldiers began targeting them with fire, too.

"Reinforcements just arrived," Sol called and began looking for a way to reach the General.

"Where are you going?" Aron asked as Sol inched along the back side of the lift.

"We'll be stronger in numbers," Sol replied.

Aron scoffed. "We're too old for this, Sol."

Sol laughed. "I'm tired of being a victim. If I go out, at least it'll be hurting them as they hurt me." He moved faster now, stopping just at the other side of the lift as his eyes searched for the safest route to dart across and join Uzah and the others. The lift bearing them had now settled to the floor and they came out firing, taking down several more enemies, as they scattered and sought cover behind ships, pillars, and anything they could find.

Sol felt energized like he hadn't in years and grinned. "The kids'll be impressed when they hear about this."

Aron shook his head. "Or they'll have us committed." Then he fired at an enemy soldier who stepped out from cover to move closer and sliced the man in two across his middle, sending him flying backward in two pieces with no time to even scream.

Sol grunted. "Nice shot."

Davi's VS20 rocked from nearby explosions slamming his shoulder painfully against the cockpit hull as he dodged enemy fire and entered the boundaries of the fleet, headed for *Reliance*. He winced but kept his focus.

Farien's amused voice came over the comm as he followed close behind. "Nothing like coming back to the fun, eh?" Then he yelped as he let loose a spray of cannon fire and decimated two enemy fighters within seconds of each other.

"Sometimes I think he enjoys this a bit too much," Davi muttered. His own cannons opened up and it took him a moment to recover from the shock as he realized Tela was controlling them from the rear. Another enemy fighter soon met its fate in a yellowish orange flash of disintegrating particles.

"Why should he have all the fun?" Tela teased.

Davi laughed as he steered his ship into a twisting dive to avoid two enemy ships attempting to lock onto his tail. At the same time, Farien braked and shot backwards behind the two enemies, firing on them with his cannons. One took damage to a wing, the other tried to dodge and inadvertently slammed into its companion, exploding them both.

"Who trains these idiots?" Farien cracked.

"Not us," Tela replied.

Davi frowned. Was this the same Tela he'd been engaged to for two years? She was enjoying this far more than he remembered. "Having fun?" he asked on their ship's private comm.

"We've had a few adventures together," she replied and he could hear the smile in her voice.

Uzah motioned for the other officers and security men accompanying him to form a phalanx around him so he could get to the two trapped Councilors and protect them as they fought together against the invading troops.

So far, the enemy numbers had dwindled a bit but Uzah felt sure they had landed a ship in the next bay over because the hull breaches weren't viable sources of entry for ground troops without compression suits, which none of these soldiers had.

As Uzah and his companions fired at the remaining attackers, Sol and Aron did their best to fire as well. Their efforts were impressive considering neither man had likely fired a gun in two decades, but Aron was clearly intimidated at the experience and Sol, while seeming confident, was clearly out of practice. He'd hit a few soldiers out of luck when they first entered en masse, but now their dwindling numbers found most of his shots missing the mark.

"Where are Joram and the others?" Uzah shouted as his phalanx hurried across the open floor toward them. Aron was soaked with sweat but Sol barely showed any sign of stress.

"In the shuttle," Sol replied.

Uzah's companions kept up a constant stream of fire until they slid in beside the two Councilors behind a couple of maintenance trailers parked in the middle of the landing bay floor. Blaster bolts landed around them as the enemy returned fire, causing smoking craters in floors and pillars or damaging the carts and surrounding tools and equipment.

Uzah shook his head, his nose detecting the smell of burned flesh and smoke from further out in the bay. "A little beyond your usual Council duties, isn't this?"

Aron nodded somberly as Sol grunted. "We took a few out, though," Davi's father said with clear pride.

Uzah laughed. "Let's get you out of here."

All three ducked as more blaster fire struck the wall above their heads. Debris and dust fluttered down around them as they brushed the smoke away with waving hands.

"If they get to the shuttle ..." Aron started to say.

Uzah cut him off with a nod to his men. "Keep the area around that shuttle clear of the enemy as best you can, until we can move closer. We have Council members aboard."

"Maybe we should toss them blasters," Sol teased.

"They might shoot one of us," Uzah joked back. Grabbing the two Councilors by the shoulders, he shoved them back toward the lift. "You'll have to lie on the floor as it rises, but let's get you two to safety."

"We want to help," Sol insisted.

"You'll help most by relieving me of worrying about you right now," Uzah said as the men laid down cover and he escorted the Councilors to the lift, pushing them along as gently as he could, all three keeping as concealed as they could manage in the process.

"Thank the Lord you arrived," Aron said. His eyes were filled with gratitude.

"How'd they get aboard?" Sol asked.

"We're trying to determine that," Uzah said as they reached the lift, despite increased fire from enemy soldiers who'd spotted their movement.

All three men ducked down on bent knees as several bolts flew overhead and hit the wall behind the lift with flashing explosions. Aron winced, but Sol and Uzah just waited calmly for it to finish.

"I've never felt more alive," Sol confessed.

Uzah smiled. "Well, Aron looks ready to faint, so get him clear."

Sol shrugged and rolled onto the lift, lying face down on its platform, then motioned to Aron. "Come on!"

Aron did his best, stumbling a bit as he tried to imitate his best friend's movements. When they were lying there together, Uzah jumped up and punched the button to take them back up to the upper deck out of the landing bay. The lift hummed to life and began moving as Uzah fired several blasts at the enemy with his blaster and looked for an opportunity to rejoin his men.

Then lifts were moving across the bay, too, and he saw armed men firing from them and other Vertullian military troops pouring in from corridors on the other side to reinforce them. Help was here.

Davi could see several small breaches in *Reliance*'s hull as he circled around toward her landing bays. With a huge flash, the battle cruiser's cannons opened up on attacking enemy fighters and Destroyers as they circled around her like vultures. Davi and Farien exchanged fire with a few as well as they prepared to go aboard.

"Alpha is closed. Looks like Beta," Farien called over the radio.

"Beta it is," Davi confirmed and lined up his nose with the landing pattern on his vidscreen.

"I'm hearing chatter about enemy troops aboard," Tela said.

"What?" Davi's body tensed with alarm. Troops where? How many? How many dead? He hadn't heard anything but Tela had been monitoring other channels in the back as Davi and Farien flew. He thought of his family and said a quick silent prayer for their safety.

"We just need to be ready," she added.

Davi nodded to himself then muttered. "Fun never ends." As he keyed the comm to fill in Farien, he slowed his fighter into an arc and headed for Beta Bay's landing gates.

Xalivar stared at the *Tarragon*'s bridge vidscreen with a puzzled look. The repositioning of several key ships had begun without his orders, and Lucius knew nothing about it either. He'd ordered his General to look into it. It would be unusual for his commanders to move their ships away from the flagship without specific orders, leaving her exposed, but it appeared that's what they were trying to do, and Xalivar didn't like it one bit.

"My Lord!" a Lieutenant Commander shouted from nearby as he hurried onto the dais, "We are launching to takeover *Reliance* this moment, sir. Troops are engaging the enemy as we speak."

Xalivar smiled. At least something was going right. "That's good, Commander. Inform me the moment we send further troops aboard and order the transports prepared to launch at a moment's notice." Gods how he loved the smell of success!

The Lieutenant Commander fired off a quick salute and hurried back to his station on the floor as Xalivar turned to Lucius. "Why is our fleet shifting positions, General?"

"The commanders claim the orders came by your private codes, my Lord, but we sent no codes," Lucius replied, looking as confused as Xalivar felt. "I have men tracing the communications channels."

Xalivar cursed. "Where is Pres?!" The female General must be responsible. No one else would dare betray him now. Not anyone on his ships. "Order them back and find her!" he bellowed, waving a fist.

"Yes, my Lord." Lucius bowed slightly and hurried off, looking agitated and lost.

*I'll find her myself if I have to.* Xalivar turned and marched toward the stairs, fists clenching and unclenching as his eyes locked on several nearby communications techs. Lucius was his finest officer but there was no time to waste. If the Boralians arrived with the *Tarragon* exposed, there was a real risk....

Uzah and the soldiers made quick end to the enemy invasion of landing bay Alpha and hurried toward the corridor connecting it with Beta Bay. Enemy bodies lay scattered across the deck as Uzah rushed past them into a small section of corridor. Doors had shut to seal off an area where a hull breach had occurred, but Uzah now had visual confirmation from one of his officers that the enemy transport had landed in Beta Bay.

As he and the others began exchanging blaster fire with the enemy troops assembled there, he took in the site. Several fighters and mech-bots had been damaged along with maintenance equipment, and several Vertullian crew and soldiers lay dead. But it was clear the enemy had not gotten to the lifts yet. A small contingent defending the bay had been joined by reinforcements much as Uzah's had and with the arrival of overwhelming support, the enemy were now facing equal numbers.

Still, the enemy held them off fairly well. Lights overhead flashed, indicating ships coming in for a landing.

*Who could be landing in the middle of this?* Uzah wondered. Then two restored VS20 fighters appeared. "More enemies," he said, motioning to a nearby officer.

"They look right out of a museum," the man replied with a puzzled look.

Then the fighter's cannons hummed and lit up, indicating they were ready to fire.

"Take cover!" Uzah called out, ducking behind a nearby work counter with several others.

The VS20s opened fire, mowing down the invading troops and racing jaggedly across the deck toward the enemy transport.

"These are our guys?" the puzzled officer beside Uzah muttered.

Debris, flesh, dust, and mechanical parts exploded or disintegrated in the cannon's path as the smell of smoke and burned flesh clogged their noses and enemy soldiers screamed and fell.

Then the enemy transport was struck, the stink of burning paint and screech of burning metal filling the bay. The transport's engines exploded as lasers tore into its hull around them. Enemy soldiers ran out, seeking cover as Vertullian soldiers mowed them down with blaster fire before they had a chance.

The transport exploded with a loud blast, a fiery mass that shook the deck below his feet as the VS20s set down nearby, facing toward where the enemy troops had been congregated. The cannons wound down with a fading whine as they shut off and the cockpit shields hummed open, revealing Davi, Farien, and Tela, all three grinning ear-to-ear.

"Did we get them all?" Farien shouted triumphantly and the troops around Uzah erupted into cheering and applause, even as a few mopped up the remaining enemy invaders with their blasters.

# Chapter Thirteen

The chirping of Ambygids and singing of Zingas filled the fresh morning air as the twin suns' rays warmed Obed's skin. He smiled, almost tempted to sing. His plans continued to progress better than he'd ever imagined. Soon, he'd be back on top, back in the position of power and influence he deserved and had always worked so hard for.

Strolling around the yard outside his office, he listened to the chattering of workers and the hum of machinery as the farm complex came to life around him. Men and women were hard at work, making money for him right now, across the planet and beyond. The gods were blessing him beyond measure. He couldn't wait to tighten the noose and be restored to the Council. It would only be a matter of weeks, he felt sure.

He heard their humming, whirling engines before the two shuttles appeared on the horizon, and then it took a few moments to identify their markings—one was a Council official shuttle and the other, LSP, Lord's Special Police, the security police commanded by the High Lord Councilor, whom Obed himself had commanded during Xalivar's reign. And they were headed straight for him.

A lump filled his throat as his smile faded. Had something gone wrong? There was nothing else out here for miles around. Gritting his teeth, he raced for his Floater and started the engine, keying the comm. "Supervisors report. Do we have problems on site today?"

The answers came back one after another in the negative.

Obed didn't wait for them to finish. The shuttles were closer now. They'd be ready to land in five minutes or less. He slipped the Floater into top gear and took off along the trails leading out toward the fields. If the Council were coming with LSP, it could only mean one thing: trouble for him. Obed didn't intend to stick around and find out. Not until he knew what had gone wrong.

He turned sharply at the first corner and raced parallel to the fence, the cool breeze blowing his hair and skin as he went. If he could get to his shuttle first, he could find out what was happening and avoid dealing with his pursuers until he had a plan.

But then he heard the drone of shuttles from behind and above and spun the Floater around another corner into a boundary road as he turned to look back.

The LSP shuttle was hovering just behind and above, keeping pace with him, the Council shuttle following a safe distance behind.

A voice came over a loudspeaker: "Stop the Floater, immediately! By orders of the High Lord Councilor!" it demanded.

Obed cursed, leaning forward involuntarily as he accelerated the Floater. He'd known he couldn't outrun shuttles in a Floater, but he'd hoped to get away before they saw him. Apparently, he hadn't.

The dash comm beeped, someone calling on a private channel. He ignored it and pushed the Floater's accelerator to the floor, while his mind raced through options.

His hands turned clammy and his stomach hardened like a rock as he kept looking around and back at the chasing shuttles, his breath bursting in and out. *Damn it. There had to be a way….*

Then the loudspeaker rang out again. "This is your last warning, halt!"

Obed clenched his jaw, swerving the Floater onto a side road in an attempt to find cover.

It took moments for the shuttles to catch up with him. The LSP shuttle began firing laser blasts that landed, exploding earth and rock around him, sending debris flying.

"Halt!" the voice overhead demanded again.

Obed cursed as the laser blasts continued and slammed the brakes, darting the Floater over under the shuttle, attempting to avoid the gunners.

With a loud whoosh, a door opened above and an LSP sniper leaned out, firing down at him.

The Floater shook with explosions as the blasts struck its fuselage and the platform on which he was standing, then it rocked and began to smoke and slow as two blasts hit the engines. The Floater was finished.

Obed coughed, waving smoke from his eyes and raced to jump over the side and continue on foot.

Jumping a fence, he raced across one of the fields now, hoping to get away or to his office to retrieve a blaster or something; anything to avoid being captured by his former men.

The shuttles arced quickly, clearly the best pilots had come along, and stayed with him, sinking lower as their snipers took aim again.

"Halt!" the loudspeaker voice said one last time, then blasts exploded at Obed's feet, sending dirt and plants flying, and he fell to his knees, winded, his hands in the air.

"I surrender," he choked out, his voice barely audible.

The LSP shuttle lowered down and allowed three snipers to hop out and circle in to surround him as both shuttles moved back toward the road to land.

In a few more minutes, ten more armed LSP soldiers and three Council members were hurrying toward him across the field. He recognized Kray, Qui and the High Lord Councilor himself, and his shoulders sank as he exhaled, his head bowed.

"You are under arrest for violation of the fair trade and agriculture acts, for fraud and misuse of funds, personnel, and equipment," Lord Kray said formally as the pursuers surrounded him.

"You've betrayed us for the last time," Tarkanius added.

Then Obed was dragged to his feet and cuffed by the LSP, and they were escorting him back toward the shuttle. He said nothing as he looked up at the brightness of the twin suns beating down on him from above. There was nothing to say. He'd hire the best lawyers, get his aides to work on hiding funds and records as best they could, and he'd wait until he had a plan. He had no idea how they'd uncovered his scheme. He'd worked so hard to conceal it and his years with the LSP had made him very skilled at such deceit. But Charlis and Boralis gleamed overhead like beacons of hope. He'd find a way around this. His heart warmed at the thought. *I'm not done with you yet.*

The three VS28s launched from *Reliance* like she was on fire and headed to rendezvous with the rest of their squadrons. Tela and Farien formed up immediately on Davi as the world exploded around them. Fighters and battling ships racing and firing chaotically filled the starfield as laser beams and cannon blast exploded all around them, filling Davi's vision with explosive orange and yellow flashes as his scanner searched for the best rendezvous point.

"Nothing like jumping right back into it," Farien muttered over the comm.

"Is no one coordinating?" Tela replied.

"Clearly it's been a mess," Davi said. "Uzah said we lost more than a third of our fighters and several transports, and two of the cruisers are all but disabled."

"If the Boralians don't arrive soon …" Tela's voice trailed off as she acknowledged what all three of them were thinking: the Vertullians were in big trouble.

"Alpha Leader to Alpha squadron," Davi called after switching channels to the squadron's battle frequency. "Need any help? Three incoming."

It took several moments for a reply as enemy and friendly fighters sparred and a few more exploded. Explosions also rocked two transports and several warships on both sides. This battle was as intense as any Davi had ever seen.

"What took you guys so long?" Virun's voice came back at him finally. "Vacation's over. Get busy!"

"Where are you?" Davi inquired.

"Coming up on your rear," Jorek replied as several VS28s closed in from behind on the scanners.

The screen filled with blips, identifying them one by one, including several enemies.

A bright explosion flashed outside the cockpit.

"Thanks for bringing friends," Farien snapped.

"They're everywhere," Nila replied. "Ruining our party."

"Well, let's ruin theirs," Tela said.

The VS28s began arcing apart and reforming in teams as Alpha Squadron reformed on their leaders. Tela had Ace on her wing, Davi had Brie, and Farien had Nila. All of them turned back and targeted the pursuing enemy fighters as chattered filled the comms.

"One on your tail, Virun," Tela warned.

"We're on him," Nila replied.

"I think I can lose him," Virun said, even as Davi saw his wingman drop back in an attempt to get on the enemy's tail, but the enemy dodged as his own wingman locked onto Jorek's fighter.

"Jorek, eight o'clock!" Ace called.

"I see him," Jorek replied, spinning his fighter and racing forward again.

Davi's cockpit rocked as his combat targeting system alerted him of ships in range and he fired within seconds, firing off multiple blasts in one fluid motion. His heart increased its tempo as blood rushed through his veins, warming his body. *At it again, Rhii. Don't screw up.* For a veteran, returning to battle was always a bit like a reawakening. Fear and excitement made an odd mix but that was healthy given how many times he'd risked his life, and how many times he'd watched friends die.

Two enemy fighters exploded under his cannon fire as Brie got one other, and another took hits to its engines.

Brie's whoops filled his ear. "Good shooting, boss."

"Let's do it again," he replied, smiling. At least the people he cared most about had survived so far. Then his thoughts turned momentarily to the transports. How many lives lost? How many were people he'd met?

He winced as he shoved away the thought. *Can't afford the distraction, Davi. You have work to do.*

He spun his sleek fighter into an arc, Brie tight on his wing, and circled around to find more enemy targets.

From the bridge, Xalivar had marched straight to his quarters and checked if someone had accessed his private communications system to send out orders to his ships. His quarters were clean and tidy, much as he'd left it. Clearly Manaen had done his work, but now the majordomo was nowhere to be found. Xalivar couldn't remember the last time that had happened.

His brow creased with frustration as his fingers danced on the keyboard. *Where are you?* He opened the private comm channel through which he and Manaen stayed in constant touch and sent a code paging him.

There was no response after several minutes.

He found no sign of anyone tampering with his comm system either.

He pounded a clenched fist on the desk and stood, cursing. *Where was Manaen and where was that damned General Pres?!*

He stomped angrily toward the sliding door, which opened as he drew near, and headed for Pres' quarters. Manaen's absence was annoying but finding Pres was the priority. Where had she gone to hide? What role had she played in the realignment of his fleet? He wouldn't stop until he had answers.

He found her quarters similarly clean but empty. No sign of her. He called her name twice, then checked the cleansing room and closets.

Empty and no one responded.

His mind raced for ideas where to search next as he marched back to the door and headed for the launch bays. There was a chance she'd gone to coordinate ground troops, although he'd have her cited for it. Such preparations should have been well underhand before the battle began. She was needed on the bridge, but it was one possibility that might explain her absence. And it would be good news. Xalivar had little faith in good news at such times. Somehow he knew he wouldn't find her, and he didn't.

Five minutes later, he was leaving the bay in a huff yet again, having seen the officers and troops assembled aboard transports, ready to launch any moment at his command.

As he entered the lift, explosions rocked the *Tarragon*'s hull. He grabbed a rail to steady himself and avoid falling to his knees, then opened a channel to Lucius on the bridge. "General, what's going on?" he demanded as he pressed a button for the fourth level and the lift began to rise with whining servos.

"The Boralian fleet has arrived, my Lord," Lucius answered haggardly. Xalivar could hear chaos on the bridge in the background.

"Have the other ships returned to position?"

"Not yet, my Lord," Lucius replied.

"WHAT?!" Xalivar's scream cut him off.

"We've tried, my Lord, but our fleet frequencies are being jammed, from one of our own ships," Lucius added quickly. "I'm afraid we are exposed."

Xalivar's fists clenched so hard his arm muscles spasmed, but he ignored the pain. "Jammed?! Our own ship?! Find the source immediately and stop it! Override!"

"The technicians are trying, my Lord, but we had no contingency for our own people jamming us," Lucius said, his voice faltering a bit now. "It's never happened before."

Xalivar let off a string of curses and shook his fist, forgetting Lucius couldn't see it. "GET THEM BACK NOW!"

"We'll keep trying, my Lord," Lucius said, sounding more lost than Xalivar had ever heard him.

"I'm on my way!" Xalivar yelled, cursing as the lift arrived at level four and he shut the comm. He pounded a button for level two, fighting the urge to pace in the lift's limited space. *May the gods strike you down, Pres!* Xalivar would not lose again. Whatever it took. He'd take them all with him, before he'd let them see him fail once more. His back arched as he straightened with firm resolve and thought of his father and grandfather and spat.

*Call me a dishonor and a fool! You're the fools!* He'd never been so delighted that they were gone.

*Reliance*'s bridge shook under an onslaught of fire even as the orange and yellow flashes of explosions on her hull lit up monitors around Uzah. He somehow managed to stay on his feet, a firm hand gripping the dais rail as he directed the counter response. Then cheering broke out all around him as the scanners lit up and alerts sounded at the arrival of numerous ships.

"They're here!" Colonel Cardno announced, excitedly, grinning from ear to ear.

The Boralians had come at last.

Uzah smiled, too, as the bridge stabilized and he moved toward the vidscreen showing the locations of all ships. "Is that the *Tarragon* still there in the middle?" he asked, looking toward a nearby tech.

The tech double-checked her own screen and nodded. "Yes, General."

"The *Tarragon*'s alone. Isolated," he said, looking at General Matheu as his eyebrows raised in question. His fellow General's eyes revealed mutual understanding then Uzah spun, raising his voice, "All fighters and all available ships close on those coordinates …" He motioned to the tech again.

"236, 427," she called out.

"We can end this right here," he muttered to Matheu.

"With God's will," Matheu responded, nodding, his lips parting slightly as his eyes looked upward in recognition of their God's involvement and constant presence in all things.

"The *Tarragon*'s wide open," Uzah said, stiffening with confidence as he raised his voice again. He licked his lips and raised a palm triumphantly. "Let's take her down!"

The bridge broke into cheering again as Uzah turned to the comm station. "Get the Boralian command ship on the line!"

Davi heard the commands coming across his comms. "236, 427, you heard them," he echoed.

"Is that the *Tarragon*?" Brie asked.

"She's all alone! Look!" Farien replied.

The fighters turned and headed toward the coordinates, engaging only enemy fighters who tried to follow or interfere. With Boralian fighters joining in, the enemy fighters had a lot more distractions than they'd had moments before and Alpha Squadron had little trouble disengaging and slipping away.

Davi saw the huge shadow looming ahead and watched as it became the large, gray hull of Xalivar's flagship. He still couldn't believe the chatter he'd heard or the video he'd seen aboard *Reliance* showing his uncle alive and well. The man had more lives than a quat, and here he was, wasting them again on revenge. Would he never give up?

He exhaled and rolled his shoulders, shifting in his seat as he prepared himself for the next attack. *Lord protect us*, he prayed silently. Mixed emotions filled his mind and heart. Despite all his uncle had done to harm Davi and those he loved, he still carried love for the man who'd helped raise him like a son. *If only things were different....*

The air in his cockpit was warm and stale but he breathed it in anyway and steeled his resolve. *They aren't!* he scolded himself, shaking off the sentiment. They had to end this. No matter what it took. The cost had already been too high. They couldn't let it continue.

He turned his VS28 into a long curve, Brie tight on his wing, as the *Tarragon* grew larger out of his cockpit shield. "Fire at will," he ordered across the comm, and Alpha Squadron closed in.

Pres sat at the main comm station on the *Tarragon*'s war bridge and waited as Manaen poured brown leaves into hot water, preparing Talis nearby. They'd discussed fleeing and hiding somewhere. There was no use leaving the ship. They had nowhere to go. Surely the Vertullians would suspect them and they were seen as traitors by the Boralians as well. So they remained.

It surprised her that Xalivar hadn't found them by now. Only three places in the entire ship could transmit his private channels—his quarters, and the two bridges. If it hadn't occurred to Xalivar himself, surely he had men tracing the codes and it would soon be discovered. Could it really be that wouldn't happen in time? She'd love to see his face when he realized he'd failed: the great Xalivar undone at last!

The *Tarragon* shook as the Vertullians began concentrating their fire on the flagship more and more. Clearly they'd noticed its isolation and revised their strategy. If the Boralians joined it, the *Tarragon* wouldn't be around much longer. If Xalivar had called the ships back to support his own, they were moving far too slowly to make a difference. She suspected, as they'd planned and hoped, that he'd wasted too much time trying to sort out who had sent out commands in his name and how. Perhaps Lucius had wasted the time, despite Xalivar's insistence. That was more likely, she surmised, but it didn't matter. Their deaths were inevitable now, she felt certain.

Manaen cleared his throat as he stepped up beside her and leaned down to offer her a cup on a saucer. Commander's China, the official service of officers, so rarely used on the bridge and never in combat. Kept there mostly for ceremonial occasions. She accepted it gladly and smiled warmly up at her compatriot. "Thank you, Manaen."

The Idolian smiled as he bowed slightly, his yellow teeth and red eyes almost sparkling from his joy and relief. "You're welcome, General."

"Please, my friend," she replied, "call me Pres."

He nodded. "I suppose it hardly matters now."

She grunted as she sipped the Talis, its warm delicious taste sliding smoothly down her throat and making her relax involuntarily. So soothing. "Never imagined it would come to this."

Manaen sighed as he finished swallowing a sip of his own Talis. His eyes were flat, narrowed, showing no emotion as he looked in her direction but past as if staring at the wall. "I think none of us did."

With that, both their shoulders slumped and they returned to silence as the *Tarragon* rocked again and they watched the unfolding path to its destruction growing on the wall-sized vidscreen before them.

Xalivar grabbed the rail beside him as the *Tarragon* rumbled from more and more explosions and direct hits by enemy cannons and lasers. "Get us out of here, General!"

Lucius stumbled to stay on his feet beside his master, nodding. "We're moving her as fast as we can. There's no room. We're surrounded."

"Blast our way through or ram them, if you have to," Xalivar demanded, reaching up to massage away a stabbing pain in his neck. "Just get us out of here!"

So far Xalivar's forces were still gaining ground, but as more and more Boralians arrived via FTL, he feared a turn in the tide, especially if anything happened to his flagship. He considered for a moment taking a shuttle to another, safer ship, but the risk was too great with the *Tarragon* under increasing barrage. Instead, they had to try and get closer to the other ships, those attempting to resume their protective positions but also struggling to find a path through the enemy swarm.

"My Lord, unless we move to the war bridge, we risk breaching the bridge hull …" Lucius replied.

"The war bridge!" Xalivar couldn't believe he hadn't thought of it before as he raced for the nearest lift, his nose wrinkling as he swallowed hard. *Of course. There were only three places where he could access his private comm channels. He'd checked his quarters and the bridge but he'd completely forgotten the war bridge!* "Have security meet me there!" He let off a string of epithets directed at Pres and whomever her co-conspirators were. *I have you now!*

He heard Lucius on the comm ordering security to the war bridge as he stepped on the lift and pressed the button to take him down three levels to the interior of the ship.

He clenched his jaw and ground his teeth, his nostrils flaring as he paced the lift floor, thinking of Lucius. The man had been his loyal officer but clearly he'd lost his focus. Failing to notice the *Tarragon*'s vulnerability until Xalivar pointed it out, and then failing to act quickly to reposition the ship. *You'd better get us out of this, General, or you'll be joining them in facing my vengeance!*

The lift rocked, throwing him against a sidewall as the flagship let loose with all of her cannons and guns at once, likely attempting to clear a path for her escape. More pain assaulted his neck and back but he ignored it. Whoever was responsible for this would pay with great pain of their own—a death that would make them wish they'd never met Xalivar!

Uzah stood at the command vidscreen as Admiral Mora Esta and her aide, Commander Tully, appeared aboard the Boralian flagship *Gryphon*. Esta, who went by Mo, had risen under General Grif's tutelage to become the highest ranked female in the Boralian military, following in the footsteps of the rebel General Pres. Big boned with piercing brown eyes and blonde hair cut so short she could almost pass for male, she was tough and demanding, intimidating almost all who dealt with her. Even Uzah at times. Tully was a foot taller, rail thin with dark hair and a tightly trimmed mustache, and pretty much accompanied her always, seeing that her orders were followed to the letter. They made a good team, and no doubt their pairing as officers had aided their mutual rise through the ranks.

"General," the Admiral barely nodded.

"We're grateful to see you, Admiral," Uzah said, smiling.

Mo Esta grunted. "It appears we arrived just in time."

"The *Tarragon* is unprotected and we are concentrating fire on her," Uzah explained. "If we can take her out, we believe the enemy will be left in chaos."

Esta raised an eyebrow in acknowledgement. "I'll order our ships to join you. We seem to be holding even with them on the perimeter and more ships are just arriving now."

Uzah straightened, shoulders drawn back as he clasped his hands behind his back. "We can put an end to this for good, Admiral."

Esta gave a curt nod and began barking orders as she turned away and the screen went blank.

Uzah turned to Matheu and Cardno. "You heard her. Coordinate movements to allow the Boralian reinforcements into position. And target the *Tarragon*'s engines. She seems to be making an effort to break away." Uzah knew he would. He was shocked she hadn't moved away as soon as General Lucius realized his ship was unprotected. The error would cost him his ship and his life. The Vertullians had to win at all costs.

Firing her cannons directly at the *Tarragon*'s hull, Tela completed her fighter's arc and headed out for another run. Explosions and debris rained out from the warship's hull as her fighter turned. She still couldn't believe what she was seeing: Xalivar's flagship isolated and surrounded and none of his fleet ships moving in to intervene. She double-checked her scanners and then her cockpit shield visual again. It made no sense.

"It's like they've abandoned him," she muttered into the comm.

"Or they were ordered off," Davi said.

"What? Who would do that?" Brie scoffed.

"Perhaps Xalivar finally picked the wrong people to trust," Davi said. "Regardless, his people don't disobey orders, knowing they'd do so at the cost of their lives. Why else would they have moved away and held position?"

Tela bit her lips, her knees bouncing against the floor. "It makes sense, if you believe that's possible. . . ." After all, nothing else did. The big enemy fleet ships had moved off before the Boralians arrived, they were now fully engaged with Boralian and Vertullian ships, and none were attempting to break free and go to their leader's assistance. Surely they saw the flagship's predicament.

An explosion close by rocked her fighter, its flash filling her blast shield, and she snapped out of her reverie in time to see she'd drifted too close to one of the *Tarragon*'s cannon batteries.

"Tela, look out!" Ace warned from his position on her wing.

Her chest tight, muscles taught, Tela flipped the joystick and put her VS28 into a roll away from the flagship, spinning 360 degrees as she did and heading to coordinates from which she could circle back and attack again. A quick glance back told her Ace followed without the theatrics, like any good wingman would.

As she settled into a steady flight path again, she finally allowed herself to breathe. *Enough second guessing opportunities, Tela. Let's take this bastard down once and for all!* She chided herself and looked again to confirm Ace was in position before arcing back for another run.

Farien and Nila spun around for another run at the *Tarragon*, targeting a cannon emplacement and scoring five hits each before arcing out again to circle back. The flagships fighters were all but destroyed, leaving the *Tarragon* on her own. That plus the fact she was now surrounded by enemy ships of all sizes, filled Farien with hope and pumped up his adrenaline like nothing he'd experienced in years. *We can actually win this right here!*

Glancing back over his shoulder as he and Nila arced away in a well-coordinated loop, he saw at least two of the four cannons rocked with explosions as orange flashes and debris shot out from them.

"Nailed it!" Nila called gleefully.

Farien smiled. "Good shooting, kid. You've come a long way."

"Nice to see you old folks haven't lost it," Nila snapped back.

And they both laughed.

Farien shook his head. Gods, it was great to be back with their friends again after all that time away. Defending the fleet, fighting the enemy, doing what they were designed to do. His biggest dread about leaving the Borali System with the fleet had been the realization that they'd likely spend isolated months bored in their cockpits with only routine patrols, inspections and scouting to occupy their time and keep their skills sharp. Oh sure, there were dangers—great risks, in fact, if they encountered unknown enemies—but Farien had long ago decided that combat was where he felt most alive, despite all its perils. Besides, he had a score to settle with Xalivar and his minions for murdering so many of his friends.

Gritting his teeth as his mind filled with the images of their faces, Farien took a deep breath and shook it off. Even the stifling air of the cockpit invigorated him, like a feeling of belonging, or home. No time for memories now. No time for reverie. He had a job to do, and by Gods, he'd make them pay!

As he and Nila arced back, they watched several more Boralian and Vertullian fighters strafe the *Tarragon.* Whole portions of the great flagship now showed battle scars and outright damage. She was in trouble, losing, and it delighted Farien to realize: Xalivar knew it.

Then he saw motion as one of the large battleships broke away from its attackers and began increasing speed, moving toward the embattled flagship. Either somebody was improvising or orders had been changed.

Returning to his focus, he turned back to his controls. *We have to make this count.*

*The Tarragon* rocked violently again and again with explosions and missile strikes as the war bridge door rose with a whoosh and Xalivar marched into the room, fists clenched, his eyes narrow and face pinched with fury.

"PRES!" he screamed as he ran towards her, armed security filing in after him like ants on a picnic.

Pres just sat calmly beside the control panel and accepted her fate. Not even her heartbeat or breathing offered any response to her Lord's presence. She'd known it would come to this the moment she decided to betray him.

Then Xalivar turned and saw his majordomo, his eyes widening and his breath freezing momentarily in his throat. The Idolian's blue skin paled and his red eyes looked white as he stiffened with resolve and faced his longtime master.

"Manaen! You?! My most trusted aide!" Xalivar's voice faded, cracking with each word.

Manaen nodded, showing no other reaction. Clearly he'd prepared himself to accept his fate.

Xalivar rushed to the control panel and shoved Pres aside, towering over her as he sent her sprawling onto the floor on her knees. "Arrest them at once!" he ordered over his shoulder as he examined the panel. "My own private codes?! My own channel?!"

Pres thought his head might actually explode, shrinking back as security men rushed her and Manaen, and dragged them to their feet, applying spanners to lock their hands behind their backs.

Xalivar worked furiously at the panel as he keyed the comm. "Get technicians to the war bridge immediately! I've found them!"

He kept working at the controls, clearly a bit overwhelmed. He'd surely been trained on it at some point, but it had been years since he'd had to operate such controls for himself. His brow creased in frustration as he pounded the keys.

Pres and Manaen were herded together but neither said a word. They merely exchanged a quick look of resolve and braced themselves as the security men searched them forcefully for weapons and anything else worth removing; Xalivar's curses providing a soundtrack to their reckoning.

Uzah couldn't breathe as he watched from *Reliance*'s bridge as the enemy warship moved to protect its flagship. They'd done significant damage to the enemy flagship but she was still fighting back and operating under her own power. If too many ships moved in …

"The enemy is repositioning, Generals," Colonel Cardno reported from nearby.

Uzah merely nodded as General Matheu grunted in acknowledgement. Uzah's eyes went to fallen pillars and damaged control panels across the bridge where the *Tarragon*'s cannons had hit home. There were areas throughout the ship with similar damage, he knew, and he only hoped the few reports they'd gotten of mostly minor losses and casualties would prove true.

Uzah took a deep breath as his command screen beeped and he turned to see Admiral Esta's face fill the screen, standing on the dais of her Boralian flagship.

"Admiral," Uzah acknowledged after reaching to open the comm channel.

"The *Tarragon* is weakening. Several hull breaches," she said. "My crew have made calculations, and we believe that if we concentrate our power in two positions, she will come apart."

Uzah motioned urgently to Matheu and Cardno, and asked, "Coordinates?" as they hurried toward him.

"Sending over now," Esta replied. "We'll take 327.651, you cover the other."

"Coordinated strikes?" Matheu asked as he looked over Uzah's shoulder at the screen.

Esta shook her head. "Unnecessary. Fire at will."

Uzah acknowledged the message as Matheu and Cardno turned and began barking orders, the Colonel working with communications techs, Matheu the weapons techs.

"Admiral," Uzah said as Esta reached down to shut off her screen.

She stopped and looked up again. "Yes, General?"

"They are repositioning their ship," he said, knowing she was likely well aware of it.

Esta nodded. "If we act now, they will be too late. My ships are moving to intercept even now." With that, she reached down and flipped a button and the screen went blank.

The sounds of the bridge went mute as Uzah's heartbeat filled his ears. *Lord, please deliver your people,* he prayed silently.

Then, snapping back to focus, he turned back to *Reliance*'s vidscreen and began issuing orders of his own, but now, his tone had a higher pitch and hopeful sound for the first time in hours.

Davi switched his comm to the main channel and keyed his mic as he reread the orders sent to his computer from Admiral Matheu. "All ships, focus your fire on the *Tarragon* at 227.53. 227.53," he repeated.

Then he arced around as he sent the coordinates into his targeting system, Brie close on his tail. As their fighter's guns let go in unison, the *Tarragon*'s hull began to glow from multiple hits and explosions. All around him, Vertullian and Boralian ships were firing at the same sets of coordinates.

Davi wasn't sure why the orders had come through but he leaned forward in his seat with excitement. Had they found a way to tear the *Tarragon* apart? The flagship had suffered significant damage already, despite still being under power and returning fire.

His uncle's face flashed into his mind. Not the evil Lord they now faced, but the gentler man who'd raised Davi—Xander—as a son. His nephew. Born of Xalivar's beloved sister. They'd laughed together, joked, even danced a few times. Xalivar had shown a childlike nature with Davi that no one else ever saw. In truth, he'd been a decent substitute father, Davi had to admit. All until the day he discovered Miri's secret: Davi's true birth as a Vertullian, a slave.

Then it had all changed. Xalivar's resentment quickly turned to hatred at both Miri and Davi. LSP death squads were sent to assassinate him, and he fled into hiding, eventually joining the rebellion and helping the Vertullians fight and win their freedom.

That all seemed so long ago, as his VS28 vibrated with the fire of its cannons and he arced up and circled around for another pass. It had only been a few years. Hard to believe.

And now, the beloved nephew, raised like a son, was helping to kill the only father he'd known as a child. A dagger stabbed at his gut as he shook off the emotions filling him. Xalivar had left them no choice. They'd defeated him twice and he kept coming back. Death might be the only way to stop him.

Still, Davi ached with regret, wishing somehow it could have been different.

Then he thought of Yao, flashing back to the horrendous moment when one of his closest friends had died, giving his life to take out Xalivar's shuttle, a shuttle it turned out the leader hadn't been aboard. Yao's death was not in vain. How many times had he told himself that?

His lips pursed, his eyes narrowing with concentration as he took a measured breath. This had to end. *God keep you, uncle.*

As his targeting computer beeped to indicate the coordinates were in range again, Davi opened fire with everything he had.

Xalivar's growl sounded like a scream as his fists pounded the war bridge's main control panel, still struggling to remember all the codes to release the communications jamming and countermand the false orders sent to his ships.

Glancing at the vidscreen he saw the Battleship *Asaro* leaving its attackers and breaking toward the *Tarragon*. For the first time ever, he rejoiced that one of his commanders actually defied orders.

"Come on! What are you waiting for?!" he shouted at the others as technicians scrambled through the door and came to his aide and security men stood behind at attention, awaiting further instructions.

The *Tarragon* rocked constantly now, and through monitors, Xalivar saw enemy ships of all shapes and sizes, Vertullian and Boralian both, letting loose barrages, then zipping past and circling back for more runs. How much more could his ship take?

"My Lord!" a technician called.

Xalivar whirled, choking down a forced breath. "Yes?"

"Comms restored," the technician said and opened the fleet channel with the press of his thumb.

"All ships return to support the *Tarragon* immediately!" Xalivar ordered, resisting the urge to scream for fear his voice would override the sensors and get scrambled in transmission. "Pull back and assist us!" he repeated. "All ships return to defensive formation around the *Tarragon* now!"

Acknowledgements began flooding the comms as Xalivar took a deep breath and turned his attention back to the vidscreen.

Then the deck vibrated as a deep rumbling filled his ears. Struggling to stay on his feet, he pressed his feet against the shaking deck and grabbed for the nearest handrail, even as Pres, Manaen, and their security guards stumbled to their knees behind him and the technicians fought to stay on their feet. A few cried out in fear or surprise.

And Xalivar knew.

His mind filled with the image of his father and grandfather berating him in the throne room.

And then his world flashed and went dark as the flagship *Tarragon* disintegrated around him. He didn't even have time to scream.

Davi winced and shut his eyes to block the fierce light flooding through the cockpit shield as he forced his fighter into a sharp turn on instinct and curved away from the enemy flagship. By the time he arced around again, only sparkling debris and smoke remained where the *Tarragon* had been.

Xalivar was really gone. He could hardly believe it.

Cheers of joy flooded the comms in celebration as it sunk in.

Tears streamed down Davi's face as he settled back in his cockpit seat, trying to wrap himself around the meaning of the moment. Xalivar was dead. They'd won. They still had enemies to defeat, yes, but without their leader, who would coordinate?

For the first time since he'd helped the Vertullians win their freedom, Davi Rhii felt free.

# Epilogue

The footsteps echoed across the hangar as the aide ran toward the table. Aron wasn't the only one who looked up and took notice, despite the intensity of the ongoing conversation. An Idolian aide approached Kanaan, leaning over to whisper in his ear. Aron watched the ambassador's face for a reaction. His face went from disbelief to amazement to shock in a matter of seconds. Then the aide stood, waiting for a response, but the ambassador only waved him away.

Farien brought his VS28 to a soft, perfect landing in the Beta Bay of *Reliance* amidst cheering and revelry from pilots, mechanics, and anyone else who'd managed to make their way down there. Laser fire scars and debris still remained from the earlier boarding incident he, Tela, and Davi had helped end, but that was long forgotten in the euphoria of the victory.

After the destruction of their flagship and deaths of their leaders, Xalivar's forces had fought on for nearly two hours, but in the end, the overwhelming enemy ships surrounding them had sent them fleeing—those who weren't destroyed. Two additional warships and most of the fighters had also ended in explosions before it was over. All in all, the greatest victory Vertullian forces had ever experienced, and everyone was in a celebratory mood.

Everyone except Davi.

Farien climbed down from his cockpit, hands slick on the ladder from layers of the drying sweat that always accompanied long hours in a cockpit. He accepted the slaps on the back, hugs, and shouted praise from friends and others around him, as he saw Davi still sitting quietly in his cockpit, head down, blast shield closed as if he were afraid to come out. Farien spotted Tela across the bay wading her way through the throng. She hadn't seemed to notice Davi yet.

Farien returned the cheerful greetings, hugs, and encouragement but began making his way through the crowd toward Davi, who'd landed two ships over from him.

Reaching Davi's cockpit, he climbed the ladder up the side and knocked at the shield. "Open sesame."

Davi looked at him through somber eyes but said nothing. His friend's deep pain pierced Farien like a sword. After all their years together, all they'd been through—even the rough spots—Farien could read him like a book. Davi was mourning. Grieving his uncle, their friends, and so much more. Farien searched for words that might help as their eyes locked together in silent commiseration.

Finally, he spoke, "You had no choice."

Davi's face wrinkled in puzzlement and Farien repeated it.

Then servos whined as the cockpit shield began to rise. "What?" Davi asked.

"You had no choice, Davi," Farien said again. "He would have never let it go."

Davi squinted his eyes and nodded, chin down again.

"You're a hero. We all are. And we're all safer now."

Tears streamed down Davi's cheeks. "I always hoped somehow I could change his mind. I wanted to save him."

Farien choked up but managed to keep his voice steady. "That's who you are, brother. You did the same for me and so many others. And we're all better for it. But Xalivar … he just wasn't going to change." Farien's chest tightened as he looked for anything he could add that might help but his mind drew a blank.

They remained there in silence for a moment, then Davi took a deep breath. "I know. You're right. We did what we had to. But I have fond memories from my childhood."

"I do, too," Farien said. "Xalivar was good with all of us."

They exchanged a look and Davi laughed. "Remember the time he caught you trying to hide behind the throne and scare us? You had that water sprayer in your hand …"

Farien laughed, too. "Gods, I have never been more scared in my life than when he came at me with that booming voice, shadow leering down at me. 'What are you doing, boy?!'"

They both laughed even harder at the memory, tears on their cheeks for different reasons now.

"And Yao," Farien added after he recovered a bit, "Yao comes running in and looks at him and says, 'Please, please, my Lord, it's only a toy. Don't kill my friend!'"

They chortled yet again.

"Good old, Yao, always the mediator," Davi said.

"He kept us alive," Farien agreed.

Davi smiled. "Yes, that he did."

Darkness fell over them again as they both turned their thoughts to their friend's sacrificial death, flying his fighter into a shuttle to save them all.

"And he's avenged, his death has meaning. We finished what he started," Farien added when he'd steeled himself again. "Don't forget that."

Davi locked eyes with him again and then reached out and squeezed Farien's hand as it rested on the side of the cockpit. He stood and Farien started back down the ladder.

Farien waited at the bottom, stepping aside, until his friend joined him. "I'm sorry, Davi. For so many times … all the times you had to save my butt. Again and again. Both of you."

Davi grabbed Farien and pulled him into a firm, warm embrace. They stood there a moment, two friends as close as brothers, and Farien saw Tela arrive over Davi's shoulder, watching them.

Finally, Davi pulled apart and smiled. "I'm sure I'll have to do it again."

"With an idiot like me? No doubt!" Farien teased.

They laughed again, Tela joining them. Then she drew near and pulled Davi into her arms. After a moment, Davi motioned for Farien to join them, and the three pilots formed a group hug amidst the celebration of their people on a battle damaged landing bay floor.

The Vertullian Council gathered in *Reliance*'s conference room forty-eight hours after the battle and the room was fraught with tension. Sol could tell right away Joram had come itching for a fight, but they all waited quietly with minor chitchat until Aron and General Uzah arrived and joined them at the table.

As always, Joram occupied the far end of the table with Lords Tamora, Hula, Klima, and Chad filling out their side. Coz, Nachor, and Sol occupied the far side with Aron at the opposite end. General Uzah took an extra chair between Aron and Klima.

When everyone had settled in, Joram cleared his throat and scowled at Uzah. "Our first order of business must be to address the gross insubordination and disrespect General Uzah has shown members of this Council—!"

"Joram!" Aron silenced him with a glare. "We haven't even called the meeting to order."

"Parliamentary procedure is your main concern?!" Joram snapped. "He had no right to treat us as he did!"

"He had no right?!" Aron's voice rose in pitch and volume with every word and he stood, hands planted atop the conference table, raging eyes locked on Joram.

Sol coughed. He hadn't seen his best friend so worked up in decades, since they were much younger, and certainly never in public. Aron had always been good at controlling his emotions, a skill which had served him well in his political aspirations. But this time, Aron's face was twisted with fury, his eyes narrow, neck corded as his nostrils flared.

"You. Had. No. Right." Aron enunciated every word.

Joram sat back in his chair, his mouth dropping open in shock. "I?"

"General Uzah and his people saved all of us, Councilor," Aron said. Sol had never heard him call anyone by that official title. They were all on a first name basis, at least in their Council sessions. He fought the urge to smile.

"Your petty pride almost cost half this Council their lives, Joram! It's inexcusable," Aron continued.

"If he had allowed us to launch, we'd have been—"

"You'd have been dead," Aron snapped. "All of you. Make no mistake of it." He glanced around, his eyes meeting each of Joram's cohorts in turn. And for the first time, they showed their leader no sympathy, instead revealing emotions ranging from fear to anger as they turned and glared at Joram in turn. "And you distracted the General from his duties in the middle of battle."

Joram looked away, shaking his head. "You are out of line, sir. I demand that you watch your tone. I am a Councilor elected by the people."

"Not anymore."

At that Joram's head snapped back around at he stared at Aron. All eyes at the table were on him, and Sol once again fought the urge to show his delight. As Joram scanned their faces, each Councilor's expression revealed the truth to him plainly: he'd gone too far. And this time, they all agreed with it.

"I am the head of this Council," Joram protested.

"As of yesterday evening, you are no longer eligible to hold such a position," Lord Tamora said then, adding her voice in support of Aron.

"We held a session to discuss your … inappropriate behavior," Lord Coz said then. "The vote was unanimous." The rest of them turned and looked to Aron then.

Aron nodded, his eyes thanking them for their support. Tension flooded from Sol to be replaced with relief, fairly bursting with pride at his friend's accomplishment. Uniting this group of determined people was a rare and difficult feat, but Aron, the former slave and starship mechanic, had managed it somehow.

"As of twenty-one hundred hours, you are removed from this Council and all authority associated with the office revoked," Aron said then. "By unanimous vote of the Council, an election will be held for your replacement, and you are forbidden from seeking office on this Council or any of its responsible offices until we change our minds."

Joram stood, exasperation shooting across his face and body. "This is outrageous!"

"So is trying to get us killed!" Lord Tamora said then, her voice brittle with emotion. "We trusted you. We helped you. And you almost led us to our deaths, Joram. It's over."

With that the rest of the Council chimed in with grunted agreement or words of acknowledgement. Then the room grew silent again.

General Uzah just sat there quietly, dignified, his face all business. Sol marveled at his ability to conceal his emotions. Surely he must be feeling a sense of pleasure at this turn of events. He had known about the secret meeting and helped ensure Joram was kept away. But he had not been told of its outcome.

"You did this … while I was visiting the people," Joram muttered. He'd gone alone to visit a few key supporters, the others he'd invited each making excuses about their need to visit supporters of their own. Given the hectic events of the past weeks, Joram hadn't even questioned it, and Uzah's security men had thus never needed to act to keep him from the meeting. But Joram's features were filled with questions now. "I … I can't believe this."

"Sit down, sir," Aron said sternly to Joram. They all stared, waiting, until the former Councilor reluctantly complied. Leaning back in shock as he tried to wrap his mind around what had just occurred.

Aron turned then to General Uzah. "General, with the Council's utmost gratitude we have unanimously voted to award you and General Matheu commendations, the highest possible—which as a new Council we fear we have not had time yet to create."

Uzah broke character and smiled then and several Councilors chuckled, including Sol.

"We'll correct that error at the soonest possible date in the future and award you with appropriate pomp and circumstance," Aron added.

"Hear, Hear!" Sol called out and the others joined him in applause for the embarrassed General as Joram alone sat in stoned silence at the far end of the table. The applause continued for several minutes, and at the end General Uzah simply bowed his head.

"I just did my duty, but thank you," he said softly.

With that, they broke into applause again.

Aron and Tarkanius met privately with Pharah Brahma and Lords Kray and Simeon, Sol, Tamora, and Klima shortly after the High Lord Councilor's shuttle arrived at the starport in Regalis. Local officials had offered them a secure private conference room for the meeting, despite being told as little as possible about its purpose, just that the High Lord Councilor and important dignitaries would attend.

Even two days after the battle, everyone was still reeling from all which had occurred. But Tarkanius tried to open the meeting on the right note by suggesting that rather than sitting at the table's head, he and Aron, the newly re-appointed head of the Vertullian Council, take seats in the middle of each long side of the table instead. That simple, humble act which placed the other attendees around them like equals, established a tone of welcoming and equality that would serve the discussion well, he hoped.

After the initial greetings and formalities were dispensed with quickly and with striking informality, he began. "On behalf of the Boralian people, our Council of Lords, the entire government, and my own family, I offer heartfelt apologies to the Vertullian people you represent for the years of wrong, mistreatment, deceit, and abuse you've endured at our hands." He paused a moment, panning those across the table, meeting each one's eyes in turn with his own. "I know simple words in no way make up for all you've endured and all you've lost, but I pledge to you now, it will never happen again. And we will do all we can to make it right."

The Vertullians exchanged surprised looks then slowly smiled, nodding to him.

"We are most humbled by your kind words, my Lord," Aron replied on their behalf.

Tarkanius smiled back, swallowing, and then straightened his shoulders as he continued, "We are here to officially invite you to reconsider your decision to leave the system."

The Vertullian contingent's smiles disappeared again under surprise. Several mumbled with uncertainty.

Tarkanius showed no reaction, having expected this response; he continued, his smile widening, his eyes shining with sincerity. "We are prepared to offer not only the full return of all Vertullian properties, businesses, and land which were abandoned but to offer government grants and assistance for the next two decades to ensure that they meet the highest standards of their industries and are capable of competing with the highest level of success."

"Two decades?!" Lord Klima repeated it with utter amazement, his eyes scoffing.

Lord Simeon joined his leader in smiling. "The Council voted to approve all of this yesterday in a private session, but we have video to show if you wish to see it."

"You brought video?" Lord Tamora's eyes sparkled with what Tarkanius hoped was being impressed. "Have we become so untrusting?"

"We wouldn't blame you," Lord Kray added, locking eyes with her female counterpart.

"Furthermore, we offer you full representation on the Council as shared with all other races and planets in the Borali System," Tarkanius continued. He'd had to apologize, even sign an agreement never to invoke any of Xalivar's secret codes ever again. In fact, he'd already issued an order ensuring that those codes were erased from the records and officially declared invalid. Then he spoke with each Council member he'd detained personally one at a time, to hear their concerns, and offer separate apologies. In the end, they'd come alongside him on this, agreeing it was the right thing. But he suspected he'd damaged his relationship with the Council permanently, if not for years, and he resigned himself to the problems that might create.

Every Vertullian there knew what that meant. Not just one Councilor, as Aron had been before they left, but several, with more and more added depending on factors such as population and influence and representation amongst the thirteen planets.

Even Aron looked stunned.

"After all this time, you come to us prepared to offer that which we always wanted and always deserved?" Sol asked. "Why?"

"It is time for the Boralian Alliance to not just claim new ideals, but embody them," Tarkanius answered. "You all know well the changes I have made since taking office. But know this: it was not enough and it will never be enough until we are all equal."

Pharah Brahma's purple eyes sparkled as his dark orange skin lightened, a sign of excitement amongst Tertullians. "The changes have already been offered to our people and accepted, and we expect the Idolians, Lhamors and others to follow. There will be true equality and full participation for all in the Borali government, for the first time since its creation!"

His enthusiasm was like a salesman and it clearly had the desired impact. The Vertullians went from cautious surprise to smiling again and nodded their heads.

"We must take it before the Council, of course, and our people," Aron said, "but given the damage done to our fleet, the terrible losses, and the further risks posed by our anticipated journey, I can promise I'd tend to lean promisingly in favor of it."

Sol, Klima, and Tamora nodded. "Yes." "We as well." "Of course."

They all exchanged pleased looks, shifting excitedly in their seats now much like Pharah and the Boralians. The tension in the room dropped immediately and everyone began chattering and laughing like old friends.

Tarkanius just leaned back in his chair and enjoyed the moment. Further details could be ironed out later. Including two speeches he and Aron needed to make on the nets to both their peoples. But for now, his mission had gone far more smoothly than he might have hoped. That the Vertullians had reached the same conclusion despite all that had been done to harm them, warmed Tarkanius' heart and he'd meant every word about not just repairing the damage but making up for it. It would be his life's legacy. If he accomplished nothing else as High Lord Councilor, this he would do. Leaving all his peoples—the Vertullians were his people, too, now, he reminded himself—far better off than they'd been when he first came into office.

What else could a leader truly expect or ask of himself?

Aron leaned across the table, extending his hand and Tarkanius leaned forward to clasp it firmly as they shook, smiling—two old friends, compatriots, and former enemies who were witnessing a realization too long coming and reveling in it.

Bordox arrived back at the pirate's base raging at having lost one more chance to kill Xander Rhii and his cronies. He cursed to himself as his ship settled down on the pad and he climbed out of the cockpit to find

Staggs, Rufa, and several pirates waiting for him.

"Well?" Staggs demanded.

"They got away," Bordox said.

"Weeks returned with the shuttle and said you went after them," Staggs replied with a scowl.

"And I chased them through the starport but lost them," Bordox said.

Staggs grunted then waved dismissively. "Rufa, go with Bordox to pack his things. He'll be leaving now."

"What?!" Bordox stiffened, fighting to control his temper. "We can find them. I know where their fleet is. We can hunt them down. They killed our Lord."

"We will handle it," Staggs said, eyes locked on Bordox's eyes with a threatening look.

"We must avenge them, Staggs," Rufa said and several others grunted in enthusiastic agreement.

"*We* will," Staggs replied, still staring at Bordox. "Not him. Etan told me the Pirate Lord wanted him out."

"He said he knows those people," Stevens said, stepping forward, his eye bruised from his struggle earlier with the prisoners. "Surely he has intel we can use."

Staggs growled and whirled to face the others. "Fine. You want to question him, go ahead. But when you're done, he leaves. He's not welcome here. The Pirate Lord wanted it."

"The Pirate Lord trusted them and paid with his life!" Bordox snapped, making eye contact with Rufa, Stevens, and the others, who looked far more sympathetic towards him than Staggs. His mind raced for words to change Etan's mind. He needed them. Staggs might be taking command, but he had no more claim than several others and that could be dealt with the way he'd dealt with Etan and the Pirate Lord. Their resources and set up would give him the advantage he needed to continue hunting Rhii down and wreaking his revenge. He had to stay. He let out a breath and forced his body to relax. Showing hostility would not help at the moment.

"He stays!" a gruff, mountain-sized pirate, torso covered in tattoos stepped forward, frowning. "They violated our sanctuary and we must make them pay."

"We must relocate and regroup," Staggs said. "They know where we are."

"They attacked us," Stevens said. "Have you no desire to face them again?"

Staggs snorted. "We will face them again. *That* is for certain." He panned their faces, making eye contact with a fierce look on his face, then motioned to Rufa and Stevens. "You're responsible for him. If he gets out of line, you'll be blamed."

Stevens nodded. "Fine."

Staggs turned and marched off, a few supporters following behind as Bordox remained with Stevens, Rufa and a few others.

"Thank you," he managed to say, softening his voice to a friendly tone. He had to keep these men on his side for his plans to succeed.

Stevens chortled. "We don't trust you either, but we do need information. You'll have to prove yourself beyond that. Be warned!" He shot Bordox a stern look, then turned and said, "Come with us!"

It was not a request, so Bordox followed. For now, he'd play along. For now. But he had far bigger plans for these pirates than they could imagine.

Davi met Tela outside her quarters, around the corner from his on one of *Reliance*'s lower decks, and they rode a lift together three levels up to spend the evening with his parents. It was the first chance the family had had to gather in weeks, and it was also the night Aron and Tarkanius would address the system about important decisions that had been made regarding reintegrating the Vertullians into Boralian worlds and life.

As the lift doors opened and they stepped out into the broad, brown corridor, Tela clasped Davi's hand. "It's good to see you and Farien laughing together again."

Davi shrugged. "He is my oldest friend."

She smiled and leaned her head softly on his shoulder. "Your best friend. I know, but it hasn't seemed that way since …"

Davi swallowed and she knew she didn't have to say Yao's name. He knew what she meant. "Yeah. We had some stuff to work out," he said, almost a whisper.

"He blames himself, you know," she added, hesitating only slightly as she searched for the best way to broach a difficult topic.

Davi's face crinkled with surprise. "It's not his fault."

"He thinks you blame him, too," she added.

David turned so his eyes met hers as they stopped in mid-corridor. "He told you this?"

Her eyes searched his, wishing she could heal the pain so obvious there. But she knew she had to just love him through it. She squeezed his hand as she replied, "Not directly. But all those months we spent scouting together he carried this burden, this weight on him."

"I don't blame him," Davi said and sighed, relaxing again as he turned and started up the corridor again and she laid her head back on his shoulder. That had been easier than she'd feared.

"I know, but does he?" she answered.

Davi groaned. "You want me to go back and talk to him again? Is that what this is?" He shot her a questioning look.

Typical men, those two never could discuss their emotions with each other. They worked through them in other ways. At least Davi had her. But Farien didn't have anyone, as far as she knew. Still, now wasn't the time, so she chuckled. "Let's eat first."

Davi relaxed beside her as they continued on. "What about us? Are we okay?"

This time she stopped, clasping his hand and pulling him around to face her so their eyes met again. "You rode in like a knight and rescued me," she said with a melodramatic flourish, then clasped his arm with both hands. "You're my hero!" Then she leaned in and planted a noisy, wet kiss on his cheek.

Davi grimaced. "Oh yay!"

Then they both laughed. And this time, in his eyes, she saw that everything really was okay, despite all they'd been through. There had been struggles, but they'd made it through together, and her heart warmed as she realized he'd proven it all by doing what had made her fall in love with him in the first place: being her hero. And what more could she ask? It was more than she'd ever expected to find, for sure.

A door slid open with a whoosh down the hall and Miri poked her head out. "It's coming on the nets! Hurry, you two!" She waved for them to come in.

They exchanged a smile, turned and hurried to join Miri together.

They gathered in Sol and Lura's living room before a large vidscreen, watching as first Tarkanius and then Aron addressed the entire system over the nets. The High Lord Councilor spoke of forgiveness and a new unity, the need to leave the past behind and move forward together for a secure and better future. Aron spoke of reconciliation and peace and a desire to contribute fully as members of society with mutual respect. Emotionally delivered but pretty much what Davi had expected.

Each spoke for around twenty minutes on the plaza in Accra before a huge crowd at the great Palace Davi and Miri had once called home. As they finished and the applause broke out, Sol, Lura, Davi, and Tela embraced and cheered while Miri sat stoically in silence just staring at the screen.

After exchanging hugs, Davi approached and put a hand softly on his shoulder. "Are you okay, mother?"

A solitary tear wound its way down her left cheek, but she nodded. "Yes. I'm sorry. I just realized … for the first time I can remember, there may actually be peace. We may not be at war. It seems surreal."

Davi chuckled. "And wonderful."

Miri smiled. "Yes, of course." She stood slowly, steadying herself against her son, who embraced her, holding her tightly for a moment and enjoying the familiar flowery scent of her perfume, the warm comfort of her touch, before pulling away.

"You two act as if you're at a funeral, for God's sake," Tela teased. "This is a great day!" Then she too hugged Miri, and Sol and Lura did as well, each in turn.

"Without a Council of our own, how will we occupy ourselves?" Sol wondered.

"I guess you just retired," Lura said and grinned. "Finally!" She shook a fist in celebration and they all laughed as her husband hugged her again.

"Not so fast," Tela said sternly. "I believe we have a wedding to plan."

They all smiled, seeming pleased, and grunted or nodded in acknowledgement with great enthusiasm.

"And since we're not going to be in space … I want a big wedding, the wedding of my dreams," Tela started in, speeding up with excitement at every word, twirling about joyfully like a young girl as the rest watched, laughing with delight.

"We'll do our best," Lura agreed.

Tela motioned frantically. "Stop moping around then. Let's get to work!"

"Can we eat first?" Davi joked and the three women shot him a look of mock warning.

"We might have to eat out, son," Sol replied, laughing.

"No, no, no," Lura said and motioned toward the table. "Everything's ready. Come! We have so much to discuss!"

And with that, Davi found himself caught up in the wave of enthusiasm as they gathered, said their prayers, and planned for the future—a future they'd barely envisioned for the past few years which now seemed possible for the first time in ages. All the while, Davi silently offered praise and thanks to God. He didn't know where life might take them, but he loved the feeling of anticipating it without dread. Perhaps like Tela, he too was feeling young again.

# THE HAND OF GOD

A Saga Of Davi Rhii Short Story

# The Hand of God

Cordelia shivered, her hull groaning as Buj McMaster pushed her engines to full and spun her into a sharp, diving turn. His hand slipped on the stick, wet from the sweat which now covered him. He took a deep breath and relaxed his grip. "Come on, baby. Hold together now."

He glanced down at the scanner to see the pirate ship echoing his dive and spin, falling back only slightly as it stayed on his tail. His instruments showed hull scarring and weakening of his shields. He cursed, then adjusted his rear shields to seventy percent. Might as well protect what needed protecting. This was supposed to be a simple honey run—basic supplies for the colony on Kempol I—nothing of interest for anyone. Except a pirate. They always needed basic stuff to survive. Still, he had to try.

Flipping the comm to an open channel, he keyed the transmit button. "Freighter *Cordelia* to raider ship, I have nothing of value on-board."

His answer was another volley of laser cannons, the blasts rocking his ship as they exploded against his rear deflectors.

"Basic supplies for Kempol I." A scratchy male voice came back over the comm: "Your ship has no markings. That's illegal in this system. Stop engines and let us board."

Buj's mind raced as fast as his heart, looking for an excuse to stall. The ship attacking him had no markings either. They couldn't be Alliance official then. Who was this guy?

"Your ship has no markings either. What right have *you* to stop me?"

"Citizen's Patrol. Keeping the shipping lanes safe for honest pilots."

"What makes you think I'm not honest?"

A blip lit up his screen and he quickly pulled back on the stick just in time for the torpedoes to fly past his left wing, a near-miss.

"Last chance to avoid disintegration."

Buj's hands moved like lightning on the controls as he pulled up quadrant scans, one after another. His eyes searched the screen for something—anything—a suitable place to hide. His heart pounded so loudly he wondered if it could be heard across space by his attackers. Then he saw them: the dwarf twins, Romulus and Remus, named after an Old Earth legend. The only dwarf planets in the system, out in nowhere land between Kronis and Plutonis. Kronis was his destination, but the chase had forced him off course and the two dwarfs were now his closest option.

Explosions rocked his ship as the pirate's lasers raked his shields again. He pushed the joystick forward into a twisting dive as he turned and headed toward the dwarf twins.

Shutting off the comm, he dropped two mines in his wake right in the path of the raider, but the pilot was skilled and deftly slid his ship between them, flying the large freighter almost like a fighter. *He definitely flies like a military pilot.*

Buj increased *Cordelia's* speed, shifting horizontally and vertically in a zigzagging pattern, trying to stay out of range of the freighter's weapons. The pirate stayed with him, hit-and-miss explosions rocking his ship as they exploded on or near his shields.

*I'm not going to make it!*

Then Buj recognized the ship and he knew for sure he was in trouble. At that moment, the pirate's laughter echoed over the comm.

Major Farien Noa was leading his squadron on a deep space probe when the alarm sounded. One of his pilots defined it for him, even as he checked his computer.

"Explosions and laser blasts—some kind of battle," Lieutenant Solanus Rhii said, sounding much like his father twenty years before.

"Anything on how many ships are involved?" Farien remained relax even as he felt the tension from his squadron. He'd been through this too many times to make any assumptions. It could be a false alarm or something minor.

"Negative," Rhii replied. "We're a quadrant over."

"Well, let's change that. Accelerate in formation, shields up, weapons armed." Farien complied with the commands even as he issued them, then laid in a course and accelerated his fighter, leading the squadron toward the targets.

"There's two of them," a young voice said—Farien's son, Yao, named after an old friend of Farien and Solanus' father.

Farien nodded as he checked his computer. "One of them's a freighter." The scan was fuzzy on the other. Farien typed commands into the computer, even as he completed his arc and straightened his VS37 for a direct approach from above toward the fighting ships.

"I've seen that signature before," Rhii said, his tone evidencing the search running in his mind. "On reports..."

"It's an odd construction," Yao said.

Farien smiled. Still so much to teach him. "It's probably employing sensor blockers as well as been custom modified to confused them."

"Got it!" Rhii called. "*The Hand Of God.*"

"*The Hand Of God*?" Yao's concerned voice echoed.

*The Hand Of God* was the name of a ship belonging to a pirate who'd been terrorizing smugglers and other commercial pilots throughout the area for six months. What was he doing out here alone? Supposedly he had great numbers. Had he stumbled onto the freighter by accident?

"He rarely works alone," Farien answered. "Where's his gang?"

"I only read two ships," Rhii said.

"An ambush?" Yao asked.

The two fighting ships came into view through Farien's blast shield as he keyed the comm. The Hand's ship was tight on the tail of the freighter, explosions rocking it as it struggled desperately to continue evading. Clearly the freighter pilot had some real skill. "This is Major Farien Noa of the Borali Alliance," Farien said into the comm. "Kill your engines and come to a full stop so we can inspect you."

The only answer was laughter over the comm. Farien shuddered. Why did he recognize that laugh?

"The freighter's barely hanging on," Rhii said. "My weapons are locked."

"Fire warning shots," Farien said, using his voice to project his own calm to his pilots. "Don't damage them. Just scare them."

His squadron slipped into attack formation around him, all seven VS37s sliding into a V-pattern, their weapons locked. Farien held back as the others fired at both ships. Explosions rocked the pirate ship with a couple other blasts singing the freighter.

"I say again," Farien repeated into the comm, "kill your engines and prepare to be inspected."

"You already shot at me!" the pirate's rasp snapped back over the channel. "Why would I trust you?"

"Trust me if you want to live."

The pirate's only response was laughter. The *Hand* fired two more blasts at the freighter, then swerved off in an erratic pattern, clearly designed to prevent further damage from the squadron's cannons.

"Stay on him!" Farien ordered. "Yao, you and Lake check that freighter."

Yao's voice was full of disappointment. "Yes, sir." The two fighters served off, leaving the formation and heading toward the freighter as the rest formed up on Farien and increased speed, chasing the pirate.

Buj listened to the chatter on the radio as his ship rocked with more explosions. Then the fighters fired too, barely missing his wings. Had they missed on purpose? Farien Noa? Where had he heard that name?

Explosions rocked his ship from behind. He checked the display and saw five ships closing fast on the pirate. Two more had turned off and were closing on him as the pirate led the others off in an attempt to evade. Buj didn't want Boralians aboard either, but they'd probably saved his life, and he couldn't outrun them.

He killed his engines, allowing *Cordelia* to drift as the VS37s closed in.

"This is Lieutenant Yao Noa of the Boralian Alliance," a young voice said over the comm. "Please identify yourself."

Another Noa? Were they related? "This is Buj McMasters of the freighter *Cordelia*," he responded.

"You're flying without markings," another voice said. "That's illegal in this system."

"I just had my ship refit. The markings will be added once I arrive at my destination." *Are you here to help me or him?*

"What is your destination?" The first voice, Yao, if Buj recalled correctly, asked.

"Kempol I," Buj answered. "I have supplies for the outpost there."

The VS37's matched *Cordelia's* velocity and settled in along either side.

"Leaving port without markings is asking for trouble," the second voice said. "And it looks like you found it."

Buj sighed. "He came out of nowhere. I don't know how he found me."

"You're lucky we came along when we did."

Buj chuckled, feeling relief again. "That's for sure. Thanks for the assist." The comm went silent for a moment. Buj assumed the two pilots were talking with each other. *Please don't let them board me.* He was already delayed because of the encounter with the pirate and the supplies were on rush. If he got them there on time, he'd gain a large bonus. He really needed the money.

"I'm afraid we're going to have to escort you to the nearest port for an inspection," the pilot Yao said.

Buj groaned, cursing to himself, then keyed the comm. "I'm kind of in a hurry. I could lose a major bonus. I really need the money. Can't you cut me some slack? You know he was preying on me."

"Sorry," said the other pilot. "Major gave us strict orders."

Switching his engines on auxiliary, Buj slowly accelerated, matching his speed and course with the escorting fighters as his mind raced for options. *There goes my bonus.*

Adrenaline raced through Farien's veins as his squadron gave chase. It had been a while since they'd seen any real action. Their deep probes generally involved encounters with merchant ships and passenger vessels either in trouble or committing minor violations. Usually they issued warnings and sent them on their way, stopping only to assist the vessels with trouble. But in this case, a mini war had been waged. He had a responsibility to find out what was going on, especially if the pirate was indeed *The Hand Of God.*

The pirate's ship rocked as blasts exploded just off his engines but he continued evading their shots like an expert.

Who is this guy? Farien knew a lot of people who'd love an answer. "Pree and Ami, cut him off. Rigel, stay with me. The other two hit him from the sides. We need to shut him down."

As the squadron broke apart, Farien fired another burst at the pirate's engines, striking the heat shield and rocking it again as the silver hull turned black from the flames.

"You want him alive, right?" Pree answered, a chuckle in his voice. The chubby veteran was one of Farien's best pilots and had a reputation as a prankster, but he was always on top of his game when he needed to be.

"The pirate, yes—his ship, no," Farien replied.

Pree laughed as Ami's high-pitched giggle filled the comm. "Let's leave enough of her to see what she's made of."

"You can indulge your fascination with starcraft on your own time, Ami," Pree teased. "We're on official business here."

Farien could almost hear the female captain rolling her eyes as she responded to her wingman. "You're the wingman, remember? Just follow my lead."

Farien watched with admiration as she skillfully accelerated then arced sharply and spun around to face the oncoming pirate, firing head on. Pree slid in beside her and did the same, forcing the pirate to dive and roll to avoid their blasts.

The dive was so steep the fighters had to abruptly change course to keep him in their sights and maintain their positions. Farien noticed the pirate was leading them toward an outer moon of a nearby planet. "His course is taking us toward that moon." Even as he commented, he launched his computer into a long-range scan. "He could have a base there."

"Or be hiding his fleet," Pree added.

"My sensors pick up nothing," said Lieutenant Hest. The youngest Squadron member and Farien's wingman sounded nervous.

"The moon could be hiding them," Ami said.

"Or the planet," Farien said. "Let's keep our eyes open and get ready for evasion if we need to."

Farien accelerated, Hest staying right with him. The pirate ship disappeared around the arc of the moon as Farien glanced around and spotted the black, sleek bodied snub nose craft of his squadron closing in. Suddenly, the pirate ship spun into a sharp arc, curving back around upside and firing its cannons straight at Farien and Hest.

"Hest! Evasive now!"

Farien tensed in his seat and scrambled with his own controls, hoping his young wingman was doing the same. His ship rocked from explosions as a blast singed his right wing, leaving streaks on the dark painted hull. As he slowed back to turn toward the pirate he caught a glimpse of Hest's limping fighter nearby. A blast had knocked out one of the engines and torn a jagged cut into the hull plating just behind the cockpit.

"You okay, Hest?"

The young wingman sounded surprisingly calm. "Fine, sir. A little shaken but I'll be okay."

The pirate ship arced back around toward the moon, following the curve of its atmosphere. It was moving so fast it would soon be out of sight. Accelerating, Farien's teeth clenched as he checked his targeting and fired blasts at the pirate ship's disappearing engines. Pree and Ami fired from above as well, then his computer beeped. The blip that was the pirate ship disappeared.

"He's gone?!" Ami's voice was almost a squeal.

Farien ignored the stabbing in his chest and typed frantically into his computer. "He can't be."

"He is," Pree said softly. Farien could sense his disgust.

"What the hell—?" Ami yelled over the comm as Farien heard the pounding of her fist on her cockpit wall. Ami always pounded when she was irritated.

"We don't have time to argue. Circle the moon and do another scan. Spread out." Farien turned, with Hest on his tail, and arced around the moon as he ran through more scans on his computer. There was no sign of the pirate ship and he knew none of the others would find any either.

In moments, they'd confirmed it. The *Hand Of God* was gone.

Farien sighed and keyed the comm. "Let's get back to the others."

The moment his scanner beeped, Buj realized they were all in trouble. In moments, his screen filled with blips and ships began popping out of lightspeed all around them—ships of the menacing kind. The *Hand's* pirate compatriots had found them.

His escort's voices revealed their panic. "Who are they?"

"Stay calm, Lake," he heard Lieutenant Noa answer.

"There's a lot of them!" The other pilot's voice cracked as it rose in pitch.

"Radio the major for help," Noa instructed. "Mr. McMasters, we have visitors. We're increasing speed, please stay with us and activate your shields."

Buj didn't even bother to respond. His shields had been on since he'd identified the blips as hostile. He increased speed to stay with the VS37 fighters and wondered how they'd survive an attack of seven ships to three.

The VS37s began to dive and Buj followed into a steep trajectory angling them away from the newly arrived ships. But then the stars ahead fizzled a bit and more ships began to materialize right in their path. Now it was twelve to three. *We're dead!*

"We're in trouble," Lake said, his voice almost a whine. "I can't raise the major on the comm!"

"Our best option is to put as much space between us and them as we can," Noa answered, leading the squadron into a turn that would arc them around the newly arrived ships.

"There's so many of them!"

"Stay calm, Lieutenant," the officer's voice remained calmer, focused. Buj hoped it matched his inner state as well.

Not waiting for further instructions, Buj typed a code into his computer, modifying his arc a bit so his tail angled back at the new arrivals. As the squadron soared past, mines dispatched from their special compartment in *Cordelia's* hull, leaving a nice string where the ships couldn't pursue without passing them.

"Are those mines?" Noa asked.

"A little extra insurance policy," Buj answered.

"You may have just destroyed any chance they're friendly."

Buj rolled his eyes. "These are pirates, Lieutenant. They're not friendly."

As if in confirmation, the ship's cannons began firing in unison, sending scattered bolts and torpedoes into the space surrounding *Cordelia* and the fighters. Explosions rocked *Cordelia*, shaking the cockpit but there were no direct hits so far. Buj had no doubt that wouldn't last long.

Noa steadily dispatched orders. "Increase power to rear shields! Evasives. Engines full! Keep heading away from them." Buj was impressed by Noa's calm in the face of attack.

*Cordelia's* computer beeped and he saw the pirate ships closing in. He punched a code into the computer to activate the mine's tracking systems. Moments later, he saw explosions on his combat screen as the mines zeroed in on the nearest targets and did their jobs.

"That ought to piss them off," Buj muttered.

Then a final ship appeared close on their tails and the comm beeped, indicating an open channel. Buj recognized the new ship as The Hand. He'd escaped and come back? Where were the major and the rest of his squadron? The comm beeped again and he flipped a switch.

"Attention freighter *Cordelia* and fighter escorts, you have twenty seconds to stop engines, lower shields, and prepare for boarding or we will destroy you." The Hand sounded almost amused this time. He had the upper hand and clearly knew it.

Buj cursed himself for taking the common shipping route at the last moment. It was faster, which is why he'd made the switch, putting aside his reservations about just the kind of trouble he was having now.

Yao Noa's voice was confident as he replied. "I'm sorry, we can't do that. We're on an official mission for the Boralian Alliance. It is you who must stop all aggression now to avoid arrest."

The Hand laughed heartily and his crew began firing again. The Hand's own missile rocked *Cordelia*, and the warning alert sounded as the shield strength lights flashed. Shields were down twenty percent.

Buj flipped the comm to the VS37's private channel. "We can't win."

"We just have to hold out until help arrives," Noa replied.

"I thought you couldn't reach them?" Now the boy's confidence was starting to get annoying.

"If the Hand is here, they'll be right behind."

Buj had never met a pilot who wasn't prone to overconfidence, but he found himself questioning the Academy's teaching methods. Realism was also a necessity for survival.

*Cordelia* rocked again, shields dropping another five percent. He saw explosions rocking the VS37s too. They were done for. His heart pounded the walls of his chest like a prisoner attempting to bust out of a cell. This wasn't the way he'd wanted to go out. He had no control. His brow creased as his mind raced, considering things he might have done differently.

The combat system beeped as Buj adjusted the controls, strengthening the rear shields. More blips suddenly appeared and he saw behind them.

"This is Major Farien Noa of the Boralian Alliance, you're all under arrest by authority of the High Lord Councilor." The voice was commanding and firm as it came over the open channel on the comm.

Buj closed his eyes and sighed a moment. At least the squadron could help them escape. They couldn't possibly win against so many bigger ships but their arrival at least meant Buj might have a chance to survive.

As soon as he came out of hyperspace, Farien's ship rocked with explosions and he had to gather himself and focus on sorting out what was going on. He sensed his squadron appearing around him and sliding quickly into formation. Farien's eyes were too busy searching for the VS37s and freighter he'd left behind. There they were—in the middle of a fleet of attackers of all shapes and sizes, evading as best they could an onslaught of laser blasts and torpedoes. Every few minutes, they'd surge toward an opening in an attempt to break free, but then a pirate would cut them off while his teammates deluged them with fire. Farien was amazed they'd held out at all.

"This is Major Farien Noa of the Boralian Alliance, you're all under arrest by authority of the High Lord Councilor," he announced over the open channel on the comm.

He switched the squadron channel and keyed the comm again. "Squadron commander, shields on full, weapons ready. Fire at will."

As his Squadron split off to obey the orders, Farien sped toward his endangered pilots. "Lake, Yao, you okay?"

Yao sounded amazingly calm. "Yes, sir. Just wondering what took you so long."

Yellow and orange flashes lit his cockpit from behind as his fighter rocked from an explosion. Farien's hand tightened around the joystick as he began turning the VS37 and visually searched the scanner.

The Hand's scratchy voice came over the comm. "Weapons and shields off. Engines full stop. And tell the freighter to prepare for boarding." The pirate sounded amused as he added: "Trust me, if you want to live."

"Not gonna happen," Farien replied, noting that the pirate's ship had closed up fast to ride tight on his and Hest's tails.

"I was hoping you'd say that!"

Farien's ship rocked again as the pirate fired torpedoes, narrowly missing his engines. He saw Hest peel off to his right in an attempt to evade, but the torpedoes stayed locked and exploded against his right wing. Hest's ship wobbled as the young pilot struggled to regain control.

"You okay, Hest?" Farien called.

"I think so, sir." Hest's voice was shaky. "She's a little hard to control."

"Fall back and assess the damages," Farien said. "I'll deal with our friend."

Matching his arc to Hest's as the wingman turned back, Farien pulled up, spinning his fighter and coming down straight at the pirate's ship from above, lasers blazing. Farien cackled as explosions rocked the pirate's ship as he spun to evade and dove up to meet Farien. *How'd you like that one, pirate?*

Then the Hand suddenly changed course and raced to follow Hest's crippled ship, firing lasers and torpedoes simultaneously.

Farien screamed inside his cockpit as he arced around onto the pirate's tail, but he could already see he was too late. His fist clenched around the joystick as he silently urged the engines to somehow defy physics and fly beyond their capabilities.

Hest's ship exploded into thousands of particles of light.

Farien winced cursed as he let go with his lasers at the pirate with everything he had. His breath froze in his throat, so intense was his focus. But then he had to breathe and he was that the Hand was already diving again and slipping out of range.

Flashes on his combat scanner and through the edges of his blast shield confirmed that the rest of the squadron was also engaged. But they couldn't last long against these ships. Farien typed into the computer, sending a distress call to the Boralian fleet. He only hoped a military ship was near enough to arrive in time to help.

"We're way outnumbered, Major," Solanus said urgently over the comm. It was the first time Farien had heard the young officer lose his cool in combat. "We need to get out of here!"

"Leave these pirates to keep terrorizing everyone?" Pree sounded disgusted.

"We can't take them on alone," Ami replied.

"We already lost Hest," Solanus added.

"I sent an alert to the fleet," Farien replied, swallowing the rage within. He cleared his throat, bile sliding back down his throat with the anger. He glanced out the blastshield to see Yao and Lake with the freighter, turning back from another attempt to break free of the surrounding pirates. Each time they tried, a ship moved in to block while the others opened fire. They'd all three taken significant hits but somehow avoided major damage. Farien knew that couldn't last. "I'm going to get the others to safety and then we can go FTL again and head for home."

Breaking off from the Hand, he spun again, racing back toward the freighter and VS37s at the center of the attack. He pushed his engines as fast as they could, firing at any enemy target that came into range.

The fighters had formed a circle with the freighter, facing outward and were somehow managing to return fire and operate thrusters simultaneously, spinning themselves in a circle, each wobbling in and out of place to evade as necessary. Farien was amazed.

"Lieutenants, break off engagement and form up on freighter *Cordelia*. The three of you follow me!"

"I alerted the fleet, but it appears no one heard," Lake said. "You didn't respond either."

"I never got a message," Farien answered, instinctually checking his communications settings. Sweat dripped off his brow onto his flightsuit.

His body felt slick inside the plastifiber material. He reached over to adjust his cockpit environmental controls.

Thoughts raced through his mind of all the men he'd lost under his command. Each one was personal, like a jagged edge ripping through his gut. He'd never forget the faces, never forget the names. Now, there was another. For a moment, he wanted to abandon everything and go after the Hand. But then he shook it off. He had other pilots to protect.

When the fighters were locked in formation around the freighter, they unleashed a barrage of laser fire, designed to clear a path through the ships. Explosions rocked some of the smaller pirate vessels, but instead of moving clear, they seemed to be closing in.

"Is it me or is this not working?" Solanus said over the radio.

"Push your speed. We have to get clear or they'll tear us apart," Pree said.

"We'll never make it," the freighter pilot commented.

"We have to try," Yao said.

Farien held back on commenting. He had to sound confident, but at the moment, he was more rattled than he'd been in ages. They were right. It was a long shot. And while the fighters could outmaneuver the pirate craft, they were severely outgunned. It would take hours to disable or destroy them all and, given the numbers, the odds were in the pirates' favor.

Explosions rocked the fighters as several of them took direct hits from pirate guns.

"To hell with this!" Pree suddenly peeled off and headed straight for a small pirate ship lying directly in their path.

"Pree! Come back! That's an order!"

But Pree ignored him. Farien tensed as he watched. Pree was a veteran, but he couldn't take on the whole armada alone.

"What are you doing, Pree?" Ami asked, almost pleading over the comm.

"Giving us a chance," her partner replied.

"You should have taken my offer while you stood a chance," the Hand's raspy voice said over the general channel.

"What do you want from me?" Buj roared. "I just have basic supplies for an outpost!"

"We need them more than those people," the Hand replied.

Pree began zipping in and out around the small pirate ship, targeting the engines, then the cockpit, trying to break through the shields. The pirate craft shifted, in an attempt to aim her guns and fire back, but Pree was too fast for her.

"I hope he knows what he's doing," Farien muttered over the comm, his eyes following the daring pilot's every move.

"He's the best, sir," Ami replied. "Let me help him."

Farien sighed. "Go. Breaking through may be our only chance."

As Ami's fighter spun off to join her wingman, Farien hoped he hadn't just sent another pilot off to die. They were his two best people, but still, it was a suicide run. Once the other pirates came to their fellow's aide, it could be over quickly, but then again, he and the others might be able to use the distraction.

As Ami and Pree worked together to attack the small pirate ship, it shifted course, moving toward two larger compatriots, obviously hoping to lead the fighters into range of their more powerful guns. In the process, Farien saw an opening was being created which the rest of them could use to clear the center of the pirate armada.

"Center your fire to keep the path clear," Farien instructed. One fighter alone wouldn't scare most of these ships, but concentrated fire from a squadron could do real damage.

Buj was fed up. The Boralians might be skilled pilots but they were clearly used to formations and planned attacks, not the improvisation required for the situation they all found themselves in. The major's decision to bring his entire squadron inside the armada to help "rescue" Buj and the others was the last straw. Of *course* the pirates let them in, but getting back out would be the trick. Buj and the two fighter pilots had been pinned down for over thirty minutes now. More than likely, the major had just signed everyone's death warrants with his commands.

Enough waiting around, Buj would show these military jocks what improvisation meant. He'd been running schematics and estimates through his computer for the past five minutes and he believed the scenario he had in mind might make a difference. The decision by two of the jocks to distract nearby pirates just aided him.

He had to figure out how to get away from his escort and lay the mines. He'd already programmed his computer to load the mines into the torpedo bays. The mechbots had followed the order without questions, an advantage of the old fashioned kind he employed over the newfangled Artificial Intelligence models they'd come out with over the past decade.

Bots that think and reason? How could anyone have considered that a good idea?

Exhaling to relax the tension, he double-checked that the mines were ready then punched in the code to activate the sequence he'd programmed. He engaged his brakes and fired his thrusters, sliding straight down between his escort and shot out around them to clear space where he could execute his plan.

As soon as the targeting computer said he was clear, he launched the sequence and the mines began firing from the torpedo tubes, homing devices activated. In their present mode, the mines would seek the largest heat signature they could find and latch onto it, waiting for his signal to explode. If it worked right, the pirates would be so surprised and distracted by the hull explosions that he and the fighters could escape. But all that wouldn't occur until Buj finished planting the mines.

He swung *Cordelia* out further to avoid one of the mines homing in on a fighter or two. Now, if those two jockeys playing games distracting the pirates would just stay clear, he'd be okay. Either way, as long as he escaped, he'd be okay with the losses. Pilots die in combat—it was unavoidable.

His radio beeped as fighters adjusted, racing to form around him again.

"Captain, what are you doing?" Major Farien demanded over the comm.

"Stay put, Major. I'm doing what I can to give us a chance. Trust me."

"You're firing devices at the pirates and making yourself a sitting duck in the process," the major answered.

"He's launching mines," Yao corrected.

"Mines?"

Buj smiled. "Yes, Major. And if the plan works, it might just give us the opening we need. Stay clear of their heat seeking tech until I have them all place, ok? Just a few more minutes."

Farien gave the order. "Lay down cover fire and keep them distracted," he said. The fighters began firing haphazardly at the various pirate ships, clearly a tactic designed less for damage and more for distraction. But Buj thought, as he continued deploying his mines, *it just might work*.

"You are aware, Mr. Masters, that heat-seeking tech is illegal outside military channels," said Lake, the other pilot who'd escorted Buj.

"Now's not the time," Yao scolded. Buj could almost hear him rolling his eyes. Every squadron had its rookies.

In a few moments, Buj finished deploying the last batch of mines. According to his computer, one or two had latched onto each of the pirate ships, except the original one. The Hand had flown erratically, zipping in and out and, so far, managed to avoid any of the mines.

It would have to do.

"Okay, boys and girls, get back in formation and be ready to move," Buj said into the comm. He navigated back toward the fighters as they formed up around him again.

The pirate's raspy voice came over the general channel. "We've tired of your games. Enjoy the last moments of your lives, pilots."

With that, the pirates began a barrage of fire unlike what they'd subjected them to before. It was as if even the freighter's survival had been taken off the table. Buj entered the command and let the mines go as he and the pilots zagged evasively, trying to keep from being hit.

Explosions rocked the pirate ships and the barrage suddenly stopped. Several of them shifted position, as if trying to preemptively evade, not realizing where the attack came from. He saw the two attacking VS37s firing at the damaged pirate ships, working to weaken them in already damaged areas. In the process, as the pirates tried in vain to evade the new threat, a large gap opened up. Buj and the fighters seized the opening and shot through.

To Farien's amazement, the freighter pilot's crazy plan worked. Despite the use of illegal weaponry, it had saved them all. Farien decided perhaps some details could be left out of his report. As he curved back to view the pirates and account for his men, he saw an explosion rock the two VS37s which had lagged behind—Pree and Ami.

"I'm hit," Pree called.

"I've got you, Pree," Ami answered.

"Too late, get clear." Pree's voice trailed off as his ship wobbled then seemed to teeter and point straight down toward a pirate freighter.

"Pull up!" Ami screamed, but moments later, the fighter exploded against the freighter's engines, stopping the pirate cold and ending Pree's life.

Farien cursed at yet another loss as he heard Ami's scream over the radio. Then Ami began firing maniacally at anything in sight.

"Ami! Get back here! Now!" Farien forced out the words. He knew how she must feel but they'd never survive once the pirates regrouped and came after them. Explosions rocked his cockpit. He glanced at his scanner to find the Hand's ship on him again.

"Transmitting coordinates for rendezvous," Farien said into the comm as he did his best to evade. "Get there and wait for me. Captain Masters, that means you, too."

"Let us help you, sir," Solanus urged.

"No, I can handle it. Get to safety!" Farien spun his ship into a loop and dove upward, curving so his cockpit was upside down from his earlier position as he looked down on the Hand from above.

"We won't leave you, Major," Yao said.

"We have a civilian to protect," Farien said. As he arced back, he saw Ami's fighter break away from the pirates and rejoin the others. The pirates themselves were regrouping, leaving their disabled comrade to drift as they did. Then he saw the Hand's ship adjusting course to intercept him head on.

"Don't sacrifice yourself, sir!" Solanus pleaded.

"I'll just distract them 'til you're clear," Farien said. "Go! Now!" He had no idea if he could get away or not, but it didn't matter. He'd lost enough men. If anyone else had to die, he was determined it would be him.

Then Lake's fighter and the freighter leapt into FTL, smearing across the stars and disappearing into space.

Farien breathed deeply with relief, then saw the remaining three turn back toward him.

"We can't leave you, sir," Ami said.

The pirate ships were racing toward them again.

"I'll be right behind you! Go before they trap us again!" His ship rocked as he and the Hand exchanged fire head-on, then dodged last minute to avoid colliding. *So that's how you want to play it, is it?*

The other fighters fired at the Hand's ship as he circled around, but he evaded their shots again, heading back toward Farien.

Farien forgot his companions and put all his focus on the Hand. *Two of my pilots are dead because of you. It's time you paid for your sins.* The Hand fired, but Farien waited, targeting, hoping for just the right moment.

Then his scanners beeped. Blips began materializing around them. Farien looked up to see the pirate armada, changing course. They were arcing back to flee. Still, the Hand kept coming. Farien fired, lasers strutting across the enemy's upper hull, then the enemy was past him and Farien began turning his ship.

"Someone call for help?" A familiar voice said over the comm.

"Commander! Are we glad to see you!" Solanus called out.

Farien recognized the markings on the new arrivals—the Boralian fleet had come to their rescue. But he didn't have time to chat. He had to get the Hand. He lost sight of the pirate as he arced around, but when he came back straight onto the position where the pirate had last been, once again, the enemy had disappeared.

"Where'd he go? Do anyone of you have a fix on him?" Farien cursed to himself, tensing in his chair with determination. Sounding panicked in front of his men wasn't going to earn him any marks for leadership.

"He's gone, Sir," Yao replied.

Farien's fingers danced on the keys, sending a code through the scanner and it searched again. The wait time seemed interminable but lasted only a few seconds. Farien cursed. What kind of technology did this guy have to disappear so fast?

The commander's voice came through the comm sounding almost amused. "Is this how you greet a Senior Officer, Major?"

Farien sighed as he keyed on the mic. "Hello, Commander. Welcome to our party."

"My men will round up these pirates. Your ship appears damaged. Are you okay?"

Farien sighed. For a moment, he considered mentioning Hest and Pree. Of all people, his old friend Davi Rhii would understand. But he shook it off. Time to lead again. "I'm fine, Commander Rhii. And so's your son. He distinguished himself today."

"Well, come aboard so we can thank you properly."

Farien sighed and turned as the other fighters formed up on him. He heard Ami sending a radio call to Lake and the freighter, asking them to return. Explosions flashed outside his blast shield as six Boralian destroyers finished mopping up the much smaller pirate armada as they fled in desperation.

*Some day, Hand. Some day.*

With that, he led his squadron back toward the command ship of his oldest friend.

# Glossary

**Agora**—One of Vertullis' two moons.

**Auto-bot**—Prototype robot created to perform basic human tasks.

**Barge**—A smaller transport used primarily to carry loads between neighboring planets.

**Boralis**—The larger of two suns in the solar system.

**Bots**—Robots designed to perform tasks formerly assigned to humans.

**Cab-bot**—Bots designed to drive air taxis and interact as tour guides with passengers.

**Charlis**—The smaller of the solar system's two suns.

**Chrono**—Watch.

**Council of Lords**—The elected body that works with the High Lord Councilor to lead the Borali Alliance.

**Courier Craft**—Round, silver craft designed to carry supplies and papers between planets in the solar system with light speed drives.

**Daken**—Large, blue, predatory birds, coveted for their beautiful feathers.

**E-post**—Messages sent over the computer, like e-mail. Usually sent via computer terminals or kiosks in public places.

**Feruca**—A black fruit with a thin skin and soft pulp.

**Floater**—A floating platform with two seats facing a control panel at the front which moves by manipulating the air underneath to float above the ground. The largest floaters have benches to hold as many as twenty troops—more if ten stand in the middle. Smaller models are typically designed for four or five passengers.

**Gixi**—A round, purple fruit grown in orchards on Vertullis and Italis with a delicious, tender pulp and sweet juice.

**Gungors**—Six-legged brown animals with yellow manes raised for their tasty meat.

**High Lord Councilor**—Leader of the Borali Alliance, elected by the Council of Lords. The post typically passes down through members of the same family until the Council decides new blood is required.

**Iraja**—Capital city of Vertullis.

**Italis**—Ninth planet in the solar system, home to the Lhamors.

**Jax**—A blue and oblong fruit with crispy pulp and a bitter taste, which becomes tart and sweeter when boiled; often used as an ingredient in salads.

**Legallis**—Seventh and largest planet in the solar system and capital of the Borali Alliance.

**Legon**—Capital city of Legallis and headquarters of the Borali Imperial government.

**Lhamor**—Native to the planet Italis. Lhamors have green-scaled skin and disproportionally large, orange eyes and four arms, the lower two extending from either side of their large, round stomachs, parallel to the arms which extend out of their shoulders above them.

**Lords**—Elected members of the Council of Lords, usually of high bloodlines from the upper echelons of Legallian society.

**Mech-bot**—Bots used as mechanics in starports.

**Off-worlder**—Person not from the same planet as a person calls home.

**Plutonis**—The 12th planet in the solar system, an icy world suitable only for natives and the Qiwi antelope. Also the location of the Borali Alliance's outermost post, Alpha Base.

**Presimion Academy**—The Borali Alliance's leading school for future military leaders located on Eleni 1, one of Legallis' largest moons.

**Qiwi**—Antlered creatures native exclusively to Plutonis, with dark brown fur and white spots lining either side of their spines. Waist high on most humans, qiwi have four long legs ending in black hooves. Their antlers can grow up to forty centimeters out from their skulls.

**Quats**—Striped creatures with long tails similar to Earth's cats but larger, like Cocker Spaniels.

**Regallis**—Thirteenth planet in the system, habitable only because of its development as a major indoor resort.

**Royal Shuttle**—Smaller version of the shuttles (see description below) reserved for the Royal family and their guests.

**Serve-bot**—Bots used for serving patrons in bars and restaurants.

**Shuttle**—White personnel transport with light gray interior. The cockpit has two black chairs facing a transparent blast shield, surrounded by controls, and is separated by a bulkhead from a passenger compartment containing four rows of seats—two lining each exterior wall and two back-to-back down the center. Each has its own safety harness. Intraplanetary models operate without lightspeed capabilities, while interplanetary models are equipped with ultra-lightspeed drives.

**Skitter**—One-man ground craft that operate on a system allowing it to fly above the planet's surface, higher than a floater. Sleek and fast, skitters are easy to maneuver through trees and other obstacles and are known to handle much like Imperial VS28 starfighters.

**Talis**—A warm beverage brewed from beans grown on Vertullis—somewhat like the old Earth beverage, coffee.

**Tertullis**—Eighth planet in the solar system, home to tall humanoids similar to humans except for their orangish tinted skin and purple eyes.

**Transport**—Larger craft used to transport supplies, food, and other loads across the solar system.

**Vertullis**—Sixth planet in the system and home to the humans known as workers, the only slaves in the solar system.

**VS28**—Sleek and black starfighters with snub noses and three wings—two longer wings out of each side, and a third shorter wing extending vertically above the fighter's four engines. Each bears its squadron's insignia, and a few bear names given them at a pilot's indulgence. They have laser cannons on each wing as well as in the nose. The cockpit lay beneath a gray, transparent blast shield through which the pilot can see the stars in space around him.

**WFR (Worker's Freedom Resistance)**—An organized resistance formed by workers on Vertullis to seek freedom from the Borali Alliance's rule.

**Workers**—Residents of Vertullis, and age-old enemies of the Legallians; they live and work as slaves for the Borali Alliance.

# Acknowledgements

The idea for this story came to me when I was a fifteen-year-old science fiction fan living in a small Kansas town where it sometimes felt like dreaming was the only way out. Over the years, I lost my original notes, but the idea in my head and the names Xalivar and Sol stayed with me as well as the opening line "Sol climbed to the top of the rise and stared up at the twin suns as they climbed into the sky." I revised it a bit when we did the Author's Definitive Edition for Wordfire in 2015 and again for this version, cleaning up some typos, missing words, logic flaws, and repetitive words. But for the most part, it is the first novel I wrote—imperfect and an example of a less mature, established author than I am now.

I made that choice because ultimately a writer can only go back and fix his flawed works so many times before it loses any meaning, and this book took me twenty-five years to write and I wrote daily through some of the toughest trials I've experienced in my life. So this book you hold in your hand is a victory in many ways, and I'm still proud of it and what it accomplished for my career (giving people an experience similar to the first *Star* Wars and making Honorable Mention on Barnes and Noble's Year's Best Science Fiction of 2011) and hope you'll enjoy it and share it with others.

Thanks go first to Lost Genre Guild for inspiring me to try writing for *Digital Dragon* and to T.W. Ambrose for encouraging me to write more space opera stories, and then agreeing to publish them. An abridged version of the prologue to this novel first appeared in *Digital Dragon*'s May 2010 issue.

Secondly, thanks go to fellow authors like Blake Charlton, Ken Scholes, Jay Lake, Mike Resnick, Leon Metz, Moses Siregar, and Grace Bridges who have supported, encouraged, and advised me time and time again, no matter how silly my questions were or how many times they'd heard them before. Special thanks to Blake and Grace for taking time to read and offer more specific advice to help me grow as a writer and to Mike Resnick for advice in figuring out this crazy business.

Thirdly, thanks to first readers and friends like Larry Thomson, Tim Pearse, Jeff Vaughn, David Melson, Todd Ward, Mike Wallace, Andrew Reeves, Chris Zylo Owens, and the members of the FCW-Basic Critique Group for actually seeming to enjoy my writing even in its roughest form and for giving me feedback which helped me to improve it greatly.

Fourthly, thanks to friends like Charlie Davidson, Aaron Zapata, Mark Dalbey, Nelson Jennings, and Greg Baerg, who, along with some of the guys above, have helped me escape from behind the desk and keyboard and laugh a little bit when I needed it.

Fifthly, thanks to Vivian Trask, Randy Streu, Jen Ambrose, Paul Conant and Darlene Oakley for their editing and advice, Anthony Cardno for proofing the latest iteration, the El Paso Writer's League for encouragement and fellowship, and Mike Wallace for the science of the Boralis solar system. Thanks also to Jeana Clark for the solar system map which brought it to life for me.

Thanks to you, the reader. I hope you like it enough to come back for more and check out my John Simon Thrillers and other works.

Thanks to God for making me in His image and giving me the talent and inspiration to do this and continually opening the doors. I look forward to seeing what's behind the next ones.

# About the Author

Bryan Thomas Schmidt is a national bestselling author editor and Hugo-nominee who's edited over a dozen anthologies and hundreds of novels, including the international phenomenon *The Martian* by Andy Weir and books by Alan Dean Foster, Frank Herbert, Mike Resnick, Angie Fox, and Tracy Hickman as well as official entries in *The X-Files, Predator, Aliens Vs. Predators, Joe Ledger, Monster Hunter International,* and *Decipher's Wars.* His debut novel, *The Worker Prince*, earned honorable mention on Barnes and Noble's Year's Best science fiction. His adult and children's fiction and nonfiction books have been published by publishers such as St. Martins Press, Baen Books, Titan Books, IDW, Blackstone, and more. He lives in Ottawa, KS with his canine bosom companions, Louie and Amelie, and four cats.

Website/Blog: www.bryanthomasschmidt.net
Twitter: @BryanThomasS
Facebook: www.facebook.com/BryanThomasSchmidt
Goodreads: goodreads.com/author/show/3874125.Bryan_Thomas_Schmidt

**To sign up for**
**Bryan Thomas Schmidt's**
**Author Newsletter**
**and get a free short story,**
**go to bit.ly/3yE13Kt**

www.ingramcontent.com/pod-product-compliance
Lightning Source LLC
Chambersburg PA
CBHW030551310726
48979CB00011B/2117/J